THE FREEWATER CHRONICLES

PEARL ISLAND

James P. Lally

First edition

This is a work of fiction. Names, characters, places, and incidents either are the product of the author's imagination or are used fictitiously. Any resemblance to actual persons, living or dead, events, or locales is entirely coincidental.

ISBN: 979-8-9857658-0-9 (paperback)
ISBN: 979-8-9857658-2-3 (ebook)

Cover art and design: © by Nevy Liang
Interior art: © by Nevy Liang
Editing: Jaime Powel
Interior Design by Tracy Atkins (The Book Makers)

thefreewaterchronicles@gmail.com

This book is dedicated to:

My wife, Susan. It was your constant love and encouragement that
provided the fertile soil this story needed to take root.
Thank you for always believing in me.

My parents, Dave and Prudie. You two have always supported
my dream to be a writer and helped me find the confidence
I needed to see this project through.

All the people out there trying to make this world a better place.
Thank you.

Acknowledgments:

I am humbled and honored by all who felt called to financially support this self-publication project. It has helped me realize that you are never truly alone in this journey through life. The publishing of this book is as much a collective accomplishment as it is an individual one. Thank you, each and every one of you, for helping bring my dream into reality. I am eternally grateful for:

Marissa Gaven, Kevin Wilson, Tanner Jensen, Sarah Jones, Deborah Tozour, Melony Sanders, Bryan Lally, David and Prudie Lally, Patricia Yount, Kimberly Spivey, Zach Evans, Haley Schnakenberg, Mary Craft, Michael Lally, Nancy Paul, Tish Yelverton, Billy Russell, Haley Dolata, Gabrielle Barriere, Brian and Marilyn Schimke, Sara Setzco, Dell Hagwood, Kari Kram, Donna White, Jessica Lam, Stephanie Tatlbot, and Sam Millard.

Contents

CHAPTER: 1

Riding the Wave

Just beyond the gaze of the naked eye, an unassuming star continues its ageless cycle through the cosmos. Caught in the gravitational wake, an array of planetary passengers accompanies the glistening spectacle. One of these passengers, a waterlogged planet called Maia, has even given birth to her fair share of sentient civilizations. Despite being the perfect proximity from the sun, few have fully appreciated the point of balance this speck in space has to offer.

A cataclysmic flood ended the strong hold of her last civilization. Some might say they had it coming. The remaining survivors cling to the scattered lands that sprinkle her oceanic body. Around the same time, a mighty storm was born at the southern pole. Partnered with the tidal-locked moon, they have teamed up to churn the angry waters for eons. The combined forces have kept the seas from releasing their grip upon the world. This watery fate has done well to inspire some inhabitants to embrace a sense of humility, but not all heed the call. Tonight, the moonlight cuts through the dense cloud cover of the night sky, highlighting a fool's quest to challenge nature's authority.

∞

"I don't understand why this isn't working, Beau!" the foolish sailor yells from the crow's nest. He smiles reflexively, gazing towards the mighty storm before him. Its ancient reign over the planet captivates the imagination of most inhabitants of Maia. Few, however, have had the chance to witness the majestic manifestation up close. Even fewer have ever wished to. Rain pours down from the sky like a hailstorm of freshly sharpened knives. Clothed in nothing more than a hat and a pair of overalls, the man's exposed flesh takes the full brunt of the abuse. Despite the seemingly obvious detriment, he doesn't appear fazed by the onslaught. He waits for his previous words to reach the ears of his grizzly companion.

The howling winds suffocate the air of the lone sailors, making such a sonic journey nearly impossible. As the call of his captain finally registers, an involuntary twitch possesses the left eye of the helmsman. Already overwhelmed with the task of navigating these unforgiving waters, he struggles to take such a comment lightly. His fatiguing restraint finally gives way to the bubbling frustration in his heart. His mind races while he shakes his head in disbelief of his captain's ignorance.

"What do you mean you don't understand?" he yells back as a streak of lightning strikes the sky. The consequential crack of thunder pulsates through the air, acting to further punctuate his disgruntled question. His uncaged frustration leads him to forego any ability to wait for a response. He fires another rhetorical question into the night sky. "What did you think would happen? That we would just casually sail into the strongest force of nature this world has to offer with no complications?! Do you even—" His words are interrupted by a towering wave crashing over the port side of their ship. Beau is stricken with disappointment for allowing himself to be distracted at such a time. He burrows his grip into the spokes of the helm and regains focus. He fights with all his might to combat the force of water crashing over them. The colossal wave quickly consumes them and buries them into the depths of the sea.

Navigating the now submerged vessel, they carve through the water with the sharpened metallic bow of the ship doing most of the work. The ship glides smoothly underwater, moving like the swing of a trained samurai. However, the splintering sound of the wooden hull echoes through the water. Just when the helmsman thinks the ship is finally about to give up, they explode out the backside of the wave, erupting into the night sky like a fired cannon.

"Yeaaaah!" the captain cries with unrelenting zest. Another bolt of lightning cuts through the sky. Thunder claps behind the flash of light like a celestial applause. The crazed captain's wet hair flaps violently behind his head. He remains perched atop his ship, unfazed by their continued flirtation with death. His eyes beam brightly with childish joy. "You are incredible, Beau!"

"Don't you try and change the subject, Brahm," Beau retorts, returning to their earlier discussion. "How can you still take this all so lightly? We will eventually die out here. Why do you insist we keep this up?!"

"The compass, Beau!" Brahm says while pulling a golden relic from his pocket. The octagon-shaped device sits heavy in his hand. He stares down at it and smiles. It's like the weight of all antiquity rests within the clutches of his fingers. With a flick of his thumb, he flips off the protective face of the device to reveal the inner contents. Three wiggling needles lay suspended in glass domes, all pointing towards the massive storm ahead.

"See?" Brahm says despite having no intention of actually showing his companion his epiphany. "All the needles are still pointing us right here! This has to be the right way! My father's compass wouldn't have steered us wrong."

"Uggh," Beau grunts, tired of fighting a losing battle. His attention shifts back to the turbulent ocean. The waves that surround them have increased their undulating intervals significantly. He can feel another mighty tidal wave emerging. "I tried to tell you before," Beau rebuttals, deciding to go against his better judgment, "we never fully understood what that instrument was used for! We just assumed it could take us back, we never tried!"

"But it got us so close!" Brahm fires back, unwilling to admit defeat. "I know it's got to be the key to getting through; father felt it too! Right?"

"You are most definitely his son," Beau says with a shake of his head. He finds himself drifting into the guarded memories of an ancient past. "But that's not always a complement!"

"C'mon, Beau! Lets give it one more shot!" Brahm says as he slams the face of the compass shut.

"I don't know why I ever agreed to this," Beau mumbles as he spins the wheel, pointing the bow back towards the storm.

"Sure you do," Brahm says with a playful smirk on his face. "Into the storm we ride!" he cries, lifting his hand holding the golden instrument high above his head. Another bolt of lightning splits the sky. This time, sensing the newly introduced metallic relic, the electrical discharge diverts from its original trajectory. Racing down from the heavens, the surge of energy strikes the golden instrument with concussive force. Serving as a perfect grounding wire, the overwhelming force discharges the full extent of its power into the unsuspecting ship captain.

"Waaahooo!" Brahm screams as every ounce of his body surges with electricity. His body glows bright, flashing between states of transparency as if hooked up to a high-powered x-ray machine. As the last surge of current makes its way through his body, he emits an intense, radiating flash before fading back into the surrounding darkness. The heroic cries for adventure fade with the dissipating light. Only the sound of pelting rains and screaming winds fill the air now.

"Brahm?" Beau asks cautiously. His captain's lingering silence grows concerning. He looks up the mast, using the flickering moonlight to catch a glimpse of the electrifying aftermath. A charred corpse now stands at the top of the mighty ship. Smoke smolders around the captain's burnt contours while a faint flame flickers atop his head. The flame dances in the wind, consuming what remains of Brahm's long hair.

"C'mon, quit playing around!" Beau shouts, seemingly unconvinced of the dire situation. He gazes back to the sea, frantically checking the changing water currents.

"Ha-a," Brahm finally says, coughing up a plume of smoke from his lungs. A bright white smile cuts through his face, contrasting his otherwise dark and dismal presentation. "Hahaha… it's going to take more than that to stop me!" he cries triumphantly. Brahm shakes his body like a wet dog, dislodging all the superficial remains of his burnt flesh. He stands arrogantly upon the vast ocean, full of pride, and without a scratch on him.

"Well," Beau says unimpressed, "if that doesn't deter you, what do you think of that coming our way?" The two men share a silent moment as they gaze upon the colossal wall of water heading right towards them.

"There's no way we can avoid this one!" Beau yells as he burrows his focus back into the helm. He grips the spokes as hard as he can, demanding as much control over their situation as possible. As the wave gets closer, Brahm can feel the frantic nature of his companion grow even more chaotic.

"You might be right this time," Brahm admits. He chuckles to himself as his resurging defiance gives way to acceptance. "Just let it go."

"Excuse me?!"

"You heard me," Brahm says while turning his back to the monstrous wave. "Let it go, all of it. Now is not our time."

"Not our time for what? To *live*?"

"Well, I guess there is one way to find out," the young captain says with an ominous tone. He smiles in the face of his own surrender. The wind suddenly shifts directions and the ship takes an uncanny plunge backwards as if grasped by the hands of God herself. Each shift in the changing direction spins the helm ever further out of Beau's control.

Brahm calls down from the crow's nest again, "Take a closer look at those ever-slipping spokes between your fingers. Now, ask yourself what force binds your hands to that helm. Why are we even out here in the first place, Beau? Truly? Are you not ready to let go of this fear that has ended up taking control of the expedition?"

Brahm's words are punctuated by another flash of lightning cutting through the night sky like a glowing tree branch. In the brief moment of illumination, a light is cast on the struggling duo's predicament. Their ship is fully lodged within the towering swell as it continues to grow and suck everything up in sight. The white foam of its crest quickly emerges from the depths of the dark waters. As the light fades back into darkness, Beau's weathered face starts to relax. That last cry from the crow's nest finally hit home. His white knuckled grasp finally releases its lingering attachment to the helm. The lasting indentations of Beau's fingers can be seen planted into the wooden spokes. He watches as they start their whirlwind spiral out of his control.

The final surrender relinquishes the ship's grasp on the ocean below. A rush of unrestricted energy now flows freely throughout the sea-bearing vessel. All resistance to the whims of the great storm has faded away. It becomes too much for Brahm to contain himself. Howls of wayward laughter pour into the night sky as the ship is flung ever further into the chaotic swell rising behind them. Beau gives into his own release of laughter as their impressive ship transforms into a rising surfboard, sailing effortlessly in sync with the wise and mysterious flow of the ancient waters.

CHAPTER: 2

Initial Contact

Known as a gem among the islands of the South Sea, The Pearl Island is well renowned by its neighboring lands but not necessarily because of any outward beauty. Most of the historic vegetation has been washed clean from its shores due to the constant barrage of the churning seas. Except for a few stubborn elephant trees known for their steadfast root structure, the island displays its stone and rocky exterior proudly. Many islands owe their very existence to this battle-scarred land. Pearl Island serves as the main shield from the repetitive storm surges and harsh weather patterns that are accustomed to the South Sea. Veterans to sea-bound storms, the intensity of this particular night's tidal surge is not unique to the Pearl inhabitants. This night would pass as any other for most, except for the select few who will bear witness to a rather peculiar 'package' being delivered by the intrusive storm.

Otto, a salvage boy of the docks, rushes to secure his viewing perch at the base of an elephant tree. With the sturdy roots in hand, he stares down the approaching storm. His poorly fitted vest flaps around his body, dancing violently with the sidewinding winds. His dusty blond hair flies frantically over his face but does little to distract his intense focus. Despite his sixteen years of life, the carved lines in his face seem to better serve someone twice his age.

Otto takes his trusty rope from around his waist and carefully tethers himself in-between two bulging roots that flow out of the mighty tree. In a world full of so much uncertainty, the elephant trees still stand resilient. They are a stark contrast to the otherwise chaotic and destructive palette nature has been painted with. The roots of the mighty trees display their strength as they splinter apart the carefully laid cobblestone streets below. Storms like the one tonight should signify danger and destruction, but for a growing number, they have become a steady source of income. Shipwrecks are a common occurrence on The Pearl and the clean up crew has become quite efficient.

Another tug on the knot of Otto's sturdy rope signifies his readiness to brace the incoming surge. He lets out a deep exhale, calming himself as he prepares for what is to come next. His weathered body stands in defiance of the elements. His confidence in his knots and the tree serve as his only protection from the upcoming storm surge. This job is definitely not for the faint of heart. One loose knot, one rogue piece of debris, one miscalculated breath and your days are done. However, necessity serves as a powerful motivator. One final tug to tighten his knots is all the time Otto has left. He glances up from his lifeline to see the encroaching tidal wave rising up over the darkened horizon.

"This is it," he says out loud, staring down his foe. "Show me what you got!" With unruly force, the once distant wave rushes over the island. The water plummets onto The Pearl, serving as a test to her might. Warning sirens scream into the night sky as the waves swallow up the polished streets with an effortless gulp. The harsh ocean water quickly blankets the protruding warning towers along the shores, muffling their sonic call for caution. The waves fully engulf all the efforts of humanity to keep their heads above water. Otto grabs onto his rope for dear life as the surge of water lifts him up off his feet, suspending him by the seemingly endless updraft of water.

Off in the near distance, he hears a substantial crash through the deafening flow of the water. He dares not open his eyes to look. He must keep his face clenched as tight as his fists. It is a constant struggle to keep the water from rushing into his saturating body. For a brief second, the intensity relaxes as the wave has reached the climax of its assault. Otto cracks one eye to peer out into the water. To his amazement, he sees what looks like an enormous ship wedged into the side of one of the fortified sea-dwellings. The ship appears mostly intact, only a slight crack in the bottom of the hull is visible. The building it collided with, however, did not receive as gentle of a consequence.

Those structures are supposed to be impenetrable! Otto thinks to himself in bewilderment. His time to ponder such anomalies, however, is cut short as the receding wave beckons his full attention once again. As the ocean calls back its destructive hand, Otto is sucked down into the surging current. His sturdy rope is the only thing holding his body back from being plastered into the cold hard ground. Otto knows it's only a matter of time before he will be allowed another breath, but how much longer can he hold out? Reaching the edge of his limits, he cracks another eye to see how much water is left to endure. Pockets of trapped air bubbles rush past him, taunting his oxygen-deprived body. *Too much!* he fears. His already narrowed field of vision starts to grow dim; the pressure of the water feels less distracting as an overwhelming peace now floods his body.

"GASP!" At the last moment the floodwaters break over his head and his empty lungs lunge to suck down the elusive air they have been starved of. Sprung back into consciousness, Otto looks again to his right, expecting to see only scattered remains of the earlier ship. He shakes his head in disbelief as he sees the strange vessel still protruding from the stone building like a casted throwing dart. Against all logical belief, the ship still remains almost fully intact.

"This is my big break! I have to make it over there before the next surge!" he cries out. With every storm comes the rush for time; there is no telling how many other scavengers are out tonight or how quickly the waves will strike again. He unties his safety line and races through the freshly washed cobblestone streets. He gazes out over the ocean as he runs. The water appears to be arching her back into another swell as she continues the recall of the previous wave.

It's going to be another big one. As he reaches the building the ship is perched in, he looks up and sees there is a good twenty feet he will need to climb. Otto starts his assent up the well-crafted stone building as the roar of the ocean signals the next incoming stampede. The toes of his bare feet flex as they cling to the slippery stone blocks with a feverish grip. Built like a spider monkey, Otto scurries up the slick wall, fueled by the hopeful payoff that awaits his climb. With a quick look back to the returning storm surge, he hastens his pace. He leaps into a gap in the hull of the ship just as the water blankets the island again.

Otto lets out a sigh of relief before taking a look within the contours of the ship. With the rush of the storm outside still ringing in his ears, he gazes around with wide eyes. He struggles to process just how the ship remains so sturdy. *This ship should be in shambles,* he thinks, as he continues his delicate plunder. The otherwise barren room has walls lined with wood-framed glass cabinets. Most of them are now shattered, holding what remains of blue and white porcelain pottery. Various cups and plates of all sizes rock back and forth with the churning blanket of water massaging the ship. In the corner, resides a wood-burning stove, its rod-iron chimney snaking into the ceiling above.

He hears a faint drip coming from behind him. Slowly turning around, he sees a leak coming from the center of the ceiling. The steady drips strike a platform holding an assortment of papers. Hoping to find some clues about the content of the ship, he makes his way to inspect the dampened parchment. On his way, he drags his fingers along the railing surrounding the platform. He holds his head cocked upward while surveying the remaining interior. Breaking his scattered concentration, he brushes his hand against something hanging from the railing. He unenthusiastically grabs hold of the object, shifting it around in his hand. As he studies his new find, he notices a dense, golden octagon-shaped box within his grasp. With a shrug of his shoulders, he pockets the find, suspecting it should be worth *something* and moves on to view the parchment.

The paper is smeared from water damage, but what Otto can make from the remains is it is a map but not one he is familiar with. The Great Storm, the source of the relentless tidal surges that plagues The Pearl, signifies the southern end point for the known world. No one has traveled past the turbulent waters and lived to tell the story. Yet right here, before his very eyes, is a map indicating a starting point from an unknown land mass beyond the storm. He hastily tries to make out more clues about the mysterious land but the water damage quickly takes its final toll. The remaining ink bleeds its secrets off the wrinkled parchment into a dark swirling pool at his feet. Riding high on a surge of adrenaline, Otto frantically scans the room in search of more parchment, hoping to find another map. However, his search is quickly cut short as he hears the sound of heavy footsteps lowering themselves from the room above.

Otto hesitates as he prepares for the unexpected guest, his mind racing. *I thought the crew would be dead from such an impact! Do I run? Do I fight?* Unable to bring himself to do anything at all, the gripping anticipation renders him frozen in place. Trapped by his own overloaded nervous system, he is left to stare at the quivering door in front of him. He slowly manages to wipe the beading sweat from his forehead right as the descending footsteps hasten their pace. The steps abruptly turn into a chaotic stampede. The mayhem erupting behind the quivering door sounds like an escaped zoo barreling down each preceding step. Otto cringes as the tumbling racket crashes into the door with a triumphant crescendo. The door bows under the impact, shaking free a breath of dust resting atop the frame. His ever-growing fear still renders him unable to make any physical movement. He stares hopelessly at the final barrier that separates him from his encroaching fate. A dangling oil lantern above the door sways back and forth. The light casts dancing shadows as the door handle starts to turn with an unnerving and rusty creak. With Otto's heart begging to jump out of his throat, the door finally swings open. The mysterious survivor takes a step onto the slick hardwood with thundering authority.

His bare feet slap the damp floor like a butcher throwing down fresh cuts of meat. He flexes his toes one after the other, as if to show off the tufts of hair that lines his knuckles like little toupees. As the man's presence fills the room, Otto feels a tidal wave of energy washing over him that harbors no other comparison than the Great Storm herself. He struggles to suck down a breath as the air becomes almost too dense to consume. Now standing directly under the swaying lantern, the man appears to be flickering in and out of the dark cast of shadows that surround his physical frame. As the light begins to slow its pendulum swing, it brings into focus the still motionless stranger. His exceedingly tall frame brings him dangerously close to knocking his head on the light above. His head harbors a well-crafted, wide-brimmed black hat that holds back his long, straight jet-black hair. He has his head tilted in a way to keep his face hidden in the lingering shadows. The simply dressed man wears tattered green overalls, held in place with a dark red shawl tied sloppily along his waist. The attire works well to complement the reddish-brown skin that resides beneath it. The shadows imposed by the lantern carve deep valleys and trenches into his frame, accenting his symmetrical muscular overture. The humble fabric that hangs off his body does little to distract the overwhelming physical perfection that makes up the stranger's composition. The man's flawless complexion leads Otto's mind to wonder if this person before him could even be human. Not a single scrape, scar, or blemish resides within the well-crafted nature of his physical form. Never have his eyes consumed a being constructed with such overwhelming grace and perfection.

With a twitch of movement coming from beneath the green overalls, Otto's heart skips a beat in anxious anticipation. The light in the room starts to dim as the man finally lifts his head, causing the wide brim of his hat to temporarily impede the light source above. A smile curves upon the newly revealed face of the stranger. His chiseled face has scattered pockets of unshaved stubble that scurries over his chin and up past his high cheekbones. Resting in the center of his face is a set of breathtaking bicolored eyes. His transcendent gaze gives off a bright flicker as if harboring its own light source. The man's left eye pops with a radiating deep and earthy green. It's a green that can be found hugging the flowing grassy fields of the most majestic of mountain prairies. His right eye shines bright with a piercing crystalline blue, tearing effortlessly into the recesses of Otto's soul. His unexpected appearance grabs Otto's full attention, dissolving all other sensory perception. Otto shakes his head but cannot find the energy or the will to look away from the tantalizing pull of the man's gaze. He finds his knees giving way into an abrupt plummet to the floor.

Unfazed by his collapse, Otto attempts to sit up, but he is sucked further into the deepening vastness of the stranger's eyes. Space and time start to bleed into variable fluid factors. Becoming more sensitive to the subtle energy that surrounds him, each audible heartbeat pounds with a force that seems to cause the very fabric of reality to rip at the seams. With his eyes still locked onto the stranger, Otto notices his own body start to melt away, merging with the permeable barriers of his environment. All remaining distinction between self and other starts to make their final convergence.

"I am ready," Otto hears himself say as he prepares to let go of his last worldly tethers. The man breaks his spell with a much-needed introduction.

"Hey!" Brahm cries. "Would you care for a cup of tea?" Otto is rocketed back into his body with crushing speed, completely blown away with his unexpected existential blast off. The room starts to spin as vomit looms eagerly at the back of his throat. "I'll take that as a yes!" Brahm exclaims as the color green quickly spreads onto Otto's face. The carefree ship captain rummages around his cabinetry, paying no mind to the broken glass exterior or the porcelain shards glistening atop the wood floor. His feet glide over the broken shards of glass and porcelain as if they were only grains of sand. He opens each cabinet inspecting them for an intact pair of teacups.

"Aha!" he exclaims. "I knew I would find at least two still together among all this mess! There is power in numbers, you know. Despite all the chaos, these two managed to survive," he says holding the cups triumphantly above his head, "and who knows how many more! Quite fascinating. It's good to hold onto hope despite the tough situations we find ourselves in." He walks over to the perfectly intact wood stove, and throws a few logs into the furnace. Satisfied with the amount, he pours some water in the kettle waiting upon the stovetop. The man reaches into the brim of his hat and finds a solidary match. He strikes it upon his pants before casting it onto the hungry logs. The tiny spark bursts into a proud flame and races to consume the dry wood. With his back still turned to Otto, he makes another attempt to spark conversation with his guest. "All right, with that warming up, I feel it's time to finally introduce myself!" He turns and says, "I'm—" but to his disappointment he is met with his stoic first mate, Beauregard Hum, standing in Otto's spot with his grizzly arms crossed.

"He ran out in the middle of your teacup allegory," he says bluntly as he shakes his head. "I think you may have came on a little strong."

"What are you talking about? All I did was offer the boy some tea; that's what any good host would have done!" Brahm exclaims with a hint of stubbornness.

"You know he ran off with the compass, one of the few things even *you* can't reproduce," Beau says as he walks towards his captain with heavy footsteps. The impact of his leather boots echo within the wooden walls of their navigation room. His black boots run about calf-high, the edges neatly rolled over a pair of dark brown corduroys. His weathered pants are held up by tight black suspenders. Under his straps rest a partially unbuttoned white cotton shirt with the sleeves rolled up, exposing his hairy forearms. Beau is a sturdy gentleman. He gazes out into the world with his stormy gray eyes. He manages to hide much of his aged and scarred features behind a thick red beard reaching down to his chest. Some gray hairs can now be spotted within the fiery fibers, but he wears them proudly. The moonlight glides through the crack in the ships hull and reflects off his glistening bald head. "So what are you going to do now?" he asks his pondering companion.

"Well," Brahm sighs as he steps away from his tea preparations, "I guess I'm just going to have to go get it!" he exclaims with a cheerful grin. "While I'm out retrieving such an *irreplaceable* tool for our journey, I guess that leaves you to work on the ship repairs!"

"Funny," scoffs Beau. "Even I should have seen that one coming. It's also funny how after riding that storm head first into this island, the only repairs that exist are in this room."

"That is funny! And during such a powerful storm! I thought we were goners. Who would have guessed?" he chuckles.

"Who would have guessed indeed," Beau says more to himself as his companion abruptly springs into action.

"All right, Beau! I got two cups of tea here so I guess this one is for you!" he says handing him a steaming cup. "As for me, I'll take mine on the road, don't want to waste any time hunting down our lost treasure!"

"Try and take this seriously; there really is no point to our trip without that compass," Beau calls out as Brahm heads towards the opening in the hull.

"Ha, if we always take things seriously, we run the risk of missing the point altogether!" he says with a playful wink.

"The point, huh?" Beau says, playing along with his captain's banter.

"Yep! The point of this journey is hardly just to reach the end of it." He takes a few calculated steps towards the crack in the hull before continuing.

"Don't you worry about me; you got your work cut out for you as well. Not going to get very far on a sailing trip with a hole in the boat, are we?" he adds cheekily. He turns and gives a final wave before jumping out through the crack into what's left of the storm. Beau watches his captain's departure with a furrowed brow on his face and a few choice words uttered under his breath. The steam from his teacup diverts his attention and he decides to take a sip. His eyes lighten in surprise.

"This is good tea," he exclaims. He laughs to himself as he makes his way back up the stairs. "Stubborn brat, you just never know who's actually looking out for who on this journey."

CHAPTER: 3

Superficial Celebrations

The Pearl inhabitants have grown very accustomed to the clockwork storm surges as well as the persistent dark skies that linger in their wake. Even on a surge-free day, it is to be expected to have the wide gamut of gray tones painted as the familiar backdrop. The Pearl sits as the closest known habitable island to the Great Storm. Although, habitable might be debatable depending on who you ask. The rough conditions render life on The Pearl a daily struggle.

The "island" wasn't always considered such. Back before the Great Flood, it existed as part of a fertile land accompanied by a towering mountain range. Sometime during that era, what some call Eden, a great storm emerged at sea. Years passed and the storm remained fixed in a single location, progressively growing in size, and with it came monumental environmental shifts the whole world was powerless to ignore. Wind patterns changed, ocean currents shifted, temperatures climbed, and the sea levels rose. Any chance of survival resided in relocating to higher ground. The higher the better, for the water just kept rising until the land became only freckles on the planetary blue face. Even though the size of the storm eventually plateaued, its existence has remained without pause for as long as memory holds. The survivors of The Pearl were considered some of the lucky ones. Without high ground to escape to, most civilizations were erased from existence. Those who survived have carried on into the current time. It has become an era considered by many as Post Eden (P.E.).

There are many stories that account the storm's existence, its purpose, and its origin. However, they all remain entrapped by the confines of myth and fable. Many of which have transpired into circulating religious groups that feel the storm has come for divine judgment. Truth is, no one knows for sure how or why that storm emerged from the sea and definitely not how it has remained. With all the different creation tales floating around, only one detail remains consistent: her name, Babel. Babel's reign on the world has forced most to live a life focused on survival. It's hard to think about what life was like before the storm, but it's clear the highest worldly peaks were not initially designed for mass inhabitation. Most survivors don't have the luxury to ponder the existence of Babel in their constant struggle to tame the unforgiving lands that remain.

There are a few circulating souls who refuse to be content with the incomplete folklore of their planet's most powerful inhabitant. Some manage to dedicate their lives to uncovering the mysteries that lie buried in the waters and forgotten times. These people are referred to as Shakers. Traveling from one speck of land to the next, their search for truth intertwines with many who are trying to put the past out of mind. For others, they bring fresh news from foreign lands; to most, they shake up undesired and repressed emotions. Regardless of their reception, it will be a monumental day if any one of them manages to uncover the nature of their sunken world. Today may very well be regarded as a transcendent shift towards uncovering that truth, but that is still to be determined. Either way, the inhabitants of The Pearl just received a new arrival that is about to shake up their storm-polished land like never before.

∞

Brahm falls swiftly from the twenty-foot perch of his wall-locked ship. He has one hand keeping his hat secure while the other holds close attention to his steeping tea. The calloused pallets of his bare feet elegantly kiss the cold morning stone as he makes his first contact with the foreign land. He stays crouched, making sure his impact doesn't spill any of his precious drink. A lingering raindrop from the departing storm falls into his tea, evaporating with a faint burst of steam.

The controlled impact of his landing has sent subtle shockwaves surging through the deep layers of the once proud mountain peak. Brahm closes his eyes and studies the vibrations flooding through the first piece of land he has seen since leaving home. The shockwaves flow all the way to the flooded bedrock below before bouncing back and returning to the surface. The mysterious ship captain reads the returning waves as if accustomed to the subtleties of sonar. He falls to one knee as he becomes overwhelmed from the disheartening stories the coursing vibrations bring back. He takes the hand that had secured his hat and places it gently onto the whispering cobblestones at his feet.

He listens to the stony streets as they sparkle with a specific sense of purity. A purity that comes from being rigorously washed clean, cleansed of the many layers of the past. A cleansing that also keeps many roots from taking hold of the harsh rock. The stones shine bright like the bleached bones of a freshly picked carcass. The land beats with a faint and distant heart, as if all that was once grand and noble has also been washed clean. The pure and polished stone gives a welcoming first glance, but as Brahm's feet tread upon the stone, a sense of hollowness starts to take hold. The sensation causes his soul to shrivel up and gasp for air, searching desperately for a sense of life and vigor.

"Such sadness within this land. You haven't given up, have you? Aye, don't let this water change who you are!" he says as if speaking directly to the island. "No. There is still a flicker of life left in you…"

A growing sense of warmth upon the right side of his face draws his attention towards the coast. He looks over to where the mountainous terrain fades into the sea. The rocky soil struggles to form the rough contours of a makeshift beach. Large boulders parade around the coastline like the outlines of an abandoned quarry. Aesthetically, the island's exterior definitely does not resonate with the sight of a romantic getaway. He sees the waves lapping the shores feverishly, but surprisingly, no monster swell looms in the distant horizon. He stands and lifts a hand to the sky feeling only a few lingering drops of rain. Noticing the wind transitioning to a delicate eastward breeze, the ship captain's attention is drawn to the peeking rays of the rising sun. The breeze brings with it a fluttering pack of birds that spring forth from a nearby elephant tree. One of the chipper birds soars into the morning sunrays before it lands without introduction on the captain's welcoming shoulder. Together they bask in the warm light that cuts through the thick cloudy veil. They watch as the clouds dismal hold on the sky slowly dissolves from the power of the light. The remaining songbirds nestle their way out of the elephant tree trunk and pay homage to the welcomed daybreak with their whimsical chirps.

"Absolutely beautiful," Brahm remarks as he watches the sky dance boldly with swirling hues of pink and orange against the fading gray. He takes a sip of his tea and stares farther out to see the emerging blue sky etching its way into focus. "I guess this means the storm is over for now!" he says with glee and starts his casual stroll down the hollow streets. Despite the intoxicating rays of the rising sun, he holds tenderly to the immense sorrow and emptiness he still feels emanating from each step along the rocky path.

Steam from the evaporating puddles quickly envelops much of the view in a wispy fog. Fortified stone buildings line the streets, resembling the backs of giant turtle shells. They hug the curb, stacked one atop another as they populate the steep hill Brahm travels. Despite the dense fog, it's still hard to find any lingering memory of the recent storm surge. The streets are washed clean and barren, with no sign of anything out of place. Squat chimneys poke out of the turtle shell buildings that start to pump smoke from the morning fires burning from within. The storm survivors clack open their fortified shutters, letting in the growing rays of light. Brahm smiles as he watches the island wake from its stormy slumber. As he continues his way down the stony street, he hears a strange, sinister voice hitching a ride within the flowing wind:

"…Consider yourself lucky."

What in the world? Whose voice was that? He glances from side to side but sees not a soul in sight. His attention eventually wavers back to his cobbled path. He watches it snake up the mountainous valley like a retired riverbed. Its final destination appears to be a giant archway at the top, but what lies past it is hidden from his current vantage point. His eyes continue to wander, easily forgetting what he was originally searching for. His gaze settles upon a peculiar metallic structure resting at the top of the mountain peak. The enormous size alone sets it apart from the uniform turtle dwellings he has seen so far. As the captain squints his eye to bring the monumental structure closer into view, the winds rustle again with a peculiar warning:

"It's time you remember why you are here."

"Who are you?!" the captain calls into the wind, quickly remembering what he was searching for so vigorously. "And what are you even talking about?" Before the winds could return with another message, chaos spontaneously erupts into the whispering streets. All hope for an answer is replaced with frantic singing that pours from the windows of the cheerful inhabitants.

"Celebrate! Celebrate! This day-y-y-y-y! Hey! Hey! The sun has finally come! Time for Babel to be done!" chant the once quiet and barren city streets. The bubbling energy from within the turtle dwellings finally explodes with a festive bombardment. People for as far as the eye can see come pouring frantically out of their homes in blissful jubilation. Colorful banners and flags hang in their hands and fly out the windows. Engraved on each flag appears to be lists of prayers to permeate the day. They flow in the wind as exuberant song and dance radiates from the Pearlites below. Hand in hand the members of The Pearl hold their neighbors as they start their dance towards the giant archway. Brahm cannot stand idol in the rambunctious crowd for much longer, as he, too, is swept into the stream of chaos.

What is the meaning behind all this excessive expression? he ponders as he is dragged along in the current of people. *This is so strange; their energy, their faces… is this a joke? They appear as hollow as the rocks they dance upon!*

An old, pale, and skinny gentleman with teeth long departed from his gums, grabs the captain's arm and gleefully pulls him along with the crowd. The crowded streets are now shoulder to shoulder, making it almost impossible to hold tight to a cup of tea. In a matter of seconds, the captain's tea takes a leap from its porcelain prison after an unexpected shoulder-check from a dancing bystander. Brahm watches his beverage floating in mid-air, still congealed and wiggling in sync with the vibrant crowd. The dancing blob quickly makes its way towards the unsuspecting head of another. Brahm takes a daring leap forward and secures the defiant drink back into its respected container. He spins around and takes a final gulp ensuring his drink is locked safely away in his bodily vessel. The crowd erupts in cheer as they mistake his antics for a blissful celebration for the still unknown call to the streets. There is no time to take a bow, as the toothless old man grabs ahold of Brahm's arm once again and marches him further down the dancing streets.

Music can now be heard coming from the other side of the archway, yet the full sound remains muffled by the stampeding and chanting herds of people. The captain is immediately drawn to the sonic vibrations. He turns an ear to the sound in hopes to pick out the hum of an intoxicating rhythm. Despite its obscure and foreign nature, it still finds a way to resonate with an odd flavor of familiarity. As Brahm continues his search for the source of music, he realizes not everyone is making their way out of their homes. Those who remain indoors open their windows and begin showering the crowd with handfuls of colorful dust. The powdered color not only brings superficial complexion to the Pearlites but to the surrounding pale stones they tread upon. With exuberant cheers, those in the streets become transmuted into a bobbing river of vibrant wild flowers. As Brahm approaches the entrance to the Plaza, it is now his turn to grab hold of the toothless old man. As the people continue to pour around them, the old man looks to Brahm for an explanation. At first he can't answer the silent inquiry. His attention is still drifting elsewhere. Brahm wipes the colorful swirls of dust from his eyes and abruptly hands his teacup to an unsuspecting bystander. Slowly, Brahm lowers his head and beckons the old man to look out into the chaos with him and fully take in all that is before them.

The archway has opened into a grand city plaza, flooding with people from every adjacent street. Each one is brightly colored with the showering dust flying in abundance. Brahm catches a name etched into the passing stone archway: Portala Plaza. The sun continues its climb into the sky, banishing the last storm cloud from view. In the center of the plaza, positioned well above the growing crowd of people, is an impressive stone stage carved into the shape of an open clamshell. The Clam Stage has been hastily painted bright colors like the surrounding Pearlites. It is further adorned with flapping multi-colored prayer flags strung along the angled stone ceiling. A quartet of musicians dance gleefully within the contours of the mollusk-inspired dwelling. They stand center stage as if representing the personified pearls of the mighty clam. Their energy pours out into the crowd, infecting all those around them with their invigorating sonic expression. Even the morning carrier pigeons feel the need to pause their migratory mail flight to bob a beak to the intoxicating sounds. A flickering flame rests in the heart of The Clam Stage, causing the projected shadows of the musicians to dance along with them on the roof of the stage.

Their shadows dwarf their physical form, dancing unrestricted, powered by the burning light. The musicians' faces pour with sweat as they feverously forge their fingers into their respected instruments. They pluck and strum, percuss and chime with riveting vigor, blurring the lines between human and instrument. Brahm is drawn into the hypnotic performance. He fixates on their ability to play in perfect harmony. It's as if they are all extensions of the same musical body. He can feel them weaving the sounds of their souls into the collective web of music. The tantalizing vibrations ensnare the surrounding crowd, trapping them within the blissful web of musical pleasure. The pulsating beat that holds the harmony together grips Brahm by the chest. He begins to notice his heart pounding along with the beat from the drum. In no time at all, the rhythms of the stage and his heart beat as one.

Why does this sound so familiar? he thinks to himself, oblivious to everything else. *I know I've never heard this song before… so why does it feel like I… I… am… home?* The sonic vibrations dive deep into his core, flowing effortlessly in-between the particles that dictate his physical form. He starts to lose himself in the moment, drifting with the music, breathing with the sonic melody and at times wondering if he has become one with the music. As the lyrical harmonies start to overlay the symphonic groundwork, he finds himself tangled up in an even deeper state of trance.

Times of past,
Moments of new…
All comprise what is you!
Woven in web,
A path to be lead…
Tangled in what is alive,
What is… dead!"

On the surface appears to be two,
Look deeper to see what is true…
One is the all and all is the one.
Know this and be the light of the sun,
Deny this and you will never be done! Hey!"

And the winds of the mind just keep whirling and twirling… Hey!
Open your eye and hear what we say!
Bring forth the sun that will dawn a new day!

This is more than just a sound. This is… a gift… a magical space… a portal to a communal sanctuary! He burrows into that thought as the music compels the urge to dance again. Relishing in the emptiness of his mind and openness to being, he welcomes yet another transitory thought. *It's as if they have found a way through music to weave a bridge from this world to the other side! One of pure vibrational solitude! Oh, how splendid! I hope they never stop playing!* His thoughts wisp away again as he gazes out to the surrounding crowd. He watches as their faces become washed with the blissful waves of the intoxicating tunes.

Brahm shifts his attention to look into the eyes of the feverous musicians, their attention intently locked onto their instruments. Their fingers glide over their respected strings and drums, flowing like the lapping waves of the churning tides. The look of complete concentration and focus permeate their vessels. *Have they tasted the fruits of the celestial planes? Is that even possible? Oh my, I must know!* Overwhelmed with joy and curiosity, Brahm finally turns to the old man and begs for a tangible explanation.

"You must tell me! What *is* all of this?" Brahm asks in complete awe.

"You must not be from anywhere around here!" exclaims the old man with a toothless grin. "It's the Fantuzzi celebration! Come buy me a drink, stranger, and I'll tell ya' all about it!"

Brahm and the old man stumble into the nearest pub and are bombarded with chaotic jubilation. They notice just as many people are rushing in for a drink as there are rushing back out to the festivities. Two stools abruptly become vacant at the bar and beckon the gentlemen to take their spots.

"Two 'Great-Spirits!'" the old man calls while slamming his hand playfully on the counter.

"What's that?" Brahm asks as the bartender solemnly acknowledges their order.

"Oh man, it's only the finest brew around! Now, granted, I've lived my whole life in the South Sea, but they say the secret to a perfect brew is the water! Aye, and it's no secret The Pearl has the purest water around."

"What makes you say that?"

"All right," the old man says with a deep sigh. He hesitates, glancing to the bartender returning with their drinks. After taking a big swig of his Great Spirit, he finally proceeds with his explanation. "So, if you don't know what the Fantuzzi is, I can almost guarantee you don't know what that giant metal flower is at the top of the mountain, eh?" Brahm just smiles and nods, taking his first sip of the embellished beverage. "That up there is the Lotus, the pride of the Pearl." The old man slams his drink back down on the counter for dramatic effect. "It's because of 'er we have good water to drink. It's because of 'er we have something worth living for around here! Beautiful. And Mune…" he says, trailing off in thought. "Uggh, ya' know, things weren't looking good around here for a while."

"Yeah?" Brahm asks as he can feel the old man's heart grow heavy. With a reluctant sigh, the old man continues.

"We were once ruled by these religious nut-bags who had us living off nothin' but the charity of our neighboring folk. They thought they were something else, with their 'planet powers' to talk to Babel; bunch of nonsense! Bunch of heretics is what they were! They had us believing we were repenting for our… past sins or somethin' like that. Like we were paying off a debt to Babel! It was pure sufferin', I tell ya, bunch of rubbish. Indebted to a storm? Ha! And to think we believed them! That's no matter, just when we all came to our senses and decided to rebel, the answer to our prayers came to us. A man named Mune was sent from Wisteria to bring peace. Oh, he did so and then some! He's the one who sent those loons where they belonged and helped us build that beauty! It sits at the top of our island and filters the waves of seawater into the freshest drinking water around! And not just us! Everyone around here benefits from 'er!

Those farmlands on Wahaka? Would be nothin' without the Pearl's high peaks and that mighty flower. So now we raise a drink to 'er and the man who helped us build 'er! He really has been the source of our salvation in all this mess." The old man trails off as he stares pensively into his diminishing spirit.

Brahm sits back and sips on his spirit as he soaks in the old mans story. "Sounds like quite the blessing to have a flower like that able to bloom in such a tough environment. She lives up to her name. So, is that what this Fantuzzi festival is all about?"

"Mostly," scoffs the old man as his second drink is sent sliding down into his hand. "I guess there was more to this festival back in the day, but nobody cares about that anymore. The light of the sun makes us think of the light of our savior, Lord Mune. He promised us there was more than enough work to go around. That's when he started that pipeline project of his, ya' know, connecting our water straight to Wahaka." He drifts off again with depressive disconnect. Brahm realizes this is no longer the time to try and lighten the mood. "So what happened?" Brahm asks, hoping to continue the tale of shifting tides.

"Lord Mune sold you all out," calls a voice along the bar. The two men shift their focus to a woman sitting at the end who is looking up from her drink. She pauses and peers intently at the two men before continuing her interjection. She prolongs her hesitation as if to first analyze her newly acquired audience. Brahm takes this time to study her as well. She sits with outstanding posture. Her long brown hair flows effortlessly past her shoulders, ending with a natural curly bounce. The beige cloak she wears covers most of her olive skin, accentuating her face all the further. Her hands rest on the bar, smooth but strong, bearing a single gold ring on her left index finger harboring an intricate crest. The gold insignia encompasses a curled dragon in-between two olive branches. A circle is carved above the dragon and an egg carved below. The meaning behind such a symbol falls flat in the minds of Brahm and the old man.

The woman shifts her position, locking eyes with Brahm. She entangles her piercing yellow eyes with his own. It's as if she is studying his very soul. Her face is rounded with some freckles sprinkled over her high cheekbones. The gravity of the bar shifts noticeably as this woman commands an overwhelming presence. Neither the old man nor Brahm dare speak before the woman finishes her analysis. Her face gives no indication of any emotional registry until her voice finally releases the tension.

"He is using you all for nothing more than slave labor, old timer," she says, now looking at the toothless man. "He's using you then losing you when you become too weak to work. Is that what happened to you, old man?"

"Don't you talk bad about Lord Mune!" the man fires back with a hiccup. "It's not his fault we are deprived for work! That pipeline is the only work still around here, and at least he gave us that! I blame those blasted Seers still running around, undermining all his great actions to bring prosperity to this land again! I thank God he is here! Anything is better than being led by those Bakuwan! Maybe we need the Wardens to return and sweep the streets once again!" The old man's face flashes various shades of red as he pants heavily from his resurfacing emotions. He desperately reaches out for what's left of his drink.

"I, of course, wouldn't dare talk poorly of Mune," the woman proclaims with a slight flavor of sarcasm. "I only choose to remember the true essence of Fantuzzi. Let us forego our present suffering for a day, old man; we could all use a reminder of what hope feels like." She shifts her attention again to Brahm. "Isn't that what this old man dragged you in here to do, stranger? Or are you content with these tangential-filled tales of the past?" Brahm stares at her for a moment, excitement beaming from his eyes. He senses a playful invitation from her inflection. The woman takes his pause as a signal to continue her monologue, "I'm headed to the docks, but I can fill you in on the true meaning of this festival along the way if you like."

"It would be an honor," Brahm says playfully, placing his empty glass on the counter. The woman smiles and throws a few coins onto the counter. She nods towards the door. The captain studies her exchange of goods before following suit. At first, he pulls out two unsuspecting stones, rough and ordinary. The old man glances down with a puzzled look on his face. He watches as the curious stranger flicks his wrist, and in a flash transmutes what were once two stones into two identical coins like the ones the woman placed on the bar. Brahm gives the old man a wink before tossing the newly conjured currency onto the bar counter. He tilts his hat to the puzzled bartender, pleased to get no resistance from his offerings. He then turns to thank the wide-eyed old man for his time. Brahm pulls out another conjured coin from his pocket and tells his elderly acquaintance to enjoy himself for a little longer.

"I'm Sophia," the woman says as they make their way to the exit.

"Brahm," he replies as he pushes open the door, flooding the tavern with rays of light from the rising sun.

CHAPTER: 4

A Walk to Remember

"So, you think you can tell a story better than that old man?" Brahm taunts as they walk freely back into the illuminating rays of the sun. The crowd continues to shift from the bars to the stage, and back again. The flow of people starts to feel like a riptide of indulgence. Brahm playfully dismisses the outward commotion and focuses back to the trench-coated woman beside him. "You know, 'cause I think he was really getting somewhere with that gloom and doom deal he was on."

"You're more than welcome to go back and get the rest of his depressing story if you like, but it's a story you will hear any day of the year. *Years* sometimes. I just figured you would like to bask in the sun before the darkness returns," Sophia cryptically replies.

Back out in front of the Clam Stage, the Fantuzzi celebration has settled into a more organized orchestration. The rambunctious crowds now surround the center stage in layers of evenly distributed rings. They resemble a human bullseye targeting a desired state of being. They sway back and forth, stomp their feet, and chant along with the musicians in resonating cadence. The energy is palpable and Brahm is pleased with his decision to be brought back into the light.

"You got me," he admits. "This story already seems to be a lot more colorful. However, you and that old man both left me at quite the cliffhanger. C'mon and tell me what this Fantuzzi thing is all about."

"With pleasure," Sophia smiles. "The Fantuzzi goes all the way back to the original leaders of The Pearl, the Seers. Believing the selfish actions of the old world triggered the great flood, they ruled with the intention to bring about peace and harmony. They even held the power to communicate with the forces of nature and Babel herself. For generations the Seers protected this land and the surrounding islands through the gift of clairvoyance. Preaching a life of repentance, they spoke of a time when Babel would come to an end if humanity were to recognize the error of their ways. Only then would the gray skies fade into the sun forever. It was a prophecy that resurfaces with each sunny day. These sunny days don't happen very often, that's why we celebrate. You never know if a day like this will be the foretold day of prophecy. No harm in hope is there?" she says with a solemn smile. Brahm stares at her quizzical expression but decides not to interrupt.

"Despite the eventual disregard of the old Seer ways, this festival resonates with such hope the people here can't seem to let it go. Most don't even remember why they celebrate, but the desire for hope still lingers on some level in their hearts. It keeps the will to survive alive. However, survival is not the only thing that motivates the soul, right? It's the desire to thrive that really gets people moving." She looks to Brahm who nods in agreement. With that notion, she pauses, lifting her gaze towards the visiting sun.

For a moment, she loses herself in the music and celestial warmth that surrounds them. She quickly drifts back to continue her tale. "No one truly knows much about Babel and maybe it's the strong cling to hope that inspires the stories that help us move forward. A Great Seer Sage by the name of Fantuzzi was the man credited for telling the Pearlites his vision. A story those on The Pearl hold closest to their hearts, but over time, the true message got lost within the plea for Babel's mercy. Fantuzzi said long ago a man was born from fire and Babel was created to shield his light from the rest of the world. The world is to remain in darkness until we are ready to face the light Babel protects us from. This story has firm roots here because I don't think anywhere else suffers as much direct punishment from the storm as we do. Every once in a great while, the island is granted a brief reprieve and we get a glimpse of the distant sun. It is on these days we celebrate. The festivities have now been perverted into a patronage honoring the leader of this rock. Before him, this was a time when we came together to celebrate the light. We celebrate Fantuzzi, and most of all, we pray this may be the day we are ready to face the hidden fire."

"That was quite the story. No wonder everyone is so excited!" Brahm points out. "Do you believe it? The prophecy?"

"Believe it?" Sophia is taken aback by his question but quickly recovers. "I believe in hope. I believe it is the hope imbued in this festival that inspires our people to stay alive. With so much pain and suffering from living here, I believe without that story to hold onto, this place would return to a lifeless sea stone." Sophia's last statement lingers with the sting of sinking silence. Her gaze shifts briefly to the stones beneath her feet as she realizes the mood has taken a solemn dive. "I also believe I am becoming no better than that old man back there. No wonder no one really talks during Fantuzzi," she says with a half-curved smile.

"What do you mean?"

"This is the time everyone waits for a brief moment to be able to forget all the misery that comes with living on this rock. I could feel his hollow sorrow seeping back into his story and I just couldn't take it. I felt like he was breaking the rules, you know? Like he should have known you just don't talk about your pain today or else it will break this spell we all put ourselves under. I guess I'm realizing now how fragile that spell really is, and how desperately we all cling to it." She pauses to soak in the light breeze sweeping its way through the alleyway they entered. Glancing back at Brahm, she raises her finger to her ear and tucks a flowing lock of hair behind it. "It may be a spell, a false hope even, but even so it is still a beautiful day, no?" she says with a big smile. Brahm takes a moment to register Sophia's attempt to salvage what is left of her hold on the festive spell. He ponders his next question carefully, unsure as to how to direct his lingering inquiry. As if being able to read Brahm's thoughts, Sophia attempts to add some relief to his pondering mind.

"Don't worry," she says, "this place won't be able to hold its secrets for much longer. They're not buried very deep. Let's try and enjoy what escape from reality we are allowed while the skies remain clear. You'll get the answers you seek soon enough." With that being said, Sophia turns to Brahm. "This is where we part for now," she says abruptly. "I need to return to the docks and assist those still coming in from the neighboring islands to celebrate Fantuzzi. You really should head back and enjoy what is left of the festival. Think of it like a snapshot of what this place was like before the Great Storm."

"I think I will, and I'll try my best not to ask any more prying questions; would hate to break any more spells," he adds with a smile, staring into her bright yellow eyes. "It was very nice to have met you. I hope our paths cross again." Sophia acknowledges his wish with a silent bow of her head, careful not to break eye contact before turning around towards the docks.

CHAPTER: 5

Breaking the Spell

The sound of the music resonates with more clarity as Brahm makes his way back to the festival center. He travels with a slight spring in his step that was absent prior to his walk with Sophia. He is quickly engulfed back into the swirling mob of people who surround the center stage. Their numbers and intoxication levels have grown as they dance in sloppy, yet unified fashion. They are completely at the mercy of the rhythmic beats, letting go of their past and pain with each cycle around the stage.

Brahm looks to the performers and senses the struggle they display with their exhausting faces and the ferocity at which they continue to play. They are the fans to the rhythmic flame, and they move as if they know it. If it was to ever go out, so, too, would the spirit of the Fantuzzi. No one is talking; the tone of the music has assumed its place as the dominant gravitational force, and all the participants bow to its mystical trance. Further and further, the residents of The Pearl are drawn into the fruitful call to forget themselves and become one with the music. All seem to hear the call, except for a solitary voice coming from just outside the dance circle. Brahm turns his attention towards the voice and hears a young woman pleading with her mother.

"Mom! Let me go! I need to at least try!" the voice cries.

"No honey, you can't! You know what happened to your father and your brother, I can't risk that happening to you!"

"What would they have done in this situation? Would they have just let all these people die? I just can't live like this anymore, not now of all times!"

Those last words must have been enough to loosen the grip of the mother. Brahm watches as someone runs through the current of people towards The Clam Stage. A young woman sprints down the cobblestones, her feverish pace causes her long brown hair to flow behind her in chaotic waves. Her dark hair contrasts her pale skin that is wrapped up in a tattered and poorly fitted dress. Her vibrancy and physical beauty easily shine from underneath the layers of rags hanging off her matured figure. As she nears the thicker grouping of people crowding the stage, she struggles to push aside the hive-minded Pearlites with her petite frame.

Though slowing her down, it does not diminish her determination in the slightest. Her cries are unheard as she burrows her way closer to the festival epicenter. Her determination captures Brahm's attention. She manages to carve a path within the multitude of oblivious people with a strength fit for one carrying a heavy burden. She makes it all the way to the edge of the stage before finally being halted.

∞

"And where do you think you are going?" barks one of the guards who surrounds the stage perimeter.

"I don't have time for this!" she says as she pushes her rustled hair out of her face. Her determined blue eyes shine bright as she stares down the guard. The man takes a step back as he is overwhelmed by her presence. He shakes his head and quickly rids himself from his momentary blunder.

"You have to let me on stage!" the girl continues as she takes advantage of the guard's pause. "You have to let me make an announcement! We are in grave danger!"

"Really?" hums the guard, now in full grasp of his earlier composure. He mockingly strokes his mustache and licks his lips with impure intentions. "Now, I have strict orders from the top to make sure no one disturbs this ceremony. Why such a blasphemous pagan holiday is still played out here is a mystery to me, but! Orders are orders. So, what could you possibly have to say that would be worth screeching this *prized* celebration to a halt?" he asks with thick amusement and sarcasm. He gives the girl an accosting look up and down as he impatiently awaits her answer. "By the looks of things, you could use a bath rather than an audience! Such a shame a beauty like you is left to rot in the slums. Maybe you could come with me, and I could help… clean you up." The girl ignores the man's hedonistic comment while giving her purpose one last mental run-through.

"The storm. The storm is on its way back!" Her words drive the guards to look to one another with disgust flooding their facial expressions. "I know we are used to these sunny days signifying an end to our suffering. I also know our last grace period lasted multiple days, but not this time. This time our parade into false hope will get us killed if everyone is not warned! One of Babel's storm surges is already on its way back. If it were to hit us during our celebration, we will all be washed clean off this island. Trust me! It's coming back today! I saw it! Please! Let me warn everyone!" Her words linger for a moment before the guard chimes back in.

"Saw it, you say? Hmm… that's very interesting. Very interesting," the guard says while gazing up at the clear sky and then to the man on his left. "Hey Claude, did you hear that? This girl says she 'saw' Babel coming back today."

"That is pretty interesting," Claude says as he leans his head into the conversation. His snarling brown eyes hone in on the girl in question. He squats down to look the girl in the eye and continues his conversation with his fellow guard. "You know, it reminds me of that 'Seer' problem we had not too long ago." His protruding grin hikes his cheeks so high they begin to impede his eyesight. The joy resonating from his vessel is enough to bring the young woman to a fit of nausea. "Those Bakuwan abominations…" Claude continues, "who subjected this island with stories and hope that were grounded in nothing but fanciful dreams and lies! When we called the Wardens in to clean it up, I thought we got them all. Looks like we might have missed some. How disgusting. What do you think, girl? Think we need to call them back and tell them we missed one?" Claude says with an evil grin growing on his face.

The two guards start to close the gap, their intentions very clear.

"Such a shame, boss. She has so much… potential," the other guard says. The girl tries to back up, but the swaying crowd she aims to protect serves only as a barrier to her escape. Unwilling to get captured without a fight, she makes a last-ditch effort for the stage and leaps with all her might. She soars through the air with the stage just fingertips away. Just as she is about to make it, a strong hand interjects her plan and rips her away from her goal. She swings her fists and strikes feverously at the head of her captor. To her surprise, she turns around to see the head she attacks is attached to a strange, dark haired man in green overalls.

"There you are, dear!" Brahm exclaims as he throws the girl effortlessly over his shoulder. "Are you bothering these good-natured gentlemen about your conversations with nature again? I thought we talked about this!" He turns to the guards as he makes his way through the crowd.

"What the—" A guard mutters.

"So sorry, gentleman," Brahm says while strategically interrupting the guards train of thought. "She's been so obsessed with talking to the water lately! Her mother and I tell her time and time again, 'cut that out or else it might just talk back one day!' Kids these days, am I right? Just old enough to rebel, too young to think of the consequences," Brahm says with a playful shrug. "Sorry to have disturbed you, we will be on our way now."

"Where did he come from?" yells Claude as he looks to his fellow guards and then back to Brahm. "Hey! You! Get back here!" he says waving his glistening spear. The lack of blemishes on the polished blade brings to question the amount of combat the weapon has ever seen. However, the opportunity to show off its fighting capability disappears just as quickly as it had first appeared. Brahm's giant frame vanishes in the crowd like smoke right before the guard's rage-filled eyes, taking the girl with him.

∞

"Get a message out to Mune immediately," Claude says heavily, "we are definitely going to need the Wardens."

"But how?" responds his subordinate. "He's on his way to the Fantuzzi Feast! Anyone wanting to keep their head wouldn't dare interrupt that!"

"That's why I'm sending you, moron! Figure it out!" Claude bellows as he stares intently at Brahm's fading contour.

∞

"Left, right, left again, now dodge! Weave and spin!" Brahm sings as he makes his way out from the dancing crowds. He's resorted to making up a dance of his own to avoid disrupting the collective groove.

"Let me go! Let me go, I said!" demands the girl from atop his shoulder perch.

"Hold on, almost there," Brahm says as he approaches the spot where he last heard the girl's mother.

"Raja!" comes a familiar cry from one of the upcoming alleyways. Satisfied, Brahm finally releases the reluctant captive. Her mother immediately runs to embrace her. "You fool!" she cries in-between sobs. "I thought for sure I was going to lose you too."

"You worry too much, mother! I had everything under control until *this* guy came along." The girl looks over to Brahm with a roll of her eyes. "Who are you anyway?" she asks with her hands mounting snugly atop her hips.

"Brahm," the captain says cheerfully.

"That was rhetorical!" Raja screams back. "And what right do you have to judge me! What was it you said… 'just old enough to rebel, too young to know the consequence?' How dare you!" she says, marching towards the oversized Brahm and jabbing her outstretched finger into his rock-hard abdomen.

"It was 'think of the consequences,'" Brahm corrects. "I'm sure you *knew* the consequence, I only meant that you didn't—"

"Enough! It is you and your act of ignorance that shows just how unaware *you* are of the consequences of *your* actions! Damn Shakers, you all come around just to mess things up for everyone actually trying to make this world a better place. Just get out of here and go back to where you came from while you still can!" The girl retracts her finger and stands with a furrowed brow. Her crystal-blue eyes swim with anger and a flicker of sadness. Her mother looks over to Brahm with both gratitude and wonder swimming in her equally crystalline-blue eyes.

Brahm takes a moment to soak in the tense silence that quivers around Raja's fury. With a respectful smile, Brahm tips his hat to the pair of women and turns to carry on his way. Raja's mother watches the man take only a few steps into the distance before feeling the need to call out to him.

"Wait!" she cries, "Brahm, was it?" Her words are enough to stop Brahm in his brief retreat.

"Mother," Raja screams, "what do you think you are doing?"

"Thanking this man," the woman says as she takes a step towards Brahm. Feeling the call for connection, Brahm turns to the woman with a warm smile.

"My name is Mufida," the woman says. "Please accept my gratitude for saving my daughter. Times have been hard for both of us lately, I can understand her desire to get involved with our current affairs, but her methods continue to be… rash."

"How dare you!" Raja says with a continued flame of fury igniting each word she speaks. "You understand nothing about what I do or why I do it! If you did, then you would join me! Have you truly forgotten your heritage, or do you just conveniently choose to dismiss it?"

"That's enough!" her mother retorts. "I have seen more of this land and this world than you ever have. And with that comes the ability to discern my actions. There is and will always be acts of injustice in this world! The answer is not to meet such injustice with brute force. Sometimes you must act by not acting!"

"Spoken like the chumps who let this land fall to the hands of Wisteria." Brahm can feel the heat of passion and rage coming from Raja's words. He chooses to lightly engage the hostile youth.

"Getting a little tense around here, isn't it?" he jests, despite the obvious dismissal of his presence. "Right. Well, I'm sorry to have gotten involved in something that does not concern me. I'll leave you to your solitary revolution if you wish. Just know, I was rooting for you," he says while turning his back to fulfill the previous request of his absence. "I thought it was great you didn't let those guards deter you from saying what you needed to say. I'm honestly not quite sure who these 'Warden' characters are, but they didn't make it sound like they were going to let you give your speech without a fight." He gives a lackadaisical wave while continuing his departure.

"The Wardens?!" cries Mufida, the emotional spike is enough to stop Brahm again in his tracks. "You didn't… Here I was blissfully assuming this man stopped you before you truly took things too far. Raja, how could you?! After everything this island has already gone through, how could you go and do something so careless!?" Tears pour out of Raja's eyes as her mother's words start to crack her defiant exterior.

"I…I… I can handle the consequence, mother! It is a necessary risk! If I don't warn everyone about what is to happen today, there won't be anybody left for the Wardens to prosecute!"

"Then what, Raja!? So you save the day only to pave the way for another massacre like before? What do you think you will accomplish by going up against the forces of God? Will you have done any good or just brought on more suffering? Think of all the Seers here still trying to hold on to what life they have been spared!"

"Wisteria hails from no God of mine!" Raja stammers, struggling to hold on to her fighting spirit. However, her emotional wall starts to suffer some damage. "I just thought… I just thought the risk of being caught was worth warning everyone! I-I didn't think about all the other Seers still in hiding! Oh God, what have I done?!" Raja's hands jump onto her face as she tries to bury herself. Her knees begin to shake under the weight of her realization. "How can I fix this?" she cries.

"Maybe I can help," Brahm offers as he abruptly sits himself down on the cobblestones. A soft breeze blows through his long black hair as he sits in deep contemplation. His hat dangles along the rope secured around his neck. The gravity of his concentration becomes palpable. "So who are these Warden characters?" he asks as he leans his torso to reflect a perfect forty-five degree angle with the ground. The women take a minute to digest their guest's odd behavior before responding.

"Brahm, was it?" Mufida mumbles with soft concern. "Are you seriously asking who the Wardens are?" "I am! They sound pretty gnarly."

"To make such jokes must mean you truly don't know what you speak of," Mufida says solemnly. "They are the abominations of man; creatures created by the scientists of Wisteria. They have been sent to hunt down and capture all of those left in this world who are considered a threat."

"A threat??" Brahm says with childish enthusiasm. "A threat to what?"

"I've never met a Shaker who knows so little of the world. It's a shame to have to pop such a blissful bubble you live in. There is currently a war against the world, Brahm."

"A war… against the world?" Brahm ponders. "What does that even mean?"

"This war… this genocide is sung under the guise of the 'Progressive Movement.' It has become a movement capitalized on reestablishing humanity's right to prosper on this planet. The first order of this movement has been to refute all those who still sympathize with Babel's existence. Wisteria views that way of thinking as detrimental to humanity's progress. The propaganda of the Progressive Movement deems such sympathy illegal. They see it as a sign of psychosis and delusion that needs rehabilitation… or death."

"Now that's actually insane!" Brahm blurts out. "Why care so much if someone is a tree-hugging planet lover?"

"A good question. You see, among those considered sympathizers, there are those they fear the most; they have been labeled the Bakuwan."

"The what?"

"It's a name Wisteria has branded to those who have derived power from Maia herself. Guardians we call them, beings who harbor special abilities that are used to protect the planet. We were once revered people who helped lead others to salvation after the time of Babel. With the Warden Project in full effect, many are being… slaughtered or captured every day." She decides to cut her story short. The weight of her words grows heavier with each utterance.

"*We*, you say?" Brahm catches. He pauses to carefully choose his next words. "Are you two Baku—… Guardians? Is that why you are so worried about these Wardens?"

"How could I let myself slip!" Mufida cries out, falling to her knees. "Please, tell no one of what I have said. I… I…"

"Get off your knees, Mother, and have some pride in who you are for once! We are Seers! The proud and true Guardians of this land."

"Raja! My god, do you truly wish for a death sentence?!"

"Please," Brahm says softly. "Don't worry. I have no interest in turning you into these monsters. Honestly, it makes me want to help you all the more."

"Help? All you can do is run! If you are not a part of the Progressive Movement, then you will surely be seen as a Sympathizer! You must be careful!"

"All you can do is run?" Raja says starkly. "Is that true, Mother?"

"Of course! You've seen what those monsters can do! And with Mune still here? There is no hope to oppose their power!"

"Then all that father and Mono did was for nothing? Is that what you are saying?! That their efforts were in vain?!"

"No. That's not what I—""Just stop, Mother! I can't believe I let you get in my head. I know my actions harbor risks and consequences; all actions do! Just because there are negative possibilities does not mean the answer is not to act! We are here to help guide the people of Maia to a new future! I think it's about time we remember who *we* are before the whole world forgets who *they* are!"

"I like your spirit!" Brahm exclaims in light of Raja's returning vigor. "You are very wise. Rash… but wise," Brahm says warmly.

"Hey!"

"You would make a great leader someday," Brahm continues, quickly clearing the tension and filling Raja's heart with unexpected warmth and compassion. "So fixing this mess will be a tricky one. It's not just about beating the Wardens or overthrowing a leader. It's about winning over the hearts of people who are scared and angry." "Exactly!" Raja says. "That is why I need to get on that stage! I need the people to remember what the Guardians are here for, and how Maia has not given up on us before it's too late!"

A faint and unexpected sound catches Brahm's ear and diverts his attention away from Raja for a moment. With further focus, the sound resonates like the stampede of heavy marching. Clanking metal strikes the cobblestone streets serving as a stark contrast to the intoxicating music that superseded its arrival.

"So… this Mune guy…" Brahm says, trying to dismiss the distraction and return to his conversation with Raja, "he's…um, he's…"

"Here!" Mufida cries out in horror, breaking her momentary silence. "Quick, we must not be seen!" She grabs Raja and Brahm and flings them into the dark veil of an adjacent alleyway. Satisfied with the protective darkness she just threw them in, she glances back to the looming threat that marches ever closer. The welcoming morning sun reflects off the marching caravan as they make their way over the hill that momentarily separates them. The once hope-inspiring rays of light quickly turn to incriminating searchlights. With a deep breath, Mufida jumps to join Brahm and Raja just as the marching feet mount the peak of the hill and make their way into the heart of the plaza. From the shadows, the three struggle to adjust their sight to the abrupt darkness.

CHAPTER: 6

Freedom's Folly

"So, what's the big idea?" Brahm blurts out. "And how did you get so strong! You—"

"Shhhhh!" Mufida scowls. "You and my daughter just became wanted criminals! Just stay quiet and wait for his parade to pass."

Reluctantly adhering to a vow of silence, Brahm looks on as the militaristic parade glides past the alleyway arch like a reel of film. Guards armed with their ceremonial spears are first to walk past. Following their lead, other guards holding large purple and green banners continue the march. Unlike the guards Brahm and Raja met earlier, these men don plates of protective armor clanking loudly with each cumbersome step they take. Their rigid stature and gait appear almost comical. They wobble in and out of cadence despite how hard they attempt to appear stoic and uniform.

As rows and rows of armed guards walk past, a significant gap forms after one group passes. Brahm takes it as a sign they are in the clear but, just as the thought crossed his mind, another wave of guards comes into view. This time, they are all bunched together, struggling to hold up a seemingly heavy load upon their shoulders. Each grasp a long pole that supports a large and brightly decorated podium reaching as high as the tip of the alleyway arch. With backs hunched and sweat flowing, they continue their march. Brahm traces his eyes to the top of the bizarre podium they carry and sees an elaborately decorated throne.

Donned with gold and precious jewels, the flamboyant purple throne serves to cradle a disproportionally arranged man. The pompous individual spits feverously as he yells at his guards to move faster. He quickly becomes red in the face from the exertion it takes to scold with such ferocity. The man is held together by a polished and shiny set of armor that appears custom-tailored to fit around his protruding midsection. His portly proportions resemble that of a dwarfed potbelly pig than that of a functioning human being. Stout arms flail around within the glistening armor plates as his men fail to hasten their pace.

Suddenly distracted, he abruptly turns his head towards the alleyway he now passes. His beady eyes squint into the darkness, giving Brahm a full view of his pudgy face. Blond hair falls below the head cap of his decorative helmet. His pale skin complexion is highlighted by the reddened nature of his overly excited nose. He aggressively flexes his nostrils, appearing to be frantically searching for something important. As his head turns more towards the ground, Brahm can hear Mufida gasp. The pudgy man locks his squinted brown eyes right where Brahm is standing.

"Get down!" Mufida whispers in haste, dragging Brahm and her daughter down further into the darkness. Brahm peeks up again from his crouched position to see the beady brown eyes scanning the alleyway as his caravan marches slowly out of view. As the remaining members of the caravan pass the alleyway without a second glance, they hear the distant cry of the man atop the mobile podium.

"I smell shish kebabs! Move men, I am quick to waste away if I don't fill my belly soon! It will be all your funerals if you dare make me go hungry a moment longer! Now march!" he bellows as he lifts a whip into the air and cracks it down upon the feeble men who hold him above their heads. As Mune's words indicate his highest priority, Mufida lets out a heavy sigh of relief. "I think we are safe for now," she says after her long exhale.

"Phew! That guy was something else!" Brahm says with a chuckle of jest. "Who was that weirdo atop all those poor guards?" Mufida is about to speak but notices a deep and pensive silence start to swirl around her daughter. Brahm notices it too. They both peer over to Raja as she slowly emerges from the dark alleyway into the light of the Plaza. She stands rigid, looking out into the celebratory crowd. She watches the tail end of the portly man's caravan carve its way through the masses. Raja curls her fingers into her palms, balling her fist so tightly specks of blood start to drip from her nails puncturing her skin. Tears swell in the corners of her eyes as she watches her fellow islanders part the waters for the man atop his human tower. They bow down to him, shouting words of praise as he passes. They grovel at his feet, welcoming any scraps of wealth or food he decides to throw down to his loving subjects. The sight becomes too much for her to bear as she turns her face away from the gut-retching reality.

"Was that the Mune guy?" Brahm asks again, twitching his nose as if he just smelt something foul. Mufida stands behind her daughter and places her hands comfortingly atop her shoulders.

"What was your first clue?" she adds with a snarky inflection. "Yep, the current ruler of this land, over-thrower of the Seers, erector of the Lotus, the savior sent from the heirs of God themselves: Bartholomew Mune," Raja sarcastically recites, wiping a rebellious tear from her eye.

"That pig-man is the leader of this place?"

"Unfortunately so," Raja confirms. "They bow to him as if he really is God's gift to the people."

"But that's just it, don't you see, Raja?" Mufida interjects with anxious panic in her tone. "That is why we must stay in hiding! To these people, he is God's gift to them! He comes from Wisteria, after all! Why can't you understand it is futile to stand up to such a man?! In the eyes of our people, he is God, and we are the devil!"

"What difference does that make?" Brahm asks.

"What difference does that make??" Mufida repeats with exasperated fury. "You've gone and done it now, Shaker," Raja says mockingly as her mother boils over with rage. Tears pour from the woman's eyes as her emotions struggle to latch onto words. Brahm feels this is a good time to clarify his sentiments.

"All I am saying is the truth will set you free. Set you all free. Let your daughter show this land what they have forgotten. Allow the people to decide for themselves who is good and who is evil."

"No," Mufida says, struggling to maintain eye contact with her daughter. Brahm can feel the internal conflict raging within her heart.

"This is not a fair match! Don't you see? What if you get on that stage and speak of your vision? It would be the work of the devil in the eyes of those you wish to save! This is suicide what you two speak of! Why can't you just listen to reason?"

"Beau asks me that all the time!" Brahm laughs.

"You still mock our situation??" Mufida stammers in disbelief.

"I'm just confident in our plan. Those Wardens are not the only bizarre creatures around here. I'll take care of them as long as Raja is still up to the more challenging task."

"You'll… take care of them? What nonsense are you talking about now? What could be more challenging than that insane claim??" Mufida asks as her head swirls into distortion.

"Well, what she's been talking about this whole time obviously! If she is willing to sway the hearts of all these people gripped by fear, then I would be honored to help her attempt such a feat!"

"Are you serious??" Raja exclaims with joy.

"You've managed to sway my heart, so that's enough for me to have the confidence you can do the same for another. So what's your plan?"

"The Seers are the Guardians gifted with the ability to communicate with nature through visions. Babel showed me in a vision that she will be sending another storm surge our way today. We have come to rely on Wisteria's technology to warn us of the surges, but this time it will be too late! Everyone is too distracted by the festival. I must try and prove to them, despite the sunny skies, Babel's storm is just over the horizon!"

"Show me," Brahm says with a commanding force.

"Show you? How?" Raja asks with rippling confusion.

"You didn't have your vision very long ago; it should still be fresh in your mind. Take my hand and concentrate on what you saw, I'll do the rest," Brahm adds to clear the confusion. Raja finds herself walking over to Brahm despite her earlier skepticism and sits in front of him. She disregards her lingering doubt and closes her eyes. Taking a deep breath, she focuses her mind before reaching out for Brahm's hand. The moment her fingertips touch the end of his, an abrupt flash erupts around them, and Raja is catapulted back into her earlier vision.

She is standing on the high mountain peak overlooking the incoming tidal surge. This time, Brahm is standing next to her holding her hand. The two watch from high in the sky as the waves sweep over The Pearl. They retract their heads back in horror as the mayhem unfolds. Festival-drunk patrons run through the cobblestone streets screaming cries of agony and disbelief. Not a soul is spared as everyone gets dragged into the unforgiving sea. As if able to sense Raja and Brahm's presence, the drowning patrons look into the sky with pleas of mercy bubbling in their eyes. Quickly, one by one they all disappear under the violent waves leaving only tattered prayer flags in their wake. The flailing fabric serves as a lingering totem for the final Fantuzzi celebration. Raja can't take it anymore and lets go of Brahm's hand. They are immediately rocketed back to their original spot on the cobblestones. Raja wipes a tear from her eye and stares mesmerized at Brahm's stoic and statue-esque stance.

"Who… are you?" she asks with newfound sincerity. "I've never seen anyone able to do that before. Are you… a Guardian too?"

"Honestly, I'm not sure," says Brahm. "Being a Guardian sounds way too noble for someone like me. Who I am, though, is actually what I'm out here trying to figure out. I'm a mystery even to myself!" he adds with a slight chuckle. "But enough about me. We obviously have more pressing matters at hand. How accurate are your visions?"

"My visions about Babel are never wrong, but I rarely have to do anything about it because everyone around here lives on lockdown; not that I can really do much about it with my very existence being outlawed. Luckily, everyone is always expecting the worst. Well, except for today obviously."

"Right, now it's a matter of convincing all these people drunk on celebration that they have to run for shelter again. How much time do we have before your visions come to fruition?" asks Brahm.

"It's always hard to say; I normally get a vision a few hours before the storm surges arrive."

"So we have time, just not much of it. We have to get you to that stage pronto!"

"You are most definitely insane, but I appreciate your offer to help," Raja says, standing tall. "Let's work together to break this spell of fear." Brahm gives a reassuring nod of his head, and the two of them start walking side-by-side back towards the clamshell stage.

"Wait!" Mufida calls out, her voice quivering slightly. Brahm and Raja stop but refuse to turn around. The sound of the band hums in the background.

"Mother! Just let it go!" Raja screams.

"Humor me. This whole time you never even discussed a single plan, option, or an idea as to how you are going to combat the forces of Wisteria! What if Mune really does send a Warden??"

"Well, if things go well—"

"Hold it! There is no plan! Is there?" Her own words bring a sinking feeling in the pit of her stomach. She falls to her knees and sinks her face into the palms of her hands. The tears are just moments away from overflowing.

"Right, so look," Brahm says as he stands back up. His gaze is purposely avoidant of any direct eye contact with Mufida. "We are gonna have to wing this thing, Mufie. It's the only way."

"Mufie?" she responds, surprised by her new nickname.

"Yep! No use worrying about what you can't control. Do your best right here and keep your heart open to the possibility of success! I'm not asking you for a miracle or anything, that's your daughter's job!" Brahm says as he peers over at Raja. "C'mon Raja, we've got a crowd to win over. Wish your mom luck!"

"Good luck, Mufie!" Raja calls with a playful nod to her mother's new nickname before they head back into the crowd. Mufida crumbles to her knees, still unable to believe what is transpiring before her. She gathers her wits and does the only thing she knows how to do in situations like these. She starts to pray.

"Please, Great Babarossa. Please watch over my daughter and this lunatic she has found. They know not what they do, and they do so with such vigor. Please keep them safe, please give them some sense, and please help me bear witness to this unfolding disaster, please, please, please."

CHAPTER: 7

An Entanglement of Quantum Proportions

"So you really don't have any idea what to do about Mune and the Wardens?" Raja asks with a hint of concern.

"Oh, it's not that I don't have an idea of *what* to do, I just don't know what I'm *going* to do!" Brahm thinks about this a little further. "There is a difference between 'winging it' and not having a plan. To me, the best way to go about this is to know what we have to accomplish and just have that intention behind everything we end up doing. Specific expectations have a way of getting the better of us."

"Sounds like a good enough plan to me! Takes a lot of the pressure off what I'm going to say, that's for sure," Raja says with a sigh of relief.

"Yeah! Don't worry so much about *what* you will say but *where* it comes from. As long as you speak from the heart the people will hear what is truly being said." As the pair approach The Clam Stage, they quickly catch the eye of the guards from earlier. They leave their post at the stage with spears in hand, making their way into the crowd to confront their returning adversaries.

"Bold of you to come back this way," taunts Claude. "Saves us and the Wardens from having to track you down." Claude moves himself even closer to the pair, putting his face a breaths length away from Brahm's nose. "Now, if you have come back to apologize, I completely understand. I would be sorry too if I were you! Sadly, that won't change much at this point. The cavalry has already been called in." Claude takes a step back and makes a sweeping gesture with his hand towards the crowd. "Take a look around you! You see all these mindless faces consumed by the tune of false hope? None of them are even remotely aware of what is about to happen to you two, and you want to *help* them? I hate to break it to you, but we are all going to be wiped out by one of those abominations of nature one day. That said… maybe I hope you are right! Maybe today is the day Babel can finally take us out of our delusional misery! 'Cause by now we must have all realized there is no relief coming! So how about it? Let's just do what we both know needs to get done." He finishes his monologue and motions the rest of his guards to enclose Brahm and Raja. Brahm stands his ground as Claude's posse proudly displays their overwhelming numbers. Appearing unfazed by this showcase of power, Brahm looks up to Raja and cracks a smile.

"Well, you heard the man. Let's get to it," he says as he lowers his tantalizing gaze towards Claude. He instantaneously pierces through the guard's narrowed brown eyes, diving deeper and deeper into his swirling blackened soul. Seemingly unfazed by the intrusive gesture, Claude shakes his head and stares back with an unrestricted ferocity.

With a bellowing cry, Claude hurls an emotional-filled strike with his spear right into the heart of Brahm. Brahm reads his rage-filled swing and takes a swift step to the left, dodging the strike with ease while catapulting Raja high into the air.

"Wingin' it!" Raja cries out as she soars high above her future audience. Anticipating the next wave of attacks, Brahm lowers his body so quickly an after-image appears where he once stood. Claude struggles to process how his opponent can occupy two different positions in space and time. Not giving the situation much thought, Claude fires a multitude of frenzy-fueled attacks at both renditions of his opponent. Waking up to a sense of urgency, Claude's backup forces finally join the fight. They launch themselves simultaneously at all angles towards Brahm's superposition. With sheer numbers in their favor, the guards sigh with relief. However, Brahm easily dances in-between the flailing guards, landing in a new position behind them. The guards inevitably strike the empty pockets of air before collapsing themselves into an entangled pile of frustration and disbelief.

Brahm glances over to the writhing pile of assailants as they scramble back to their feet. They struggle to salvage what composure is left to their disposal. Without breaking his attention on his foes, Brahm stretches out his arms and catches the now falling Raja.

"Holy cow," Raja exclaims. "I'm going to need you to teach me how to move that fast when this is all over."

"Let's do what we came here to do before we worry about what comes after," Brahm commands with stern concentration. Raja nods with understanding, suppressing her distracting excitement.

"So what's next?" she says, mirroring Brahm's radiating aura of determination.

"The stage. It's time. Slowly make your way up the stairs behind us. With all this commotion, the band will unfortunately realize it's time for an intermission."

"Unfortunately?!" Raja banters. "Just whose side are you on?"

"The side of harmony, my dear. It's a shame it has to come at the cost of ending such beautiful music." Brahm takes a longing look at the enamoring musicians as he soaks in the final bit of sonic sap that drips into the bucket of his heart.

"Okay… now, let's go!" he shouts, jumping into action. Raja nods and makes her way to the stairs as the guards finally reassemble their positions.

"You're not going to be so lucky this time," Claude calls out before shifting his attention to his men. "Put an end to this charade once and for all, whatever you have to do! Dead or alive, make sure they do not get on that stage!" The guards rush towards Brahm who stands ready for their next move. A spear jettisons from the mob towards him, this time with much more concentrated force. He takes a step back while dodging the strike. Spear jabs are coming from all directions as Brahm continues his pacing backwards towards the stage. He is pushed back to the point where his foot lands on the bottom step of the stairs.

"I thought you were going to keep them away from the stage!" Raja cries with concern.

"Don't you worry about me! I told you I would handle these guys. We are still wingin' it!" he says with a wink of his eye. Raja gains the confidence she needs in her partner in crime and continues her climb.

"This is the end of the road!" shouts Claude as he resurfaces as the primary aggressor. The persistent barrage of attacks leads Brahm further up the stairs. Consequently, his upward move forces the mob of guards to streamline their assault as they, too, make their way up the narrow stairwell.

"Damn it!" exclaims Claude as he realizes the trap they have fallen into. "All you in the back, break off and climb the other stairwell. Get that girl while we stop this guy! Go!" The remaining guards on the initial stairwell push Brahm further up his climb to the point where he backs into Raja.

"Seriously! What's happening down there?!" she cries.

"Just preparing your audience," Brahm replies cryptically as they finally emerge on the stage floor. Brahm reaches up and grabs ahold of the loosely hanging prayer flags surrounding the stage. As he removes the flags from their casual perch, he repurposes their decorative function into a more restrictive one. Now armed with combat-ready prayer flags, he weaves his new weapon in-between the encroaching guards. With each slash of their spears, they are only wound further into the binding force of prayer. Brahm turns to face the guards approaching from the flanked position and quickly renders them incapacitated. He easily ties them up along with their fellow brethren. Now tethered and powerless, the guards look out with disbelief as they realize their comical capture has been put on full display for the whole Fantuzi celebration to see.

"I can't believe this!" Claude cries as he wiggles helplessly in his prayer-bound prison. The wide-eyed crowd gazes towards the stage with bewildered curiosity. The musicians silently look on with their awe-struck audience awaiting answers to the unexpected interruption. With the tension building, the band is forced to end their performance. They gather their instruments to quickly retreat off the stage.

"You were amazing!" Brahm calls out to the band as they scurry down the opposing stairwell. "Sorry to have to cut it short!"

Raja steps over one of the limbs of a tethered guard and walks to the center of the stage. The crowd stands motionless, still in shock. Raja clears her throat and takes a deep breath before initiating her moment of truth.

CHAPTER: 8

A Moment of Truth

A deep, profound silence rushes over the crowd. They gaze upon the unexpected pearl in the center of their beloved stage. A lump of fear starts to bulge in Raja's throat as she stares out at the anticipatory eyes burrowing into her vulnerable vessel. Feeling the bulge in her throat trying to move into her heart, she decides to swallow it and take in a deep breath of fresh air. The breath of the very planet she wishes to represent fills her lungs and gives her strength to speak her truth.

"Brothers and sisters, I stand before you knowing full well of the atrocities I have just committed. Not only have I rebelled against our sworn protectors, I have also interrupted our most cherished ceremony. As much as it pains me to have ripped this celebration from your bones, I do so with the sincerest of intentions. This festival represents our heritage, our call to purpose. With all the changes that have befallen our island, this festival is one of the few things we have been able to hold onto despite the changing times. This festival does so much more than provide an escape from our daily suffering. It is supposed to serve as a reminder that there will come a day when Babel will eventually end! Have we let go of that hope and replaced it with futility?" Raja takes a breath and pauses for a moment to read her captive crowd. She sees an overwhelming number still wearing their vacant gazes. As she looks into the eyes of those closest to her, she sees a small spark twinkling in their eyes. She takes that as a sign to continue.

"Our land has been taken over by a foreigner who promised peace and prosperity. We fell on every word Mune broadcasted because of how beaten-down we have become from these relentless storms and our internal fights with one another. I don't think anyone can fault us for acting in desperation. As a Seer, I understand why we were thrown from power and why you all are upset." An audible rumble of banter now fills the crowd at the unveil of Raja's identity. A flicker of worry ignites in her heart, but another deep breath of perseverance extinguishes the moment of doubt. "Living on The Pearl has taken its toll," she continues. "Now, I ask you to take a moment and reflect on life since Mune took over. Has it brought any real prosperity? Mune has put a price tag on our water, put us to work on the Lotus, alienated us from our neighbors and left us to fall into poverty unlike anything we have faced before. Many of us have been forced to salvage scraps for a living. Despite all of this hardship, I stand proudly as a Seer of this land. You may still shun me, you may still hate me, but I ask you to at least listen to me before you make your next move. No matter the outcome, my job as a Seer is to protect my people and I am here to tell you that Babel is making an abrupt return. I have seen what will become of us if we do not heed this warning. If we don't take shelter right now, this could truly be the end of us. Please hear my words and let us live to see another day!" Raja takes another pause to assess her audience, and witnesses the earlier spark starting to flicker and sputter. She quickly runs through her mind for a strategy to more directly connect to her people.

"I understand the threat of Babel on a clear day like today seems comical, but please trust me enough and join hands? If my words are not powerful enough, I will personally show you what is about to befall us!" Each one of the participants look to one another with silent processing, the wheels of contemplation spin feverously. In a miraculous move, one by one, they slowly grab ahold of their neighbor's open palms. As Raja watches this gesture of hope, she yells frantically to Brahm, "All right, that thing you did earlier… I need you to bring everyone with me this time! Can you do it?"

"One way to find out! Just tell me where you need me," Brahm says as he walks away from his dumbfounded guard-pile. Raja grabs Brahm's hand and runs to the edge of the stage.

"Everyone hold on!" she yells and without thinking twice, takes a leap into the crowd below. Brahm jumps after her and lands safely with Raja in his arms. He looks to her awaiting her reckless explanation. "What is a speech about hope and trust without a leap of faith?" she replies with a playful smile. Scanning the front row for a willing participant, she locks eyes with a gentleman on the edge with a hand still vacant. "Perfect!" She rushes Brahm over to the man's corner. "Hello! You are about to play a critical role in the efforts of saving your people. Now take this stranger's hand and hold on!" Raja finishes by flinging the two men's hands together before grabbing ahold of Brahm's remaining one. "Okay, time to do the thing!" She closes her eyes and says a quick prayer before diving back into her earlier vision.

Just like before, she is teleported back to the same rock Brahm visited her on, but now she is accompanied by more than two thirds of her Pearl brothers and sisters. Together they watch the destructive force sweep over their unsuspecting island. Raja can feel all their conflicted hearts start to crack open as the severity of their upcoming reality begins to hit home. The waves of observable tragedy weave their distant hearts together as the power of Raja's vision washes over them. The collective vision eventually fades, bringing them back to their original starting points. This time, however, with a newfound clarity of their impeding future. Raja takes a deep breath and looks to Brahm with a warm smile before releasing a deep sigh of relief. "Let's hope that worked!" she says.

There is a chattering hum among the returning festival goers as they digest the collective vision. Unsure how to swallow the intense download of information, their humming and mumbling progresses in volume and chaos. Reaching a tipping point, one voice finally breaks through the turbulent chatter; the words capture what's on the forefront of everyone's mind: "We've got to get out of here!"

A stampede is triggered, and everyone scrambles like wild beasts for the nearest exits. Amidst the chaos, Raja is almost trampled by the very people she came to save. Brahm reaches out and pulls her out of the way of her frenzy-fueled brethren right in the nick of time.

"I guess it worked!" Raja exclaims, completely unfazed by the growing pandemonium.

"It's probably time to go check on your mom, this crowd looks to be getting a little out of hand."

"I think you're right! It's like they have never evacuated for a storm before! Granted, these clear skies are pretty convincing… for now—"

"For now is right," Brahm says cutting her off. "We need to hurry if we are going to heed your own warning." Raja nods in agreement and they rush off to find Mufida. They dive into the rapid currents of the frantic crowd. They weave in and out of the waves of patrons rushing to safety. As Raja breathes a heavy sigh of relief, tears of joy erupt from her eyes. Brahm looks down at the proud young Seer and gives her a warm smile.

"Thank you," she says. Her words carry an emotional resonance that transcends the boundaries of language.

"This was all you," Brahm responds. "I knew you could do it. Now, let's find that mother of yours. Hop on my shoulders and see what you can find," Brahm says as he lifts Raja onto a higher vantage point. Together they race along the current of people, trying to keep up with the fast paced scurry. She looks out over the congested crowd and notices a parting of bodies near the southern gate.

"Up ahead, everyone seems to be moving around something stuck in the street. Let's check it out, maybe someone has fallen!"

"Good thinking!" Brahm picks up the pace and races to the source of the divide. As they rush to the potentially fallen patron, Brahm screeches to a halt once they reach the roadblock.

"Mother!" Raja calls out as she leaps from Brahm's high perch. Mufida slowly looks up from her crouched stance, unfolding her long prayer-bound prostrations.

"I prayed to the Great Sage the moment you left to keep you and this man safe. I prayed and prayed and prayed, and I finally heard a voice telling me to 'stay here and wait.' I didn't know what else to do but listen. People started pouring over me, but I stayed! I just kept praying and praying and here you are! My baby! It looks like you did it! I'm so proud of you, Raja!" she calls out, tears flowing like a levee break. "You did it! You really did it! I-I owe you the biggest apology," she says as she locks eyes with Raja. "You were right about all of this. This whole island would have been wiped clean if it wasn't for your brave efforts."

"You mean it, Mother?" Raja exclaims with a heavy heart.

"I do. You did what I couldn't bring myself to do and face my fears. Warden or no Warden, you never let your fear turn you away from what you knew was right in your heart. Your father and brother would be beyond proud of you." Raja soaks in her mother's words and falls with outstretched arms into her mother like never before. The world seems to spiral in the opposing direction as they hold each other in swirling bliss. Each passing moment allows all the lingering tension they have harbored to dissolve like the ever-eroding shoreline. They release their embrace and look at one another with silent recognition before turning to Brahm. "I think it's time we evacuate ourselves," Mufida says. "Brahm, you can come with us. Someone has been gracious enough to open their home to us. I'm sure they will give you shelter too until this storm passes. I feel it is the least we can do to thank you for all you have done for us."

"That is very kind of you. I am truly honored to have been able to meet you both. This island is riddled with such amazing people." He smiles, pausing to ride the waves of the flowing energy around them. "To have witnessed the opening of your hearts in the face of such adversity is truly inspirational. I wish it was time for me to seek refuge, but there is someone else I have met here who needs to heed your words." He thinks about his departure from Sophia earlier, wondering if he can remember which direction she walked off to. "Please, you two make your way to safety," he continues. "We will meet again after all this is over. For now, I must head to the docks."

"You better come back and find us!" Raja cries out as she rushes to hug her new friend. "Thank you." She buries her head into his chest. Brahm bows his head down and joins in the embrace.

"Thank you for staying true to who you are. This island is very fortunate to have you here looking out for everyone." Raja wipes the lingering tears from her eyes as she peers up to her departing friend. The three of them share one last silent moment of recognition before Brahm turns and makes his way towards the unsuspecting dockside.

CHAPTER: 9

Event Horizon

Nearing the docks, the hasty steps of Brahm's bare feet echo through the cobbled streets. His trepidatious pace serves as a steady reflection of the chaos still bubbling atop the city plaza. A conflicting calm starts to bear an ominous tone as Brahm gets closer to the water's edge. The few souls who casually roam the streets stare quizzically at the urgency Brahm radiates with. *Raja did a good job at alerting the majority*, Brahm thinks to himself. *Despite how drunk that old man from before was, even he got the message, but there are still so many who were not at the plaza!* Brahm studies the remaining oblivious Pearlites. *Hmm... I wonder if Beau knows a storm surge is coming back. Meh, I'm sure he will be fine, he's definitely been through worse. I need to find Sophia first! I'm sure she knows how to reach the remaining stragglers on this island.* Brahm laughs at the thought of his loose-fit plan. *And to think I don't even know where she is, the 'docks' cover the whole bay-side!* He gazes out over the daunting maze he must navigate in order to find Sophia. Ships and piers line the entire crescent bay. Countless dry docks follow the banks of the canals. They cut through the mountainous terrain like meandering ocean veins. The majority of the ships still at the docks are tanker-like vessels carrying large containers filled with what appears to be water.

The mountainside view resembles a ghost town with minute activity flowing through its grid-like streets. The stillness ripples slightly as a hard-to-miss wooden ship abruptly emerges out of the light fog creeping into the docks. The large ship gently drifts down one of the canals towards a cylindrical dwelling that rises high above the uniformed structures that surrounds it. Brahm stops and watches the surprisingly small crew fastening the sails at a blistering pace. Before the sail is completely rolled up, he notices a unique symbol etched onto the black sail. Marked in white, there is a thick 'X' shape above a humanoid character made up of geometric shapes. A triangle for the face, a circle for the core, two lines for legs and a 'U' shape that resembles arms reaching upward. The figure looks like it is breaking free from a collection of strings. *A puppet?* Brahm thinks to himself, m*aybe an angry puppet? Proud puppet?* He shakes his head, unsure what to make of the bold symbol coiling up before his eyes. Brahm catches a light twirling around the top of the cylindrical building, revealing its purpose as a lighthouse. The ship ties in at the dock and four cloaked people emerge out of the vessel. Three of them head into the lighthouse while one stays back, appearing to stand guard. Brahm grabs ahold of his overall straps and arches his back as he ponders his next step.

"Well," he says, shifting his weight back and forth, "doesn't seem to be much else going on. I bet the people down there might know where Sophia is. At the very least, I'm sure they would want to know a storm is coming." Finalizing his plan of attack, he slaps his straps back into place and jets off towards the only sign of collective activity. A strong breeze cuts through the new street, signaling to Brahm the impending storm is getting closer.

Need to hurry, he thinks before picking up the pace. However, just as he makes his first conscious footstep at the new speed, a chaotic ball of energy erupts out of the adjacent street, running right into him. The impact knocks Brahm to the ground bringing him to a screeching halt. In the process, the force whisks his hat clean off his head, only saved by the dangling strap that hooks around his neck. His jet-black hair is now free to tickle the sky as it flows unrestricted in the lingering breeze. Brahm takes his hand and combs through his unruly locks in an effort to tame them. He looks for the chaotic wrecking ball that ran into him. It finally reveals itself to be a frantic young boy, no older than sixteen, who resides on the ground only a few feet from where Brahm sits.

The boy's clothes are tattered, and he wears a thick rope slung over his shoulder. He picks himself up and dusts off his ragged jeans before looking over to Brahm. The boy opens his mouth to apologize but Brahm cuts him off.

"Ah!" Brahm exclaims. "I'm so happy to have run into someone out here. Well, I wasn't intending on *literally* running into someone, but it was a nice added effect!" The boy simply stares blankly, unable to understand the unexplained enthusiasm. Luckily, Brahm continues his monologue to fill the void of confusion. "I'm looking for someone by the name of Sophia; long brown hair, yellow eyes, and likes to wear a raincoat during a celebration of sunny skies. Ring a bell?"

"Well," the boy says with a stroke of his chin, "there is a Sophia who works at the Bay-6 lighthouse down there and it looks like her light is on. Probably your best bet."

"That's great news!" Brahm exclaims as he jumps to his feet. "That's right where my intuition was leading me. Not sure what made me question it! Thanks kid!" Brahm reaches back for his hat and places it securely on his head before extending his hand to thank the boy. His outstretched hand is met with some unexpected resistance. The boy stares at Brahm with his mouth gaping open.

"Y-y-you… you're… you're…" the boy stutters. Brahm tilts his head to the right, then the left, studying the boy for clues to the situation he clearly is not volunteering willingly. About to give up and leave the boy to his mysterious stupor, his glazed and bewildered stare finally triggers his memory.

"Aha! You're that kid from earlier! The… the one who ran away before I had finished making tea! I was hoping I would see you again! Sorry about your tea, I had to give it away once you left. Can't waste good tea. Anyway, there is this thing I—" once again Brahm is cut off, this time by an abrupt departure as Otto collects himself enough to fire off an emergency-exit dash into the adjacent alleyway. Before Brahm can finish his last thought, Otto is well out of eyesight with dust trailing behind his footsteps.

"Well darn," Brahm huffs, "he must really have a thing against tea. I do admit it can be a bit strong. What should I do? Beau is really going to be mad if I don't get our compass back. Oh well!" Brahm throws his hands up in the air along with his general sense of concern and continues on his way to the lighthouse.

∞

The streets around the docks remain scarcely populated. They resonate with a continued lack of awareness of the anticipatory beast looming over the horizon. Brahm witnesses a few darkened clouds rolling towards the island as he reaches the lighthouse. He worries it won't be enough of a warning for the remaining people left in the dark. The sun is slowly starting to set; the ominous clouds in the distance trade in their dominating gray tones and adopt a pink and orange palette. The mirror image is reflected in the rippling pool of the crescent bay. The gentle waves lap effortlessly onto the shore. All indications of encroaching danger now reside shrouded in deceptive beauty. Brahm makes his way to the red wooden door of the lighthouse and realizes it hasn't shut all the way. He slowly creeps closer and takes a peek inside, careful not to give any sense of alarm to the residents, not yet anyway. As Brahm peers even closer, he can overhear a familiar voice in the middle of a conversation.

"…I know this is not what you originally came here for, but we must redirect our focus for the time being. We will eventually carry out our initial investigation. I just can't believe they would come now of all times, they were just here! No matter, most of our job revolves around anticipating the unexpected. Does anyone know what time they were called?" Sophia hesitates a little longer than would be expected, "…What? What do you mean someone is here?"

A lump forms in the back of Brahm's throat. He can feel an overwhelming shift in energy towards his general location. Taken aback by this unexpected concentration of hostile energy, he panics. Unable to salvage the situation in a sophisticated fashion, he manages to trip and fall into the door, flinging it wide open with a loud crash into the adjacent wall. He wobbles with his lingering momentum but eventually succumbs to the pull of gravity. He spills onto the floor, sprawling out on all four limbs. Brahm looks up at his scowling audience and attempts to ease the tension with a toothy grin.

An abnormally large gentleman stands closest to Brahm. He towers over the rest, his frame extending at least ten or twelve feet off the ground. Brahm recognizes the man's full-body cloak as the same style Sophia wore at the bar. Most of his larger-than-life features lay hidden behind the cloak. All except a metal plate hanging off his ears like a reversed crown. Long spikes go down both sides of his cheeks and end a few inches below his jaw line in curved points. The man takes a step closer, resulting in the whole room quivering with the sheer impact of his foot colliding with the floor. The impact unsettles some dust from the rafters above. The dust floats down in-between the remaining floor space that separates Brahm and the mysterious giant.

"There is no telling how much he has heard. Let me just dispose of him now," the giant says to the crowd behind him.

"No, not just yet," Sophia says as she removes the hood from her matching cloak. "Unfortunately, I know this man. Honestly, I just met him earlier today and assumed him to be a clueless Shaker."

"Hey!" Brahm remarks but is quickly cut off by Sophia.

"More importantly, he obviously is not from around here. With him making his way down here of all times, he is clearly more than who he alludes to be. He could be a spy. We need to question him before we get rid of him so quickly. Izak, will you please?"

"With pleasure, m' lady," comes a distant voice from the rafters. A faint hiss can be heard coming from multiple directions, but before Brahm can make sense of the strange noise, it is too late. In a flash, his body is wrenched into an upright anatomical display. His hands and feet become bound by thread so thin it takes a second glance to even register anything physical is there at all. Brahm assesses what movements are still available in his newfound prison. He chuckles at the realization of his almost complete immobilization.

Another cloaked figure emerges from the shadows above. The figure lowers himself to the ground while lifting Brahm further into the air at the same time. The man stops his descent a few feet off the ground and hangs in controlled suspension looking eye-to-eye with Brahm. He tilts his head while examining his new prize. Brahm struggles to keep eye contact as the man's actual eyes remain hidden behind his thick goggles. The goggle straps reside snugly behind his flowing white dreadlocks that dangle down past his shoulders. He reeks of cigarette smoke. It's a smell so strong it strangles the breathable air surrounding him. The man reaches above himself and grabs ahold of the almost invisible tether that suspends them both. Without removing his veiled gaze from his prey, he pulls out a knife from under his cloak and cuts the tether below his hand. He falls neatly to the floor as Brahm jostles slightly from the removal of his counterweight. Still suspended in the air, Brahm is hoisted up further as the man from the rafters ties the severed end of the chord to an exposed support beam. Now about ten feet off the ground, Brahm gets a good look at his defensive audience. Unable to look up and see for himself, he feels now is as good of a time as ever to explain his situation.

"Ah, well, now that I have your undivided attention, I have some very important news to tell you! Ahem," he clears his throat. "I have come to warn you that you are all in grave danger!"

"I think you may have your situations mixed up, stranger," says Izak, the man from the rafters. "I suggest you reassess your predicament. You are the one bound, suspended, and currently on trial before your swift execution."

"Right, you're not the most welcoming bunch, I got that already, but no matter! I have recently befriended one of your renowned Seers. Lovely girl, great spirit, high-strung mother, but she is doing the best she can; aren't we all though? Oh, I digress! She is desperately trying to inform everyone of the impeding storm that is to return. Well, any minute now!" The reaction to his dramatic pitch is cut short as his floating prison adopts a slight spin. He now has his back facing the contemplative and silent crowd. Unwilling to let silence get the better of him, Brahm continues his pitch to the wall he now faces.

"So, she gave a wonderful speech at your Fantuzzi celebration. We did have to interrupt that beautiful music. Such a shame. I hope they will forgive us, but it really was for a good cause! She got everyone to see what was about to happen, and they all ran off to safety! It was wonderful! Except I remembered you, Sophia, wouldn't have heard the warning, seeing as you came down to the docks and all. I also thought you might have a good idea on how to alert everyone else who didn't either. So, what do you think? Want to work something out so a bunch of people don't die?" His gradual spin has now realigned him with the still silent jurors who have dissolved their faces of any emotional registry. This lack of connection drives Brahm to distraction. "C'mon! At least say something before I spin around again!"

Sophia finally steps up. "You are telling me not only does a Seer remain on this island, but she commandeered the most public celebration so she could inform them of one of her visions?" she questions with a harsh tone.

"So you *were* listening! Wonderful, so do you—"

"No wonder the Wardens are on their way back here!" she barks as she turns her back to Brahm.

"Ah! So you already know about the Warden part. That's great! Ha, I almost forgot about that one! Got so caught up with the destructive mega-storm warning. It's fine though, I told Raja not to worry about it. I'll take care of them after this storm passes."

"Take care of them?" Sophia turns back to address Brahm directly. "No offense… well, frankly I don't care if I offend you or not at this point. You are in no position to 'take care' of anyone as you are dangling up there like a helpless gnat caught in our web. We will survive a storm surge, like we have countless times before. The Wardens on the other hand… you clearly don't know what you are talking about. Never should they be taken lightly. I should kill you now for such blatant disregard for reality."

"I'm sure you will survive, you look resourceful enough, but what about all the people who didn't get the warning? Clearly your pretension of having a cold heart can't glaze over that fact, right? Don't you know of some way of alerting everyone else before it's too late?" Brahm asks while omitting the threat on his life.

"What difference does it make to you?" Sophia says, the quiver in her voice indicating his words hit a soft spot. "You are not from this island. Why bother with this 'save the people' charade? You are clearly trying to save your neck and it's not working."

"Well, what about you?" Brahm says while eying Sophia's distinctive olive skin. "Compared to the pale skin the sunless days create around here, clearly you aren't from here either, yet you seem to care. Why can't I?"

"You just arrived on these shores! Don't you dare claim to know the first thing about these people… or me!" Sophia bellows with anger.

"So the difference between us is just the amount of time we've spent here?" Brahm responds mockingly. Sophia bites her lip in frustration. Unable to respond quickly enough, she stews in her caustic stream of consciousness. Before her rebuttal surfaces in her mind, the attention in the room has shifted to the window.

"Lady Sophia, you might want to take a look at this," calls another cloaked figure standing by the window, facing the sea.

"Lady, huh? Didn't know I was speaking to royalty!" Brahm says as he spins to face the wall once again.

Ignoring his last remark, Sophia walks over to the window while doing a poor job at concealing her obvious irritation. "What is it, Em'?" she snaps.

"See for yourself," the man remarks, as he moves to give Sophia full view of the window. As the content of the window comes closer into view, Sophia struggles to make sense of the combined horror that presents itself. Staring back at her is an enormous air ship emerging over the horizon heading towards their location. The swirling vortex of Babel's storm clouds follows closely behind. Sophia hesitates for a moment. The sheer shock of the dual calamities pulls at her attention like an unavoidable black hole. Eventually gathering her composure, she turns to address the room.

"All right; looks like this guy wasn't lying. Babel will be returning to our shores any minute, and just as fate would have it, the Wardens are just over the horizon. They are only a few clicks ahead of the storm."

"The Wardens are flying during a Babel storm flare? Are they so consumed by their 'rehabilitation' project that they have disregarded all logic and common sense? Have they completely lost their minds?" Izak yells, hardly able to believe what Sophia has reported from the window.

"*We* weren't even aware of the storm until just now; I doubt they were either until they were already mid-flight. We have no other options right now, we have to factor this in," Sophia says, proudly displaying her regained composure.

"I tried to tell you!" calls Brahm.

"What do you want us to do?" the giant asks, trying to ignore the spinning peanut gallery.

"Odds are the Wardens are going to try and make a hasty landing near our docks… if they make it before the storm hits. I'm going to have to ask you and your crew to remain here and await their landing. We can use this situation to our advantage. We can make it look like the storm took them out, but whatever you do, make sure they do not make their way inland. Stall them. I know we are no match at defeating them, but we cannot run from this one. We have to buy ourselves as much time as we can to complete our mission. Understood?"

"Yes ma'am," the giant remarks with a slight bow.

"As for me, I'm going to ask you to trust me on this one. Izak, I need you to cut this man down." Izak lifts the lenses of his goggles as if to better hear what Sophia has asked of him. The look in his eyes clearly begs for further explanation.

"I know we still do not know the origins of this man, but I'm not going to leave him here to die knowing he came here to try and warn us. Also, we won't learn anymore about his intentions if he is dead. I will take him with me while I go to sound the storm siren. With the sun almost set, there is a good chance many of these islanders still don't know what's about to come our way. I'll keep him in my custody until the storm passes, and then we will meet back here. We can decide what to do with him afterwards. Understood?"

"As you wish," Izak says reluctantly as he walks over to Brahm with his knife drawn. He strolls up to his dangling prisoner and gives him one last scowl before cutting him free. "If she doesn't return tomorrow, consider yourself the most wanted man on the sea. We will find you, and we will kill you, no questions asked." With that made clear, he leaves to reunite with his fellow cloaked comrades.

"Phew!" Brahm exclaims paying no attention to yet another threat on his life. "I thought you were going to leave me up there until I got dizzy! Thanks!" Brahm says with childish enthusiasm.

"We were going to leave you up there until you were dead, you imbecile." Izak scoffs.

"Enough," commands Sophia. "We don't have any more time for this. You all know what needs to be done. God willing, I'll see you back here when this is all over." With her plan set in motion, she leaves the lighthouse along with her mobile prisoner to alert the lingering masses.

CHAPTER: 10

No Pain, No Gain

Outside the lighthouse, the winds have started to pick up. The clouds can be seen making steady progress towards the mainland. Brahm and Sophia catch the last twinkles of dusk before the sun departs, allowing the rolling storm to blend into the encompassing darkness.

"C'mon, follow me," beckons Sophia, "and I promise, if you try and make a run for it…"

"I'm not going to run away," Brahm responds calmly. "I'm not quite sure why we had to go through all the theatrics earlier; this is exactly what I came down here to do. Of course I'm going to stick around and help you."

"I really wonder how you have survived in this world this far," Sophia says with a sigh. "Anyway, you see that large tower behind the shipyard?" Sophia points further up the shoreline. "That is one of the primary alarm towers that will activate all the sister towers on the island. Any one of them will trigger the cascade. There are others, but this one is the closest. Should take us just a matter of minutes to turn it on. Afterwards, we brace the storm before returning to the lighthouse in the morning. Think you can handle that?" "As long as someone doesn't come flying out of the rafters again and hang me up on display, I think I should be fine!" Brahm says jovially. Sophia is quick to express herself.

"We could have easily killed you for breaking into our meeting like that! If I hadn't met you earlier today, you probably would have been killed on the spot! I don't think this is a matter to be taken lightly."

"You are right! No matter should be taken lightly! The cosmic significance of *every* moment harbors the accumulating impact of the entire universe collapsing into itself, ya' know?" Sophia stares at Brahm with questioning disgust. "I guess what I'm saying is I am just glad things played out the way they did! I've found there really isn't any point in wallowing in the hypothetical. It only distracts you from the beautiful mysteries unfolding in this ever-present moment," he concludes.

Sophia shakes her head and tries to hide the smile she is fighting back. "You are an odd fella, but your life! Of all things, wouldn't that be worth worrying about? Not many 'beautiful mysteries to unfold' when you are dead."

"Now I wouldn't go that far!" Brahm says without holding back any of his excitement. "Such vast mysteries and adventures reside outside this plane of physical existence. Our physical body is defined by limitations. Only five senses? C'mon now! You have to know there is so much more out there than what this body can process. Physicality seeming the most 'real' is merely an illusion. Death releases the restrictive barrier this body harbors, freeing our soul from its illusionary prison. Funny how that works, yeah? 'Death,' in the physical sense, can open the door to the true limitlessness of our reality!"

"I stand by my claim you are odd. I don't know if I can necessarily agree with your wild enthusiasm with death. Though, it does help explain your careless nature. All I claim to know is you have this life we are living right now, and it is your responsibility to make the most of it. Thinking about what comes next, if anything, seems like imagination wasted."

"What comes next? You still mean death?" Brahm asks while he soaks in Sophia's statement a little further. "I guess it's a matter of experience. Death is just a process, not a destination. Nothing ever stops existing, just always changing. Once you can accept that, nothing appears meaningless, insignificant… or wasteful." Sophia struggles to continue the conversation with her exponentially existential prisoner.

"I've met some really strange people in my days, but you are quickly starting to take the top prize. I want to ask you what island you come from, but I feel I should actually ask you what planet you come from!" Sophia says trying to make light of their very confusing conversation topic.

"Well, I was born on this planet to the best of my knowledge! However, I don't really know much about my past. I never really knew my parents. A family friend raised me on some lonely island, but I don't have much grasp on my origin. Something tells me the answers I'm looking for lay inside of that storm you call Babel. I thought it would be easy enough to just sail right through it, but here I am! Proving it isn't as easy as one would imagine!"

"You've *got* to be kidding me. *No one* would imagine it would be easy in the slightest regard," her shocked expression displays proudly on her face, "... except you, obviously. You purposefully sailed into that monstrosity?! And lived? Obviously you lived. What were you thinking? Right, you probably weren't, just out enjoying the life-threatening experience?"

"Yeah! Exactly! Didn't go quite as expected, but therein lies the problem with expectations! It has truly been a wonderful experience thus far; no use worrying if it doesn't play out the exact way I want it to! Just evidence there is so much more I have to learn about this world!"

"You definitely talk like you are from another planet."

"So what about you?" Brahm ponders. "Do you have a better grasp on your origin story? You must come from somewhere where the sun shines more than once a year!" he says, in reference to her golden-bronze skin. Sophia opens her mouth to answer his question but quickly stops herself.

"What's wrong?" Brahm asks.

"You almost had me, but I think you have already forgotten the predicament of your situation. Until I figure out if you are a threat in hiding or not, you will be the one who remains on the witness stand, understand? The only thing you need to know about me is by the end of this, I will be the deciding factor if you live or die."

"Must be exhausting to keep shifting back from hot to cold, but whatever you want to do... I am at your mercy," Brahm says while holding out his hands as if cuffed by invisible shackles.

"I may have to end your days due to your consistent mockery alone!" Sophia yells without disclosing the level of sincerity of her threat.

"Hey now!" Brahm yells. Sophia turns only to see it is not her he's addressing any longer. A young boy abruptly emerges from one of the alleyways onto the main street in front of them. The boy looks like he is in a panic, sweat pouring down his face, his body clearly trembling. In his right hand, shimmers a gold artifact, mostly hidden by his fingers locked tightly around it.

"Otto?" Sophia calls out, "What are you doing out here? You need to take shelter. Babel is on her way back earlier than expected!"

"You know this kid too?" Brahm says with a raise of his eyebrow. He turns to Otto again, "I agree you need to take shelter, but before you do, I think we have some business to take care of first."

"What could you possibly be talking about?" Sophia asks.

"He knows," Brahm says with a devious smile. "You managed to slip away twice now, but not this time. I think it's time we settled our little debt, don't you think?" Otto takes a step back, his mouth hanging open with no words able to break free. He stares with the same flabbergasted look that gave him away during his last run-in with Brahm. He takes another silent stumble backwards, clearly indicating a cordial conversation will not be in the cards. Brahm takes the initiative.

"All right… Otto, is it? I'm gathering very quickly nobody here has very long to discuss this due to, well you know…" Brahm says while waving his hand towards the rolling storm now casting streaks of lightning into the rippling bay.

"We all seem to be on pretty time-sensitive schedules, so I'm sure you will understand if I make this brief. That gold box you have in your hand is very important to me, and it's very unfortunate you decided to steal that of all things on your way out. 'Cause honestly, everything *but* that would have been totally fine to steal, encouraged even! I mean… who *needs* stuff anyway? Well, I guess you do if you're stealing it." Brahm lets out a deep sigh and glances over to the ticking time clock of a storm.

"So, let's just be done with it. Throw it over and let's both head to higher ground before we all get washed away. No hard feelings," he adds with a large grin.

"I-I can't!" Otto squeaks out as he clutches the compass to his chest.

"Oh, good lord," Sophia mumbles as she buries her face into her hand.

"Oh-ho, so he does speak! Well, I understand you *think* you can't, but I promise you it is definitely in the wide range of possible answer choices."

"You wouldn't understand!" Otto cries out with a little more gusto moving to further separate himself from Brahm.

"Exactly, you wouldn't understand," calls a voice emerging from an alleyway further back. A kid a few years older than Otto emerges, his face appearing to have aged a lot quicker than the rest of his body. His tattered clothing reveals a skinny, yet wiry build, topped with a head full of frantic, curly silver hair. The kid holds a metal pipe. He swings it in and out of his right hand, making a loud whacking sound like a judge's gavel.

"This no longer is a matter that concerns you, old man. Otto is here to do business with me. Whatever claim you have to this artifact is now void. It belongs to me now."

"Oh, for crying out loud!" Sophia calls out with a complementary eye roll, "I hate to use your own words, Brahm, but we really don't have time for this. Whatever that thing is, I'm sure it's important, but we have to go! If you can disregard concern for your own life, I'm sure you can happily apply your principle to that thing too." Brahm stands motionless, soaking in the evolving situation.

"I suggest you listen to the old lady, it's safer for the both of you to just leave while you have the chance," the kid from the alley remarks.

"Old? Just who are you calling old, kid?!" Sophia yells with raw emotions boldly reverberating in her cry. "I am not *old*, thank you very much! You are just young, a child even! Get that through your arrogant head!"

"It's all relative, lady," the alley kid jabs.

"You know, he's got a point," Brahm says with a shrug of his shoulders.

"Oh, shut it," Sophia snaps. "Let's just get out of here. I'm done with this."

"I can't. I wish I could just walk away from this, but that compass is significantly more important than even my own life. It's the ticket into Babel."

"You've seriously got to be kidding me… '*into* Babel?'" Sophia repeats back while mirroring a pretty good rendition of Otto's flabbergasted face.

"Yep, first attempt didn't go as planned, but it wasn't the compass's fault! So if you don't mind loosening the reigns on your prisoner for a moment, I'm going to go retrieve that compass. I promise it won't take long," Brahm says as he makes his way towards Otto and his mysterious alley friend.

"You take too long here, that thing really will be *all* of our ticket into Babel… and not the way I think you intend it too!" Sophia yells as Brahm makes his move to retrieve his prized artifact. The alley kid makes his move as well. He walks next to Otto and snatches the compass from his hands and slings it around his neck.

"Hey!" Otto cries as the kid walks past. "I don't think this is a very good idea!" But the kid doesn't stop moving. The alley kid continues his march to meet the advancing ship captain. The two stand toe-to-toe, silently sizing each other up. The storm has moved closer now to where the cracks of lightning have become audible. After each illuminated crack, the roaring thunder reverberates triumphantly through the bay.

"You're big," the alley kid proclaims with smooth arrogance, "but you're unarmed. I've been watching you and I've taken down bigger. I hope you are prepared for what comes next if you make another move forward," he threatens with his metal pipe held firm with both hands.

"As I hope you have prepared yourself," Brahm says solemnly as he makes his fated step.

As the kid strikes the advancing traveler, it's hard to tell if it is the sound of thunder or metal striking bone that echoes through the bay this time. Brahm falls to one knee with his head cocked to the side revealing a throbbing indentation on his temple.

"Such pain," Brahm remarks.

"Just wait," calls the alley kid. "It has only just begun." He rears up his weapon of choice up over his head before slamming it square onto his opponent's head. Brahm's mind swims violently with a flood of images that pour into his stream of consciousness. So much is happening at once, but he does his best to pick apart the scattered images. There is a flash of a young child being held by loving parents. The scene quickly shifts to a golden puppy jumping in the background. Another strike comes reigning down, this time triggering the stolen memory of a scrambling family struggling to make their way to a stone dwelling. Rising flood waters start rushing down the streets. The scene transitions to a brave father securing his family before being caught by the receding currents. A tear swells in the corner of Brahm's eye. The next strike brings visions of a desperate woman trying to reach for her husband before an unexpected current carries her away too. The young boy watches helplessly as his parents get washed into oblivion. The attacks now increase in velocity, hailing down with rapid fire intensity, but they are powerless to hold back the image of a now older boy with his dog staring down some street thugs; the thugs raise a metal pipe and the dog rushes to protect the boy. The scene shifts one last time to the boy crying while holding his motionless golden savior in his arms.

"Such immense pain," Brahm says from his slumped position upon the cobblestones. Blood pours from multiple concussive wounds, his arms, ribs, and face are indented from the repetitive blunt traumas. He lifts a mangled arm and props himself up high enough to stare the alley boy in the eyes. His gaze penetrates his rough exterior before diving deep into his soft and emotional core. He swims in the same turbulent waters that flooded his mind earlier with each swing of the pipe. The alley boy, becoming aware of Brahm's intrusion, involuntarily starts to surf on the repressed waves of his own soul. He takes a step back, drops his pipe and grabs his head on either side as if he is writhing in physical pain.

"AHHH!" he cries out. "Get out of my head, old man!" He grips his head tighter, attempting to pull Brahm out of his mind, but to no avail.

"Maybe it's time you look further into this pain before inflecting it onto anyone else," Brahm remarks as he lifts himself to his feet, his wounds still clearly displayed as blood drips from his face and collects in small pools at his feet. The alley boy watches as his beaten and battered adversary walks calmly towards his cowering position. He falls to the ground, as he is still overwhelmed by the bombarding images of his past.

"Make it stop!" he cries out in agony. "This is not fair, make it go away!" Tears stream down his cheeks.

"These memories can never truly go away," Brahm says as he kneels and puts a hand on the boy's shoulder. "Even when they reside in the most repressed places of your heart, they still bleed out with every action you make. Instead of opening to this pain on your own, you transfer it onto others. No matter how many times you swing that pipe, does your pain ever truly lessen?"

"I… I don't know! AAHHH!! What does it matter?!" the boy screams.

"These memories and the people who populate them are a part of you," Brahm continues with a soothing tone. "You tear yourself apart by trying to remove these aspects of yourself and that only causes further pain. Let the memories of those you loved live on as cherished rather than repressed. Hold each of their sacrifices as a testament of what they saw in you. Who knows how much their memories could help you grow into the man they all saw you to be."

"Okay," sobs the kid. "Fine. I will, now please… make this stop."

"Like I said, I can't do that. However, what I can do is help you face this pain," Brahm bargains. "Are you willing to do that?"

"Yes, anything! I'll do anything!" the kid begs. "All right," Brahm says while bringing his free hand to the kid's shoulder. "Brace yourself." Just as Brahm's hand connects to the kid's other shoulder, the two blast off through a swirling wormhole of radiant and exploding colors.

$$\infty$$

The swirling vortex stretches the explosions of colors into trickling trails of beautiful geometric patterns that scatter throughout the mystical portal. The overwhelmed alley kid tries desperately to make sense of his catapult into the seemingly infinite array of celestial fireworks. Soon a bright light triggers his attention. He stares fiercely at the bright indigo swirl appearing before him. He watches it shatter into the most splendid arrangement of repeating hexagons and triangles. As he stares deeper into the lingering geometric ripples, the shapes appear to be merging into a large, uniform rectangle. He focuses a little further, and the shape starts to resemble more of a door than an undifferentiated polygon. As this thought pops into his mind, he sees a small circle manifest on the rectangle where a doorknob would exist. The kid reaches out and touches the makeshift knob, turns it to the left, and is amazed as the structure opens like the very door he envisioned. As he makes his first steps through the celestial doorway, he is immediately blinded with an overwhelming ray of light. He reaches his hands up to protect his eyes, but quickly realizes no harm has befallen him. He cautiously opens his eyes and cannot believe what exists before him.

"Hi honey," calls a familiar voice. The kid wipes his eyes one last time to make sure he is not mistaken. With his sight as clear as it was before, the kid feels himself succumbing to the surreal reality that has manifested behind his door.

"Mom? Is that really you?" the kid asks as he patiently awaits her answer. In the wake of her silence, he casually glances over to her right to see what looks like his father. As he pans further, he sees next to his father-figure, rests a dog that bears the striking resemblance to his canine companion. The woman just nods to his question. She smiles so brightly the kid is washed over with overwhelming waves of love and compassion. He is brought to his knees as these emotions surge into his core. The tears start pouring from his eyes once again. His well-constructed emotional dam is no match for his resurging emotions. Such a barrier is quickly demolished from around his heart. Unsure what to do with this flood of emotions, he starts saying the first words that come to mind: "I'm so sorry! I'm so sorry for everything— what I've done, what you all did to keep me safe. I blew it! I wasted it! I'm not worthy of all this love. And to think you still love me like this after all I've done? How blind have I been? I don't deserve any of this," the kid says as he trails off into a drowning pool of self-pity.

The kid's family glides over to his depressive slump, surrounding him with their presence and gently infusing him with even more loving awareness than before. As desperately as the kid tries to remain in his self-loathing slump, he can't help but be lifted by the overwhelming support of his family. He gazes around and studies each of their beaming faces. He goes to speak again but stops himself. He realizes no words are necessary to translate what they are conveying. The kid finally lets his guard down and allows his family's love to come pouring into every fiber of his soul. His body lifts even further as he momentarily glides alongside his guiding spirit family.

"Thank you," he finally says, "for everything. I love you." His family returns their love with another blanketing wave, this time pushing him back towards the door.

"Wait! I'm not ready to leave you again! I just got here! I can't do this without you." He thinks for a moment. "I won't be doing this without you, will I?" An enthusiastic bark erupts from the otherwise silent bunch. The kid smiles as he drifts back through the doorway. The next thing he remembers is Brahm's hand receding off his shoulder. The kid looks into Brahm's glowing eyes, reaches his arms out, and pulls him into the warmest embrace of his life. "Thank you," he muffles as he pulls Brahm even closer. "Thank you."

∞

"What's your name, kid?" Brahm asks sincerely.

"Domino. Domino Fritz," the kid replies. "I'm so sorry about everyth—" Domino hesitates with his apology as he studies Brahm's face a little more closely. "Your wounds!" he cries in shock. "They have already started to heal!"

"It looks like yours have as well," Brahm replies with a smile. "So what do you say, Domino? Otto?" he calls out behind him. "We are running a little low on time still, how about you guys come help us activate this alarm tower?"

"Of course!" the two say in unison. Otto comes rushing over to where Brahm and Domino remain seated. Sophia slowly stumbles over to their location as well, fighting to regain her composure once again.

"I think it's about time you get your box back," Domino says as he lifts the golden lanyard over his head and holds out the compass. Brahm reaches for it but before the compass completely leaves Domino's hands, he looks up again at Brahm. Brahm smiles in a very similar way as his parents did earlier, and just like before, he is washed over with a familiar wave of love and compassion. He smiles and wipes the maturation of a tear from his eye.

"So that was real, what you showed me earlier?" Domino asks.

"It's as real as you want to make it," Brahm replies cryptically. Domino nods, accepting the fact he isn't going to get any direct answers about his recent experience.

"All right, so have you guys decided to just let the storm come flying in without a proper introduction or what?" Sophia barks as she stands over the emotional heap on the street.

"What do you say, guys?" Brahm asks his new friends.

"Let's get the hell out of here!" they cry.

CHAPTER: 11

The Tower and Babel

As the band of four close in on the alarm tower, Sophia glances back to check on the status of their other threat. The Warden's airship remains a consistent eye-sore with the howling storm complementing its destructive foreshadowing.

"How's it look back there?" Brahm calls out as more of a reminder that Sophia's pace has slowed down.

"Bad," she responds paying no attention to his jab. "Judging by how much distance they have covered since we left the lighthouse, I think it's safe to say they will make landfall before the brunt of the storm surge hit."

"Judging by your description of these guys, it doesn't sound like there is anything *safe* about what you said at all," Brahm responds out of playful reflex.

"Oh, get off yourself," Sophia scoffs. "Someone who can't even take a single conversation seriously can hardly judge someone on their semantics!"

"Hey now——" Brahm starts his rebuttal but is interrupted by Domino.

"When you two are done bickering, you might want to check out that airship again." Considering the hierarchy of importance, all four stop and turn to assess Domino's observation. The airship can now be seen clearly against the darkened backdrop, thanks to the large flames now erupting around its back rudders.

"Looks like it was struck by lightning!" Domino calls out with joy. "At this rate it's only a matter of time before——" Domino is interrupted this time by a concussive explosion emanating from the airship's envelope catching fire and erupting right before their eyes.

"No way!" Otto cries out as his hair is blown back by the explosion's shockwave. "That's got to be a good thing, right?"

"It doesn't hurt," Sophia says with a dash of emotion as they watch the airship plummet into the bay, "but it's not a guarantee we are safe just yet. These guys have shown to be nearly indestructible. I doubt being sunk by Babel would be enough to get them off our tail for good. Let's count our blessings for now and focus on getting to that tower in time." Her words strike the air like a fired gun signaling the start of a race. They take their mark and launch into their final sprint to the tower.

∞

The gusts of wind have made another significant shift in gear as they propel the hurried crew even quicker than expected towards their intended destination. As they reach the approaching doorstep, Brahm reaches out his hand and catches Otto as he is almost blown past his mark while still riding on the barreling winds.

"Thanks," Otto says while patting down his hair. "But I would have made it just fine on my own! It's not my first time out in Babel's induction, you know."

"My apologies! I'm learning more about you with every passing moment! You sound like quite the storm veteran. Make sure I don't get in your way again!" Becoming overwhelmed with the unexpected dose of praise, Otto turns his back to Brahm and lets out an audible exhale, "Humph!" His exaggerated antics serve as a ploy to hide the uncontrolled smile growing on his face. Sophia struggles for a moment to get the key to the tower door out of her pocket. The delay gives Brahm enough time to analyze the growing force of the storm winds.

"With the wind picking up as much as it has, is this not enough of a warning for the rest of the island?" he asks.

"It's easy to think that standing down here," Sophia says with her hand still rummaging around in her pocket, "the winds blow off the bay and hit the dockside the hardest. The steep angle of the mountain cliff causes the higher altitudes to be oblivious to the build up... or Babel's induction period, as we call it around here. Those higher up on the cliff normally don't notice the initial shifts in weather at night until the waters start to rise. That's why the warning towers are located down here. It's been the adopted job of the dockworkers to also serve as the first responders to Babel's induction. Ah! Here it is," she says while pulling out the desired key.

Sophia slides the key into the metal lock; with a swift turn of her wrist, the monumental steel door flies open with the help of the whipping winds. They walk in the open room and are initially taken aback by how quiet their surroundings have become. The howling winds have been dampened to sound like a muffled breeze thanks to the thick stone walls of the tower. Sophia brings the crew over to one of the few installments in the large, undecorated room. Their footsteps echo as they move towards a metal-plated device along the wall, extending around the curvature of the room. The device is large enough for six seats to be mounted in front of it, and a handful of thick pipes extend out the sides in various directions heading further up into the tower.

Brahm is first to take a seat on one of the mounted swivel chairs and decides to break the enveloped silence. "This thing sure is huge! Takes up almost the whole room! You even got dials and buttons all over it! Hmm, looks a little too rigid to be an art piece…Oh, but it could be!" he corrects himself, realizing he could have offended someone's handiwork. "So… what is it?" he asks Sophia as he spins his chair around to face her.

"Definitely *not* art, you simpleton. It's the radio receiver for the storm siren! These towers we use for Babel are one of the few pieces of technology this island has. It's amazing Mune even allowed such expensive machinery to reach the hands of the commoners. However, once the Seers were removed from power, even someone like him had to realize we needed some alarm system for Babel's storm surges. Coming from Wisteria, I thought they would have brought with them some more impressive technology, but any tech is better than no tech. They are convinced it's more reliable than anything the Seers could ever do."

"Except for this time!" Brahm says playfully. A warm smile from Sophia gives away her true feelings about her earlier statement.

"Now, let's turn this thing on!" Brahm shouts with a wave of enthusiasm, bringing an end to Sophia's solemn history pitch. She gives him her best death stare, but he shrugs it off.

"You said we were in a hurry, right? Like ten times already. Might have missed one though," Brahm says as he wiggles his fingers as if actually counting.

"Hopeless," she scoffs under her breath as she decides to give up the fight for now. She sits down and starts bringing the tower's gargantuan control panel to life. After a few switches are flipped, a loud hum can be heard coming from inside the metal device. Buttons and dials shine as they come online, and the whole tower seems to start vibrating. Brahm can hardly contain his excitement any further.

"This thing is so cool!" he blurts out. "How do you power this monstrosity?!" With Sophia clearly maintaining her focus, Domino decides to take on Brahm's new line of questions.

"Babel," he states directly, grabbing Brahm's attention. "With the amount of destructive force she holds, it has become pretty obvious her power could be used for something more… productive. We have huge paddles in the bay hooked up to generators that bring power to these towers. They also double as the initial warning trigger that sounds the alarms. As often as Babel swoops by, these towers never have a shortage of power."

"That's amazing! So how come the technology has to stop at these towers? It seems like you would have enough power to light up this whole island!"

"You're right; it definitely would look like that from the outside," Domino says trying to hide his sense of defeat, "but technology like this is hard to come by. The only other technological fruit we are allowed to taste is those LRCs."

"LRC?"

"Yeah, Long Range Communicators. They are pretty much really beefy radios. So far Mune is the only one around here who gets one. He'll roll it into the plaza when there is news sent from Wisteria."

"Propaganda you mean," Sophia interjects while still working on setting up the alarm tower.

"Whatever, some people are just afraid of the progress Wisteria offers." Domino looks to Sophia to see if she took the bait for a fight, but she remains glued to the control panel. "Well, I think that stuff is fascinating!" the eager youth continues. "It's a shame most of the Eden tech has been lost in time. Only a few islands harbor people who remember the ways of our past. As the stories go, before Babel, all the lands above the water all had the most amazing techno-gadgets! It's one of the reasons I'm sure we call the time period Eden. The technology was said to do everything for you. It was almost like it was magic! But…" he trails off with a darkening cliffhanger.

"But what?" Brahm asks eagerly. "You can't just keep someone hostage like this!"

"Have you no respect for the dramatic pause?" Domino banters back, confident his strategic story telling should of landed appropriately. "You *are* hopeless… Anyway, those who still do remember how the old technology works are essentially owned by Wisteria. They are forced to keep their trade a secret from the masses and contracted out under the supervision of a Wisterian official. If anything goes wrong with these towers, we have to pay an arm and a leg to have someone come and repair them. There is no way we could rely on this power for anything else. We could never afford the maintenance bills! Luckily, these things have remained pretty reliable. Makes you wonder though. This technology must have really been quite something before Babel came along, you know, for Wisteria fighting to keep it under such lock-and-key."

"Yeah, that is pretty interesting." Brahm interjects. "Maybe they are like spoiled kids in the sand box hording all the good toys."

"Um… Maybe? Or could it be because technology was the downfall of the old world, and they are saving us? Who knows. Hopefully this Progressive Movement will work out and we can finally tame this planet. Maybe we can do things better this time. You know, it would be nice to taste the fruits of Eden again in our lifetime—"

"This can't be happening!" Sophia yells, interrupting Domino's captivating history lesson. She slams her fists onto the machine in defeat, prompting the full attention of the crew.

"What happened?" Brahm inquires, quick to shift his attention.

"I've activated this thing *a million* times and never had a problem. I hate to burst your reliability claim you just pitched, kid, but this thing finally decided to play hardball," she says as she walks away from the machine. "We tried, but now I think it's time to save our own skins. This place will be underwater in no time."

"Let me take a look," Brahm volunteers.

"Right, you are without a doubt the least-qualified individual on the planet to even touch this thing," Sophia says with frustration. Brahm tunes her out for a moment as he scans the machine's vibrant operational panel. The various lights all illuminate with oscillating patterns as if each is dancing to the beat of their own drum. Brahm becomes mesmerized with the flooding patterns of light. His eyes dance along with the fluctuating patterns until they fall upon a display screen showcasing two specific vibrating lines of light.

"What's this?" he asks Sophia. "It looks as if they are fighting for who gets to take center stage!" Sophia rolls her eyes but decides to sit back down next to him.

"Uggh, it would be my luck that you would go right to the source of the problem, but it still doesn't mean you fixed it. That screen is supposed to show the frequency this tower outputs. There is only supposed to be *one* frequency! Whatever this other frequency the tower is picking up is causing a disturbance in the transmission. The tower doesn't know which frequency to transmit, so it's just stalled in limbo! I have no idea where this other frequency is coming from and it doesn't really matter, unless…" Sophia drifts off, failing to include her audience on her growing insight. Enough time goes by that Brahm finally feels inclined to stir the pot.

"What's with all the dramatic pauses around here?" Brahm says interrupting her train of thought. He huffs a heavy breath like an impatient child. "All right, I'll bite. Unless what, *Ms. Mysterious*?"

"Nothing, don't worry about it," she says with a shake of her head. "There is nothing we can do about it now anyway."

"What about the manual trigger at the top? Would that still work?" Otto interjects, taking the focus off Sophia's poor attempt at secrecy.

"What do you mean?" Sophia asks, happy to change the subject.

"Well, these towers are a great spot to secure yourself to when Babel is coming in. Makes it so much easier to look for incoming debris. A while back, I noticed a lever near the antenna at the top… and of course, I had to pull it. Next thing I knew, the whole island was blaring with the warning siren all over again! I've climbed to the top of a few of these towers, and they all have the switch at the top. I don't know if turning it on that way would bypass the other frequency problem, but do you think it's worth a shot?"

Sophia thinks for a moment while pacing. "It's true if we can just get this tower activated it would trigger all the other ones to follow suit. I wouldn't think the other frequency would matter then, but I can't know for sure. Honestly, it's too risky for anyone to climb the tower at this point, you're liable to get blown off it at any moment!"

"If that's all we need to do I could—"

"No!" Otto shouts, cutting Brahm off. "Sorry. I'm sure you could do it, you've done some pretty remarkable things so far, but I've decided I'm done relying on others when I finally realize what is in my power to accomplish. I am finally getting a grip on all this madness that has transpired and now realize what I can do to help! This is something I can do. Last time I checked, I have the most experience battling this storm at its worst moments. If there is even a remote chance to sound this alarm by climbing up this tower, then I'm doing it!" Otto gives a tug on the coil of rope hanging from his shoulder as an additional statement of resolve. "I've got all I need." Sophia starts her plea to talk him out of his dangerous proposition, but Brahm jumps at the opportunity to encourage Otto's vigor.

"Sounds like you really are the right one for the job! I promised to stay out of your way, so the path is yours to venture! Go out and save the day, kid!" Brahm cheers. Realizing the gravity of their situation, Sophia decides to withhold her lingering concerns. Otto smiles and takes a deep breath, inhaling the essence of his long-forgotten confidence. He sizes up the exit door and calls to the crew, "follow me!" They charge towards the door in haste-fueled unison. Otto is the first to round the bend and looks out through the vacant doorway. His refurbished confidence is quickly put to the test as he stares down a barreling surge of water racing towards them. Otto slams on the breaks and turns to the rest of the crew.

"Quick! We've got to shut this door!" The crew scrambles behind the large steel storm door and muscle it closed. The roar of the raging waters grows louder, triggering lingering doubt in the structural integrity of the door before them. Sophia rushes to get the support beam for the door. She slides it into place right as the roaring wave slams into the tower with a tremendous and ruthless crash. The door buckles slightly, allowing some of the bay to slip into the room. They watch through the adjacent window as the wave washes past the bottom layer of the tower. The water flows up a few more blocks before receding slightly towards the bay. The surge leaves the tower surrounded in a few feet of water, blocking their intended exit.

"We really are running on borrowed time," Otto says more to himself than the group, "There's got to be another way to get to the top."

"Well, above this room is just solid stone. Babel makes having structural cavities any higher a risk too great to gamble. It's not the biggest opening, but that's really our only other option," says Sophia, as she points to the lone window now showcasing their new watery prison. "We got lucky that it's high enough above the waterline. Someone small could still fit through, but we run the risk of the water levels rising any second."

"I got this," Otto chimes in. "I'm the perfect size, just need help getting up there."

"We are seriously counting on you, kid. The next surge that hits us is surely going to trap us down here for the remainder of the storm. You have to make this count," Sophia adds.

"I won't fail," Otto proclaims, wearing his tested resolve proudly. With that settled, the four race to the window and together they lift Otto to the greatest test of his resolve to date.

"It is no accident you are the only one who can fit through this window," Brahm says giving some last words of encouragement. "You were right, this is your challenge to overcome. Trust in yourself."

"Yeah kid, we are all counting on you," Sophia adds.

"Don't fall," Domino chips in right as Otto reaches the window. Otto looks back at him and displays an unfazed smile. He turns back to the window and locks eyes with his own reflection. He studies the reflected face representing his entire existence up until this very moment. With a deep exhale, he releases the firm latches that adhere the window to the inner wall of the tower. The window abruptly flies open and crashes against the outer wall, shattering the pieces of glass into the churning waters below. He catches a glimpse of his broken reflection within the glass drifting away with the current.

Otto takes a deep breath, sucking down the howling winds of Babel into his expanding lungs. A final push from Brahm leaves him now completely supported by his own grip, dug firmly into the creases of mortar. A flash of doubt strikes through his mind. "What about this hole in the wall now?!" Otto exclaims with panic in his voice.

"Don't worry about us," Brahm reassures him. "You focus on flipping that switch and we will focus on staying dry! Now go!" Otto gives a sturdy nod and starts his monumental climb. Once Otto ascends out of the view of the shattered window, Sophia turns to Brahm. "So what exactly is your plan for avoiding this room turning into our deathtrap?"

"We're going to wing it!" he says proudly.

"What does that mean?" Domino asks.

"It means we are all going to die," Sophia responds with her face embedded deep into her sorrow-filled hands.

Out on the tower's unforgiving exterior, Otto, with each advancement skyward, fights the relentless winds whipping back and forth. The years of repeated storm surges have left the tower's bleached stone walls polished and smooth. Luckily, Otto scales the side facing away from the bay; otherwise, there might not be anything left to grip. He looks up and counts the layers of stone that reside between him and the upcoming flat plateau. *I can do this! I can do this!* With the skin nearly shaved off his shaking fingertips, he eventually locks his hand on the flat edge he's been waiting for. With a mighty push from his feet, he flings himself onto the plateau and takes a breath of relief. It's short-lived however, as a look skyward reveals the true test of his might.

Otto stands on the only flat surface that wraps around the tower. The edge depresses about a foot into the tower before the solid stone starts its gradual spiral into the night sky. Accompanying the upward swirl are imbedded steps that have only been used when maintenance is in order, or for an eager scavenger looking for the perfect vantage point. Favoring the latter, Otto is all too familiar with this perilous climb. However, being used to making this assent before Babel's induction period, this is his first time braving the climb during the most unpredictable period of the storm.

With there being no intention of doing repairs during a storm, the original architects saw no problem with placing the beginning of the spiral steps over the main tower door. With no time to deliberate the added risk, Otto prepares himself to leave the protective far side of the tower. With arms extended, he inches his way towards the bay side, his back grinding like sandpaper against the sturdy stone. The roar of the returning tidal surge rings louder and louder in Otto's ear as he rounds the bend to reach the stairs. He leaps onto the first step of his spiral climb and feels the tower vibrating under his feet. He quickly glances back and sees the rising full moon illuminating the next incoming surge. The next mighty wave rises out of the water like the poised tail of a scorpion ready to strike. Having no guardrail to hold onto, Otto puts all his faith in his tested balance and sprints up the spiral stairs. He hopes to make it to the far side of the tower again before the wave connects its deadly strike.

Water erupts on either side of Otto in a violent display of power. The tower holds its ground and cuts the incoming wave in half. He grabs ahold of what mortar edging he can find and presses his body as far into the tower as the laws of physics will allow. His whole body vibrates with the intensity of the oceanic onslaught. As he feels the water start to recede, he makes a quick dash to the edge to check the status of his trapped companions below. As the water plateaus its recession, he sees the water level has already risen well above the broken window. A slight indentation can be seen in the settling water as it pours unrestricted into the room below.

"NOOOO!" he cries out in defeated despair. His mind races with a flood of images of his new friends drowning to death right below his feet. As he sinks deeper and deeper into his sorrows, an inner voice bubbles to the surface. *Brahm said they will find a way to survive. They all trusted you to make it to the top of this tower; you can stand here and let your doubt get the best of you, or you can learn to trust them as they have trusted you… even if they don't make it out alive, let their sacrifice matter! Go and do what you came here to do!* Otto shakes his head, breaks the spell of his depressive plunge, and races full-speed up the unprotected stairway.

"Honor their trust!" he bellows. "Trust in your friends and trust in yourself!" His feet slap against the damp steps, leaving no room to worry about the growing danger with each progression into the night sky. As he rounds the bay side for the fifth time, his foot slips on one of the slick steps. His momentum launches him off the side of the tower and he narrowly avoids his plummet with a well-placed grab onto the fated step that triggered his fall. Otto dangles alongside the tower with all his attention shifting to his throbbing forearm. He carefully turns his body to face the tower and digs his feet into the slick side trying desperately to gain traction. Realizing his struggle is in vain, he shifts his focus towards his outstretched arm. *This is my only choice*, he thinks to himself as he channels all his strength into the lone lifeline of an arm. He grinds his teeth with the combined agony of pain and fear of failure. "If I can only reach with my other arm…" Otto bears down, and with a depth of unforeseen power, his body miraculously lifts towards the desired stair. "Ahhh! Give… it… all… you… got!" With a tremendous battle cry pushing him the last few inches, Otto finally takes a breath knowing both of his arms are now firmly supporting his dangling body. Paying attention again to the sound of Babel churning, he digs back into the depth of his strength and pulls himself back into place.

"No time to waste!" he says as he picks back up where he left off. The time it takes to circumvent the tower grows shorter as the spiraling steps narrow into the top platform.

"I can finally see it!" Otto says as the peak starts to come into view. With just a few more steps separating him from his goal, Otto manages to pump even more speed out of his already feverishly flailing legs. Trying to manage the unnerving anticipation and urgency, he skips the last few steps and leaps towards the antenna with outstretched hands. His remaining strength pours into holding onto the antenna as his momentum spins him around a few times before he settles to his feet. "I made it! I actually made it," he says with tears pouring down his face.

"But I'm not done yet!" he reminds himself as he scans the narrow platform for the desired manual switch. He panics at first, unable to locate it, but can't help but chuckle as he finally finds it located right between his feet. He gazes out towards Babel and notices the next tidal surge already hurling towards him. He sits down next to the switch and soaks in the growing reality of his situation.

"There is a good chance none of us will make it off this tower. Our purpose was to alert the remaining people of this island, and that is exactly what we are going to do." Settled with his resolve, he wraps his hand around the manual switch and pulls it into its active position. Otto can hear the hum of the antenna firing up. In a matter of moments, he hears the all too familiar roar of the storm siren blaring through the mountain streets above him.

"We did it," he says as he lifts the rope off his shoulder. "This very well might be my final resting place, but I'll let whoever finds me know I didn't go down without a fight." He ties his rope around his waist and secures the opposing end around the base of the antenna. "I'm giving you all I got,

Babel," he says to the storm. "So you're going to have to give me all you got in order to rip me from this tower!"

Not one to back down from a challenge, the incoming tidal surge rears up into the familiar scorpion tail formation. As it reaches closer to the tower, it grows further in height, sucking up the pooling water left in the streets. For a brief moment, time appears to slow as Otto looks out at the gigantic wave reaching up over the height of the tower. The wave ripples from the sheer weight of its own being, struggling to maintain its impressive heights. Unable to hold its position any further, the wave comes crashing down over the tower with unrelenting force.

Otto is ripped from his perch and flails in the skyline currents like a fluttering flag. His barrage is short lived as the majority of the wave's concussive mass falls on the streets below. Otto dangles from his tethered perch looking down at where he assumes he first exited the tower. With the water only a few feet below his dangling limbs, there is no telling how much air his companions have left. "Hold out as long as you can!" he calls out. "It's all we can do at this point. Whatever becomes of us, just know we succeeded!" Expecting to be overcome with thoughts of his own demise, Otto is surprisingly bombarded with thoughts of all the clueless islanders who are now scurrying to safety. He shifts his weight to look over at the roaring storm surge, waiting for the next wave to come. There is a refreshing peace that swells within him, despite being in full view of the violent beast of destruction.

The moon holds her position as a steadfast beacon of light despite the swirling darkness surrounding her. Her defiant rays shine down in sporadic flashes as the dark clouds try to disrupt her illuminating presence. With the help of the moon's determination, Otto catches what looks like a large piece of debris floating towards him on his right. Expecting nothing to come as a surprise at this point, Otto initially pays it no mind. As it gets closer, he reaches up to refresh his eyes, but it does little to help him believe what is coming into view. Casually sailing towards him is the very ship he watched impale a seaside dwelling the night before. *I must have already died and didn't know it*, he thinks. *There is no way that ship is seaworthy.* Unfazed by Otto's misfiring perceptions, the mysterious ship continues to move further into focus.

Eventually the ship's sharp, sword-like metal bow comes into view, cutting through the choppy water with ease. The elongated hull displays its dark wood paneling extending into the back living quarters. The flat roof of the living quarters provides a perfect platform for the open navigator's deck. Scattered throughout the ship are various sails that seem to sprout from the ship's main masts at random. The collective conglomeration of sails looks like a floating cloud resting above the sturdy streamline ship. Unsure of what to expect from the approaching anomaly, Otto struggles to gather what composure he can from his dangling position. Sure enough, the powerful gusts from Babel propel the sword-like ship right towards him and the submerged tower. Otto stares down the reflective bow-blade of the enormous vessel, which shows no sign of slowing. Unable to cut himself down, he turns to face the tower wall and braces for the imminent impact.

A huge rush of water flows over him, and he is flung from side to side while still tethered to his dangling perch. As he catches his breath, he can't help but wonder why he hangs like a wet rag and not a mangled corpse. Assured of death, he opens his eyes, ready to meet the celestial gatekeeper. However, he is met with the dark brown exterior of the gargantuan ship residing patiently before him. Otto's mouth hangs open as he struggles to understand how a ship so large and moving so fast could have come to such an abrupt stop. Footsteps can be heard coming from the ships deck, but Otto's overloaded mind refuses to absorb any more sensory perception.

"Interesting way to go fishing," Beau's voice calls out as he comments on Otto's bizarre presentation. Otto manages to close his mouth but can only bring himself to stare at Beau with his trademark flabbergasted gaze.

"You weren't much for words when I first saw you," Beau says to the youth. "It's no matter. To be honest, I'm not much either. Let me just get you cut down from there." Beau flicks his wrist, producing a knife out of thin air. He throws the knife with blistering speed, easily cutting through Otto's rope. Triggering the youth's abrupt plummet, the severed rope flails around Otto like a startled snake. Beau reaches out his hands as if coaxing the animated rope towards him. Appearing to heed his call, the rope slithers towards the impromptu snake charmer. Beau clenches the falling rope as it nears his position. Taking a heavy step, he pivots his massive body and casts the rope over his shoulder. He maneuvers the tethered chord with sublime grace, appearing to be fly-fishing for the heavens. Consequently, Otto's plummet is abruptly rerouted back into the sky, appearing like Beau's makeshift celestial bait. He floats in the air for a split second, immersing himself in the momentary state of airborne bliss. He stares downward and follows the extended rope down into Beau's firm hands. As his momentum straightens out the arching tether, he watches Beau's solemn face twitch into a cynical smile.

"Hold on, kid," Beau calls out.

"Whoa, whoa, whoa! J-J-Just wait…" but it was too late. With another fierce heave of the lifeline, Beau reels Otto towards the ship with blistering speed.

"I'm going to die! I'm going to die! I'm *really* going to die!" Otto cries out as the tears are sucked out of his head from his rocket-powered removal from the heavens. Beau drops the rope and positions himself directly under Otto's reentry point. He bends his knees and holds out his hands as he waits for the moment of contact.

"Ahhhh! I'm still going to die!" Otto howls as he flies head-first into Beau's unconvincing arms. Summoning his super-human reflexes, Beau reaches out and grabs ahold of Otto by his shoulders. Powered by another heavy pivot, Beau directs the falling momentum into a swirling spiral. The skin on Otto's face ripples to one side as he struggles to maintain consciousness. Beau's grip clenches a bit more firmly as he burrows his feet into the deck of his ship to slow their nauseating whirlwind. Otto's face slaps back into place as his spin cycle finally comes to a halt. However, the rotating trails of emesis that follow show Beau's flashy rescue didn't come without consequence.

"I-I-I've lost count of how many times I have been faced with death these last few days; it's becoming as anticipated as the wind shifting directions," Otto says to himself as he still struggles to find his equilibrium. "And to think I was so afraid of death before."

"Sounds like you got a lesson hidden in there somewhere," Beau says as he walks over to Otto's stumbling position. "What are you doing out here, kid? I figured Brahm would be the only person crazy enough to be out in a storm like this. Honestly, seeing you scurrying around that tower, I thought for sure it was him." The sound of Brahm's name stops Otto's unbalanced stumble dead in his tracks.

"Brahm!" he cries out.

"Sounds like you two finally got acquainted," Beau responds as he bides his time for the rest of the epiphany-struck realization.

"H-H-He is trapped under the tower! Under the water! There was a leak! I had to keep going! There are others, but I don't know if they are even still alive, can you help?!" Otto's mind races in so many directions it is a miracle any thoughts made their way out of his traffic-jammed thought process.

"You need *me* to rescue *Brahm*?" Beau says as he rears his head back in disbelief. "Ha! Now it's been a long time since I've been in this situation. Wonder what kind of mess he's gotten into now."

"Please! You have to hurry, he's not the only one down there! There is a woman and a boy about my age; I don't think they have much time left!" Otto says as his thoughts swirl in the pitting currents of apprehension.

"Right, right, I'll take care of it. But I wouldn't worry if I were you. If your friends are with Brahm, I'm sure they are all right."

"Please, just hurry!"

"Geez, I said I would help. Just give me a second," Beau says as he lifts his foot into his hand. "Here, hold these," he says handing Otto his thick leather boots. Beau throws his hand up in the air and stretches his back out before walking towards the water. "I won't be long, but please try not to steal anything while I'm gone," Beau says with a wink. Otto is unfazed by his attempt at humor. He simply stands there, ringing the boots in his hands as the anticipation builds to unbearable levels.

"Just go already!" Otto cries in desperation. Giving a final chuckle, Beau turns to the water and watches the violent ripples crashing against his motionless ship. He wiggles his barren toes freely as he searches for an optimal entry point. One by one, his toes wrap around the ship's edge, clenching the dark wood with a firm grip. With a swing of his arms, he thrusts his massive body into an elegant dive. He glides effortlessly into the choppy waters below leaving just a slight ripple in his wake.

CHAPTER: 12

Diving in, Falling Out

The liberated moonlight breaks free from its cloudy barrier. The rays of light shine bright, illuminating Beau's descent towards the sea-bound trio. Each stroke of his massive arms propels him deeper into the waterlogged streets. A steady hum can be heard coming from his propeller-like feet as they slice through the water with unrestricted ease. The penetrating rays of the moon highlight the trails of air bubbles cascading off his body. The swirling bubbles bob with the churning currents, floating back to the surface to release their encapsulated breath.

Fully aware time is of the essence, each stroke serves as a well-calculated pivot towards his descending mission. Outside of his goal-locked gaze resides a plethora of uprooted wildlife that has quickly claimed the city streets as their oceanic oasis. A rainbow eel circles around Beau's rigid frame, playfully flashing his bioluminescent patterns. Schools of frantic fairy fish scurry around his deepening trail of air bubbles. Their reflective scales radiate bright shimmers of red and orange when struck by the moonlight. As one manages to pop a bubble, the school frantically disbands as if exploding with fright. They quickly regroup and return to the bubble stream to eagerly pop another. Their playful efforts are soon disrupted by a herd of giant ray-fins charging through the converted streets. Their thick, muscular fins forcefully brush the tiny fairy fish out of their way.

Disinterested in the colorful sea life, Beau quickly nears the base of the alarm tower. He goes for the main door but is met with unexpected resistance. He swims around the tower, inspecting its structural integrity. Along the far side, he notices the port window's bronze frame fluttering in the swirling currents. With a sturdy kick, Beau launches himself toward the only apparent entryway. Peering through the glassless window, he scans the barren room. He spots three lifeless bodies casually floating into view. Taking a calculating moment, he compares the tiny porthole to his massive lumberjack frame. He decides to make some necessary structural adjustments.

Beau floats back slightly and lines himself up with the stone wall surrounding the window. Calibrating careful precision, he rears back his right arm, locking his forearm into perpendicular alignment with his torso. With an abrupt flash, he fires his fist out of its well-crafted chamber. The force completely destroys the once solid wall of the tower. Blocks shatter in all directions as they are abruptly displaced from their sturdy formation. The view into the tower becomes shrouded with dust and debris from the erupting fragmented blocks. The obscured view quickly washes clear from the churning currents, revealing the still lifeless bodies unaffected by Beau's remodeling. Beau swoops in and places Sophia and Domino securely under each of his arms. Struggling for a moment, he tries to figure out what to do with Brahm. Giving into his limited option choices, he bites down on his captain's overalls. With his jaws locked and hands full, he turns to head back to the surface.

A sudden cracking sound thunders through the water, directing Beau's attention towards his peripherals. He watches a splintering fissure race around the circumference of the tower. Falling debris reappears as the base of the tower finally succumbs to the combined assaults from Beau and Babel. Letting go of the years of structural endurance, the tower starts its implosive descent. With his opening quickly deteriorating, Beau concentrates all his energy into his powerful legs, swinging them back and forth with growing intensity. Ignoring the restrictive forces imposed by the surrounding water pressure, his legs quickly fade into a vibrating blur of fury.

Another crack is heard further up the tower. Assuming no time is left to build up any more momentum, Beau positions himself into firing position. He pauses for just a moment longer, watching the falling bricks, waiting for his unobstructed opening. As the stones finally align, Beau's propeller-like legs erupt with explosive force. He flies out of the crumbling tower, spiraling around the countless falling obstacles. Clenching tighter around his precious cargo, he makes sure they are secure before triggering the afterburners of his rocket-powered propeller feet. His legs oscillate so quickly they appear as a dark smear above the cloud of bubbles populating from their turbulent churning. The gallivanting sea life scurries to safety as they make way for the sentient-torpedo. As the surface nears, Beau straightens out his spiraling maneuvers to line up with his patiently awaiting ship.

What was that? Beau catches sight of a dark figure emerging into the scope of his peripheral radar. He is taken aback as it is clearly unlike any of the sea life he has encountered so far. The humanoid figure radiates with distracting concern then disappears as quickly as it had appeared back into the murky waters. Beau is forced to put it out of mind for the time being as he can feel the life quickly fading from his limp passengers. As he nears the rippling surface, he deciphers the wavy outline of Otto's head protruding over the edge of his ship. Beau can't help but smile between the overall straps as he feels the genuine concern radiating from his eager passenger.

Sure enough, Otto clenches his fingers firmly around the ship railing as he leaps frantically with nerve-racking anticipation. Staring down into the vast floodwaters, he awaits some sign of reassurance that he has not witnessed another victim fall to Babel's wrath. Eventually, he sees some strange bubbles emerge near the spot Beau first entered the waters. The bubbling quickly transitions to a ferocious boiling mass. Steam radiates off chaotic undulating mounds of water fueled by the immense pressure being exuded by Beau's assent. Otto squints to focus on the odd mound and sees a black silhouette racing into view from the dark depths. The mound of water starts to swell like an expanding balloon until the tension explodes into a magnificent geyser. Otto's gaze trails high into the sky. He watches awestruck as Beau explodes out of the floodwaters into an elegant aerial spiral. His momentum pushes him up and over Otto's perch along the railing and lines up squarely with his landing-pad of a deck. Almost as if in slow motion, Beau lands his descent with both feet securely planted, his passengers still cradled in hand and mouth. The trailing floodwater finishes its ride on Beau's momentum, crashing overhead like delayed rainfall.

Otto once again struggles to maintain his composure as he is forced to process yet another outlandish display of reality-bending ingenuity. He watches, paralyzed by his own disbelief, as Beau makes his attempt to revitalize the rescued trio. He gently places Sophia, Domino, and Brahm's motionless bodies next to each other on the now gently rocking ship deck. He kneels next to Sophia first, closes his eyes, and takes in a deep breath. In sync with his exhale, he reaches out his right hand and leaves it hovering slightly above her motionless chest. A faint hum starts to emanate from Beau's body. The audible frequency turns visual as Otto catches rays of green light dancing around his frame. The youth watches the aura of light move down Beau's extended arm and flow into Sophia's chest. The flow of energy pours into her like water hitting a thirsty sponge before evenly dispersing around the contours of her body.

With the radiating green light around Sophia mirroring his own, Beau's chest swells as he takes in another deep breath. He channels a new wave of accumulating energy back into his extended hand. Holding the vibrating energy in his palm for a moment longer, he concentrates on aligning the frequency with Sophia's weakening pulse. In a flash, Beau's eyes open wide. Following a powerful exhale, he fires the concentrated ball of energy deep into Sophia's heart. She bounces violently off the deck from the impact. Her chest arches towards the sky, hovering for a moment in mid-air as the enormous wave of energy flows through her every vein, artery, and capillary. Beau hits her again with another blast of energy, this one demanding breath to be brought back into her lungs. Her eyes burst out of their eyelids as she simultaneously gasps with a new breath of life.

Sophia turns to her side and coughs up the lingering water still trapped within her. Satisfied with her survival, Beau wastes no time and moves over to Domino. His glowing green aura still radiates strong as he reaches out his arm once again. With another flash of light, Domino's chest arches towards the sky, suspended by the feverish current of Beau's life force. Domino's eyes spring open as air floods into his lungs once again. Beau now looks over towards his motionless captain. With lips pursed, he lets out a nasally sigh as he kneels over Brahm. Beau's energy swirls in his hand, vibrating with a more chaotic pulse than before. He extends his arm, and with a lightning-quick flick of his wrist, he drives his open palm into the still-damp cheek of Brahm's face. The impact relocates his face to the other side of his body before consciousness reassumes his vessel. Brahm opens his eyes as water pours out of his nose and mouth like a pressurized faucet. He hesitates to speak, still in shock as Beau lines up his hand for another revitalizing strike.

"Whoa, whoa, whoa big guy! I'm alive! I'm alive, all right!" Brahm shouts with his hands in the air. "So let's just put that thing away for now, okay?"

"Fine by me," Beau responds. "Now let me just get out of the way. Seems I'm not the only one with the same idea." Brahm stares blankly at him walking away, confused by his odd statement.

∞

Hastening footsteps can be heard pounding the deck as they scurry towards Brahm with the answer he seeks. Another open palm strikes Brahm's face, this one belonging to the now very alive and furious Sophia.

"That?! That was your genius 'winging it' plan?!" Sophia screams with her hand still primed, eager to strike again.

"Ha, well, you see…" Brahm says while scratching his head, trying to think of how to explain himself.

"We saw, alright! We saw you dive into the mind of a complete stranger, somehow force him to come to terms with the horrible sins of his life just so you could get a stupid compass. We also saw you when we were trapped like rats under a flooding deathtrap. It would have been a perfect time to use your crazy magic tricks to do something productive, and what did you do? Nothing! Not a damn thing! I can't believe you just sat there while we struggled to find a way to survive… laughing! Like this is all one big joke!"

"Sophia…"

"No, I'm done with this. I'm done with you. Maybe this is all one big joke for you, but not for me. I'm done pretending you are any prisoner of mine. I'm ready to be rid of you. You're free to do whatever you please, as I'm sure you always have been. Just leave me out of it from now on." Sophia drops her gaze as she swims in the current of her own rage. A thought rises to the surface as she looks up to address Brahm again. "You know, some parts of life deserve more attention than just moving through them 'winging it.'" She stares down again and shakes her head in disgust. Without any need to validate her conclusive feelings, she turns her back to Brahm. "The one who saved us, what is your name?" she asks without turning around.

"Beau," says the burly bald-headed man.

"Thank you, Beau for coming after us… for cleaning up this mess."

Brahm silently watches Sophia walk towards the stern. Getting out of earshot, she sits down next to one of the staircases leading up to the navigator's deck. From the south, a strong gust of wind rips through the ship from the bay. Otto and Domino are taken off guard and are blown like tumbleweeds into the ship's massive tree-like mast. Brahm and Beau remain planted, shifting their focus to the howling storm beckoning their attention.

"We have to act fast. What's your call?" Beau asks.

"Man the helm. I'll take point on the sky-sails," Brahm responds as he places his soaked hat firmly back on his head.

"Ah, going to take another crack at riding this beast, are you?" Beau asks playfully.

"Exactly. This time we leave no room for error."

"Error? Now that is a word I don't hear from you very often," Beau says with an enthusiastic chuckle.

CHAPTER: 13

No Room for Error

Otto and Domino struggle to regain their sea legs after their abrupt collision with the ship's mast. They stumble like a pair of drunken sailors unable to guess correctly which way the world is spinning. The swirling currents from Babel make it hard to determine if it is the storm or the lingering concussion that provokes the unsteady footing. Otto is the first to conquer his wavering gate. Finally, standing square-footed, he takes this time to assess the monstrous mast in front of him.

"This is unreal," he says as he tries his best to digest the unexpected sensory input pouring into his eyes. "Domino, do you see this?" he calls out, his attention unable to be pulled from his skyward gawk.

"See what?" Domino calls back, as he still struggles to recover from his recent cranial collision. "I'm still trying to figure out which of these six hands are the real ones."

"Man, you need to get it together quick. I've never seen anything like this. It's like being inside a cloud of kites!" Otto circles around the mast, losing count of the plethora of kite-like sails. He rubs his eyes to try and clear his vision. *There's no way they are really just floating up there… is there?* Upon his second glance, he notices a network of thin cables connecting all the strange sails to the mast. The highway of cables run skyward, leading to the top of the mast which branches off like the canopy of a tree. Resting atop the confines of the canopy exists a small hut with a flat roof. "A… *tree* house? Really?" He shakes his head in disbelief, wondering if his concussion is in need of medical attention. Resting on the roof of the bizarre hut lies a large, rolled up sail dangling below the canopy. "That thing is massive. I wonder what it—"

"Hey," Brahm calls down from the navigator's deck, "have you two ever worked a ship before?"

"Uhhh…" Otto mumbles, running his fingers through his hair as he fumbles to procure the most accurate answer.

"Of course!" chimes in Domino with inflated vigor. His earlier cognitive concerns quickly dissolving.

"Sure, but nothing like this!" Otto scans the contour of the sail rigging once again.

"Oh, right," Brahm says scratching the scruff of his chin. "Don't worry about all the sky-sails whizzing around, I can manage those just fine back here. However, if you two can work on untying the main sky-sail up top, the stratus sail, it would help get us moving a lot quicker. It's the… the one rolled up on top of the crow's hut."

"All right! Sure!" Otto yells back with an unconvincing tone. The two boys peered up at what Otto imagined was a tree house. Unsure as to the best route to climb the mast, they run off full speed in opposite directions. They circumnavigate the lower deck in a zigzag pattern before returning to the point at which they started. Beau strikes his face with an open palm.

"Guys," Brahm calls down before they start the next scattered search. "The netting?" He points to either side of the navigator decks.

"Right, right! That's what we were looking for!" Domino responds with unwarranted reassurance. The two boys now concentrate their hasteful sprint towards the aft of the ship. They race single-file up one of the two matching stairwells leading to the main navigator deck. Their shoe-bound feet strike the steps like a hoard of hammer-wielding carpenters. Halfway up their assent, a harsh wave slams into the side of the ship. The impact flings the boys through the air towards different parts of the stair railing. Domino bounces off the floor and crashes into the sturdy spokes holding up the railing. Otto manages to rotate in the air just enough to direct his impact into the railing's edge. He lands abruptly along his waist, momentarily knocking the air out of his lungs. He reaches out to grab the smooth and intricately crafted spokes as his momentum is determined to fling him onto the deck below. He bears down on his grinding grip and manages to pin himself securely to the ridged railing. As he lets out a sigh of relief, his eyes rest on his once projected point of impact below. He watches as Sophia sits motionless, unfazed by the violent rocking of the ship. At first, he thinks to call out to her, but he is drawn into the thick aura surrounding her defeated slump. She stares into the swirling skies in front of her, eyes half-mast, emotions washed clean from her hollowing face. It's as if she has already accepted this ship as her final resting place. The gravity of her emotional demise pulls at Otto harder than the forces governing his near-plummet to the deck.

"Hey! What's gotten into you?" Domino asks, right before he slaps his companion on the back of his head. Otto forgoes the initial reaction of anger and is thankful to have his attention brought back into focus. Domino gives a quick scan of his friend to make sure all his faculties are still in place. He gives an approving nod, then turns to lead the remaining race up the stairs. The boys quickly reach the first navigators' deck, occupied by Beau and the ship's main helm. As they start to slow down, Beau motions for them to continue up to the smaller platform behind him. A single staircase leads the boys to the second navigator's deck where Brahm awaits.

Aside from Brahm, the only other occupant on the final layer of the ships deck is a strange, pipe organ-like instrument that Brahm is currently standing in the middle of. The boys take a step towards the acutely focused ship captain. His attention is completely unwavered by their presence. The moment of silent concentration gives the boys time to catch their breath. They pause and study the bizarre contraption displayed before them.

Several brass pipes of various lengths are mounted around Brahm in the shape of a half moon. Long cables run through the top of each pipe and attach to wooden handles below. The network of cables runs along thick wooden beams jutting out of the furthest corners of the navigation deck. They flow with a skyward arch, merging into a central point before connecting to the top of the main mast. Otto follows the network of cables under the arching support beams and realizes they become the same cables he saw tethering the peripheral sky-sails. As if to confirm Otto's observation, Brahm gives a firm pull on one of the wooden handles and immediately one of the sky-sails draws in closer to the ship's midline. Brahm lifts his right foot, drawing attention to the row of pedals jutting out of the half-moon structure. After a few final adjustments, he slams his foot on the desired pedal until he feels it lock into place. Satisfied, he drops the wooden handle leaving the maneuvered sail locked in its new position.

"What are you two waiting for?" Brahm asks while simultaneously scanning the swarm of sky-sails.

"Well, we uh… you see, we don't…" taken off guard by Brahm's abrupt address, Domino struggles to explain their lingering confusion. However, he is cut short by the swift extension of Brahm's arm. A single finger emerges from his outstretched fist, beckoning the boys to turn around and follow its direction. Awaiting their discovery ruffles the extensive netting that hangs down from the arched support beams. With images of the strange pipe contraption still running through their mind, the boys take a moment to register why this netting is important.

"Ah! The stratus sail!" they cry in unison.

"You guys forgot already?" Brahm asks with his attention still directed on the peripheral sky-sails.

"Of course not!" they cry out as their spell is broken. "We won't let you down!" They rush to embark their skyward climb.

"Just remember," Brahm calls out right before they make their first step, "it's not me you need to worry about. Your own survival depends on this climb. Don't lose focus. That storm isn't slowing down for anybody." The boys take a collective gulp as they register the gravity of their situation.

"C'mon!" Domino calls to Otto with inspirational vigor, "let's do this!" Otto gives a faint smile and takes a moment to study Domino's vibrating hands. They shake uncontrollably as they clench the wind-ravaged netting. *He's scared too,* Otto thinks, *but he's not letting it get the best of him, and I won't either!*

"Let's go!" Otto screams into the night sky, signaling the start of their race against the storm. As the boys carefully scurry up the net, Beau turns to his captain with a deep sigh.

"No room for error, eh?"

"None," Brahm responds with his gaze now shifted to the still motionless Sophia below. After a lingering moment, he gazes up at the boys as he watches them wrestle the flailing netting for each advancement forward. "No matter what does or doesn't happen, we are all making it out of this storm alive. Whatever it takes," he finishes with a harsh cracking of his knuckles.

"Is that so?" Beau wonders while stroking his beard. "Haven't seen you this focused in a long time. I wonder what could be the inspiration?" His jest-filled question falls flat in silence, eventually turning rhetorical. "Ha, no matter. Either way, this should be interesting," he finishes with a bright smile. Paying him no mind, Brahm shifts his focused attention towards Babel.

The storm has consumed the moon once again, leaving just a dim glow to shed warning of the next assault. Dark clouds race to further choke the limited illumination. Their payload of rain can be seen pouring down furiously in the distance like an impenetrable curtain. Brahm watches as a swirling wave leaps out of the bay as if suddenly provoked by the shrinking shoreline. The wave races towards The Pearl's mountain peak and unleashes its bottled-up fury along the barren streets. The wave crashes its essence into the awaiting Lotus above before bending back towards the bay from which it was born. Not willing to retreat in silence, the wind lets out a mighty howl like it was summoned to voice the wave's detest. The bay sinks into a deep crater as it molds around the force generated by the falling avalanche of water.

"Quick, pull up the anchor!" Brahm calls to Beau. "The shockwave that will emerge from that impact will definitely wash this boat clean. We have to ride it out!"

"Whatever you say," Beau says lightly. "Need I remind you, the last time we tried this, we wound up in the very mess we are still trying to clean up?"

"Don't worry about that," Brahm responds as he waves his hand for Beau to hurry. "I got a few tricks up my sleeve I wasn't willing to try before."

"That's the spirit! Now, just try and make sure we finish up in the same dimension that we started in, all right?" Beau says with a chuckle. He lines his thumbs under the straps of his suspenders as he heads down to the bow to retrieve the anchor.

With the help of the rapid-fire cracks of lightning, Brahm watches the concave crater in the bay start to bulge back towards the surface. As it races to establish its equilibrium, it brings forth the first round of towering shockwaves. They rise out of the bay like an inflated bull's-eye sprawling out in all directions. Brahm peers up to see how far the boys have advanced. They are near the merging point of the two support beams and the mast, but Brahm fears it's not far enough.

"Domino! Otto!" he yells, competing with the deafening howls of the wind. "Hold on to where you are for now! Get ready to brace for impact!" The boys nod and tangle themselves into the netting as best they can. Brahm glances to the bow and sees Beau single-handedly pull the massive anchor out of the water and resting it gently alongside the starboard hull.

"All right! C'mon back and let's ride this wave!" he calls down to Beau. "Sophia! Be sure to hold onto something, this storm is about to put us to the test!" Brahm looks on awaiting some registry of confirmation, verbal or nonverbal. Nothing. Sophia remains motionless, a solitary blip residing along the rocking deck.

"Looks like you will have to steer very carefully," Beau jabs as he returns to his position on the helm.

"So be it!" he cries as he grabs ahold of the wooden sky handles. A quick look behind brings awareness to the impeding wall of water heading straight for them. "Here goes… everything!" Brahm shouts as he kicks the brass pedals out of their locked positions. The cables start to hiss and the pipes rattle under the pressure of all the sky-sails collectively soaring into the sky. They penetrate the dark layer of clouds and fly into the more stable air currents above. Despite the encroaching wave of destruction, Brahm closes his eyes to better concentrate on the sky-sails, feeling for the optimal current to ride.

"You better find one quick. This ship can't stay stationary much longer," Beau points out as the wall of water forces some feelings of urgency.

"Almost got it," Brahm whispers as he clenches his already closed eyelids. "The storm's impact on the higher air currents is unreal. I'm starting to wonder if we even have enough cable for… ah! There!" Brahm launches his eyelids back into his head and sets his sight on their narrowing escape route. He grips the pair of wooden handles in his hands and pulls back on the reigns to slow the advancing sky-sails.

"C'mon man! Punch it!" Beau bellows.

"Haha, here we go!" Brahm stomps the pedals back into their locked position and immediately launches the ship into motion like a spit-fired rocket. The ship skips along the ocean's surface with the rippling wall of water hot on their heels. Beau latches himself to the helm, making sure to keep from flying off the deck. With the ship leaping in and out of the water, much of the navigation relies on Brahm's control over the sky-sails. He frantically runs from one side of the half-moon instrument to the other, releasing, pulling, and then locking the various cables. Each adjustment in the sky equates to an abrupt shift in the ship's position on the sea. The boys remain tangled in the netting above as Sophia sloshes around the deck like a foregone mop bucket. As Brahm struggles to stabilize the ship, Beau points out their next quickly approaching obstacle.

"You better get control over those sails quickly! We've got another one of those towers I saved you from dead ahead!" Brahm stares down the encroaching tower and quickly processes the possible courses of action.

"The speed at which we are going… the girth of the tower… the closing distance—"

"Are you talking to yourself again?"

"Yep! And we're going over it!"

Beau shakes his head and smiles, "I should have guessed that one." Brahm releases the brake pedals on the pipe reels, sending the corresponding sails soaring further into the sky. As the cables hiss and scream, he grabs as many handles as he can and plants his feet with grizzly force to the port side. The ship lifts its keel a little further out the water, but still grips onto the comfortable familiarity of the waves.

"You have to do better than that! We are running out of time!"

"I'm doing the best I can without the stratus sail! I'm going to push these sky-sails to the max!"

"This is it!" Beau says as the looming tower envelops most of their forward view. He bears down on the already-indented spokes of the helm and whispers a prayer. Brahm runs to the port side, handles still in firm grasp, and slams his weight on the open pedals. The latches lock, and the pull from the higher current finally lifts the keel out of the water. The few feet gained finally allow the ship to be considered airborne but is not enough to clear the approaching obstacle. The sharpened steel blade of the bow crashes into the tower, carving it in half as the ship barrels through its stony adversary like a drunken lumberjack. The impact sends stone blocks flying in all directions, raining down like a hailstorm from Hell. Beau studies their trajectory, anticipating their chaotic flight patterns to turn quickly into hostile projectiles. As the ship starts its plummet back towards the sea, Beau catches a rogue stone heading right towards Sophia. He leaps from his navigation perch and glides through the air, held by the momentary lull in gravity. As the ship's bow connects with the water, Beau extends a calculated kick to the falling stone just as gravity makes an abrupt return.

After displacing the stone from its deadly path, he lands with heavy footing beside Sophia. He turns his back at the last second to shield her from the spray erupting from their oceanic reentry. Splashes of water fall like rain, surrounding the two like a spring shower. Slowly turning her head, Sophia makes her first conscious movement since they set sail. She looks at Beau with eyes full of wonder and confusion.

"I thought that was going to kill me," she says solemnly.

"As grave as our situation may look, I promise you, we are all getting out of this alive," Beau says with a reassuring smile.

"What about that?" Sophia asks slowly pointing to the towering wall of water looming directly overhead. Drops of water rain down, striking the ship deck like the salivating drool of a hungry giant.

"I got this!" Otto yells as he untangles himself from the safety of the ship's netting. "If I can just open up the stratus sail, we should be able to get out of here!"

"You fool! This is no time to be a hero!" Beau cries out with a parental scolding. He watches in horror as Otto crawls into the mast's canopy to wrestle with the tethered sail. The wave closes in on the frantic crew, blocking what little moonlight remains on the already-darkened situation. Beau's piercing eyes penetrate the enveloping darkness and stare directly at Brahm. A moment uncharted by time passes between the two men as they process their crumbling situation. A silent decision is reached and Brahm nods his head with unspoken understanding.

Brahm drops his collection of handles and brings his hands together at his chest. He carefully breathes in deeply and closes his eyes upon his exhale. An indigo light now dances around his frame, flickering like a burning ember. With each passing breath, his burning aura grows in intensity. His hands depart from his chest, flowing upward above his head before separating outward, circling back around to his chest. A multitude of shadowy arms suddenly appear in the wake of his movements. They quickly condense their questionable apparitions into solid form, causing a stampeding shockwave to erupt from his glowing chest. The cascading force washes over the crew and surrounding area like a blanket of raw energy.

∞

Sophia's eyes widen as the unexpected surge of energy causes an unusual sensation throughout her whole vessel. The unexplainable vibrations pulsate through her body like blasts of echolocation, bringing acute awareness to the hidden processes within her. With each pulsating ripple, Sophia gains momentary awareness of every organ system tucked away in her chest. She notices the blood swimming through her constricted veins, the stress hormones surging from her brain, down to the very spaces in-between her steadily vibrating molecules. All of her heightened sensations trigger an unprecedented awareness of the limitless vessel she inhabits. Sophia hastily peers down to study her hands, flipping them back and forth to make sure they are still attached. Her sense of self is beginning to expand as vast as the spaces between her molecular makeup. Just before she is about to lose herself completely, the intensity of the shockwaves starts to lessen. The disoriented return to ordinary consciousness inspires a wave of intense emesis that is quickly expelled. Thankful to still be alive, she desperately looks to make sure the rest of the crew survived the vibratory onslaught.

Content the crew is still in one piece, Sophia glances back at Brahm with mixed emotions and a nauseated gut. She studies him with both awe and disgust swimming in her eyes as the hovering band of arms flutter like the sprouted wings of an angel. One by one they open their clenched fists, revealing an emerging eye awakening in each of their palms.

∞

Brahm's whole body starts to adopt an indigo hue that matches his dancing aura. His toes kiss the deck farewell as he floats in a hovering trance. The eyes on his face finally reopen with a third opening in the center of his forehead.

His swarm of eyes all shift and lock onto the quivering cables still tied to the sky. He floats closer to the half-moon instrument and reaches out with his plethora of hands to grasp each cable independently. The indigo flame radiating from his body pours through the extended cables and flows up into the clouds. The tethered stratus sail that Otto desperately tried to unravel also adopts the indigo glow and unties itself right before his eyes.

The sail bursts into bloom, stretching its four corners into the sky as if waking from a prolonged slumber. Glowing cables extend from the stratus sail as it soars into the clouds to join the others. The cables dance through the air, flowing down through the canopy spokes above the mast like a threaded needle. They float gently into each of Brahm's remaining hands, making him now personally connected to each navigational apparatus on the ship.

The impeding wave harbors no mercy as it closes its distance from the ship with shattering speed. Beau and Sophia duck out of reflex as Otto and Domino look on helplessly as the contours of the wave begin to engulf the hull of the ship. With no time left to spare, Brahm gives a flick of all his wrists as if commanding the reigns of a heavenly steed. Struck by the chord of Brahm's intention, the ship lunges towards the sky like a chariot of the gods. With a second wrist flick, the ship catapults towards the clouds, narrowly avoiding being devoured by the collapsing shockwave.

CHAPTER: 14

The Kiss of Death

The howl of the ravenous wave echoes in Otto's ears. In-between shrieks of horror, the ocean clamps her sea-bound jaws on the ship's once-accessible position. Her cries intensify as she realizes her desired prey has escaped into the sky. Not used to being deprived of her destructive hunger, she calls to the turbulent skies, demanding the return of her elusive target. As if gravity has chosen to conspire with the Babel-possessed waters, Otto feels his body being summoned back to the watery executioner below. He can feel an overwhelming force start to pluck his fingers, one by one, from their already loose grip upon the mast. Time appears to slow as he is abruptly forced to realize his path to safety was as secured as his departing grip.

His body adopts a feeling of weightlessness, as all tethers to security quickly fade away. As the final splinters of the mast slip from his outstretched fingers, a moment is spared for him to contemplate his unexpected and approaching demise. He resides suspended in aerial purgatory, watching the elusive indigo chariot continue its ascent to the heavens with out him. Emotion feels like a wasted vehicle of expression at this point. The bizarre lull in time allows for an uncharacteristic sense of peace to flow into the core of Otto's heart. He takes this peace and decides to embrace the unexplainable forces at work over his being. He allows the existential musings once held back by emotional blockages to flood his consciousness.

Possibly, he contemplates, *this is it: a window into the space between moments in time. The space where heaven and hell exist as equal possibilities and not exact realities.* He can start to feel gravity slowly move to secure a stronger hold on his body, desperately trying to break the suspenseful ponder of his predicament. *So, this must also be so...* Otto thinks as he continues to make sense of his situation. *This is a place we can never stay in. Time for us must move on.* His musings bring a smile to his face. *Our concept of time, of different moments, is just an illusion. There really is no place to 'go' that is not also 'here.' I see now its all just one continuous moment.. The possibility for heaven and hell exists in every moment! Even this one... for there can truly be no other moment! And who's to say what is what? When is now? Is this heaven or hell? It has always been up to me!*

"So c'mon!" he calls to Babel. "Spin me around so I can look my fate in the eye! This may be my final moment, but it will be *my* moment and not yours!" The winds rustle a slight chuckle as a gust is summoned to heed the request of the falling youth. Otto embraces the helpful nudge and makes his flip to face the encroaching waters below. His smile remains as a fixed totem to his newfound state of mind.

"Heaven and Hell are not above or below us! They are possibilities that reside within us! No place, no event, no person, and no storm can ever decide that for us! That has always been for us to decide. You can take my body, but you will no longer be allowed to take away my heaven!" Otto's cries of revelation ring loud for all of Babel to heed. As if manifesting a test of resolve, a bolt of lightning comes crashing down from the clouds, lighting up the sky with an electric explosion. Its path cuts through the air, coming inches from Otto's body. The hairs on his head stand on end from the surging current racing past them. Otto's smile only grows a little wider as he closes his eyes, marking his resolved claim of peace.

Suddenly, the familiar pull from gravity starts to lessen and the feeling of suspension returns. Otto opens his eyes in bewilderment, searching for an answer to this unexpected interruption. His attention is drawn to the sky as he watches the glowing indigo ropes of the ship wrap themselves around him in a warm embrace. He immediately soaks in the energy from the spellbound cables and is brought right back to his peaceful space between time. His body rotates back towards the sky and his arms dangle as a lingering reminder of his anticipated path. The glowing ropes tighten their hold and begin to reel the fallen comrade back into the sky.

The ropes hasten their retrieval and Otto leans further into the embracing tethers, producing a deep sigh of relief. Still swimming in his newfound revelations, the sigh lingers on his lips for a moment. The departure is ensnared by his continued contemplation.

So, it looks like I'm not going to die after all. I can feel the anxieties of life racing to fill my vessel once again. It's funny… funny how deeply we can become centered and at peace when faced with death, but then feel that resolve slip away the moment the impending threat seems to fade. But does the reality of death ever truly fade? Hmm… You may have slipped away for now, Death, retreating back in the shadows of my mind, but mark my words, I no longer fear you. Next time we meet, I will be ready for you.

The lingering sigh of relief finally makes its full departure. Otto's resolve now swims in the growing turbulence of his chaotic mind coming back online. Even though he can feel the impact of his musings starting to fade, he rests comfortably knowing the peace he had found is still in there, somewhere amidst the chaos. The wet wisps of the clouds float behind him as he emerges to face the glowing sky awaiting him. The moon hangs boldly, accompanied by her many starry companions. Her light reins unrestricted by the fierce storm that bellows below. She welcomes Otto with her warm, radiating silence. The glowing rope from the ship sends him further into the sky than he expected. The vantage point allows him to look down at the ships new position among the clouds.

The sky-sails hang scattered amongst the higher air currents, quivering under the harsh winds that impregnate them. Brahm manages to tame the currents for a moment, allowing the ship to rest just above the cloud's exterior. From Otto's perspective, it casts an illusion that the ship is actually sailing in a sea of storm clouds. He hovers above the ship until making eye contact with one of Brahm's many ocular extensions. A floating crown of eyes has emerged around Brahm's head, a fixture which was absent when Otto last saw him. One of the eyes appears to be tracking his descent and gives him a wink. Immediately, a knot forms within his chest. An overwhelming desire to reunite with his friends consumes him. The indigo ropes collaborate with his desire and pull him towards the inner confines of the ship.

Domino is the first to come into focus as Otto nears his upcoming landing spot. He jumps around the deck like an over-cranked windup toy. His face glows with anticipation. A tear hangs from his cheek as he locks eyes with his approaching companion. No sooner after Otto's feet hit the deck does the now fully sobbing Domino tackle him to the ground. Sophia and Beau look on with a shared radiance of relief as they watch the two boys' long-awaited reunion.

"I thought you were dead!" Domino bellows in-between sobs. "I saw your hand slip and I was powerless to do anything about it! Before I knew it, we were already into the clouds and all I could assume was you were swallowed up by Babel!" He wipes the restrictive flow of snot from his nose. "Are you okay?"

"I'm fine!" Otto cries out, in slight shock from the overwhelming welcome. "I'm more than fine; I couldn't be better!" Domino seems to fail to register his friend's contentment and just shakes his head as if he didn't hear him.

"I was so worried about you!" Domino says with unrestrained emotion. "I couldn't stand the thought of losing… of losing y-y-you!" The tears start to flow again like a rampaging monsoon. "After all this time of being a complete jerk to everyone around me, I didn't think I was allowed to have a friend anymore. I know you were one of the people I may have been the worst jerk to. You came to work for me so you could pay back that foster family of yours. I knew that, and yet all I did was take advantage of you… worked you like a dog! Oh God, I was horrible. Of all people, it was your friendship I felt I deserved the least. Then I started to think about everything we've been through today, and that I might actually be able to call you a friend!" Otto's face starts to wrinkle, the tears hardly being held back from his feeble attempts to sustain composure. "That's all I could think about after being saved from that tower. To think you could be taken away before I could ever tell you that… I don't think I could have lived with myself if you didn't come back!" Domino grabs Otto by his shoulders and lifts him back on his feet. "So," he continues with sweat beading upon his forehead, "do you think it is possible… someday, some way, you could ever see me as a friend?" Otto takes a step back and clears his throat in reaction to the abrupt formality of Domino's question. He tries to buy himself a few moments to process the weight of his friend's testimony. The growing anticipation for his answer is reflected by Domino's quivering frame. Otto quickly realizes his hesitation could be easily interpreted as rejection.

"You fool!" he cries out, unintentionally striking Domino like a sea of daggers. "We *already* are friends!" The tension finally dissipates and the two boys rush towards each other to wrap themselves into a teary-eyed embrace. Sophia and Beau watch with warm smiles reigning ear to ear. Something catches Beau's attention, shifting his focus towards the ship's bow. Sophia stretches her neck to catch sight of the abrupt distraction.

"Were you scared?" Domino finally asks after letting go of his new friend. "Honestly," Otto says while making sure to choose his words wisely, "no, it wasn't fear I felt. I know I've been afraid or overwhelmed by just about everything that has happened today, but I just couldn't bring myself to feel that way when I started to fall. It was like I felt everything at once… everything and nothing at the same time. It's hard to really put into words, but when I finally faced the fact I was going to die, I was at such peace! I wasn't afraid of anything anymore and I felt so free! To think, I was more at peace with dying than I ever have been with living! How crazy, right?" Domino smiles with silent recognition. Their silence hangs for but a second longer before Beau calls focus to another development.

"Your words ring all too true, kid. You just never know what is going to happen in this life." His comment holds the weight of a double meaning, drawing the boys and Sophia to rush and join him at the bow. They collectively stare out in awe as their curiosity is met with a swirling whirlpool churning the dense clouds in front of them.

"A-A whirlpool," Domino stammers in shock, "up here? How is this even possible?"

Without an immediate answer surfacing among the four stunned onlookers, they simply wallow in the sight of the massive hole in the clouds as it devours everything in sight. Winds scream as they are pulled off their intended course. The wisps of cloud condense to thick mats of braided water vapor along the contours of the growing black hole.

"Can't we just fly over it?" Otto asks, holding firm to his realigned composure. Beau thinks about the valid question while stroking his scruffy beard. He glances back towards his captain, still engulfed in indigo flame. Even with the aid of his celestial extensions, Brahm appears to be struggling to maintain control of the overtaxed sails.

"If this was just a 'normal' cyclone, possibly, but as I'm sure you all know, Babel is unlike any storm you will come across at sea. At this point, we are at the mercy of our captain. There is no telling what wrath that storm is capable of. Granted, there is also no telling what glow-man back there is capable of either. So, we will have to just wait and see," he says while plopping himself down onto the deck in a seated position. "All we can do is put our trust in him and hope for the best." He stretches his arms above his head then slaps them down on either one of his folded knees. He smiles in an attempt to alleviate the festering tension he senses. Otto mirrors a carefree smile of his own before sitting down alongside Beau. With a playful shrug, Domino cheerfully follows suit.

Sophia remains standing, still staring at the approaching whirlpool and then up at Brahm. Her face is stern, holding a veil to her true feelings about their open-ended situation. She carefully walks to the tip of the bow and notices their course towards the howling vortex in the sky shows no sign of slowing down.

Twitches of panic start to surface on her otherwise emotionless face. She glances back again at Brahm who appears to be struggling even harder with the flailing sails. The exposed muscles of his array of arms start to swell, his veins bulge, and despite his engorged heavenly exterior, the dark vortex appears to be winning the tug-of-war. Brahm grows another pair of glowing arms to make additional adjustments on the crescent moon instrument. However, he cannot manage to remove the sails from the draw towards the whirlpool. A bead of sweat appears to trickle down his glowing face.

All his corresponding eyes collectively shift towards the sky, intently studying the patterns of the war-torn sails. The rest of the crew instinctively shifts their focus to join his. Despite the frantic nature of the sails, the grounding tethers of the cables remain rigid, quivering slightly at their points of tension along the line. To everyone's horror, they start to splinter as the tension finally forces their structural decline. Brahm's face shifts to a disappointed scowl. He moves his hands along the crescent instrument towards a lever that has yet to be pulled on their trip. Unable to stand the growing anticipation, Sophia looks behind her again to judge the distance between them and the whirlpool.

A yelp escapes her pursed lips as she realizes the ship's bow is now kissing the outer edges of their adversary. Brahm releases a breath of reconciliation and makes the decision to pull the awaiting lever. To the crew's surprise, every one of the ship's many sails uniformly collapse like folded paper and enter a streamline slither back towards the ship's midline.

"What the—" is all Sophia can manage to expel before being ripped from her perch by Beau's firm grasp. He dashes towards the ship's mast with Sophia tucked under one arm and the boys collectively under another. Each step comes with a new angle of adjustment as the ship enters its downward spiral into the whirlpool. Beau manages to grab ahold of some extra cables tied at the base of the mast right before the ship becomes fully engulfed in the shadow of darkness.

CHAPTER: 15

Torn and Scorned

"Doo-o-o-onnnnn't yoo-o-o-oouuuuu daaarreeee leeeeet goooo-o-o-o-o," Sophia cries to Beau as she is whipped around in the sea-bound funnel. Heeding Sophia's plea, Beau tightens his grip on the cables strung to the mast. He focuses on keeping the boys and Sophia tucked into his core as tightly as possible. The centrifugal force increases as the crew furthers their corkscrew course towards the ocean below. Amidst the darkness of their spiraling descent, the radiating glow of Brahm's mystic form is all that illuminates the center of the whirlpool.

Brahm's celestial extensions have receded, and he resides in a seated position, hovering slightly above the deck with his eyes shut in deep contemplation. He sits, seemingly unfazed by the immense turbulence surrounding him. The swirling winds draw up the vengeful waters below. Together they shriek with joy, trying desperately to pry the defenseless ship apart. Its unhinging planks slap against the hull like a cacophony of gunfire. Scattered debris swirls around the ship, sporadically striking the deck like an angered hornet's nest. Various sea creatures have emerged, plucked from the depths below. A plethora of fairies, eels, and rayfins dance along the disorienting currents, frantically searching for the direction towards safety. Interlaid among all the outward chaos, is the constant cry from Sophia, ringing ever louder in Brahm's ear.

"Find a way o-o-out of thi-i-is messss!" Her cries fall on seemingly deaf ears as Brahm's attention appears to be elsewhere.

"Ugh, so much commotion!" Brahm bellows before letting out a deep sigh. The hold on his concentration is becoming as faulty as the planks lining his ship. "I know the answer is to just let it go, but I can't expect that of everyone involved here!" he mumbles to himself. "There has to be another way… think!" He peers around the wall of water quickly closing in around him. He can't help but shed a smirk as he quickly realizes the vortex very easily could be the outer reflection of his inner turmoil. "There is a law about stuff like this… what was that law of… Law of Correspondence? As above, so below… as within, so without. Is that how it goes?" he remarks as he tunes his senses further into the chaos. "So then, this mess reflects where my mind is at? How troublesome!" He closes his eyes once again and listens to the undulating churning of the currents as they continue their climb towards the sky. He filters through the exasperated sea life, the displaced debris, and the swirling waters, struggling to find what part of the equation remains elusive to his awareness. "Maybe if I… hmm…" he mumbles again, but with still no clear grasp of a solution. "Quite the pickle we are in!"

Allowing himself to let go of his present pondering, he dives into a deep stretch with arms thrown overhead. Unfolding into a standing position, he takes another elongated stretch before embarking on a stroll towards the center of the ship. His gaze falls onto his glowing feet as he continues to forge through the wedded internal and external turbulence. So consumed in thought, he doesn't even notice walking past the struggling bundle of bodies the crew has merged into. They cling to each other in desperation, flapping in the wind like a tethered flag of surrender. Even the rapid onslaught of obscenities firing from Sophia does little to break his chaotic musings. The bundle of bodies looks on through winced eyes as Brahm stumbles side to side like a drunkard, narrowly avoiding the pelting debris being hurled at him.

"W-w-what in the world a-a-are you-u-u do-o-oing?" Sophia manages to shout towards their unreliable savior.

"What *am* I doing?" Brahm repeats back to himself, still avoiding direct connection to his fluttering crewmembers. "Am I going to let this mess consume me? Is this really the extent of my abilities?" Looking down at his glowing hands, he turns them over and examines their bioluminescent qualities. "Now that I think about it, I've been so afraid to see what power these hands are truly capable of manifesting; always worried about the consequences of what would happen if I ever really tried. The consequences of such actions could be catastrophic! So then, what are the consequences if I do nothing?" He looks back, finally soaking in the predicament his crew has befallen. He first makes eye contact with Sophia; her fierce yellow eyes align perfectly with his despite her flailing body. The fire of her gaze dives straight into his soul, dissolving the lingering tribulation impeding his next decision. He turns back around to the wall of water surrounding them and lets out a deep sigh.

"Your power and purpose have always left me baffled, Babel," he says to the storm as he runs his fingers gently along the wall of water hugging the ship. "But then again, so has my own. Maybe that's why I'm so determined to understand you. So what do you say? How about we get a little more acquainted?" Turning his wrist so his fingers start to dig into the currents, he brings his opposing hand to follow suit. Water sprays like a ruptured fire hydrant as Brahm burrows his fingers deeper into the enclosing wall. His body jerks back and forth as if he just latched ahold of something heavy floating in the upward currents. In an effort to brace himself, Brahm plants his feet into the deck with such force they appear to merge into the deck like the trunk of an ancient tree. Glowing root-like structures start to flow from his imbedded toes, weaving their way into the wooden planks below. Suddenly, Brahm's maneuvering brings the ship to an abrupt halt in its centrifugal spiral. The waves slap against the hull, desperate to regain control but prove to be momentarily powerless in reaction to the firm grip Brahm has on the situation.

"I hope you're ready!" Brahm shouts into the storm. "There will be no more holding back!!" With preparations finalized, his glowing aura erupts into a magnificent flame as if gasoline was suddenly poured onto his furnace. Brahm clenches his waterlogged hands with focused and concentrated will power. He triumphantly grabs ahold of the water after forcing it into a solid form. The swirling waves slither in all directions, trying desperately to break free of the abrupt binding. Brahm holds firm and with a mighty heave, he hurls his fists to his side, peeling back a slice of the wall of water as if it was a stubborn tuna can. The winds rush in with fierce howls, scorning the glowing sapient for his blasphemous actions towards the mighty Babel. Still holding firm to the slice of water, Brahm leaps from his rooted perch on the deck, sending the ship back into circulation along the spiraling inner wall that remains. He skates along the wall himself, his bare feet skipping along the mortified waters. The ship flows along the consistent currents, leading it back around to where Brahm has made his opening.

"Reluctant as you may be, Babel, it looks like you might be assisting in our escape after all!" Brahm calls out as he watches his ship circle around and head straight towards the opening he created. Propelled by the very currents that aimed to entrap them, the ship flies out of the watery vortex like a fired cannonball. A smile carves deep into Brahms glowing face as he watches his friends break free of the intended death trap. The flap of water whips even more violently as it aims to pry itself from his grasp. "I'm surprised I was able to hold you back this long," he says to Babel with a respectable tone. His smile remains as his fiery aura dissipates and his eyes gently glide shut. His fatigued fingers finally give way to the call of exhaustion, loosening their bind on the scornful storm. The howling winds grow silent as the slice of water falls back into place. Brahm's body skips along the edges of the storm's eye like an elegantly-cast stone before fading into the swirling chaos as just another piece of ragged debris.

∞

"All right, guys! Hurry up and find something to hold onto!" Beau shouts to his crew nestled under his arms.

"What do you mean?! What about… I thought you…" shouts Domino, unable to decide what to be most concerned about: their sacrificial companion or Beau's unexpected command. His pondering is quickly brought to focus as Beau abruptly flings his nestled cargo into the air. With the ship hurling towards the ocean below like a clunky frisbee, gravity starts to feel like it was left within the cyclone. The three freed companions float frantically in free-fall, desperately flinging their arms trying to hold onto something solid.

"Apologies for the abrupt departure, but I need to open that stratus sail back up," Beau says as he elegantly positions himself up along the mast. His feet align along the wood as though he is setting mark for a track race. "We need to use it like a parachute or else our narrow escape will be short-lived. Be sure to find something to hold onto, quick!" he says with a smirk before launching himself like a rocket towards the ship's stern.

His body swirls along the swift air currents. Wispy jet streams erupt along his protuberant features as they react with the air friction. He quickly lands a hand along the desired navigation railing, spinning himself into place along the crescent moon instrument. The boys start to float further into the sky as their flailing arms do little to stop their growing distance from the deck below. Sophia gently floats over like a veteran skydiver to help them regain their focus.

∞

"C'mon, boys. We aren't out of the woods yet," she beckons with a motherly tone. "If we make it over to the netting along the stern, we have a chance of bracing our impact."

"But how??" Domino cries as he flaps his arms even harder like an overly ambitious ostrich.

"Not like that," Sophia says, trying to sooth the commotion. "Make yourself streamline, go *with* the wind. Angle your body and point your head towards where you want to go; it's falling with style!" To further elaborate, she tucks her legs together, points her toes and brings her body rigid like a board. Her arms rest along her side, serving as the rudders for her bodily air ship. She gives the boys a reassuring smile before turning her attention towards the desired netting. Tucking her head slightly and angling her body, she eloquently drifts to the stern. A couple rogue bursts of wind do little more than add some cadence to her otherwise streamlined flight to the net. After safely securing herself, she waves her hands for the boys to follow.

"C'mon, man. This looks a lot more fun than the last time I went skydiving!" Otto says with a playful grin. "Let's do this together!" He grabs Domino's hand and waits for him to clumsily get his body into position. The two boys take one last look at each other, and with an affirming nod, they angle themselves towards the awaiting Sophia. Their flight starts off without a hitch, gliding smoothly towards their desired landing pad. Domino's flustered composure relaxes as he allows himself to enjoy his friendly free-fall.

"This is amazing!" he cries. "We are actually flying… falling?? Fly-falling!" The boys share a chuckle as they casually drift along the currents. Nestled in the background of thought and perception, the Babel-fueled waterspout lets out a blistering howl as if accelerating into a higher gear. A blast of wind washes over the ship, forcing Sophia and Beau to bear down on the sturdy surroundings. As soon as Sophia can pick up her head, she immediately looks to the sky in search of the untethered duo. At first glance they are nowhere to be seen. She calls out in desperation, hoping to hear their reciprocal cries.

"Boys, where are you?" she cries with panic quivering in her voice. Silence fills the spaces between gusts of wind. Sophia can feel her heart sink deeper into her chest. She frantically searches all around her, hoping to catch a glimpse of hope.

"S-Sophia!" comes a ghostly cry from the sky. "Up here!" Sophia squints her eyes to focus towards the skyward call. She quickly springs them back open in shock as she catches sight of the boys hovering along the distant cloud line.

"Get them down here quick," Beau shouts from the navigation deck. "I need to pull this sail now!" Sophia squints again to assess the bleak situation, only to notice the boys remain hand in hand. That's all the hope she needs.

"Boys," she calls with all her might, "remember what I told you earlier! Align yourselves with where you aim to go! Trust the fall and don't let your sights waver! Do it now!" Otto grips the hand of his quivering friend and immediately leads the plummet towards their intended safety net. Domino quickly aligns himself properly, setting his sights on his highest desire.

"I'm never letting you go again!" he cries into the wind, his hand burrowing further into his friends'. The duo dives deep into a feverish freefall with the wind sucking the breath out of both of their lungs.

"They are coming in too hot," Beau says with a matter-of-fact tone. Sophia stares on helplessly from her nestled perch in the netting. She closes her eyes and decides to try her best at the only thing she has left to offer: a prayer. Beau looks to the encroaching water below, back up to the kids, then to his two hands along the crescent-moon levers.

"I'm not as good as Brahm at this," he says out loud as his racing thoughts flow out of his mind. "Let's hope the sky holds you two in favor," he says as he pulls down one of the levers governing a stabilizing sail. The sail fires into the sky as the releasing pressure launches it from the mast. Slithering towards the boys, the sail appears to be heading right into their trajectory. "Close enough," Beau says as he stomps on the release peddle at his feet. The cable springs taught as the sail fully blossoms, wrenching the ship into its hold onto the sky. The sail's bloom is quickly interrupted as the boys make a mad dash into the center of the sail, slamming into it with the hopes of slowing down their fall. As they deflate the sail, the ship pivots back into its earlier flight pattern. The boys, however, scamper frantically to salvage their own alignment.

"Let's roll to either side!" Otto shouts. "If we grab the corners, we can open it back up to slow our fall!"

"I-I don't know if I can!" Domino says with a quiver as he looks down at his hand still entangled with Otto's.

"You have to let go of me!" Otto says, trying to calm his petrified companion. "It's the only way, but we are still going to do this together! I need you to trust me!" With a deep sigh, Domino nods and watches their hands separate. The two roll towards the ends of the flapping sail and latch onto the corresponding corners. They lock eyes right before rolling over the undulating edge. Their collective weight quickly drops them below the sail and sure enough, the wind catches the pocket created by their plan. Jerked back into the sky by the sail, Beau flips a leaver and reels the boys back into the deck with faces glowing.

"Now hurry and grab ahold of that netting! This is going to be a rough landing!" Beau commands. Wasting none of their borrowed time, he pulls on the lever holding the stratus sail with all his might. The enormous sheet of cloth leaps into the sky like a reborn phoenix spreading its wings. With time still of the essence, Beau locks the sail into place as soon as it gets fully airborne. The ship creaks and moans under the immense pressure being summoned to halt its' free fall. The ship rocks back and forth like a pendulum, challenging the integrity of the crew's grasp on their impending fate.

"This is it!" Beau informs as the ship nears its impact with the eagerly awaiting waters. Walls of water erupt from the impacting interjection of the ship. The bow dives deep into the bay before finally bobbing back to the surface. Water quickly starts to seep between the cracks of the fatiguing planks, but for the time being, the mighty ship stands triumphant in its battle with Babel.

∞

One by one the boys and Sophia fall to the deck from their netted perch, crippled with an uncontrollable release of laughter.

"I can't believe we just did that!" Domino shouts in-between belly laughs. "I thought we were goners!"

"I did too!" Otto says with a pleasant vigor.

"Ha! No wonder you were so calm and focused then!" Domino says as he takes a jab at his friend's earlier statements concerning death.

"Oh wow, I guess you might be right!" Otto says while taking heavy consideration of his friend's observation. "I still don't fully know why that is!"

"Either way, it all worked out! That's what is important," Domino concludes, trying to keep things light. "Just had to keep that unwavering alignment! Right, Sophia?"

"Sounds like you took my advice to the next level," she says with a bright smile. "I'm so glad you guys are safe, and that was quick thinking on your part, Beau! It was like you had done that maneuver before," she says in light jest.

"Well," Beau starts, as he walks down from the navigator deck, "when you have been with Brahm as long as I have, conventional solutions to problems rarely serve much assistance." The lighthearted chuckles start to wind down into solemn silence at the mention of Brahm's name. The thought of his absence stings like an acid bath for the heart. It triggers their minds to feverously scan the recesses of possibility, searching for any likelihood of his survival. Sophia is first to speak to the collective pondering.

"So, what are we waiting for? Let's start looking for him."

"You can't be serious," Beau blurts out. "After all he just did? Whether he is still alive or not, the last thing he would want is for us to sail right back into the deathtrap he just freed us from." The four of them take a moment to look at the ever-growing waterspout that clearly has not let go of its pursuit of the crew. The water has started to churn around the spout, turning into another whirlpool like they saw in the sky. As the intensity of the spiral increases, so does the pull back into is reaches. "The only step left for us is to get as far away from here as possible; this is what Brahm would have wanted!"

"No," cries Sophia. "If anything, what he did was to show us the answer is *not* to run away! We must stand and fight! That's what he did for us! Now it's our turn to do it for him! I just can't accept that he could be…"

"Sophia, please try and listen to reason. I know you are upset, but Brahm sacrificed himself so we could escape. We don't have time to just sit here and deliberate our fates or else they will be chosen for us!" Beau points his finger towards the center of the bay for a further example. "The currents are already pulling the ship towards the vortex again, it's only a matter of time before we are sucked back into the very situation we just escaped from! We have to move now; we have no other choice!" Sophia shakes her head, taking a step back from their conversation.

"No," she responds with an ominous tone. "There are other ways to challenge the unruly forces of nature." Her words hang heavy. Beau is forced to raise an eyebrow at Sophia's strange remark. "It's true," she continues. "Brahm may be special, but you clearly have more of this world to explore before you can say a statement like that in confidence." Sophia stands tall and drives her hand into the pocket of her fluttering cloak. She shifts around various items before slowly unveiling a cylindrical wooden artifact. It's imbedded with elaborate carvings covering every square inch of the surface. Her hand wraps around the bottom-half of the piece, leaving only a portion of the mural carvings visible. The three onlookers gaze intently, studying the tool Sophia displays as the source of her mysterious confidence. Beau's eyes widen as a flood of impossible explanations start to come to the forefront of his mind.

The head of a bird can be clearly identified with long wings carved around the circumference. The piece is complemented with intricate geometric shapes around the bird, some resembling lightning bolts. Beau is about to interject his thoughts on what she has just displayed, but Domino's eagerness takes the very words out of his mouth before he can speak them.

"Is that… what I think it is?" he blurts out in bewildered excitement. His brow furrows as he studies the displayed artifact more intently. Sophia oddly does not acknowledge his growing intensity, but it doesn't stop his onslaught of questions. "Does that mean you are that crazy… sorry, that *weird* shadow buyer who bought up all those artifacts that washed up on the shores years back? I totally recognized that one! It's got to be you! Isn't it?" His face turns to eagerness as he awaits Sophia's confirmation. His excitement is too much for Sophia to ignore any further.

"I don't think 'weird' or 'crazy' is any way to describe your most lucrative investor. I doubt anyone has paid you as handsomely for your washed-up rubbish… or your *silence*." The tone grows tense as Sophia's words pierce the atmosphere, but Domino grows too excited to notice.

"I knew it! And yeah, I know I was never supposed to say anything, and I haven't! Until now, but shoot… I doubt anyone here is going to endanger your 'secret shadow plots' or whatever your weird cult organization is up to," he says with a childish scoff. "Look at me! I got my super-secret cloaks and my super-secret magic wands! I'm going to rule the world! Muhahaha!" he mocks while prancing around the deck as if being puppeteered by a child who was just gifted their first marionette.

"That's enough. We don't have time for any of this now," Sophia commands.

"I agree," Beau chimes in, "I never thought I would see one of those things in person, but this is not the time for show and tell. Hurry up and explain how that is going to help us or else I'm plotting my own course out of here."

"Just stand back. Once you see what is locked inside this beautiful Totem Wand, the answer will be clear enough." Sophia elevates her hand and stretches it out taught so it is perpendicular with the deck. She widens her stance and takes in a deep breath.

"Oh great Father of the Sky, your presence is needed to aid in the suppression of the tormented water beast. Let your wings kiss the sky once again as you are called to defend your name! Come forth, Alagon!" Sophia's hand quivers from the gravity of her request. Time starts to slow, yet only silence lingers after her triumphant call to action. The three bystanders look to one another, debating how long is appropriate to wait for the anticipated outcome. Sophia lets out a deep sigh and is about to drop her arm until the Totem Wand begins to shake uncontrollably in her hand. She grips the wand with both hands as it quivers like a flopping fish. A bright light emerges at the tip of the wand and the quivering slows to a manageable cadence.

Sophia regains her composure and calls again, "Now come, Alagon, mighty Thunder Bird!" The wand erupts in blinding light cutting through the thick clouds and murky waters. The light is so bright the submerged structures of The Pearl become momentarily visible. From within the light, a dark shadow now takes form at the base of the illumination. Growing in size, dark winged structures protrude from the light folding into an elaborate arrangement as the head of the shadow emerges. As the head molds into the familiar bird shape on the wand they saw earlier, the onlookers step back as the reality of the phenomenon takes hold. Enormous taloned feet step out from the light and kiss the stationary ship deck. As they take another step away from the blinding light, the shadowy form starts to solidify. Bold colors of brown, red, yellow, and turquoise start to paint over the dark contours of the mighty silhouette.

CHAPTER: 16

Alagon

The ship's bow dips under the unexpected weight of the solidifying shadow. The wings stretch into the air as they fill with geometric patterns of elaborate color. The still darkened head dips low, inching itself towards Sophia. She stares intently towards the encroaching form, taking extra precaution not to shed even an ounce of concentration. Her brow starts to bead sweat as she watches the waves of patterned color start to flow up the neck of the mighty creature, systematically bringing to life the darkened face staring her down. White feathers give way into a yellow beak. The colors fold inwards, detailing fractal-like turquoise pyramids and deep red circles along the cheek. The unfolding pattern encircles the fierce brown eyes of the now fully emerged bird of legend. Alagon remains stationary except for a deep breath that is expelled into Sophia's face. The warm burst of air blows her hair back but does not fault her exceptional concentration.

Alagon shifts his head from left to right, analyzing the human who decided to summon him. With his assessment assumedly complete, he lifts his head towards the sky, straightens out his spine, and expands his wings towards the east and west. The crew collectively stares in awe as they soak in the magnificent creature before them. Alagon tucks his wings into his sides and gazes down again at the beings below him.

Before Sophia is able to utter another word, Alagon's attention abruptly shifts to his left as he hones in on a school of rayfins leaping out of the water. The enormous fish desperately flap their fleshy fins in an attempt to escape the pull of Babel's growing waterspout. Their smooth bodies dive in and out of the churning waves, expelling a breath from their blowhole with each break of the surface. Although they may be just out of reach of Babel's predatory pull, they have unfortunately caught the eyes of another type of predator. Alagon's sights narrow as he turns his body to the unsuspecting school. As his eyes start to dilate and his mouth is drawn to salivation, Sophia fears her control over her summoned guardian is slipping.

"Alagon!" she calls again, "the mighty storm of Babel aims to destroy us! Please lend us your strength to defend us!" Her earnest pleas fall on deaf ears as the mighty bird spreads it's massive wings and with one heavy flap he lifts himself into the air. The ship bobs back and forth with the released weight of the thunderbird. The crew seems unfazed by the undulation as they watch the impressive beast circle the sky for his dinner. The tips of his wings glisten with the penetrating rays of the moonlight, triggering golden shimmers to mark the trails of his swooping flight patterns. As he approaches his selected target, his feathers start to quiver as an electrical current flows throughout his frame. As the charge comes to completion, an enormous lightning bolt fires from his exposed abdomen. The bolt strikes right through the unsuspecting rayfin, flash frying the delectable seafood.

Alagon licks his beak as he makes his dive towards the choppy waters. The charred fish floats to the surface, presenting its sacrificial body to the heavenly creature preparing to devour it. All but Sophia, look on, struggling to fully register what their senses perceive. Never before has the existence of such a creature even advanced past the imagination of Beau and the boys. Free from the inspired trance of Alagon, Sophia falls to her knees, drowning in defeat.

"I thought for sure this time would work," she tells herself. "I know it was a huge risk bringing him out, but he was our last hope! Does he not sense that? Does he not care?" Her mind races with other possible explanations. "Maybe it is me," she ponders as her defeat bleeds into self-loathing. "I must still not be ready to harness such power, it's no wonder he doesn't respect me." She glances over to the mouth-gaping trio. "I have failed everyone." Picking up on Sophia's sinking situation, Domino shakes his head, freeing himself from Alagon's mystic trance. He bends a knee to join her on the rocking deck.

"You know, sometimes things don't always go as planned. Maybe he will want to help us once he gets done eating!" he says with hopeful promise.

"That's really nice of you to say, kid," Sophia responds as she picks up her head and attempts to smile. "But I don't think we are going to be so lucky. This is not my first time trying to summon Alagon. Honestly, despite the show I just put on, I can't even get him to come out of the wand most times. When I do, the results are pretty much the same." She hesitates for a moment but decides to allow Domino to travel further into her mental musings.

"I came across a book washed up on the shores when I first came to The Pearl. It was strange; despite being at sea for who knows how long, there wasn't a speck of water damage on it. It spoke of these mystical creatures imbued in special wands with powers that rivaled the gods… you know, moved mountains, parted seas, or took you to other worlds. It was just the kind of thing that could make some real change in the world if in the right hands… and if they were real. I thought I was silly for believing a thing could even exist until you found those wands that washed up last year. They *had* to be it, I thought! And sure enough, they were. However, it is becoming growingly apparent, my hands might not be the 'right ones' after all."

"Maybe you… maybe you just don't know what you're doing!"

"Ha, thanks, kid. You really have a way with words."

"No, no, no. What I mean to say is—"

"Don't worry about it," Sophia says cutting him off. "I appreciate you trying to make me feel better. Now, how about you help me get him back."

"No! Let me finish!" Domino shouts, cutting back in. "I may not be good with words, but I think you do have the right hands! I know I don't know you that well, but from what I've seen so far, I wouldn't trust that power with anyone else! Well, except for me of course…" he says as he starts wringing his hands. "Whoa! Definitely not the point!" he says as he catches his egotistical spiral. "You just don't have the right know-how. Maybe if you ever find out who wrote that book you could find someone to help teach you how to use them!"

"Maybe you're right, but that still doesn't help us right now. If we ever make it out of this alive, I can keep the search going. As for now, let's try and get this bad boy back inside his wand." She looks over to Beau with defeated acceptance. "All right, you win. I admit this was a bad idea. Let's get out of here."

"Way ahead of you, sister," he responds with his hands tangled in the remaining cables attached to the sky-sails. "Most of these things were damaged beyond use, but we got enough that should get us out of here; but *where* is the question. I was hoping you might have some thoughts on that."

"Well, about that," Sophia says, turning towards the waterlogged Pearl for a reference point. "We are near the far east end of the bay. If we continue to hug the shore, it will wrap us around to the backside of The Pearl. That should act as a natural deterrent to the storm surges."

"That will be enough?" Beau asks skeptically.

"It is the natural phenomenon that blocks the brunt of these storm surges from the other islands in this sea," Sophia answers. "That route comes with its own set of challenges though. Considering what we are dealing with here… it's definitely the lesser of two evils. If we can make it there, we might be able to survive until morning."

"Good enough!" Beau says, slightly more confident in their charted course. "Now you worry about getting that thing—"

A shrieking bolt of lightning strikes the scattering school of rayfins again, interrupting Beau's request. The bolt continues to trail along the water, coming only inches from the ship. Static electricity runs rampant, creating some exotic hair perms that even extend to Beau's now poufy beard. The electrified crew gazes up at Alagon who is tracing chaotic flight patterns, mirroring the dance of an escaped convict. Lightning bolts discharge from his wings in all directions, appearing to double as his own personal firework display.

"This is always the hardest part," Sophia moans as she tries to flatten her still-sparking hairdo.

"Next time you have an urge to conjure an untamed celestial beast to assist us—"

"Hey!" she shouts to Beau, quickly triggered by his defamatory tone. "No one's got time for your attitude. I'll handle him, you worry about getting us moving again."

"Humph," is all Beau decides to respond. He locks the remaining sails into place and walks down with heavy footing to his preferred spot at the helm. Many desired words go unspoken; his silence echoes his commitment to the classroom of compassion. *Not all schools are conducted in buildings. Not all teachers are even aware of their lessons,* he thinks. Beau grips the spokes of the helm hard enough to supply even further indentations. Sailing with Brahm has provided a multitude of undesired, yet apparently necessary classrooms. "It only makes sense he would pick up another *teacher* of compassion for me," Beau says under his breath. *When do you ever graduate from this class?* he ponders for a moment. "Ha!" he blurts out, gathering further attention from those around him. "You don't! Do you? Always a refresher class to be taken, always time for refinement, eh? Ha!" He stares down at the wide-eyed and frozen collection of crewmembers staring at his bizarre conversation with himself. Soaking in the oddity of the situation, he smiles and tips his hand towards Sophia as if removing an invisible hat. "That can't be the strangest thing you've seen this trip!" He responds playfully. The three look to each other and easily nod in agreement. "Now, let's get out of here!" Beau bellows with a residual chuckle.

Sophia turns towards her daunting task in the sky and decides to shake off whatever she just witnessed. "Those two must have been at sea for way too long. They have both lost their damn minds."

"What do you think he was talking about?" Otto asks Sophia as the two boys gather around her.

"Does he actually think we are in school?" Domino feels the need to ask.

"Who knows what he thinks. All we have to think about right now is pretty simple. Get that spirit bird back in this wand before he fries us all like those fish."

"All right!" the boys shout in unison.

"So how do we do that?" Domino asks cheerfully.

"Well, there is a simple return spell you can conjure with this thing. All you have to do is line up the beam of light that emerges with the conjured creature and bam! Back in the wand he goes."

"Sounds easy enough," Otto chimes in.

"We will soon see," Sophia remarks as she holds the Totem Wand towards the sky. "Return! Alagon!" she shouts into the night air. Her command travels to the mighty bird and perks his attention. He looks down at Sophia just as the retrieving light emerges from his previous prison. A hard dive towards the water, and Alagon narrowly avoids his capture. Sophia frantically shouts her return spell with sporadic rays of light firing in all directions. Alagon proves to be the more agile contender, remaining free from all attempts to be captured. He shifts his attention from dinner to preservation, locking his sights on his next target: Sophia. Rapid-fire discharges of lightning bolts erupt back-to-back towards the crippling ship's direction.

"Do something, Beau!" Sophia cries as she continues to fire silent beams of light back at Alagon.

"That's what I should be saying to you!" he shouts back in-between evasive turns of the helm. "Ugh! Get it together, Beau! Compassion… the lesson here is in compassion. See her in a compassionate light. See all of this as an opportunity to widen your concept of compassion! There you go. Breathe. It's not like this is all her fault. Oh wait. Isn't it, though?" he shakes his head furiously. "Ahem… compassion. Compassion is what will see us through—" Another bolt of lightning comes reigning down, narrowly missing their position.

"Better steering is what will see us through! Pay attention, Beau! That one almost hit us!" Sophia cries from the upper navigation deck. Compassion slips through his fingers once again as Beau's eyes involuntarily roll tightly into his head.

"I can see you will be a very challenging teacher," he scoffs, but his remarks fail to register with his audience. Sophia has already reconnected with her encroaching foe. Her rays of light appear to be getting closer to hitting their mark but continue to be avoided at the last possible moment. Beau skirts the ship back and forth with equal evasive prowess as the bolts of lightning rain down feverously. The boys look on at the escalating predicament, wondering who will win this competition of endurance. Sophia stares down her elusive target, her piercing yellow eyes taking no thought of distraction, not even to blink. She watches Alagon reposition each time the ship avoids one of his lightning strikes. "From the left he just came, to the right he adjusted. He dives mostly up or down to avoid my recall light; here he goes." She watches him roll up into the sky, getting ready to fall back into his now predictable attack formation. "He will come out of that roll and line up parallel with the port bow… Now! Return! Alagon!" she bellows and a stream of light darts straight for Alagon's anticipated move in the sky. As he unrolls from his last skyward maneuver, he sees the light already heading right towards him.

"This is it, I got him!" She says while watching the discharged magical light head right towards her desired location. Unfortunately, Alagon's reflexes prove to keen. He erupts out of his barrel roll and heads straight into the concealing safety of the clouds. "I-I lost him. I thought I had him. I thought…" Sophia mumbles as she falls again to her knees. "This is bad, this is going to be real bad." She watches helplessly as the shifting predicament develops overhead. The continuous cries from Babel are momentarily overwhelmed by the ferocious squawks coming from inside the already electrically charged storm cloud. Bolts of lightning can be seen skating in all directions along the lumpy exterior. The cloud now pulsates with light, showcasing Alagon's silhouette flying frantically throughout the cloud's contours.

"What is he doing?" Otto asks with a hollow tone.

"It looks like he is absorbing the energy from Babel's storm cloud," she says, unable to fully believe her own words. "I don't know what he plans to do with all that energy exactly, but I have a feeling I know who the target will be."

"CAACAWWWWW!" Alagon bursts out of the cloud like an electrified battering ram. He is now accompanied by trails of lightning trapped within his clenched talons. The bolts of unrefined energy quiver under the restrictive binding from the mighty bird. The bolts bellow with crying cracks of thunder. Alagon angles his wings in a streamline position and flies like a bullet straight towards the struggling ship.

"Can we dodge him? Tell me you can dodge that! Oh my, Maia, what if you can't dodge that?! We are all going to die!" Domino whimpers as he collapses to the deck.

"I don't know, kid. We might not have to this time," Beau responds cryptically. He smiles to himself, making sure to keep his attention on the helm. The rest of the crew scatter their sights in search of Beau's sense of reassurance. Suddenly, Sophia notices an all-too familiar wave of sensation flooding her body. Pulsating shock waves ransack her presumably solidified body, causing her to now question all that is tangible and physical. The stern focus on her outward predicament becomes possessed to turn inward as she revisits the vast spaces in-between her molecular arrangements. Her sense of self falls into an eruption of cosmic proportions.

"Ugh, not again!" she mutters with the last ounce of conscious control.

"Look!" cries Otto through his disoriented state, as he spots an odd mound emerging from the water. Sophia picks the mesmerized Domino off the deck and rushes him to the stern to catch sight of the hopeful phenomenon.

"Here he comes!" Domino shrieks, still held in Sophia's arms. His sights remain fully locked on Alagon's electrified path of revengeful retaliation.

"No… freaking… way," Sophia utters unconsciously as she drops Domino back to the deck with a heavy thump. She stumbles forward to the railing as she watches in awe as the mighty Alagon is suddenly swatted away by a giant watery hand extending out of the bay. He skips along the choppy water, failing to maintain control over his pulsating lightning bolts. He eventually is forced to discharge his electrified fury in every direction except towards his intended target. Quickly gathering his wits, he directs a powerful flap of his wings towards the water and catapults himself back into the sky. Sophia and Otto continue their paralyzed stare into the rippling waters as Domino finally gathers sensation back in his legs. He stands to join the transfixed pair.

"What? What is it? Are we dead? Are we alive? How? Who? Why? Oh! Oh." Eventually, he, too, bears witness to the sight demanding transfixed paralysis.

"I told you we might not have to dodge him!" Beau calls with a lingering chuckle still in his voice. He turns around to catch sight of their saving grace. Everyone takes a moment to look upon a glowing fifty-foot oceanic-hand. Complete with a wrist and forearm extending back into the ocean below, it turns to face the ship and gives a friendly wave. The kind gesture does little to break the awe-inspired trances. In efforts to bridge connection, the hand bends down towards the lapping ocean surface and pushes off the now abruptly solidified contour. Waves of water swirl around the extended arm as it lifts itself further out of the oceanic depths. Soon a connected elbow emerges from under the sea, then a shoulder that eventually gives way to a protruding torso and head.

The crew on the ship can only watch as the remaining body parts of the unexpected water giant are born from the bay of The Pearl. The swirling currents commanded by Babel's waterspout are diverted to fuel the growing giant that is now knee high out of the water's surface. The giant towers hundreds of feet above the bobbing ship. The deep currents holding the magnificent creature in place have split into a plethora of micro-currents collectively making up the extensive details of the evolving sea beast. The small detailing waves flow over and under, on top and in-between each other, developing various muscle groups of the giant. The sound of the rushing water currents is like a cacophony of waterfalls collectively crashing into one another. The concussive acoustics of the water pressure causes the boys to reflexively cover their ears. Suddenly, the original waving arm lifts itself up towards the giant's face, rotating around the watery wrist as if observing itself for the first time.

"Great, let's just add one more mysterious god-like entity to the list of things going to destroy us!" Otto yells over the sound of the water. "We have Babel churning in the background, sparky-bird charging back up in the clouds, and now we have Mr. Water Giant springing up from the ocean floor! That's it! I'm ready to wake up already! This is absolutely ridiculous! This is insane! This is… Brahm?!"

Turning its head to face the crew, the giant reveals its pulsating, glowing face to be carved into the unique shape of the very sea captain they assumed was lost to Babel's wrath. "No… freaking… way," Domino chants, mirroring Sophia's earlier exasperation. Brahm, in his new watery form, smiles and waves again at the mesmerized crew. It's all they can do to muster a makeshift smile and wave back at the unprecedented variation of his physical form. Brahm's attention drifts skyward as the scorned Alagon emerges once again from the clouds with thunderbolts held firm. With a new target in sight, he charges at Brahm with fire in his eyes. As if called to dance, Brahm moves with graceful elegance, avoiding the multitude of hostile advances. As Brahm continues to distract Alagon with his evasive maneuvers, Sophia turns to Beau with a flame of her own flickering in her eyes.

"All right, I think it's time we finally talk about some things. That man, if you can even call him that, out there, we left for dead, right? So what gives? Don't think it has gone unnoticed you have remained *exceptionally* calm as your captain has spontaneously transformed into a glowing, eye-juggling peacock. And now when he comes back from the dead as a carefree dancing water beast? Oh! And how about the whole 'molecular-vibrating-reality-questioning-pulse-wave' that just happens to conveniently discharge out of his chest every time he decides to … do whatever it is he is doing? So enough is enough. What is his deal?" Beau hesitates for a moment as he stares out to the still churning waterspout drawing them closer with every passing moment. Satisfied it still appears as big as a threat as ever, he glances back to Sophia. He is surprised at his hesitation to decide which storm is a more formidable adversary.

"Well," he says, finally making his decision and turning towards Sophia, "seeing as though we are still pressed for time, and for some reason this seems stranger to you than a uncontrollable magic-bird erupting from a wooden stick, what I can tell you is neither Brahm nor I truly know *exactly* what he is—"

"Enough of that crap," Sophia cuts him off. "That's what he told me, and I don't buy it. He should have died back there! You don't seem the least bit surprised. I've heard enough of what you *don't* know. It's time someone tells me what you *do* know!"

"All right," Beau says as he caves further. "Right now, Brahm is performing a skill we have come to call 'dimensional bridging.' I guess you could say he is connecting this dimension we are in with a 'higher dimension' for energy. He is doing this in effort to counter the unique energy emitting from Babel. The consequence of doing such a thing... well, one of many I should say, is that 'reality-questioning, vibrating, pulse-wave-thing' you mentioned. It's the reactionary ripple this plane has when another dimensional energy is introduced. It hyper-excites the molecular framework that maintains the physical nature of things in this dimensional plane."

"Right..." Sophia says as she starts to regret her line of questioning.

"Now, it normally isn't a huge problem to play around with energy native to a dimension," Beau continues, trying to soften the blow of his info-dump. "However, if not done right, the dimensional interactions can become... caustic. Mixing for too long or in a careless orchestration can disrupt the point of equilibrium that constitutes a particular dimension."

"Caustic?" Sophia interjects forcefully.

"Yeah, that's... going to have to wait for another time. Basically, time is literally of the essence, so can we get out of here now?"

"Wow," Sophia sputters, not expecting that kind of answer. Her brain feels like it has emulsified and just poured out of her ears like the contents of a churned meat grinder. "That's... that's... yeah... other dimensions... right. So, um, quite the gamble he's taking, juggling the fate of our entire dimension, right? What in the world... worlds? And how? How exactly is he doing all of this?"

"Look, I told you this wasn't the best time to dump all of this onto you," Beau says. "There is no easy way to answer your question. At least there is no easy way *I* can answer it. All I can say right now is we are not sure how Brahm can bridge dimensional energy, only that he can, and he is. That's one of the main reasons we are traveling this world. We don't claim to have all the answers. We are searching for them just like everyone else."

"Right, right, ugggghhhh!" Sophia grunts as she squeezes her hands into either side of her head, attempting to keep the overload of information from pouring out.

"We really should focus on getting to safety," Beau interjects carefully. "The longer Brahm feels the need to juggle in-between dimensions, the more dangerous it is for everyone."

"Right, I understand… ish. Thank you, Beau. I'm sorry I've been so harsh towards you," Sophia says with a renewed smile.

"It's quite all right, this has been a lot for anyone to try and make sense of without an explanation. I must commend all of you for enduring this adventure thus far. Neither Brahm nor I intended for civilians to get involved, but it appears it cannot be avoided. Now, let's beat this storm!"

"Agreed!"

"Oh, hey now. Looks like your friend out there has suffered from a change of heart," Beau says with playful obscurity. Sophia whips her head around to illuminate Beau's observation. With widened eyes, she once again stands transfixed in bewilderment. Even compared to her most recent conversation with Beau, she still cannot believe her eyes as she looks out to see Alagon peacefully perched upon Brahm's watery shoulder. He bobs his head, playfully cooing as Brahm scratches the underside of his chin.

"This is my chance!" Sophia blurts out as she rushes her hand into her pocket. She grabs ahold of her Totem Wand and points it towards Alagon. She pauses only for a moment, but long enough for Alagon to slowly turn his head around and look her in the eyes. Her hand starts to quiver as she is now unsure of what to do. She looks from Alagon to Brahm, unable to deny the bizarre relationship the two have developed in such a short period of time. Against her better judgment, she takes one more look at the pacified thunderbird before slowly putting her wand back into her pocket.

"Interesting choice," Beau remarks with a playful inflection. "Intuition get the better of you?"

"Ha! I guess you could say that. I think my mind would explode if I kept trying to think through everything that has happened so far. I hope I don't come to regret it. Maybe in time I can make sense of all this insanity."

"Well said!" Beau says with a chuckle.

The mighty head of Brahm turns towards the ship, diverting his attention from his new feathery companion. He looks to Beau, opening another inaudible conversation pathway. A moment passes and Beau nods in understanding.

"Sophia!" he calls out with glee. "The backside of The Pearl… you said getting there comes with its own set of challenges… what exactly are we talking about?"

"Well, most of us refer to that area as 'The Jaws of the Pearl,' and for good reason. Most people who get caught in the waters are chewed up, swallowed, and never seen again." Beau looks at her with a dumfounded and blank stare. Sophia chooses not to acknowledge his silent concern and continues. "Countless tectonic shifts have caused large boulders to fall from the top of the mountain peak and scatter towards the waters below. Their elongated and jagged nature makes them appear like the teeth of a ferocious beast. Navigating those waters is almost impossible on a clear day. It's like traversing a labyrinth from hell. When the storm surge is high, the pull from the current leaves countless whirlpools in-between each boulder outcropping. Our odds of smashing into one of those boulders are only slim margins above being swallowed up by Babel's currents here in the open waters."

"Guess that depends on who is navigating," Beau interjects, noticing a slice of hope within her words. "And it sounds like you have a pretty good idea of what is back there; have you sailed those waters before?"

"Yes," she responds, taking a pause as she struggles to keep her awareness from getting lost in the darkened recesses of her memory. "It was a long time ago. I was being chased and saw this route as my only way to avoid capture. I figured I would either make it out alive or die trying. I swore I would never face that labyrinth again. I don't know what I was thinking to suggest taking such a route," she says as her words spiral into the sea of doubt.

"But you said it yourself," Beau interjects, "it's our only chance at this point, right?"

"Ugh," Sophia says with her hand pushing into her face, "unfortunately so."

"Perfect! Sounds like we have our navigator and our destination! Now you take the helm and get us through there!" Beau says as he leaps from the navigation deck.

"Whoa, whoa, whoa! What are you talking about? What about you? I don't know how to navigate a ship like this all on my own! What are you going to do?"

"You'll see soon enough! Now let's beat this thing!" Beau turns to his captain and gives another gleeful nod. "We are counting on you, Sophia. Don't worry, you will soon see you are never truly 'all on your own' with anything." He smiles before leaping with otherworldly force into the branches of the crow's nest. The boys look on with uncontrolled excitement as they watch him grab ahold of the ropes tethering the ship's main sail to the mast. He spirals back down towards the deck, unraveling the fluttering sail. As soon as his feet hit the deck, he grips the ropes with all his might and braces for some form of impact.

"Hold on, everybody!" Beau yells as Brahm's giant form inflates like a balloon as he engulfs the air around him. "This is it!" With a mighty heave, Brahm releases the accumulated breath, projecting the howling winds directly into the unraveled sail. The sail appears to choke, struggling to engulf the immense load being demanded on it. Beau's grip remains steadfast, causing the ship to be lifted once again from the oceanic perch.

"What have I gotten myself into this time?!" Sophia cries as she clings desperately to the already indented helm. The crew holds on to whatever they can as they are catapulted back into the air, skipping along the waves towards questionably safer waters.

CHAPTER: 17

Going Toe to Undertow

"All right Babel, no more distractions," Brahm says in-between pants of exhaustion. His energy is quickly depleting with every passing moment he holds onto his higher dimensional form. He turns to face the ravenous cyclone with a smile, confidently masking his fatigue. "It's just you and me now. Let's finish this."

"Squuuaaakkkk!" Alagon lets out a mighty cry from atop Brahm's shoulder, signifying his momentary allegiance with the formidable water golem.

"Ha!" Brahm chuckles to himself. "Looks like I stand corrected! I'm sure you won't mind a little company during our reunion." The winds pour in-between the spaces that separate the two competing forces of nature. Their sporadic rustlings carry with them the sound of a sinister laugh lingering within harsh gusts. The winds double back, carrying with them yet another message:

"You can call upon all the armies of the Heavens and it still would bring you no closer to surpassing me." Bellows the sinister winds of warning. *"You are a fool for trying to take me on by force yet again. You have learned nothing, but soon… you will."*

"Ah! So that has been you all this time!" Brahm exclaims with excitement, remembering the voices in the wind when he first arrived at

The Pearl. "It's true, it was foolish of me to try and sail through your mighty storm before. I had no idea how powerful you are! I am still ignorant to your purpose and place, but right now you stand in the way of the safety of my friends. That, I'm afraid, I cannot look past. Even if it results in my own termination, I will show you your will is not absolute! Mark my words, I am going to stop you right here, right now!"

With the winds carrying his message back to the mighty storm, Brahm initiates his assault with a full-on charge towards the howling cyclone. His watery feet pound heavily into the ocean's surface as it reluctantly holds sturdy footing for his barbaric barrage. Alagon flies high into the clouds, giving Brahm a clear shot at his intended target. Babel doubles down on her grip of the ocean and the sky. She magnifies the size and intensity of her unifying waterspout before hurling it at her incoming foe.

As the two forces advance towards impact, Brahm increases the space between his steps. He leaps further and further into the air, covering even more distance with each elongated pivot off the rippling waters. With his last monumental leap into the air, he lingers for a moment roughly midline with the swirling vortex. In a heroic display of might, Alagon reemerges from the clouds harboring an enormous lightning bolt clenched within his talons. Sparks radiate in all directions from his torpedo dive as he hurls himself in the direction of the hovering golem. He breaks his streamline descent just in time to fling his electrified cargo into the now outreached hand of Brahm.

"Kakawww!" he cries as he makes a last-minute dive back into the sky. His call lingers in the air as he leaves the final blow for his co-conspirator to deliver. Electricity courses through Brahm's conductive form, but he pays it no attention as he quickly drives the heavenly bolt deep into the heart of the storm with all his might. Upon impact, the winds howl once again, pouring from the center of the aggravated water spout. The turbulent winds carry the cries of the storm as it screams in pain. Babel can do nothing to stop the discharged bolt from unleashing its full wrath. Brahm lands on the other side of the vortex, watching the storm struggle with the electrifying nightmare.

The drowning remains of The Pearl are momentarily illuminated in the backdrop from the vengeful lightshow. The vortex slows its rotation for only a moment as it works to dispel the radiating charges. With the final sparks dissipating from its sluggish form, Babel quickly regains her strength and charts her course yet again towards the awaiting giant.

Brahm decides to stand his ground as the advancing column of wind and water moves ever further from the struggling island in the background. Sensing no sign of resistance, Babel accelerates her onslaught.

"You fool!"

Brahm curves a smirk as he cannot help but agree with the cries of the wind. With a mighty inhale, he consumes not a gulp of air, but a gulp of the seemingly infinite pool of water beneath his feet. His glowing form expands to almost twice his original size as the ocean races to fill the demands of his well-calculated defense. There is no time left to alter her course as Babel launches herself right into Brahm's outstretched arms. At this point, his wingspan has grown to the full circumference of the cyclone. As Babel makes contact, he barrels down on either side of the miscalculated vortex. Babel surges from side to side but lacks the leverage to pry herself from Brahm's burrowing grip. With his hands buried deep in the walls of the storm, he channels all his remaining strength to throw the unworldly manifestation into the horizon. The winds scream like never before as the funnel visibly rips apart from the clouds above. The vortex falls into a gravity-ridden arch as it is completely pried free from its claim to the sky. With his watery muscles swelling to their maximum capacity, Brahm lets out a soulful battle cry that momentarily drowns out the sobbing winds.

The final tethers to the ocean are ripped clean from Babel's clutches as her vengeful cyclone is held triumphantly above the head of the opposing golem. A final heave launches the adversary deep into the darkened void of the skyline. Brahm watches the proud extension of Babel unravel itself by its own broken momentum. The proud storm reluctantly returns back into its original construct of wind and water.

"Do not think you have surpassed me. You have lifted but a finger of the hand I hold this world with."

"That was more than I could have ever hoped for," Brahm says. His glow fades and his watery form starts to shrink back into the ocean. "Maybe someday we can come to understand one another."

"You understand nothing."

"Ha! That may be so; I hardly even understand my reckless desire to save these people I just met! Here I thought you were all that was left to discover! Thank you for showing me my ignorance. I will honor your lesson, great storm!" With the final words leaving his breath, Brahm's eyes close with his heartfelt smile still embedded across his face. His consciousness fades while his human form is left to contain his overwhelmed spirit. With no energy left to protect his fragile vessel, he slips quickly into the depths of the raging sea.

The surface of the water above his sinking body flattens under the downward gust that propels the approaching thunderbird. Alagon dips his talons into the water like a rescue helicopter lowering its safety line. Circular ripples stamp the water below as the powerful flaps of his wings get closer to the water's edge. With gentle precision, his cargo becomes safely secured in his grasp. The bird of legend quickly returns to the sky and sets his course towards the retreating ship.

CHAPTER: 18

A Final Farewell

The lingering remains of the unraveled cyclone struggle to regain its earlier glory. Babel feverishly commands the winds to summon the ocean back into the sky. However, her attempts sputter and deflate as if the winds themselves are too exhausted from their earlier showdown. The unexpected calm makes for a quick getaway as Alagon takes full advantage of the momentary clear and passive skies. In-between each flap of his massive wings, he looks down at his limp cargo tucked safely between his talons. The prolonged pauses following Brahm's shallow breaths appear to be taking longer and longer to bring life into his fatigued body. The mighty thunderbird pours all the remaining strength he has into a mad dash to get his new friend to safety. The ship and crew that once served as an imprisoning adversary now appears over the horizon as a landmark of hope. Fighting off his own growing fatigue, Alagon tucks his wings into streamline alignment, allowing gravity to pull them across the finish line.

"Sophia! Look!" Otto shouts from the upper navigation deck. "It's Alagon! And he's holding something in his talons! Oh… and he is coming in fast! Yikes! Real fast." Sophia turns and quickly processes the unexpected arrival. His descent is gaining more and more speed with no signs of slowing down. She whips her head vigorously back towards Beau for assistance.

"Beau…" she starts but is met with immediate reassurance.

"Say no more, I've got this," Beau responds as he finishes tying down the last tether of the main sail to the mast. He rushes to meet Otto and Domino on the upper navigation deck and prepares for the thunderbird's hasty arrival. As Alagon maneuvers further into view, Beau struggles to register the reality of the situation. His assumed invincible captain now hangs lifeless within the bird's careful grasp.

"This is bad, you pushed yourself too far this time," he mumbles to himself. He grinds his teeth in anxious anticipation. "Hang in there just a little bit longer, we got you." Sophia and the boys all sigh heavily as they sense the gravity of Brahm's arrival sinking in. Beau locks eyes with Alagon and quickly tunes in to the bird's frantic plea for assistance. With no time left, Beau nods his head with understanding. He widens his stance and positions his hands like a World Series baseball catcher.

Alagon's bulleted approach is abruptly halted as he spreads his elegantly painted wings at the last second like a pulled parachute. Just inches from the boat, he carefully flings open his talons and releases Brahm. The well-calculated release launches his precious cargo safely into Beau's awaiting hands. His feet slide back on the deck from the impact, but he manages to stay upright. A sigh of relief penetrates Alagon's beak as he watches Brahm fully embraced in the arms of his companion. His wings drop to his side, and he soars just inches past the ship, crashing from exhaustion into the awaiting waters below. He tumbles frantically, bouncing along the unforgiving waves like a skipped stone. As his crash landing enters its final spin cycle, his wings spread apart doubling as convenient flotation devices. He floats peacefully on his back, gazing whimsically into the swirling clouds above.

"Hold on, everybody!" Sophia cries as she flings the helm towards Alagon's fallen position. The ship abruptly alters its course, sending the remaining crew tumbling to the port side.

"Sophia!" Beau calls from the deck, still clutching his fading companion. "We have no idea how much time Brahm has bought for us; there isn't any room for detours! We have to get to the backside of this island now. Just call your bird back with that wand and be done with it."

"No!" Sophia barks, maintaining her control over the crew's current direction. "This is something I have to do, and this is the way I have to do it! I realize now he is not *my* bird. He's not anybody's anything! I saw him look at Brahm as an equal and unless he can look at me the same way, I don't deserve to have any association with him! I won't take advantage of him while he is down. He comes with me if he chooses, or he is set free. I'm done hauling a prisoner around in my pocket." Sophia's words fall heavy on Beau's chest as he hesitates to utter a counter argument. He watches as the defeated woman he pulled from the depths of the ocean just hours ago stands atop his navigation deck solid in her resolve to direct their course. She now holds the fate of all their lives in the palms of her hands and the whims of her heart.

"Okay," Beau says as the reality of the situation starts to settle in. "I get so caught up in the old way I used to see things. I tend to forget it's not an alignment with the right direction or speed that will save you but alignment with the right intention." He stares down at his captain fading fast in his arms. "I didn't fully understand why I thought you would be the one to guide us to safety," Beau says to Sophia. "I see it a little more clearly now. I'm going to take Brahm below deck and do what I can to make sure he stays alive. I trust you will do the same for us up here."

"There is no room for error, for either one of us," she says eerily without removing her gaze from the sea. Beau gets a run of chills flooding through his body as the words of his dying captain pour into his ears once again. *Who is this woman?* He shakes his head and chuckles, realizing there are no more words needing to be exchanged. Suddenly, a strong tail wind roars through the ship, bringing attention back to the elements. Beau takes a moment to hold out a damp finger into the wind and calculates its direction carefully.

"C'mon, boys!" he calls out. "Come with me below deck. I have an idea on how you two might be able to help increase our chances of survival." Domino and Otto spring to their feet with rejuvenated vigor as they scurry along the deck to meet Beau at the descending stairwell. The boys run ahead below deck as Beau takes his time to look out towards their lone navigator. She pulls a leaver alongside the helm that drops a counterbalance to the main sail. As the sail recedes up into the canopy, the ship starts to slow as they approach the floating thunderbird. Confident in his decision to leave her in charge of their fate, he finishes his descent with Brahm carefully slung over his shoulder.

∞

Slowing to a crawl, the bow of the ship glides carefully past Alagon's mighty tail feathers. His enormous stature rivals the very vessel that approaches him. His stillness projects a contrasting calm to the storm as it chaotically struggles to rebuild its earlier momentum. Sophia makes the necessary adjustments to keep enough distance separating them so as not to disturb the mighty creature. Slight ripples flowing from the ship pulsate under Alagon's peaceful frame as Sophia pulls the ship nearly parallel to his position. His beak remains pointed towards the sky as Sophia stretches her head over the railing with the hopes of making eye contact. She pulls the ship to a stop and the two float in silence together in the open ocean. With their faces aligned perfectly, Alagon's attention remains distant from his uninvited companion. Sophia takes a breath in preparation to say what she has come to say. However, before any words can escape her mouth, Alagon abruptly turns and captures her open gaze deep within his tantalizing brown eyes. Sophia is taken off guard and quickly realizes she is powerless to break the trance that has fallen over her.

This is what I came for, she thinks, but is still blown away by the gravity pulling her further into this majestic creature. *What do I do?* Her last thoughts burn bright and quickly fizzle out before her mind is rendered completely blank. She scurries through her head, attempting to string words together or find any personalized thought at all. She is only left with raw, undefined vastness. The vacancy that has fallen over her mind frightens her, and for the moment she is left to soak in the indescribable pulsating eyes of Alagon.

The fear quickly subsides as she builds comfort in her shift of awareness. Emotions stir, sensations of light, touch, sound, and smell flow through her vessel without becoming stuck in her web of habitual mental labeling. The only thing that remains steady in her awareness are those deep brown eyes. A new feeling emerges that she cannot label, even if she wanted to. Waves of pain, agony, mistrust, and abuse, soar into her perception, but none of these projections feel as if they are her own. Visions begin to flood her mind as she imagines herself soaring through the skies. A freedom that is unlike any human experience washes over her. A man rides on her back in-between her mighty wings. She feels deep love and admiration for him. He is a friend.

Right before becoming completely lost in that unexplainable memory, a cascading sensation of restriction and binding befalls her. She can feel herself being pulled back towards the ground. Sophia watches as the man from atop her back is torn away from her and placed in a cage surrounded by men with bright yellow eyes. They turn towards her now and slowly start to walk closer. As much as she struggles to save the man in the cage, a strong binding keeps her trapped in place. Helplessness and rage overcome her as the approaching men start singing incantations that feel like chains encasing her heart. One of the men steps out from the group and holds up a very familiar wooden wand that starts to emit a bright white light from one end. Sophia can feel herself being pulled into the light like a vacuum as the chanting rings louder and louder in her ears. As the helplessness now completely overcomes her, she looks back to the man in the cage. His flooded eyes stare back at her with tears streaming down his face as she is sucked deep into the darkened prison of the wand now residing in her coat pocket.

"WOOOAAHHHHH!" Sophia bellows as her personal awareness floods back into the current timeline. She falls to the deck and desperately peers around to gather clues to her reality. The plaguing stream of her personal consciousness soars back into her mind like a derailed freight train: *What was that? Where was I? How was… whatever that was… was it… possible? Was it real? Those yellow eyes! Could they—? No! Yes? What in the world! Wait…* She takes a deep breath and collects herself to the best of her abilities.

"There is no time for this," she says with a deep sigh. She gathers what is left of her wits and stands back up to reconnect with the fallen thunderbird. As she stares out over the railing, she locks eyes once again with his awaiting gaze. There is no earth-shattering pull that erupts between them this time. Silent acknowledgement flows effortlessly, giving a natural quieting to the bullet train of thoughts that have returned to Sophia's bewildered mind. Without knowing how much time the two have left to share, Sophia decides to speak of her earlier feelings.

"I am sorry," she begins. A light breeze flows between them, carrying her words down to Alagon like a fallen olive branch. "My intentions up until this point have been no different than those of your original captors. Our similarities are very clear. I never even stopped to think about how you became entangled with that wand. I don't know if I can apologize on behalf of the past, or if that would even matter. I hope to at least right the wrong they have imposed upon you. From now on, you are free."

Sophia reaches into her coat pocket and displays the elegantly carved wand honoring the mighty thunderbird. Alagon's eyes twitch at the sight of his long-standing prison, but he does not look away. Sophia grabs either end of the wand and holds it over her head. With a swift snap she slams the wand over her knee, splitting the ancient wood in two. With the shackles now severed, she casts the wand into the ocean. Alagon watches the severed prison float casually past his head and off into the distance. He looks back again at Sophia who musters a shaky smile.

"Thank you for helping us," she says as a tear forms in the corner of her eye. Alagon tucks one of his wings to his side, using the other to slowly roll himself off his back. Floating on the ocean like a poignant swan, he shakes his head to rid the water trying to flow into his eyes. Lifting his mighty wings above his head, he gives a powerful thrust, but his waterlogged feathers prove quite the adversary for flight. With two more swift thrusts he makes himself airborne enough to lift out of the water and perch momentarily on the stern of the boat. Sophia rushes off the navigator deck to meet him but is forced to brace herself as Alagon produces a controlled convulsion to rid himself of the excess water covering him. His convulsions rattle the entire boat with such ferocity it causes some unexpected distress.

"Not again! Brace yourselves, we are under attack!" cries Domino from below the deck. A heavy thud can be heard as the youth throws himself onto the floor. "Ouch…" Sophia can't help but smile.

"Everything is fine, Domino! It's just Alagon—"

"Just Alagon??" the exasperated youth repeats back. "How is that supposed to make me feel better?"

"Relax, everything is going to be fine. We are going to set sail shortly." She glances back at Alagon, the smile remaining on her face. He picks through the lingering feathers that refuse to fall back into place with his beak. Once he is satisfied with his feathery arrangement, he spreads his wings wide and flaps them gently to finish airing them out. He returns his glance towards Sophia, a softness resonating in his eyes. With another thrust of his wings, he launches himself deep into the night sky. A glistening shimmer resonates from his tail. It soon becomes all that can be seen of him as he quickly vanishes into the roaring storm clouds.

CHAPTER: 19

Choose or Lose

"Beau! What is happening to him?!" Domino cries from below deck as he rejoins the others by Brahm's bedside. "It looks like he is trying to disappear!" Otto looks to his friend with an empty expression, then back at Beau who sits motionless with eyes closed. Brahm's once solid body now appears to be fading in and out sight within flickering waves of transparency. "Is he going to die?! Oh, for the love of God, say something, Beau!" Domino wails as he clings onto Otto's arm, flinging it around dramatically.

"Enough already!" Beau finally responds, his eyes slowly opening to address the frantic commotion. "I'm trying to concentrate. I brought you down here to help, not to make a racket. Now be patient." He takes a deep breath, attempting to re-center himself, but he is plagued with another thought. "Sophia!" he yells through the ceiling, "have you made peace with your bird yet?"

"I told you already, he's not my bird!" comes her muffled response through the floorboards. "I thought you said you trusted me. I'm getting the sails repositioned as we speak so we can get out of here! You have no patience!" Beau smiles at the irony and grabs ahold of a broom resting against the wall next to him. He uses it to strike a small square door above his head that snaps open with a sharp *pop*. A surprised Sophia glances down through the opening only to see Beau's toothful grin.

"Sorry, old habits die hard," he says with an apologetic chuckle. "I'll leave this hatch door open so communication can be a little easier. I got a plan in order for the boys to help you out, but you have to get this thing going as fast as you can, all right?"

"Yeah, yeah. I got it. You just focus on keeping 'magic man' alive. Oh, so what about all these extra sails no one else knows how to use but you two?" she adds with a scoff.

"Check the rigging again," Beau chimes playfully. "When we were making our escape while Brahm was wrestling that storm, I tied up the sky-sails and left just the traditional sails for you to use. Figured we might run into this problem! If you need any of the other sails for more power, I'll send the boys up to help you out."

"I think I'll make do with what I've got," she says dryly, remembering how well their last attempt at assistance went.

"All right, that should be everything. I'm counting on you, Sophia!"

"Right, here goes… well, everything, I suppose." She lets out a huge puff of air and shakes off what nerves she can. "You've been through hell and back countless times already, and you managed to make it out alive. What's one more trip down the demon road?" She shakes her head. "You can do this. You got this." With the main sail fallen back into position, she spins the helm to have the ship face The Pearl. The tailwinds from earlier start to pick up and quickly engulf the hungry sails. With a healthy jolt, Sophia leads the crew headfirst towards the foreboding Jaws of The Pearl.

"Okay boys, I really need you to pay attention to what I'm about to say," Beau says while turning his attention to the eager kids vibrating with anticipation. Even as he hears himself say those words, he already foresees a menial reception rate. He can feel their conscious attention firing in all directions, but he decides to follow through with what he has to say anyway. "Even though we don't quite know what we are getting ourselves into this time, we do know it's at least one more daunting hurdle to pass before we can rest this ship safely… hey!" he shouts, snapping his finger at Domino who has returned to staring at Brahm's fading physique. "What part of 'pay attention' didn't you understand?"

"I think he's disappearing even more now!" the distracted youth responds passionately, rocking back and forth on the floor. "I think we are losing him! What are we going to do?"

"You could start by listening!" Beau barks loud enough to jumpstart Domino's attention. "Sophia is doing a great job getting us out of here, but she is going to need our help soon."

"What makes you think we can make any difference?" Otto asks sincerely.

"Yeah, I feel like we just keep getting in the way," Domino adds.

"If it wasn't for your sprint to the top of the tower where I first met you, Otto, I doubt we would all be this far into our journey. Brahm trusted you then, and I trust you now. We all have a part to play in this, I'm sure of it," Beau says while looking down at his translucent captain. The boys nod together in agreement, but Otto hangs his head low for a moment. The overwhelming weight of their situation appears to be anchoring into the youth's heart. Doubt bubbles into his mind as he wonders if he can even handle what comes next. As he observes Domino's face consumed with pride and excitement, he decides to bury his uncertainty for the time being.

"So, what do we do?" Domino asks, unaware of his friend's troubled pondering.

"We will get to helping Sophia in a moment. Right now, I want you to stay right here. Brahm is in a critical state, and he is going to need help finding his way back into his body."

"What do you mean? Is he lost somewhere?" Domino asks, still vibrating with excitement.

"Gather around closer, boys, and place your hands over Brahm. We are going to put some of that youthful energy of yours to good use. Try and envision sending energy out of the palms of your hands into his body. In a way, he is lost. You could say he is 'everywhere' and yet 'nowhere' at the same time. We are going to be like a homing beacon to illuminate the way home." The boys scoot closer and do as Beau asks. They look to one another with confusion now overriding their previous emotions. With arms outstretched, they raise a questionable brow to the lack of observable change coming from their uncomfortable gesture.

"I don't see anything, Beau," Otto says as he squints his eyes, still desperately trying to see energy flowing out of his hands. "Are we not doing it right?"

"Don't worry," Beau laughs. "In time you will learn how to train your eyes to see the flow of energy. If it makes you feel any better, you are doing a great job."

"So what exactly is going on with this guy?" Domino asks eagerly.

"Brahm's ability to manipulate energy comes at a cost," Beau starts, making sure to choose his words carefully. "He needs to remain focused at all times, or else he loses connection with his body or even who he is all together. That recent maneuver he pulled drained a lot of his energy. As he grows tired, it becomes harder to focus."

"Focus on what?" Domino asks.

"Well, focus on… *everything*. Who he is, what he is, where his body starts and his environment ends… it even can extend to what planet, universe, or dimension he is in!"

"Wait… what?" Otto asks with an involuntary interjection. "There are other… dimensions?"

"Yeah, there are many 'layers' to this reality most of us are not aware of. Our body limits our ability to perceive the nearly infinite dimensions of reality out there. Those human limitations keep us safe and honestly, allow us to actually experience this human condition. It's kinda like blinking."

"Yo… blinking?" Otto repeats with a healthy serving of doubt.

"Well… yes!" Beau responds warmly. "You can consciously make yourself blink, but more often than not, your body just does it automatically. Could you imagine how hard it would be if you *had* to think about blinking each time? Or breathing? Beating your heart? It's kind of like that for him all the time. Brahm is someone who has reached past those limitations and has tapped into incredible power."

"That is wild!" Domino says. "Someone as aloof as that guy is constantly thinking about every aspect of his body functioning all the time? That is insanity! How on Maia does he manage to exist in such a way and not just… disintegrate every time he sneezes?"

"Ah, you bring up a good point. It takes a lot of effort on his part, but there is a secret of sorts that helps keep everything together. With as chaotic and messy as this existence can be, there are universal constants that hold everything together. It's how we can start to make sense of the seemingly randomized reality we find ourselves in. We have come to know them as Universal Laws."

"Not very original," Otto remarks coldly.

"Ha! You're not wrong, kid!" Beau says while letting out a genuine laugh. "However, where these concepts may lack in originality they definitely make up in practicality. Mastering these Laws means you become the master of your own reality. It is through these Laws that Brahm got himself lost. It will also be through these Laws that we will be able to help him find his way back."

"Alright!" Domino nearly squeals. "Now we are getting somewhere! This sounds like some 'secrets of the universe' kind of spiel. I'm so ready for it!" The youth rings his hands together like he is plotting a diabolical scheme. Beau silently nods his head back to the flickering ship captain to indicate where his attention should be focused.

"Learning too much too fast could spell disaster, so I will only tell you what you need to know."

"Disastrous?" Otto squeaks.

"It can be," Beau says with a warm and fatherly tone. "Knowing about a Law makes you responsible for upholding that Law. Once you know, there is no way to un-know. With more awareness comes the need for more responsibility. Should I continue?"

"Yeah… I don't know about that," Otto says, "I think I'm better off not knowing."

"Nonsense! This is it, man! This is real! Don't you want to know how to make sense of the universe?" Domino pleas.

"Oof… I mean… I guess it wouldn't hurt to understand a little bit." The youth exudes an extra long exhale as his nervousness becomes physically palpable. Beau looks to him with a questioning glance. Otto notices the silent gesture and gives him a reassuring nod to continue.

"The first two Laws tell us all we need to know about how to find Brahm," Beau continues carefully. "The Law of Oneness dictates that everything in our reality is ultimately connected. The energy that makes up… *everything* just appears on the surface to us to be a bunch of separate things, but deep down, there is no inherent separation. We are all one. Understanding this Law, we can gather that no matter how 'far' away Brahm might be, he is still connected in some way to us, to this reality and ultimately to his body."

"Yeah, ok… sure, that makes sense in some degree, but how does that account for people? Or animals? Clearly the voice in my head is not the voice in your head… right?" Domino asks earnestly. "How does that still fit into these Laws of yours? Clearly some things have to be separate from other things, right?"

"Ah, very good. You are already knocking on the door of Universal Law number two: The Law of Vibration. Despite everything being ultimately connected as one big energetic soup, the various aspects of that soup distinguish themselves through vibration. You could think of it as a giant cosmic concert. A concert is made up of many individual instruments, people and sounds but when played together, it creates one unified piece of music. You and I appear different because of our unique vibration but that doesn't mean we are not an integral part of a larger 'concert' so to speak. It's how we can appear different on one level and yet the same on another. We each have our individual part to play and Brahm is no different. However, in his case, he has lost touch with his unique sound and has become lost in the cosmic concert."

"That is freaking nuts!" Domino says, his mouth slightly ajar. He looks to his friend for some kind of collective reassurance. Unsurprisingly, all he can register from Otto's presentation is sheer panic and disbelief. He turns back to Beau for some further answers.

"And that is why you are sitting here with your hands extended," Beau continues in effort to smooth things over. "Brahm may have forgotten his own vibration but with all of our unique vibrations surrounding him, there is a chance he will pick up on our energetic transmission and find his way back."

"A… a chance?" Otto manages to mutter. "When you say 'a chance' that also must mean there is a chance he can't, right?"

"That's no way to think about it, Otto!" his friend shouts, "You have to stay positive! What kind of attitude is that?"

"A realistic one," Beau answers heavily. "The risks are real, and we are doing everything we can to help fix the mess Brahm has found himself in."

"So, what happens if he can't…" Otto asks wearily, "… if he can't return to his body?"

"Well," Beau starts, shifting his body back and forth, "best-case scenario, he gets stuck in that other dimension and his body fades away."

"*That* is the best-case scenario?" Domino asks dumbfounded.

"Well… the different dimensional energies don't mix very well. If Brahm isn't careful with the return to his body, he could bring fragments of the other dimensional energy back with him. If that happens, a dimensional rift can erupt from his body. He essentially would become a giant vacuum that will pull the dimension of lower frequency into which ever one was higher."

Sweat pours profusely from the boys' faces. Their bodies start to vibrate with nervous energy as they look to Beau for some signal of reassurance.

"Not to worry, boys! Brahm got us this far, and he wouldn't have chosen to take this risk if he didn't think it was the only way to keep us all safe."

"Wait just a minute," Otto asks with a pondering look on his face. His earlier feelings of repressed doubt mixes with his crumbling understanding of his physical reality. His eyes flicker with a spark as if his mind were just struck by Alagon's lightning bolt. "Don't worry? Are you really asking me not to worry about the very nature of our reality crashing down on us because this guy might not get his 'vibration' right?"

"Hey now," Beau tries to interject unsuccessfully.

"No…" Otto continues. "What the hell gave him the right to take such a risk? I was minding my own business until you two just showed up and decided to… to… what? Go to the casino and gamble the entire fate of this universe on a freaking joy ride? How dare you?!"

"Whoa, whoa, whoa. Slow down, kid," Beau says trying to soothe the flabbergasted youth.

"No! You speed up and hit me with some *real* answers… if there are any!" he screams as he abruptly makes a move for the door leading to the adjacent room. He puts his hands on the door handle and pauses before entering it. Otto looks to the left of the door and sees a potted flower resting on a shelf. He immediately takes ahold of it and throws it against the opposing wall, narrowly missing Beau's head. "How did you like that? Huh?! Me taking a risk of harming you without ever telling you I was going to do it?" The fragmented pieces of the pot pelt the ground as Otto falls to his knees. His mind shatters into its own disjointed pieces as tears bubble in the corners of his eyes. "I'm losing it," he says in-between sobs. "I'm done with all of this. I just want to go home. I just want to wake up and be done with this dream."

"There is no waking up from this, Otto," Beau says seriously. "I know we didn't ask you if you were ready for all of this, but we also didn't come searching for you either. Meeting each other has been consciously out of either one of our hands. The question now should not be 'how do I stop this' but, rather, 'how can I make the best of this?'"

"Okay, 'Mr. Guru.' Please, tell me… tell me how I am so wrong, and you are so right." Otto slowly looks down at the floor with a defeated aura surrounding him. Silence ensues for a while before he looks up to Beau. A plea for help lingers in his eyes.

"I can tell you are overwhelmed," Beau says while trying to summon as much compassion into the words he is about to manifest. "I know you can understand this if you want to. This is not a joke. Maybe you wish this day never came, but I promise you, everyone gets a day like this, a day that makes them question the life they have been living. These are the moments that define us and it's okay to be overwhelmed. It's okay to be scared. Just know if you decide to run away from this reality, it will never disappear. You can't 'un-experience' something, so you are left to make a choice. Do you give up? Or do you rise up?"

Babel reminds the crew of her persistent presence as a harsh wind roars through the ship, getting tangled up in the open sails. The ship jerks forward as the winds suffocate the already saturated sails. As the ship roars onward, Otto is knocked back down to his knees. He holds firmly to the doorknob to avoid sloshing around the room. Beau lunges over Brahm's flickering body, embracing it to keep him locked in place. Domino, with no immediate refuge, is catapulted into the air. His abrupt takeoff is quickly transitioned into a cataclysmic crash landing. His head makes a significant collision with the ceiling above before plummeting into the wall next to Otto. As he rubs his head, he braces himself with his other hand as the ship continues to speed along the rocky waters.

"I hope you guys are having a grand bonding moment down there, but if you had any plan to help me ensure our survival, *now* would be the time!" Sophia shouts through the flapping hatch door.

"What's happening up there, Sophia?" Beau asks casually. "Are we getting close to the Jaws?"

"Yeah, we are, right as Babel decided to catch her second wind… literally. These currents are propelling this ship almost beyond control. I'll never snake through the minefield of boulders like this! I hope you really have a plan, or else we are speeding head-first to our own graves."

"All right then, you heard the lady!" Beau says while turning his attention towards the boys hugging the adjacent wall. "Time to make those choices! So, what is it going to be? Domino? Otto? Do you give up… or rise up?" His eyebrows narrow as he leans forward. His head blocks the lantern behind him, causing his facial features to become carved with deep shadowy accents. Another harsh wind ransacks the ship, causing it to crash violently into the waves below. This time, nobody moves. There is a ripening fog of tension simmering in-between the silent pause. Otto grips the doorknob in his hand so tightly the fastened screws start to rattle loose. He stands slowly to his feet, making sure not to take his eyes off Beau's tantalizing face.

"I'm going to carry on with this madness for now, but when this is all over, I'm done with it! I've learned enough to know I don't want any more of this. However, I'll do my part to finish this mess," he erupts sharply. His choice words echo off the walls, dissipating the festering tension in the room.

"I'm glad you have made your choice," Beau exclaims.

"Just know," Otto adds quickly, "I think you expect too much of me. I'm still just a salvage boy from the docks."

"Oh dear boy, you wouldn't be here right now if you couldn't handle this. You are so much more than you think you are," he says with a full belly laugh. Otto stares at him blankly, trying his best to make sense of all that has transpired.

"What do you say, Domino?" Otto asks, turning to his friend still seated on the floor. "Are you still willing to go along with all this?" Domino shakes his head with a bewildered look in his eyes. He springs to his feet with an exuberant bound.

"Are you kidding me? I have finally found people I can call friends! I'm going to do everything I can to keep them safe. I don't care if I don't understand everything else that is happening. I think this is all so fascinating!"

"Yehahaha!" Beau bellows. "That's the spirit! This is really starting to get interesting. Now, if you two are ready, I need you to turn that handle you hold so firmly, Otto, and make your way through that door. This ship has an ace up its sleeve that will hopefully be just what we need."

CHAPTER: 20

The Hydrofoil

As the ship thrashes around in the tumultuous sea, the boys gaze down a dimly lit staircase leading into a deep, open chamber. From what they can make out, the chamber stretches all the way from aft to bow. The full content of the room remains shrouded in wisps of dark shadows. The hollowed out room amplifies the surrounding acoustics, accenting the shifting and creaking wood planks lining the ship. The ominous plopping sound of trickling water festers in-between the cacophony of creaks and cracks.

"What is down here?" Otto asks, still reluctant to walk down the foreboding staircase. He feels entitled to more explanation before blindly venturing into the unknown.

"Don't fully trust me?" Beau responds with a chuckle. "No matter. This might help illuminate some things." With a flick of Beau's wrist, gas lanterns, previously shrouded in darkness, ignite with vigorous flames dancing around in their glass chambers. The lanterns light up one by one, lining the railings of the deep staircase and all around the hollow hull of the large chamber room. The boys gaze around in awe at the two huge pillars extending from the lower deck to the hull. Chains, pulleys, and leavers hang off the massive contraptions, rattling in response to the continued bombardment of the sea. Along the flanking sides of the chamber, the boys see firsthand the battle scars the ship has suffered from Babel's wrath. Countless loose panels slap against the hull, allowing the eager waters of the sea to flow effortlessly into the heart of the ship. The boys' own hearts sink as they lock eyes upon the growing pool of water at the base of the room.

"Oh my, looks like we took on a bit more water than I had expected!" Beau exclaims with significantly less concern than anticipated. "No matter, what I need you two to do should fix this mess along with the one above deck!"

"Are you serious? Wait, how did you… What is this room?" Otto asks, rephrasing his question.

"This is the hydrofoil room," Beau answers. "It encapsulates the majority of the ship's interior. It's also the other hallmark feature, along with the sky-sails that is!"

"H-hydrofoil?" Domino brings himself to ask.

"Yes. It's technology that appears to have not reached these waters yet," Beau says as he is taken aback for a moment. "However, it's constructed in a way that will be easy enough for you two to operate. Hydrofoils are a nifty trick to navigate difficult sea currents. They are wings that extend from the hull of a ship into the water. Once lowered, the shape of the wing causes the ship to be lifted out of the water! Isn't that amazing? The ship has to be going pretty fast in order for it to work properly, but thankfully Babel has helped us out with that part! Are you listening, Sophia?" he yells through the hatch above him. "We are about to unleash our secret weapon!" Splashes of water spray down through the hatch door as Sophia continues to struggle with maintaining control over the ship.

"Yeah, I heard you all right. So how exactly does that help our situation?" she asks. "We got the ship airborne before, and that's half the reason why we are in this predicament."

"Well, that may be in part true, this should help with those tricky water currents you mentioned. So, whereas the sky-sails work well to pick up additional speed or navigate tricky air currents, the hydrofoils give the navigator immaculate control over the ship's position on the sea. Lifting the hull out of the water, the ship rests completely on the hydrofoils! It makes for quick and precise directional change one could never accomplish with a hull this large!"

"How do you think it would handle navigating whirlpools?" Sophia asks.

"That's quite an extreme situation, but I assume they should help us glide right through them. I've honestly never tried before. Why do you ask?"

"Well, at risk of being overly dramatic, we have one right in front of us. Babel is pulling the current back towards The Pearl. Like I told you before, the large boulders create pockets of suction when this happens. I'm sure there will be plenty more whirlpools for us to 'glide right through' if we can survive this one. Oh, and just in case you didn't realize, we are not slowing down at all, and I am losing ability to steer this thing! Hurry up, will you?!"

"She makes a good point, boys. I think it's about time we get this plan into motion!"

"What do we do?" Domino asks eagerly.

"Each of you need to get to one of those pillars! There will be a platform to stand on which will allow you to release the hydrofoils."

"What do we do once we get up there? Otto asks.

"Don't worry about that yet, just yell when you get there. Now go!" The boys' eyes widen as they receive a jolt of adrenaline coursing through their veins. A sense of urgency rings loudly as they feel the fate of their survival fall into their reluctant hands. They frantically scramble down the stairwell, fueled by the hope to live another day. Their feet splash through the encroaching waters well before they leave the confines of the stairwell. They churn through the waist-high waters with all their momentum quickly plucked from their eager descent. The boys look to one another for unspoken support before diving head-first into the mission at hand. The creaks and moans of the ship fill their ears as their heads reemerge above the flood waters. Without knowing how much time they have left to spare, they put all their energy into turning their bodies into efficient powerboats. Their cupped hands pierce the waters with elegant poise, gliding as far out in front of them as they can.

Sweat blends with the already salty waters as they strive to produce as much force as possible with each stroke. Feverous kicks produce a bubbly wake propelling them even further in-between each stroke. With a relieving gasp of air, Otto is first to reach the nearest pillar. He waves his hand for Domino to continue towards the one close to the bow. Otto circles the pillar until he finds a ladder located on the port side. He pants lightly as he scales the steps with his eyes. He locks his sight on a platform that looks like what Beau had mentioned. He holds onto the step and waits to make sure his friend has secured the same position before making the climb. With only a few strokes separating them, Domino secures his position at the pillar and looks back to Otto.

"Let's go!" Domino shouts. Waterlogged hands and feet maneuver their bodies one step over the next until they reach the summit. They slap the flat deck with their hands, digging their fingers in-between the wood planks to help pull themselves off the ladder. With no time to pause, they turn their heads towards the open door from where they started and call to Beau, "We are here! What's next?!" They pant with their exhaling breath.

Beau hears the call and looks up from his still translucent captain. He drops his gaze again and shakes his head. "I wish you would hurry up and get back here," he mumbles to his captain.

"What was that?" Otto cries, trying to make out Beau's muffled direction.

"Never mind," Beau says more clearly as he gets his focus realigned. "Good work, boys! The next step is the easiest part! Look to the center of the pillar and you should see a leaver positioned near the ceiling. You will need to release it to unlock the system. Then carefully pull down on the chain to the right of it, which will lower the hydrofoils into the water. The hydrofoils are positioned in the pillars you stand on like a telescope. They release in three stages, each time locking itself into place before lowering to the next level. You will feel a distinct 'click' when it falls into place. Get the foils fully submerged and we will leave the rest to Sophia! You got this, boys!"

"What about all the water down here? Won't that weigh the ship down?" Otto calls back.

"You'll see soon enough why you won't have to worry about that! Now hurry! Sophia is driving me crazy with all her concern about our *impending doom...* or whatever she called it."

"Hey!" comes an unfriendly call from above deck. Beau laughs and returns to his attempts to guide Brahm back to his body. Down below, the boys turn to one another, hands primed on the release lever. They let out a simultaneous sigh and nod their heads in unspoken understanding.

"On the count of three!" Otto dictates.

"One!" Their hands quiver with growing anticipation.

"Two!" Sweat clams their already waterlogged hands.

"Three!" Fists clench as they slam the leaver into the unlocked position. A tremendous clacking sound echoes through the room as the telescoped hydrofoils now rattle loosely in their chambers. Without the need for further dialogue, the boys rush quickly to the dangling metal chain resting next to them and start to pull on it with all their might. The chains hum with each pull as it spins the gears located at the top of the pillar. All of a sudden, they hear a heart-stopping crunch like the sound of splitting wood. The ship jerks heavily and they angle further into the sea.

"What's happening now?!" cries Sophia as the ship moves further out of her control. The boys look on in horror as two bottom planks of the hull break off and plummet out of sight into the waters below. The ocean waters flood the room even further and quickly wash away any confidence the boys had in their survival plan.

"What happened, Beau?! Did we break the ship?! What do we do??"

"Not to worry! I forgot to mention the foils double as hull planks when not in use. You'll take on some water for a moment as they detach, so whatever you do, just don't stop! Otherwise, then we really will be done for." Beau adds cheerfully.

"Is there anything else you forgot to mention?!" Otto calls back, his heart still beating in his throat.

"I hope not!" rings his carefree response. Realizing the only thing they can do to alter their sinking fate lies with the metal chains in their hands, they work even quicker, placing hand over fist until they hear another *clack*!

"That must be the first stage! Keep going! We haven't sunk yet!"

"And we are not going to!" Domino says with confidence. They continue their hand over fist method of releasing the chain until another *clank* reverberates throughout the hull.

"That's two!" Domino calls out in-between chain pulls. "Has the water gone down yet?" "I don't know, just keep going!"

"My hands are bleeding!" Despite the outcry of pain, the boys persist. The sound of the whizzing and rattling chains consumes the sonic registry.

"Just keep going!"

"I don't know how much longer my hands are going to hold out!" As both boys are nearing their collective breaking point, a resounding *clank* finally signals the end of their pursuits.

"That's three!" they cheer together as they fall to their backs in exhaustion.

"Good work, boys! You did it!" rings Beau's praise from upstairs. The boys eagerly look down and happily watch the water finally start to drain out of the precious hull. With the last lingering drips of seawater evicted, they gaze down through the openings left in the hull into the choppy waves underneath. The rattling lanterns cast eerie shadows on the hostile waters trying to jump back into the hull. As the lights illuminate the dark depths below, they reflect a glowing flash that resembles a pair of watchful eyes. The event goes unnoticed from the boys, as the next flicker of light shows whatever anomaly poked up from the depths has disappeared back into the darkness.

The boys' attention has been captured by the ship transcending the grip of the ocean's surface through the power of the hydrofoils. The swirling waters can do little more than kiss the bow goodbye as the ship glides smoothly out of reach.

"This is amazing!" cries Sophia as she gently maneuvers the ship around the outer rings of the whirlpool and through the first set of jagged tooth boulders. "I can't believe this actually worked! We might just make it out of here alive!"

"Ha! I think that's what we all want to hear," laughs Beau. His lighthearted remark quickly fades as the dense atmosphere of the daunting Jaws takes center stage. Navigating the Jaws comes with its obvious physical perils. However, the emotional turbulence is something Sophia never foresaw having to endure again. Her heart starts to throb so intensely she can hear its beat ringing in her ears. She throws her hand upon her chest as a precautionary move in case it decides to leap from her chest. She takes a deep breath, preparing to endure the most challenging part of their evasive endeavor.

"It's not like before," she tries to reassure herself, struggling to maintain focus. She clenches the helm with a tightening grip and burrows her fingers deep into the previous indentations. The pressure brings a throbbing pain to her left index finger. Looking down at the glimmering gold ring brings forth more pain than her heart can bear. She tries to shake off the weight of her past, shifting her focus onto guiding the ship back and forth between the boulder outcroppings. Her precise skills mirror the elegance and grace of a downhill skier. Regardless of her successful navigation, her attention continues to drift. Her heartbeat pounds its thunderous rhythm like a tribal drum preparing for war. She feels her focus slipping away as the past creeps further into her field of view. Her heart screams to turn back, but her mind holds firm to the task at hand.

"I can't let it get the best of me! I've worked so hard to forget! Just get back in there, just a little bit longer. I promise I'll deal with you… eventually," she bargains with her emotions. A tear streams down her cheek as the painful memories overwhelm her conscious repression.

"You must survive, Sophie." a voice from the past calls out. *"No matter what the cost, we all shall pay it gladly… it's up to you now; we are counting on you. The 'I's of the world' will not close today."*

"S-Samuel…" she mumbles as tears race down her cheeks. The painful past finally comes up for air after its decade long suppressive dive into her subconscious.

CHAPTER: 21

Ten Years Ago

"Sir! Sir! They are gaining on us!" calls a frightened bearded man as he runs along the deck of the Hathor. "We can't get the ship to move any faster! They will catch us at this rate!" The man trembles at the sound of his own words. "Captain, what will you have us do?"

∞

The year is 1746 Post Eden (P.E), over 1,700 years after the estimated arrival of Babel and almost ten years before the current time. It was on this fateful day that Sophia first arrived at The Pearl. She rides upon the speed freighter named the Hathor, the fastest ship in the Resistance fleet. Today, the Hathor is put to its ultimate test of speed and endurance. Just off the coast of The Pearl, it is being pursued in a high-stakes chase by one of the dreaded Warden.

∞

"I don't even know how this is possible! Their ship is twice as large as ours, yet they keep gaining traction on us!" cries the bearded man. He becomes too impatient to wait for his captain's direction. "I know we are no match for a Warden on land, but I thought we would at least be on an equal playing field out on the sea!"

"You've never directly encountered a Warden before, have you, Miguel?" Captain Tiger finally responds with a calming tone.

"N-no sir." Miguel immediately feels his heart rate start to slow. "I've only heard stories… horrible stories. Too outlandish to possibly be true!" He glances up at his nearly seven-foot captain for some reassurance. Captain Samuel "Tiger" Spearhead stands firmly at the helm of his ship. He exists as the current leader of the underground movement known to many as the 'Resistance.' His uniform beige cloak flaps loosely in the wind, complemented by his thick dreaded locks held in place by a red bandana. His long sleeves have been rolled up past his elbows, proudly displaying the unique birthmark that gives fuel to his nickname. A rare pigment condition has left horizontal bleached stripes all over his otherwise bronzed skin.

"Well Miguel, today you will see firsthand where those outlandish stories originate from. Odds are, the stories you heard aren't stretched far from the truth," Tiger responds with a characteristically jovial tone. "We are being pursued by lab-rat monsters unlike anything our imagination could prepare us for. With the price on our heads, it was only a matter of time before they tracked us down. Luck will be on our side if we manage to make it out of this one." An audible gulp can be heard dropping in Miguel's throat as he stares cautiously back at their fearsome pursuers.

"So, Sophie, how lucky are you feeling today?" Tiger says turning to a young, thirteen-year-old Sophia who holds a quivering map in her hands.

"Um, well, I'm not sure, Captain! Samuel…" Sophia stammers as she struggles to find the correct answer.

"Please, Sophie, we've been over this, call me Tiger! You know I don't like authority! What kind of rebel would I be if I became attached to my own hierarchy! Hahaha!" His laugh carries the same calming effect Miguel felt earlier. Sophia's heart starts to slow, and her thoughts return to their usual cadence in her mind.

"But no one calls you that!" she throws back with a smile back on her face.

"Hahaha, that might be so! Sounds like they all have their own issues with authority! Anyway, if I'm not mistaken, you've done some reconnaissance around this area, no?"

"Yes! I've mapped out the area as a potential hideout. There, of course, are some pros and cons to consider. The conditions there are really harsh, which makes this an undesirable location for anyone, even those who live here. They are one of the closest known islands to Babel which causes nearly permanently overcast skies and habitual storm surges that wash away everything that isn't secured by stone and mortar."

"Yikes," Tiger responds. "I can see why this would make a good hideout. You would be crazy to vacation there! How do the people there survive? Would *we* even be able to survive there?!" he chuckles.

"Well, it wouldn't be easy, that's for sure. However, that also is what makes it a good hide out. If we can make it there, we might shake anyone who wouldn't want to tough out the harsh conditions to look for us. We could blend in and work on the giant desalinator they are building."

"Sounds like you did your homework! What do you know about who leads this island? Think they would have any sympathy for our cause?"

"The island *was* governed by a religious democracy led by their sovereign 'Seer' people. They were gifted Guardians who could communicate with the forces of nature."

"Was?" Tiger responds with a heavy heart.

"'Was' is right. A Wisterian official now oversees this island after a civil uprising did away with the Seers' leadership. They are not *officially* taken over by Wisteria, not yet anyway, but it will make blending in a bit more difficult."

"Wisteria, huh? Their power grows like the plague! No wonder one of those devils is lurking in this sea. It's getting harder and harder to find land not infected by their influence. Looks like we have sailed right into a trap!"

"We could always go straight to Wahaka! They remain independent for the time being and have vast deserts they call the 'Rough-Lands' that we could hide out in until—"

"Unfortunately, I think we have run out of time. I doubt our pursuers would allow us to make such a detour unnoticed." The two look casually behind them at the continually advancing Warden ship. Tiger strains his eyes a little further and locks onto a lone man standing at the bow of the ship. The man stands boldly, with hands in his pockets, wearing a pleated black suit with matching black glasses. A spiked mohawk rests upon his head, contrasting his otherwise formal exterior. Catching the curious eyes of his onlookers, the man slowly peels the glasses from his face and stares intently at the curious Tiger. Tiger's eyes widen involuntarily as the darkened gaze of the Warden starts to take up his whole field of vision. Behind the sunglasses, reside even darker eyes, if you could call them that. Black, hollow voids exist where eyes would have been preferred. Specks of light scroll through the darkened sockets resembling circulating celestial constellations.

"How can this be?" Tiger hears himself saying as he is drawn further into the tantalizing gaze of his pursuer. Confident he has assumed the full attention of the meddlesome Captain Spearhead, the Warden reaches his hand towards the residing cannon by his side and points it towards the Hathor.

"What's going on?" Sophia asks.

"Whoa! Thank you!" Tiger exclaims as Sophia's words shake him free from the unexpected spell he fell into. "We need to act quickly. Evasive maneuvers, everyone! We are in range of their cannon fire!" The men of the Hathor immediately scramble to secure their posts along the sail rigging. Tiger spins the helm towards the port side to start his zigzag tacking defense route. A loud explosion can be heard from behind followed by an accelerating crescendo of the incoming cannonball. Tiger spins the helm to bend their course even further but to minimal effect. A splintering snap can be heard from the front of the ship as the cannonball makes its initial impact.

"Sir! The foremast is hit!" Miguel reports as the gigantic mast falls with another crash like a lumbered tree.

"Freemont! Assemble the sharpshooters and prepare the cannons to return fire once in range! They are gaining speed; it won't be long now!"

"Aye, Captain!" Freemont calls as he rushes to the aft of the ship.

"Miguel, you take the helm, I have an idea."

"Aye, sir!" he responds as Tiger leaps with magnificent force to the bow of the ship. He lands with a heavy thud right beside the fallen foremast.

"She's dragging in the water, slowing us down! We will be caught in no time!" reports one of the crewmen.

"Not on my watch," Tiger replies as he flings his cloak and button up shirt off his body. They flap violently in the wind before crashing into the turbulent waters. His striped markings can now be clearly seen, woven all over his bronzed muscular frame. They carve into his pigment with beautiful symmetrical patterns throughout, appearing as if he is fused with the mighty spirit of the noble tiger. He claps his hands together before placing them on either side of the mast.

"My god, sir, what are you thinking about doing?!" cries a flabbergasted crewman.

"Buying some time for our marksmen," Tiger says as he rotates his body towards the aft of the ship and locks his sights back on the formidable adversary behind them. With his hands firmly planted on the mast, he takes a deep breath, fully inflating his torso. Following his mighty exhale, he flexes his already impressive muscular definition to inhuman proportions. The crew looks on with eyes widened as their captain pries the enormous mast from its splintered connection to the deck, holding it firmly overhead. Taking another moment to align with his target, Tiger burrows the fingers of his right hand deep into the confines of the wooden pillar. Concussive cracking grows louder as he sinks his fingers deeper into the wood. A stern look washes over his usual playful demeanor as he steadies his aim. He lets out an enormous battle cry before launching the mast like a missile towards the Warden's ship.

The projected mast whistles as it penetrates the restrictive force of the surrounding air. Despite the impressive speed of his attack, the enemy ship quickly reacts to the impending projectile. With a last-minute maneuver, the Warden's ship glides slightly to the starboard side, avoiding the hurdling mast all together. Tiger's crew looks on in horror as their Hail Mary of hope sinks into the unforgiving sea.

"Prepare yourselves, men!" Freemont bellows from the back as he commands his marksmen. The clanking sound of calibrating cannons can be heard shifting into position.

"Now give them hell! Fire!" Freemont yells as the cacophony of cannon fire quickly drowns out his battle cries. The Hathor's cannonballs screech through the sky as they carve through the air on their way to the Wisterian battleship. Tiger and the rest of the crew look with eager anticipation as they trace the cannonball's trajectory with their eyes. Assured of a clean hit, their hearts leap prematurely with renewed hope. However, as quickly as their hearts leapt, they come crashing down in heartbreak as the Warden finally displays his magical might.

"H-How is this possible?" a man behind the lenses of his binoculars asks as he watches the cannonballs erupt into colorful confetti at the casual wave of the Warden's hand. The Resistance members feel their hearts sink even further as they watch their act of defiance conclude in comical celebration. They turn their attention to their captain, who stands slumped over gasping for air, struggling to catch his breath. Overwhelmed by the force he just exerted, he falls to one knee. Glancing around to his fearful comrades, he gathers enough breath to address his eager audience.

Is this really it? Tiger thinks to himself. He can feel the hope starting to fade from his crew as he struggles to contain what is left of his own.

"W-we all knew w-what we signed up for when we aligned ourselves with this organization," Tiger says painfully as he finally addresses his crew. "We saw a cause that was… m-more important than our own personal wellbeing. Together we have fought to keep the spirit of independence, hope, and future prosperity alive… and that will not die with us tonight!" The captain's usual calming effect on the heart has transitioned to inspire the pounding chests of all those who surround him. Pride and honor course through the veins of each man and woman on the deck of the Hathor. They gaze at their captain in awe, awaiting his next words.

"We will not go down without a fight. No, we will rage with defiance into our approaching fate. I have a feeling we have one more trick up our sleeves, and I believe that trick resides with our young navigator. Sophie, is there anything unique about The Pearl's terrain that might help us out?"

"W-W-What?" Sophia stammers as she takes a step back. The attention of the whole ship turns and focuses on her. She can feel the hope, the desperation, and the pleas for solace pouring through their bodies into hers. She struggles to gather her wits as she takes a desperate glance towards her captain. Tiger closes his eyes and smiles brighter than she has ever seen. *Why does he believe in me so much? What have I done to deserve such confidence? No one has ever believed in me… not until him. What does he see in me?* As Sophia's troubling thoughts course through her mind, she can't help but realize her breathing has become more level and her posture stands more erect, like a blossoming flower. She glances around to the awaiting crowd and finds herself calming the quiver in her hands and in her throat. Taking a look down at the map she still holds, she realizes the solution Tiger was referencing.

"T-There is an area located on the backside of this island directly in front of us. It's named 'The Jaws of the Pearl.' It is one of the most treacherous areas in the surrounding seas, riddled with boulders and whirlpools that can pull any ship that sails into that area to their doom.

Every story of someone traveling those waters ends with them being swallowed up by the Jaws and never seen again." The crew looks to one another, wondering how her words lend any solution to their predicament.

"Our c-captain is the most skilled helmsman this world has ever seen. Countless assailants have tried to chase us down and never to any avail! If anyone can navigate those waters, i-it is Captain Spearhead!" Sophia says with a fist clenched above her head. A rambling murmur falls upon the crew. Their collective reception fails to mirror their young navigator's enthusiasm. Realizing the struggle at hand, Tiger climbs the stairs back to the helm to lend Sophia some assistance. He braces his right arm but shines a youthful glow from his face that makes them look past his injured state.

"It's Tiger, Sophia! Tiger! How many times… ahem," he clears his throat before addressing the crew. "If what Sophia says is true, this may be our only hope of survival. A thread through a needle for sure, but it's a risk we have to take. However, remember that death is not the worst fate that can befall us. We all have within us the knowledge that could either rebuild civilization… or destroy it. It is our responsibility to the ancestors to make sure that knowledge does not fall into the wrong hands. I appreciate Sophia's words of encouragement, but know I cannot guarantee our survival. What I can guarantee, however, is that those abominations of creation behind us won't make it out of there! This may or may not be our grave, but we will make sure it will be theirs!"

A dark glow radiates around Tiger. His feral energy is palpable. His word serves as the law of the Resistance and the crew makes the emotional transition from doubt to unified hope. "Who's with me?!" Tiger bellows into the crowd. Without a moment's hesitation, a resounding howl of cheer floods the deck. The course has been set. Tiger takes back the helm with his one good hand and spirals it towards the hungry Jaws that await them.

Tiger looks back to the Warden still positioned at the bow of the enemy ship. His glance captures a smirk now covering the adversary's once emotionless face. With the Warden's glasses still removed, Tiger whips his head back around to avoid another episode like before. As the Hathor skips along the encroaching waters of The Pearl, Sophia takes this time to run below deck. Unable to divert his attention, Tiger remains fixated on the pounding waves clashing against the awaiting Jaws of destiny. Sophia reemerges on deck with a white cloth dangling from her hand.

"Miguel, give me a boost," she calls out as she runs headfirst to the first mate. Before he can even process Sophia's vague request, she leaps into the air with the safety of her descent depending on Miguel's quick thinking. Miguel reaches out his arms at the last minute and catches the spontaneous youth. He takes a step back to stabilize himself. Meanwhile, Sophia takes it upon herself to climb on top of his vacant shoulders.

"Watch yourself!" Miguel calls out. "If I'm going to be used as a ladder, at least give me forewarning!"

"There is no more time for forewarnings!" Sophia calls back playfully. "We are currently engaged in a high-stakes death race. The fate of our lives and our entire organization is up in the air and our narrowed survival is at the whim of the destructive potential of uncharted waters! We got to learn how to just… roll with it, you know? Now move me closer to the captain." Miguel catches a quick eye from Tiger before he diverts his attention back to the Jaws. It's enough of an invitation for Miguel to initiate conversation.

"She's taking this pretty well," he starts out, ignoring the fact Sophia can clearly hear his words. "Probably a lot better than most of us are taking it." As he gets closer to Tiger, Sophia dangles the end of the white cloth in her hand below his injured arm tucked across his torso.

"Wrap it under his elbow and hand the end back to me," Sophia commands Miguel.

"But of course," he responds, mimicking his best butler impression. As Sophia works on tying a sling for her captain, Miguel attempts to finish his earlier dialogue. "Most of us questioned your sanity when you picked up this girl years ago. Abandoned, left for dead. We assumed she was damaged goods that would just weigh us down. Shoot, she didn't even speak for the first six months she was with us! Now look at her." The two men pause and gaze upon the glorious light that radiates from the jovial youth. "She has blossomed into the flowerily light none of us knew we needed," Miguel continues. "It's a dismal life we live, hiding behind the shadows. I'm sure you know as well as any, it's been mainly this girl atop my shoulders who has illuminated our darkest days. She gives us hope for the future. Watching her grow into the person she has become makes me feel like a… father, or an uncle or something like that, you know? We all feel it. It's that glimpse of life and family we thought we would never see again. Thank you… for allowing us to experience that before our time is up."

A few drops of water fall on Miguel's head as Sophia wipes the trickling tears from her eyes. She avoids any eye contact by continuing to pour her focus into securing her captain's sling. Tiger remains silent as well, allowing Miguel's words to resonate a moment longer.

"All right! You should be all set," Sophia calls down from her perch with a slight quiver in her voice. "Nice and tight. Should give you one less thing to worry about." She taps on Miguel's head to signal her desire to be put down. As Miguel transitions into a personal elevator,

Tiger steals an emotion-filled glimpse of the beautiful young woman kicking to be put down faster.

∞

Tiger's mind flashes back to the time he found her. The poor girl was slumped over in an alley, barely covered with filth-ridden rags. She was left in a dumpster, to be discarded with the morning trash. Those golden eyes though… they shown through the darkness like a lantern, pulsating with life despite her dismal situation. Tiger shakes his head as he dives deeper into contemplation. *Look at her now! She appears to be living the life those eyes had always intended for her. Full of energy! She can smile a smile that warms even the coldest of hearts. This can't be where her path ends,* Tiger thinks to himself. *And it won't be,* he decides as he grips the helm a little tighter.

∞

"So, how does it feel?" Sophia asks after departing from the human elevator. Her words startle her mighty captain as if he was just awoken from a trance.

"It feels… phenomenal," he responds warmly, coming back to reality. "You have quite the knack for first aid. You will make a great healer someday!"

"Maybe someday I will, but first you have to get us through this Jaws place!" she says, with all concern of the impending danger absent from her inflection. With the Jaws quickly approaching, Tiger turns his attention to his first mate.

"All right, Miguel, it's time. I want you to go out on the deck and make sure our men are giving it all they have. Everything depends on this trip. Oh, one more thing." Tiger nods his head for Miguel to take a step closer. They share a private word before Miguel goes to carry out the original order. Sophia struggles to make out their conversation, but they prove to be pretty good at keeping secrets.

"Understood?" is all Sophia can hear from her captain as the two men separate from one another.

"Understood, Captain," Miguel calls back on his way down the stairwell. "I think that will bring us all a greater sense of relief," he adds before walking out of sight.

"So what was that all about?!" Sophia questions with hopeful resolve.

"Just a conversation between men!" Tiger responds as he ruffles Sophia's wavy hair. "Nothing to concern yourself with. Now, let's take a look at that map, shall we? Hopefully some of these boulder outcroppings are charted."

"You and your 'men talk,'" Sophia scoffs as she pulls the map out of her pocket. "Luckily, the entrance of the Jaws is clearly marked on either side; probably not farther than what can be seen from a distance, but at least it should show us the best entry point. I got this map from a local trader. He said they are hard to come by. I assume it's more than what that Warden has at their disposal!" Sophia adds cheekily.

"Safe not to assume anything at this point, Sophie," Tiger says with a fatherly tone. "You already saw what they are capable of and I'm sure you've heard even worse stories."

"But none of those stories have you in it! They may have avoided your first attack, but they won't last the whole round with you! No one can defeat the mighty Tiger!"

The surrounding waves give a threatening roar as they crash up against the massive boulders of the approaching 'Jaw line.' The ocean spray coming off the rocks shower the crew with the damp reality of their situation. The Hathor enters the treacherous labyrinth with the fate of a revolution at stake.

"Let's hope you are right!" Tiger shouts over the roaring waters as he sneaks another look back at the Warden. As expected, he is still hot on their heels, showing no sign of being scared away by the formidable path.

"This is it!" he calls to his crew as he turns back around. "Make sure you stay secured to your posts on the masts! Tie yourselves down; this will not be a smooth ride and keep a close eye on your sails. Any loose lines, any broken tethers need to be replaced as soon as it breaks free! We need the wind choking these sails. Do you all hear me?!"

"Ooooh-yaaahh!" The crew chants with fists held high. Sophia watches as her captain hunches over and streamlines his focus. With full confidence in his crew, all his attention is directed to his navigation abilities. Single handedly he maneuvers the helm, narrowly avoiding each approaching boulder. He skates the hull inches from each obstacle, looking back periodically to see if it's enough to shake the Warden. A game of endurance has been initiated. While the Warden still closes the gap, Tiger controls the pace. Any misstep at this point is game over. The Warden proves its worth once again, shaving it's ship just as close to the outcroppings, yet still gaining in speed.

Another ominous cannonball comes flying overhead. The crew watches it sail above them, powerless to alter its course. The preceding explosion ripples in the crew's ears as it collides with the upcoming boulder. Sediment of the obliterated rock rain down on the crew as Tiger is forced to deviate from his projected course. Sophia shakes the sediment from her hair and looks to Tiger as worry seeps into his eyes.

"They are changing the game," he answers Sophia's silent question. "It's like they can tell what move I'm going to make next. That boulder they just targeted was the one I was planning to sail around. Blowing that one up forced me to turn the other direction. Ahhh! This is unbelievable. Those things truly are monsters."

"You can still make it, r-right, Sam? Tiger?" Sophia asks as worry works its way further into her body.

"Of course!" Tiger responds with exaggerated flair, realizing how his dismal expression is impacting Sophia. "My plan is foolproof, no matter what tricks they manage to pull out. I've had my own ace up the sleeve the whole time!" A smile returns to Sophia's face. She opens her mouth to ask a question but is forced to take cover. Large debris falls from another exploding boulder, altering their course once again.

"They're not targeting the ship, sir!" Miguel calls from the bottom of the stairwell, "I think they are trying to trap us in the falling sediment!"

"I get the same impression!" Tiger calls, "I think it's time, Miguel; it's our only hope at this point. The 'I's of the world' will not close today."

"Ha," Miguel painfully laughs. "So it is. She's been our source of hope for quite a while now."

"Wait… what? What are you guys talking about?" Sophia asks as she takes a step backwards. The energy of the situation has clearly shifted, and she doesn't know what to make of it.

"I need you to go with Miguel, Sophie. You will understand soon."

"No!" she cries, stomping her foot. "I'm not leaving until you tell me what's going on! Tell me! What is this 'ace up your sleeve?' That should be enough not to worry, right?! Right?!"

"Hahahaha," Tiger laughs unexpectedly.

"This is no laughing matter! Tell me, Samuel!"

"It's you, Sophie! You are my ace. You always have been. You have been like a daughter to me, and I couldn't be more proud of you. After taking one look at you, I knew you deserved better than what you had. You are destined for great things, Sophie. Your road is not going to end here." He takes a heavy breath while checking on the enemy behind him. "We have gotten you this far," he continues while turning back to Sophia, "but we won't hold you back from the bright future we all see in you. You are the light in all our lives. We would be honored if you take our memories to live on with you."

"W-W-What are you saying?"

"You must survive, Sophie," he says, looking intently at her with eyes on fire. "No matter what the cost, we all shall pay it gladly. All we ask is for you to carry our message along with our memories. The Resistance will live on with you." He slips a gold ring from his finger. "Whenever the day will come, this will prove who you are and will bring your allies to light." "No! I won't take it! You are talking crazy! We are all getting out of this alive!" she says as she strikes her captain's rigid torso. Tiger grabs ahold of her hand as her next punch plans to connect and plants the ring deep into her palm. "We are counting on you. Live, for us." Sophia's mind races too fast to make her next move. Tiger takes the initiative.

"Miguel!" he bellows. Miguel comes bounding up the stairwell, grabbing Sophia along the waist and lifting her off her feet. As she kicks and screams to be set free, Tiger turns to her. He lingers for a moment, soaking in every aspect of her being. The heaviness of their situation starts to weigh on his heart. Taking a deep breath, he decides to share one last sentiment. "You are the daughter I never thought I deserved. Today I will prove to the gods that brought you to me I did in fact deserve your grace. I love you, my little Sophie." With tears pelting the deck, Miguel takes his cue. He turns and sprints down the stairwell with Sophia safely in hand, just as another cannonball flies overhead. The residual debris from the impact adds to the buildup already piled high on the deck. However, it provides no resistance to his purposeful descent to the escape boats. Reaching the end of the steps, he sees a single dinghy that remains tethered to the port side.

"You have meant more to all of us rough and forgotten sailors, more than anyone could hope to put into words. It's been an honor to call you family, Sophia," Miguel says as he struggles to strap the flailing youth to the tiny boat. "I know it doesn't look like much, but the small size should aid in your favor. You should be able to sneak away as we cause a distraction."

"I don't want to leave you!" Sophia cries. "You are the only family I know!"

"We live our life by the choices we make." Miguel wipes another tear from his eye. "We will always be family, Sophia. We have made our choice today so you can still have your choices to make tomorrow." Another cannonball explosion breaks their concentration. Miguel looks to the boulder residing beside him and notices a crumbling crack forming at the top. It begs to collapse at any moment. He glances to his captain who quickly gives an affirming nod. Turning back to Sophia, Miguel places both hands on either side of the escape boat.

"You have been the light in all our lives. It's time for you to share that light with the world! It's now or never, Sophia! Stay alive!" he bellows as he cuts the cord and launches the boat into the choppy waters below. Sophia's screams do little to slow her descent. Smashing into the water, it's all she can do is watch in horror as her family turns the corner of the crumbling rocks. As the momentum carries her past the boulder, the compounding cracks and fissures give way to plummeting dagger-like fragments. The debris quickly piles up, creating a barrier between the fading past before her and the uncertain future waiting behind her. With the last of the debris nearly falling into place, Sophia watches through the small gaps that remain as the Hathor takes its turn and slams directly into the Warden's ship.

The battle cries of the crew can be heard reverberating through the rocky Jaws as they sandwich the enemy ship against the nearest boulder.

The two ships make their dive into their collective watery graves as the impact detonates the entirety of the remaining explosives with a cataclysmic eruption. The concussive force ripples through the Jaws and shakes the loose debris further into place, finally obscuring Sophia's painful vantage point.

"Noooo!" she cries out in vain as the horrific reality of her situation brands itself into her mind. The rumble of the crumbling boulder drowns out her cries for a different future.

The newly stacked stones serve as a heavy reminder of her solidifying reality. Sophia reluctantly looks down at the ring still planted in her palm and examines it. The etching of a coiled dragon in-between two olive branches is imprinted in her palm from holding it so tightly. In that moment, it appears the two dragons are staring each other down. She thinks of the dragon in her palm as her past meeting the golden dragon of her future. They find themselves co-existing in the lingering space of the current moment. Watching the dragon in her palm start to fade, her heart sinks deeper into her chest. She digs deep, finding the courage to do what is necessary. Wiping the lingering tears from her face, she slams the ring onto her index finger and goes to work preparing her tiny ship. Unfolding the sail of the mast, she notices a small bag underneath. Expecting to uncover an extra sail, she is surprised to find her adored sundresses Tiger always loved to get her. Under them resides a large ration of food that could easily last four or five days. Tears flood her already saturated eyes. *Did he have this planned all along?* she thinks in between sobs. *Did he always know they were going to die like this?!* The roar of the raging waters demands her attention to resurface from her intrusive thoughts. She wipes the tears from her eyes for the last time and hoists the folded mast of the dinghy. With teeth clenched and emotions repressed, she weaves the sail into place. The wind takes its cue, engulfing the sail as she makes her first move into her uncertain future.

The current takes no hesitation to overpower the gusts of wind carrying her sail, drawing her ship closer and closer into the upcoming boulders. The navigation skills she picked up over the years with the Resistance becomes her saving grace in the labyrinth from hell. *Tack left! Tack right! Got to align the jib! Double check the boom… Go!* She proves her might with each successful pass by a jagged tooth of the Jaws. However, the current continues to draw her towards an unknown destination, pulling her ever closer to each passing tooth. She looks down at her fatiguing hands, the rope slipping ever so slightly from her grasp.

"I'm going to be swallowed up at this rate if I can't think of something!" she calls out to her vacant surroundings. She desperately scans the environment with each break between the boulder teeth but is met with the same dismal results. There is no beach. Only rocks and horizontal cliffs rising to the island peak for as far as the eye can see.

"I can hardly even see more than one step ahead of me!" she scoffs, staring down the dense fog blanketing the already dark and dismal labyrinth. "I can't let them have died for nothing! What would even possess them to put so much faith in me? No matter!" she answers herself, shaking her head to clear the painful visions of earlier. "I'm going to make it out of these jaws! I don't care how hungry you are!" Sophia can hear her battle cries echo through the boulders. A rustling of loose rocks draws her attention to the top of the boulder on her right. Quickly dashing out of sight, she catches a flash of movement before hearing the plop of the rustled rocks falling into the water. She swishes her head from side to side. Her attention is quickly commanded back to her laboring navigation maneuvers, but the sliver of wonder still lingers in her mind. *What was that?*

"Oh no!" Sophia cries as the port side of her vessel grinds against the passing stone. She leans all her weight to the opposing side, desperately trying to salvage her unintended collision. "Hold together!" she pleads with the dinghy. She manages to pull herself away, but quickly realizes the severity of the damage acquired. Leaning her head over the side, she makes note of the gashing battle scar, leaving only a paper-thin barrier between her and the hungry waters. Scanning the inner confines of her lifeboat, she notices a repair kit tucked under her seat. Despite the discovery of hope, she responds with a defeated shrug of her shoulders. "What good are you if I can't stop moving!" She looks again to The Pearl and is met with the same grim rock face that beckons no welcoming break from the chaos. "I really don't know how much longer I can hold on," she says with doubt creeping into her voice. She stares down the upcoming boulder tooth and wonders if it is worth her remaining strength to avoid it. "So what if I miss it? There will just be another one, and another one and who knows how many others. What are my chances of making it out of here anymore? They were already slim to begin with!" As her words settle into her heart, they rustle up a visceral rebuttal to her own doubt.

"What are you even saying?! The only life I have ever known has resided on slim margins!" She stands tall, ready to take control of her wavering resolve. "I will not die here, damnit! I won't! You hear me?! The Resistance will not meet its end today!" Her echoing calls reverberate within the fog, rustling up a familiar sound. A shadowy creature soars elegantly through the fog towards her. Sophia's eyes widen, trying to make sense of the unexpected guest. Wing tips clip the outer edges of the fog as the creature gets closer. Shimmers of vibrant color contrast the gray fog with mesmerizing brightness as they poke their way out of the veil. With color flooding the dismal scene, it's as if the feathers of the winged creature are entangled with an array of crystal prisms. Sophia wipes her eyes, wondering if what she sees transcending the fog could possibly be real. With the advancing boulder racing closer, she is forced to recalibrate her attention back to securing her safety. As she pulls on her remaining strength to hold onto life, the mysterious creature glides overhead.

"A crow?" she remarks, studying the outlining features of the winged creature, now back in the darkening fog. "So, those colors were just my imagination!" she says with relief. Looking ahead to the next obstacle, she is settled with her dismissal of the extraordinary.

In an instant, she is forced to shield her eyes from a blinding ray of light that comes pouring out of the fog. Out of necessity, she pries one eye open and locks her sight on the most unbelievable of manifestations. "So much color!" she says, drawn back into to the ecstatic spectacle before her. "It's like every color is shining at once!" All her worries of survival, danger, turmoil, loss, and grief are all swept away in the blissful moment. She struggles to categorize exactly what she is witnessing. "You must be a… a…"

CHAPTER: 22

The Present Moment

"…Rainbow Crow!" Sophia shouts, skyrocketing back to the present moment. She shakes her head in disbelief as the very creature that visited her in the past sits perched upon the upcoming boulder. "I was beginning to wonder after all these years if I would ever see you again!" she calls out, wiping a tear of joy from her eye. "It was you who guided me to safety all those years ago! I wasn't sure if I should count on being so lucky a second time! Please!" she begs, gasping on hyperventilating breaths. "Lead me to your sanctuary once again!" Upon hearing her request, the Rainbow Crow slowly spreads his radiant wings, flooding the dismal surroundings proudly with his array of vibrant color. "Thank you," is all Sophia can manage to say while another tear swells under her eye.

"What's going on up there?" Beau calls from below. "It got really bright all of a sudden!"

"That's hope, Beau! That's our ray of hope shining down on us!" Sophia calls down with a full grin stretched across her face.

"Cryptic! I like it," he laughs. "Don't lose sight of it!" He shifts his weight back and forth, getting himself situated to dive back into his role as a homing beacon.

"Hey! Beau!" Sophia calls down through the hatch. "We might make an unexpected pit stop. Tell those kids to get ready to pull up those sea-wing things when I give the signal."

"Is that so?" Beau responds with a jest-full flavor to his tone. "I thought you said there were no places to stop along this course. Forget about one, did you?"

"I knew you weren't going to let me sneak that one past you!" Sophia responds with a newfound lightness in her voice. "It's not that I forgot, it's just that I couldn't bring myself to count on being so lucky twice in a row! The last time I sailed these waters, I was saved by a miracle! A creature I thought only existed in legends helped guide me to a hidden haven I could never have found on my own."

"Well, out with it already! What is your miracle?"

"Haha, a Rainbow Crow!"

"A what?"

"Rainbow Crow!" she cries again. Her words are overflowing with blissful cheer as she races along the choppy waters after her mystical companion. "Ten years ago, when I was here, I thought all hope was lost. I was trapped in an endless fog and surrounded by a deathtrap in a damaged boat. Out of nowhere came this bright and illuminating bird of hope that guided the way to this cavern in the rock face. The cavern provided enough protection so I could rest and repair my boat. I don't know where he is leading us this time, but I trust he will make sure we get out of this alive! Beau! This is incredible! Tell those kids to prepare for anything!"

"You got it, sister!" He settles back into place, basking in the newfound radiance that emits off the once angry and edgy Sophia. "All right, boys," he shouts down the corridor, "we might have to bring those hydrofoils up sooner than expected! When I give the word, pull those chains the opposing way to reel them back into place. Speed is of the essence! I know you can do it!"

"We are ready!" Otto calls back from the foil chamber. The boys rest their hands on the rustling chains, eager to be called back into service.

"Sophia, bring us home! We are ready on your signal!" Beau yells. With their newfound strategy in place, Beau shifts his attention again back to his captain. He places his hands over his fading frame but not before shaking his head. "You are missing quite the show over here. You've done so much to set the right conditions for these people to grow. You're like a farmer who's walked away from his garden as the first flower starts to bloom. Your parents would be so proud if they could see you now. I know I sure am. Now hurry up and get back here! This can't be the day when your worldly journey ends. Not today." He pauses to inhale a drip of congestion. "I'm not ready for that day."

∞

Back on the deck, Sophia glides effortlessly through the water, chasing behind her guiding rainbow light. The hydrofoils cut through the water with ease, allowing the ship to tack through the network of obstacles with laser like precision. With each passing boulder, she can feel the emotional weight of her past start to slough off her calloused exterior. The further she sails into the treacherous waters, the more it feels like a soulful exfoliation.

"I can't believe how freeing this feels!" Sophia exclaims. "To think I had rationalized that this pain could never be alleviated. I buried it so deep that on most days I convinced myself it could never resurface to hurt me again. How ironic to think that bringing it back to the surface was just what I needed to be free of it!" She easily succumbs to an involuntary chuckle. The deepest of smiles emerges onto her tear-dampened face.

"This!" she says, referencing the furthest extensions of her being. "This is so… wonderful! I feel like a brand-new person! I feel like the 'me' I use to be. The 'me' Tiger and the others sacrificed themselves for me to be. I didn't realize that until now. They didn't sacrifice themselves so I could weigh myself down with their pain! They sacrificed themselves so I could lift myself up with their hope and love! It took me so long to realize this. I see that now and I won't let you all down!" she shouts into the reverberating rock faces.

"Aaah-ah-aa-aaah!" cries the Rainbow Crow, calling for Sophia's full attention. The bird makes a wide dive to the left, heading closer to the vertical cliff face.

"I think this is it, Beau!" Sophia calls down. "I'm being guided closer to the cliffs; Rainbow Crow might be taking us to that cavern after all. It will be a great place to wait out the storm! Tell the boys to get ready!"

"Yes ma'am. You heard the lady!" he says, turning towards the foil room. "We are counting on both of you!" A sense of pride swells in the boys' hearts as they prime themselves for action.

Rainbow Crow's rays of light continue to cut through the dense fog and dance upon the polished white rocks of the Pearl. He flies with such elegance, like he's drawing his air-bound suspension from a celestial puppeteer. Sophia hunches over the helm and grips the spokes with added security, mirroring the final moments she remembered of her noble Captain Tiger.

"We are *all* making it out of this one," she hears herself say, setting clear distinction between the two moments. "There have been enough sacrifices made in these waters. I will not add anymore." A dense cloud of fog appears ahead and Sophia watches as even the luminescent Rainbow Crow gets swallowed up in its obscurity. Trusting her colorful guide, she pushes headfirst into the unknown obstacle. Wisps of damp fog wash over her face as she penetrates the barrier. Beading specks of water collect all over her exposed hair as she continues her course.

"Oh wow," she utters as she takes a look around her damp surroundings. The Rainbow Crow's radiating exterior returns to sight, this time creating even more of a visual spectacle. His emitting rays of light become trapped in the beads of water in the air, bouncing fragmented rainbows all throughout the fog. Sophia squints to keep the source of light in sight. Gusts of wind can be seen trailing in his wake with each flap of his wings. The churning air currents cause the plethora of rainbow prisms to dance along in playful cadence as he swims through the darkened sky. The crow flies further ahead, making it difficult once again for Sophia to keep him in sight. Just when she thinks she can't squint any harder, a bold beam of white light pours out of the crow. The light shines down, illuminating the adjacent cliff face.

"This is it!" she calls down to Beau. "Pull up the foils! We are making our pit stop!" Her relayed message is quickly registered as she immediately feels the jarring return of the telescoping foils. A huge shock rumbles throughout the ship, signaling the first stage became locked. She continues to keep her speed steady as the ship wobbles under its quivering support. Another shockwave hits, indicating the second stage has been secured. She slows the ship as she gets closer to the hovering beacon of light. "All right, one more." The final returning stage rocks the boat before it locks the foils back into the hull. The ship slows dramatically as the familiar pull from the ocean returns to greet the vessel. "How did the landing go?" she calls down, quick to assess for any unforeseen complications.

"Hold on… okay… the boys are giving me a thumbs up!" Beau responds. "Wait… we took on some water… it's good? Yeah? Yeah!

Awesome, we are looking better than when we started! Thank God! What was that? Yeah, of course we can always drain it when we stop. You did a great job, boys! I'm proud of you. All right, all clear down here. Bring us in Sophia!" As she nears the stationary crow hovering purposely in the air, she follows his concentrated beam of light to a specific point on the rock face. She turns the ship to face the cliff, still unsure as to where the opening lies.

"This isn't quite how I remember it," Sophia says with doubt sneaking in. "But I've come this far trusting Rainbow Crow! I won't stop now!" She pushes forward, full speed into the solid cliff. Aligning herself with the beam of light, she sheds her last fragments of doubt before surrendering control to the call of the crow. Sophia is forced to shield her eyes as the light suddenly grows in intensity, cutting through the lingering obscurity the fog still possesses. As her eyes grow accustomed to the added illumination, she can see a deep crack emerging along the eluded cliff surface. "Yes!" she cries with relief. "This is it!" She slows the ship to a crawl, gently entering the familiar sanctuary.

The bright light from the Rainbow Crow shines far into the cavern, highlighting the steep walls that calm the waters flowing inside. Overwhelmed with relief, Sophia's knees buckle, causing her to collapse onto the deck. Her hands remain steady on the helm, gripping tightly to the mission at hand. The ship glides silently along the waters, carving casual ripples in its wake. The only sound in the serene sanctuary comes from the occasional plucking of dropping dew falling from the dampened cave walls. As the crew becomes completely submerged within the womb-like cave, Rainbow Crow flies on ahead, casting dancing shadows along the glistening walls with each elegant flap of his wings. He makes a triumphant landing, perching upon a chiseled-out embankment further downstream. The light grows dim around the entryway, causing an eerie hush to fall over the already silent scenery. The light of Rainbow Crow bounces in the distance like a freshly lit candle flame, beckoning them to continue further into the heart of the cave. Sophia pulls herself back onto her feet, determined to finally pay her respects to her brightly feathered guardian.

With Beau relieving their duty below deck, Otto and Domino quickly emerge to join Sophia next to the helm. The boys gaze around silently with widened eyes, the sacredness of the situation resonating deeply. Humbleness grows heavy in their chests as the reality of their survival finally starts to sink in. Safety and security echo boldly off the dripping cave walls.

Their eyes are quickly drawn towards the flickering beacon in the distance. The bright light of the crow has shifted back to a prismatic color palette, radiating like an enticing flower to a diligent bee. Realizing Beau has not seen Rainbow Crow, Otto runs to the open hatch to ask him to join them, but as their eyes connect, Beau silently shakes his head no. His gaze drifts to face Brahm and then back up to Otto as if to highlight his priority.

"Be careful up there," Beau says solemnly to the youth, confirming his decision to stay on board. "Something has changed since we entered this cave. I can't say what, but something has started to interfere with my energy work. It just feels… wrong. I don't know, just don't let your guard down, okay?" Otto nods with understanding and returns to join the two at the helm.

Collective pupils undergo further constriction as they approach the bank where the illuminated crow continues its perch. The boys take their cue and throw the rope from the deck to tether the tired ship. Safely secured, the ship is finally allowed to rest. The resilient planks shift and compress, as if letting out a sigh of relief as Sophia and the boys cautiously embark onto the slippery rocks below. With hand in front of foot, they slowly climb up the few remaining rocks that separate them from the light.

Rainbow Crow gently turns his head from where his attention resided to greet the approaching trio. Emerging from the climb onto the flat surface, their hands are forced to shield their eyes. His radiant glow is still too much for their struggling eyes to process. With a single flap of his wings, the crow adjusts his perch to a rock outcropping a few feet above their heads. He dims his light to relax their sight. Irony quickly creeps in as the dimming light brings even more into sight. Deeper still into the recesses of the cave, a pulsating force can be seen that was previously overshadowed by the encompassing darkness. A large, eerily colorless pole protrudes out of the dark waters, extending all the way to the top of the high rock ceiling. Despite the inherent lack of color, an aura of distorted light from the crow wraps around the edges of the phallic structure. Its paradoxical visual nature appears to be warping the light around it like a trapped black hole. Tree-like root structures extend at various points of the pole and latch onto the surrounding rock faces as if growing into them. Each root harbors the same internal darkness, outlined by a distorted field of white light. With each pulsation of the pole, the structure seems to be consuming what light still exists in the cave. This would have been more than enough to fully capture their inquisitive attention, if it weren't for the unexpected blood-splattered man lying at their feet. His coughing gasps for life take center stage as Death appears to have located Her next patron.

CHAPTER: 23

The Beginning of the Inevitable

"My God!" Sophia exclaims, bringing her hands to cover her mouth. Her knees buckle and she falls with a heavy *thud*. Regaining some muscle control, she inches herself closer to the dying man, stretching her hand out to rest upon his blood-soaked chest. His breathing is shallow; each labored breath rustles the ceremonial bone and beaded breastplate that lies loosely across his chest. His darkened bronze skin proudly displays a plethora of thick black tattoos scattered all over his exposed torso. Their bold tribal symbols remain a mystery, obscured by copious amounts of dried blood crusted over them. His eyes start to slowly open as he lifts his right hand to meet the foreign fingers upon his chest. Sophia jolts at his touch but quickly tries to recover. His extended fingers are ice cold, an ominous sign his remaining blood supply has already shunted to his core. Despite his chilling presentation, a warm smile glides onto his face as he brings into focus the yellow-eyed lady that resides above him.

"So, there is more to this journey after all," he says with a voice that booms with authority.

"Please!" Sophia begs. "Try not to speak." A chuckle ferments inside his chest at the sound of Sophia's words. It brings to surface a reluctant cough of vital blood that splatters onto the smooth stone that supports them.

"My dear," he continues regardless of the plea, "my words are the only thing I have left to give." He smiles again. "Every preconceived intention I had coming here was… ahhh… thwarted from completion. But here you are, looking at me with those bright yellow eyes… as if you don't even know where those golden gems come from." His words linger in the tense air. Sophia's face fails to register the meaning behind the dying man's words. She just shakes her head out of confusion. "It's no matter," he continues, fighting back the pain with a grimace. "You will find out where those came from in time. For now, we… eeeh, we have more important matters at hand. That look in your eyes… it may not recognize who you are, but if I'm not mistaken, I feel you recognize me, no?"

"Yes!" Sophia blurts out with tears streaming down her face. "There is no mistaking you are from one of the lost Condorian tribes of Wahaka!"

"Lost?" he responds with a quizzical tone. "Well, I guess that is one way you could put it."

"Good lord! The rebellion! You all were massacred! I mean, that's what we were led to believe when we arrived! The Warden had already left by the time we got there, erecting Wahaka as a new ally in the Progressive Movement. They boldly advertised it in the new propaganda plaza: the complete eradication of the 'demonic Condorian tribesman.' I sent forces to look for any sign of survivors, but they found nothing! We failed you! I am so, so sorry." Her overwhelming emotions drown any remaining words in blubbering sorrow.

"Now, now, this is no time for tears," he says while patting her hand. Sophia wipes her eyes and waits intently for his explanation, silently begging for a reprieve from her resurfacing regret. "You must be part of the Resistance we had contacted for help." Sophia nods in agreement. "Ah, thank you," he says sweetly.

"But we were too late! We did nothing! We—" another tap on her hand ushers a call for silence.

"Just because you couldn't find us, doesn't mean we are lost or even dead for that matter," he says with a twinkle in his eye. "My dear, y-you showed us there are allies to our cause that exist off our shores. You and your Resistance are the answer to our prayers, and it was Hanu that brought us together… then and now."

"Hanu?" Sophia asks as she tilts her head to the side. The man braces his battered abdomen while carefully pointing to the radiating bird above them. "I have a feeling this is not the first time the two of you have met."

"Oh wow," she says, shifting her focus towards the light. With her full attention locked onto the mighty bird, she bows her head immediately in condolence. "No, it surely is not." She drifts slightly back into the time capsules of her memory. "Thank you, Hanu."

"It was almost ten years ago that Hanu begged me to leave the wand and travel on his own. It was so unlike him. He never told me where he was going or why. Tell me. Do you… ah, do you believe in chance?" the man blurts out.

"Well, I'm not sure." Sophia responds, remiss to shift her focus from Hanu so quickly.

"Don't," he says sharply, paying no mind to her interrupted moment of gratitude. "Everything is connected. Everything. Nothing is an accident. Remember that. You, dear… What is your name?"

"S-Sophia."

"What a beautiful name. I am Namaka. Well, for however much longer I can lay claim to it."

"Don't say tha—" Sophia tries to dictate but a wave of Namaka's hand silences her dismal cry. His movements trigger a spontaneous coughing spell. He leans into his arm to try and muffle his violent hacking. His audience looks on in horror, unsure how to help the dying man.

"I have come to peace with my time… ehhh… on this planet. Soon… I will return to her. On top of that, you have given me an opportunity to realize one last act of purpose. Ahhh… It is time I pass the baton." He rummages through his leather pouch along his waist. "Here." He slowly hands Sophia a familiar wooden wand with a unique set of carvings.

"This… This… is…" she stutters, gliding her fingers over the winged carvings of the wand.

"Yes, a Totem Wand. I heard Alagon's battle cries earlier this evening. Never thought I would live to hear him take to the skies again. I take it you had a hand in summoning him?"

"Yes! But I set him free; I couldn't control him."

"Ha! Did you now? Very interesting indeed," he says with a cryptic tone. "Well, no one can tame Alagon. Not forever anyway. Aeeehh!" he cries out, clutching his ribs.

"Oh God! What can we do?" Sophia cries. Namaka waves his hands to dismiss her helpful advancements. He pauses, gazing into the wide, concerned yellow eyes staring back at him. Slowly moving his left hand, he props his failing body upon the rocks to better face Sophia and the boys. He winces in pain but strikes out another hand to ward off any advancing help.

"D-do you know what that dark abomination is behind us?" Namaka asks with a heavy inflection.

"A Power Pole. Or that is what we have come to call them," she says backtracking, clearly displaying her familiarity with the structure. "We have sent scouts to study these things, but few ever return from those expeditions. Earlier, I had picked up a strange frequency that was jamming one of our alarm towers. I had a hunch it was from one of these things. I assembled a team to find it and shut it down before it became operational. Looks like we were too late… again."

"Mhmm… sounds like you and I are on a similar path," Namaka says warmly. He takes a deep, wheezy breath before making his attempt to speak again. "Much like you, I came here to destroy-y this one in particular." He pauses for a moment to catch his shallow breath. "We call them Dark Serpents. After they were placed on our soil, our people started getting sick. We went into the Spirit Realm to try and study them, thinking we would be safe there," His voice trails off as his next words seem to bring him more pain than his failing body. "W-we… ahh… were wrong." Sophia and the boys look on with horror, eagerly awaiting his painful testimony. "Our spirit guides were afraid to get too close, but we persisted. Eventually, as it would be, one of our reckless warriors did get too close and was… *consumed.*"

"Consumed?" Domino repeats back with exaggerated flair. "Wait, these things eat people now?"

"N-no. Not quite," Namaka responds slowly. "He disappeared. We waited for him, but all that came to meet us was one of those Wardens—Ahhh!" Namaka cries as he doubles over, clutching his side. Sophia and the boys crowd the man, helplessly placing their hands on him as if it will heal his wounds. The Wahaken struggles to find the energy to ward off their sympathy. His breathing grows heavier, each inhale sounding like it's being dragged across a cheese grater.

"Yo! Don't die, old man! You gotta tell us what happens next!" Domino cries out carelessly.

"You idiot!" Otto yells, slamming his elbow into his friend's rib cage. "Do you have no shame? This man *is* dying, show some respect!" Just before Domino is about to retaliate, Namaka lifts a delicate hand and ushers another moment of silence. Sophia gives a disgruntled look to her rag-tag companions before shifting her focus back to Namaka.

"We were chased out of the Spirit World by that monster," he continues with a gurgling undertone to his voice. "W-when we returned to our physical bodies, we saw that our lost warrior had disappeared in the physical world too. Each time we ventured into the Spirit World looking for him, we were met with the same Warden guarding our entry." He clenches his face, contorting it into a makeshift snarl. "We had seen too much. The next day a Warden arrived physically on our land. The Warden, together with our Eagli brothers, sentenced us to a fate worse than death—"

"Worse than death?" Domino reflexively interrupts.

"Yes… we were banished to the forbidden Forest of Amenti."

"I am so sorry," Sophia says softly as she soaks in the weight of the Wahaken's words. His labored breath appears to grow heavier with each expansion of his lungs. "You don't have to say anymore," she calmly asserts, brushing her hand gently across his forehead. "You have done enough; you can rest now."

"Rest?!" Domino involuntarily blurts out. "On that kind of cliff hanger? That's rude! What's the deal with that forest?"

"Rude?!" Otto screams. "I'll show you rude!" The youth leaps from his perch and tackles his friend, slamming his back into the cold hard ground.

"Boys!" Sophia bellows like a reluctant mother. "I will personally feed each one of you ill-mannered sacks of flesh to the Jaws if you do not cut your crap! Show some *DAMN* respect!" Her commanding voice echoes through the cave, reverberating her threat into the hearts of her audience. Even Namaka's eyes widen in response to her intimidating declaration. "I am really sorry. I'm still not sure what they are doing with us," she says while turning to Namaka, paying no mind to her own volatile presentation.

"N-no, my dear, I-it's quite all right," Namaka says, careful not to anger the beast beside him. "I do not plan on leaving this rock. I'll tell you all I can."

"That's what I'm talkin' about!" Domino declares triumphantly. Sophia and Otto cut him with disapproving glances, but he shakes off their attack knowing he has already attained victory.

"Sounds like quite a story, old man," comes a dark voice among the rocks behind them. The four turn to face a mysterious man crawling out of the dark water. He steps elegantly onto their flat rock outcropping.

Towering over the four huddled on the ground, he stands nearly seven or eight feet tall. His large stature accentuates even further as Hanu's light casts his shadow against the full height of the adjacent wall. The man takes a waterlogged step towards them while ringing out the bottom corners of his black dress shirt with both hands. He brushes off the lingering moisture from the pin-striped suit jacket that covers his shirt before tightening the white tie hanging from his neck. The tie bears a unique symbol, a skull-like design made up of two mirroring lightning bolts for eyes, a triangle that rests at the base of the bolts marking the nose and five downward pointing triangles appearing as a jagged tooth mouth. A steady drip of seawater continues to flow from his expensive fabrics. Hanu squawks with defensive cries.

A devious smile forms onto the man's face as he adjusts his displaced sunglasses.

Taking another step forward, he slides his hands over his mostly shaved head, pulling to attention a drenched slump of hair hanging to one side. Sandwiched between his hands, his hair stands straight up, as if instantly dried, erected into a midline mohawk. Wisps of steam erupt off his frame as the water starts to evaporate from his sweltering body. As he continues his slow advancement, the heat radiating off his body quickly becomes physically palpable.

"Ah, should have known not even Babel could put an end to a god-forsaken Warden," Namaka calls out with spite. Sophia is lost for words as her eyes stay glued to the familiar flair of the aggressor's hair spike. Her mind races back to that gut-retching day, ten years ago. *Could he be the same one?* she thinks to herself, as the encroaching heat causes her to gasp for breath. Domino and Otto tuck themselves closer into Sophia despite the added body temperature. They grip each one of Sophia's hands as they await the next card of fate to be dealt.

"Well, that storm did separate me from the other Warden they sent; no telling if he made it out alive, not that anyone would care. Babel sure gave *me* quite a run for my money though! She really messes with my abilities. Almost made me feel… normal! Strange, huh?" the Warden exclaims with unexpected exuberance. "Looks like you had a similar run in with the storm. Meh, serves you right. You probably would have managed to die here in peace if it wasn't for that convenient vessel right there." He points back to Brahm's ship. "Good thing this beauty decided to come give me a lift. It was like a gift from God, showing up out of nowhere to allow me to hitch a ride. And quite a ride that was! Crashing through towers, flying through the sky, swirling in a cyclone, having a front row seat to a… what would you say? Water-beast-sumo-match? Yeah. Now, I must say, that was pretty interesting to watch. What's even more interesting is where all of this has led, Bakuwan." He places his burning finger right on Namaka's sweating forehead. "Right here to you and—" He cuts himself off, shifting his attention to Sophia. His eyebrows rise as his internal musings become audible. "… and judging by that ring… could it be? A new head of the Resistance? I thought I put an end to your nuisance years ago. It appears the 'I's of the World' have still been watching. I'll have to make sure to close them for good this time."

"Eyes?" Sophia mumbles unconsciously, her mind racing to what the Warden could be eluding too, but he pays her no mind.

"After I take care of you two, I still have to go settle this 'Seer' problem they told me about," the Warden continues. "Uh, so much to do!"

"You will never succeed!" Namaka cries in rage.

"You'll never know," he scoffs as he drills his burning finger further into the Wahaken's forehead. A fiery crack of light erupts from his fingertips, effortlessly penetrating Namaka's skull. Time slows to a disorienting crawl as Sophia and the boys struggle to register what has just transpired. Namaka's spirit springs from his bodily prison well before his lifeless flesh hits the cold damp floor.

As the huddled trio focuses their attention on screaming out his name in disbelief, Hanu springs into action. He flies in-between the trio and the Warden, spreads his wings, and with an exuberant battle cry he emits the full force of his blinding light into the eyes of the unexpecting Warden. The Warden's sunglasses do little to shield the celestial light as he takes a step backwards in a brief moment of distraction. The trio gathers their composure and makes a mad dash to the docked ship. Hanu continues his blinding cover until he is sure the three are well on the move. He takes one last look at Namaka before dissolving into a stream of pure light. The light flows into the tip of the exposed wand Sophia has haphazardly stuffed into her coat pocket. With the cracking sound of the Warden's attack still ringing in their ears, all other sensations have become severely dampened. The boys run ahead of Sophia in a disorienting fog, desperate to find safety.

∞

The overall shock causes every conscious movement to be an outright battle of will. As the boys make it back to the ship and mount the rope ladder leading up to the deck, they look back only to see Sophia nowhere in sight. They fling their heads from side to side in a frantic scurry. They finally look up towards the deck only to see their worst nightmare manifest before them. The well-dressed Warden stands at the top of their ladder with Sophia held tightly under his arm. He gazes out to the opening of the cave and notices the storm from Babel has finally settled down. The rising sun brings a sliver of light into the cave, cutting through the thick overcast skies.

"Ahhh, with Babel finally done with her temper tantrum, it will make this so much easier," the Warden says to the boys. He touches two fingers to his forehead and gives a makeshift salute before dissolving his physical form, Sophia and all, into a wisp of the wind.

∞

"Beau! Beau!"

"Oh my Maia, it's terrible!" "Beau! Are you still alive?!" Otto cries as he flies up the deck and continues into the hatch next to the helm. He fires his head through the opening and lets out a gasp of momentary relief. "Thank God you're still alive!" he says. His words do little to disrupt Beau's meditative concentration. The youth lowers himself back into Brahm's recovery room, carrying with him the vibratory wake of chaos and fear. Otto tries to catch his breath as Domino makes his way into the room. His eagerness unfortunately gets the better of him as he overshoots his trajectory, landing first onto Beau's unsuspecting head before falling not-so-gracefully onto the waxed floor. He slides smoothly until he brushes up against the adjacent wall. Forced out of his deep meditation, Beau rubs his head as his consciousness is abruptly called back to the physical realm.

"That's quite the entry, boys. What in the world happened out there?"

"Beau! It was terrible!" Otto starts.

"There was this dying guy on the rocks!" Domino chimes in.

"But first there was this glowing bird that saved us…" "Twice!"

"Boys…"

"Yeah, twice! And then…"

"And then…"

"BOYS!" Beau bellows, quickly growing tired of the tennis match of information. "Just spit it out!"

"Sophia's been kidnapped!" they cry together.

"Kidnapped?"

"Beau! It was awful! A Warden came out of nowhere!" Otto tries to start again.

"Well, he apparently was riding under this ship this whole time!" Domino feels the need to correct.

"Right! Oh man, we spent all this time trying to stay alive through Babel and in the process, we managed to rescue one of the most dangerous creatures on the face of the planet!"

"He killed the man in the cave!" "Then he took Sophia! Saying she was… a Resistance member!" "The *leader* of the Resistance!"

"And now it's all our fault she got captured! Beau! We carried Sophia to her doom! What do we do?!" Otto asks while tears of fierce anger and guilt pour down his cheeks. "We can't let him get away with this!"

"Yeah!" Domino cries, siding with his fired-up friend.

"This Warden guy must be pretty scary. He was under the ship this whole time? Through everything we've been through tonight?" he asks, specifically recounting the nosedive through an alarm tower. "How could he have survived *that*?" he thinks out loud to himself. His mind drifts further into his memory as he recalls the dark, shadowy figure he saw in the water while going to rescue the crew from the tower. *Could that have been him?*

"He's been with us through *everything*, Beau!" Otto says. "They are monsters! Some say they are indestructible! Nobody that ever stands against them lives to talk about it!"

"Not a very reassuring factor when trying to plan a rescue mission," Beau mumbles to himself.

"But we have seen what you and Brahm are capable of! You two can bend reality and stuff. I mean, come on! Just look what we went through tonight! Brahm *wrestled* an ancient storm spirit!"

"And you… can like, heal people and stuff!"

"That is not normal! The Wardens are not normal! *You're* definitely not normal! There has to be a chance!" Domino pants as his exasperated explanation causes him to forgo his urge to breathe.

"I wish I knew more about what we were up against—"

"Monsters!" Domino blurts out.

"Right, give me a minute, Eager Beaver. Even if I wanted to help Sophia, and I do! Don't get me wrong, but my hands are still tied here at the moment. Brahm still hasn't returned to his body and I'm starting to wonder what it's going to take to get him to come back. If I leave him now, he might never return."

"Ugh, we don't have time for this," Domino huffs as he rolls up his sleeves. Beau and Otto watch with curious eyes as Domino marches right over to where Beau and Brahm lay. Beau's eyes widen as he is pushed out of the way while Domino takes it upon himself to straddle the chest of the transparent ship captain.

"Umm, what exactly are—" Beau tries to say before the sound of an open palm striking flesh cuts through the room.

"Did he just—" Otto mutters.

"Wake up already, you buffoon!" Continuing his assault, he times his strikes to land when Brahm's pulsating form becomes most visible. "There is no time for this anymore! Sophia has been captured and they will eventually kill her if you don't do something!" He punctuates his statement with another slap. "Do you want that on your conscience? Letting her die while you lie here taking a freaking spirit nap?!" Another strike connects to the still flickering ship captain. "Get a grip already! Sophia needs you! So-phi-a!" Domino thrusts his hand back to make another strike, but this time his palm does not connect. Domino looks down at the once translucent hand now firmly gripping his wrist. He slowly turns his attention to the now very solid face of Brahm. Brahm bears a furrowed brow and devilish glow behind the whites of his eyes. His jaw is clenched so tightly you can almost hear his unsuspecting teeth cracking under the immense pressure. Domino's body shivers with waves of fear crashing into his soul. He freezes, afraid that an unmarked move could make him the recipient of the accumulating rage that builds below him.

"Where is she?" is all Brahm asks as he lifts himself to his feet. Still caught up in the moment, he continues to hold onto Domino's wrist, subsequently lifting him up as he makes his stand. Domino kicks his feet as they struggle to reconnect with the distancing floor. Brahm pays the struggling youth no mind while he moves around as if he has completely forgotten what he holds so tightly.

"Well, if I had known that was all it was going to take, I could have easily—" Beau says in efforts to lighten the mood but is quickly cut off.

"I asked a question," Brahm responds firmly with no reaction to Beau's lighthearted attempt. He takes a step closer to Beau, finally letting go of Domino. He hits the ground like a sack of discarded potatoes. Domino nurses his swollen wrist, thankful it is still attached. Otto rushes to aid in the relief of his friend.

"We don't know," Beau responds, taking heed of the commanding atmosphere Brahm exudes.

"We saw her and the Warden dissolve into dust and fly away in the wind!" Domino calls out, trying to be helpful. Otto rushes to cover his friends' mouth, afraid that any misplaced word could tip the energetic juggernaut into a fit of rage.

"Which way was the wind blowing?" Brahm asks, paying no attention to Beau's unhelpful comment. Domino strokes his chin for a moment, trying to recall the events to the best of his memory. He confidently takes ahold of Otto's hand and gently moves it aside.

"There was a breeze blowing out the mouth of the cave. The fog was moving towards the east," he recalls calmly. Brahm nods with understanding and makes his way to the door leading to the navigation deck. As he makes his silent trek up the stairs, Beau and the boys take heed to follow his purposeful steps. The trio trail behind the deafening pounding of Brahm's footsteps as they echo ominously throughout the stairwell. As Beau reaches the top deck, he looks out at his captain staring intently at the mouth of the cave.

"She could be anywhere, Brahm!" Beau calls after him, trying to slow the abrupt jump to action. "Let's think about this before you go off and do anything reckless."

"Reckless?" Brahm asks without turning around. His tone is eerily calm. The wind continues to bellow out into the cave opening, rustling his unkempt hair under his fluttering hat. He takes the time to choose his next words carefully. "Would it not be reckless to wait around here pondering while allowing her fate to be decided by another?" The steady wind dances between the two paradigms of thought. "You can do all the planning you want, but I'm leaving *now*."

"Have you thought of anything?!" Beau asks with hands extended like a street beggar. "How do you plan to find her? How do you intend for us to find you or her after you bound out of here like a lovesick loon?" Brahm finally turns to his concerned friend. A bead of sweat pools on Beau's forehead as he looks to his emotionally unstable captain.

"What are you insinuating? That I don't know what I am doing? That I can't handle this without you holding my hand?" Brahm says with a burst of ferocious energy fit for a wild animal.

"Whoa, whoa, whoa there!" Beau says with his hands now up in surrender. "I'm insinuating nothing, I just want to know what your plan is. That's all."

"I've already set my intention to find her. That will be enough to guide me where I need to go," he says with a slight settling of his energy. "I made a promise to her and her people we would meet today at her lighthouse by the docks. The boys know which one it is. Her people know this land and I'm confident they know the ramifications of what it means to be captured by one of these Wardens."

"How did you—"

"I know enough. There has been some strange activity in the ethereal realms that kept me distracted earlier. There is something going on, Beau. It's not good. I'm not sure what yet, but it's somehow connected to those people they call Wardens. Their energy signature is tied to a dangerous pocket of dimensional energy I have never come across before. It might even be a merger of energy from multiple dimensions. Either way, something is channeling it… sending it to them in a way that does not automatically interfere with the vibrational octave of this dimension. It's unbelievable to think how any of this is possible. It's breaking all the rules I've ever known to exist. I need to put an end to it at all costs."

"Well, what about the weird pole that's right here?" Beau asks, nudging his head towards the pulsating Power Pole. "Does that have something to do with it? I felt it when we first came into this cave; it's definitely not fit for this world. Why not just get rid of it now and see what happens?"

"Get rid of it?" Brahm asks with detest growing in his voice. Beau silently looks side to side; not aware his question was out of line.

"Think about it," Brahm continues. "If that thing is channeling energy from outside this dimension, how do you think we would… 'just get rid of it?!'"

"Well, I guess when you put it that way—"

"Not knowing what we are doing, we could end up bringing any level of destruction upon this world!" Brahm feels the need to yell. "And if not that, we don't even know what dimension it originates from! How do you suppose we go about putting something back when we don't know where it comes from? Oh! Maybe I can go ahead and create an interdimensional rug we can just sweep this thing under? Maybe that would work!"

"Yeah, I guess you are right. You've made your point," Beau concedes. "I didn't think about that."

"Now who's not thinking things through?" Brahm says with a hostile bite.

"I get it, okay? You've made your point and then some. I'm sorry. So, what's next?"

"We act. I'm counting on you to gather Sophia's people," Brahm says. "They are a testy bunch so act quickly and honestly. Just tell them what happened, and the rest should unfold after that. I have a feeling we are going to need all the help we can get."

"Those are concerning words coming from you."

"If you saw what I saw, you would be concerned too," Brahm responds flatly. Beau soaks in his captain's words and produces a light chuckle at the thought of what is about to unfold.

"Do you regret leaving our quiet and remote slice of rock on the other side of the world?" he asks. Brahm finally lightens up as a chuckle forces its way to the surface.

"Hmm, we couldn't stay secluded forever. Not even Babel could keep the dramas of this world from eventually knocking on our doors. This is the beginning of the inevitable, my friend."

"Well said, captain," Beau responds with a hint of jest. "Well, get on with it. Guess you have thought it through after all. I'll rally the troops and keep a lookout for the nearest explosion. I'm sure that is where we will find you."

"You know me all too well," Brahm says as he tips his hat to Beau. Turning his attention back to the mouth of the cave, he gets a running start before taking a mighty leap off the stern. The ship bobs back and forth, forcing Beau and the boys to brace themselves from the violent undulation. They watch as he bounds effortlessly from side to side of the cave before latching on to a low hanging cloud at the base of the cave entrance. He lingers for a moment, suspended by his supernatural grasp on the whimsical cloud. He sways back and forth as the rays of the rising sun fight their way through the dense cloud cover. As if emulating a celestial monkey god swinging from heavenly vines, Brahm flings himself through the dense clouds until he bounds over the horizon and out of sight.

"All right, boys," Beau rallies. "This is getting real. Time for us to get to work."

CHAPTER: 24

A Heavy Choice

"This is the last one!" Domino calls out as he reels in the final rope Otto has untied from their makeshift dock along the rocks. Without getting an immediate response, Domino turns to see if Beau received his relayed information. His eyes catch sight of him up on the higher navigation deck wrestling with the cables of the sky-sails. Domino scurries up the curved steps to inform his struggling leader of their completed task.

"Beau!" Domino calls with more vigor as he pivots off the last step of the stairwell. "Did you hear me? We finished untying—" Beau's frustrated foot kicks the brass contraption holding the sky cables in place. "I heard you, kid. Uhhh," he grunts as he scratches his head. "Now just give me a minute to get these things straight and then we will get out of here." He moves a step closer to the cables. "Which one was I messing with again?" he mumbles to himself, mentally dismissing Domino's presence.

"Are you really going to be able to get us out of here?" Domino chimes in, not one to take heed of inferred boundaries.

"Don't you worry yourself," he says under his breath. "I was flying these things before Brahm was even a twinkle in his father's eye. I just need a minute to get reacquainted." He dives his hands back into the tangle of cables as he thinks of another way to get rid of his eager cabin boy. "How about that friend of yours, where did he run off to?" Beau strategically asks. Taking the bait, Domino runs over to the railing and hangs his head over to scan the rocky beach. Quickly assessing Otto is no longer where he last remembered, he returns to Beau for direction.

"He's not on the bank anymore! Where do you think he went? Doesn't he know we are in a hurry?" Beau grumbles as the lack of insight grows more apparent.

"Well," he starts, reserving only a sliver of sarcasm, "why don't you be useful and go look for—" The two jump at the sound of the unexpected door leading below deck slamming shut.

"Ah! That must be him!" Domino exclaims with joy. "I'm going to go check on him!" he calls out as he makes his way back down the stairwell. "Hurry up and get those sails figured out, Beau! We've got a lot riding on this mission!" Domino's head bobs out of sight as his words linger like an uninvited house guest. Beau shakes his own head out of reflexive frustration yet can't help but notice a smile blossoming.

"I don't know how he holds onto that enthusiasm after all we've been through, but I'm sure we are going to need every last ounce of it. Now, where was I?" he says, returning to his growing knot of cables. "This one?" As he pulls back the stubborn cable it suddenly snaps, breaking off above his quivering hand. "Well, so much for that…" He holds back a sense of defeat as he watches the flailing cable slither haphazardly up into the mast.

∞

Below deck, Domino scurries down through the ship's unexplored corridors in pursuit of his distant companion. Without any idea as to where his friend would have wandered off to, each door he passes presents a possible end point to his search. The initial door leads him back to Brahm's old recovery room. The broken pot Otto threw is still scattered on the polished floor. The next opens into a discarded laboratory. Dust lines the shelves and a stale smell permeates the atmosphere. Further down leads to a room of assorted beds and hammocks fit for a crew of thirty. His search leads him deeper and deeper into the heart of the ship, all the way to the end of the spiraling stairwell. As he reaches the last remaining steps, a final door emerges into sight. As Domino picks up his pace, his carelessness leads him to trip over his own eager feet. Head over heels, he tumbles down the remaining steps until he crashes with a triumphant *thud* into the final door. Rubbing his throbbing head, he uses his other hand to slowly turn the bronze doorknob. A slight push produces an eerie creak from the rusty hinges holding the opening door.

Otto stands pensively in the center of the familiar navigation room. His head is sunk over as he dramatically retraces his first steps in the strange ship's quarters. The cabinets that line the walls have been fully restored with pristine porcelain pottery. They hang from the racks inside, shifting slightly from side to side. The chatter-like rattling settles down into hushed silence as Domino makes a careful step into the room. He quickly becomes aware of the dense energy that surrounds his friend. He hesitates, unsure as to what words to use to break the heavy silence. As if sensing the internal conflict, Otto turns to his worried friend and addresses his unspoken concerns.

"I had a feeling you would come find me," Otto finally says.

"What are you doing down here?" Domino asks, taking another step closer. His face wrinkles with concern. He can feel the distance between them intensifying despite his advancement forward.

"You know, this is where all the madness started for me," Otto starts, avoiding a direct answer. "Everything used to happen in a predictable, clock-like fashion. My purpose within that clock seemed to be pretty simple and I was okay with that. I was a salvage boy. I did what I could to put food on our table. That was it. That is, until this ship comes flying out of nowhere and changed everything overnight. Now everything is energy? Reality is malleable? People are being murdered? I know I said I would finish this thing out, but this has all become too much." Otto looks back to his hands, running his fingers along the polished wood framing. Not knowing what to say, Domino takes another step forward with his eyes glued on his troubled companion. Before either can find the next words to speak, they are both forced to brace themselves as the ship makes an abrupt jolt.

"Ha," Domino laughs nervously. "Must be Beau finally testing out the sky-sails. I don't think he's very good with them." Otto regains his composure, adjusting his stance to adapt to the ship's undulating dance through the water. However, it is not enough to shift him from his solemn demeanor.

"We just saw a man die, right before our eyes. Murdered, Domino! That's what this adventure has led to," Otto says definitively.

"I know. I was—"

"But look at you!" Otto cuts him off. "You stand there with a smug look on your face, making light of all this like everything is going to be just fine. What gives? Did Brahm give you some magical exorcism or something? You were this arrogant prick I could count on to make money, and now you've turned into this happy-go-lucky nut job!"

"Hey!" Domino says, cutting him off as he takes yet another step forward. His face takes on a more serious tone as he prepares to defend his defiled image. "Look! Watching that man die is tearing me up too, trust me! It's not my fault I am working through this differently than you." His fierce words cut through the air like a knife. Otto takes a deep breath as he finally stares his advancing friend in the eye. "But I will say this," Domino continues, "I was changed after that moment by the docks, and I am not ashamed of who I have allowed myself to become since then. I may not know who that person is yet, but I do know he is free."

Another violent jolt from the ship forces the two to brace themselves once again. This time, the pull into the floor sends the message that the mighty ship has gone airborne. A flash of cheerful relief strikes across Domino's face, but he quickly realigns with his situation at hand.

"You know, you talk like Brahm is this savior sent here to free us from all our suffering," Otto starts again. "I can't help but think how he could have easily come to bring more suffering upon us." His words take a challenging tone. "He may have helped you, and that's great and all, but look at you! You didn't just have a change of heart, you had a whole 'change of person!' I could never see you going back to being who you were after all this."

"Why would I want to?" Domino asks sincerely. "Why would anyone want to go back to who they were after being given so many opportunities to change?"

"I still have a family, Domino. People who depend on me being 'me!' The 'me' I was before all this madness. They need me, and the longer I stay adrift on this maddening adventure, the more they suffer."

"Suffer?"

"They can't work! You know that! They took me in when I lost everything. I owe my life to them. I realize now it's selfish for me to stay out here any longer." Otto clenches his fists as the incoming thoughts boil to the surface. "It's easy for you. You don't have anyone but yourself. You are lucky. You can become someone else, and nobody is going to suffer because of it." Domino's once careful advancement turns to haste as he stampedes towards Otto. With his hand extended, Domino slams his open palm into the chest of his friend and grips him by the scruff of his shirt. With his fingers clamping tightly into a fist, he lifts his much shorter companion off the ground. Dancing on his tiptoes, the shocked Otto stares helplessly into the burning eyes of his enraged aggressor.

"Lucky?" Domino growls through clenched teeth. "I'm lucky for having my whole family die as I helplessly watched them get washed away into oblivion?"

"Domino I—"

"No!" Domino cuts him off. He flexes his arm, straining to maintain his grip. "I know who I was before, what my cling to pain had shaped me into; what it's shaping you into! But I have decided to let go of my past and better myself. Can you say the same? You stand there preaching like a martyr, claiming you 'can't change.' That's crap. You're just scared." He punctuates his statement by finally releasing his friend. Taken by surprise, Otto struggles to gain his footing before falling to his knees.

"Scared?!" Otto nearly screeches as he tries to regain his bearings. "Of course I'm scared! Scared of losing myself! I can't do that to my family. I can't take that risk like you can!"

"Enough!" Domino bellows. "You listen to me! You can pretend you can't change all you want because of your 'responsibility to your family.' However, as someone who still considers you to be my friend, I cannot stand here and let you blatantly lie to yourself with such conviction! This isn't about a man dying anymore! This isn't about you helping your family. You're afraid of change and you're just hiding behind the facade of responsibility."

"You have no idea what you are talking about!" Otto fires back, with anger swelling in his throat.

"You know," Domino says with a deliberate pause now permeating the room. The shift in momentum strikes a confusing nerve in his audience. "Despite all the hell I have given you all these years, I was jealous of you."

"Jealous?" Otto stammers as he struggles to pick himself back onto his feet.

"Yeah, jealous. We may have both lost our parents but there was something about you that made someone *want* to take you in. Someone wanted to give you a second chance at a family. You see your new family as a burden, but it's all I ever wanted." A heavy pause resonates after his last words. Otto can feel his friend's pain, but he still can't let go of his own. Domino senses the resistance but realizes he has lost the will to fight any longer.

"As for me, I've already made my choice. No matter how scary it gets out there, I'm going to see this thing through and become a better person because of it. I won't let that man die in vain. With or without you, this is what I've decided to do," Domino says as he turns to head back to the door. "I don't know what I expected to find when I came down here looking for you, but it wasn't this. Regardless, you've helped me so much whether you know it or not, but I have to let you go if you wish to return to the past. That's the one place I know I cannot join you." After exhausting the words that swelled into his heart, Domino makes his way to the door with a cleared conscience.

"Wait," Otto pleads, finally bringing himself back onto his feet. As a strong breeze strikes the sky-sails above, another reverberating shockwave runs through the ship, knocking Otto back to the ground. Domino, having maintained his composure, watches as his friend falls with a defeated look still in his eyes.

"I'm done waiting, my friend." With his final words hanging in the air, he takes to the stairwell, making his return climb to the deck above.

Otto frantically flails his hands in search for something to hold onto, something to assist him back to his feet; but he remains sprawled out on the floor watching his friend ascend out of sight. He burrows his hands into his face, overwhelmed with doubt, worry, and the growing awareness of his own fear. As if to personify the building pressure in his head, he hears the whistling of a boiling tea kettle. He flings his head around in search of the source. Tucked in the back corner of the room an unacknowledged kettle sits upon a small wood-burning stove. Its whistling steam bellows up into the ceiling. Otto wipes his eyes with disbelief. He was certain it wasn't there prior to his entry to the room. He quickly brings himself to his feet and walks towards the enticing spectacle. As he nears the kettle, he looks to the wall behind the stove and sees two empty cups on a hook, begging to be filled.

CHAPTER: 25

An Unexpected Arrival

Back on deck, Beau looks away from his tangled mess of sails to register the heavy heart reemerging from below deck. He watches as Domino takes a deep exhale before carefully shutting the cabin door behind him. Running his fingers along the banister, Domino makes his way to the high navigation deck to join Beau. Having grown accustomed to the constant shaking from Beau's subpar sky navigation, the two stand side by side like silent bobble head dolls. Beau is first to break the thickening silence.

"So, did you find your friend?" he asks, fishing for the root of his uncharacteristic mood.

"I did," Domino responds without any hurry to divulge what happened below deck. He peers out into the clouds they sail through with his attention clearly drifting elsewhere. "Watching that man die really shook him up. It shook us both up, but he's in a darker spot than I had imagined. He's somewhere I think he has chosen to be. Somewhere he thinks he *has* to be. Somewhere, no matter how much I am hurting, I cannot bring myself to return."

"I see," Beau mumbles, unsure of how to console the youth.

"I think all this has really gotten to him, not just what happened with the Warden," Domino continues. "Granted, it is a lot to take in. Out of nowhere you and Brahm have come and turned our lives upside down. He's afraid. I don't even think he fully knows why. What's worse is that he doesn't want help. That fear is going to destroy him eventually, and I just can't stand by and watch that."

"I thought he had gotten over his fears," Beau says heavily.

"I'm sure he thought he had too," Domino responds flatly. "I said my piece, but ultimately it is his choice to bury himself further into that hole or climb out of it. All he was doing was trying to bring me down with him, so I had to walk away."

"I'm sure that wasn't an easy thing to do," Beau remarks. His heart swirls with mixed emotions.

"No, it wasn't, but it feels like the right thing to do."

"You have to do what feels right in your heart. And who knows, maybe your friend will come around."

"Maybe. But I can't hold on to that hope."

"No, but you could still keep your heart open to the possibility."

"I came up here with the intention to see this thing through. Whatever it is we are getting into now. That's where I need to focus."

Domino's words resonate in silent recognition as they both continue their pensive gaze into the clouds. The abrupt sound of a muffled door closing now begs the attention of the two upon the navigation deck. Beau sneaks a peek below to see Otto attempting to tiptoe his way onto the main deck. His hands cradle two semi-full teacups that he holds close to his chest like newborn children. A stain runs down the front of his shirt, alluding to the location of the other half of the cup's contents. Beau's diverted focus leads into another violent jolt felt through the ship as an unnoticed gust rattles one of the sky-sails. Otto stumbles, spilling more of his precious tea onto the polished wood at his feet.

"Not again!" he whines reflexively. With exasperated eyes, he peers into the depleted cups to see if anything remains of his precious offerings. With a reluctant sigh, he continues his careful journey up the winding stairwell. Taking the hint his attention is best served undistracted, Beau returns his sights to the sky. He contemplates informing Domino of the advancing situation but decides to let things play out naturally.

Nearing his intended destination, Otto peers over the last remaining steps to scout out his best course of action. As his hands quiver with anticipation, he turns to take a heavy look down the stairs he climbed. Turning around now would still offer the opportunity to avoid the approaching hardships. Shaking his head, he realigns his focus forward and burrows a deep breath into his chest before announcing his presence.

"H-Hey…" At first, the howling winds are all who greet him. Domino and Beau remain fixated on the clouds in front of them, each for their own reasons. Worried he just made a huge mistake, Otto quickly digresses back into the comfort of doubt and turns to retreat back below deck.

"How nice of you to join us!" Beau says, ignoring his earlier decision to stay out of the budding drama. The potential for a resolution was just too much to let pass by.

"T-Thanks," Otto responds, unsure what to do with his position of indecisiveness. Caught in mid-turn, his right shoulder faces the beckoning stairwell, his left shoulder points to the still distant Domino. Otto anxiously peers into his teacups as if they hold the answers to his situation.

"Are one of those for me?" Beau asks playfully.

"Um… well, yeah, sure. You can have this one," he says with eagerness, hoping offering the cup he made to share with Domino will be enough to please him.

"Ha! No need, kid, I just can't help but mess with you. Luckily, I already had my tea earlier," he says as his memory drifts back to his first encounter with the polished Pearl below.

"Uh… okay…" Otto stammers, clearly unsure what to do about Domino's reluctance to acknowledge his presence. Beau finally turns his head and connects eyes with Otto. He starts aggressively nudging his head towards Domino with silent coaxing. He throws in a couple dramatic eyebrow raises to reiterate his message to initiate contact. Finally taking the hint, Otto directs his full attention into his original goal.

"Ahem, Domino. I…" But before he could get another word out, Domino immediately turns around and faces his friend with the same burning eyes he displayed below deck. The winds he was originally peering into now blow his silver hair frantically into his face. It does little to disrupt the intense gaze erupting underneath the fluttering strands. A lump swells in the back of Otto's throat as he feels the opportunity to speak his mind slipping away.

"I was thinking about what you had said earlier, and I… I wanted to say—" Otto's words are disrupted by the violent detachment of one of the sky-sails from its tether to the ship. Beau quickly jumps to make some adjustments to the remaining sails. The adjustments lead to an even more violent jolt than any of them would have expected. As they struggle to regain their footing, the ship reluctantly makes its first dip below the cloud line.

"Hurry up and finish your tea, boys," Beau grunts through clenched teeth. "Looks like we are about to improvise this landing!" He clenches the remaining sails with all his might. Releasing the latches with his feet, he burrows his fists into the cables and manually adjusts them to stabilize the fall. The boys rush to stretch their heads over the railing, reconnecting their sights on the storm-polished island. Horror strikes Domino's heart first as his eyes awaken to the streets of his homeland erupting in chaos.

"Beau!" he cries in shock, completely forgetting about Otto's sputtering testimony. "What's happening down there?!" All Beau can do is summon a grumble under his breath as he, too, is unsure how to register the unexpected turmoil. He peers down at the plumes of smoke erupting from imploding buildings and the people pouring into the streets in panic. Their cries for help reverberate in the chill morning breeze. The ship's vantage point remains too high to make assumptions of the mayhem below.

"We have to do something!" Domino calls out.

"Damn right we do!" Beau reaffirms. "But before we do anything about the streets on fire, we need to put this ship down as close as we can to that lighthouse Brahm mentioned!" Sneaking glances at the incoming lands, Beau huffs a breath of frustration as all the polished buildings do little to distinguish themselves from one another.

"Gaahhh, which one is it?!" Beau bellows dramatically. "Why does everything around here have to look the same?" Another failing sky-sail severs its connection with the ship. The freed cable slithers like a hungry snake through the mast before it, too, disappears into the cloudy fog above. The quickly approaching island gives a clearer view to the boys who desperately scan for the most appropriate landing point. Lifting a finger from his precious teacups, Otto draws an imaginary line around the curved Bay of The Pearl. He finds a specific canal and follows it with his finger about mid-way inland before he stops his tracing. A reflecting ray of light bounces off a piece of polished glass that solidifies his confidence.

"There!" he exclaims, finally regaining his voice. "Third canal from the left side of the bay. Their ship isn't docked there anymore, but I'm sure that's the lighthouse Sophia works at!"

"That's her lighthouse, all right," Domino confirms, "and if these people are really with the Resistance, then there is no way they won't be there. They are monsters in their own right!" he concludes matter-of-factly as he throws a side-glance over at Otto.

"Phewww!" Beau says while adjusting the few exhausted sky-sails that remain. "I hope you two are right, because we are going down quickly!" The boys watch helplessly as the ship plummets towards the ground; the sails feel like they are doing little to slow their hasteful plunge. Domino grips the wooden railing as the horror of the war-torn streets mixes with his own potential pitfall. Unable to part with his precious teacups, Otto falls to his knees and watches the approaching land advance through the parallel spokes of the banister.

The veins of Beau's grizzly arms pulsate with his elevating heart rate. They surge into his expanding muscles, swelling with commanding force as they start to tear through his shirt. Despite all his energy being directed to slowing their descent, the sails can't trap enough air to bring solace to their situation. Beau takes a deep breath of acceptance as he realizes the exhausted ship has reached the end of her abilities. With little time left for a backup plan, he lets go of the sky-sails and leaps from his perch, landing with a heavy thud next to the boys.

"Hold on tight!" he says as he wraps his arms around them. "We are coming in hot, but I'll make sure we survive this!" As he closes his protective human shield around them, his attention is drawn once again to the mast. He squints his eyes as he watches an unexpected thin thread weave itself through the main mast and even float down through the spokes of the helm. As he turns his head, he notices there are, in fact, multiple micro-threads silently whizzing all around them. Before he can process the oddities any further, the boys draw his attention back to the incoming impact.

"Don't you let us go, Beau!" Domino screams as he clenches his eyes, preparing for the collision. Beau locks his grip around the quivering boys, tucking his own head into his protective fortress.

"I won't! And whatever you do, don't let go of one another either!" Beau commands. Somehow, with teacups still in hand, the boys embrace one another as they await their impending fate. The abrupt landing unleashes unapologetic ripples of destruction upon the tightly bound trio. The huddled bundle of bodies bound unrestricted through the ship's contours as the grinding impact uproots their foothold, sending them flying in all directions. Crashing into the mast, back to the deck, then into the railing, they volley around the ship like a rampaging pinball. Impact after impact, the three still hold onto one another, refusing to loosen their grip despite the repeated opportunities to sever their bond.

The three finally roll to a stop as the ship completes its merger with the unforgiving surroundings. Scrapes and bruises mix with the falling dust and debris as they take their first steps among the wreckage. Wood planking lies scattered along the splintered deck and all throughout the cobblestone streets. Fallen masts and writhing cables make up the tangled jungle above. Creaks and moans from the dilapidated ship perspire with every move the trio makes as they gather their wits.

The boys look themselves up and down and are amazed at the lack of damage upon their own fragile bodies. Shifting their attention to Beau, they bombard him with beams of gratitude radiating from their eyes. Taking the majority of the damage, Beau stands with clothes tattered and stained with blood. Deep gashes line his back and arms where he absorbed their fall from grace. He gives the boys an enthusiastic thumbs-up to deter any worry on his behalf. The feeble gesture of assurance does little to alter their concern. Beau takes a deep breath while rotating his arms to assess their remaining range of mobility. Satisfied with a few successful revolutions of his shoulders, he moves on to his lower half. After producing a couple hobbled steps, he becomes joyfully aware of his ability to still bear his own weight. He brings his blood-bathed mess of a body to stand fully erect. With a sigh of relief, he looks to the boys with a satisfied grin on his face. Domino and Otto rush to embrace their tattered savior, tears of joy pouring unrestricted down their cheeks. The three make moves to the edge of the wreckage to see how close they managed to land to their target. Domino reaches the edge of the dismembered ship first and a gasp of surprise fills his lungs before he can turn to address the others.

Otto and Beau come to join him and the three stare upon their impromptu landing strip. Waves of polished stone rise to greet the wooden railing of the ship's deck. The once flat and level stones buckle upward, wrapping around the hull like a frozen ocean wave. The steel blade that makes up the helm remains intact, serving as the saving grace of the ship and crew. However, the cost of their safety becomes growingly apparent. The boys look back into the ripples of destruction left in the wake of their landing and see a deep gully etched as far as the eye can see. Both buildings and streets alike lay crumbled in helpless heaps of carnage where the ship's sharp blade made contact. Domino slaps his sweaty palm into his face as he realizes his arrival has only caused additional turmoil to the land he was so eager to assist.

"Ah, the great Serapis Bey shows off her prestigious might," Beau says melodramatically. The boys stare at him with curious eyes. "Great protector through and through. Despite her defeated form now, she stayed strong during the toughest of obstacles, harboring mercy and protection over us all! She really showed her stuff today!" Beau says proudly, disregarding the mutilation of their landing strip.

"Maybe the 'great Serapis Bey' could have been more merciful of our homeland as well," Domino says, referencing their path of carnage with his eyes.

"Yeah. I guess we could have been a bit more tactful," Beau says, ignoring the emotional inflection of his statement. Beau places his hands on either of the boys' shoulders, quick to realign focus to their mission. "Go ahead and finish what is left of your tea. I'm sure our arrival has not gone unnoticed. We have to be prepared for anything; we essentially have no idea who we are going to meet, or what kind of welcoming we will be met with."

The boys look to one another. Otto's eyes drown with sorrow and display the remorse he desperately wants to share. Domino gazes back at such eyes with ferocity and emotional callous. Unable to find the words to express his feelings, Otto extends a cup of tea to his friend. Domino merely looks at the content and then back at Otto with a disapproving shake of his head. Otto eagerly jumps at the opportunity to inspect the source of disapproval. His heart sinks as he becomes aware his peace offering has inevitably been emptied of its contents.

Unwilling to accept the empty and deaf apology, Domino turns his head away from him and glances to Beau. Aware of the failed communion, Beau leans down and picks up each youth and places them on his shoulders. With his new cargo in tow, he makes his way to the port side of the ship. Caught in the middle of the boys' emotional turmoil, he takes one more look back at the wake of physical carnage he has caused with his landing. Unsure what to expect next, he turns back to face the still unturned stones in front of him.

Taking a mighty leap, he soars off the decrepit deck. He floats through the air before gently meeting the solid ground below. Carefully setting the boys down, he scans his surroundings with radar-like senses. He quickly catches an eerie vibration within the chaos running amuck. Beau extends an outstretched hand in front of the boys, involuntarily manifesting the cautious tendencies of an overly protective parent. Despite all his senses on overdrive, he manages to run face-first into an unexpected obstacle with only a few careful steps forward.

Violently shifting his weight back and forth, he is surprised to realize his body has become trapped in some kind of invisible web. Before he can warn the boys, they, too, walk face first into the ethereal trap.

"What is this?" Otto cries as he struggles to backtrack. "I can't move at all!"

"Me either! What is this, Beau?" Domino cries.

"I don't know, boys! Just try to relax, struggling never helps at all," he says, in efforts to calm his own nerves. "Just what have we walked ourselves into?" Taking a deep breath, he focuses his attention to try and uncover the bizarre binding that entraps them. Brief rays of light cut through the rolling clouds, casting a momentary illumination of thin fibers that run across his torso. Straining his eyes a bit further, he notices the whole street is full of these micro fibers. They stretch from building to building and run all through their ship behind them. As the clouds roll back the rays of light, the strands of fiber drift back into visual obscurity.

"It's like what I saw on the ship as we were falling!" Beau mumbles loudly to himself.

"Beau!" the boys call out together.

"Someone…"

"A bunch of someone's…"

"…are coming for us!" Otto finishes. Beau looks onto the silhouettes walking slowly towards their position. There are four of them, ranging from a giant on the left to one who appears to be walking with a cane on the far right. Their full figures still remain obscured by the morning fog that fills the streets.

"Oh my, they are going to kill us!" Otto shouts out. "I should have just stayed on the ship! If only I could go back. What was I thinking? I knew I should have stayed put! I'm going crazy! Why can't I just wake up from this nightmare!?"

"Shut up, will you!" Domino shouts over to his flabbergasted companion. "There is no 'going back' to anything! This is it! Just face your destiny with at least a shred of dignity!"

"Boys!" Beau bellows. "Enough. Just be quiet and don't make any sudden moves. I got a feeling first impressions are going to be very important here." He looks on as the shadowy figures start to emerge one by one from the fog. He studies what he can in order to start planning his next move.

A man bearing a head of niveous white dreadlocks is first to walk through the fog. A pair of rugged goggles line his head, keeping the rows of dreaded hair pulled neatly back behind him. He is a young man, somewhere in his mid-twenties. He walks with an air of confidence, holding a still-smoking gun over his shoulder. It resembles nothing like any firearm Beau has ever seen. The man looks side to side and down the alleyway, scanning for some unknown blunder. Seemingly satisfied with his search, he turns to the trapped trio with a smug look of accomplishment on his face. His other hand reaches up to pull a lit cigarette from his mouth, triggering a plume of smoke to come pouring from both his nose and mouth. A long beige cloak complements his dark, midnight complexion. The cloak renders further detail obscured except for the thick boots that line his feet.

Next emerges a slender woman to his right who busts out of the fog as if emerging from the curtain of a fashion runway. She, too, dons a beige cloak she has left unbuttoned to flutter in the wind behind her. Black leather tights wrap around her long and powerful legs. Her quad muscles bulge slightly with each carefully placed step of her high-heeled covered feet. Ropes and chains dangle along her waist, strapped securely along a thick belt that holds them all in place. A sheathed sword also rests along her waist, tucked along her backside. Her shirt, or what is left of it, is cut like a Victorian corset. Black leather straps adhere onto large buttons along her ribcage and tie behind her back. Its purpose leaves little to the imagination. Her overextended cleavage is clearly intended to be her desired focal point. Despite her visual display of immoderate beauty, her porcelain skin is riddled with burn marks that are all in various stages of healing. Tucked behind her pierced ears, her head dons long, silky black hair with the tips dyed a bright green. Her face is plastered with layers of makeup, making judging her actual age nearly impossible. The only wrinkles allowed to emerge extend from her cheeks as she excessively chomps her macerated bubble-gum.

Quietly making his debut after the flamboyant woman, a bald man flows out of the fog as if manifesting from the eloquent wisps of moisture itself. He walks with immaculate posture. His bare feet move with effortless grace. Displaying hypnotic elegance, he appears to be floating just above the cobblestone streets. He, too, wears a matching beige cloak, buttoned down the middle. In his left hand he holds a long black pole, possibly a walking stick, which he taps on the ground periodically. His expressionless face is carved with high cheekbones and a smoothly shaved complexion. Despite the predictable overcast skies, the man harbors an unexpected and seemingly unnecessary pair of dark sunglasses. Asides from the peculiar spectacles, the man's otherwise simple presentation is complemented by a strong aura of energy that radiates around him. Beau can feel the pulsating vibrations of his aura reaching out and flowing over his still-trapped body. The sensation reminds him of how insects use their extended antenna to assess their environment. A lump of concern swells in his throat.

Finally, the shadow of a giant takes his first steps from behind the fog curtain. His enormous frame dwarfs his companions that line up to his left. The woman peers at him with an unreciprocated glance of enamor before returning her focus to Beau and the boys. The giant surprisingly walks with refined control. Following suit with the matching beige cloak, he emerges as the only one with the hood extended over his head. Deep shadows obscure most of his facial features. Despite the obscurity of the cloak, bizarre bulges extend along his arms, shoulders, and torso. The bulky features can be clearly seen as they draw the cloak taught over their protruding structures. As he makes his advancing steps, the unexpected sound of metal clanking together can be heard rattling under the cloak. His bare feet grace the street stones, gripping them so strongly the indentions of his toes are left imprinted into the ground with each step. As a strong breeze rips through the alleyway, it knocks the cloak hood off his head.

Beau's reactionary face starts to snarl as he stares into the smoldering eyes of the ferocious giant. A furrowed brow lines the dark gray eyes that lie sunken into his chiseled face. They flicker with animalistic ferocity, begging for any sign of confrontation. His mostly shaved head harbors a strip of long hair down the center that is pulled back into a thick single braid. It flows behind his head, wrapped in rows of binding leather. The polished plate of metal on his face extends on either side of his jaw, over his ears and tucks behind his head. It sits on his face like an upside-down crown, held in place upon two large metal plugs above his ears. Beau squints to bring further detail to these nodules. His eyes widen as it appears the man's skin flows around the metal pieces, adhering possibly to the man's own skull.

Could it be? Beau thinks to himself as he studies the unique trademarked features of the giant. *Those metal plates, his size? He's most definitely one of the giants from Kopala. But what in the world is he doing here? They are supposed to be the sworn protectors of Wisteria! Has he gone rogue? Could he still be working on Wisteria's behalf? No matter what it is, this is not good.* Beau's focus quickly shifts back to being on-guard as the four strangers stop their advancement only feet away from their trapped position.

"Ha! Looks like everything went exactly as planned!" the man with dreadlocks exclaims proudly.

"What are you going on about, Izzy?" the woman to his right cries out with excessive flair. "Are you trying to say you anticipated an entire ship falling out of the sky right on top of us? Get off yourself. Don't even try to pretend you were prepared for that."

"Well, no! Of course not!" he back peddles. "But I was the only one who did anything about it! Who knows who these characters are? You should be thanking me."

"I'm surprised your paranoid self even left them alive to question!" the woman barks. "Shoot, you're so trigger happy, if someone sneezed unexpectedly you would probably sling them up with your webbing and execute them. It's a miracle you didn't blow up the whole ship as it came at us."

"Enough already, Aya! One more word out of you and I will have you tied up and hanging from that building behind you! Don't think I won't!" he shouts, pointing his bizarre gun in her direction.

"Mmhmm, you would like that, wouldn't you," Aya says as she seductively lowers her chest in-between the gun's barrel.

"Still warm," she remarks with a devilish smile.

"You witch! Don't think that will work on me!" Izak stammers unconvincingly, while his finger remains steady on the trigger.

"Izak, you do seem a bit jumpier today," the man with sunglasses says as he puts a caring hand on Izak's shoulder. "Did you take your medicine today?"

"What does that have to do with anything?!" Izak shouts.

"You know what we had to go through to get those for you. You're the one who told us how important they were," Emmanuel tries to reason.

"So what, now you're on her side? This is getting way out of hand! I'll have you all tied up alongside this freak show from the sky and leave you to rot!"

"Izak, Ayananda, Emmanuel. That is enough," comes the bellowing command of the giant. "We have more pressing matters at hand," he says, his attention unwavering from the trapped trio before him.

"Of course, Jeeven! How could I have been so careless?" Ayananda says sweetly, stepping back into her previous alignment. "So, is this the guy we have been waiting for? The one who barged into the tower and has been gallivanting around with Sophia?" she asks anyone willing to answer.

"That's 'Lady' Sophia to you!" Izak feels the need to interject. "And you would know if you were at the meeting!" he says reactively.

"I said that's enough," Jeeven repeats before Ayananda can rebuttal. "And no, this is not him, but I think it's about time we find out who exactly he is." Jeeven takes a calculated step forward. "Speak stranger," he says, directing all his attention to Beau.

"My name is Beauregard Hum, and these two boys are natives of this island who sailed with us during the storm. I was sent here by my captain, Brahm." His eyes refuse to blink as he stares down the threatening giant. The two have been trading silent blows of analysis since they first laid eyes upon one another. "I was told my captain made a promise to return to this lighthouse after the storm had passed. I am here to uphold that promise on his behalf."

"Why is he not here himself?" Jeeven asks coldly.

"We were met with one of the Wardens during the storm who ended up taking Sophia captive. He left to go rescue her, but not before sending us to meet with you."

"That's bull, Jeeven, and you know it!" Izak blurts out. Beau can feel the tension growing as he realizes he did not choose the right words. Jeeven waves a hand to silence his trigger-happy companion before continuing his trial.

"There is a problem with your testimony, Mr. Hum," Jeeven says with an eerie lightness. "You see, the one who is supposed to have been captive is your alleged captain, Mr. Brahm, was it? His imprisonment was to be a consequence of meddling in affairs that did not concern him. It was not his promise to return here; that was Lady Sophia's. She was last seen with your captain and now we hear she is missing along with him? This is not looking very good for him, or you, Mr. Hum. Not at all." He takes another step forward looking Beau up and down, analyzing his every twitch and grimace as he takes full advantage of his immobile state.

"We don't have time for this!" Beau blurts out, causing Jeeven to raise a questioning eyebrow. "Your friend is in danger, and we have risked a lot to come here. I assumed we came here to gather your help!"

"You know, your captain had a similar problem. He, too, spoke to us with the assumption he was in control. Like him, you both spout ignorant statements despite your obvious powerlessness. We were stopped from acting before, but no restraint exists in this moment; maybe you need a reminder of where you truly stand," Jeeven says as he places one of his mighty fists in his other hand and takes another step forward. A grin erupts onto his face as he knowingly moves into striking range. Beau's fists clench but he makes sure not to break the critical eye contact between him and his advancing foe.

"Neither one of us has time for this," Beau continues, disregarding the giant's threatening glances. "I am aware of our situation, and I have nothing to hide. We didn't have to come here! We could have left you to figure out on your own what happened to Sophia! But no! Here we are. Our existence alone should give us some collateral!"

"So, our Sophia was captured by a Warden, you say? Possible, I'll give you that. But what proof do you hold that you are not the ones responsible for giving her up?"

"What?" Beau says with a confused shake of his head. "Why would we come here if that was the case?"

"You are quite dense; I am starting to quickly see the growing similarities between you and your captain. We are wanted men, Mr. Hum. Whether you claim to acknowledge that or not is not important to me, but our criminal status is truth. Many people want us dead or worse, captured. We are enemies of Wisteria. You must understand our reservation to trust you, especially when your words bring news of our leader's capture. This would not be the first time we have had to deal with traps laid out for us. And that is exactly what this is smelling like."

"Take him out, Jeeven! He's definitely lying! Give him a chance and he'll try to capture us too!" Izak yells from behind. His goggles from atop his head have now shifted over his eyes. He stands quivering with excitement, ready for battle.

"It is pretty obvious he is lying," Ayananda chips in, unclipping one of her chains from along her hip as she, too, becomes infected by the elevating tension. "It's not often I agree with 'Paranoid Patty' over here, but it does seem like they have taken out Sophia and now they have come for us. Case closed. Someone must have tipped them off about our mission."

"Exactly!" Izak cries out with crazed conviction.

"This is insane!" Beau yells as he becomes overwhelmed with the growing hostility surrounding him. "Sophia has sailed with us all night! We have battled that unruly storm and worked together to survive it! I'm not sure how or why she wound up sailing with us, but we took her in as one of our own! I have no idea, nor do I care about her past or if she is a wanted criminal!"

"She is our friend!" Domino calls out unexpectedly.

"Quiet child, you have already slipped too far into this mess," the giant bellows, quick to sever Domino's weak grip of confidence. Domino swallows a heavy gulp as he stares into Jeeven's eyes of judgment. "Don't make this any harder for yourself. It's unfortunate you had to be associated with this man, but it's time you all meet your fate," he says as he steps even closer to the trapped trio. He peers down at the smaller-statured Beau with a devilish smile pulsating on his face.

"I will not let you harm these children," Beau says with growing ferocity burning in his eyes.

"It is a shame, it truly is. I hope you can eventually understand, it's a game of survival and you just happen to be on the wrong side. Our mission is way too important to risk keeping the likes of someone like you alive. I can at least promise you I will make this quick," Jeeven says as he lifts his bandage-wrapped left arm from under his cloak. He massages his thundering bicep, warming it up like a wind-up toy. White bandages line the entirety of the unusually shaped appendage, folding over squared protrusions along his forearm and upper arm.

"Go for it, Jeeven! Knock them clear off the island!" Izak calls from the peanut gallery. The giant rears back his massive arm and pauses for a moment to lock onto his target. He looks deep into Beau's fiery eyes and feels he is right in his assumption of danger.

"Raaaahhhhhh!" comes the battle cry of the massive warrior. He hurls his mighty fist right at Beau's stationary head.

"No way," Ayananda stammers as she struggles to believe her senses. She watches as Beau dodges the fatal blow by ducking to the side and subsequently tearing apart the mighty threads that held him in place.

"Impossible!" Izak shouts as he takes a step back. "There is no way he could have broken my thread!" His mind starts racing, searching feverously for the most critical move to make next. With a decision quickly found, he rips apart his cloak, revealing his faded black overalls atop a tattered orange shirt. A metal exo-skeleton outlines his upper torso. In well-calculated haste, he drives his finger into one of two pull chords dangling off the metal structure. A parachute erupts above from the pack resting on his back. Just as the shoot starts to fall back to the ground, he pulls the other chord along his chest. Immediately the roar of gas flames can be heard igniting. On either side of his shoulders erupts a steady blue flame. They pour out of primed canisters that are adhered to the metal exo-skeleton. The flames quickly funnel the warm air up into the parachute, lifting Izak into the air in a matter of seconds.

"I'll cover the sky, you know what to do, Aya!" he shouts from above.

"Of course!" she calls back with a serious tone. She pulls out a lighter hidden within her hair and quickly ignites the kerosene-soaked tip of her long chain.

"A flame dart?" Beau thinks out loud, surprised by her unveil. "I've only seen those as instruments of show. Is she going to use it as a weapon?" Ayananda swings the dart in well-controlled spirals around her body, wrapping and unwrapping herself with the flaming instrument, displaying pristine mastery of the weapon's momentum. Beau soaks in the growing danger of his situation.

"Run!" Beau cries to the boys, now freed from their binding. "I'll hold them off!"

"You will do no such thing!" Jeeven roars as he shifts his weight and channels his momentum into his right hand. He moves with such speed and grace he allows no hesitation in-between his first strike and the one already in motion. The amount of air he moves as he swings his arm imitates the sound of a howling wolf.

"We shall see," Beau says calmly as he closes his eyes and channels his energy into grounding his feet into the cobbled streets. He lowers his arms into a primed fighting stance along his waist. He waits patiently for the next strike to come into range.

"You're finished!" Jeeven yells at the awaiting stranger. Beau opens his eyes at the last second, staring right into the howling fist. He gently moves his hand to meet the side of the vengeful strike, redirecting the flow of energy ever so slightly. Self-assured of victory, Jeeven unexpectedly finds himself punching the adjacent building to his right instead of his elusive enemy. He looks back to Beau, unmoved from his previous location. Fury ignites in the giant's eyes as he watches Beau patiently awaiting his next move.

"Who is this guy?!" Izak yells from above, still unable to fully believe his eyes.

"Clearly an enemy and that's all we need to know," Aya says matter-of-factly as she continues to twirl the dart chain around her body. "Em', are you going to do anything or just stand there?" she asks the cloaked man in sunglasses.

"He could have attacked, but instead he just diverted the strike," Emmanuel states, disregarding the question asked of him.

"So what is it, Mr. Mystery? It's like pulling teeth to get a straight answer out of you," Ayananda snaps.

"I will act when the time is right."

"Suit yourself," Aya says, brushing off his comment, "but don't expect me to protect you while you stand here enjoying the sights."

"I never expect anything from you, Ayananda," Emmanuel says as he places both hands on the long stick he holds.

"Hopeless," she scoffs, leaving her stationary companion while making her move into the battle.

"Who… are… you?!" Jeeven grunts from between clenched teeth. He finally releases his fist from the hold of the stone building, sending rock and mortar flying sporadically through the air. The tightly wrapped bandages now have come loose, revealing an uncanny sight. Beau tilts his head unconsciously as he studies the thick metal plates attached along his massive arm. Large bolts appear to hold them in place like the ones on his face.

Absolutely incredible, Beau thinks to himself. *I never thought I would have to face off with such a force of nature. It's hard to believe they are surgically implanted with those metal plugs the day they are born… all to carry the weight they will train with for the rest of their lives. What an honor to see one of them in action… but to be their target? I need to end this quick before someone really gets hurt.*

"I told you already! I am not your enemy! We came here to work together!" Beau says, trying to bring peace to their escalating situation. "I don't want to hurt you!"

"That's fine by me," Jeeven grunts. "Stick to your lie. It just makes my job all the easier." Jeeven leaps from his spot and charges towards Beau. Beau is thrown back by the unexpected speed blitz of his sizeable adversary. With no time to dodge, he decides to face the giant head on. With his fist loaded along his waist like a holstered gun, he unleashes his impromptu counter measure.

Shockwaves rattle the alleyway as Beau intercepts the impressive attack. Shock strikes the giant as the two men now stand eye-to-eye and fist-to-fist. Pride races to the frontline of the battle as it becomes clear the first to back down loses more than just a fistfight. Continued shockwaves pour from the point of impact, ripping the breath from the bystander's unsuspecting lungs. As the friction between the two fists intensifies, the crackling roar of thunder slithers from between their grinding knuckles.

"What are you waiting for?!" Izak shouts from above, finally regaining his voice. "This is your chance, Aya!"

"Right!" Ayananda calls back with a shake of her head. Regaining her focus, she sends her fiery dart back into a fierce twirl around her body before launching it at the stationary adversary. Beau catches the advancing projectile out of the corner of his eye but can do little to avoid it. He reaches his available arm out to counter the attack, but his efforts are in vain. The chain easily constricts around Beau's now outstretched appendage.

"Not good," Beau murmurs to himself, the burning head of the dart now singeing his exposed flesh.

"I did not tell you to interfere!" Jeeven cries out to Ayananda with fury.

"I'm sorry Big Je'! I don't think we have the luxury to take chances with this one!" And with a mighty heave, Ayananda puts all her strength into recalling her chain. The force is just enough to pull Beau off his center of

gravity, thus releasing the buildup of energy between the two fists. With nowhere else for the energy to flow, the two men go flying into the building behind them. The mighty stone dwelling erupts into cobblestone confetti.

Thinking quickly, Ayananda heads into the falling rubble to take advantage of the chaos. Unwilling to release the binding she already has on Beau, she twirls the remaining slack in her chain like a lasso over her head. Waiting for the right moment, she fires her lasso just as a large piece of

falling stone lands behind Beau. Before the dust has time to settle, Beau returns once again to a state of bondage. The mighty Jeeven stands to his feet, dust and rubble falling off his back. Snarling bursts of aggression fire through his nostrils as he looks for an appropriate outlet for his rage. He looks to Beau, his first worthy opponent in years, yet feels the fire in his eyes start to dwindle.

"This is not how I wanted it," Jeeven says apologetically.

"I get that sense," Beau says calmly. "You are a man who holds honor with his personal strength. It's what defines a Kopala Giant, is it not?" His heart flickers at the thought of a reluctant camaraderie growing from the colliding fists. The giant grumbles at the mention of his origins but does not deny the remark. "So, what will you do now?" Beau prods, hoping a resolution is coming soon. A moment of further hesitation begs the whims of the onlookers to be heard.

"Don't get caught up in his head game! He doesn't know you! Kill him, already," Izak pleads from the sky, a new gun aimed at the tension-filled standoff, "or I will!"

"Seriously, Je', I won't be able to hold him like this for much longer," Ayananda grunts. "Just get this over with while we have the chance." Despite the clear intention of his followers, the rage of the beast inside Jeeven continues to dampen as he gazes into the eyes of Beau. He takes a step forward, still unsure of how to act. However, at that very moment, an unexpected, yet purposeful nugget of debris knocks the contemplative giant on the side of the head. Silence ensnares the situation as the fire in the giant's furnace starts to rekindle.

"Oh no…" Beau says as he shakes his head with disbelief.

"Get away from him!" an unexpected Otto calls from behind the safety of the adjacent alleyway. He stands in the open, his adrenaline surging so strongly he can hardly catch his breath.

∞

"Now?" Domino yells from the same alleyway that spit out his crazed companion. "*Now* you find your fighting spirit? What is with you and your bizarre death complex? Are you that afraid of the tides of life that you have become so willing to throw it all away?" Unable to hear his friend, or anything for that matter, Otto stands transfixed on the giant before him. His fist clenches another piece of rubble, ready to launch a follow-up attack.

CHAPTER: 26

Baba and His Blanket

Drifting along in the sky as if a child of the wind, Brahm continues his unique monkey-like maneuvering through the thick clouds. He swings back and forth in his airborne trajectory to the Portala Plaza. A faint murmur of commotion entangles his ears, leading him to drop lower to assess the noise. His feet are first to drop below the cloud line, carving an expanding wake within the cumulus wisps. His toes wiggle in the open air before gripping the underside of the cloud like clenched monkey paws. Satisfied with his footing, Brahm releases his grip on the sky with his hands and pivots head-first towards the ground. Steadily swinging back and forth, his feet prove to have an adequate hold on things. The gentle breeze wrestles with gravity, fighting for control over what direction his tangled hair will flow. Paying no attention to the battling dance atop his head, Brahm searches for the source of the disruptive commotion.

With eyes fit for a falcon, he quickly zooms in on the turbulence coursing through the streets below. People can be seen running out of burning buildings, stores are being looted, and children are screaming for mercy. Brahm tries to analyze a pattern of movement, but each person moves with the same chaotic frenzy as the next. Zooming in a bit further, he sees men draped in familiar green and purple garb. The Wisterian guards act as the only people navigating the streets with any perceived direction. The rest of the frantic people are running both away and towards the decorated guards, still giving no real answers to the cause of commotion.

"I must get closer if I am to find any clues to her location," Brahm decides.

Relaxing his bare toes, he releases his grip on the sky and plummets like a missile into the quickly approaching ground. He remains poised and rigid as the wind whistles around his bony prominences. Cutting through the air like a sharpened blade, his plummet barely casts a ripple through the morning breeze. With a few hundred feet separating him from the approaching stone street, he opens his eyes and rotates his body like the hands of a clock. Once upright, he notices a space amongst the tempestuous crowd opening below him. Dust rustles under his feet as he makes his physic-bending touchdown. Despite his mass and the speed of his fall, he touches the ground like a departed feather from a skyward bird. The buildup of momentum from his fall seems to dissipate as quickly as his abrupt arrival, blending seamlessly into the chaotic flow of people around him. His heavenly dissention doesn't go completely unnoticed; as it abruptly catches the attention of the frantic man he lands beside.

Already overcome with the panic of the streets, the man stares bewilderedly at the enigmatic force appearing before him. He registers a cold, determined, unworldly being that could easily be an angel or a demon. The look in Brahm's eye sparks with a fire burning with unrelenting ferocity. It gives the man on the streets an unnerving shiver down his spine. Unable to fully process the man from the sky into his already stressed psyche, the Pearlite is quickly sucked back into the rush of the crowd. Brahm's unexpected presence fades into the saturated realms of disbelief.

Possessed by concrete intention, Brahm returns the favor of disregard to the man and surrounding crowd. He moves forward against the flow of electrified chaos, walking towards the center of the city plaza. His steps are firmly planted, heavy, and calculated. He weaves his body in-between the countless cries for help with only one thought swimming through his mind: Sophia. The numerous people he must navigate around to get to his desired vantage point add to his growing frustration. Their collective anxiety starts to infect Brahm's unexplored states of consciousness. The harder he grips on to his goal to find Sophia, the more the pain he inadvertently adopts from the surrounding chaos.

Pushing forward, despite the calls for urgent reflection, he finally makes his way to the Portala Plaza. His hawk eyes scour the streets, prying desperately for a clue pointing to Sophia or the Warden's location. His sight captures just another angle of his previous skyward scan, except the pain of The Pearl now pounds even louder into his senses. Children fall from their mothers' grasp, and the crippled or careless tumble only to get trampled by their hurried neighbors. Buildings crumble under the failing mortar, raging fires pour soot and smoke into the foggy sky, and not one single sight of Sophia or a Warden. Brahm grows tired of the distractions to his search and is about to turn and find another spot to explore. That is, until his keen eyes catch ahold of something that abruptly stands out amongst the chaos.

An old man covered in a plaid blanket sits comfortably in the center of the plaza. He rests his back up against the crumbling stage that Brahm and Raja had climbed to help save the very people he now tries to ignore. The man is far along in age as the wrinkles slide eloquently down his shaven head and nestle neatly around his plump cheeks. A thick mustache grows under his nose and provides a nice balance to the bushy eyebrows that rest over his soft eyes. His calm presence brings such a strong contrast to the turbulent frenzy within the plaza, Brahm feels compelled to study the man further.

What is he doing? Feeling the earlier sense of urgency starting to fade, Brahm makes his way to the old man in search of answers to questions not yet populated inside his mind. *What am I doing?* he now asks himself as he questions his new direction. Brahm's whole sense of purpose starts to become blurry and muddled. He stumbles through the crowd like a lost zombie. Despite his disorientation, he continues to head towards the old man. For whatever reason, the mysterious figure exudes a level of clarity and composure Brahm desperately wishes to regain.

Brahm sits himself down beside the man, but his presence is not immediately acknowledged. The man scans the crowd with an unexpected twinkle in his eye, watching the turmoil as if he has glanced upon the most beautiful countryside. The silence that surrounds him takes on a note of sacredness. Brahm struggles to find the right way to speak to the enigmatic being. He studies the silent cadence that drifts between the two of them. Looking for his opportunity to speak, he finds himself acutely aware of the breath flowing in and out of his own lungs. What was once a benign, controlled operation, now becomes the new center of his attention. The old man, the chaos, the plaza, and even Sophia drifts from his focus as he becomes intimately connected to the lifeline of breath that flows in and out of his body. As his rhythmic breath builds, a flickering thought bubbles to the surface. *What is happening to me? Who is this man?*

"Do you not know who I am?" the old man says. Brahm is immediately thrown back with surprise, confident he was not speaking. He wonders if somehow, he uttered his last thought out loud.

"Did I…" he starts to say. "No," he corrects himself, shaking his head. "No sir, I don't know who you are. I—"

"Hmmm," the old man hums as he swims in a moment of ponder. "So, do you not know who you are either?" he says without taking his sight off the crowd.

"Excuse me?" Brahm says with a flutter of frustration creeping back into his chest. "Are you really asking if I know who *I* am?" he repeats with a bitter tone.

"Well, *do* you?" the man asks with a flash of intensity and turns to Brahm with his eyes fully ablaze. His smile is poised in a curious curl. "Normally, one introduces themselves when they wish to make a connection. Makes me wonder if you even know who you are enough to introduce yourself!" he says with a chuckle, and then returns his sights to the crowd.

"My apologies!" Brahm says, jumping to the defense, forgoing the explanation of his unwillingness to disrupt the earlier silence. "My name is Brahm! I-I… Well, I don't really know why I came to sit next to you. I was looking for someone and then, well, and then I found you," he says, but can hardly believe the words coming out of his mouth. "What am I talking about?" he says more to himself. "I sound like a complete loon!"

"Brahm?" the old man repeats. "You are the man who helped a young girl, Raja? Right here, no?"

"Yes!" Brahm exclaims as his thoughts swirl with wonder about her wellbeing. "How did you—"

"The same people who hosted her and her mother during the storm also extended a helpful hand to me. Such wonderful people, aren't they?" he asks while radiating a warm glow. "They sure had an interesting story to share with me." Brahm struggles to remain focused on their conversation.

"A-Are they okay?" Brahm manages to ask.

"Raja spoke very highly of you. They said you were a very special person. I've been wondering when you would come to find me."

"But I wasn't looking for you. I… I still don't even know who you are. I-I…" Brahm stutters as he continues to lose grasp of his words.

"Have you come to save them?" the old man asks.

"Who?"

"Raja and her mother, of course."

"Well, no. I—"

"No?" the man asks with a heavy inflection. "That's interesting."

"W-Why?" Brahm back peddles. "What happened to them?"

"Them? Why not ask what has happened to everyone? I'm starting to wonder how you managed to find me with such narrowed sight." Feeling the desire to earn the man's approval, Brahm chooses his next words carefully. He finally takes a good look around and makes note of the fragrance of suffering that fills the nostrils of their peaceful state of observation. All the commotion he pushed out of his field of awareness comes crashing into his sensations. Pain, loss, anger, confusion, hate, jealousy, and vengeance surge into his chest and grip his heart like a primed grenade. Tears start to pour out of his eyes as just a peek outside his blinders overwhelms him with emotion.

"What *has* happened to everyone?" Brahm asks with a heavy sigh and a heavier heart.

"That ocean storm brought with her the seed of yet another storm for this land," the old man says, avoiding a direct answer. His words leave Brahm on the edge of his seat. A moment of silence begs Brahm to take a guess at the man's riddled words.

"Is this all… all because of the Warden?"

"To a degree," is all the man needs to say to prime Brahm to start firing back on his earlier cylinders. The thought of Sophia swells back into his mind as he becomes eager to return to his search.

"This person you were looking for earlier, is she the reason you pushed away the suffering of everyone else?"

"Uhh…"

"I figured so," he says, finally turning back to face Brahm. He speaks like an authoritative father, yet his face glows with the love and warmth of a welcoming mother. Brahm is frozen in place as he wonders if he should defend himself or rush to embrace the man. "What are you going to do?" he asks with a curious tone that leads Brahm to wonder if he already knows the answer.

"If I remember correctly, when the Wardens came here before, their purpose was to round up all the 'Seers' and take them away," Brahm says as he works to decide what his next steps will be.

"That's true!" the man says with bizarre enthusiasm. "They really thought they got them all! Thanks to you and Raja, they realized their search was not yet over." His tone confuses Brahm. He squints his face unconsciously as he wonders why it sounds like the man is pleased with this happening. "An interesting move, for sure! You help them avoid one storm just to walk them into another! Lots of responsibility comes with that decision, I imagine. Did you think that one through?"

"Well, no, not exactly." "I see. Not a strong suit of yours, is it?" The words resonate with such bizarre familiarity it is almost as if the old man switched places with Beau for a moment.

"No," Brahm feels willing to admit. "It never has been."

"Wonderful!" cheers the enthusiastic man from under his blanket. "Now is your chance."

"To do what?" he mumbles like a lost child. A swift hand from under the blanket connects with the back side of Brahms head.

"You tell me!" the man says as Brahm nurses the lump forming from the surprise strike.

"Hey!" Brahm shouts with surprise. "Just forget about me for a moment! What are *you* going to do, old man? You keep asking me what I'm going to do, but it doesn't look like you are doing much about all this mess either!"

"What do you suppose I do?" the man asks playfully. "I'm just an old man, after all." Brahm, getting the sense he is being purposefully provoked, still allows his frustration to get the better of him.

"Something! Anything, I imagine!" he yells back with a vein pulsating across his forehead. "From the stories Raja told me, the Wardens will stop at nothing until they find every last Seer!"

"Is that so?"

"I think so!" Brahm responds with an equal level of certainty and uncertainty. His own emotional state is lost to his own understanding. It is in the following moment the two men are called to bring awareness to the shift of energy to their left. A space has emerged from the chaotic crowd as they make way for a group of advancing Wisterian guards. They walk the streets with a casual cadence, looking to the crowd as a wolf would gaze upon a grazing flock of sheep. The man in front points to his right, instigating his fellow guard to reach out and capture a passing citizen.

"Bring him in for questioning," a familiar voice booms. The captured man squirms and screams as if his life has just been sentenced to the gallows. His efforts to overpower the guard are futile.

"Is that—" Brahm starts to ask himself as he looks closer to the squad of guards.

"That's it!" the old man shouts as he stands to his feet in a seamless bound. His old age and protruding belly seem to cause no interference to his graceful movements. The man's whole body glows as he looks to the guards with an aura of love.

"What is it?" Brahm asks. "What are you about to do?!"

"You said they would stop at nothing until *every* Seer is captured, *no?*" The emphasis of the totality brings a lump to Brahm's throat.

"Yes. But—"

"So that's it! That is what I can do. I'll give them one less to look for!" he says with bounding joy as he walks casually to the approaching guards. "Wait," Brahm calls after him, "you are a Seer too? There has to be another way! Let me help you!"

"Oh, now you want to help?" the old man says turning back to face Brahm. His eyes glow with a penetrating light fit for an expanding star. Brahm feels the radiant light flow all through his being, intoxicating every cell in his body. "Wonderful!" he boasts as he continues his way to the guards. Brahm suddenly feels a heaviness in his legs he has never felt before. He struggles to stand to his feet. He hunches over, having to brace the weight of his torso with a hand on his knee. Exasperated, he looks to the old man while struggling to catch his breath. He watches powerlessly as the man walks right up to the first guard.

"I'm so glad I found you!" he says with exuberant cheer.

"What are you doing, old man?" the guard says. "Get out of the way if you don't want to get hurt."

"But I've come to turn myself in!" he says, extending his arms to be handcuffed.

"What game are you playing? This is no time for jokes."

"Hold on, boss," the third guard interrupts.

"What is it?"

"I think this is… it couldn't be…"

"Out with it!"

"Sir, I think this is the Great Seer Sage, the one who always eludes our capture… Babarossa!"

"What?" the lead guard sputters, shaking his head with disbelief. "What are you waiting for! Cuff him!" Jumping to follow orders, a guard quickly whips off the cuffs from his waist and goes to bind the extended arms of the old man. He does so carefully to not harm him, all while triple checking the clasps have locked securely.

"If you think this will stop us, Baba, think again! We won't stop until every last one of you Seers are sent off to be rehabilitated."

"So I've heard!" Babarossa responds. "And you are doing such a great job at it. I just wanted to do my part to help."

"If you really want to help, you can tell me where all your other Seers are hiding so we can stop tormenting these innocent citizens!"

"Gladly!" Babarossa says cheerfully. "Right over there is one!" he says while lifting his cuffed hand to point to Brahm's direction.

"What?" Brahm yells as his eyes bulge out of his head.

"Hahahaha! I like you, old man!" the guard says with a heavy belly laugh. "Get him!" he yells to his men. As they rush to apprehend him, Brahm finally brings himself to stand fully erect. His breath is still heavy, but he feels there is no reason why these guards would pose any threat to him. The first guard reaches him with hands outstretched. Brahm makes his move to dodge the easily perceived maneuver. However, he finds his body failing to respond with the speed his thoughts command.

"Got him!" the guard yells with pride.

"Hey! What gives?" Brahm yells with anxiety-pounding confusion. He tries to shake the guard off but no matter how hard he struggles, he can't find the means to overpower him. "What's happening to me?!" Brahm blubbers frantically, unaccustomed to his will not being honored. He glances for a moment at the captured Seer Sage who looks at him with a warm smile and flashes Brahm a playful wink.

"What did you do to me?!" Brahm directs with fury at the old man.

"Quit trying to resist, it's futile," the guard tells Brahm. "It's over, you're outmatched. Just give up and come quietly." Brahm looks to the guard with a snarl on his face but turns his attention back to the old man. His eyes widen once again as he watches the Sage take advantage of the growing commotion. With one step, Babarossa fades into the swarm of people who surround the guards and disappears into the chaos without a trace. The smile on his face lingers for a moment where his body once stood.

"You can't leave me like this!" Brahm calls after him. "Come back!"

"Enough already," the guard says with a forceful nudge towards his leader. As Brahm is dragged reluctantly towards the man in charge, he starts to get a sinking sense of familiarity.

"You!" Claude exclaims with overwhelming glee.

"You?!" Brahm exclaims with matching surprise.

"Today is truly my lucky day!" Claude boasts as Brahm stares into the face of the arrogant guard from the day before. "Never thought I would see you again! Oh my, I can hardly contain myself! With what you did to me and my squad the other day, I've been dreaming about what I would do if I ever found you again. Looks like some dreams do come true! Come on men, let's take this guy and the other two back to the containment chambers."

"Boss," the guard responsible for Babarossa says with a quiver in his voice.

"What?" Claude barks with a lack of patience.

"I don't know how to say this…"

"Damnit man, I'm tired of your stammering! What is—" Claude turns around to see the guard holding the empty cuffs that once held the Great Sage.

"You let him go?!"

"Of course not! He escaped… somehow! I checked the lock three times when I put them on!" Claude's small mind spins with the thought of how to proceed. With deep pity, Brahm looks at Claude's squirming face, indicative of his racing thoughts. With an excessive amount of time dedicated to a simple task, he finally reaches his decision.

"It's fine, it's just one old man. We have an unexpected treasure on our hands that isn't going anywhere!" he says looking to Brahm. "We are going to have fun with this one. I think the Warden will be very pleased with what we have found."

"The Warden?!" Brahm says with excitement.

"Oh yeah!" Claude says as sinisterly as possible. "But don't worry, you and I will have some fun together first! Ha! Only after I have taught you my lesson will that monster teach you his. Your life, as you know it, is over!"

"Oh my god! Please let me go!" cries the man captured earlier. "I promise you I am no Seer! I swear!"

"And maybe you're not!" says Claude. "But maybe you have some information about where some might be!"

"I don't know anything! I promise!" the man pleads with Claude with water swelling in his eyes.

"Ahh, that will be for us to decide! We can't possibly let any of these blasted Bakuwan to continue hiding among these good-natured citizens! Anyone who looks even remotely suspicious *must* be interrogated for the sake of progress! Hahahaha!" Claude laughs with gut-churning gusto. The man's face sinks into a sea of desolate despair; his faith in God's supposed chosen people shatters as the shackles surround his wrists. The remaining guards tighten their grip on their captives and turn towards the high cliffs supporting the mighty Lotus desalinator. As they walk past the archways of the plaza, a large metallic tower-like castle comes into sight.

The excessive building is carved into the protective mountain, using the sturdy land mass as the primary source of structural integrity. Its eccentric presentation is a contrasting eye-sore when compared to the simplified stone architecture known to The Pearl. Taller than it is wide, the castle stands cylindrical with large swirling decorative pillars on either side running halfway up the structure. Where the decorative swirls cap off, leaf-like extensions drape down over the bottom layer of the castle like petals of a blooming flower. At the top, a dome rises to a peak like a dollop of whipped cream. The whole castle is lined with glistening green and purple stones, highlighting the trademark colors of Wisteria.

"That's Master Mune's private quarters!" Claude says without prompting. "It will be where you will await your fate with the rest of the captured Seers. And don't worry, your judgment will come soon enough! We have ways of making you talk…" his monologue drifts off into a chuckled laugh that his companions fail to reciprocate. Brahm stares at the approaching tower while his mind swims in doubt and disbelief. *I don't know what that old man did to me! My strength is gone, my body feels heavy and unresponsive, my connection to the other dimensions is severed, and my soul feels trapped and claustrophobic inside this flesh body!* For the first time that he can remember, Brahm starts to feel the waves of fear flow through his veins. *Is this… what it feels like to be… human?*

CHAPTER: 27

Back Alley Brawl

"Otto! What are you doing?!" Beau screams from his chain prison. "Get away from here while you still can! I can fend for myself!" Beau makes a desperate move to loosen the chains that surround him, but with no effect.

"No, no, no, 'Mr. Burly Man,'" interjects Ayananda as she tightens the chains even further. Beau is sucked back to the stone debris and stares scornfully at the taunting woman. "Trading blows with Jeeven and living to talk about it is no small order, mister," Ayananda continues. "Don't think I'm going to risk letting you go until we have this little fiasco under control. You just stay right here and watch the show."

"He's just a child!" Beau yells to her, pleading for a seemingly obvious pardon.

"Tisk, tisk," she responds with a wave of her finger. "A *foolish* child. I don't think any of you have registered the gravity of your actions yet. It's a shame, but nonetheless, a fool must still pay the price of their shortcomings. No one can avoid Jeeven's judgment," she says as she buries her knuckles further into the chains, pulling them even deeper into Beau's chest. His fingers fan out involuntarily while he coughs up the residual breath lingering in his lungs. The lit flame continues to burn freely as it dangles at the end of the chain resting dangerously below his waist. The ball of fire kisses his inner thigh, bringing the smell of burnt flesh into the air. Ayananda can't help but let out a playful chuckle as she watches her captured prey suffer. Beau turns his breathless attention back to the brewing standoff. He struggles to come up with a plan. The hissing sound of gas overhead now diverts his attention to the sky as he watches Izak inch his way closer to the impromptu standoff.

Otto grips another piece of rubble in his hand so tightly his knuckles have accumulated white caps at their peaks. A slight tremor can be seen in both of his knees as his body struggles to contain the high levels of adrenalin flowing through his being. Despite every involuntary impulse screaming to run, Otto holds firm to his resolve, much like the clenched rubble in his hand. A distant rumbling can be heard vibrating through the streets behind him. The cries of exasperated Pearlites inch their way closer to their location. With all this in mind, his focus does not waver. He has locked eyes with the giant and refuses to look away.

"All I wanted was to wake up from this nightmare and return to my life," Otto says to the snarling giant. "Even if all this really is a dream and you are some really, *really* messed up manifestation of my subconscious, I still can't bring myself to leave my friend to die. Not while I could do… something! I know I'm not much, but I'm not going to wake up a coward.. I've finally made my peace, you mindless beast, so bring it on!" he taunts, taking a critical step forward.

"Insolent child," Jeeven grumbles.

"I've already looked into the eyes of death!" Otto continues. "Babel couldn't kill me, so let's see if you've got what it takes to finish the job!"

"Otto," Domino utters with his mouth ajar. He continues to watch, frozen in disbelief. *Does your flirtation with death know no limits?* he thinks to himself. *It's one thing to face death when it presents itself, but it's a whole different thing when you seek it out! This is going too far!*

"Why can't you find this resolve in life?" he yells. "Can you only see who you are when you feel your life is on the line?"

Jeeven finally makes his move. He takes a heavy step forward, calling the full attention of all immediate bystanders. The unraveled rattling plates on his arms become taught against his muscles as they engorge and flex with unconscious rage. Ayananda and Izak wince with anticipation. The giant's ferocity is palpable and intrusive; a swirling vortex of energy begins entangling everything in his wake. Beau can feel himself being drug through the chains towards Jeeven as if his rage has shifted the very focal point of gravity. He notices Ayananda's grip on the chain loosening ever so slightly, as she, too, is shifted from her firm footing. Even Izak struggles to remain airborne. He tugs on his pull chord once again, triggering another roar of gas to flood his parachute. The added fuel is just enough to shift his position away from the black hole of energy surrounding his leader.

Clearly no match in terms of physical strength, Otto surprisingly does prove himself on par with Jeeven's intense focus. His feet drag along the ground governed by the supernatural pull of the giant, but his posture remains upright and rigid. Otto rotates his fist holding the debris and cocks his hand back, ready to strike.

"It's now or never," Beau says with the breath granted by Jeeven's gravitational distraction. The slight slack in the chain is all he needs to cook up a battle plan. Thinking quickly, Beau grips the loosened chain with his exposed hands. With a mighty flick of his wrists and a quick hip flex, he takes control over Ayananda's chain and flings it up into the sky. Panic strikes as Ayananda notices the chain is still wrapped securely around both of her wrists. Unable to adjust in time, she is ripped from the ground and soars helplessly into the sky towards her weaponized companion. Beau grins as he contemplates the chances of taking out the quintessential 'two birds with one stone.' Izak's eyes metaphorically protrude through his goggles as he struggles to comprehend what is coming at him.

"Heeellppp meeee!" Ayananda screams as she races through the air. Desperate to intervene, Izak can't do anything but shift out of the way of her destructive path. The two lock eyes momentarily as they pass each other. Bulging eyes of surprise mirror each other as they struggle to process how the proverbial rug got so quickly pulled out from underneath them.

Beau plants his feet firmly back into the ground and continues to swing Ayananda through the sky. The grip of the chain loosens around him with each cyclic revolution. With calculated precision, he moves his hands down the chain and creates even more slack. Each rotation sends Ayananda further and further into the sky. It is all she can do to hold on for dear life. The sweat pouring from her hands brings added realization that she is one slip away from becoming a human projectile. Nearing the fire-tipped end of the dart chain, Beau shifts his weight once again, analyzing his counterweight in the sky.

"Raaaahhhhh!" Beau cries with a mighty roar. He rips Ayananda from the sky and sends her hurdling straight at Jeeven's position. The force behind Beau's recall folds the flawless skin of Ayananda's porcelain face into distorted crevices fit for a storybook witch. She cuts through the air like a trash bag drug under water, flying at break-neck speeds towards the ground with no hope of slowing down. Tears transpire from the corners of her eyes as her cries for help are quickly stolen from her emptied lungs. Anticipating a quick victory, Beau lets a smirk slide across his face as Ayananda and Jeeven near their moment of impact.

"Ahhhh, nooo!" Beau cries out in unexpected disappointment. At the last possible moment, Jeeven rotates his gaze behind him and leaps out of the way. At nearly the same time, at the point where consciousness should have been a fading afterthought, Ayananda manages to shift out of her head-first dive and lands flawlessly on her feet. Her leather-bound calf muscles burst through their binding upon impact. The torn fabric spreads apart to reveal bulging veins working quickly to pump an exuberant amount of blood to fuel the seemingly impossible landing. The force from Beau's swing has drilled her feet deep into the solid stone streets, sending rippling cracks and deep fissures racing through the alleyway. Some fissures even reach the surrounding dwellings, crumbling their storm-tested foundation in seconds.

"I've been far removed for too long!" Beau says. "I've forgotten just how scary the people in this world can be!"

Despite the excessive destruction from her landing, Ayananda seems to have suffered no personal damage. She slowly stands from her crouched position, exuding a feral rage pulsating from her aura. Her head hangs below her shoulders causing her hair to flow over her face. Heavy breathing is all that can be heard under the veil of hair as she pants like an awakened demon.

"Just who are these people?" Beau mutters to himself as he is blown away from Jeeven's and Ayananda's display of superhuman abilities. He shakes his head and decides he doesn't want to find out what new monster has awakened from the battle. A quick look to the left shows Jeeven has already returned his unnerving attention back to Otto. Leaving no room for Ayananda to catch a second wind, Beau takes a step forward and lunges the chains still bound to her wrist in a horizontal strike towards Jeeven's new position.

"Think fast!" Beau yells, as he rips Ayananda from the ground and sends her flying back to her leader once again. Jeeven snarls with disgust as he effortlessly leaps over the strike, leaving the momentum carrying Ayananda to send her crashing into an adjacent stone dwelling. The building erupts in dust and rubble as she completely destroys its sturdy integrity with her deceptive durability. Her mighty chain falls slack upon the ground. With no further movement detected from within the deteriorated building, Beau assumes he has vanquished at least one beast. He drops the flaming end of the dart to the ground with a heavy *clank* and redirects his attention back onto his initial focus.

His tattered leather boots stomp the disjointed cobblestones as he rushes to intervene in the continued standoff between Otto and Jeeven. As he looks ahead, a snarl and a forceful puff of breath storms out of Jeeven's mouth.

"You stand there, little one, as if you have any chance of inhibiting my will," he remarks. "Your fate has not changed in the slightest. Not even your strong man can stand against me, and yet you speak of vanquishing your fear, but I promise you…" his words linger as he lowers his face closer to Otto's, "I will have you screaming for mercy before I finally wipe your insolent existence from the graces of this unruly world!"

"Enough talk, you clown! Let's do this already!" Otto cries as he extends his arm, preparing to launch his clutched piece of rubble.

"No!" Beau cries as he finally steps into striking distance. He leaps into the air, hurling himself at the giant at blistering speed. Indented craters erupt into the street as a result of Beau's superhuman takeoff. Jeeven turns his head slightly and gives an unamused grunt. From the sky, Izak's keen eyes track the rampaging blur.

"Not so fast, baldy," Izak mumbles to himself as he slides his finger onto the trigger of his weapon. The sound of his fired projectiles erupts through the air. Luckily, Beau knew better than to direct all his attention on the giant. With Izak still in position, an aerial strike was predictable at the first move against their leader. Beau spirals his body to the right to avoid the shots in mid-air. By the time the sound of gunshots fully registers, Izak's bullets are already sailing past Beau's repositioned body.

"Your fight is with me, giant!" Beau bellows, as he feels confident in dismissing his skyward enemy. He readies his fist to make contact with the giant. "Wait! What?" The earlier projectiles ricocheted off the ground and have rebounded right back at his new position. Beau narrowly avoids the first two. "Oh no!" He can't rotate far enough to avoid the final shot in time.

"Gaaahh!" he screams as the shot cuts deep into his left shoulder. He keeps moving forward despite the pain, but thoughts of bewilderment flood his mind. *How was that possible? They were moving even faster after the ricochet, and right at my shifted position! Was that by chance? Did he anticipate the ricochet? Anticipate my dodge?* Shaking his head to clear the nagging thoughts, he puts his attention back in focus. A surge of energy swells around Beau's clenched fist as he continues with his vengeful attack. "This is it!" Beau screams as he releases his fist from alongside his waist. His muscles throughout his abdomen clench in unison as they work together to assist the projected strike heading straight into Jeeven's face.

"Hahahaha!" Jeeven clenches his belly, acting as if his laugh is in need of support. The brightest grin stretches across his face.

"N-Now what?" Beau stammers as he struggles to assess the situation. He watches as the piece of rubble cast from Otto's hand falls to the ground after its brief contact with the metal plating across Jeeven's chest. It rolls to a stop a few inches from the giant's feet.

"As I told you, little one," Jeeven says as he continues his earlier monologue, "not even your strong man can stand against me. Not even, in fact, to a single woman with a chain it seems! Bahahaha!" Beau glances down at his fist that was inches from completing its mission. His intended weapon is now bound with the same chain he thought he left behind him for good. The burning head of the dart nestles securely along his wrist, causing his screaming flesh to bubble and ripple from the immense heat. Beau strikes a grimace across his face, but it's not the pain that fuels the contortion. Not since the days before Brahm's birth has he ever found himself in such an overpowering situation. *Have I truly become this weak?* he wonders to himself as he shakes his head in disgust. *All those years watching over Brahm, did I let myself fall this far from grace? I can't even protect this small child! How have I convinced myself for so long I could protect someone like Brahm? I've clearly underestimated this journey back into the world.*

"B-Beau…" Otto stutters as his shaking knees finally give way. The release of his scornful toss has relinquished the emotional energy that fueled his mighty standoff. He takes a deep breath as he comes to grips with his unfolding reality. "I-I'm s-sorry," he says with tears starting to pool in his eyes. "This is all my fault."

"No!" Beau calls back. "Don't say such things! If anything, this is my fault! I brought you along thinking I could protect you and Domino! I *should* have been able to protect you from all of this! If anyone should be sorry it is me!" he yells with such gusto that his words find a way to penetrate Otto's self-loathing heart. Otto turns to look at him with an aura of gratitude swelling upon his face. "Be proud of everything you have accomplished!" Beau continues. "We must all meet our end someday, and if today is our day, then know you are one of the bravest men I have ever sailed with!"

"T-thank you," Otto says with a heavy sigh.

"Well then, I'm glad you have all come to your senses," Jeeven says, disrupting the emotional connection flowing below him.

"No!" Domino yells as he throws himself in-between Otto and the giant.

"Damnit!" Beau spits with anger, "Damnit, damnit, damnit! I can't believe you right now! How can you look at all this sacrifice and still throw your life away!?" he asks the foolish youth.

"How could I?" Domino re-asks the question, "How could I not?!"

"What?!"

"How could I look at such sacrifice and run away?!"

"You have your whole life ahead of you! You are a fool for throwing it away unnecessarily!" Beau rebuttals. "Run while you still can!"

"I understand I may be a fool!" Domino pleads. "I've thought Otto to be a fool for the same reason, but I've got my own reasons! You two are the only family I have in this world. I'm sticking it out with you through this no matter what!"

"Damnit. You are impossible! Both of you!" Beau calls back, rage bubbling through his defeated core. His will to fight is now rekindled by the youthful ignorance. He makes a move to step forward but is stopped as if tethered to a ten-ton weight. He looks back at his arm as the flame continues to burn around his wrist. He follows the taught chain into the rubble pile where he disposed of Ayananda earlier. Large boulders of debris part ways as she reemerges from the pile with the demonic aura from earlier radiating from her body. Her wild hair still flows in front of her, obscuring her face. Her petite hands cling to the end of the chain with a ferocious grip, easily holding back Beau's attempts at advancement.

"He's coming," Emmanuel says, breaking his meditative stance. The stick he once held steady now shakes with an anxious rattle.

"What in the world?" Beau mumbles in awe as he tries to process what has emerged in place of the porcelain doll he fought earlier. Primal grunts and snarls flow from her throat, growing louder as she tries to reel in her catch. Beau plants his feet sturdy and makes an effort to overpower the demonic woman. As he puts his freed hand on the chain to stabilize it, a glimmer of light catches his attention. He looks down at the fire upon his flesh and is met eye-to-eye with a clearly defined face protruding from within the flame.

"Bahahahaha!" Jeeven laughs again at Beau's bewilderment. The face in the flame gives a peculiar wink before cranking up the heat.

"Gahhhh!" Beau cries in pain as the flame finally triggers a response he can no longer ignore. He shakes his head and tries to overpower the chain holder. His fading strength is easily matched by the figure in the rubble. With blood pouring from all his open battle wounds, his remaining strength quickly fades from his overtaxed muscles. As the smell of burning flesh permeates into the air, Beau digs deep and calls upon his only recourse he has left: prayer. "Please, if anyone is out there, anyone at all, please don't let these boys die here today." He puts all his remaining energy and intention into his words. "I know I'm no religious man by any means, but I've seen enough in my days to know something is out there; something in-between all the energy and matter. So, please, if you are out there, we could really use a miracle here."

"Getting sentimental in your final moments, are you?" taunts the giant. Un-triggered by his words, Beau continues to keep his eyes closed with his vision turned inward, remaining deep in meditative prayer. The boys hold onto one another as they await their fate. Looking into one another's eyes, they both reflect an uncanny smile, marking their resolve and acceptance of the decisions they have made.

"Domino, I'm sorry," Otto says as the words flow through his lips with sincerity and conviction. "I'm sorry you are in this mess and I'm sorry for everything I said earlier. You were right. I have been afraid to change and afraid to live. I see that now. It may be the end, but I'm glad I get to live these last moments with you."

"Damnit!" Domino says with tears streaming down his face. "Get over here!" He embraces his friend with all his might. "There is nowhere else I'd rather be." His earlier detest dissolves completely from his heart.

"Hey! Over here!" comes an unfamiliar voice from the alleyway where Domino was hiding. "Yeah, this looks like the place he told us about! It looks all clear! C'mon everyone!" The foreign voice is followed by the stampede of countless feet racing towards Jeeven's area of judgment.

"Uhh, what now?" Jeeven scowls as he pauses to question the unexpected cacophony. Suddenly, the archway that marked the barrier of the once quiet alleyway gives birth to a sea of people running frantically, possessed by the chaos infused by the Warden's presence. They run at full speed, screaming for their lives and desperately looking for a way out of their suffering. The chaos of The Pearl has finally caught up to the feuding foreigners. Wave after wave of people pour around Beau before swarming in-between the boys and Sophia's companions. They fill the area like a freed river racing out of a demolitioned levy. Their overwhelming internal turmoil keeps them focused on getting as far away from the island officials as possible. They pay no mind to the unusual circumstance they happened to stumble upon.

Jeeven takes a step back as he is forced to process this new occurrence. The surrounding bystanders inspire an uncomfortable reflection upon his decision to execute a pair of children. He glances from side to side, feeling this must be some kind of joke or strategic ploy to further hinder his mission. Met with no sign of foul play, he grunts while looking back to Otto and Domino as the crowd starts to thin. Just as all the unexpected patrons have made their way through the battlefield, an old man trips over the two boys sitting motionless on the ground, falling in-between them and the giant.

"So sorry, boys!" the old man says. "Didn't see you there!" A warm glow emanates from his eyes. He smiles brightly, curving his thick mustache around his rounded cheeks. He dusts off his plaid blanket that he has wrapped around himself and looks up to the giant standing over them. "Oh my! What a big fellow you are!"

"Get out of here, old man!" Domino pleads. "He's dangerous!"

"My patience is running thin, old-timer, do as the boys say and get out of here while I have an ounce of it left," Jeeven commands.

"My, my!" the old man responds. "You must be pretty strong! I'm sure you're used to getting your way when you flash those mighty muscles around, aren't you?"

"What did you say?!" Jeeven bellows with quick-tempered rage.

"You best do as he says!" Otto begs. "He'll kill you!"

"Kill me?" the old man asks with surprise in his voice. "Is that what is going on here? A man as strong as him would lower himself to harm an old man like me? And children no less?" He smiles as if his blanket was an impenetrable suit of armor. "Now that just sounds silly! What have we done to anger you, strong man?" Fury builds in the giant's body to the point where steam appears to be pouring from his ears like a heated kettle. His skin turns a shade of red as his whole body falls into a cascade of tension-fueled rage. He takes a step forward, his eyes blinded red as he aims to destroy everything in sight. The old man gazes at the smoldering giant with his smile still beaming brightly. Jeeven pulls back one of his mighty fists, driving his fingers even tighter into his palm. His lip quivers slightly before firing his emotionally driven strike at the defenseless trio below.

"Boys!" Beau calls out involuntarily. The smoke screen of dust casts a dramatic cliffhanger to the results of the strike. By the sound of the destruction, Beau can't help but assume the worst. As he looks on, the dust starts to settle, first revealing a giant crater created by the headstrong giant. His heart sinks as he tries to inch himself closer to see what remains of the boys and the old man. To his surprise, the crater appears empty. His heart leaps out of his chest in joy, but quickly settles back in as his mind starts racing. *That's great and all, but where are they? There is no way the two kids and an old man could have avoided that strike!*

"That's enough, Jeeven," comes the calm voice of Emmanuel from behind the lingering shrouds of dust. His silhouette can be seen through the dust and as it falls, the boys and old man can be seen safely behind his protective frame.

"You dare get in my way, Emmanuel?" snarls Jeeven, priming his fist for another strike.

"This is no ordinary old man," Emmanuel continues, with no reverberation of fear. "If you were not so angry, maybe you, too, would see the light this man emanates."

"I do not care!" Jeeven says as he takes a threatening step forward.

"Please try to relax," Emmanuel says lovingly as he reaches out and touches the giant's right hand. Immediately the waves of anger and rage that have defined the beast of a man for so long dissipate from the enormous vessel like the changing tides.

"I will have you pay severely for this," Jeeven says, trying to summon his earlier rage but to no avail.

"Please try and forgive me, you left me no choice. If my senses have not failed me, this man here is the true leader of this land; the Great Seer Sage, Babarossa. His aura blossoms with a radiating beauty I have never seen before. I was compelled to protect him. I could not risk you harming such an important person."

"Seriously?" Jeeven asks earnestly. "The same man Sophia couldn't stop talking about?" His energy has calmed so dramatically, yet he insists on holding onto what anger he can. "Regardless, don't you ever perform your blasphemous 'magic tricks' on me again or I *will* kill you."

"Understood," Emmanuel says with a head bow before turning to the old man. "Please forgive our rudeness. We are under a great deal of stress. Our leader has recently been captured, and we believe it was done by the hands of these people here. I'm sorry you got mixed up in our affairs." Emmanuel closes his statement with a deep bow of respect.

"You have a kind heart, young man, but it is a bit misguided," Baba responds.

"I don't understand," Emmanuel says, inching his way back to a standing position.

"You can recognize who I am, but you cannot recognize these people are not your enemy?"

"Ha, so this is the Great Seer Sage?" Jeeven interrupts with uncharacteristic glee.

"It appears so," Emmanuel responds with a defeated tone.

"Cheer up, boy, your sight will improve in time," Baba responds warmly.

"I have my doubts."

"It's no matter, it will get better. You will *see.*"

"Will I now?" Emmanuel responds with heavy inflection as he hangs on the Sage's choice words. Baba just smiles, ignoring the urge for clarification.

"For now, I feel there is someone else in need of your services," Baba says as he nods his head towards the dilapidated building behind them. Emmanuel nods back in agreement and leaps into the rubble. Ayananda's demonic aura flickers like a burnt-out lightbulb. Forgoing the tug of war with Beau, she drops the chain held with such conviction and throws her hands into her shrouded face. She shakes her head back and forth as if trying to remove a foreign body that has lodged itself in her face. Beau lets out a sigh of relief as the burning chain finally falls slack. He frantically scurries to remove the painful tether from his body. Bloodied, broken, and burnt, he collapses to his knees. As he succumbs to fatigue, he watches Emmanuel soar over to meet the tormented Ayananda. She backpedals, turning to run away from her advancing companion. He places his hand on her like he did Jeeven, causing the waves of chaotic energy to immediately dissipate from her being.

"T-Thank you… Em,'" Ayananda manages to say before collapsing to the ground. Beau shakes his head, unsure of what to make of the whole ordeal. Slowly bringing himself to stand up, he walks back to the boys with his right arm heavily supported.

"Beau!" the boys call out together as they run to greet their battle-torn hero. They embrace warmly, exchanging their collective feelings of relief and gratitude. They look at one another with moistened eyes before coaxing Beau towards the Great Seer Sage. Able to clearly read the shift in energy, Beau pays no mind to the once-vengeful giant next to him. With eyes stretched wide, Otto looks intensely from Jeeven to Beau, wondering what to make of their wordless dialogue. With a heavy sigh, Beau throws himself onto the ground with an unrestricted *thud* and settles himself into a relaxed meditative position. Otto decides to follow him to the ground. Jeeven stares down at the defenseless adversary with questioning eyes. They don't go unnoticed.

"Now's your chance, big guy," Beau says without making eye contact. "I'm a sitting duck. You can take out the old, the young, and now the broken all in one shot."

"Humph," Jeeven grunts. "If this Sage says you are no enemy to us, I will honor that." He sits himself onto the ground as well.

"Ha!" Beau bellows. "Where was this guy when we needed him earlier? Well, looks like thinking for yourself isn't your strong suit. Good to know."

"What did you say?!" Jeeven banters, struggling to rekindle his familiar rage. The effects of Emmanuel's touch seem to still be in effect.

"Relax, Big Je,'" Emmanuel says as he walks into the growing circle with an unconscious Ayananda in his arms. "You'll be back to your emotionally-stubborn ways in no time. Why not just enjoy the inner peace for a moment?"

"Damn magician," Jeeven grumbles, but shrugs his shoulders with momentary acceptance. "All right, Izak, the fight is over. Head back down," Jeeven calls to his skyward subordinate. "We are going to reevaluate our plans." Izak gives a nod of acknowledgment before turning off the gas canisters along his shoulders. Drifting delicately back to the ground, he nestles neatly in-between Emmanuel and Jeeven. His parachute collapses behind him, gently blanketing the cobblestone streets. With a pull from another chord along his waist, he triggers a cascade of mechanical devices that wind the shoot back up into his pack. A final click from the device signifies its completed packaging. Izak lifts his goggles from his face and immediately lights a cigarette. He draws in a heavy drag and after exhaling a billowing plume of smoke, he diverts his attention to the silent crowd before him. Making the most of the silent pause, Beau situates himself so his spine is in perfect alignment. He closes his eyes and starts quietly humming to himself. This maneuvering grabs the attention of Emmanuel.

"Great Sage Baba, we have caused great harm to this man," Emmanuel says after a moment. "Will you please help in restoring his health? He—" Emmanuel is cut off by a surging stab of energy that fires from Babarossa's now outstretched hand. The rush of energy steals the very breath from his lungs. With his hand still raised, Baba looks over intently at Beau and then turns back to the eagerly awaiting Emmanuel. A large smile blossoms upon the face of the Sage.

"There is no need," he finally says.

"But Baba—"

"If you just *look*, child," Baba coo's, "you can see why you need not to worry." Emmanuel crinkles his face at Baba's words, but he adjusts his focus towards Beau as instructed. He notices Beau is now humming louder than before. The vibration from his voice permeates into the air between them and the crumbling stone below them. Everyone conscious takes notice of the bizarre feat. Well, all except for the energetically oblivious Jeeven who has moved on to re-wrapping his metal plates.

As the hums grow louder, waves of auric vibration flow from Beau's stationary vessel. The waves appear to some keen eyes as beautiful geometric patterns of light. As each breath brings in a new tone to his hum, new colors and sensation dominate the perceptive field. To their amazement, the boys squint their eyes and are overjoyed that they, too, can make out the faint outlines of beautiful rainbow shapes flowing out of their friend. After a while, the boys can't help but bring attention to what else they can see.

"Look!" Otto cries out. "His wounds! They are starting to disappear!" Everyone inches their heads closer to watch Beau's miraculous self-recovery. The burns along his arms and legs, the cuts and scrapes from his crash landing, and the scars from his recent fight start to fade from sight. Even the lodged bullet from Izak's gun flows out of his vibrating muscle and falls to the ground. Jeeven turns his head away once again, eager to dismiss such energetic feats of wonder. After a few more moments, Beau brings his humming to a rest. He opens his eyes and smiles at his onlookers. His breath is heavy, clearly exhausted from his recent maneuvers.

"See?" Baba says playfully. "No need to intervene."

"Whoa, hold on a minute!" Domino blurts out. "If you could do that this whole time, why have you never put your hair back on your head?"

"Yehahahaha!" Izak laughs, with overwhelming pleasure. He inadvertently shakes his snow-coated dreadlocks proudly behind his head. Beau narrows his eyes and gives Domino a dirty look. He is about to tell him what else he can do if he's not careful, but Baba decides to interject his thoughts on the matter.

"What's wrong with a bald head?" he says with a childish tone, slapping his own hairless dome.

"Well, I… well, I didn't mean to offend," Domino stammers. Baba laughs a huge belly laugh and waves his hand to dismiss Domino's feeble attempt at an apology. Beau turns to the old Sage with a bright smile on his face.

"What is your name, old man? Could have used your help a while ago," he says endearingly.

"You sure could have! But you never asked until just a moment ago," he says cryptically. Beau opens his mouth to ask some clarifying questions, but Baba moves on with the conversation. "You can call me Baba," he finishes with a warm smile. With curiosity etched all over his face, Beau reaches out to shake his hand, causing Emmanuel to go into a tizzy.

"You can't touch him!" he cries out. "No one can—" his words are abruptly halted at the merger of the two hands in a brief but powerful handshake. "I-I don't understand," Emmanuel mumbles to himself.

"Judging by the reaction of that guy over there, you must be someone quite special," Beau says, opening himself to any volunteered background information.

"Nonsense, I'm just a happy old man," Baba replies. "But you on the other hand…" He inches himself closer to Beau. "Hmm…" He gazes deep into Beau's bright green eyes. "So it *is* true," he says, drawing all the surrounding attention to his next words. "You have been there… to the place Babel protects." Gasps can be heard from everyone in earshot. They look eagerly to Beau for his response.

"Ahh, I don't know what you are talking about, old man," Beau says, as he clearly grows uncomfortable. He inches himself away and tries to distance himself from the Sage's prodding gaze.

"But you have!" Baba exclaims with joy as he follows his feeble retreat. "You have stepped foot on the Holy Land. How wonderful!"

"Can it be true?" Izak says with sincere curiosity.

"No one has ever stepped foot past Babel's reaches," Emmanuel mumbles. "But Baba wouldn't lie about such things." Izak takes an extra-long drag of his cigarette as he contemplates the paradoxical report.

"Look, I appreciate what you did. I really do. You know, helping bring some sense to these 'judge-first-ask-later' mercenaries or whoever they are, but I really don't know what makes you think you know anything about me. I don't know anything about what lies behind that storm." Jeeven grumbles at the derogatory statements but decides not to say anything further. "Plus, we have wasted way too much time here. Our friend, and I'm assuming she's your friend too," he says directing his attention to the giant, "is still in danger and we intend to help her. I thought these guys were supposed to help, but it appears even my captain can be wrong sometimes. C'mon boys, we—"

"No, he was right," Baba interrupts, folding his arms across his chest.

"Excuse me?" Beau says, his tone harboring a slight note of annoyance.

"He was right," Baba repeats. "All of you are going to help her and the rest of the Seers."

"Are you asking or telling, old man?" Beau fires back, clearly displaying a lack of interest in playing any more games.

"I'm telling you your captain is already on his way to engage the situation at hand," Baba responds, unaffected by Beau's brash energy. "He will keep the Warden distracted while all of you can get your friend out of Mune's castle."

"Hold on," Beau asks, dropping his disgruntled tone. "How do you know all this?"

"Please," Emmanuel interjects, "the Great Babarossa does not need to be subjected to any more questions. He has helped us out enough already." Beau gives the man still donning sunglasses a sideways glance.

"Right, so what makes you think we plan to rescue her?" Jeeven asks, disregarding Emmanuel's plea. "Her capture jeopardizes our mission. She could be anywhere. She knows the mission comes first."

"Jeeven," Emmanuel remarks with a heavy sigh of defeat.

"Just remember your original intention for coming to this island. If you can do that and figure out how to work together, I'm sure you all will find what you are looking for," Baba says happily.

"So, she's mixed up with the Power Pole then?" Izak interjects in-between puffs of smoke.

"How could you? That is not a matter we speak of out loud!" Jeeven bellows.

"Didn't you hear the Sage?" Izak rebuttals. "Aren't we supposed to work together or whatever? Who cares anymore? Let's just get this thing going already."

"You," Jeeven grumbles with his returning rage as he makes a threatening motion to stand and fight.

"Hahahaha!" Baba laughs uncontrollably, rolling onto his back in a full-belly roar. "Oh my! Bahahaha!!" Tears stream from his eyes. His antics are enough to disrupt the bubble of tension that manifested. "How wonderful!" he cries in-between chuckles. "You all are going to work splendidly together!"

"Aaaahhhhhheeeee," yawns the newly awakened Ayananda. She stretches her fists above her head and comes to a seated position next to Emmanuel. Izak flicks the remainder of his cigarette and looks eagerly over at her, analyzing her wellbeing. The devilish aura she emitted before has completely disappeared. "What's going on, Big Je'?" she asks the standing giant.

"Well," he says, trying to take in everything that has transpired since her fall from consciousness.

"C'mon Je-Je," taunts Beau, picking on Jeeven's hesitation, "we don't have all day now."

"Quiet you!" Jeeven bellows. "We are going to finish this mission." He returns his attention to Ayananda.

"All of us?" she asks, looking around questionably at Beau and the boys.

"Yes," Jeeven responds.

"All of us," Beau says with the follow up. He stands side-by-side with the mighty giant, signifying their momentary truce and partnership.

"Whatever you say," Ayananda responds with a sarcastic eye roll. "But I get the feeling I just woke up into another dream. Just make sure it's not a nightmare, will ya?" As the newly aligned forces start to work out the details of their plan, Baba makes his silent removal from the group. Unnoticed, he drifts into the wisps of fog still surrounding the edges of the alleyway. The fog grows thicker around where he stands; with the help of an incoming breeze, his presence completely fades into the passing wind.

CHAPTER: 28

Sandpaper for the Soul

"O-ooof!" The impact of the cold concrete floor knocks the breath out of Brahm's defenseless chest. He hits the ground with such force he bounces into the air before falling back onto the unforgiving slab. He lies sprawled out like a helpless rodent awaiting a science class dissection. Fueled by residual rage, he pours the last remaining strength into his quivering arms. Despite summoning all his conscious will power, his limbs struggle to lift his torso off the ground. The shackles around his wrists limit his mobility, but he pushes aside any thoughts of further restriction. With arms fully extended, his head now hangs low, reluctantly attached to the flaccid neck atop his shoulders. A drip of blood falls from the gash upon his busted lip as he slowly turns to see the guard standing at the doorway. The guard proudly slaps his hands together as if he just tossed out the daily garbage.

"You think that beating was bad?" the guard says mockingly. "You just wait until that madman Claude has his way with you! And if you survive that, well, then there is the Warden to look forward too. Lucky you." The poorly lit room hides most of the man's face in the shadows, but his gleeful smile shines bright into Brahm's furious heart. Brahm gives his throat the command to yell out but is halted by the continued inability to bring air into his lungs.

"You're nothing but scum! All of you!" the guard yells from behind his grin. "And to think we gave you all the opportunity to get help! Why would anyone turn down such a lucrative offer?" The silence that surrounds his words leads him to carry on with his rant. "While we clung to what's left, working tirelessly to find a way to rebuild, you Sympathizers did what? Made *friends* with the storm?" He takes another step back and snarls his lip in disgust. "You all are on the losing side of this war. You think this world won't bring another calamity upon our heads and wipe out what is left of us?" The guard slams the barred door of the prison cell closed as he ends his tirade. His keys jingle with an echo as he pulls them from his waist. With a definitive *click* he takes a key and secures the lock binding the prison bars.

Brahm's strength finally gives out as he sprawls back onto the ground. The footsteps of the guard grow faint, fading into the distance. Brahm's mind races to find a solution to his situation. Unfortunately, even thinking drains too much energy from his depleted body. Dispelling a heavy exhale of defeat, he lets his exhausted mind quiet and settles into a depressing slump. With the right side of his face firmly planted to the floor, his eyes move to scan what limited surroundings are in view.

He is surprised to see his cell populated with at least thirty grown men. They don tattered clothes, easily showcasing their scarred and battered skin underneath. Most of their wounds remain undressed, left out in the open on gruesome display. Despite the allure of pain and suffering, they all sit quietly as if in a meditative trance. Brahm becomes confused at the lack of attention he is receiving and begins to grow uncomfortable. *Why are they just sitting there?* he thinks to himself. *They look so peaceful, like nothing out of the ordinary is going on! Do they even know I'm here? Do they even care?* Brahm grows disgusted with his company's lack of attentiveness. *Maybe they are all fine being locked away here! But not me!* He forces a wave of vigor back into his body. *No matter what, I need to get to Sophia.*

"I will not let this place get the best of me!" he yells out loud. The continued lack of movement from his crowd further fuels his rage as he clenches his fists, ready to make another attempt to stand. While he struggles to force his body to heed his commands, he misses the opening of a few eyes from his meditative onlookers. Curiosity seems to swell in their minds as they must wonder what their mysterious guest plans to do. They watch as Brahm screams and yells at his body. He repeatedly berates his physical vessel, slapping his flesh like the horse of a second-place race jockey. Brahm looks through the bars surrounding the prison from his crouched position and flings himself as close as he can to the barrier. His feeble legs spring his body in the intended direction, but he flops back onto the floor like a freshly caught fish. A sick grin of misplaced satisfaction races across his face as if this was his intention all along. Gripping the iron bars, he uses them as a prop to finally inch his body back onto two feet. His knees shake, begging to be decommissioned. Ignoring the pleas of his body, he holds tight to the supporting prison bars as he prepares to summon the guard to return.

"Hey!" he shouts into the damp darkness. He has to pause to catch his breath, but one breath is all he will allow. "Y-You think you can just throw me away and forget about me?! Do you even know who *I* am?" He is forced to pause his banter as his lungs desperately gasp for another breath. His eyes glow red as his body huffs and puffs, wheezes and pants, desperately trying to maintain consciousness. Brahm grows even more furious. "How dare you betray me?!" he yells at his body in-between breaths. "Of all the times to decide to fail, you pick now? Now?! I can't believe you!" The meditative onlookers flash glances to one another with furrowed brows, growing even more curious of this strange man talking to himself.

"I'm not done with you!" he yells back into the darkness. "I'm not going to stop until you show yourself again! I want you to look into the eyes of the man who will bring this whole organization of yours down! You will pay for what you have done to me!" Brahm returns to his desperate gasps of air as he awaits the response to his taunting. He stares longingly into the darkness, eager to reunite with his foe on the other side. His exhausted and debilitated body weighs heavy in stark contrast to his desire. Desperate to disregard such an inconvenience, he prefers to stay locked inside his mind. Revenge anchors itself as the only thought worthy of holding on to. His face snarls with glee as he fantasizes sending the guard flying to the next island when he reemerges.

Finally, in the distance beyond sight, comes the sound of a door opening. The hinges squeal as the door is flung open. Footsteps can be heard making their way to the prison cell, accompanied by the sound of something dragging on the floor. Brahm squints his tired eyes with the hope of forcing more light into his retinas. Eventually the guard from before comes into sight. He pauses in front of the cell for a moment, displaying his pressed and pristine purple and green uniform. He stands tall and confident, holding a barely conscious man in his right hand by the scruff of his tattered shirt. He smiles as he makes his way back to the cell door. The familiar jingle of his keys echoes through the prison chamber. With a swift turn of the key, the door flings back open as he throws the prisoner in his hand to the cell floor. The meditating men turn their attention to the new arrival. Brahm, on the other hand, places all his attention onto the guard remaining in the doorway. His snarls become audible, his rage palpable. The guard turns to Brahm and smiles a bit wider.

"I'm feeling generous today," the guard says, taking a step back from the open cell door. "I'll give you your chance. Here! The door is wide open. Make your great escape. Come get your revenge. I won't even stop you."

"You…" Brahm grunts under his breath. "You will regret this. I will show you no mercy!" he yells as he makes his first step towards the door. His legs shake even more feverishly as the demand to stand and walk proves to be overwhelming. Still, Brahm pushes forward. He has one hand still holding onto the prison bars for support as he maneuvers one foot in front of the other. Feeling confident in his stability he lets go of the bar. Sheer determination and boiling fury charge the next step as Brahm advances his foot towards the beckoning door of freedom. However, despite the best of intentions, his body plummets back to the ground as gravity holds tight with a secure embrace.

Brahm's head smacks the ground but falls in a way where he can still see the guard standing before him. His ears start to ring, and his vision begins to narrow. *What has become of me?* His fading consciousness ponders. In-between the escalating ringing he can hear the faint sound of the guard laughing uncontrollably. The curtain of his vision starts to pull closed as the guard puts the lock back on the cell door. Once again, he hears the familiar footsteps fading away as his consciousness follows suit. He lies motionless with deep restorative breaths pouring unrestrictedly into his unconscious vessel.

∞

"Hey, shhhh, keep it down."

"I think he's starting to move!"

"Step back! Give the man some space."

"Yeah, you never know, he might wake up swinging." "The only person he could harm at this point is himself."

"Quiet already, give the man some peace. We all know he could use it." Brahm struggles to lift his heavy eyelids as the voices of his fellow prisoners stir him back to wakefulness. His vision fades in and out before focusing on the multiple faces hunched over him. Their eyes peer over his excoriated exterior as if examining a new animal species. His arousal causes the onlookers to take a step back, slowly returning to the corner to join the rest of the prisoners. Brahm inches his head to bring the whole group into view. Most have remained seated like Brahm remembers before he lost consciousness. A few surround the man the guard recently brought in, wrapping his wounds with liberal amounts of what shreds of fabric remain of their clothes. Some others surround the man being cared for with heads bowed, mumbling repetitive chants under their breath. Brahm is overwhelmed with the amount of peace that permeates the atmosphere. His mind races to figure out what could be driving these people to act in such a way; but like before, his mind cannot keep up with the demands of his prying consciousness. Quick to mental exhaustion, he is forced to lie there and experience the serene scene unfolding without the energy to judge and analyze.

As he watches the man be nursed back to health, Brahm finds his own strength start to rekindle. He immediately cashes in what energy he regained and spends it on exhausting his negative emotions. His recharging mind races with fury once again. *How can they act like this is no big deal?!* Brahm ponders. *Where is their anger? Where is their fighting spirit? Has their will to be free been broken?* He peers out at the men with disgust in his eyes as he feels even more confident about his last musing.

"H-How?!" Brahm yells, finally manifesting his thoughts into speech. His face contorts and snarls as he bends his elbows to prop his torso off the ground. "How can you just sit there, pretending like nothing is happening?!" he asks as he inches his way to the men in the corner. A few of them look over at him with rekindled curiosity, but most pay him no attention. Their dismissal of his assumed words of reason infuriates him even further. "Am I the only one who doesn't want to die here?" he continues, inching further and further towards his unenthused audience. Brahm can hear their chanting start to grow louder; he assumes it is to drown out his call to action. "Well, I'll tell you what! You all make me sick, giving up like that! It's like you are just handing over your lives, allowing them to walk all over you like you don't even exist anymore! Where is your pride?! Where is your will to live?!"

"I'm sorry, sir," a young man says, casually breaking off from the group and walking over to greet his advancing prison companion, "but the way we see it, it is you who is giving yourself away to this prison." The young man crouches down to look Brahm in the eye. Compassion swelling from the depths of his soul, but it does little to extinguish the rage that has been festering in Brahm's heart.

"Excuse me?!" Brahm belts back, displaying no interest in filtering his emotionally charged expression. "You all look like a bunch of complacent bumps on a log, content with the dismal fate imposed on you! You all should be ashamed of yourselves." Brahm shakes his head. "I have more to do in this world than be bound by these bars. I just figured you all would too."

"We do!" the young man says, pleasantly dismissing Brahm's harsh words of criticism. "We all strive to be free from this place. However, what you call our complacency, well, we consider our last gem of freedom!"

"This place must really be getting to you; either that or the brain washing has kicked in. All that mindset is doing is making it easier for these guards to stay in control! Don't you see? You are giving them all the power!"

"That's where we differ, mister," the young man continues with a smile across his face. "What you suggest we do, what *you* want to do… fight them, act in rage and anger… to us, that is how we give them the last bit of power we have left." Brahm gives a disapproving glance but does not interrupt the young man. "Don't you see? With everything they have taken from us, there is still a spark that resides within us. That spark is what encompasses our freedom of will, the calmness of our hearts, and the love we share for all things. It's the spark no one can take; it can only be given away, and that's why we do what we do here! Our peace is our defiance." Brahm looks up with a wave of curiosity washing over him while a silence hushes over the crowd. The chanting stops, eyes have opened, and many have turned their attention to the energy surrounding the debate. Many of the men nod their heads with a silent agreement. Others sit motionless with smiles blooming on their faces. Brahm struggles to find the words to continue his fight. He is torn. The words the young man said hold a resonation of truth he cannot dismiss. On the other hand, the rage in his heart still burns with equal validation. In the midst of his turmoil, another guard enters the prison room.

By the sound of his footsteps, Brahm can already tell it is a different man from before. As he gets closer, the dim light shows that he carries a metal tray holding multiple bowls of assumedly food. The smell that permeates from the individual bowls is strong, as if one notch away from being completely spoiled and rotten. The guard appears more focused on not dropping the large amount of food he carries than the prisoners he has come to feed. He places the tray of food on the ground and slides it through the bars onto the other side. He stands back up and walks away, uninterested in even addressing the humans he has come to nourish. This triggers the rage still tormenting Brahms heart. He quickly army crawls to the tray and grabs ahold of one of the slop-filled bowls. He holds it in his hand for a moment before launching it towards the guard.

"Let me see you eat this slop!" he cries as the bowl goes flying in the air. However, Brahm's limited strength barely gets the bowl out from behind the prison bars. The guard stops as he listens to the loud *clack* of the bowl strike the ground and roll around before toppling to a stop. The contents of the bowl splatter with an expressive smear, but land nowhere near its intended target. The guard lets out a snort of comical relief before continuing his calm pace out of the prison room. Brahm watches helplessly as his anger tries to overpower his growing sense of defeat. A tear rolls down his face, but he wipes it away as quickly as it emerged. He turns back to the crowd of the other prisoners to see the young man passing out the remaining bowls to his companions. The young man makes sure everyone is fed before going to retrieve his own bowl. Brahm turns his head away in disgust as he flops his torso back onto the ground in a feeble attempt at a temper tantrum.

"Excuse me, sir" comes a familiar voice. Brahm turns back around to see the young man crouched with his bowl of food extended towards him.

"What are you doing?" Brahm asks flatly.

"Please. Try and eat so you can regain your strength." Brahm is momentarily taken aback by the extension of kindness, but continues to foster his commitment to his anger.

"I already ate mine, kid." He gestures to the splatter on the ground. "No need for a second helping," he says sarcastically.

"No, that bowl was for him and this one is for you," he says kindly before placing the bowl in front of Brahm.

"I cannot take your food. Please, just leave me alone."

"And I cannot let you give up on yourself!" the young man responds with zest. "Let your anger pour out of your heart like the porridge that lies splattered on the ground. Open yourself up for something greater to fill your vessel! You have such a fight to live, but it's so misplaced! If you can just find a way to empty your heart of all that constricts it, it might finally be able to beat with the rhythm you feel has been taken from you."

"Why are you trying so hard, kid? You don't even know me."

"But I do! We are brothers of Maia. We are all in this together," the young man says with a tear running down his cheek. "Love people. Serve people. Feed people. All people. That's what it is all about. That is how you maintain your humanity. That is how you help others maintain theirs." Brahm looks up at the young man, compelled to face the source of fire that has ignited within him.

"Feed people?" he asks, desperate to harp on semantics rather than give in to the swelling surge of emotion in his chest.

"Yes," the young man replies softly, "and no, I am not *just* referring to the action of filling one's belly, rather that of their soul." His words tip Brahm's emotional tightrope dance over the edge. As he teeters into the depths of his opening heart, he struggles to believe what his eyes perceive. For a moment it appears the old man from the city plaza is swimming behind the young man's eyes. The thought alone is enough to summon the final crack in the emotional dam of his heart. He falls to the floor in a puddle of his own tears. As he weeps and sobs, the young man puts a hand on his back to comfort him. A deep sigh of relief can be heard from the onlooking crowd.

"Thank you," he says, "even though I don't deserve your kindness—" "Stop right there," the young man interrupts, causing Brahm to dramatically stop mid bite. "We *all* deserve kindness. Even the guards you despise so much. They of all people need it the most."

"Who are you?" Brahm asks as he decides to return to his meal.

"My name is Mono, a Seer of this land. Who might you be?"

"M-Mono?" Brahm stutters, spitting out what food has passed through his lips. "Are you Raja's brother?"

"Raja!" Mono exclaims with joy. "Guys, do you hear this?" he calls back to his friends in the corner. "He knows Raja! Yes, yes, I am her brother! How is she? Is she still alive?"

"I'm afraid I don't know," Brahm says as he looks dramatically down at the floor, unable to continue eye contact with the young man. "I met an old man in the Plaza today, someone named Babarossa, who asked me if I came to rescue her. A Warden has come back to finish the purge of the Seers... which I'm coming to realize is all my fault!" Brahm says with tears starting to swell back into his eyes. "If I hadn't gotten involved and helped her climb to that stage and announce to the whole island who she was, she wouldn't be in this mess! It was so careless of me! I had no idea what the ripple effects of that decision would be!"

"Please, sir, don't be so hard on yourself,"

"How can you say that?! I practically assisted the capture or worse, the murder of your sister!"

"Trust me, I've known my sister for a long time. If she wants to do something, rest assured she will find a way to do it!"

"Are you not worried about her?" Brahm asks.

"I mean, I would prefer her to be safe; but like I said, I know my sister, and this was bound to happen eventually. However, if it was Baba who told you about her, just knowing he is involved brings me peace. He will make sure this all works itself out." He gives Brahm a reassuring smile before continuing. "So, tell me again, mister, who are you? I'm starting to get the feeling you are not here with us by chance."

"My name is Brahm. I came to your island two nights ago, riding in on one of Babel's storm surges."

"Yoo, did you all hear that!?" Mono yells back, "This guy was sent by Babel and then by Baba?! Tewari, doesn't he sound like the guy from your dream—"

"*Sent* by Baba?!" Brahm yells while rearing his head back defensively like an offended ostrich. "That crazy old man. He's the one who took away my... my... everything!" His words create a dramatic stage for him to proclaim the pain of which he blames the old man for. "I was soaring through the clouds before I met him, and now I've been reduced to this feeble shell of flesh and bones! I would have never wound up in this mess if it weren't for him. If I ever get out of here and see him again, I'll... I'll... I'll..."

"Thank him," Mono interrupts happily.

"Not quite where I was going with that…" Brahm trails off sarcastically.

"No, but I imagine that's where you'll end up once you learn why you are here."

"All right, smart guy, so why am I here then?" Brahm asks defiantly.

"We will soon find out; Baba has a way of hiding what you rely on in order to show you where your true strength lies."

"Is that why you think you are here?" Brahm asks with the layers of sarcasm piling high.

"Exactly!" Mono responds, paying no attention to Brahm's jest. "You are a quick learner!" he says with a playful wink. Brahm takes the moment to finally have a bite of the already cold slop of food. He winces in anticipation of disgust but is delightfully surprised by the revitalizing sustenance flowing into his vessel.

"See?" Mono says as if he were peering into Brahm's mind. "Some things may not always be as they appear on the surface, just like this prison, just like with Baba and just like this reality. My stay here has allowed me to settle my senses. Without the distractions of the world, I can now see behind the veil of physical reality. I can finally see the web of light that connects us all. That web surrounds our world and unites all things within it. Everything is important. Everything has purpose, even my situation here, the situation with my sister and even the loss of your powers. I'm thankful to this prison for teaching me what it has. I'm sure you will receive a similar lesson."

"Speak for yourself."

"You see your suffering as a limitation. However, you could think of it like sandpaper for the soul."

"Sandpaper?" "Exactly. Our experiences here work to gently wither away the false aspects of self. They keep refining us until we are left with a smooth and polished understanding of reality. The process looks different for everyone, rough and painful at times, but the purpose is all the same! It can be a tricky course to navigate, but once you stumble upon the force that drives this refinement, there is no turning back."

"What force is that?" Brahm asks eagerly. Mono opens his mouth to answer, but the sound of the heavy metal door crashes open, interrupting the invigorating dialogue. The two turn to watch as the previous guard strolls back into the room. He peers down at the emptied bowl of porridge still on the floor and gives a light chuckle of pleasure.

"All right, new guy, it's your turn now!" the guard says with demonic delight.

"Wait, what's happening?" Brahm says as he quickly becomes aware of the target on his body.

"You are about to be tortured," Mono says calmly. "But don't panic. This is your chance to let go of what is not."

"What are you talking about?" Brahm says frantically as the guard starts to unlock the prison door. "You've got to help me!"

"This is your moment of truth," Mono says compassionately. "Look for that underlying force that brings all things together. Once you find it, no one can harm you. No one can hinder you, because they all become you."

"Time's up!" the guard yells as he lifts Brahm's hands into the air by the chains that bind him. The echo of the guard's heavy boots reverberates with a painful sharpness. The rattling of Brahm's shackles add to the dismal symphony of suffering. The guard turns to walk out of the prison cell with Brahm kicking and floundering as he is dragged to his upcoming trial.

"What is the underlying force?!" Brahm pleads as he gets dragged further out of Mono's sight. Mono takes a deep breath, concentrating the full extent of his energetic being.

"*Love!*" he yells back, his words echoing triumphantly through the chamber. The guard slams the prison door in Mono's face, but it does not stop his momentum. "It's all bound together with love!" he continues to yell through the bars. "That's what this vantage point is here to show us! Everything! Everyone! It's all connected by love! If you can see that, if you can feel that, you will see you already hold the key to your prison!" Mono watches as Brahm drifts into the shadows that shroud the door to the other side. The heavy metal door closes with a solidifying crash. Silence quickly resumes its reign over the prison.

Mono takes a solemn look over his shoulder to see all his Seer brothers looking out into the same shadows with warm eyes.

"I wish I had more time with him," Mono says openly to the crowd, with a wave of defeat flavoring his words.

"You said everything that needed to be said. Now it's up to him to realize his own truth," an older Seer says with an authoritative tone. He walks carefully, bracing his recently incurred injuries while coming to stand by Mono's side. The man harbors a husky build, his skin defined by a plethora of intersecting wounds and scars. He is clothed like the rest with a few remaining shreds of fabric hanging off his frame. His weathered face dawns a salt and peppered beard and crystal blue eyes. A deep scar stretches down his forehead, over his right eye and onto his cheek.

"What if he doesn't get it, Tewari?" Mono says to the man after a while in silence.

"We can't worry about such things," Tewari responds lovingly.

"How can you say that? He *must* be the man you've been dreaming about! You have been talking about the importance of the energy that man harbors for weeks now! If he can't rekindle his connection with the web, then what does that mean for the world?"

"The fate of the world is not decided by an individual," Tewari responds sternly. "We all have our role to play. Remember, with love comes faith, Mono. Don't lose sight of either."

CHAPTER: 29

The Severed Marionettes

Beau and the boys weave in-between the scattered remains of the frantic crowds as they advance with their new companions to Mune's castle. The growing silence from the thinning crowd is a pleasant welcoming to Beau's ears. He drifts just far enough behind Jeeven to still see his head above the crowd. As they interact with less and less of the inhabitants of The Pearl, the silence beckons a buildup of suspense for the boys. Their chests tighten as they meander through the vacating plaza, the final checkpoint before the foreboding castle makes its way into view. Not above devising a distractive ploy, the boys shift their anticipatory anxiety towards their newly acquainted celebrities.

"I can't believe it, Otto! Do you think it's really them?!" Domino asks with inflated vigor.

"Of course it's them! You heard it yourself! Sophia is their leader, so they have to be a part of the Resistance!"

"Do you think they came here to save us?"

"I sure hope so!"

"Let's go ask!" As the boys make their pivotal step to poke at the thin veil holding together the recently acquired truce, Beau attempts to intervene.

"Choose your words carefully," Beau advises, stopping the boys in their tracks. They look up with questioning eyes. "You saw how quick they were to react to the slightest hint of a threat. Don't go starting another fiasco with your careless questions."

"Don't worry, Beau!" Domino cries out confidently. "I mean, if you think about it, I've been dealing with the Resistance for quite some time now. I'm sure they wouldn't mind getting to know their Totem Wand dealer!"

"Cocky brat," Beau scoffs under his breath. The boys give themselves reassuring grins as they run up to the silent giant. Jeeven glances to his periphery as the sound of eager footsteps break into his bubble of personal space. He gives a grunt of acknowledgment but does not slow his pace. The boys are forced to jog to keep up with him, but they don't seem to mind.

"Hey! So, I know you don't know me, well, other than being someone you almost smashed into the ground," Domino starts off, "but I just want you to know I've been a big fan and have supported your cause for years now! Well, I didn't know Sophia was an undercover Resistance leader, but now that I do, it's clear we are all on the same side, right??" He looks up to Jeeven who just gives out a deep sigh from his nostrils. "Right, right, I don't mean to say I'm a part of the Resistance or anything, but I have helped! Uhhh…" Domino finally gets the hint that his words are not connecting. He decides to get straight to the point. "So, about your mission here… have you come to save us? You know, from Mune and his people? How about the Power Pole? We saw it, you know! Maybe we could—"

"Enough!" Jeeven bellows. The boys watch in horror as the giant stops his march and turns to them directly. Ayananda and Izak place their hands on their respected weapons, ready to heed the call of their leader. Jeeven stares into the quivering eyes of the overeager boys. He takes a deep breath and lets out a reluctant sigh through his snarled lips. "Don't pretend like you know anything about us or our mission. If you know what's best for you, you will stay out of my sight!" The boys remain frozen in fright, unsure of what to do in the presence of the formidable beast. "Ugh," Jeeven grunts in disgust. "Get out of here!" Realizing they have outstayed their welcome, the boys quickly run back into the safety of Beau's presence.

"I tried to warn you two," Beau says with an unexpected fatherly tone. He shakes his head with the thought of falling into such a parental role.

"I-I'm sorry!" Domino stutters.

"Yeah! Me too!" Otto chimes in. Beau shakes his head.

"You're lucky all he did was yell at you. I would think of all people you two would be more careful around someone who *just* tried to kill you." As the boys soak in the reality of their poor choices, Beau flairs his nostrils as a strong whiff of smoke makes itself known. He looks to his left and notices Izak falling back to walk alongside him and the boys. At first, the gunslinger doesn't make eye contact. He takes a long drag of his cigarette while Beau eyeballs his plethora of weapons and gadgets hanging from his metallic exoskeleton. They rattle as he walks, loosely blanketed by his long cloak flapping freely in the wind behind him. He plucks the cigarette from his mouth and dramatically spews a flume of smoke from his charred lungs.

"So, is it true?" Izak says.

"Is what true?" Beau responds defensively. He reflexively reaches up to guard his exposed left shoulder.

"These kids, have they really seen the Power Pole?"

"Ah, I'm not sure. There was this cave where—" "Yeah, we saw it!" Otto chimes in, with Domino hot on his heels, eager to prove their worth.

"Do you know where it is?" Izak asks.

"Kind of!" Domino exclaims. "We were sailing through the Jaws, and we found this cave hidden in the fog. We were below deck, so we don't know exactly where it is, but we saw it pulsating in the cave!"

"Yeah!" Otto butts back in. "There was this huge dark pole thing that pulsated like it had a heartbeat! There were these vein-looking things crawling off it onto the rocks! It was super strange looking, like it was darker than black if that is even a thing!"

"How do you *know* that was a Power Pole?" Izak challenges in-between cigarette drags.

"Well," Otto says, slipping into somber memory. "We met someone there, a shaman from Wahaka. He called it a Dark Serpent."

"Now I know you are full of it, I know for a fact the Condorian's were all wiped out," Izak says, his attention now turned to the boys.

"Yeah, facts can be weird like that. Sophia thought the same, but it turns out they are in the… forbidden forest or something."

"You're kidding. The Forest of Amenti? Without proper training that is mental suicide!"

"He alluded to something like that. He was going to tell us more but, then…"

"Then, what?"

"A Warden showed up," Domino says, aware the story is becoming too challenging for Otto to recap alone. "He killed the shaman and took Sophia captive once he realized she was a part of the Resistance. Something to do with that ring she wears." "So, one of the Wardens we saw earlier survived the storm after all? Should have known it wouldn't be that easy. This is going to be a problem," Izak muses as he turns his attention back to his cigarette. He puffs away in silence until Beau feels compelled to pry.

"You said earlier your original goal had something to do with these Power Poles. What's the deal with those things?"

"Ehhh," Izak starts, but stops as Emmanuel walks up from behind them.

"I doubt Jeeven would appreciate you saying any more about that matter," Emmanuel says with his nose pointed to the sky. He keeps his pace brisk as he walks past the gossip group to join Ayananda and Jeeven.

"He's probably right," Izak sighs.

"Didn't stop you from talking about it before," Beau prods with some gambled hope.

"Yeah, guess it didn't. I'm not a fan of being told what to do anyway. All right," he says, eagerly rolling up his sleeves and stretching the creases of his face in thought. He pauses briefly to prepare an answer to Beau's questions without signing his death warrant. "All you really need to know is those Wardens are powerless without those poles. We can't beat them head on, so destroying their power source is the only chance we have to take them down. Wisteria is trying to create their own version of the Mountain Gods with these things in hopes to destroy Babel once and for all. That's what they tell the people anyway, but we don't trust it. The consequences of tampering with such forces are just too great, Baldy."

"Baldy," Beau mutters under his breath before he forces out a cordial response. "That's quite a tall order. Do you really think these things could rival the Mountain Gods?"

"Who really knows anything about the Mountain Gods anymore? They have drifted into the exaggerated fables we tell our children. This Warden project is just another one of mankind's attempts to play God. No matter how close they might be, such endeavors never end well," Izak says coldly.

"Humanity has been plagued with the desire to challenge the gods since our first breath upon this world," Beau says heavily. "Our obsession with power leads us to always want to have it all. We seem to have the hardest time making peace with our place among divinity. Maybe someday we will realize it might not be a force to conquer like we've kept trying to do lifetime after lifetime…"

"Yeah, I like what you are saying, Baldy. That obsession is going to get us all blasted into oblivion, that's why we have to do something to save us from ourselves." Izak lifts his cigarette to his face and watches the trail of smoke drift into the sky.

"I can sympathize with those sentiments," Beau says with a lingering pause. "It reminds me of a world I once ran away from."

"Ah, that world wouldn't have anything to do with that tattoo on your arm, would it?" Izak says while playfully pointing his thumb at Beau's exposed left shoulder. Beau slaps his right hand over the incriminating tattoo again, but not before the symbol of a lightning bolt cutting through a ring of expanding circles gets stamped into Izak's memory. Beau drops his hand, realizing there is nothing more he can do about his reveal. The boys look on eagerly as the two men continue their conversation.

"That's the mark of the Babel Research Team, if I'm not mistaken," Izak says, confidently. Beau tries to remain stoic, but his quivering facial expressions would easily contend for one of the world's worst poker faces. Izak smiles at the reaction his words manifest. "What a refreshing symbol of Wisteria's peaceful era. A symbol I'm sure they hoped died with the project twenty years ago. Everyone who knew of the B.R.T operations knew they were conducting suicide missions. Sending people directly into the storm? Ha! Never thought I'd get to meet one of the infamous suicide sailors! Well, I guess there always is that rumor floating around—"

"That's enough," Beau says violently. Accompanying waves of hostility lap defensively around his frame, threatening Izak with immediate confrontation. "Enough about me. Just tell me, what is your plan to stop all of this?" Izak draws in a prolonged drag of his cigarette before deciding how next to engage. The tantalizing allure of Beau's mysterious past remains an attractive hook. As if feeling his prying companion's intention, Beau stops his march and stares intently into Izak's dusty eyes. He does nothing to hold back the aggressive fury in his heart. Izak allows his hand to drift closer to a firearm along his waist as he processes the growing hostility. The dramatic tension surges between the two men locked in silent warfare as they wait for the other to make the next move.

"Oh well, I guess rumors will remain rumors," Izak says with a defeated tone. His hand drifts away from his weapon and he slides it innocently into his side pant pocket. "For our plan, it's simple," Izak continues from behind his cigarette cloud. "We storm the castle, blow it to smithereens. The hope is we take down the Power Pole with it."

"Are you serious?" Beau nearly shouts. "That's it? And the Warden? What if the Power Pole is not where you think it is? And Sophia? Are you mad?"

"Mad?" Izak remarks with heavy inflection. His hand slips out of his pocket and reaches towards his firearm once again. Taking a moment to process his situation, he decides to holster his flash of hostility for the time being. "This situation is bigger than any individual, can't you see that? Sophia hired us to complete this mission and we intend to do just that. We decided to play it carefully with Wahaka and that didn't pan out well for anyone. If there is any hope left in taking down this Power Pole, we are going to take it. We would all rather die than be the reason we fail; Sophia feels this way more than anyone." *God, I'm glad Brahm is as focused on Sophia as these guys are about this mission,* Beau thinks to himself as he soaks in the cold rationale of the trigger happy gunslinger. "You can turn back now if you're scared," Izak adds.

"Ha!" Beau laughs, quick to dispel the flash of tension. "My captain seemed very certain that staying involved with you lot was crucial. He placed his bet on you, so I'll do the same."

"That careless man-child? Ha! Good luck following his lead. Life is all about choices, and just so you know, I judge you severely for that one."

"Bold, but I don't mind," Beau says with no resentment in his tone. "It's a complicated relationship to say the least. It is true he has some maturing to do, but that will come with time. He's worth betting on."

"Suit yourself, but don't forget the true wager is your life, Baldy," Izak says. "And those boys..." he glances down at Otto and Domino. "Why include them in any of this? They seem to just be a walking liability." He flicks his exhausted cigarette to the ground.

"There may be some truth to that, I cannot lie," Beau says to try and save face.

"Hey!" the boys shout together in protest.

"But in the short time we have spent with these boys," Beau continues, "I have come to realize there is an even greater reason they have stayed with us all this time."

"Yeah? What might that be?" Izak says with a hint of sarcasm. The boys stretch their heads like hungry baby birds as they await his answer.

"Transparency."

"What the hell is that supposed to mean?"

"All too often the truth of the world, the same world they share a part in, is translated and fabricated by people like us who face it head-on. The youth are left waiting for us to report back only versions of the truth… the versions we think they can best handle. It doesn't seem right. Think of these kids as our investment in the future. If we want to have any hope for a future worth living in, we have to start trusting our youth to be able to comprehend the present struggles."

"Your investment in the future could risk all of our lives, you know?" Izak says somberly. "I hope you have thought this through."

"I've probably thought it through as well as you have thought out your blitz and battle mission!" Beau jabs. Izak looks at him with unamused eyes.

"Is that so?" Izak asks as he reflects on his assessment. "Fine. I'll let it go for now. Just remember, when things get rough, which they will, they are your crew. Your responsibility! Got that?"

"Ha, you can relax. I didn't need your permission to accept such a responsibility. I've already accepted that a long time ago." Izak smiles at Beau's remark. Seemingly satisfied with his analysis, Izak extends his stride, casually making a move to return to his crew up ahead. Beau notices the shift, inspiring one last lingering thought. "Hey," he calls out. "Just who are you guys anyway?"

"Just a bunch of misfit Shakers trying to save the world," Izak remarks without turning around. Beau is desperate to know more but remembers his early resistance to his own past. Just as he decides to let go any further prying, Izak turns around and throws Beau's hungry curiosity a few scraps. "We call ourselves the Severed Marionettes, recent allies of the Resistance. Back in the day it was Jeeven's idea we raise a flag to represent our cause, a call to welcome all the rejects and rebels of the world. We see ourselves as freed puppets with the strings of our fate back in our own hands. Paints a nice picture, eh?" Izak says with an added wink. He pops his cigarette back into his mouth and hastens his pace to meet up with the other members of his crew.

∞

"Hey…" Domino says timidly, seemingly unsure if he wants to share the words populating in his head. Beau looks down at the youth and gives him the space to collect his thoughts. "Thanks… ya' know, for saying those things about us. Never really had anyone believe in me like that before."

"Everyone has potential, kid," Beau says with parental flair. "Now it's just a matter of if you believe the same about yourself." The boys look to each other with a tidal wave of emotions ready to be expressed, but Beau has shifted his attention back to the band of Severed Marionettes. "They have stopped," he says heavily. He watches intently as he continues to walk towards them. They stand at the top of the hill marking the end of the Portala Plaza. All their heads are tilted to the high rock faces that make up the backside of The Pearl. The giant Lotus desalinator rests upon the high peak, sitting proudly after purifying the previous night's storm surge. As Beau and the boys make their way closer, a large metal structure comes into view under the Lotus. The pointed roof of the structure gives way to long pillars that stretch to the ground. A multitude of shuttered windows line the rounded wall facing them. The storm shutters swing open upon the group's arrival. Armed guards hang from their strategic perches, ready to protect the unsightly structure.

∞

"So this must be it?" Beau asks the Marionettes as he walks up beside them.

"Yep," Izak says. "Disgusting, isn't it?"

"The castle?" Beau asks, unsure of what Izak is referring to.

"If you can call it that," he says as he violently shakes his new cigarette at the cylindrical eye sore. "I don't know what it is with cowardly men in power and their obsession with phallic structures. I mean, come on! Just look at this thing! What's he got to prove? Compensating, I'm sure! It's like someone erected a giant d—” “I think they get the picture,” Ayananda says to cut off his crass description of Mune's dwelling. She gently maneuvers her face right next to Izak's ear. “I mean, maybe he's just really proud of what he's got,” Ayananda adds, clearly showing she harbors the same level of maturity on the subject.

“That's enough from both of you,” Jeeven says to end the conversation. Ayananda leans over and gives Izak a provocative wink before standing up straight. Beau watches as Izak shakes his head in disgust. On a second glance, Beau notices a faint blushing of his cheeks, which he clearly is trying to hide.

Beau raises an eyebrow while he thinks about the interesting interaction. His eyes eventually scan over to Mune's castle, which is showing signs of movement from inside. The once barricaded windows now display the brightly colored guards poking their heads out with guns pointed in all directions. The bottom floor also opens its doors with a few more of the guards surrounding the entrance. Their uniform spears have been replaced with long barrel rifles. A few of the men look uncomfortable holding the large firearms that rest in their palms.

“That's a lot of guns in one area,” Beau says, wondering if this changes their plan for a direct assault. “From that vantage point they will see us coming from whatever direction we choose. It could be a problem to rush the castle.”

“It might be, “Izak says calmly, “but the question we must ask ourselves is: despite the number of guns, do they even know how to use them?” His inquiry results in a pregnant pause that is carried to full term. The uncomfortable silence progresses into painful contractions of situational awkwardness. As the hope of a natural delivery grows increasingly unlikely, Beau decides to cut the unnecessary tension and help deliver the incubating thought.

“Okay, I'll bite,” Beau says with a roll of his eyes. “What makes you think they don't know how to use them?”

“Oh, just look at the way they hold such a precious instrument… untrained swine!” Izak responds with inflated glee. “It's like they don't know the stock from the barrel. Half of their safeties are still on, their hand placements are all off, and none of them are taking note of the directional changes of the wind! Such novices. They are a fitting defense for such a joke of a leader. They just harbor the illusion of security, just like he harbors the illusion of authority," he says as he pulls his own firearm from its holster.

"So what now, Big Je'?" Ayananda says, her tone reflecting no regard for Izak's recent testimony.

"It's clear they know we are coming," Jeeven says with his eyes still studying the castle intently. "I'm sure they have kept Sophia alive to bait us." "Or at least that's what they want to make it look like," Izak adds with a strong inflection of skepticism.

"Babarossa told us she was here," Emmanuel says defensively.

"Hate to burst your bubble, but he definitely did *not*," Izak fires back. "All he did was give us some vague riddle and we made our own assumptions of the matter." Jeeven waves his hand to end their conversation.

"What intel we have leads us to believe the Power Pole is located either inside or behind that castle," Jeeven says with his booming voice. "Our plan remains the same, we storm the castle and bring it to the ground, uncover the Power Pole, and destroy it. We will pray Sophia finds her own way out of this mess."

"What if the Warden is already there?" Beau asks.

"Then some stay to hold him off and act as a diversion while the others continue with the mission," Jeeven answers, looking directly at Beau. The implication is clear it will be the two of them leading the distraction. Beau laughs to himself but accepts the giant's silent proposal.

"That's fine by me," Beau responds.

"What will you do with the children?" Jeeven adds. "Izak tells me you are not willing to part with them. That is a problem for me." There is a long pause as Beau thinks carefully about his response. He lets out a deep sigh before taking a knee to address Otto and Domino.

"I need you to listen to me very carefully," Beau starts. "There are a lot of moving parts already in motion right now. I need to make sure you two are in the best place you can be in order for all this to work out with the greatest chance of success." He pauses again, leaving the boys biting at the bit for news of where their important roles reside. "I need you to stay here."

"What?!" Domino belts out.

"Yeah! After all you just said?" Otto adds.

"I know! I know! I know what I said, and I still mean that."

"So what's with this, 'stay here' crap?! You don't think we can hold our own anymore? You better not let these mercenaries get into your head!" Beau nods and turns to Otto.

"You all saw what happened to the shaman who was killed by the Warden. With one finger you said, right?" The boys immediately go quiet. "Everything felt like it was in our control until that… *thing* showed up. I don't even know enough about what it is capable of or even if it is human. There is a limit to the lifeline I am willing to risk when it comes to you two. It's because of how important you are! If you don't survive this and tell your stories about what happened here, this will all be for nothing, regardless of if we succeed or not! Please try and understand that."

"So what are we supposed to do?" Domino jumps in. "Just wait here and twiddle our thumbs while you all go off and save the day?! We want to help Sophia too! She's just as much our friend as she is yours!"

"That is true," Beau consoles. "However, what you can bring to the table has always been very different and right now we need to make the most of that. We haven't seen Brahm for quite a while and seeing how relatively quiet things are, it's safe to assume he probably got himself into some kind of trouble. He knows how to find you. If anything happens to me, I need you to be able to help him find himself if it comes to that again. Can you do that?" There is another moment of silence while the boys deliberate what Beau has asked them. The extended pause starts to frustrate Ayananda.

"Good lord, just tell them what to do and be done with it!" she blurts out. "They are just kids, why give them any option in the matter, anyway? This is pathetic."

"That's enough!" Izak unexpectedly yells. He clearly is taken aback by his own brashness. He quickly diverts his eyes from her location after the words leave his mouth. Ayananda takes a step back and looks intensely at Izak's closed-off body language. She licks her lips with a level of excitement before reengaging the situation.

"I didn't know you felt so strongly about these little kiddos, Izzy," she says seductively. "Thinking of settling down and starting a family of your own, are you?"

"Grrr…" Izak grumbles, trying to ignore her insensitive banter.

"How touching to see this sensitive side of you!" she continues. "Got a nice woman picked out already?" Beau watches as Izak balls his fingers into a fist so tightly, his knuckles resemble primed volcanoes ready to burst. Izak grumbles more to himself, unable to retort Ayananda's web of mockery. He finally flips the safety switch of the weapon he holds and cocks the device into commission. The sound of his guns abrupt engagement shifts the tides of the conversation. He burrows the stock of the gun into his muscular shoulders as he turns to face the castle once again.

"So our plan is to still storm this castle and see what happens?" he yells out with a slight quiver in his voice. Jeeven gives a silent affirming nod of his head. "Well, what are we waiting for? Let's just do this and get it over with already." Beau and the boys watch as his final words transition to a triumphant, emotion-fueled shot from his gun heading right towards the castle. The smoke sizzles from Izak's barrel as he lowers his gun after just one shot. Everyone looks over the hill as the single bullet takes a rather unexpected trajectory. The bullet flies as if governed by a mind of its own. Landing first on the slanted frame of the lower roof over the main entrance, it bounces straight up to the highest level where a guard hangs out the window. Bouncing again off the lip of the roof, the bullet soars into the exposed window. Screams of confusion and horror ring through the castle as the ammunition assailant tears through the top floor. The guards scurry with panic and confusion but it provides them no resolve.

Guns fire in all directions as they react to the unexpected adversary. The single projectile can be seen striking everyone and everything in its path without ever decreasing its velocity. Izak watches his bullet fly intently with his goggles now shifted over his eyes. He holds a triggering device in his right hand as his thumb hovers over a large red button. Beau watches the bug-eyed gunslinger while he soaks in the expanded capabilities of the weapon that struck him down earlier.

Did he actually calculate the entire trajectory of that bullet? Beau thinks to himself. *The angles? Geometry? Velocity?* Just as the last man remaining in the room falls, Izak studies his bullet's bloody path as it bounces a few more times before exiting the window. It strikes the lip of the roof again then heads down to the iron door on the ground floor. A faint sound resonates as his thumb finally connects with the anticipatory button. The triggered bullet explodes with a vibrant fury, detonating right in front of the main door, tearing apart the feeble barricade. Iron fragments and stone rubble trickle back to the ground as the dust from the explosion starts to settle. A handful of guards that were stationed on the ground floor fly out of the detonated door frame like a team of electrocuted synchronized swimmers. One by one they finish their expressive routine with a lifeless dive into the cold stone ground. There is a brief moment of total silence before the sound of marching footsteps can be heard resonating from deep inside the castle.

"You all can wait here as long as you want. I'm going in," Izak says stoically as he marches down into the valley where the castle resides.

"I do like a man of action!" Ayananda squeals to herself. "C'mon Jeeven! Let's not let him have all the fun!" She skips down into the valley herself.

"Do something about the kids," Jeeven says before he makes his own way into battle. Emmanuel silently follows suit, leaving Beau and the boys alone on the hilltop.

"It is very important we navigate this obstacle on our own paths," Beau says while he still has a knee to the ground. "I promise you I am not leaving you here to forget about you. I meant every word I said earlier. I want you to see for yourself what happens here today. However, you must still stay alive so you can light the torches of the future."

"Uhh, just go ahead and go, Beau!" Domino says with a smile on his face. "We will wait here for you or Brahm or whatever. You are so worried about us being safe, you better make it out of this alive too, got it?!"

"Thank you for understanding, boys," Beau says as he stands up tall. "I promise to come back alive!" He turns and walks down into the valley, drifting slowly out of view with the rest of the Marionettes.

"Did you really mean that?" Otto asks, turning to Domino with curiosity burning in his eyes.

"Mean what?"

"That you were okay with just staying up here and waiting?"

"Of course not! Let's go 'light the torches of the future' now!"

CHAPTER: 30

Into the Valley of Death

As Beau rushes to reach the others, he notices his feet slapping against the soles of his torn and damaged boots. They flop lifelessly with each hurried step he takes into the valley, begging to be put out of their misery. Realizing the increasing odds of tripping over himself, he hops hastily on each foot, relieving his damaged footwear one by one from their supportive duty. Casting aside the unnecessary resistance, his bare feet race to join the four members of the Severed Marionettes.

"I see you left the kids behind," Jeeven says without turning his head.

"We all have our own role to play in this," Beau says proudly. "Not everyone is meant to be a warrior."

"We all must be warriors, if we are to survive this world," Jeeven says reflexively. "We all fight our own battles, whether that be with our fists or not." Beau nods his head in agreement, surprised by the giant's expansive viewpoint. Jeeven's words inspire Beau to bow his head in a silent prayer for the boys' safety.

"They have proven themselves in my eyes," Beau says as he lifts his head out of his prayer. "I trust they will make it through this ordeal."

"Do you have the same trust in yourself?" Jeeven asks. Beau feels the impulse to give a quick-witted response but takes a minute to reflect on Jeeven's question.

"I didn't make the decision to join you lightly," Beau responds. "Partly I did so due to the wishes of my captain, which I honor. The other…" he trails off in thought for another moment. "The other is for me. I've renounced my commitment to this world for a long time. This is my chance to give back to what I have previously neglected. I had my reasons, but their relevance to this situation is absent. My time of hiding in the safety of the shadows is over."

"Well said," Jeeven says approvingly. The five warriors walk boldly and silently, stretched out side-by-side to Mune's fortress. Flies have already started to congregate over the dead guards who were struck down earlier by the single bullet. Beau can feel a heavy knot start to wrap itself around his heart. As they get closer, he is forced to step over the lifeless bodies that surround the castle entrance. He looks to the others who move past the human bodies as if they were just piles of dismissed debris. Just before a flavor of judgment is about to stamp his impression of the Marionettes, he witnesses Izak stick his hand in one of his many pockets. Beau watches with a heavy heart as Izak pulls a flower from his pocket and places it on the chest of one of the fallen guards. The peddles of the flower emerge wrinkled and faded. Izak does what he can to flatten out the wrinkles as the flower rests upon the guard's chest.

There is hardly any greenery on this island, let alone flowers! Beau thinks to himself. *How far has that flower traveled? How long has this man known what he picked that flower for?* The gesture strikes a chord in Beau's tangled heart as his mind races with the profound symbolism just displayed. Both the flower and the guard have been severed from their source of life, yet their color remains for the moment as a reminder of the life they once lived. In time they will both fade back into the ground. *Did he mean to cast such a message?* Beau's mind races further, *or is the gravity of all this starting to get to me?*

"Is that a normal custom of yours?" Beau finally asks, thankful his grim impression of the gunslinger has been altered. Izak glances to the guard now carrying his flower one more time before answering the question.

"It has become a way of coping with the unfortunate sacrifices of our duties. No one signed up to be a murderer, but death is an unavoidable aspect of this game we play. There is no way around it. Those who lie here are not the ones who deserve to be at the receiving end of our strike, but here they lay. Why is that?" he asks rhetorically. "Because of those cowards in power who hide behind them. It forces us to ride the tides of war. Otherwise, men like Mune can remain hidden in the shadows. Now that we have drawn blood, we cannot stop until Mune is thrown from this tower and everything he has built comes crashing down. Otherwise…" he stops to shake a reluctant tear from the corner of his eye. "Otherwise, each and every one of these men will have died for nothing." Izak gives a sunken glance at Beau. His eyes open wide, extending welcoming invitation to any further questions he may harbor before they cross the threshold. Beau understands all he needs and tilts his head with an empathetic nod.

"This blood is on your hands as well, Baldy," Izak adds. "With our hands already stained, we work from now on to wash clean the sins of our actions. May the heavens have mercy on all our souls."

"Ah-ho!" the remaining Marionettes recite in unison.

"Ah… ho," Beau adds as he takes in a heavy gulp of the dense atmosphere. The five warriors stand in the decimated doorway as they each clear their mind and prepare for the battle that awaits them. The sound of thundering footsteps can be heard overhead. Ayananda unclips her chain dart from her hip and ignites the steel wool. The crackling flame dangles in the air, swinging side to side like the ticking hands of a clock. Beau watches as Emmanuel places both hands on his walking stick and bows his head. His face twitches with intense concentration. Beau's eyes widen as he can see the fierce aura he sensed in the man erupt again from his body like a raging bonfire. The energetic flames quickly condense into a thin, pulsating field around his frame. Izak reloads the fuel canisters of his makeshift jet pack, casting aside the emptied ones onto the ground. A cigarette quickly returns to his lips. Ayananda reflexively lifts the end of her dart to his face so he can light it. The two stand together, completely in sync and ready to face Mune's reinforcements and whatever else may come their way. Jeeven stands stoic and motionless, giving no reason to think he needs any further preparation.

Beau lets out a heavy sigh and takes a look at his hands as he turns his palms up towards his face. He imagines the blood from the earlier guards dripping off his fingertips, allowing Izak's words to pour through his mind. He clenches his fingers into tight fists before returning his gaze to the room in front of him. The spiral stairwell is flanked by bright purple and green accented walls. They are lined with elaborate paintings hung in intricately carved gold frames placed in-between each window. Each frame holds a portrait of the same mustached man that Beau assumes to be the fated Mune. His pudgy face covers every wall, greeting the uninvited guests with his smug, buck-toothed smile. Multiple statues of the same man rest upon the polished marble floor. The glossy stone glistens from underneath the scattered remains of the decimated front door. Beau notices his eye gives an involuntary twitch at the sight of such exuberant and excessive flair. The ornate stair railing starts to rattle under the force of the incoming guards, breaking Beau's contemplative processing. He takes another deep breath to clear his mind.

"This is it," Izak says as he lifts his weapon to face the stairwell. "And remember, Baldy," he says without turning his head, "if you start to have thoughts of showing mercy, the only way that looks now is to give them a quick death."

"I know," Beau says. "As much as I don't want to admit it, this isn't my first time on a battlefield."

"Good," Izak says as he cocks his weapon into firing position. Beau continues to try and steady his heart rate with deep circulating breaths as the stampeding march of leather boots progressively rings louder in his ears. He looks up in-between breath cycles as the stairwell starts to quiver under the pressure building from above. The rattling of guns now accompanies the symphony of footsteps. Soon, the tips of the men's shiny boots round the bend and make their collective appearance. The guards take center stage, coming to a halt within the confines of the stairs leaving about ten steps between them and the first floor. They stand at attention, their fully loaded firearms placed across their purple and green uniformed chests. The men look frightened. Their faces quiver, struggling to front a fearsome and formidable presence.

It's anyone's speculation as to how far up the stairs the men stand ready to defend. A man bearing gold-pleated shoulder pads pushes his way into view. His face strikes a more composed awareness of his duty and purpose.

"This is your first and only warning," he says before initiating a dramatic pause. A smile blossoms upon his face as he soaks in the silent tension building in the room. Unfortunately for him, the tension he feels comes from within his own terrified men. "Drop your weapons and surrender. You are clearly outnumbered. If you can do that, I can guarantee you will make it out of this situation alive." The gold-shouldered general appears very pleased with his display of firepower and assumed authority. He eagerly awaits the acceptance of the Marionettes surrender.

"I bestow upon you the same condition," Jeeven says, his face remaining as stone cold as the plates scattered over his body. "Do not pretend you did not see the departure of all your earlier brethren from a single shot," Jeeven continues. "That was our warning. Do not be fooled by our small numbers. There is no need for you to lay down any more of your lives for a cause that does not concern you. Our fight is with Mune. Just tell us where he is, and we will leave you in peace."

"This is pointless, Jeeves," Izak whispers in the silence that follows Jeeven's speech. Jeeven produces a deep growl from within his throat that leads Izak to let go of any further rationalization. The general snarls so profoundly the ripples of pampered flesh upon his face start to resemble more of a shriveled raisin than a human.

"Absurd!" the general finally retorts. "We will never back down to the likes of you rebellious Shakers. You're Resistance is just a thorn in the side of progress! The world will be restored back to her earlier glory, and we choose to stand on the right side of history! You cannot scare us! Am I right, men?!" he bellows to his plethora of guards.

"Aye!" they respond, as if the switch has been flipped for their pre-recorded answer.

"Told you," Izak mutters under his breath. "The sheep would rather be herded off a cliff than to think for themselves."

"This is coming from the man who brought flowers for the sheep he knew he intended to slaughter?" Beau fires back, unable to withhold his flair of judgment.

"Excuse me?" Izak says with his head cocked back.

"Maybe I did get you all wrong after all. I thought you would have more compassion for the people still lost in this maze," Beau says with disgust in his throat. "I thought you knew what you were getting yourself into! You seem to know nothing about battle, after all. Don't get it twisted! They came here to kill us!! So, what are you even talking about, Baldy? I obviously don't *want* to kill them, but they are leaving us no other choice! It's fight or die, don't you see? I told you not to go soft on us!"

"How are you any different?!" Beau rebuttals, his voice quivering from his reflexive anger. "There are many layers to compassion, you fool, and hypocrisy is not one of them! I understand the need for sacrifice and even death! What is the point of even winning a battle like this if you have lost the heart for why you fight?" A guard upon the stairs takes a large, audible gulp as he soaks in the unusual conversation taking place in front of him.

"How dare you question my integrity! And to think I opened up to you!" Izak says, turning his gun towards Beau. A deep scowl strikes across his face. "Don't even pretend to know what we have been through, what we sacrifice our lives for every day!"

"Is it not all for a better future?" Beau says with his hand reflexively resting over his heart. "Is it not for those who have already sacrificed themselves to pave the way? And what's the point in looking down at those still lost, trapped in the reality you are trying to change? Do you not also fight for them? Or do you just fight for yourself?" Beau says, staring deep into the eyes of the mad gunslinger. Izak's growing rage has taken ahold of his voluntary responses, inhibiting his ability to forge the right words to defend himself. Only his smoking gun is presented to speak for him.

"Maybe I don't know why you fight," Beau continues, following a heavy exhale, "but I know I came here to help rescue Sophia despite your reluctance to factor her into your equation! If we end up toppling a tyrant in the process, so be it, but the world is full of them! What happens if we survive this, and you keep overthrowing tyrants with your raw sense of justice? What if you succeed, ending their reign of corruption one by one? Change is difficult. What is keeping those who survive from hating you, hating those like you or hating the process of the future that is being built? My God, man, without compassion in times like this, what makes you any different than the oppressors you fight to overthrow?" Jeeven's attention is drawn to the heated debate to his left. He turns his head, removing his fixed gaze upon the rows of guards that have come to execute him. He looks sincerely at the two men quarreling, feeling the need to interject his own thoughts into the debate.

Unfortunately, the opportunity to take advantage of the momentary distraction is too much to pass up. A premature shot is cast at the stationary giant despite no order being called. It cuts through the air like a sharpened blade before striking the center of Jeeven's chest. The sharp sound of the bullet striking his metal breast plate resonates ominously before falling to the ground. The room descends into silence as everyone watches the dented bullet roll around on the floor at Jeeven's feet. A deep sigh of disappointment fills the giant's chest as he looks down at the hole in his shirt then slowly back up into the eyes of the guard who shot him. The guard takes a step back, his legs quivering with fear and regret.

It's too late, Beau thinks to himself, his fixation on Izak's resolve shifts to the discharged tension now permeating the room.

"I never said to fire! Ugh! You worthless lot could hardly figure out how to hold the damn weapon in practice! I'm surprised any of you know how to pull the trigger!"

"See?! I told you!" Izak blurts out like a newly appointed bingo winner.

"Whatever! There is no turning back!" cries the gold-shouldered general from within the herd. "They had their chance! Fire in all directions! Maybe you'll hit something that way!" A fury of bullets comes pouring from the stairwell flying in every angle possible towards Beau and the Marionettes. Evasive maneuvers are triggered like a born reflex. Beau and Ayananda rush to the far edges of the room, just out of reach of the rifle fire. Making his own mad dash, Izak's legs fire like a coiled springboard catapulting his body high into the air. His parachute is quickly deployed and dangles behind him. It hangs in the air, waiting to catch the rising heat from his ignited fuel canisters.

Beau takes a moment while protected by the guard's blind spot to study the Marionettes in action. Izak quickly returns fire, leveling the first few rows of Mune's men before they could even register his airborne assent. Ayananda, with her flaming dart in full swing, snakes her weapon around her body like a swirling shield. Those without guns storm off the stairwell with swords drawn, ready to take down the deceptively dangerous woman.

As the men get closer, Ayananda makes dramatic angular maneuvers with her chain. She flings the head of the dart high into the air, then rips it down and wraps it back around her waist. She twirls upon the floor, becoming one with her weapon. She flings the chain off her waist towards the men, pulling it back right before it would strike the first man in the chest. Around and around, she twirls, never revealing where she will swing her chain next. Her movements become hypnotic, drawing the guard's attention to her weapon and away from her. Lured in like possessed zombies, she picks them off one by one. As the guards are forced to keep stepping over their fallen brethren, the spell begins to break. With regained focus, they start their assault once again.

"Get her!" an eager guard yells to his comrades. As if anticipating their next moves, Ayananda launches the deadly weapon into the ceiling directly above them. The uniformed men reluctantly look up, wondering what plot has just been initiated. Just as the flaming head of the chain carefully cuts through the ceiling, she recalls the weapon back into hypnotic twirl around her body. Large fissures ripple across the once-pristine mural work along the ceiling. The weight of the awaiting guards above proves to be too much for the damaged structural integrity to support. In a flash, the room becomes filled with dust, debris, broken support beams, and more frantic bullets discharging from the sea of unexpected falling guards.

Shots from the first level stairwell continue to fly in all directions, despite the obscured view from Ayananda's evasive smoke screen. Jeeven and Emmanuel remain standing in their previous positions, unfazed by the chaos. Rogue bullets bounce effortlessly off Jeeven's multitude of protective metal plates. His gridlocked stance gives no registry of urgency. Emmanuel on the other hand, appears transfixed in a personal dance with the plethora of projectiles hurling at him. Beau squints his eyes, focusing all his attention on this bizarre reaction to their situation. A field of energy extends roughly ten feet in all directions from the warrior's body, swirling and vibrating with exuberant tenacity. Beau watches closely as Emmanuel waits for the very moment a bullet enters his extended bio-field before contorting his body to avoid the projectile. Even when more than one bullet enters his field of perception, Emmanuel quickly calculates the additional danger. Beau's eyes widen as he is convinced, for a brief moment, he caught a slight smile emerge from the cold and emotionless Marionette.

"Incredible," Beau utters to himself, overwhelmed with the profound mastery the man displays with his life aura. "There are so many amazing people in this world… so much still to learn." Suddenly, a loud concussive *crash* is heard high above. The sound causes the guards on the stairs to momentarily pause their frantic firing. An eerie silence ripples within the wake of warfare. Even the guards appear confused with what just happened. The crashing sound returns, faint and distant at first. However, the compounding crashing can be heard breaking through each floor of the castle, growing louder and louder. The sonic anomaly hastens its descent with each reciprocal crash, quickly approaching the ground floor. The men on the stairwell grow frantic, breaking formation with their own self-perseveration as priority. Just as the dust starts to settle, another plume of dust showers the room as the plummeting anomaly finally falls right on top of the guards defending the stairwell.

A sea of screams and moaning emanates from the blindsided guards. Almost all Mune's forces have been crushed by the unforeseen tragedy.

What was once a grand stairwell has transitioned to a hollowed-out graveyard. Beau looks on in horror as a silhouette of a fallen guard tries to crawl out of the fresh crater. His hand reaches out of the plume of dust and debris, revealing his bloodied and disfigured appearance. Despite his fading cling to life, he desperately reaches for a way out of his unfortunate fate. As he claws his way to safety, a dark swaying shadow rears out of the thick veil of dust behind him.

The guard appears to have no awareness of the mysterious entity, as all his focus remains dedicated to escaping the unforgiving battleground. The shadow gives way to the contours of a tall and slender human silhouette. The arms of the humanoid figure rise and erect what looks like a shark fin atop its head. The figure continues to move casually out of the crater, swaying side to side like the predatory fish Beau was imagining. The guard on the ground has contracted a premature smile on his face, certain he has moved out of danger's way. Suddenly, a swift polished shoe extends from the swaying shadow and out of the veil of dust. The shoe is thrust unexpectedly, yet intently right into the retreating guards back.

"A-a-a-ahhhhh!" The crushing and splintering sound of bone echoes throughout the battlefield. The guard's cries of agony do nothing to stop the continued penetration of the shoe deeper into his spine. The shadowy figure quickly expunges all life that clung so desperately to the guard's physical form. With a flick of the shadowy figure's ankle, it flings the lifeless body off the tread of its prized footwear.

"This is bad…" Beau can hear Izak mumble above him, in-between bursts of gas from his reversed parachute. Before another thought can be processed, the dust settles and gives the full reveal of the unexpected guest. A thin-framed man dressed in a well-tailored suit now stands arrogantly before them. He dons a pair of thick sunglasses and a slicked-back mohawk that Beau imagined to be a shark fin. His white necktie contrasts the otherwise uniform color of his wardrobe. A black lightning bolt skull design on the tie is displayed proudly upon his chest. The man takes another step out of the crater and to Beau's surprise, causes Jeeven to take an unexpected step back. The once stoic and statue-esque giant now fumbles with a look of uncertainty and panic. His eyes bulge as they soak in the sight of the sharply dressed man. Choking and intoxicating waves of cold fear permeates from his dilated pours. The suffocating emotions quickly flood and infect the whole room.

"So, we finally get to meet!" the Warden speaks, his voice boisterous and full of cynical vigor. "The remaining essence of Tiger's Resistance! Or, should I say, *Sophia's* Resistance now? I can't believe ol' Mune was going to make me wait for these pawns to have shooting practice before I got to make your acquaintance! How silly, don't you think?" he asks Jeeven, who stares at him with a scowl. "I think you all should be very offended. I know I would! To think Mune actually thought these lowly men of hire could even stand a chance at scratching you special specimens! But! Not to worry! As soon as I heard you had arrived, I had to come greet you myself, because I, unlike my tacky overseer, have an appreciation for the finer things in life!" He pauses with arms extended, anticipating a pleasant reaction from his crowd. Everyone just stares at the strange man, afraid to make a single move. He gives a reluctant shrug at the dismissive silence and decides to continue. "Now, with that said, if I had my way, I would take you all on a welcoming trip to the Ward right now! Bypass all this unnecessary riff raff and lead you right to the real party! I would show you off as the honorary guests you would be, then we could take a deeper look at just how special you all are! But… ah… but, but, but, you see," he says, waving his finger dramatically, "free will is not one of my strong suits! Mr. Mune made it very clear he wanted, oh, how did he put it, 'every last one of those blasphemous Resistance abominations brutally destroyed!' So, as you see, my hands, and your fate have been sealed." He lifts his hands up in a helpless gesture, rising to meet his already shrugged shoulders. "No hard feelings, right?"

"Izak, Ayananda, Emmanuel! Run! Now!" Jeeven screams at the top of his lungs. The bellow from deep within his core rattles through the remaining contours of the room, causing the fallen rubble to dance upon the ground. The Marionettes scatter at once in different directions. Izak looks at the window to his left and makes a skyward dive into the welcoming exit. Emmanuel dips behind the bellowing giant and sprints to the obliterated front door. Ayananda hesitates, stumbling for just a split second. It was just long enough to capture the attention of the Warden. Realizing the shift, Jeeven lets out another bellowing cry, this time evoking the shattering declaration of war, "Raaaahhhhhh!" Following his declaration comes a full stampede towards the coy Warden. Heavy feet pound into the already excoriated floor, leaving cratered footprints in his hasteful wake. The Warden readjusts his focus and stares down the raging juggernaut.

The giant's grisly grasp latches onto the Warden and runs him right through the adjacent wall. The other Marionettes continue their maneuvers to safer ground. Ayananda looks back with tears in her eyes as Jeeven's sacrifice resonates heavily in her heart.

"Don't die, you big lug!" she cries out in-between sobs as Jeeven pours all his focus in restraining their cocky adversary. Jeeven studies the Warden, who is pressed deep into the rocky mountain cliff directly behind the walls of Mune's castle.

"That was quite a maneuver!" the Warden says with complementary jest. "As to be expected from a Kopala warrior! But I must ask, do you think your strength alone will *ever* be enough?" His words strike a quiver of doubt in Jeeven's grasp. As the giant's mind swirls with contemplation, the Warden's limbs start to slither and wobble like an electric eel.

"Let's see what the runaway man from Kopala can do about this!" the Warden says playfully as his elongated limbs erupt from his torso. They stretch and slither through the air towards Jeeven's retreating companions.

"Damn sorcery!" Jeeven cries out, powerless to defend the unexpected attack. One by one, the extended limbs sail through the air, aiming to latch ahold of the dispersing Marionettes. One appendage soaring towards Izak flies right overhead Beau, who watches the air bound mercenary's attempt to out fly it. It is no contest. The Warden's arm reaches Izak right as he is about to exit the open window.

"I have to do something!" Beau cries as he leaves his hide out to intercept the trap. With his fingers clenched tightly, he leaps into the air, firing his fist at the unsuspecting snake arm. A sensation of satisfaction resonates through his body as he initially makes contact with the bizarre extension. However, just as he thinks his attack connected, he feels the Wardens arm begin to vibrate out of its initial state of matter. Within a flash, the once-solid arm dissolves into dust, causing Beau to crash into the ceiling from his own unrestricted momentum. The fazed arm quickly regroups its elusive molecules and secures its entanglement of Izak.

"Damn!" Beau blurts out as he falls back to the ground after his deflected assault. "These Wardens are no joke! I wonder if—" Beau's thoughts become distracted as he watches the Warden effortlessly faze through the very solid Jeeven much like he did his own fist. Regrouping his particles, the Warden reconstitutes himself back into his physical form. He floats above the ground, suspended by his extended appendages. The

Marionettes try desperately to break free of their imprisonment, but to no avail. Jeeven turns around and starts swinging madly at the Warden's seemingly defenseless position. Despite putting all his might into each strike, he manages to hit nothing but air. The giant digs deeper into his anger and fires an even stronger fury of punches. As he is fixated on swinging at the apparition of his once-physical adversary, the Warden slowly turns his head around to face his exasperated foe.

"Does it bother you that you cannot hit me? Maybe you will like this better," he says, indicating he has made some unseen change to his presentation. Jeeven rears up his next punch, oblivious to anything the Warden has said. He swings his fist with all his might, but this time is met with a shattering and concussive impact.

"Aaaahhhh!" Jeeven cries out in pain, cradling his pulsating fist. He stares down at his shattered hand in disbelief. His mangled fingers are crushed, like they just connected with a bed of diamonds.

"Was that any better?" the Warden asks, his coy smile returning to his face. "You seemed so frustrated swinging at air, I thought maybe you would like something more solid to swing at!" As the Warden appears distracted with Jeeven, Beau takes this time to study his molecular behavior.

"So he can fluctuate between different states of matter?" he thinks out loud. "This is bad. Real bad. God knows what else he is capable of. I wonder though, if he still exists in this plane of reality, he must still be governed by the Universal Laws!" he exclaims with a sense of hope. "I don't know how much energy I have left, but I have to give *it* a try." He lifts his hands into the air and gazes into his open palms before taking a deep breath. On his exhale he clenches his fingers tightly into a fist.

His breathing takes a deep cyclic pattern as he focuses intently on releasing something deep within his core. A swirling orb of energy begins emanating from within his bio-field. The field pulsates with each inhale and exhale Beau pushes through. The free-flowing force quickly condenses, narrowing its energetic focus on the ends of Beau's own appendages. His hands and feet start to glow with red and blue tinged orbs of light. His panting breaths remain cyclical while a bead of sweat slithers down his face. Looking up from his color-tinted hands, he sinks his sights into the motionless Warden. Bending his legs, he triggers a flicker of red light that completely fills the energetic orbs around his feet. In a flash, he repels off the ground with nearly twice the force of his previous leap. He reaches his fist up towards the extended arm that still traps Izak. Beau can feel the molecules of the arm start to dissipate like they did before, but this time, he's ready for it.

He opens his fist right as the arm fluctuates in-between states of matter. Just as the orb of light around his hand flashes blue, he latches his fingers securely onto the elusive arm. The molecules start to involuntarily scurry back to their physical state, right where his fingers lock down. He reaches up with his other hand and clenches the Warden's arm with all his might. With both hands securely locked into place, a flash of blue from his feet wrench him back to the ground with blistering speed. The Warden whips his head around, but it's too late. Beau brings the Warden's snake-like appendage down with him. Using the momentum granted by gravity, he hurls the Warden to the far side of the room. The impact startles the Warden just enough to loosen the grip on the imprisoned Marionettes. They waste no time scurrying back to their intended points of exit. Izak is first to escape out the window; he looks back at Beau and gives him a silent head nod of appreciation. Emmanuel flies out of the main door and makes an abrupt turn towards the side Izak flew out of. Beau watches as Ayananda tries to make the same maneuver out the main door, but the Warden has already regained his composure. A furrowed brow of anger now populates the once-boisterous foe. He now rushes to fling his snake arms back at the retreating Marionette.

Beau's feet flicker red right before he flings himself back into battle. He flies at rippling speed to intercept the Warden's strike. His narrowing field of vision warps the whole room into a blinding blur. Only the freakishly outstretched arms of the Warden populate his gaze. Ayananda looks back as the slithering hand has almost caught up to her. Accepting her fate, she turns and faces the approaching beast with her chain ready to attack. Beau seizes his opportunity and dives in-between Ayananda and the Warden at the last second. Right before contact is made, Beau's outstretched hands flash a deep red. The snake-hand reacts to Beau like hitting an electro-magnet and is immediately repelled up into what's left of the ceiling. The force of the impact also sends Beau flying into the adjacent wall. However, the chain charmer is spared for the moment. Ayananda hesitates once again to check on the status of her unexpected savior.

"Don't stop!" Beau yells from the rubble. "Run! Jeeven and I will hold this guy off!" Not knowing how to process the surprise moment of assistance, Ayananda struggles to respond. Anger and gratitude flood her vessel with conflicting currents of validity. She settles for a silent head nod before running to meet up with the others outside. Beau pushes aside the rubble created from his impact with the wall. His breathing remains cyclic but heavier than before. His hands and feet continue to flicker with orbs of blue and red light. He walks with heavy footing back into the battlefield. The Warden looks over to him with a curious smile as he retracts his arms and legs back into their regular human-like proportions. Jeeven, on the other hand, glances to Beau with a deep scowl of resentment that would better serve an enemy. The giant's glare goes unnoticed while Beau's gaze remains gridlocked with the Warden's. Beau circles the room, charting a course to join Jeeven at his side. The Warden produces no resistance to his movements.

"I must say," the Warden finally says, "I was not expecting that. Oh my, no, not at all! And how I do love surprises. You must tell me! Where did you learn such a useful trick?"

"I'm wondering the same thing," Jeeven grumbles unexpectedly. His tone is brash and condescending. Beau is shaken by the negative response from his supposed ally.

"Excuse me?" Beau asks, reluctant to divert any attention away from the still very dangerous adversary in front of them. "What is your deal, man? It's going to take working together if we have any shot at stopping this guy!" Beau pleads.

"More damn sorcery," he grunts, disregarding any direct line of communication.

"Sorcery?!" Beau blurts out, his focus wavering even more from the watchful Warden. "What? With what I just did? Are you kidding? That was *electromagnetism*. Everything carries an electrical field. I just manipulated the polarity of my bioelectric field to repel or attract our surroundings. Despite this guy being able to alter his physical make up, his molecules are still governed by bioelectrical properties. If anything, this is more science than sorcery. Not that it should matter at all!" Jeeven turns and fires a ferocious grimace at his reluctant companion. Beau can feel his control over his emotions slipping as he lets loose his boiling banter. "We have to get creative if we are ever going to land a hit on him! Were you seriously just going to keep swinging your oversized fists at him, hoping for a different outcome?" "I don't need you or your damn magic," Jeeven says taking a step towards the Warden.

"That sounds insightful," the Warden says with a heavy serving of sarcasm.

"Right?!" Beau shouts, inadvertently agreeing with his aggressor. "Do I need to define the term insanity to you??"

"You are no better than this abomination," Jeeven proclaims, ignoring the collective call for reflection.

"Oh my, my, my. I'm sure you didn't mean any offence by that," The Warden responds playfully.

"You two are what is wrong with the world these days. Damn magic and sorcery tearing apart the very fabric of our society! I will show you. I'll show both of you what the epitome of true strength can do in the face of your magic tricks," Jeeven says as he lifts his hand to grab the metal plate resting upon his head. He lifts it up off the metal plugs on his skull that held the plate in place. Jeeven holds the headgear in his hand, ready to transition the piece into a weapon. "It's those who have dedicated themselves to physical mastery that will reign victorious in this world. Your cheating magical ways won't last."

"I can't believe you've gotten this far with such ignorance!" Beau calls out to the giant. "You really think you can just bulldoze your way through this life relying on your brute strength alone? Wake up, man!! Hell, your own crewmembers harbor exceptional mastery of energetic manipulation! Can you not even see that?" Beau hangs his head, shaking it with a sense of defeat. "Are all of you Marionettes this self-centered?! I can't wait to be done with you damn imposters when this is all over."

"I think you are overestimating yourself, magic man," the Warden taunts.

"Shi—" Before Beau can recoup from his relaxed focus, an extended hand from the Warden comes flying at his chest. Beau recovers enough to place the palms of his hands where the Warden's fist is lined to make contact. A flash of red light flickers before the Warden sends Beau flying back to the other side of the room. Beau's body skips along the tattered floor, his consciousness struggling to remain tethered to his physical body. The Warden's extending arm remains in hot pursuit. Beau turns to face the strike head on, hoping his repelling electrical charges will soften the next strike. Shrouded in a cloud of dust and rubble, Beau and the extending snake arm collide with unrelenting force into the awaiting wall.

$$\infty$$

"Good riddance," Jeeven grumbles.

"Funny, I thought that would have been my line," the Warden says mockingly as he slowly retracts his arm. He strikes a sinister smile and walks ominously towards the stationary giant. His gait sways his shoulders back and forth, displaying unyielding confidence.

"Now it's your turn," Jeeven continues, his rage amplified by his opponent's carefree demeanor. The giant takes a heavy step forward and hurls his headpiece at the Warden at break-neck speed. The Warden easily phases through it, but watches as the point of impact leaves an unexpected ripple in his otherwise smooth material transition. The sound of the metal headpiece impaling the castle wall rips through the room like a symphonic demolition ensemble. The headpiece not only goes through the Warden with ease, but the fortified metal castle as well, creating a devastating crater in its wake. Slowly giving way to the call of gravity, the sheer weight of the seemingly insignificant item crashes into the ground upon its landing.

Jeeven leaves no room for hesitation. He continues his advancement, aggressively disposing the metal plating from his body one by one. He fires each piece like an erupting cannon right at his adversary's fluctuating position. With the weight being lifted with each removed piece, each toss becomes faster and stronger than the last. The Warden continues his evasive molecular phasing, but realizes his molecules struggle a little bit more each time to fully evade the impressive barrage.

Jeeven picks up the final plate from his left leg and tosses it gently up and down like a pebble in his hand. He bounces freely off the ground, shifting his body back and forth like a buoyant boxer. His large frame dances deceptively like a leaf caught in the wind. His bare skin is on full display, showing off his enormous and impressively carved muscles that hold his body together. The flawless lines and contours are contrasted by the plethora of metal plugs that once held all the discarded metal plating. His anger surges once again as he grips the metal plate from his leg so strongly, he indents his precious and protective armor. Sensing no added danger, the Warden gives a taunting wink.

"Take this!" Jeeven yells as he hurls his final projectile at the Warden. Jeeven's aim is spot on. In a blink of an eye, the plate strikes right in the center of the Warden's torso. As before, the Warden phases his material body out of the way of the projectile, leaving the plate to meet the same fate as the others. This time, however, it didn't remove the smirk still resting on Jeeven's face.

"What is so funny?" the Warden asks, confused. "You are all out of ammo!"

"Maybe," Jeeven chuckles, "but you just showed me your sorcery is not invincible."

"What are you talking about?! I… oh…" the Warden gazes down to his torso and notices an unexpected tear in his suit.

"Don't get cocky now, so you tore—" the Warden is cut short as Jeeven blitzes his position, firing his fist abruptly into the contours of his still very physical face. The speed at which Jeeven launches his attacks repeatedly breaks the sound barrier with each machine-gun strike. Concussive explosions erupt throughout the castle walls as fists fly in rapid fire all around the defensive Warden. He tries to manipulate his molecules to dodge, but Jeeven keeps moving at increasing speeds. The Warden quickly finds himself unable to accurately predict where the next strike will come from. Jeeven continues his unrelenting assault, which is proving to have a near fifty-fifty accuracy. Beau watches from the rubble as the enormous giant darts around the room like one of Izak's ricocheting bullets. The relinquished weight the man was always carrying has given him access to unprecedented speed and agility. The Warden continues to phase in and out of physical materialism but shows no progression of regaining the upper hand over Jeeven's firework frenzy. Just when Jeeven's speed appears to be an advantageous strategy, the tables turn once again.

"That's enough!" the Warden cries. He puffs out his chest and takes Jeeven's next attack straight on. The Warden is surprisingly knocked back slightly, but his impenetrable form proves to be just as damaging as it was before. Jeeven takes a step back and nurses his re-crushed hand.

"Damn you," he says while trying to shake off the damage.

"Don't hate me, hate the game, bucko," the Warden replies with a cocky flair. "What you call magic and despise so greatly, I happen to absolutely love! Makes the game so much more interesting!" He walks over to Jeeven with a sinister smirk back on his face. "You looked like you had fun for a minute there. And you even surprised me for a moment! The physical strength you pride yourself in isn't completely useless! You'll make a great adversary for my tailor," he remarks, followed by a slow, condescending clap. "But, unfortunately for you, even the extended limits of human strength won't be enough to turn this in your favor. So sorry." The Warden extends his arm, and it begins to wiggle again like that of a snake.

"I've seen this before," Jeeven remarks, still shaking off his injured hand. "It won't work again."

"We'll see," the Warden says passively as he is paying more attention to his other arm. Both arms now wiggle through the air, slowly extending their length until they fall upon the floor like discarded water hoses. They slither around the ground frantically as a bulge from the Warden's torso emerges out of each of his shoulders and flows into the palms of his writhing hands. The bulges merge with his hands and quickly morph into the head of a snake. Jeeven cocks his head to the side as he tries to make sense of his adversary's newest magic trick. Each arm now bares a head of their own. They slow their movements and start to rise from the ground like charmed cobras. They weave back and forth as the contours of their faces become increasingly more detailed. Eyes, a mouth, and tongue become etched into the once humanoid appendages. The mouths echo one another, each opening to cartoonish proportions displaying rows and rows of razor-sharp teeth. They repeatedly bite down, making a clanking noise like that of clashing sword blades. The dueling snakes start to mirror their host's facial expression. Three snarling smirking faces now taunt Jeeven to make his next move.

"I will not let your trickery get the better of me. I am still faster than you!" he cries out.

"Let's test that," the Warden remarks calmly. His two snakes soar off to meet Jeeven who immediately takes to the defense. He bounds all around the room evading and swinging but strikes nothing but air. Taking every solid surface as a springboard, Jeeven flies through every inch of the room with impressive grace and tenacity. The snake arms soar after him, making sure to take advantage of any minute misstep. The quickly crumbling room makes coming into contact with any apparent solid ground a gamble.

Jeeven narrowly avoids a double helix snake attack by diving in-between the cycling heads right as they close down on top of him. His momentum carries him to the far side of the room, where he plants his foot on a compromised wall. He watches with sheer agony as the dissolving platform gives way ever so slightly. The momentary shift of stability acts like a drop of blood in a pool of sharks. The chomping mouths of the snake arms resonate through the room as they race back to his location, coming just inches from severing one of the giant's burly limbs.

"How long can you keep up such a feat?" the Warden comments on Jeeven's evasive maneuvers. "I'm sure that takes quite a toll on your still *very* human body." Suddenly, Beau can be heard picking himself out of his pile of rubble as the prophetic words of the Warden inspire him back into action.

∞

"Ugh," Beau mumbles, rubbing the swollen areas on his head. "How long *can* the big guy keep this up?" He watches the impressive, yet exhaustive maneuvering of the giant with a heavy heart. "I need to be ready to make my move when the timing is right. I can't let this meathead meet his maker today." He watches as Jeeven continues his dance with the dueling snakes. The Warden is clearly at a stamina advantage as Jeeven's prized speed notably begins to fade.

"Damn!" Jeeven blurts out, as the skin of the snake grinds against one of his legs like it was made from layers of razor blades. The blood of the giant begins to pour freely upon the ground.

This is it, Beau thinks as he watches intently. Jeeven skirts around the room, avoiding the next few attacks but is quickly met with the blunt head-butt of the left snake. The concussive force sends him hurdling into the same wall Beau was cast aside to, but this time the Warden is not letting up. The right snake comes in for the finishing blow, snarling and hissing through the air towards its prey.

"Now!" Beau yells as the fading orb of light around his hands erupts into a deep red hue. Immediately affected by the repelling force, the bulleting strike is diverted slightly, crashing into the wall next to him. The momentum from the Warden's attack, however, does not stop. Beau flips the charge in his hands to blue, eager to take the offence. Trapped within the pull of Beau's now attractive electrical field, the snake arm circles back into the room, right into Beau's grasp. The Warden pulls back on the diverted snake, forcing Beau's feet to be ripped off the ground. Unable to overpower the recall, he lets go of the snake arm. A quick flash of polarized energy brings a blue glow to his feet, anchoring his molecular makeup back to the ground below. Beau's knees buckle under the pressure as he struggles to endure the force of his own maneuver..

The newly freed snake returns to take advantage of the moment of vulnerability. It opens its razor-toothed jaw, ready to consume the seemingly careless warrior. Just as the beast is inches from its target, Beau flips the polarized charge of his hands to red. Angling his now repulsive charge, he sends the snakehead hurling back to his owner. The orbs around his hands glow brightly as they struggle to overpower the slithering beast. The Warden is reluctantly forced to dodge his own attack.

"Good, but not good enough!" the Warden taunts as his left snake arm is already in full speed towards Beau's fixed location.

"You're becoming predictable!" Beau calls out proudly as he quickly flips the charge of his feet to repel, narrowly avoiding the deadly snake attack. Beau soars through the air as both snake arms crash into adjacent walls. He gently brings himself back in contact with the ground right in front of the crater Jeeven is in the midst of crawling out of. Beau stands in a fighting stance, ready to serve as a shield for his defenseless companion. His cyclic breathing has transitioned to cyclic panting. His bodily fatigue is clearly on display, alongside the copious amounts of dust-imbued sweat pouring down his face. Disregarding the physical toll just paid, the energetic orbs around his hands and feet glow as brightly as ever. Jeeven is surprised to emerge and see the man he just cast aside as a heretic standing guard, protecting his vulnerable state.

"Why are you still helping me?" Jeeven asks as his mind races with empty conclusions.

"Neither one of us truly knew what we were going to be dealing with when we partnered up," he says in-between his heavy breaths. "I'm a magician and you are a bigot. So what?" Beau responds firmly, giving Jeeven no time to retort. "We got into this mess together and we are going to get out of it together. Need I remind you, we have a lot of lives at stake here? I don't know about you, but that's more important than all this crap we are squabbling about. After this is over, then we can have the luxury of going our own ways." Jeeven studies Beau's words within a heavy sigh.

"You are right," he eventually responds. "But mark my words, there is no way in hell I'm going to be buried next to a damn magician today."

"Good," Beau says with a playful smile. "I would hate to have to put you both in the ground."

"Cocky brat," Jeeven remarks as he takes a step forward to stand side-by-side with Beau. Together, the two of them narrow their sights upon their awaiting adversary.

CHAPTER: 31

Into The White Light

Boot-strapped footsteps echo throughout the long, dark corridor. Each step is so precise and meticulous; the guard's march could double as a momentary metronome. Brahm's flaccid flesh drags upon the dusty floor, filling the sonic spaces between each carefully placed step. The normally quiet corridor now shakes with restlessness, forced to echo the not-so-distant drum of turmoil below. It's dimly lit walls quiver under the structural stress. Glass from the kerosene lanterns rattle around in their rod-iron frames, sounding like an anxious waiter cradling a teacup and saucer. Dust and soot shake free from the ceiling, raining down upon the lone guard and his prisoner like a snowy night. None of the commotion proves to be a worthy distraction for the guard. He maintains his prideful pace in the midst of the rumbling symphony of chaos. His mind remains set on delivering his prisoner on schedule.

Love… Brahm's mental musings ruminate on this lingering concept. *It's all bound together with love you say?* An involuntary cough is triggered from his lungs. The taste of iron fills his mouth, striking the urge to spit. He looks down to see a speck of blood from his battered gums splatter upon the ground he scrapes against. He's not given long to contemplate his mark as he is quickly dragged away by the marching metronome. He dives ever further into his reluctant path of reckoning. "Humph," he grunts. "Where is the love in this?"

The precision march finally comes to a halt. The guard pounds his fist against the anticipatory metal door. A latch on the door springs open with a dramatic *clack*. The space that opens is just wide enough for a bulging eye to eagerly poke its way through. The eye looks up and down at what has been presented for its viewing pleasure. An approving hum can be heard through the thick metal door before the latch is closed shut once again.

A plethora of bolts and chains can be heard sliding around the right side of the door, starting at the top and working its way to the bottom. A final *clunk* is heard as the remaining bolt faceting the door becomes unlocked. Deep creaking fills the corridor as the impressive door swings open to welcome Brahm and his guard.

A familiar man stands in the doorway, ringing his hands together, putting minimal effort into restraining his overflowing excitement. He takes a step to the side, ushering the guard into his prideful chambers. The guard returns to his slow and precise pace as he makes his entry. The man waves his arms in hasteful dramatic circles with the assumedly bizarre expectation that it will expedite the delivery of his package. The guard pays no attention to the man's eccentric behavior but turns to him in order to receive direction.

"Captain Claude, sir, where would you like me to place the prisoner?" the guard asks with tone and inflection that mirror his monotonous marching.

"The chair! The chair!" Claude chants, "How many other places could you possibly put him anyway? Put him in the chair and fasten the locks then leave already; I've got work to do!" he says sinisterly. The guard returns to his march, following Claude's instructions like a well-crafted robot. Brahm's head continues to hang low, lost in depressed apathy. To even give a scowl to his awaiting torturer seems to demand too much energy to summon. Claude watches intently at the perfect execution of his demands; each limb of Brahm is placed in a steal cuff that adheres to his torture chair, but he still swells with anxiety and restlessness. "Hurry up!" he cries out, unable to contain himself. The guard gives a disapproving glance at Claude as he secures the final latch.

"Is there anything else I can assist you with, sir?" the guard remarks flatly.

"No! I mean, no thank you. That is all. Now please, leave me to my work," Claude says, his hands returning to ringing an imaginary dishcloth.

Claude stares down at his delivered prey and pays no further attention to the guard exiting his torture palace. Even the loud slamming of the closing door does little to shake Claude's devilish attention. The sound does prompt Brahm to lift his head and scan his new surroundings. He now resides in a stone room, polished clean with the smell of recent disinfectant still tainting the air. As he rotates his head to the right, he registers the multitude of various weapons and tools hanging on the wall. He gives an apathetic shrug as he can only assume they are there to assist in his torture. As his head continues its full trajectory to the right, Claude finally comes into full view. His toothy grin shines almost as bright as the kerosene spotlight that quivers above them.

"You," Brahm says with no real intention of sparking conversation. He immediately regrets his involuntary decision to speak.

"Yes! Me!" Claude says gleefully. He inches closer while shadows dance around his contorted face from the swinging lantern. The light sways side to side, moved by the destructive rumble reverberating from below. The flame in the lantern reflects off Claude's glossy eyes, oscillating in and out of his vengeful orifices. The metronome-like movements trigger Brahm to prepare for the start of a new symphony of suffering. In this brief moment, Brahm contemplates protesting his reality. *Call for help? Spout a discouraging word? Make an attempt to break free? No.* The fire flees from his chest just as Claude's burns even brighter. His head falls low while Claude's smile stretches even higher into his cheeks.

"Why the long face?" Claude asks. "I thought you would be glad to see me!" Silence fills the spaces between the shockwave rumbling. The lack of engagement aggravates Claude, but he tries his best to stay in character.

"You know, I like it when things come full circle," Claude continues, despite his disengaged audience. "I feel like this is the epitome of justice, you know? The universe is punishing you for your acts of defiance and I feel so fortunate to be the vehicle to provide such justice! Poetic, don't you think?" Silence. Blank hollow silence. The sound of death taking ahold of a person would ring louder than the apathetic atmosphere surrounding Brahm. Claude's lip starts to quiver. "I know… I know… you must feel horrible for everything you have done. I would be sulking too if I were you. Everyone's candlewick has got to run out at some point! Luckily, mine is burning bright! Maybe we can ask some of these tools along the wall to assist our conversation… get our spark rekindled, what do you say?"

Claude heads over to the wall of torture weapons. He runs his fingers along the various devices as if he is feeling which one wants to be called to action first. The hairs on his arm start to stand on end when they glide over the leather whip. His whole body quivers as he imagines how much damage such a device can provide. Even the tip is lined with small spikes, just to add an additional sting at the end. Perfect. "Ahhh… what about this one, old friend? Does it speak to you like it speaks to me?" Claude asks as he carefully transitions the weapon into his eager hands. He practices flicking the whip in the air as he turns his head to face Brahm's fixed location. The unexpecting air particles become tossed away as the tip of the whip violently displaces them. A splintering crack accosts the duo's delicate eardrums. "Speaking loud and clear!"

"Just get it over with," Brahm spontaneously interjects, dissolving Claude's failing attempts at emotional torture. Claude grips the end of the whip with both hands, ringing the weapon so tightly one could imagine a drop of water emerging from the constricting tension. A deep breath fills his lungs as he forces himself to regain his composure. "No matter," he says out loud, dusting off his emotional flare up. "This is what I've been dreaming about anyway. I'll make you beg for mercy one way or another." Brahm looks up in apathetic anticipation. His breath is shallow but even. His hat hangs by a thread around his neck, leaving his hair to cascade over his face. His hollow eyes open wide, looking intently at Claude. Their once-enigmatic blue and green beacons of light have transitioned to monochromatic gray tones of their once previous vigor. Claude looks into Brahm's defeated eyes and raises the whip above his head.

"Do you have anything you would like to say before we get started?" Claude asks, assuming further silence to permeate.

"Love…" Brahm mutters, his mind still wrapped around Mono's last words to him.

"What did you say?" Claude remarks as he finds himself taking a step back.

"Love, haha," Brahm repeats. "Do you… love me?"

"You sick freak," Claude retorts. "Far from it! I despise every last morsel of your being! I'm going to show you right here and right now how much I hate everything about you!"

"Ah… that's what I thought," he says with a dismal smile appearing on his face. "All right, that's all I needed. Carry on."

"Do you not take anything seriously?!" Claude roars.

"I'm beginning to wonder that myself."

"I'm going to make you regret everything!" Claude cries with emotional wailing.

"Way ahead of y—" The whip finally comes into contact with its long-awaited victim, cutting into his flesh like a hot knife through cheese.

"Your decision to come to this island!" Another strike comes reigning down, ripping apart Brahm's epidermal dam. Blood begins to flow like a meandering river. "Insulting me!" The next attack ignites all his pain receptors to light up like a raging forest fire. "Even… being born!" As Claude enters a malicious frenzy, Brahm watches the carnage erupting along his physical being from a disassociated vantage point. The sound of the whip starts to deafen, the rumbling of the building settles, and the swinging light fades out of focus. Brahm sinks further out of his body; still aware of the registry of physical pain, but it resembles too closely his emotional defeat. *How much pain can this body tolerate?* Brahm wonders, *my heart is already full of suffering. There isn't even room left to welcome this additional pain. Even if I survive this, there is no going back to who I was. There is no love. Not in this. Maybe there never was to begin with.* Brahm pauses his thoughts for a moment to watch Claude's next strike carefully. He watches the whip burrow into his flesh, crisscross another fresh wound before flying back, ready to return with fresh vengeance. He bears witness to the flames of pain shooting through his being as it flies into his mind and screams that danger remains. *Do something!* His neurons cry. *Do what?* He haphazardly responds. *What's the point? Let's just get this over with. I was finished before I entered this room. Let's hope this guy can really seal the deal.*

"Hey," Brahm calls out calmly, disrupting his aggressor's flow. Claude looks at his blood battered victim, his color drifting into a dull and lifeless gray. Brahm's voice registers no connection to the pain Claude assumed to impose. "So, I'm not sure how else to ask this," Brahm says as he ponders on the right words, "but… uh, I don't know, can you… hit me harder?"

"E-Excuse me?" Claude mumbles, his lower lip starting to quiver involuntarily.

"Yeah… yeah, I know it sounds weird, given the situation and all, but do you think you could… you know… try harder? I was hoping you could step it up a notch."

"How dare you! You… you…" Claude calms his irritation as he reminds himself there are plenty of tools to assist in his pursuits. "You know, you are right!" he says between exhaustive panting. "There is still so much more pain I was saving for you, but since you asked so nicely, I will reward you!"

"Cool," Brahm says flatly. Claude hangs up the blood-drenched whip and makes his next selection: a spiked club. He lifts the weapon, displaying some hesitation maneuvering the device due to its unexpected weight. Claude drags the weapon on the ground as he returns to his prisoner. With a smile of satisfaction, he lifts the weapon with a grunt of difficulty.

"This should do the trick, don't you think?"

"I hope so," Brahm responds. "Let's see what you got."

"Insolent prick!" Claude screams as he plows the heavy club straight into Brahms chest. The force knocks the buckles right off his overalls and dives deep into his flesh. A faint crunching noise can be heard from Brahm's compromised rib cage as it crumbles under the concussive blow. A gasp of air jets out of Brahm's mouth as Claude recalls the mighty weapon. Brahm's full awareness flows completely into his escaping breath. He observes his concussed diaphragm firing the residual breath of life out of his lungs. The breath travels through his throat and out of the limiting confines of his dismantled body. For a moment he feels free; free as the breath that is quickly becoming one with the surrounding air, dissolving its individuality into the collective atmosphere.

"Auuuhhhhaaa!" Brahm cries as his diaphragm reluctantly draws back another breath, gasping desperately to return life to his vessel. "Traitor," he says to his body. "I was almost there…" He spits a wad of blood onto the ground, a good sign of heavy internal bleeding. He looks up into Claude's eyes, this time with a glisten of hope shining through his otherwise hollow gaze.

"That was good!" Brahm says in-between gasps of air. "Real good. Phewww… I think you almost got it. How many more do you think you got in you?"

"You taunt me even while your body crumbles into oblivion?!" Claude shouts in rage. "I wasn't going to kill you! I'm not supposed to kill you! But damnit, I'm going to wipe that smug look off your face once and for all!"
"Bring it on!" Brahm yells back, begging to be put out of his own misery. "MAKE MY DAY!"

"Aaaahhh!" Claude yells as he puts all his strength into his swing of the mighty club. Tears reluctantly pour from his eyes as he appears to have imbued not just his strength, but all his unresolved feelings into his attack. A wake of his inner inadequacies trails behind the swift strike before every ounce of his being crashes cathartically into Brahm's face. Skull bones crack, consciousness fades, and emotions are finally released with a decisive and concussive strike.

Claude retracts his club and takes a step back to reassess his situation. His panting is labored and irregular. It takes all his strength to remain standing and not to let the weight of the club draw him to the floor. There is a feeling of lightness in his chest, a moment of emptied emotions that quickly starts to fill back up. "W-What have I done?" Claude says to himself as he looks onto Brahm's limp and lifeless vessel.

∞

Inside the boundaries of Brahm's body, he can feel the restrictive element of his being starting to lessen its grasp. The room grows uncharacteristically silent; the forest fire of pain has been reduced to smoldering ashes. The dread of being contained to this life lifts as he feels himself float gently out of his body. He glances at the swaying lantern that illuminates the room. Its dancing flame roars before his eyes. Growing with intensity, the flame turns blue then to a bright white. The illumination devours the lantern it resides in, taking on a unique form all its own. Brahm is drawn to the tantalizing glow. He experiences no resistance to his essence drifting closer and closer to the beckoning spectacle. He does, however, take a moment to look down at his body as he floats in-between the light and his physical shell. In this moment he feels he could return to his body if he wanted to.

"Why bother?" he says to himself, quickly shaking off the notion. "It's about time this suffering came to an end. Such a drag." With his thoughts solidified, he soars into the phosphorescent portal with arms held open, welcoming the assumed realm of relief that awaits him. His astral chest makes contact with the white light, allowing his ethereal essence to be fully consumed by the welcoming luminosity. *I can almost hear the angels calling my name,* Brahm thinks right before he is swallowed whole.

∞

"What … is … this?" Brahm remarks as he emerges on the other side. A realm with no horizon presents itself for him to soak in; it is unlike anything he has ever encountered. There is too much sensory information to take in all at once. Vast arrays of swirling color soar in all directions within the infinite black backdrop. Rays of white light crisscross the realm with no sign of an end or a beginning. Concepts of up and down are quickly dissolved as Brahm loses sense of all cardinal direction. The realm is densely populated by a plethora of humanoid-like creatures, all harboring the same rainbow palette of color to outline their outlandish and cartoonish appearances. The bizarre beings whiz around him like fast-paced intergalactic commuters on their way to a celestial nine-to-five.

At first, they don't seem to notice Brahm's presence, possibly because they are too busy to notice anything out of sorts. Brahm takes this moment to study the beings, watching them soar from some distant vantage point to another. *What are they doing?* Suddenly, as if that thought gave away his location, he notices the once-oblivious beings making sly glances out of the corners of their bubbly eyes. Unwilling to stop their travels, the beings only throw further disapproving and concerned glances at the floating soul. Brahm looks back to the illuminated spot he entered through, wondering if something has gone wrong. White light still shines behind him, but it is not how he remembered it. His single point of entry now shines as a part of the whole connected series of light threads that encompass the bizarre space. As he further studies this arrangement of light, he notices each thread tethered to other various threads. They all appear to be co-creating a web-like pattern that goes on forever. The web extends well beyond the three-dimensional world he emerged from. It soars in multi-dimensions of fluctuating fluid beauty, encapsulating and weaving together everything in sight.

The movements of the rainbow-beings start to come into clearer view. They appear to be emerging from one strand of web-light before flowing into another. "Is this…" Brahm wonders aloud, "… the web Mono was referring too?" Brahm looks on in stupefied wonder. "How have I never seen it like this? Surely I've been here before?" He floats next to his entry point on the web and places his hand on the thread of white light. He becomes overcome with warm feelings of love and acceptance. "Whoa… where was this a moment ago? Could have totally used some of it before I got here." To his surprise, a shadow emerges on the other side of the light, placing its hand upon the barrier that separates them. The shadow appears like a dark reflection in a mirror. "Yikes!" Brahm shouts, as he quickly drifts away. The shadow gives a childish wave as it watches Brahm float off in a flood of fear. Brahm turns around and notices he has carelessly drifted into the congested traffic flow of the surreal, multi-colored dimensional beings. They bump into him, pushing him back and forth, casting continued disapproving grunts and glares with each run-in.

"You're not supposed to be here!" he hears one say with a voice fit for a baritone rodeo clown. He watches the being float away, its head rotating like an animatronic owl. It waves its finger like a scolding mother as it scoots into a vanishing point along the web. Following suit, all the other surrounding beings raise their bubbly block fingers and wave them in the same disapproving fashion as they continue to soar past the troubled soul. Growing overwhelmed, Brahm desperately tries to get out of the flow of traffic but feels himself sinking further into the chaos.

"What is happening to me?" he asks himself in a panic. "Someone… anyone! Please! Help me!" He closes his eyes and balls himself into the fetal position, unable to fathom another strategy. He quickly realizes eyelids serve him no relief in this place. He is left to bear the full weight of the overwhelming emotional and sensory input. "I'm sorry… I'm sorry… I'm sorry…" he hears himself utter aloud, unsure as to what he is even apologizing for. Then, out of the corner of his eye, he notices a being coming towards him. With emotions already running high, Brahm is unsure how to react to such a sight. Unable to move, he tries his best to settle into his bizarre predicament. As the being gets closer, he struggles to make any sense of its outward appearance.

The being has an exaggerated head, but even calling it a head is a risky description. In the space that, at best, might be a head, exists what looks like makeshift facial features stacked on top of a bright yellow chin resembling a 1950's Cadillac bumper. The nose shines bright blue, slithering slightly like a baby eel. The eyes, if you can call them that, appear like car taillights, red in color with the pupils shining with a bright green glow. There is a spiky purple adornment on top of the eye-like features, making up what might be hair. The face is positioned on top of a very disproportionately small torso that harbors very tiny appendages. The leg-like features don oversized clown shoes that light up with each step. The light produced by each step harbors profound patterns of arrows, squares, and circles of various colors erupting in all directions. The concept of the being 'walking' also strikes him as odd, as there are no roads, streets, ground, or anything solid for that matter anywhere to be seen. The ruling on the concept of 'up' and 'down' is still debatable. Everything around him at first seemed separate, but as he watches the flow of light from the being's shoes, everything appears to be swimming into one big collective soup of color and light. Odd quickly becomes the new normal. The being finally stops its movements and looks at Brahm. What he thought was a chin flexes upward and pivots like a makeshift smile. *Maybe that is a mouth then?* Brahm ponders. *Wait… that definitely doesn't matter right now.*

"Who are you?" Brahm asks, "If that is even a concept here…"

"Do you not recognize me?" the being asks with a masculine tone, opening the Cadillac-bumper of a chin-mouth to speak. It stays open, allowing a slithering, oversized purple tongue to pop out of its contours. It hangs out of the being's head, dwarfing the size of its own torso. It wiggles around and almost appears to be waving at Brahm, existing as if its own separate being.

"Definitely… not," Brahm manages to say as he struggles to register anything as even remotely familiar.

"Well here, let me try this instead," the being says, but not through his bumper-chin mouth. No, that would be too easy. This time he speaks through the purple tongue, which spontaneously developed its own separate mouth, because you obviously can't have too many mouths in this place.

"What the—" is all Brahm can say, unable to dive further into his feelings of being overwhelmed. The being pays no mind to Brahm's exasperation. He takes the tiny finger upon his miniature hand and stretches it up to his blue-eel nose, eagerly pushing it like a child would push an enticing oversized play toy. The eel-nose slithers vibrantly around the face with the push of its button, developing a face of its own which smiles brightly. It leaps into the air, in a direction that can only be assumed as 'up,' before diving back 'down' like a trained Olympic diver.

"Weeeeeeeee!" it squeals as it readies itself for impact. As the eel-nose nears the spiky headdress hair combo, it opens its mouth wide with disproportionate dimensions and consumes the whole entity in one gulp. The eel-nose proudly displays its inflated and gorged belly. It produces a substantial burb of satisfaction and looks to Brahm with a playful smile. Opening its mouth, it appears to start speaking, but ends up sneezing instead.

"Aaaacchhhheewwww—wo-wo-wo-wo-wo-wo-wo-wo-wo!" The prolonged sound vibrates so loudly it distorts all means of perception. Brahm covers his ears, but it does as much as closing his eyes earlier. He swirls around within the disheartening sound until suddenly, it stops. Just like that. Lowering his hands, he looks out to where the snake-nose use to be and now sees a *very* familiar figure in its place.

"Recognize me now?" Babarossa says with a heavenly glow surrounding him.

"You?!" Brahm screams.

"Me!" Babarossa screams back, clearly having fun with his shouting match. His body resembles the very human appearance Brahm last remembered him harboring. He even has his plaid blanket wrapped around him.

"Wow… that was definitely one of the strangest things I have ever seen. Honestly though, was any of that even necessary?"

"Energy manifests in different patterns here. My apologies, I just assumed you could see through it!" Babarossa says playfully. A whirlwind of thoughts flood Brahm's mind. Questions, comments, threats, concerns… too many to choose from. He takes a deep breath despite not having any lungs, but the concept remains comforting to him. His mind quiets as he attempts to reengage the old man from the Plaza.

"So," Brahm starts, "am I dead?"

"Hmm…" Babarossa hums. "No. Not quite."

"What?" Brahm shouts again. "Why not?"

"Odd question! You either are or you're not. And right now, you're not! Lost though? Yes, I would say you are more lost than dead."

"Well, what are we waiting for?!" Brahm yells with strong emotion. "This is all your doing anyway, let's just get on with it! I'm ready!"

"It's not your time," Babarossa says calmly.

"All right, wise guy, then why am I here?!"

"Hahaha! Do you even know where *here* is?"

"Well, no, but I'm sure I just died! Or should have anyway! I left my body at least!"

"You've left your body plenty of times before without dying."

"Sure! I don't know how you know that, but I never wound up here!"

"Even though you don't know where *here* is? How would you know if you did?"

"Enough with the mind games, old man! I think I would remember this place if I came here before."

"Maybe… if you were paying attention that is," Babarossa says, his words drifting off, alluding to further awareness under the surface.

"Fine, I'll bite. What's going on here?"

"Ahh," Babarossa says, "a little bit of openness goes a long way! Here! Sit!"

"Wha—" In a blink of an eye Brahm finds himself sitting comfortably in a multi-colored chair made up of chevron patterns. It resembles the rough shape of an old leather recliner despite the neon blue, green, orange, and red chevrons that rotate through the chair like a revolving roulette wheel. The buttons, however, remain stationary, giving Brahm a playful wink every time he makes eye contact with them. Babarossa manifests a chair of his own and they sit in a bizarre moment of comfort, still surrounded by the whizzing chaos.

"You are not dead," Babarossa continues. "But you've managed to wind up in a very peculiar predicament nonetheless."

"Go on."

"Yes. This is the space between spaces. The Void, some call it. The transitional space between dimensions. You have in fact been here, plenty of times but never saw it as a space to stay. Rightfully so, it rarely is a place to stay stagnant. I've watched you countless times zip around like one of our friends here," he says, pointing to one of the dimensional beings flying overhead. "We are in-between the threads of the web that connects all things. We always are in fact!" he says, unable to contain his laugh.

"Is this why you brought me here? To show me this?"

"Silly boy, you brought yourself here! You just happened to stay long enough for me to have a chat with you."

"But…" Brahm stammers, "but I would have never wanted to come here if you hadn't taken away my powers!"

"Silly… silly," Babarossa says shaking his head. "You couldn't be here if you didn't have your powers! Don't you see? Mono was trying with all his heart to tell you such things can never be 'taken away.' Sure, I hid them from you but if you only explored what you thought was left you would have easily found your true power! But what did you do instead?"

"Well, I-I …"

"Begged a very angry man to beat you with a club?"

"Yeah, I guess you could say that," Brahm says, ashamed of himself.

"Another way to say it is you got consumed by your ego. That's what I left you with: your ego. I felt it might finally be time to have a nice sit with yourself. Doubt, anger, distrust, fear, pain… all those feelings and aspects of yourself you discard at a moment's notice when they become unbearable. You retreat to this place in order to dive into another world and forgo dealing with yourself!"

"That's not why I leave my body!" Brahm shouts back.

"No! Of course you didn't think that was why you did it, but… you did! Without dealing with these very important aspects of who you are, your power is reduced to nothing more than an escape pod. How much energy do you think you put into hiding from yourself?"

"What do you mean?"

"Well, how much energy and power have you put into bettering yourself? Bettering others? Doing anything other than removing any hint of an obstacle or difficulty?"

"For myself? I don't know. Maybe none, but Sophia…" Brahm says, followed by a long pause. "Domino and Otto too, I… recently it has been different."

"Yes! Look how much you have benefited from your interactions with them. So tell me, what made you decide to forgo your selfish nature to help them?"

"I… like them, I guess. Didn't want to see them suffer."

"Like them?" Babarossa questions with a playful tone.

"Like them, well, maybe it's more than that."

"How much more? Do you—"

"Love them?"

"Do you?"

"Yeah, I guess I do. I do love them! All in different ways, and yet the same! Wow, it feels good to say that out loud. Beau too! God knows he has put up with me through all my selfishness!" Brahm says with a swirling flood of warmth pouring into his chest.

"So, what about all this? This mess I'm in? What do I do about it all?"

"Well, what seems to be the theme here?" Babarossa responds.

"Love, it seems!" Brahm says with light laughter.

"Yes. Do you love yourself?"

"Love myself?" Brahm repeats. "Well, I think so!"

"What do you love about yourself?"

"The freedom! The power! The, oh…" Brahm quickly falls into a puddle of shame. "That's what I love. I love this power of mine."

"Yes, you do. But that isn't who you are, is it?"

"No, I guess it's not," Brahm says, starting to crack open the revelation Babarossa is attempting to foster. "Honestly, I don't even know who I am without my power. I spent a few hours with myself and wound up begging to die! Ugh! What is the deal with this power anyway?"

"First things first," Babarossa consoles. "There is a reason for this power of yours, but in order to understand that you must first understand the being who harbors it."

"Me?"

"Yes, you. The real you. Once you come to figure out who you are, the reason this power follows you will reveal itself. Once you stop using it as an escape or a cheap parlor trick you will learn what you are truly meant to use it for."

"Okay," Brahm says with a heavy sigh. "I feel like I've really messed up here."

"There is still time to fix things."

"How?" The eagerness in Brahm's voice is welcoming. Babarossa smiles and points his finger at the thread of light that brought Brahm to the Void. The shadowy figure Brahm saw earlier is still standing on the other side, waving to him.

"What is that?" Brahm asks.

"It's you of course!"

"Me?"

"Yes. The 'you' you don't want to deal with. The ego. The emotions. The pain. The memories. The attachments. He is the *you* behind the powers, behind all the flair and distractions. He is the aspect of you that was born into that world in order to be refined and purified. He is the shadow you have been running away from your whole life. Everyone in that world you just came from is working together to help each other figure things out and come to peace with their own shadows. Some know that, most don't. But that's okay. It's a process of refinement."

"How do we avoid all the pain that comes from figuring things out?" Brahm asks with a quiver in his throat.

"Sometimes we need to experience pain to understand we don't want to inflict it." Babarossa shouts proudly. "Someday you will be allowed to die. Shed your body for good and travel on in this vast realm of existence, but not before you do the work on loving your shadow. Because… well tell me, of all the times you used your power to run away from your body, the very vessel which casts your shadow, why did you return?"

"Well…" Brahm stammers, "I thought… I don't know! It just felt like home base, ya know? That physical world was where my father was. Where Beau was. It was… home."

"Cherish that home. It's where most first learn where the love is. Love is all around you, but you don't always feel it, do you?"

"No, I guess I don't."

"What do you think will happen when you come to fully love your shadow?"

"I'll always feel the love?"

"Ha!" Babarossa shouts. "You'll *become* love! Don't you see? Suffering is what drives you away from wanting to be in that world, but *suffering is just the resistance to love!* Once you see through that, there will be no pain! No more suffering! No more resistance! No more *you*. No more shadows. Just love. You will see."

"Yeah, I hear you," Brahm says, trying to soak in the Seers words. "But from this vantage point, that is a pretty easy thing to say. When you are not in pain that is; when you are not suffering, then it all seems so simple. So then, what happens if I go back? If I still *can* go back, will I remember all of this? Or will I go back to my old ways?"

"Some. Doesn't matter. Your true self never forgets. It's what remembers what stage of refinement you left off at! It remembers everything, so don't worry about forgetting. You will do so in order to remember again later. It's a dance. It's all a dance!"

"And the pain? I've got a lot of pain waiting for me."

"There was a great deal of resistance before you came here."

"Right, oh man…" Brahm says, contemplating jumping back into his earlier predicament. "There is *a lot* of pain waiting for me."

"You have *a lot* of resistance to work through!" Babarossa says, falling back into laughter. "Ah-hahahaha! Embrace it! It's all you, after all." Babarossa slides back into his chair looking for Brahm to make the next move. Even his chair buttons dance around and smile, looking like they are overflowing with love themselves.

"So, earlier, you said I still have my powers? Always had my powers?"

"Yes."

"So I can still use them when I go back?"

"Of course."

"Could I use it to take away the pain?"

"You could…"

"But it would defeat the purpose, wouldn't it?" "You said it!" Babarossa says with a loving hum. "So go do it, embrace it all and don't forget the Universal Laws you love to disregard so proudly."

"What are you talking about?" Brahm says with honest confusion.

"Oh, you know what I am talking about," he says with a playful wink. "They are the foundation of the world you are about to reenter. They are the fundamental framework for reality itself. To disregard them is to disregard ascension. The Laws are meant to help you, to guide you. They are what will keep you from doing *this* over and over again. They are designed to liberate. Energy, attraction, cause and effect, compensation, correspondence, gender, transmutation, polarity, relativity, rhythm, vibration … you must master them all if you wish to master yourself. And if you think back far enough, I know you will see this is not the first time someone has tried to tell you this."

"You're right, of course you're right," Brahm says with a nervous laugh. "Beau and my father both tried to teach me the importance of these Laws. All I could ever do was show them how well I could bend them! Break them sometimes! I loved to see the look on their faces when I could alter the fabric of reality just when they told me it was impossible!"

"And where did that lead you?"

"Yeah, I hear you," Brahm says dismissively. "I do though. I do hear you. So now what?"

"Get back to work!"

"Right now?"

"There only is *now*, silly boy!"

"Right, right, of course!" Brahm says, poorly trying to play off his ignorance.

"So I just go over there and… what? Dive back into my shadow?"

"That would be a lovely start!" Babarossa says. Brahm gives him a nod and lifts himself out of the chair. The buttons grow little hands and wave to him as he floats away from their comfortable seat of safety. Brahm locks his eyes on the waving shadow behind the light and decides to wave back. The shadow jumps for joy, waving his arms in dramatic swooping patterns, beckoning his other half to come closer. Brahm smiles and begins to drift out of the flow of traffic and back towards the light. He stops, pulled by a moment of hesitation. He looks back and sees Babarossa still sitting comfortably in his chair, watching him drift away.

"Who *are* you?" Brahm asks. Babarossa smiles wider and wider until his toothless gums pop out of his lips. Waves of loving acceptance crash over Brahm to the point where he is immediately brought to tears. A flame ignites so brightly in his chest he places his hand over it to make sure he is not actually on fire.

"Who I am is not important," Babarossa says warmly. "Now is the time for you to get to know yourself. Just know I will always be with you. I will be in that space between you and your shadow. Anytime you wish to find me, just bridge that gap a little more!"

"Thank you," Brahm says, with tears streaming down his face. He turns to continue his drift back to his exuberant shadow. As he nears the white light, he slows his advancement. He looks deeply into his shadow as it starts to flail with ecstatic dance. The shadow eventually begins to follow Brahm's movements more closely, slowly mirroring one another perfectly. Brahm lifts his hand up and reaches for the light. He can feel a deep resonating pulse coming from the other side. The closer his hand gets, the more he can feel the pulsation within his own chest. With a heavy sigh, Brahm places his hand on the surface of the light, his shadow doing the same on the other side. With one more push, Brahm falls into the light and into his shadow. Everything dissolves into a blinding flash of love and light. All aspects of existence begin swirling, flowing, dancing, and weaving together as one.

CHAPTER: 32

Back to the Body

A flash of cosmic lightening comes crashing into the physical realm. It races through the paradoxical restraints of reason and reality, binding its ethereal essence with the lifeless flesh of Brahm's recently vacated body. The surge of electrified consciousness ignites a flame inside the body as if connecting with the dry brush of a forest in a drought. The combustible cosmic fuel jumps with excitement as the hungry flame races to consume all within reach. Within the darkness of his once-vacant vessel, the forest fire of energy burns inside every dormant nerve ending. The wild flames race down his neural network, scorching his flaccid appendages and torso with equal parts of life and pain. The heat and burning pulsation from the fire brings focus to the circulating consciousness drifting back into his battered body.

"Uhhhh," he gasps, wheezing under the restrictions of his collapsed lungs. He fights to force down the beckoning breath of life. His breaths are labored and shallow, yet he still works through the pain. Despite the urge to give into his suffering, Brahm brings focus to his desire to see more clearly into the reality he has been reborn into. *Just take it all away,* Brahm can hear his subconscious pleading, *you know how.*

"No," Brahm says out loud, advertising his inward struggle to the world. "This pain is what I came back to learn from." Satisfied with his claim, Brahm draws deeper and deeper breaths into his chest, stretching his lungs back into the proud containers of life they once were. He winces his eye in pain but continues to push through it. As the oxygen saturates the starved blood within his body, his color starts to return to his once vibrant complexion. The wounds from his injuries weep from the returning circulation, flowing like a flooded river delta.

∞

One could expect a pin drop to trigger a heart attack within the profound and heavy silence dominating the chamber of Brahm's resurrection. As the sole witness to such a cosmic anomaly, Claude stays fixated upon the floor. His eyes transfixed on the miracle of life before him. He watches with mystified horror as his once-expired victim of torture regains his life more and more with each cycling breath. The unusual silence hastens its grip on the room, allowing the pounding beat of the two men's hearts to bellow like a pair of thundering drums. Claude grips his chest, as if to try and quiet his boisterous heart. He listens to the rhythmic dance of the beats, hearing his own and then his victim's. As they continue to beat, the pace begins to alter. Brahm's heart palpitates louder with each beat; the ringing lingers in the reluctant confines of Claude's ears. The sound echoes throughout the chamber, dominating the sonic registry. Claude can feel his own heart start to skip beats, as if yearning to become one with the dominating frequency. He grips his chest even tighter, silently begging his heart to maintain its own independence. Powerless to inhibit the merger, Claude winces in defeat as his heart surrenders its own rhythm to the mangled man before him.

The deep pounding of the unified hearts becomes too much for Claude to bear. He struggles to regain his footing, attempting to put an end to the maddening metronome. However, each attempt to stand is halted by the concussive pounding of each successive heartbeat. An animalistic ferocity ignites behind Claude's sunken gaze. He stares upon the totem of his externalized source of hatred— the being he took every effort to destroy for good. Searching for answers, Claude burrows his sights into Brahm's face. He notices his victim's face swelling with surges of bodily fluid flowing eagerly back into their interstitial spaces. His matted and untamed hair falls over his face, covering the majority of his facial wounds under a convenient veil. The wincing and twitching that continues to follow Brahm's resurrection brings a flight of joy to Claude. He begins to strike an involuntary smirk as he soaks in the very human demeanor of the godly man before him. A moment of hope starts to take root; a moment encapsulated with the thought that this resurrected man could still be tarnished and defeated.

Just as the devilish thought takes hold in Claude's mind, a deep resonating sickness churns in his gut. Claude moves his hand from his chest to his mouth; the sensation of vomit feels eminent. Confusion swims alongside his internal discomfort, as the source of such sickness is not clearly understood. He stares back into Brahm's face, assuming he has something to do with it. This time, his gaze catches a distinct shimmer radiating from Brahm's left eye that erupts with illumination. The vibrant blue eye casts swirling waves of light that seem to spiral into fractaling rays of varying color. The whole room begins to glow despite the source of light originating from such a small aperture. The light contrasts the weeping wounds that once served to define Brahm's humanity. Claude takes a heavy gulp as his internal dialogue populates an unpopular thought: *How is this possible? Is this man… more than just a man?* As if able to hear his thoughts, Brahm turns his head away from his own internal focus and looks completely at the sickly man sitting before him. Powerless to look away, Claude locks eyes with his prisoner, captivated by the light and love radiating from his heavenly aperture.

"S-Stop it…" Claude pleads, as he tries with all his might to resist the pull into the warm and nurturing light. Giving no recognition of Claude's plea, Brahm continues to turn the rest of his body to face his singular audience.

Careful not to disrupt his intense ocular lock on Claude, Brahm easily removes himself from the chair, placing his two feet upon the welcoming ground. He stands tall directly below the stationary lantern, the single physical source of light for the room. The angle of light that hits Brahm casts a long shadow from his bloodied feet. His shadow reaches the tips of Claude's fingers, which remain planted on the ground for support. As Claude looks down at the dark and ominous casting, his eyes expand in fear. For a moment he thinks the elongated shadow just waved at him. Eager to ignore such a thought, he follows the two-dimensional darkness all the way back to the glowing source of light it originates from. Brahm stands motionless, his glowing eyes continue to pour rivers of internal light and love into the room. With the pounding of unified hearts still echoing the chamber, Claude begins to notice another sound permeating from the silence between beats.

A sweet, angelic hum churns the air, seasoning the silence with heavenly charm. With the light becoming too bright to bear, Claude can hardly make out any of Brahm's physical characteristics. He is left to focus on the unique sound that penetrates his senses. As he becomes lost in the melody, Claude still feels the need to fight back and regain control. Like a quivering stone at the bottom of a raging river, he resists the rapture washing over him.

"You are an abomination!" Claude yells in desperation. He is forced to hold back the resurgent urge to purge as his anger boils to the surface. He grips the handle of the club still by his side. "Don't you see?" You are the reason we must rely on the Wardens! They are the force that will rekindle humanity's claim to this soil! Ugh!" Claude hunches over as the sickness starts to overpower him. "You are a freak of nature! Your existence threatens all of humanity! Just like the damn Mountain Gods and their Bakuwan spawn! The Wardens will end the likes of you celestial devils. In the name of progress, all you freaks will be cleansed once and for all!" With his words still ringing in the air, he chucks the heavy club at Brahm's stationary frame. A defensive vibratory pulse immediately erupts from Brahm's core, pouring out of his chest like a triggered tidal wave. Claude's senses fail to distinguish whether the vibration exists as light or sound. The possibility of both forces acting simultaneously flashes through his mind, but registers no higher insight. He watches as the paradoxical pulse wave knocks the club out of his hand like a swatted fly. The oscillating wave of light and sound continues to flood the room, bouncing off the walls and flows with the cadence of the beating hearts.

Overwhelmed by his sensory overload and bubbling sickness, Claude folds into a fetal position, clutching his chest and gut simultaneously. He feels the internal darkness from within him start to congeal and center itself into the core of his being. He can feel his dread, hatred, and anger being pulled from his muscles, tissues, and eventually his mind. The pool of negativity knocks violently upon his chest like a frostbitten vagabond trying to find refuge from the cold. Each desperate pound strikes a new and more profound wave of sickness. Eventually, the desire to keep such a caustic force bottled up inside becomes too much to contain.

"Yeeeaaaakkk!" With heavy panting, Claude stares down at the stone floor now painted with his thick and dark green emesis. He looks into his expelled darkness in wonder. Its physical nature never revealed to him until now. With his first breath after his purge, Claude feels a rejuvenating lightness in his chest. Thoughts of early childhood flood his mind, his only memories of a time not bound by fear and hate. As he exhales, a smile floats upon his face and tears start pouring unrestricted from his closed eyes. Drifting like a fallen leaf in a river, he loses himself in the waves of celestial bliss and floats gently onto his back. He begins to sob heavily, but his deep smile remains stretched across his face.

Brahm glances over at his blissed-out adversary, rolling around on the ground laughing and crying as if he had been reborn as a child. The dark emesis still upon the floor catches his eye. He takes a deep breath as he contemplates the significance of the expunged content of the misguided guard.

"I see now," Brahm says while looking at the dark emesis. "*That* was my true adversary all along. If anything, this man and I have both been fighting that same darkness which festers in us all." He takes a deep breath as he listens to his own words. "Starved of light, it was allowed to grow inside this man. Just like so many others. Just like myself. This must be what the old man was talking about; what can happen when you close yourself off to the Light." A loud rumble shakes through the room, disrupting Brahm's train of thought for a moment.

"It's getting louder… closer even," he says out loud. "I have to act quickly. Whatever is going on below, it can't be good." He glances over to Claude one last time and dips his head in a respectful bow. Claude remains too wrapped up in his own bliss to notice the gesture of kindness. Brahm smiles at the youthful display of joy before turning to the exit. As he opens the thick metal door, he welcomes the dark and dingy corridor. Its dismal demeanor contrasts with his radiant light flowing from his aura. He walks with feathered steps along the same bloody trail he was dragged along just moments before. He can feel the pain of his earlier self echo with each footstep. He breathes in the memory of his past suffering and holds it gently within his chest. The pain squirms around like a caged animal, desperate to escape its entrapment. With a deep exhale, the light in the room grows even brighter as Brahm expels the animalistic energy. He can feel the angst and dread that defined him become purified as it exits his body. He watches with joy as the expunged energy drifts alongside him like an accompanying friend.

His bliss follows him down the remaining length of the corridor until he reaches the end. He casually places his hand on the door leading to the still captive Seers. Sharp, vibrating pulses course through his fingertips and race into the rest of his body. The sensation leads him to shutter with an unexpected chill. "What is this?" Brahm asks out loud. He looks down at his hand, still resting on the door handle, searching for clues. His eyes drift up to the door itself, leading his mind to fill with images of what lies on the other side. A sinking feeling fills his heart as his memories return of his last interaction with the men of the Seer clan.

"Am I really about to just walk in there and act like everything is fine? Disregard all the rude and unseemly things I did and said to people who only were trying to help me? I know the right thing to do is to free them, but how can I bring myself to even look them in the eye? How can they even bring themselves to look *me* in the eye after how horribly I treated them?" Doubt and regret race into his heart. The light from his angelic aura dims as the dark shadow wrapped around his feet starts to squirm. His head sinks low as he allows himself to drift into the self-loathing seas the tides of memory have brought to his shores. With his gaze fixed on the ground, his mind racing, an unusual image captures his diverted attention. *What is that?* he wonders as the dark contours of his shadow catch the periphery of his sight. He turns his head around to see his own shadow jumping up and down on its two-dimensional platform. The shadow waves its hands like a castaway trying to flag down a passing ship.

"Ha," Brahm says. "Even back in this world you act like you have a mind of your own!" The shadow stops its frantic waving and puts its hands on its hips. Brahm smiles at the animated presentation. The shadow takes one of its hands and points to his head and then to Brahm. "Trying to tell me something, are you?" he asks playfully. The shadow dramatically stretches its arms out with open palms, shaking them frantically. "Ha, Baba said that that's what you are here to do. Am I already missing something?" A dramatic thumbs-up takes the place of the open palm. "That didn't take long," Brahm chuckles to himself. With a deep breath he forces himself to reflect honestly on his predicament. "I'm letting the anticipatory judgment of another divert my actions," he says, thinking about what the Seers will say when he reappears after such a dramatic display of self-loathing. "I don't deserve their praise, but do I deserve their judgment either? Wait, how do I even know *what* I deserve?" His shadow throws its hands over its head and dances upon the floor. "I suppose it's not up to me to decide what I deserve. Worrying about what comes next is only keeping me from moving forward. Phewwww!" he exasperates as he processes his own words. "All I can do is ask for their forgiveness. Whatever comes after that is what I deserve and it's about time I open myself up to whatever that may be. No more running away." Brahm nods his head in agreement with his own dialogue, and his shadow gives another complementary thumbs-up in approval as well. "So it's settled," Brahm says to his shadow. "Let's move forward!"

A loud *clank* accompanies the unlatching of the door that has been standing between Brahm and the Seers. The heavy door creaks open and welcomes the newly ignited light from Brahm's aura to fill the room. The caged Seers turn their heads towards the light. They watch the once torn and angered captive floats over the floor as if the weight of his anger has been cast aside. Their eyes start to water as they peer into the human candle casting such a rejuvenating light. Wasting no time, Brahm makes his way to the caged door. He places one of his glowing hands on the metal bars and gently removes it from its hinges. Standing in the doorway to freedom, Brahm lowers himself to the floor and folds into a kneeling position. He bows his head to the floor and places his palms face up along the cold stone.

"I was a broken man when I first arrived here, full of hate and anger for myself and the world," Brahm starts. "I have come to apologize for the way I treated all of you. Regardless of my callused and hostile appearance, you all were able to look past that and still treat me with compassion and respect. Especially the young man, Mono, who gave so much of his heart to a man who cast his own aside. I realize now the pain I was inflicting was a projection of my own pain I wasn't ready to face. Despite that, I cannot take back what I did. I don't know if I even deserve the right to ask for forgiveness, so I can only commit to my apology. I am sorry. I hope you will find others outside these gates more receptive to your love and kindness." A warm hand places itself gently on Brahms exposed back. He looks up to see Mono standing in front of him, smiling deeply.

"Your apology comes from the heart, and we thank you for your kind words and for opening the door to our physical prison," Mono says. "Know that we hold no ill will towards you, we never have. We only ask that in your resolve to apologize you also carry it on to yourself."

"What do you mean?" Brahm says from within his kneeling stance.

"Without the ability to forgive oneself, you can never truly move forward. You would only move in the orbit of your regrets. Forgiveness is what will allow you to truly grow from such a fertile experience."

"You are wise beyond your years!" Brahm says with a smile returning to his face.

"Well, what are you waiting for then?" Mono says playfully. Brahm looks at him, confused.

"Go ahead and forgive yourself already!" the youth shouts.

"I have!"

"Then say it!"

"I don't want to!" Brahm pleads.

"Do it! What, are you afraid we will laugh at you?"

"NO!"

"Then say it!"

"Baaahhh! I forgive myself! I forgive myself! I forgive myself! There!" Brahm yells into the stone floor, his words reverberating through the chamber.

"Ahahahahaha!" the Seers laugh out loud with joy.

"You said you wouldn't laugh!" Brahm calls out in a childish tone.

"Oh, c'mon. Someone's gotta work on toughening that skin of yours," Tewari says from within the crowd. He hesitates for a moment after his words hit his own ears. Looking at Brahm's disfigured body, he wonders if his comment was a little too on the nose. Figuring his words still hold true, he slaps Brahm's bloodied and battered back and makes his way out of the cage. "Now get off the floor and come help us find the women. I had a vision earlier as to where their prison cell is. You can make good on your apology by helping us break them out."

CHAPTER: 33

Out of Sight, Into Mind

"Wow! Would you just look at that?!" Domino calls over to Otto as the two boys lie in their protective hideout, observing what they can of the battle with the Warden. They watch as a giant serpent-like creature erupts out of the first floor, its mouth open wide, howling with disappointment. It weaves in and out of the thick layers of fog that surround the first few floors of the castle. Its dark black complexion easily penetrates the fog's concealing nature. The creature slithers around in the air as if having no regard for the call to gravity. Its eyes dart to the castle wall before crashing back into the room it just ejected from. The castle shifts slightly under the compromising structural integrity. Concussive explosions fire off from seemingly every floor inside the building, leaving the boys to wonder where the epicenter of the battle even exists. With only flashes of the battle permeating outside of the castle walls, their imaginations race to fill in the blanks.

"What in the world is that thing?!" Otto asks his overly excited companion.

"Who knows!" Domino responds without taking his eye off the carnage the creature has created. "Whatever it is, it's putting up quite the fight! Neither Beau nor the Marionettes have been able to stop it yet!"

"Do you think they are alright?"

"I doubt they are picking flowers in there!" Domino responds, agitated at the distracting questions. "I mean, I'm sure that thing wouldn't keep attacking if Beau and the others were not still putting up a fight!" he says, trying to smooth over his calloused response.

"True, true…" Otto says to himself, bringing a sliver of reassurance back into his vessel. "Well, we should still be looking for a way to help! I'm sure that—"

"Whoa-ho!" Domino cries out as Izak unexpectedly comes flying out of the fourth floor. He soars through the air without any assistance from his assortment of technology. The boys' eyes widen as they notice his exoskeleton is badly damaged along with the rest of his body. The canisters to his jet pack sputter with fading power despite his desperate yank on the pull chord. Fumes are all that expel from the canisters, covering his tattered body with dark soot and smoke. As he falls with no sign of recovery, a metal chain comes firing out of the hole, following his point of descent.

"Ayananda!" Domino yells out as he watches the familiar chain wrap around the falling gunslinger right before he dips into the cloud of fog below. They squint to see Ayananda slide to the edge of the erupted hole that dispelled Izak. She leans over the edge, holding on tightly as she struggles to bear the weight of her fallen comrade. The hole in the castle wall gives the boys a much-desired window into the battle raging inside. As Ayananda begins her attempt to pull Izak back into the building, the glowing eyes of the magical serpent appear from within the darkened contours of the room. The serpent flares its tongue as it inches its way closer to the seemingly defenseless duo. Its body swishes silently back and forth with a dismantling dance of death.

"Oh no! What are they going to do?" Otto yells out. "Get out of there! Run! Oh God, I can't watch!"

"Get a grip, man! We've wanted to see what's happening this whole time! This is our chance! Keep a good look out so we can find our opportunity to get in there!"

"Ugh!" Otto squeals, falling back into his doubting thoughts. "What do you *actually* think we can do against that beast?"

"Try! That's what we are going to do! Now stop crying and look for our opportunity!"

"Fine! Bahh, but I *will* continue to cry if that's what I need to do!" Otto says reflexively as he refuses to wipe the tear from his eye. His need to defend his emotional expression surprises even himself. He looks stoically at Domino, tears and all, boldly awaiting his response.

"Wow. Yeah, sure, whatever floats your boat. Alright then, let's use our heads… *and* our emotions to help out with this one!"

"Exactly! So… oh God! Oh God! I can't watch!" Otto cries out as he covers his moistened eyes. With a shake of his head, Domino pushes his conflicted friend out of the way to get closer to the scene unfolding. The serpent's eyes glide out of the darkness and its head rises, looking ready to strike.

"C'mon…" Domino says under his breath to the Marionettes. His eyes flash with heightened vigor. "Show us what you've got, make it out of this." He watches Ayananda remain stationary, holding tight while Izak fumbles with the plethora of devices along his chest. Pulling out a small gadget that fits within the palm of his hand, he looks up to Ayananda and nods his head. Just as the serpent lunges to make its strike, Izak pushes off the wall with his feet and throws the device below him. Pulling a gun from his holster, he fires the weapon at the receding device. A small mushroom cloud of fire and smoke erupt with concussive might, consuming everything in a swirling ball of incendiary mayhem.

"Whoa!" Domino yells. "That's what I'm talking about!" As the shockwave fires him up into the air, Ayananda digs in her heals and directs his assent with her chain. With a well-calculated pull, she draws Izak back into the room as he opens fire at the lunging beast.

"Raaahhhh!" his battle cry bellows all the way into the boys' ears as his trigger-finger flies with fury, spraying the serpent with a myriad array of exploding rounds. The creature charges the attack with no attempt to dodge, detonating the blinding flashes of light harbored in each projectile.

"Ka-aaaaaa-hhhhaaa…." the serpent cries out in a high-pitched shriek. The boys watch the creature slither back into the darkness as Ayananda unhooks her chain from around Izak. Some customary bantering can be heard before the two head back into the obscured contours of the room.

"Yeah! I knew they could do it!" Domino cheers, lifting his friend up off the ground by the scruff of his neck. "They are amazing!"

"They sure are," Otto agrees as he still dangles from his friend's grasp. His new vantage point directs his attention to some unexpected activity below.

"Hey," Otto starts to say.

"Oh, sorry!" Domino says as he abruptly drops his friend onto the ground.

"Ugh, seriously? You could have saved that apology for dropping me!" he says, dusting off his clothes. One look at Domino's unapologetic demeanor says enough. "Forget about it. Just look over there! What do you think that's all about?" Following Otto's outstretched finger, the two of them spy on a lone guard carrying an old man towards the castle. The distance is too far to make out any further details. The guard and his prisoner move hurriedly along the flat rock face of the mountain that flanks the castle on the right side. After watching so many guards fleeing the area earlier, it is an odd occurrence to see one racing into danger's way.

"Let's get a closer look!" Domino suggests. The misty fog has regained its foothold on The Pearl, making long-distance viewing now almost impossible.

"Y-Yeah!" Otto agrees reluctantly. The two race down from their safety perch to get a better look at the guard and his prisoner.

"Something feels fishy about this guy!" Domino calls out as they run down the embankment.

"Something is fishy about a lot of the happenings around here!" Otto replies in-between panting breaths. "But you're right, this guy is *extra* fishy! Like, a rotten fish carcass gutted and left on the shore… that's been chewed up and spit out by a rabid seagull only to—"

"Dude!"

"Oh! Right, too far. Anyway, maybe we can get some answers from figuring out what he's up to!" Domino gives a reassuring nod before pointing to an outcropping of boulders a few feet down the hill. The two boys slide behind the rocks like they are stealing home plate. They carefully poke their heads out from the rocks and peer eagerly at the guard and his prisoner from their new vantage point. The guard continues his travels to the point where the castle intersects with the mountain cliff with no sign of noticing the boys' presence.

"Domino! That's—" Domino is forced to quickly cover his friend's boisterous realization. "Heyymmm… stommm-eett… I cammp brefff…" Otto tries to mumble from behind Domino's strategic muting.

"I'll let go but you have to be quiet! You'll give away our position!" he says as he finally let's go.

"Ahhhhhh." With a much-needed gasp of air, Otto returns his concern to the pressing matter at hand. The two boys look back at the scene unfolding. They notice the prisoner the guard is carrying is none other than the old man who saved them from Jeeven's rampage.

"B-Babarossa," Otto says with a sense of bewilderment, remembering this time to whisper his external musings. "What do you suppose they are going to do with him?"

"Well, he is one of the most-wanted Seers on the island and supposedly the most powerful. He'll probably end up worse than that nasty fish you were picturing earlier. Let's just wait a little longer and see how this unfolds before we make our next move." After his words leave his lips, Domino stares into the dismal demeanor that has now become the great Seer Sage. He hangs like a wilted flower, his head bobbing between his shoulders like a lost sea buoy. His plaid blanket is torn and frayed, but somehow still attached to his body. His hands are outstretched and shackled in cuffs. The guard looks afraid, as he is constantly checking over his shoulder. Upon a second glance, it appears he is actually sneaking frequent glances at the man he drags behind him. With one hand firmly clenched over the chains of his prisoner, his other hand rests securely over his firearm. Babarossa's overwhelming spirit appears broken, causing a wave of worry to wash into the boys' hearts.

"Uhh, I don't know how much more of this I can watch," Otto whispers, his back-and-forth battle with fear is starting to favor his rash impulsivity. "I feel like we should do something."

"I hear you, but the guard has a gun!" Domino whispers as loudly as the concept allows. "We need to make sure we think this one through! If we just run out there without a plan, we are bound to wind up in a worse fate than him! Do you want to prove everyone right who thinks we are useless baggage?"

"I'm going in," Otto says coldly, his mind gridlocked with focus like a hungry eagle who has spotted his prey. He stands up, clearly dismantling his cover as he makes his move.

"Don't you dare!" Domino yells as he grabs his friend and forces him back to the ground.

"Uhhhff!" Otto grunts as he is thrust into the dirt. Domino pays him no mind, lifting his head carefully to see if their cover has been blown. He notices the guard peering around frantically, clearly aware of the chaotic uproar. The now extra hyper vigilant guard continues his course with a hastened pace.

"It absolutely amazes me you have managed to survive this long!" Domino aggressively whispers to his friend. "You are either crippled with fear or you become a rash gunslinger who runs to a shootout without a weapon! Get it together, man!"

"I don't care!" Otto cries from under Dominos wrestling hold. He slithers to try and break free but remains overpowered. "Do you think I like being afraid all the time?" he mutters in-between grunts. "I feel like I'm always trapped in a prison, bound by fear! I look around and see all these things I want to do, people to help, a life I want to live, yet I stay bound by my personal prison. So often I see something I want to do but can't bring myself to do it, because I am afraid! I can admit that now! So, when I finally do break out, why would I ever want to look back?" Domino's grip starts to loosen as Otto's words penetrate his heart. "When I finally break out of that prison, I want to make sure I never go back! I want to run towards the things my fear has kept me from! Don't you understand?"

"Yes," Domino says heavily. "I do."

"Great! Now let me go!"

"You know, there is nothing wrong with wanting to escape that prison, but maybe you don't have to do it alone."

"What do you mean?"

"What do I mean?! You always seem to forget about me when you bust out of prison like a mindless buffoon! You forget everything when you get like that! Bring me with you! Let me help you think through this call to action! Let me help you from falling back into that prison when you finally get your senses back!"

"I was afraid you would try and talk me out of it," Otto responds, his resistance to Domino's hold weakening.

"I *am* trying to talk you out of what mindless nonsense you were about to do! Let's at least think about this before we act. Here," he says, dusting off his friend. "Look back and see what we would have missed if we just ran out there and missed our chance to get into the castle!"

"What?"

"See for yourself," Domino responds playfully as he motions for his friend to look out at the transpiring events. The guard slows his pace, stopping at a point along the cliff near the castle flank. He looks even more feverously from side to side before lifting his hand to knock on a particular spot on the stone cliff.

"What is he doing?"

"Just watch, I think this is it!" Domino fires back, demanding their attention to be focused. The guard knocks again, looking skittish, like he is about to make a run for it if something doesn't happen soon. To the boys' surprise, an unmistakable creaking sound starts to transpire from the cliff face. The sound of a rusty door hinge twirling on its axis fills their ears. As the secret door in the cliff fully opens, another guard emerges to greet the one carrying Babarossa. His hands appear to be holding something, but the poorly lit doorway leaves the content to the boys' imagination.

"Hurry up and let me in!" the guard with Babarossa says with a quiver in his voice. "I got the guy Mune asked for! What the—" Suddenly, a rogue piece of debris comes flying off the castle, and lands dangerously close to the two guards. The first guard jumps in the air with fright while Babarossa stands motionless, despite the rubble coming inches from landing on top of him.

"This place is falling apart, hurry up already! It's too dangerous out here!" the first guard continues.

"Are you kidding me? That's all the more reason to get *out* of here!" the guard emerging from the cliff responds. "The Warden has gone mad fighting that rogue Kopala giant! He's even killing *us*! Before long, there won't be anything left!"

"Whoa! Has anyone ever managed to put up a fight with a Warden?"

"Who cares? Obviously that giant has got some fight in him! I don't want to stick around and see what is left of this place when the battle is over! I've heard the Warden already killed more of our men than the intruders have!"

"We can't leave now! We would be abandoning our posts! We will be punished if we are caught and surely not paid!"

"There won't be anyone left to pay or punish us! Don't you see? The *Warden* is killing *us*! This goes far beyond what I signed up for!" the guard in the cliff says proudly. "Leave that guy you got there and let's get out of here while we still have the chance! Plus, I managed to snag some compensation on my way down here." The guard in the cliff walks out of the doorway, revealing handfuls of gold treasures within his clutches. "This should be more than enough to snag a boat out of here! Now, are you with me or not?" A wide smile emerges onto the face of the guard holding Babarossa as his eyes soak in the enticing golden trinkets held before him.

He nods his head and throws Babarossa to the ground. The two guards go running off into the fog toward the docks, leaving Babarossa and the door in the mountain unattended.

"See! Now's our chance!" Domino yells proudly as he springs out of their hiding spot. The boys run with all their might to aid the fallen Seer Sage. Sliding into the dirt, they bring themselves to their knees as they check the status of the fallen man.

"Babarossa!" Otto calls out. "Are you okay?"

"Ugh," Babarossa mumbles as he tries to lift himself into a seated position. "I was just fine until that man threw me to the ground! Couldn't you two have helped me before he did that? These old bones can't bounce back like they use to!"

"I-I-uh… I——" Otto's mind immediately races to regret for not jumping to action when he felt the call.

"What Otto is trying to say here," Domino interrupts, "is we got here as fast as we could! We saw that guy mishandling you and we rushed to your aid!"

"Did you now?" Babarossa's words fall heavy onto Domino's soul. The old Seer Sage opens his eyes wide as he looks straight at the young boy giving his testimony. His warm brown eyes ignite in flames as he consumes Domino with his presence. An urge to vomit rises from within the youth's throat. As he leans over to purge, he is surprised to discover what flies out of him.

"No! That is a lie! Otto wanted to come help you, but I stopped him! I told him that it wasn't safe! It's all my fault you got hurt! I am so sorry! Please forgive me! Wait, what?" Domino raises a hand to his mouth as if he means to capture the word vomit that just was expelled. "How——" he tries to ask.

"You are forgiven!" Babarossa says with a cheery tone before leaping into the air without the use of his hands. Otto traces the old man's trajectory through the air, watching him land softly on both of his feet. Babarossa walks over to the gawk-eyed Otto and reaches out his hand.

"What the…" Otto cries out as Babarossa smacks him on the backside of his head.

"That's for being brash and not thinking through your actions. You are lucky to have such a thoughtful friend with you."

"But… But…" Otto babbles as he nurses the welt on his head and the confusion in his heart.

"No need for further apology, you are forgiven too. Now then," Babarossa says as he adjusts his plaid blanket securely around his shoulders. "I must be going; I have some business to attend to in the Plaza. Come find me there when you are done with your little adventure."

"How do you know—" Domino tries to say.

"Your mind is not the best hiding place. More slips in and out of it than you ever realize! Now go!" The boys give the Sage a puzzled look as he turns and starts to walk into the fog towards the Plaza.

"Do you think that was all an act?" Otto finally says. "You know, to make sure we found this doorway?"

"Who knows," Domino responds with a heavy sigh. "You never know what to believe when you hear about him. You don't even know what to believe when you *actually* meet him!" the youth says definitively.

"Yeah! Shoot, you could say the same about Brahm!"

"True! There is so much more to this world than I ever thought possible. Let's make sure to make it out of this debacle alive so we can see what else is out there!"

"Yeah!" Otto cries with glee.

"All right then, let's take a peek to where this secret passageway leads!"

"Oi, Em', are you sure the Power Pole is even in this castle?" Izak asks with an irritated tone. He walks alongside Ayananda as the two continue to follow their quiet companion through yet another supposed path to their goal. Brick and mortar fall around them like sporadic spring showers. It serves a constant reminder of the ever-worsening structural integrity of the crumbling castle.

"I am getting the sense you do not trust my direction," Emmanuel says with a flat tone.

"Wow! You figured that out all on your own? Must be those keen senses of yours! I wonder what could have ever made me lose faith in you?!" Izak fires back, his emotions pouring into his words like a drunken patron who was just thrown out of his favorite bar. "Hmm, maybe it was the first dead end. No! I'll give you that one. Where are my manners? We all make mistakes! Maybe it was the third or fourth path you took us down that only brought us face-to-face with that demonic snake thing. I'm starting to think you really are working for Mune, trying to lead us on a suicidal death trap! Is that it! Huh?! That's got to be it! Just whose side are you on? I've almost died *at least* three times because of your directional hunches, you conniving, double crossing—"

"Izzy," Ayananda says in a soothing voice, attempting to dampen the fire burning inside her comrade.

"Oh, don't 'Izzy' me now! You've seen it too! Where the hell are we even going in this crumbling maze? And how can we even trust 'Mr. Super Sight' here when he doesn't seem to know where he is going any more than we do! Unless this really is a trap! I never trusted that guy since the first time he set foot on our ship."

"You know that's not true," Ayananda continues. "Plus, he was part of the crew even before you joined us, remember?"

"Is *that* even true?" Izak fires back, his head cocked unnaturally to one side. "Maybe he's been playing mind games with us the whole time to convince us of his innocence… leading us to this moment here where he takes us all down, serves us up as a sacrificial platter, and pledges his allegiance to Wisteria and the Progressive Movement!"

"This might not be the best time to remind you, but you haven't taken your medication in quite a long time," Emmanuel says from up ahead.

"You're damn right, it's not! How dare you!" Izak roars, his hands quick to grab what weapons remain along his waist.

"Yes Em', it's definitely not the right time and you know that," Ayananda says with a flair of frustration penetrating her purposefully calm tone. "You just keep looking for the Power Pole's energy signal and try to be sure of it this time. I don't know how many more spare lives we can cash in on this blind mission."

"Was that a joke?" Emmanuel responds, with a hostile aura erupting around him.

"Look, we are all tired and it was just a phrase, you know that. I think this whole thing has got us all riled up. We've spent the better part of our time together running away from these Warden monsters, and here we are confronting one head-on. The last thing we need is for us all to attack one another. Especially while Jeeven is down there making the greatest gamble with his life for us."

"Understood," Emmanuel says, putting his hostile aura back in the holster.

"Izzy?" Ayananda asks, turning her head while looking warmly into the mad gunslinger's eyes.

"You can quit the act, I'm not going to kill him," Izak replies with a flair of his lip. "Not now anyway."

"Good, I am just about tired of having to act like your mother."

"What did you say?!"

"Hey!" Emmanuel yells, dislodging the verbal onslaught behind him. "I think I figured something out."

"Oh? I wonder where we have heard that before?"

"Quiet!" Ayananda shouts, jabbing Izak in the ribcage. Emmanuel walks over and places his hand on the stone wall nearest the mountain cliff that the castle rests upon.

"Master Baba was right in assuming Sophia would be near the Power Pole. My sonar picks up the two very distinct energy signals almost right on top of each other."

"But Jeeven made it very clear we are to target the Power Pole and not Sophia!"

"He did, but why not target both if we can? Baba would not lead us down the wrong path. They are together. I can sense it."

"Maybe *Baba* wouldn't lead us down the wrong path but you sure—"

"Enough!" Ayananda interrupts. "So what is keeping you from getting us there?"

"Even though my sonar can pick up the energy signals, the way this castle is designed, I can't seem to get us any closer than we are now. Each room, each level we go to leads me to the same dead end. It's like there is a whole separate part to this castle that remains hidden from plain sight. It's as if Sophia and the Power Pole are inside the mountain itself! But I just can't find the way into it."

"Why haven't you said something until now? Just point in the general direction they are in, and I'll start blasting away at the wall until we tunnel our way to them! Easy," Izak says, feeling like he contributed a worthwhile solution.

"Easy way to blow up our leader in the process. I'm not going to unnecessarily endanger her any further. I don't believe Baba would have said what he did if it was impossible to fulfill our mission and keep Sophia alive. If Mune got her back there without blowing up his castle, then we can do it too."

"Believe what you want. Just hurry up and fine-tune that radar system of yours before that serpent comes back. What is that dude's deal with snakes anyway? I'm sure he could conjure up anything he wanted, but snakes? Guess it's only fitting. We are running around like rats in a maze, after all. A perfect meal for a hungry snake," Izak remarks.

"I did sense a life force that appeared to be running through the walls earlier," Emmanuel continues. "But it happened so fast, I'm not sure, but now what is this? There is something or someone else in the walls!"

"Sorry to disrupt your pondering, Em'," Ayananda says with urgency ringing in her voice, "but we are going to need all the focus on that other lingering problem of ours." The three Marionettes turn to face Ayananda's warning. They stare into the giant hole the Warden carved through the middle of the castle. Smoke and dust from the battle below continues to obscure any worthwhile view the window of destruction could showcase. However, from below, the familiar yellow eyes rise back into focus.

"I'm getting tired of this thing!" Izak cries out, flipping the safety switch off his gun. "I'm starting to wonder if it can even die!"

"It's a part of the Warden," Emmanuel responds, his hands and feet now in a defensive stance. "All we can hope for is to continue to evade its strikes and hope Jeeven and Beau can divert its attention once again."

"This is maddening! I'm tired of running!" Izak whines. "Plus, I think the last attack we tried might have done something!"

"Seriously? Earlier you were tired of almost dying," Ayananda chimes in. "Now you want to flirt with it? Just pick one and stick with it. We don't have any chance of defeating this beast. You either go throw yourself in the jaw of that thing or keep running."

"Oh, I'll throw something in its jaws, all right," Izak says with a sinister chuckle. He places a hand in one of his pockets and pulls out two grenades.

"Think this through! You've tried that already! It didn't work!" Ayananda tries to reason.

"It did something before! Now it's time to see how far we can push our luck."

"Test your own luck, you jer—" Ayananda's words are cut short as she watches Izak hurl his prized grenade into the swirling dust cloud that still consumes the yellow-eyed serpent. The grenade bounces along the floor, generating compounding tension with each metallic skip upon the stone floor.

"Shield your eyes!" Izak yells, pulling his goggles over his own. Just as the serpent rears its head out of the dust, an explosion of blinding light fills the room. The surge of illumination causes the creature to balk its head back from the explosion. Rushing to the offense, Izak returns his finger to his weapon while firing shot after shot into the blinding light. Swirling vortexes of his compact webbing come flying out of his weapon. They spiral out of their condensed projectiles and expand into an impressive circumference. The webbing takes hold of the serpent, adhering it to the boundaries of the hole it reared its head out of.

"It's no use!" Ayananda screams. "It's still just an extension of the Warden! It can phase through objects just like he can! Let's just run while it's distracted!"

"Just listen to her for once, Izak!" Emmanuel pleads.

"Nonsense, I'm not running until I see just how much advantage I can take of the only weakness we've uncovered! Take this!" he yells as he hurls his other grenade into the open mouth of the howling serpent.

"Ha! This is it! This is… Oh no," Izak back peddles. "This is bad." The distracted serpent quickly regains its composure, as if it predicted what was to come next. With no attempt to break free of the webbing, the serpent opens its mouth a little wider and calms its thrashing. A strange gurgling noise can be heard generating from deep inside the beast. The serpent seems to give a playful wink to the trigger-happy weapon's master before unleashing a wave of fury from within.

"Everyone! Get down!" Izak yells as he hurls himself to the floor. A tidal wave of flames comes roaring out of the serpent's mouth, aimed directly at the three Marionettes. Ayananda hits the ground in time but immediately peeks out of her crouched position only to see Emmanuel didn't heed the warning.

"Emmanuel! What are you doing?!" she cries in horror as her quiet companion leaps heroically in front of Izak and herself. Emmanuel concentrates his energy and quickly erupts a makeshift force field from his aura, surrounding himself and the two behind him.

"That grenade you tossed, it's not another flash grenade, is it?" Emmanuel asks just as the flames start to wash over the swirling vortex of his protective force field. His aura serves as a reliable barrier from the fire but lasts just long enough for Izak to realize the consequences of his actions. The high explosive grenade Izak tossed detonates in mid-air, triggered by the intense heat from the serpent's breath of fire. Emmanuel braces himself, as he prepares to take the brunt of the explosion. He burrows his feet into the flaking tiles of the floor. Expelling all his energy into the barrier, he strains his body to the very limits of his ability. His legs quickly buckle, forcing him into a crouched position. The flesh on his arms starts to ripple from the continued barrage of energy crashing around him. He holds his position steady with proud resistance, pouring his soul into protecting his comrades. His aura swirls with violent and vibrant colors as his rapid cycling emotional state is put on full display for his protected onlookers. He tilts his head to face Ayananda and Izak as he puts the final bit of his energy into maintaining the barrier. A smile flashes across his face just before his hands drop to his side.

"Em'! Nooooo—" the barrier quickly fades and the two on the ground shout cries of grief and disbelief; however, their calls are drowned out by the roar of the fierce flame. Ayananda and Izak watch in horror as their friend loses his battle with the explosion and flies through the air like a discarded rag doll before crashing into the adjacent wall. Even though Emmanuel blocked the brunt of the explosion, the continued flame forces the two remaining Marionettes to grip the warping stone floor tiles with all their might. Their fingers burn with the combination of the lingering heat and overwhelming strain being demanded of their grip. The serpent finally closes its mouth, ending the momentary reign of fire. The room harbors an eerie silence. Only falling debris and the occasional sizzle of charred timber echo through the decimated chamber. The serpent takes one last look at the two flame-broiled humans lying motionless on the floor with the third nowhere to be seen. Satisfied with its work, it phases through Izak's webbing and slithers back to the battle below.

"How insulting," Izak mumbles as he lifts himself off the ground. He dusts off the charred pieces of his clothing and peers around the room. "That thing thinks so lowly of us it didn't even wait around to see if we were really dead. We are nothing to him."

"We never have been! Maybe now you will understand why Emmanuel and I urge you to keep running! We are no match for a Warden!" Ayananda responds as she, too, springs herself back to her feet.

"I had to at least try."

"Well, I hope you're happy," she says dismissively, her attention directed at a pile of rubble covering where Emmanuel's body should be visible. "Now, help me save Em'… that is, if he didn't become incinerated while protecting us from *your* mistake."

"Wow, yeah, Aya, I—"

"Save it," she interrupts, her hand outstretched as if she is blocking a physical attack. "If you really care, you'll put all that energy you are about to waste with an apology into searching for the man who just saved your life. For your sake, you better hope he is still alive or else I'll bury you next to his remains."

Ayananda's words linger within the death stare that punctuates her threat. There is a quiver in her right eye, possibly from fighting back the tear that resides just under the surface. Izak's eyes bulge as he swallows a heavy knot swelling in his throat. Without another word, Ayananda turns and heads towards the ominous pile of rubble. Izak watches her walk off, her high heels clicking with each step along the crumbling stone floor. He is about to make his first step to join her, but a paralyzing jolt runs through his body just as his foot lifts off the ground.

∞

Oh no… he thinks to himself as he feels the control over his body quickly slipping away from him. Forcing down a shallow breath, he tries desperately to regain his composure. Sweat pours down his brow; his facial muscles clench as he strains his efforts, but no amount of willpower seems to match the ungovernable sensations. To follow suit, his vision begins to blur, and the contours of the room start to sway and converge. Shaking his head does little to dislodge the disorientation, but he still persists. Stuck within the failing confines of his body, Izak begs his eyes to squint: the last remaining sense of control he still possesses. His focus pinpoints on the pile of rubble Ayananda is walking to, but even that quickly becomes infected by the field of sensory disorientation. The pile starts to dance, colors merge, and boundaries of individual stones and sheetrock bleed into one another. Izak's eyes widen as he gives into the horrifying sight of the rubble taking the form of an oversized gravestone.

"Not now," Izak says to himself.

Oh yes… now indeed, comes a sinister voice from the dark recesses of his mind. *You really did it this time.*

"Shut up!" Izak yells to the intrusive voice.

You should know by now that won't stop me. Just like you know that man is dead, and it is all your fault.

"Lies!" he screams. His heart swells with fear and guilt. He starts to think the voice might actually be speaking the truth. He looks up and sees Ayananda's petite frame hurling oversized boulders from side to side. Blood drips from her mangled fingertips, mixing with the dust and dirt now covering her porcelain skin. Her frantic digging hastens with each unproductive toss. She pauses only to wipe the tears accumulating on her cheek. Izak's guilt shifts to his paralyzed predicament. He berates himself for falling into such an internal distraction. "Maybe I should have taken those pills," he says in defeated hindsight.

You mean that poison? the voice counters. A rumbling laugh follows the poignant response. *You know you are better off without it. It only clouds the truth. You are lucky we have returned to help you.*

"We? You brought the others with you?" he says with a sense of disgust.

But of course! They will be joining us shortly. You've kept them away for so long, they drifted off to our other worldly companions. the voice says gleefully. *Not I though! I know you are special. I've been keeping a close eye on you, waiting for you to open your doors again. We could be friends you know… if you just stop pushing us away.*

"Ha," Izak scoffs. "You would like that, wouldn't you?"

So would you. You know you can't do this alone. How many more people must you kill before you realize you need us?

"Damn you," Izak says, clenching his fist. A wave of returning guilt fills his heart. He feels his insides start to crush and constrict under the emotional pressure. Just before he completely gives into the enticing feeling, he remembers this happened the last time the voices came to him. "This is their tactic; this is them trying to make me weak." A surge of intrinsic willpower floods his nervous system. A smug smile emerges on his face as he feels himself start to regain a sense of control. He brings his attention to his feet and slowly manifests movement in his extremities.

What are you doing? the voice responds, a quiver of doubt reflected in its tone.

"I may not be able to shake you out of my head, but I'm still the one in control of this body. You are going to watch me prove your words wrong. My friend is still alive, and I'm going to help dig him up."

Dig him up from his grave? the voice says with rekindled confidence. *That's morbid even for me!* Izak looks ahead and sees the hallucinatory gravestone has grown in size and now dances back and forth, making it impossible to not be aware of its ominous imagery.

"Your tricks might work on a weaker mind, but not this one," Izak says, pushing through the crushing guilt. He puts one heavy foot in front of the other, slowly making his way to the dancing pile of boulders.

Ka-hahahahaha! the voice cackles. *You know we always win in the end. Your efforts will only weaken you further. Just wait until the others arrive, then you truly will be powerless!*

"Bring them all!" Izak manages to mumble, his outward pace quickening. "I don't care what you do or what you think will break me down. I'll make them all think twice before they knock on my door again. You all are nothing more than parasites, forgotten shadows of a meaningless existence, hitching a ride on the best ship out of your dismal Hell!"

How dare you.

"And you know what?" Izak says, pushing the voice's words aside. "That you did get right. I *am* the best ride out of your Hell, but mark *my* words, you devilish whisper, this ride will not go the way you want! The flames that burn in my soul will singe your words until they crumble away into wisps of ash and dust. You will beg to return from where you came, and then it will be *my* laugh that rings in your pathetic ears!" Empowered by his own words, Izak starts to regain more control over his body.

Now whose words are hollow? the voice responds. A foreboding silence hangs on its last word.

"Izak!" Ayananda calls out, disrupting Izak's internal struggle. He peers up and notices she has stopped her feverous hurling of debris. She stands hunched over, her breath labored and has a hand covering her mouth. Her gaze is fixated on the small hole she has managed to dig out of the rubble.

"Get yourself together and get over here," she says without looking away. Tears spring from her eyes like flowing rivers that wash through the layers of dirt and soot covering her face. Izak's sense of control remains in check as he finishes his sprint to her, but the conflicting internal dialogue continues with each step.

Why so eager to get to that man's grave? the voice taunts.

"He is alive, we will see!" Izak refutes, unwilling to dampen his stride.

Ah ha, interesting word choice; yes it is we *who will see.* The foreboding words fail to hit their mark as Izak screeches to a halt, completely enamored by Ayananda's distraught presentation. He takes a careful step closer to the revealing hole she has painstakingly carved out on her own. The scorch marks that line the walls and rubble paint a dismal and doubtful picture in Izak's mind. He shakes his head violently as if to remove such thoughts by force before they take root once again. He looks to Ayananda for reassurance. Her soot-splattered face has increasingly more streams of tears etched under her eyes. Her hand remains over her mouth. As she notices Izak's probing glance, she only nods her head towards the rubble, giving no emotional inflection for him to read. Taking a step back she forces Izak to bear the full brunt of the reveal. He clears a heavy gulp from his throat before peering into his friend's fate.

"Oh wow…" he mumbles as he looks down a gaping hole that leads much deeper than the dimensions of the room should allow. "Did you really dig this deep, Aya?"

"Just keep looking," Ayananda says. Izak blinks heavily, trying to force his eyes to adapt to the darkness. He leans over further and further, eventually sticking his head as far into the cleared hole as he can.

"This is insane! Just how far does this go? Is he even in here?" Silence falls upon his questions. "Aya?! Are you still there? What is this?" Frustrated with his momentary isolation, he pulls a lighter from his pocket and brings his thumb to strike the starter. "This isn't funny, Aya! What did you find in here? Where is Em'? Ugh…" He thumbs his finger over his lighter. A failed first attempt drives his frustration to the next level. "C'mon already!" he yells to the unassuming device in his hand. He strikes the lighter again, this time with more concentrated vigor. "Aha! There it is," he says to the flame now dancing in his palm. The flame quickly dispels the darkness, leaving only a hollow cavern at the end of Izak's sight. He looks desperately left to right, his weight fully pivoting on his waist above. He inches himself as far into the hole as he can, waving the lighter violently from side to side. "This is some really messed up joke, Aya! What is—"

"BOOO!" comes an unexpected cry from the depths of the cavern.

"Oh my god!" Izak screams as he reels his head back so fast he slams it hard on the rubble pile directly above him. "What is this? Damnit that hurt! What are you doing here?" he cries out to the unexpected apparition. Bulging eyes from deep within the darkness come dancing into the light, belonging to none other than the cheerful Domino.

"Fancy meeting you here!" he says with sarcastic suave.

"Ah-hahahaha. HA-Ahahahaha!" comes the shrieking laughter of Ayananda, as she can no longer contain herself.

"You cruel woman! How dare you joke about such matters?"

"Serves you right, you selfish prick," Ayananda responds. "Just because you got lucky doesn't mean you don't deserve what's coming to you."

"What are you saying? Is Em' all right? Where is he?" Izak says, waving his head back and forth in the hole looking for clues of his friend's whereabouts.

"I'm right here," Emmanuel says from the darkness behind Domino. Waving his lighter in that direction, his flame puts a spotlight on his battered friend. Emmanuel is hunched over, held up by a very concerned Otto.

"Thank God you are still alive! And you too, boys? How is any of this possible?"

"T-these boys saved me, Izzy," Emmanuel responds with a labored hesitance in his voice.

"Yeah!" Domino chimes in. "We were climbing through this tunnel that we found and after getting lost a few times, we heard this loud commotion from the other side. We stopped to wait it out, not knowing what was going on and then… *bam*! the walls implode, and this guy comes flying into our tunnel! We hear this roaring noise getting louder and louder and decide to grab him and pull him further back in the tunnel. Good thing we did, too, or else this guy would be roast duck!" Domino turns his chin up as he finishes his story, clearly displaying the pride fostered by his rescue.

"You kids really did save the day," Izak says with a huge sigh of relief.

"They at least saved Em' from your selfish antics," Ayananda throws in from above. Izak shakes off her words and continues his conversation with the members of the tunnel.

"Em', so are you alright? Here, let me take a better look at you." Inching himself even further into the hole, he holds his lighter up to Emmanuel's face.

"I'm alive, Izzy, that's all that should matter for now," he responds, shielding his eyes from the glowing flame that now resides inches from his face. Izak pays him no mind as he floats his lighter around, looking for injury. The light from the flame showcases the harsh scorch marks on his cloak. The smell of burnt fabric mixes with the sizzling flesh from the multiple burn marks all throughout his arms and legs. Izak hesitates when he returns his attention to his friend's uncovered face. A knot tightens in his gut as he forces down a deep breath. Emmanuel's glasses have blown off his face, unveiling a haunting display once hidden from view.

"Your glasses!" Izak shouts, full of surprise. "Oh man, I'm so sorry, about… well, everything obviously. But hey, let me try and find something to cover that up. I know how you feel about it."

"No, it's ok," Emmanuel responds, waving his hand to dismiss Izak's efforts. "There is no point in hiding it now. We have more important matters at hand here. I can at least put my past behind me while we finish this mission."

"What is he talking about?" Domino says bluntly, unable to have seen Emmanuel's face until now. He turns around to look at the charred Marionette, his face now fully illuminated by the flickering flame of the lighter. "Yikes! Oh my Maia! What happened to your eyes?!" Domino screams as his own eyes nearly fly out of his head. The youth lets his mouth drop open as he locks sights onto the unexpected disfiguration that stares back at him. "It looks so creepy!"

"You insensitive brat!" Izak yells defensively before striking the youth over the head with his hand that holds the lighter. The flame's light dances with the shadows of the tunnel as Izak keeps swinging at Domino. The light eventually settles back into steady hands after a few emotional strikes, returning focus to Emmanuel's unrestricted face. His previously hidden scars now take their place on center stage. In the sockets where his eyes used to reside, exist pockets filled with silver. The polished nature of the precious metal reflects the dancing fire bilaterally, giving the illusion of Emmanuel harboring flaming pupils. At the corners of each eye socket streams a thin overflow of silver that glides down each cheek. As the boys stare into Emmanuel's face, they gawk with unintended intensity. With a quick first glance, it would appear the man was crying tears of silver. Feeling slightly sensitive to the energy directed at his uncovered face, Emmanuel struggles to formulate a makeshift smile to offset the depressing reveal.

"D-Did that just happen?" Otto says, as quivering concern flavors his words. His whole body starts to tremble. "Your eyes are gone! Oh my God! This is horrible!" He reaches out to Emmanuel as if he somehow holds the remedy for missing sight. "Did Izak do this to you?"

"Hey!" comes a brash cry from above.

"No, no, young man," Emmanuel says while extending one of his arms to calm the youth, "This happened to me long ago, a wound harboring more emotional pain than physical."

"So, does that mean you are—"

"Blind? In one way, yes. In another way, no."

"What do you mean?"

"When time is of the essence, you must settle for the briefest of explanations. Long ago my sight was robbed from me. The precious metal that now covers my face serves as a constant reminder of that fateful day. However, whereas one set of eyes may have closed for good, another was allowed to open."

"Another?"

"Yes. Our eyes perceive only the most minute reflection of sensory information. My quest to regain my sight allowed me to uncover a field of vision far surpassing that of our limiting physical eye. Our world dances with energetic vibrations, a 'sight' none would strive to see if their vision was already considered fulfilled. Desperate to get out of my restricted darkness, I pushed through and became aware of these vibrations… the true makeup of our world. So, even though I lost the physical beauty our eyes depict, I traded them for a deeper line of sight. I tapped into a sight that is not restricted by physicality, distance, depth, or matter. I see all things as they are, dancing harmoniously together and without separation. It has taken years for me to be able to work backwards from this vision and dissect it in a way that I can distinguish separate parts again. It can be a struggle still, seeing things that others cannot."

"Did a blind man really just say that?" Domino blurts out in jest.

"You insensitive brat!" Izak rallies as he strikes the youth atop his head once again, feeling the continued need to defend his friend's dignity.

"Yes, I am aware of the irony," Emmanuel continues despite the commotion, "but it has become even more of a challenge to convince others of what you see when it is you who is the 'blind man.'"

"Hey, are you talking about your mysterious path to Sophia that has kept leading us to dead ends?" Izak interrupts.

"Exactly. Thanks to the reveal of this tunnel, my sights now finally make sense! Tell me boys, how did you find this passageway?"

"Well, we saw Baba being taken to this weird hidden door in the cliff behind the castle. The guards deserted their post and we decided to check it out, and now we are here!" Domino responds cheerfully.

"Ah, I should have known Baba was connected to this. Very good, boys, this was just the break we needed!"

"So, does that mean this tunnel will lead you to Sophia and the Power Pole?" Izak asks.

"It should. The energetic frequencies I was seeing inside the mountain makes sense now. I knew I sensed that caustic energy from the Pole within the rocks, but I just couldn't put the pieces together. There are a group of humans near it too. This is why we kept running into dead ends! The Power Pole is not in the castle at all, it's *inside* the mountain!"

"Good. Now we can finally get out of this crumbling death trap," Izak responds, his tone drastically shifting to a somber cadence. He tosses the lighter to Emmanuel before lifting himself out of the hole. Emmanuel rotates the smooth metal packet of fuel within his hand as he ponders Izak's abrupt energetic shift.

"Hey!" Emmanuel calls out. "What are you thinking about doing?"

"There is still a chance the Warden will send his snake thing back to look for us," Izak says stoically as he lifts himself out of the hole in the wall. "I feel we should not take this advantage lightly. I will stand guard and distract the beast if he comes back here. I'll hold him off as long as I can to buy you all as much time as possible. I owe you that much," he concludes before lighting a bent cigarette against a part of the wall still on fire.

"Nonsense," Ayananda says while crossing her arms across her chest. She walks through his thin puff of smoke and stands right in front of him, making her presence unable to be ignored. "You think I will let you stay up here and die alone for your heroic pity party?"

"You wretched woman! Will you not allow me to have any retribution? I swear you live just to see me suffer, so what, you think you have a better plan? Huh! Well, do ya?!"

"I do, as a matter of fact. You are no match for the Warden on your own. You will be crushed the instant he returns. That won't buy us any time at all and would only leave us down a man."

"How dare you…" Izak's fury bubbles to the surface.

"That's why I'm staying up here too," she says, uncrossing her arms. "Emmanuel, take the boys and finish the mission. The two of us will stand guard. Leave the snake charming to us."

"Very well, I will keep an eye on you two as well," Emmanuel says.

"Did he just…" Domino starts to say but receives a blunt strike from Otto.

"Hey!" Domino retaliates, unsure why he is the only one able to enjoy the sea of ironic puns. Turning to the boys, Emmanuel smiles as he reflects upon the purposeful irony of his statement, allowing Domino to breathe a sigh of relief. He stands up and dusts off his tattered cloak. "Now, whatever happens next," he says to the boys, "don't you two dare fade from my sight."

"Okay, now it's getting excessive," Domino responds flatly.

CHAPTER: 34

Mune

"Sir! The rumbling from the castle has subsided for some time now, do you think the Warden has finally taken care of the intruders?" The guard looks eagerly to his superior officer, hoping to receive a confirming suspicion. A moment of prolonged silence fills the room as the guard is forced to wade in the debilitating suspense. Unfortunately for him, his fate is held by the aloof clutches of his Lord of Wisteria, Bartholomew Mune. Mune slides his fingers around his pudgy cheeks, gliding them repetitively over his chin. A bead of sweat starts to accumulate on the eager guard's forehead as his mind swims within the suffocating silence.

"S-Sir…" the guard repeats again, trying to summon some direction from his commander. Mune turns his head dramatically, causing his freshly polished armor to rattle and clank around him. The light from the encompassing torches dance and glide along his reflective exterior. His sunken eyes flicker like the very flame that illuminates them, peering out of the swollen flesh that makes up his portly face. He looks at the guard with fierce intensity. His face turns even redder as his teeth clench and grind back and forth. A mumbling snarl begins to emerge from his quivering mouth.

"How dare you rush the decree of your Lord!" Mune bellows as he abruptly rips the sword and sheath off his waist. As he tries to pull the sword away, he is met with immediate resistance. A faint clanking sound can be heard with each failed attempt to release his weapon. The guard gulps, unsure of what to make of his confusing situation. "Damn you!" Mune yells at his stubborn weapon. Unable to hold onto his patience any longer, he strikes the guard before him with the blunt end of the rebellious sheath, sending him toppling to the ground. Mune huffs and puffs with heavy breaths. The exerted force has taken a quick toll on his poorly conditioned body. Trying to regain his composure, he puts the sword and sheath back along his waist and turns to address the rest of the guards in the room.

"Anyone else have something to say?" he remarks with cold, unearned authority. The room swims with silent headshakes, conforming to Mune's desired dominance. Satisfied, Mune walks over to a bundle of guards. They congeal around a prisoner they have shackled to the smooth stone wall behind them. The clanking of his metal-plated boots echoes with each clumsy step he takes. At best, Mune appears to be a bright silver duck, waddling back and forth like it's his first time upon dry land.

As Mune passes the halfway point of the chamber, the shadows upon his face start to grow bolder, consuming the vacating light that races off his features. The unnatural pocket of anti-light momentarily shrouds Mune in a sheet of abrupt darkness. A devilish grin appears on his face as he looks onto the pulsating Power Pole radiating alongside him. Small venous extensions from the Pole creep along the polished stone, plastering themselves over the intricate drawings covering the chamber. With each pulsating beat, the dark void swells and flows, appearing to ingest a bite of light with each thump. Light warps around the strange device as if one was looking at it through a fish-eyed lens.

"Beautiful, isn't it?" Mune says to an unspecified member of his audience, his back still facing the other inhabitants of the chamber. Everyone remains quiet, unsure if the question is rhetorical or if there is an expected response. One could even assume Mune spoke of the very chamber they reside in. Its ancient beauty surrounds the inhabitants with art and history of a time lost to the ages. Alternating light and dark brown tiles line the floor of the octagon-shaped room like a chiseled checkerboard. Along the elegantly decorated walls are seven giant humanoid statues, each positioned to face the center of the chamber. In the central focal point exists a magnificent carved structure. At the large base is a thick cube made up of a shimmering black material. On top of the cube sits three chiseled steps supporting an oversized white vase. Seven marble pillars surround the whole configuration, each painted with a different color of the rainbow. At the top of each pillar exists its own precious colored gem. The ceiling arches upward, carved with repeating octagon depressions, resembling the inside of a beehive. Despite the overwhelming beauty that surrounds him, it is the enigmatic black void that captures the enamor of the Wisterian official. It warps the beautiful contours of the chamber with its light bending manifestation.

"It's what you have come all this way in search of, is it not?" he asks, turning his attention to the prisoner shackled to the wall. The guards let out a breath of relief as they are glad his attention is aimed at another. A slimy smile inches its way over his crooked teeth while he continues his trajectory to the captured Resistance leader.

An involuntary wince strikes across Sophia's face as the full concentration of Mune's caustic energy disgusts her to the point of nausea. Her feet dangle off the ground, bound by the chains that hang her arms up over her head. Her toes slide along the floor as any shift in her body causes her to sway side to side. Disrobed of her beige cloak, she hangs exposed, displaying her patchwork sundress hanging lightly off her curvy, hourglass figure. The tattered dress is made of several bright and floral patterns, clearly suffering light damage that would come from being over-worn. Judging the size of the sewn patches, they each could very well have served to cover a small child. The stitch work appears to be handcrafted by a novice, yet Sophia wears her adornment with pride. She looks stoically at her captor as if she is dressed in her own protective armament. The overall assortment of bright colors strikes a beautiful contrast upon her perfectly bronzed skin. The dress flows off her right shoulder, crossing over her collarbone, leaving her left shoulder intentionally exposed. The fabric bunches along her waist where it has been reinforced securely with a faded orange sash. Her arms are bare and uncovered; the remaining fabric flows neatly down over her knees ending about mid-shin. The thin-soled sandals lining her feet scrape the floor, eager to reconnect with the ground. Her tribal beaded jewelry hangs in full view off her neck, capturing a wide array of muted color tones woven in intricate and foreign patterns. The bright colors of her dress further accentuate the golden yellow irises sitting at the seat of her powerful and glowing eyes. Those same eyes widen as they connect with her casted cloak that lies indiscriminately along the floor. A spot that is unfortunately right along Mune's projected path.

A sense of concern quickly consumes her heart as she can't help but worry what horrors would arise if Mune were to explore the contents of her cloak. Her exasperated presentation brings joy to Mune, as he mistakes her level of concern for his own inflated sense of intimidation. Unaware of the very cloak in silent question, his metal-plated foot strikes the inner pocket of her prized clothing. He drags it along the floor, marching like a hasty bathroom patron tailing an unsuspected roll of toilet paper upon their shoe. Finally becoming aware of his own spectacle, he reaches down in disgust, inadvertently bowing to his prisoner while removing the unsightly addition to his wardrobe. His guards gasp at such a gesture. Easily frustrated, Mune hastily casts aside the bothersome fabric, eager to return to his calculated march. Before he can get too far, a strange sound catches his ear. Sophia's Totem Wand strikes the stone floor from inside the safekeeping of her cloak pocket. The sound intrigues the paranoid Mune as he scurries to investigate the incriminating noise.

"What is this?!" he says like a spoiled child pretending he hasn't already spied on their Christmas presents. "Oh my, my, my, whatever *do* we have here!" he continues, waving the Totem Wand harboring Hanu, swinging it frantically like he is trying to write his name upon an invisible chalkboard. Sophia channels all her willpower to appear unamused by his dangerous antics. "A secret weapon, perhaps?" Mune says, casting slanted eyes towards Sophia, eager to catch any shift in her demeanor. Unsuccessful, he tries again. "You thought you were slick, didn't you? Sneaking in such a… a… treacherous devise into my inner chamber! I bet you thought this was going to be your ace in the hole, am I right?! I'm right! Aren't I?!" Mune screams, desperate to get confirmation from his deranged accusation.

"If I had known you would be that threatened by a piece of carved driftwood, I would have rethought my original strategy. It appears a splinter is all that is needed to take down the mighty Mune," Sophia says flatly.

"You foul woman, you…" Mune says with a snarl in his throat. His whole demeanor shifts to feverous fury in a split second. He tucks the mysterious device into his armor and stomps his clunky frame over to Sophia. He advances with his outstretched hand up over his head. Reigning down with a swipe of fury, his stubby hand makes contact across Sophia's flawless cheek. Her head whips to one side, causing her brown hair to fall in scattered strands across her face. "How dare you mock me," Mune says, huffing and puffing from already exhausting his limited energy supply.

"Please, you mock yourself." Sophia says bitterly. Her anger is amplified by Hanu's inadvertent capture more than her own.

"Excuse me?!"

"You are an overindulgent, quick-tempered man-child who stands to represent everything wrong with the direction humanity is going," Sophia retorts. Gasps can be heard from the guards rushing to conceal their involuntary expression. Mune gives a snarled scan of the room like a feral dog defending its dinner. His men quiver with the anticipation of retaliation. Satisfied he has regained control over his minions, he turns back to Sophia.

"It matters not," Mune continues, trying to regain his composure. "There is nothing you can do at this point to stop me. With this Power Pole under my control and the Warden tied to its power, I will soon fulfill Wisteria's mission and regain the honor I deserve!"

"You have no idea what atrocities you and your people have brought to this land, Mune," Sophia says calmly. She turns her throbbing face slowly back to address her enraged abuser. "Have you ever thought of the consequences of allowing such chaotic energy to flow freely in our world? What you see as a source of power will ultimately be the source of all our destruction. Yours included! Don't you see? What good is gaining control over the world if you need to put a ticking time bomb on it in order to do so?" She looks to Mune who only smiles, clearly not sharing her same level of concern. Sophia is now forced to watch the unsightly man waddle back and forth in front of her again. Moving closer with his waddled trek, he gets within inches of Sophia's face. The breath from his disfigured mouth penetrates her personal space with pungent violation. She winces at the disheartening smell of his most prized orifice. The stench alone harbors more pain than her previous physical assault.

"Funny, isn't it?" he says while gently stroking the reddened skin upon her cheek. "To be so close to your goal of stopping me, only to realize you never had a chance. You remain blind to your overwhelming insignificance. I could almost applaud it," he chuckles to himself, preparing for a desired reaction from Sophia that never comes. Her silent gaze is all that follows his childish banter. Her composure infuriates him. He looks to her again, ready to unleash his anger upon her but is stopped dead in his tracks. The eyes he looked upon a moment ago now glow with a radiance he did not notice before.

Their faint yellow hue from before has erupted into a pulsating golden beacon that sinks his throat into his chest. Enamored, Mune's mind starts to race. He scurries around in thought, desperately trying to make sense of his ocular entrapment. His eyes widen with sudden realization; it's as if he is staring into the face of a ferocious beast guarding her newborn offspring. She rattles within her shackled prison, radiating caustic waves of rage and fury. Despite being bound to the wall, her presence ignites fear into the heart of her captor. Mune takes a step back, shaking his head and refreshing his sights on his prisoner. Mune is happy to see the spell has been broken for now.

"You are a scary woman, you know that?" he says with a nervous chuckle. "That look must be how you command those barbaric Bakuwan of yours. How else would you govern such an irritating thorn in the side of progress?" Sophia's choice to remain silent causes an involuntary curl of his lip, but he chooses to disregard her lack of engagement. "Makes me think you and I are not all that different in that regard. Fear is such a wonderful way to maintain control, wouldn't you say? Maybe we are just two sides of the same coin, you and I."

"You make it sound like you know everything there is to know about me," Sophia responds with a sarcastic flair. "So why not just cut to the chase, shall we? No need for lengthy monologues if we are so similar. Let's flip this coin you say we mirror and see who winds up on top."

"Ha!" Mune bellows dramatically as he takes a step back and looks to his guards. "HA!" he repeats with hands on either side of his bottomless belly. "Do you hear her, men? She makes it sound like she is challenging me!" His boisterous banter quickly turns to a scowl as his men do not immediately join him in comical appreciation. A nervous laughter emerges from the guards as they look to one another for reassurance. It's enough to satisfy Mune for the moment. "You think you stand a chance at challenging me?" he says, quickly switching his rapidly fluctuating mood to that of anger and detest. "I will mop the floor with that arrogant mouth of yours, woman!" he snarls as he takes his hand and grabs Sophia by her jaw. He forces her to look into his eyes as he continues his banter. "The coin flip has already been won. It was won the moment you set your eyes on overthrowing my claim to this land. You were a fool to ever think you could make a dent in my plans here." With a flick of his wrist, he flings her face up against the rock wall she hangs from, causing a streak of blood to pour from the abrupt abrasions. He proudly walks over to the Power Pole, his boots clanking with their metallic echo.

Sophia slowly turns her head back around to study her flamboyant captor. She notices he is standing still, staring at a particular part of the Power Pole. She squints to make out a white box strapped to the pole she hadn't noticed before. The interwoven wires that extend on either end of the box resemble one of Izak's prized explosives.

"An explosive, huh?" she says, hoping to get some kind of insight from his reaction. "Seems like a strange strategy to blow up your trump card… unless it isn't you who applied such a piece of reassurance…"

"Ha," Mune chuckles calmly, his back still facing Sophia, "I'm not surprised you recognized such a device. Nor am I surprised your interpretation of the situation is completely wrong," he says, quickly turning back to see the disappointed look on Sophia's face in full view. "Being sentenced to this rock was not my idea, I'll have you know. It was my only choice to save face," he says with unexpected openness. "No one in their right mind would come to this place. However, having fallen out of favor with the Wisterian family due to… *creative differences*… coming here was my only way to make things right. They get their treasured Power Pole right where they want it, and I get to return to high graces for making it happen. Everyone wins."

"Why are you telling me this?" Sophia interrupts, overwhelmed by the unexpected transparency. "I'd rather die than become your therapist. If you have issues with your homeland, take it up with them."

"Ah, you see, you are going to help my situation, but not in the way you think. The Warden never truly imprinted its loyalty to me; I saw that from the very beginning. I'm sure Wisteria planned all along for him to be reassurance *their* plan worked out. They were naive to think I wouldn't see through that! That explosive you see is *my* reassurance, dear Resistance leader, and this is *my* plan. The Warden may still bend his wavering will to the Wisterian High Family, but with his power source in the palm of my hand…" he says as he lifts a detonation device from alongside his waist, "he wouldn't dare cross me. Or else… *kaboom!*" he yells, throwing his hands up in the air with the detonator still in his clutches. "Who has played who?" he asks sinisterly. "Then you come in, as if playing into my hand. What better way to regain my nobility and rise even higher than to present the

High Family with Spearhead's replacement?! And to do so while taming the power of the defective Warden I was given! It's almost poetic."

"Tiger," Sophia says boldly. "His name was Tiger."

"It doesn't matter what you call that abomination. Soon that dog of a Warden will show back up here with the bodies of your men in his hand, drop them at my feet, and take us back home. I can't wait to finally leave this worthless rock."

"I must say, it appears you have thought of just about everything." Sophia's calm tone strikes a nerve in the overconfident commander. "It would be a shame if you underestimated my forces, or an even bigger shame if you failed to factor in any unexpected hang ups to this brilliant plan of yours."

"You mean that Shaker who washed up on these shores the other day?" Mune says, triumphantly making his emotional chess move. He can almost feel Sophia's heart skip a beat. "I had received word he was captured on the Plaza by a few of my most worthless guards. They should be in the middle of torturing him until he begs for his own death as we speak. Is he the unexpected hang-up you were betting on?" A slash of fear-flavored doubt cuts through Sophia's heart.

"There... that must be a mistake... there is no way..." Sophia mumbles unconsciously.

"Ah, but there it is," Mune says as he moves in for checkmate. "You've been playing with a game piece that has already been taken down, my dear." Sophia soaks in a heavy sigh. She shakes her head and regains her confidence in her own forces.

"The members of the Resistance who sail with me are the best of the best," Sophia responds. "Together we can overcome your defective Warden."

"So naive," Mune says with pleasure as he leans in to further dismantle Sophia's confidence. "You lead a force full of Bakuwans as if you harbor the same threat level as they do. Granted, you do manage to organize such unruly brutes, but... look at you! You are a shell of your predecessor! You are nothing compared to Spearhead and you are nothing with out your Bakuwan back up. *You* are essentially powerless, *are you not?*" He takes a step back, pleased with the power of his words. The fire in Sophia's eyes has noticeably dwindled. "You sway there, bound like a sack of flesh at a meat market," he continues, ready to nail the coffin of his prisoners dying spirit.

"You harbor no higher threat than the flies that will soon feast upon your discarded carcass!" Sophia has come to a loss of words, her mind drowning in the sea of self-doubt. As the metaphorical coin continues to flip through the air, it it remains unseen if the tides of fate will be tipped in her favor.

"S-Sir…" one of the guards says reluctantly, hesitant to address his leader.

"What is it?!" Mune barks, his hand already making its way back to his sword.

"Please sir, I mean no disrespect. There is just… there is just a peculiar noise coming from the other side of the door." Mune huffs a deep exhale at the news his guard brings. He looks to the steel door separating him from the rest of his crumbling tower. Taking a few steps closer, he begins to hear a faint banging coming from the other side. The sound lingers in the air like a reverberating gong.

"Who would be dumb enough to try and break into here?" Mune ponders out loud. "Hmm, maybe it is the Warden returning with those worrisome Resistance intruders!" he says, trying to talk himself into a more realistic scenario. Unsure what fate resides on the other side, he stops his progression towards the door. A flame from the torch standing next to him crackles with its flickering embers. The light captures the deep creases of Mune's face as it contorts with a sinister solution. He turns and walks back to the center of the room.

"You," he says as he walks past the guard who first mentioned the noise, "go open the slot and see who is trying to gain entrance."

"M-Me?" the man says with a noticeable quiver.

"Why, of course you!" Mune says warmly. "You wouldn't want to risk any harm to come to your leader now, would you? Now go serve your duty and deal with that nuisance." The guard slowly walks to the door as the banging from the other side gets louder and louder. He desperately looks around for some source of salvation. His eyes widen as he stares upon the intricate wall carvings that the flickering flames illuminate around him. The guard's head circles around as he takes in the ancient imagery for the first time. He studies the markings depicting what looks like warriors meeting their end by the various forces of nature, be it water, wind, fire, or bolts of lightning. A hand reaches out of a swirling vortex that looks like a hurricane, casting judgment upon those below it. With the sense of doom and destruction surrounding him, his body involuntarily quivers as he nears the large metal door. Taking a heavy breath, he looks to the metal clasp that opens a small slit to peer into the other side. Going against all natural instincts, he places his clammy hand on the clasp.

"Waaaahh!" the guard screams as the door starts bellowing from the repeated banging from the other side. The unexpected hammering continues to ripple through the door, putting visible stress upon the hinges that adhere it to the mountainous cliff. Slowly, the guard pulls the latch back, bringing to view the source of the disturbing racket.

"No way!" the guard yells. "It can't be! It's—" Before the guard can continue his report, a swift hand extends through the opened slit and grips securely around the frantic guard's throat.

CHAPTER: 35

Double Vision

Brahm walks in the middle of the Seer brotherhood as they make their way to recover their female counterparts. His illuminating glow cascades off his body and bounces around the once dark and dismal corridor they travel. The destructive ripples from the battle raging below have brought the castle to near ruin. All the decorative lanterns that once hung from the ceiling now cover the floor, shattered and entirely void of their original glow. The bare feet of the men who now walk over the remains must maintain vigilant so as not to strike one of the many threatening shards of glass. The walls creak and moan as they struggle to hold up the layers of building that exists above them. Distant murmurs of destructive warfare can still be felt in the quivering hall that encompasses them. Dust shivers from between the crawling cracks among the walls. The rumbling has diminished substantially since it first started. Brahm grows a bit concerned about the fading pulse of the battle, curious as to what foreshadowing rhythm the weakened beat harbors. He tries to tap into the energetic surroundings to get a better read of the unfolding events. However, as soon as he opens his inner sight, he is bombarded by an unexpected vision.

"Ahh!" He struggles to focus his inner eye to see the scrambled information clearly. From within the vision, a dark shadow emerges into view. It radiates with a sinister energy making his skin crawl on end. Feeling like he is walking right into the mouth of a hungry beast, an overwhelming sensation compels him to turn around. He shakes his head, trying to ignore the vision and push further down the castle corridor. His stomach knots with each advancing step. His intuition screams for him to change directions. He grips either side of his head as the pain of his vision becomes physical. Most of the Seer brethren have now stopped to stare at his bizarre behavior. Their collective attention becomes to distracting to ignore. They unintentionally gawk, struggling to make sense of his troubled demeanor. With a heavy sigh, Brahm looks around and centers himself back in the physical world.

Their troubled eyes study Brahm's outward brutality. Covered in blood and bruises, he appears as a dead man walking. His strange antics do not help dispel the Seer's growing concern of his well-being. With the troubling vision removed from his mind, Brahm can easily bring a smile back to his face, but it's not enough to dispel the worry of his onlookers. Gashes of flesh remain open, while streaks of blood pour down his body. The drips of blood that strike the floor cast a disrupting and haunting rhythm. Brahm decides to address the silent inquiries.

"I promise you my injuries are only physical in nature. There is no need to worry," Brahm says with a warm smile. "They are… how did you say it before… *worldly*."

"A-As much as we want to believe you, how can you say such things as you appear to us in such a state!" Mono says with unrelieved concern. "You glow like you come from the heavens, yet you look like you've just escaped the tortures of hell!"

"If you were to put more trust in the vision of your mind's eye rather than your physical eye, you would see there is nothing to worry about," Brahm responds calmly. Mono smiles brightly as the hairs on his skin stand at attention. He looks around to his brothers who all nod with collective understanding. Just as the atmosphere lifts and lightens, Mono is first to notice Brahm's abrupt expressional shift.

"Whoa, what's wrong now, Brahm?" Mono asks with rekindled worry. Brahm appears as if he has misplaced something very important, searching the room with a panic-stricken intensity. It takes a moment for him to register Mono's question.

"It's… noth—" he says, his attention quickly drifting back to scanning his environment in all directions. He studies the wall to his left and gazes at it as if staring through a window. Placing his hand upon the stone wall, he leans against it as if trying to push open an unseen door. Exasperation and confusion flavor his facial expressions. The surrounding Seers remain at an impasse, finding themselves more worried than motivated. Tewari decides to intervene and assess his halted companions.

"Why do you stop?" he questions with authority. He walks into the center of the crowd, nearing Brahm with a serious tone resonating with each step. With no one able to answer his question, Tewari snarls slightly with disapproving resolve. "I asked what is the meaning of this standstill? Need I remind you all of the ticking time bomb we all currently reside in? What could possibly be more important than saving our sisters? Speak!"

"My apologies, Tewari," Mono finally says as he looks away from Brahm. "It's just, you see…" His unanswered remark encourages Tewari to look upon Brahm for himself. Brahm continues to lean up against the wall. His eyes remain closed as he thrashes his head from side to side, appearing completely lost in another world. Sensing his brothers' apprehension to interfere, Tewari takes it upon himself to disrupt their guest's bizarre theatrics. With an outstretched arm, he reaches to grab Brahm's shoulder in order to snap him out of his trance.

"What in the world are you—" Tewari starts to ask but is immediately interrupted by an unexpected shriek of pain.

"Ye-eeaaaahhh!" Brahm screams. He turns and grabs the shoulder with his other hand as if cradling a serious injury. Tewari steps back as he, too, is now lost for words. Brahm slides down to his knees and turns his head away from the wall. The Seers watch as Brahm's eyelids lift only to expose the pupil-less whites of his eyes. His head begins to vibrate with nauseating vigor, while his hand grips his shoulder with unrelenting force. He digs into his own flesh as if trying to stop something from entering his body.

"Brahm!" Mono screams, terrified of his new friend's presentation. Triggered by the resounding call of his name, the pupils roll back from within head and look onto his very concerned audience. Before addressing everyone, he looks down at his shoulder, appearing completely surprised with what he sees, or rather, doesn't see. He rotates his shoulder around as if he wasn't aware it could move in such a way. Distracted once again, he forgets the awaiting audience that stands motionless before him.

"What is the meaning of all this?" Tewari demands. His words distract Brahm from his shoulder fixation. Dropping his arm, Brahm places his hands upon the floor and lifts himself back off the ground. Dusting himself off, he nods his head with a level of acknowledgment that he is ready to explain himself.

"What I am about to say will be challenging to accept."

"Get on with it, we do not have time to waste," Tewari pushes.

"I agree," Brahm says softly. "So allow me a moment to try and convince you we are going the wrong way."

"Excuse me?" Tewari says with a snarling face full of emotion. "Are you questioning the validity of a Seer's vision?"

"I am," Brahm says flatly.

"On what grounds? The visions of the Seers are the pride of this land and have been the source of salvation and sanctuary for hundreds, if not thousands of years! Tell me why we should even humor your musings any further?"

"Because I am led to believe your visions have been tampered with."

"Impossible! Who would have the ability to do such a thing?"

"Someone who is equally as powerful, if not more so," Brahm says, locking his eyes into those of Tewari, fully aware he has struck a nerve with the prideful Seer. "The pulsating energy from everyone's desire to save your people is palpable. It would be easily perceived by anyone who has the ability to sense subtle energy. With a malicious intent, it would not be hard to manipulate your visions to see that which you desire rather than that of the truth."

"I appreciate you freeing us from our chambers, stranger, but this is where you cross the line. To question our visions now would be to put to question the very nature of who we are. We cannot start to doubt ourselves in such a critical time. I will leave this debate to be solved by the brothers who have heard our testimony. Brothers!" Tewari says as he turns to face his people. "What do you say? Do you place your faith in the hands of this mysterious stranger who has come to us, or do you place it in the hands of your ancestry? Will you bring yourself to doubt your God-given abilities? Speak with action, my brothers, for I stand with our ancestors and believe our visions are incorruptible and granted by the highest of high. I will continue to walk the path we been shown that will lead us to our sisters. Follow me if you wish. Stand with this man if you must. I will not force your hand." With his words finalized, he takes one last look at Brahm before continuing his path down the rattling corridor. The remaining Seers look to one another with silent inquiry, wondering what to do next. As their leader slowly drifts away from Brahm's illuminating glow, his contours fade into the engulfing darkness.

"I am sorry, sir," a man says to Brahm as he turns to follow Tewari. "I thank you with all my heart for freeing us, but I must leave you now. My place is with my people."

"I completely understand," Brahm responds. "I wish you the very best." With nods of acknowledgment, the man scrambles off to join his leader. One by one the remaining Seers follow suit, with Mono being the final one to make his decision.

"This is not fair," Mono says. "I trust both of you. I know neither of you would steer us wrong. So why must you two conflict in direction?"

"We each walk our own path into the still-malleable future. We each have to speak our own truth if we wish to see the best future unfold," Brahm says with a smile on his face. "I know this is hard. It's hard for me as well. I had a feeling my words would inspire such a polarizing effect."

"So why say them? Why implant doubt and distrust if you knew it was just going to push everyone towards the same direction they were going anyway?"

"Because it was still important. Now your people walk with the awareness that there could be another way. This will become vitally important in the continued understanding of the gifts your people possess. Maybe I am right. Maybe I am wrong. Either way, now you must work on trusting *yourselves* as much as you have trusted your gifts. Has one ever contemplated the possibility of your most cherished gift being used against you?" "No, I don't think anyone has, but I still don't understand how it could even be possible," Mono says as he looks back to his people fading in the darkness. An anxious tone reverberates within his voice.

"That is okay. As things unfold it will become clearer. We must walk the path of our choices to fully understand why we make them. Come, let us go together."

"Wait, are you coming with us? After everything you just said?" Mono asks with exasperation.

"Yes, I see my time with all of you is not quite over."

"But what about Tewari? I'm sure he is still very mad at you for questioning his vision."

"I'm sure he is, but our paths have become too intertwined at this point to part ways now. For better or for worse, we will all see the sobering truth soon enough." With his final words hanging heavy, Brahm makes his way to join the others. His radiating light illuminates those before him who were obscured by darkness. Mono hurries to catch up, his mind still racing to make sense of Brahm's decision.

"You make it sound like we are making a mistake… and you are willing to make that mistake with us. Why not try harder to stop us if you know what is going to happen?"

"The future is a funny thing, Mono," Brahm says with his sight still pressing forward. "No matter who claims to *see* the future, they only can capture a *potential* outcome. The future remains fluid and malleable regardless of the pressing vision of others who try to lock it down one way or another. What Tewari and I have seen are two potential outcomes of our awaiting future. Out of respect of his own free will, I must allow him to move forward with his resolve. The rest of your men all share the same choice, as do you. What I have seen leads me to believe my place is still here with all of you."

"Even if you feel we are being led into a trap?" Mono asks.

"Just because I feel your leader is making a mistake does not mean I have to abandon you. I've said my piece, and whatever happens, happens. I will stand by all of you and see this decision through… and pray that I am wrong." A heavy gulp swells in Mono's throat as they near the group of Seers that hang tightly to Tewari. Brahm's bright light is hard to ignore.

"I hope you are not here to try and stop me," Tewari says without looking back. A wave of dominant hostility wavers in his tone. The Seers whip their heads back to Brahm to see if he takes the bait.

"I never tried to stop you," Brahm says calmly. "I only spoke my truth as you have spoken yours. I respect your decision to move forward as I can only hope you respect mine to follow you."

"Ah," Tewari says with a boastful hum. "Change your mind, did you?"

"Not quite," Brahm says chummily. "I just realized how lonely I would have been without all of you!" His unexpected playfulness cuts the atmosphere of hostility like a swift blade. Many of the Seer brethren take a heavy exhale as they release their own internalized tension.

"So how much further until we reach the chamber you believe your other Seers are located?" Brahm asks.

"I *know* it to be only a few more rooms away," Tewari says matter-of-factly. Brahm resigns the temptation to continue their emotionally layered conversation. Silently, the group moves through the crumbling hallway, begging the attention of the resurging hostility emanating from below. The walls creak and moan as if begging to be put out of their misery. The pace of the group hastens to a steady jog. The light from Brahm bounces with each carefully placed step as the floor beneath them also starts its crumbling plea of surrender.

"There!" Tewari shouts with a finger outstretched, pointing ahead to the anticipated room of reckoning. "Let's see whose vision holds true, Shaker!" Tewari calls back.

"I hope it's yours!" Brahm shouts ahead. The group huddles around the door as it is silently decided Tewari will be the one to open it. He looks down to the lock only to see it has fallen to the floor, broken into pieces.

"That's strange," he says, feeling waves of doubt starting to creep into his heart.

"It's no matter!" one of the overly eager Seers claims. "With all the falling rubble around here, it could have easily broken the lock! Let's just go and get them out before they are crushed to death!"

"You're right, Fowani" Tewari says to the eager Seer, "No time to waste! Let's go!" Pushing the steel door open, a loud creaking cry from the rusted hinges announces their presence. The men rush in with hopeful anticipation. Brahm steps into the room and casts his light into the veil of darkness.

"Somlia!" cries a man.

"Orina!" cries another.

"Sheela!" a man shouts with tears in his eyes.

"Raja!" Mono cries, his eyes unable to convince the rest of his senses of what he sees. A familiar face turns and locks eyes with the overeager youth. Mono can hardly contain himself. He wipes a tear from his eye as he runs to his sister and the rest of the Seer women still locked within the prison cage. Joy fills the room as the men become overwhelmed with emotion. One by one they follow Mono's lead to reunite with their sisters, mothers, daughters, and wives. Tewari stands back as his men run forward, leaving only himself and Brahm resisting the urge to crowd the cage.

"I guess some people have to see it for themselves," Tewari says proudly, "that the Seers' visions go unmatched." He looks to Brahm with a smile on his face. Brahm stares intently at the cage and its contents. The women are surprisingly silent but the look in their eyes is that of relief and loving gratitude. A vein in Brahms forehead twitches as he tries to make sense of his lingering uneasiness.

"No hard feelings, right?" Tewari says, trying again to engage conversation. Brahm continues to look on, watching Mono be the first to reach the locked gate. His sister makes her way through the crowd of women to join her brother at the prison bars.

∞

"I'm going to get you out of here!" Mono promises as he surveys the ground for a tool to break the lock. Raja inches her way closer to her brother, a glowing smile taking the place of any dialogue that would normally precipitate in such a situation. Mono does not pay the oddity any attention as he finds relief in discovering a sharp fragment of the stone floor broken apart near his foot.

"This should do the trick!" he says as he begins to strike the metal loop that binds the lock to the cage door. Strike after strike, he hammers away at the thick metal clasp. The sound resonates through the room as Mono puts all his might into each liberating pelt. With the encouragement of his brothers who surround him, Mono attacks the lock harder and harder each time. Sweat pours from his brow as he focuses his conscious attention in hitting the same spot over and over again. Small chips can be seen in the metal loop from his efforts, which push him to go into overdrive with his zealous assault.

"I think he's almost got it!" cries a man from the crowd.

"Yeah! Hold on tight, sisters. You are almost free!"

∞

"Surely you can't still be cautious?" Tewari says to Brahm. "Anybody who might have been here to try and intercept us probably fled in worry of the building falling down on them! At the very least, someone would have come to stop us by now if they were still here, right? Isn't it time to celebrate already?" Brahm lets out a heavy sigh as he does register Tewari's words, but still cannot let go of his concern. He strains his eyes to study the women awaiting their rescue. Their continued silence weighs heavy on his mind. Brahm concentrates on Raja who keeps inching her way closer to her distracted brother. Her glowing smile creepily starts to curve into a sinister twist that causes Brahm's heart to skip a beat.

"What is it?" Tewari demands, very aware of the shift in energy but not of the growing irregularities from inside the cage. Raja's arm lifts above her head; her outstretched fingers taking the shape of sharpened blades.

"No!" Brahm shouts as a quick flicker of Raja's eyes give away her true intent. Her once crystal-clear blue eyes fade into deep dark pits of shadow upon her face. A golden glow emerges with a serpentine slit cutting through the now yellow orbs. Her ire smile opens to reveal rows of razor-sharp fangs behind her lips. As her hand begins to lower itself into striking position, Brahm wastes no more time before taking action. Tewari's eyes widen as Brahm brings himself into a crouching position so quickly the transparent after-image of his original position still linger as a wisp of visionary memory.

"H-How is that…" Tewari stammers, as his words start to choke up. Brahm's physical existence appears to be smeared by a celestial knife, spread across a slice of multi-dimensional toast. Various outcroppings of his transparent body extend like a trail of quivering ghosts on their way to the prison cage. They flicker in and out of existence, flowing inside a vacuum of timeless space. In reality, Brahm has pushed his particles past the boundaries of speed, distance, and time. Bypassing the limits imposed by the physics of this world, he imbues his bodily existence to move with the only force capable of competing with the speed of light: thought.

Pouring all his conscious energy into manifesting himself next to the prison cell, his law-abiding particles are overridden by the unbounded command of his will. He soars towards his intended target with absolutely nothing standing in his way. His particle existence ripples along the conscious trail of his travel, appearing to the untrained eye to look like a phantasmal blur. Just as quickly as the thought popped into his mind, Brahm's hand materializes in-between Mono's head and the incoming attack of his imposter sister. His hand grasps firmly around the encroaching daggered assailant. The impact from the colliding force sends a shock wave rippling through the room. The unsuspecting Seers are blasted away from the concussive epicenter.

"W-What is going on?" Mono stammers as he struggles to pick himself up off the floor. He glances up at Brahm's solidary hand floating in the air as it holds tightly to the reformatted arm of his sister. He watches as the rest of Brahms body quickly materializes in physical form around his floating hand. With the threatening daggers of his sister's doppelganger receding back to their normal human proportions, Mono is left unable to understand Brahm's intervention. "Let go of her!" he cries. "What are you thinking?! That's my sister!"

"This is no sister of yours!" Brahm cries as he struggles to maintain control over the deceptively strong beast emanating from Raja's body. Long talon-like daggers slowly reemerge from her delicate fingertips and start to sink into Brahm's quivering forearm. They slide effortlessly through his flesh, sending more streams of blood meandering down his arm. "Take a good look and see for yourself!" Brahm shouts as he winces from pain. Mono complies, and quickly notices the serpentine features hidden behind the guise of his sister. A slithering tongue emerges from her mouth. Her glowing yellow eyes scan over his baffled body, looking as if it is ready to devour him.

"Hurry up and get out of here!" Brahm cries, "There is no more time!" As Mono and the others run from the cage of imposters, Brahm looks into the cage and locks eyes with the being possessing Raja's body. He watches as the remaining Seer women start to adopt the same serpentine features that plaster Raja's face. Their collective crystal-blue eyes shift into pulsating yellow orbs while their bodies float like a fluttering curtain in the wind. Eventually, they all fade away, turning into a blanket of black smoke. The remaining wisps of their existence congeal into one point, merging into Raja's growing body.

"Who are you?" Brahm demands of the emerging beast.

"Who am I?" The beast responds with a deep male voice emanating from Raja's contrasting feminine frame. The waves of black smoke wash over what is left of Raja's image and blankets her with dark obscurity. From within the blob of darkness begins to emerge a tall, slender humanoid form. The more physical the being becomes, the more its strength increases.

"Ahh!" Brahm screams as the claw still penetrating his arm releases itself and floats up to the figure's developing head. Brahm takes a knee as he watches the claw gently mold back into humanoid hands. The newly reformed appendage meets its corresponding counterpart, and both hands rise atop the figure's head. Together they push the black smoke upward into a sharp point, creating the proud hairstyle of the materializing Warden. His erect mohawk peaks with such perfection, its sharpness could cut the growing tension in the room.

"Phew! I was wondering when I was ever going to get out of that debacle downstairs!" the Warden says to himself while brushing off his suit jacket. "Those two sure know how to put up a good fight! I have to give them that. Too bad they just couldn't keep up." Brahm can feel his body tense as he contemplates speaking to the beast once again.

"You still wish to know who I am?" the Warden says before Brahm's thoughts materialize into speech. A sly curl of his lip slides up into his high cheekbone. The statement takes Brahm aback, unsure if the thoughts in his mind have become vulnerable to perception.

"You must be a Warden," Brahm responds heavily.

"Very good," the Warden says as he takes a threatening step forward. "You know, it's a shame I am only known by such a vague title. Do you know how many 'Wardens' are out there? I doubt you do. It's a lot, I can tell you that. Put us all in a room and say, 'Hey! Warden' and we would all look as if you were speaking to us. To exist, void of any true individual personality can be very powerful, and awfully frustrating at times. But you…" the Warden says with a slithering change in energy. "There is only *one* of you, Mr. Brahm-El Kumara *Freewater*!"

"How dare you speak my name!" Brahm says, cracking under the weight of the unexpected jab. His heart races as his mind struggles to grasp any possible explanation for how such a sensitive piece of identity became available without his consent.

"Oh, the things I know about you… you would probably kill to find out. But trust me, it's by no choice of mine that I am abreast to such knowledge, especially knowledge of a man that concerns me no more than a toy for sport. But! That's my non-existent ego talking! Who am I to say such things?! *Nobody* of course!" The Warden begins to chuckle from his own word play. "The master is very interested in you, Mr. Freewater, and seeing as I am nothing more than an extension of his being, I am forced to be interested in you as well."

"Mune," Brahm says definitively.

"Ah, no, but trust me when I say I totally get why you would think that. It's really quite embarrassing to be associated with that guy. I mean just look at him, will ya? More animal than man, wouldn't you say? Ugh, the things I must do because I have no *choice* in what I do. The plot here is much thicker than it appears. My true master is the mighty creator of my existence. He and I are one, yet I am but a finger of his mighty hand. Mune is merely the bane of my existence I am sworn to assist. My actual master sees you through me and is very pleased. He is very ready to make your acquaintance." The Warden removes his glasses to reveal the dark spiraling voids that rest inside his eye sockets. Brahm is drawn in by the unexpected gravity of their existence. Each 'eye' is sprinkled with what appears to be bright stars amidst a dark black backdrop. The stars orbit around a large central sun that glows brighter and brighter, appearing to consume the entirety of their ocular galaxies.

Brahm can feel a strong force behind the two suns; a collective and sinister identity rests within the cosmic spheres. Its existence is definitely different than that of the physical Warden before him, yet it feels like he is meeting the very puppeteer hidden atop the strings of his toy. The puppeteer's prying nature reaches out as if trying to pull Brahm into the growing gravitational field of the dueling galaxies. A binding and suffocating force starts to wash over him. He can feel the will of the puppeteer trying to penetrate his consciousness.

"Enough!" He shouts, thrashing his arms to his side as he severs the binding from the distant foe. He stands with defiant poise, looking the Warden and his distant puppeteer directly in their cosmic eyes.

"Very good," the Warden responds calmly, as he places his glasses back over his eyes. "I… we… would have expected nothing less. Gosh, I really need to let go of this desire to have an identity! But where does that desire come from? Who's to say? Me? There is no 'me' to even ponder such a query!" Brahm no longer finds himself interested in the Warden's banter. He looks behind him to the stationary Seers and decides to act fast.

"Tewari!" Brahm shouts. "You must get your men out of here, fast!"

"Agreed, but how? Where?" Tewari responds quickly, ready to take action.

"Do you trust me?" Brahm asks, his words falling heavy onto Tewari's heart.

"I do. Show us the way," he says, exhaling the last remaining essence of resistance.

"Tewari!" one of the Seers shouts. "How can you—"

"Not another word!" Tewari commands, holding his hand out in front of him while demanding an overwhelming call of authority. His voice bellows through the prison chamber and echoes in the hearts of his men. "A true leader must be willing to accept his mistakes. I was wrong before and I admit that. I now choose to listen and trust. Follow me or find your own way. Make your decision now." The Seers look to one another and quickly nod heads in compliance. Brahm nods his own head and raises his arm towards the wall behind them.

"Take your brothers and seek refuge with your sisters! I have seen they are safe for now; I will hold off the Warden while you make your escape!"

"You will do what?" the Warden responds, cracking his knuckles with a satisfying crunch.

"You heard me," Brahm says coldly, not even bothering to look back and address his foe. With eyes closed, his focus is drawn completely inward. His breathing becomes deep and cyclic; the blood weeps from his wounds as the circulation of fluid in his body starts to increase. Directing his other arm at the Warden, he spreads his fist into an open palm. To the untrained senses, it would appear the bloody and battered man was simply pushing against two invisible walls. However, to those with a deeper sense of awareness, a swirling vortex of energy has started to resonate outward from within Brahm's core.

"Oooh?" the Warden hums with amusement. He watches as the vortex of energy expands further and further out from Brahm's body, inching its way in every direction. With no sensation of hostile intention, he allows the swirling waves of energy to wash over him. With heightened senses aroused, a faint vibrational hum starts to tickle the Warden's inner ear as Brahm's energy now completely fills the room.

"What could you possibly be playing at?" the Warden mumbles to himself. To his bewildered amusement, he watches the particles of the material environment around him start to dance and move to the rhythm of Brahm's vibrational orchestration. The particles slowly distance themselves from their molecular bonds, merging into new and unique patterns.

"Oh my!" the Warden exclaims, as he turns his heightened sight inward. He notices the once well-managed molecules of his body begin to mix and mingle with the surrounding environment like they just joined an impromptu contra dance. The rapid shifting of arranged particles cause the once defined boundary of self and other to dissolve around him. "Incredible!" the Warden shouts, as he feels himself fading into oblivion. The Seers stand dumfounded, looking to their own hands and feet expecting to suffer a similar fate. Noticing they are still all put together, they soon realize this flooding vortex of energy is only directed at the Warden.

"What an amazing sensation!" the Warden cries out from the swirling dust of dancing particles. He floats freely in the dissolved essence of the very prison he emerged from along with the surrounding castle debris. "Oh how I've longed for such an adversary to knock on my door! The master has not disappointed! What fun! Wa-hahahaha!"

"This," Brahm says, finally turning his head to the Warden and opening his eyes with a burst of primal intensity. He immediately clenches the open palm that faces his foe into a tightly bound fist. To everyone's amazement, the powerful gesture commands the dance of energy to seize into a screeching halt. In a sudden flash, the free-flowing particles that were once iron bars, well-tailored fabrics, bones and skin now congeal into one smorgasbord of material mess. With a twist of his wrist, he commands the jumbled mass of particles to violently contort and condense itself into an even denser and smaller existence. Opening and clenching his fist over and over again, he continues to mash the mass of particles into a perpetually shrinking sphere. Now, nothing more than a tiny shiny pebble, the material amalgamation falls gently to the chamber floor as Brahm releases his will from its binding.

Brahm shifts his attention back to the stupefied Seers, still frozen in disbelief as to what their senses were just subjected to.

"You must go, now!" Brahm yells at them, breaking their frozen spell. They all look to him with wide eyes. "There is no telling how long that will keep him at bay, you must all hurry!"

"But to where?" Tewari asks. "Where could we possibly run to in this crumbling castle?" Ignoring Tewari's questions for the moment, Brahm closes his eyes and returns his cosmic awareness inward. He takes a deep breath, centering himself into the moment. As his eyes spring back open, a gust of energy erupts from his hand and blows past the Seers. The energy rushes into the hallway and through the stone mountain behind them. Chills run down their spines, as they immediately look to their hands in panicked uncertainty.

"Oh my Maia! I'm going to be turned into a marble!" one of the Seers shouts involuntarily. He drops to the floor in a curled up fetal position, appearing to already be adopting the cylindrical traits of his anticipated transformation.

"Fear not," Brahm says sternly, clearing the growing anxiety of his companions. "I am creating a straight line for you to follow. I am working on building you a tunnel through the mountain to their location. Once you see the opening, you all *must* hurry, I cannot stress that enough! If I am distracted for even a moment, the walls I create around you could reformat in an instant, trapping you like this beast on the floor. Do you understand?"

"No!" the Seers cry out, as they struggle to make any sense of their predicament.

"There is no more time! Ugh… look behind you!" Brahm says as he strains himself to complete the final stages of his manifested tunnel. They all eagerly look behind them to see yet another miracle of reality-bending unfold. The walls and stone behind them start to pixilate into individual cubes. The cubes wiggle free from their original structure and zip around the room, unrestricted by the demands of physics or gravity. They appear like a swarm of bees dashing around their hive. What first presents as random movements quickly starts to adopt intellectual design. The cubes move outward from a central space and stack themselves neatly on top of one another. The pixilated cubes align to create a tunnel that burrows deep inside the mountain. At the very end, the Seers can see an open clearing with an elaborate metal door waiting for them. They look back to Brahm and are met with the face of a man struggling to maintain a grip on his altered reality.

"Go! Now!" Brahm grunts, his body quivering under the pressure and concentration required to hold such a position.

"But, but, how…" a Seer attempts to ponder.

"You heard the man! Do not waste the opportunity he has presented us!" Tewari shouts, commanding his troops. "Run! Now! Run like your very lives depend on it!" His men jump to attention and sprint off into the newly fabricated tunnel. "Better yet," Tewari adds, as he waits to make sure all his men have entered the tunnel, "run as if your sisters' lives depend on it! Run as if the fate of your entire home depends on it! Run as if the very future of everything you hold dear depends on it!" His words spark vigor in the hearts and bodies of his people. They race through the tunnel, focused on putting one foot in front of the other as fast as possible. Just as the last man makes it into the tunnel, Tewari looks back to Brahm.

"Thank you," Tewari says as his heart bursts open from the Shaker's gesture of support. "You really are the man from my vision. I couldn't see that until now." Tewari's words wash over Brahm with a wave of love and admiration. Brahm smiles and lifts one eyelid to make visual contact with the Seer leader. Locking eyes in a brief, powerful moment, Brahm gives Tewari a hopeful wink before doubling down on his concentration of maintaining the mountain tunnel. A bright smile strikes across the grizzly Seer's face as he now turns to jump into the tunnel himself. Following his own advice, he races with an explosive stampede to join his brothers. As the Seer's stake their claim to safety, a faint rattling noise draws Brahm's attention behind him.

"Ugh… seriously?" Brahm puffs out of exasperation. "So soon?" With no choice but to juggle even more precious attention, he looks upon the once-immobile marble now bouncing playfully upon the floor. "I need more time," he mumbles to himself while watching the marble quiver faster and faster. It increases its vibrational frequency exponentially until an exploding force of matter erupts from the tiny spectacle.

Long, winding, root-like appendages erupt from the sphere like branches bursting from a tiny seed. The marble continues to fracture as further eruptions of sprouting matter expel from its grasp. The root-like structures grow outward, flowing in five independent directions. As the speed of their development hastens, long fibrous filaments emerge out of the five main outcroppings and begin to fabricate the more intricate arrangements of the human form. Slowly, the very familiar image of the once marble-imbued Warden reemerges into the room.

His exposed body begins to dawn his trademark suit from the remaining particles residing in the deteriorated marble. His swirling galaxy eyes lock onto Brahm as he takes in his first breath since being reborn. Fire ignites from the central suns that make up his galactic pupils. The gravity from the swirling vortices pulls Brahm towards the enigmatic creature with overwhelming ease. The migrated cubes of his makeshift tunnel start to quiver under his wavering concentration. The drowned-out voices of the Seers can be heard yelling to one another to hasten their pace. The Warden smiles at the growing turmoil he caused before he lifts a finger to the tip of his nose. His glasses casually materialize while he slides his finger up between his perplexing eyes. Brahm is released from the Warden's pull, just before his attention slips too far from the scurrying Seers.

"I've been a lot of things," the Warden says calmly, but I can safely say I've never been a marble. Such a bizarre experience! And yet… invigorating! I feel so indebted to you. Ahh, to have shared such an experience with me! However will I repay such a favor?" he finishes with his fangs emerging from behind his tight-lipped smile.

"Damnit," Is all Brahm can muster; he remains paralyzed by his predicament. His powerlessness is further highlighted by the Warden's casual stroll towards him.

"Tisk, tisk. You seem to have let your guard down at the most crucial time," the Warden says cheekily. "As much as I want to continue playing with you, you appear to have met the bitter end of your own gamble," he says while patting Brahm on the shoulder with a belittling hand. Brahm looks up at his overconfident adversary with a silent scowl. The Warden pays him no mind, leaving his hand upon his shoulder like a victory flag planted upon a freshly conquered land. "Orders from above, I'm afraid," he says while extending his other arm to the tunnel. Concentrating his energetic will, the Warden quickly molds his outstretched arm into his serpentine companion. Glowing yellow eyes emerge from the evolving appendage before turning back to face its master. The manifested beast looks into the Warden's obscured eyes, eager for its destructive instruction.

"Go, my friend, and round up these pesky Bakuwan. But try not to kill them, their spirits need to be broken in much more creative ways! Death would be such an unfortunate outcome for such precious creatures." The snake nods and turns to the tunnel once again. Coiling it's still attached frame around the Warden's arm, it contorts its body into a spring, ready to erupt at any moment.

"No!" Brahm screams, but it's too late. The snake fires into the tunnel at full force.

Cynical laughter can be heard echoing throughout the tunnel as the Warden proudly announces his claim to a second victory. The Seers look back in horror as the serpentine abomination hurls itself at them at a breakneck speed. Bouncing sloppily off the walls, the snake knocks loose the already-quivering stone blocks with each careless, pinball impact. Seemingly out of all possible options, Tewari musters a borrowed moment to send a prayer for anyone who might be listening. He can feel his pounding heartbeat all the way in his feet, feeling each step might very well be his last.

Unable to accept the twist of fate any longer, Brahm doubles down on his gamble and plays the final card in his hand. Reaching out with the hand not maintaining the tunnel, he diverts a critical amount of energy and burrows his iron grip into the Warden's snake arm. His fingers puncture the serpentine flesh, snapping bones in the wake of his destructive intrusion.

∞

"Yyyyy-eeeee-aaaahhhh!" bellows the high-pitched squeal of the animated serpent. Cries of pain now echo through the tunnel chamber, deafening the ears of the traveling occupants. The beast flails around the confines of the tunnel with an intensified destructive frenzy. The oversized creature smashes into the walls, desperately trying to shake free from the source of its pain. Unfortunately, all the flailing accomplishes is shaking loose further blocks of reformatted mountain. Dust, debris, and the screams from the monster surround the Seer brothers. Their sense of hope starts to crumble along with their deteriorating surroundings. Tewari takes notice of the budding doubt and reminds them of their second chance.

"The beast is distracted! Hurry men!" Tewari cries. "We must make it out of here before it regains focus or tears this whole place down!" His words snap his men back into hopeful reality. They pick themselves back up and race down what's left of Brahm's tunnel.

∞

Back at the prison cell room, Brahm twists the body of the beast around his arm, reeling it in like a hooked fish. The amount of effort needed to subdue such a creature requires more power than he had anticipated. Looking back into the tunnel, he watches his own deviated attention causing more destruction than possibly the Warden's beast.

"Oooh? Willing to risk it all, are you?" he asks with a calm and poised tone. He glances down and smiles at his profusely sweating adversary.

"Such a shame," the Warden decides. "I was really hoping to keep these fellows alive. But! Because of your hasty actions, I'll make sure their blood is on your hands and not mine; all necessary consequences of the games we play, no?" the Warden says cryptically. He raps the fingers of his hand on Brahm's shoulder one by one as if playing the delicate keys of a prized piano. Brahm looks to the unsuspecting gesture and can only assume the worst.

"Aaahhhhh!" Brahm screams out in pain as he drops his head in agony. The Warden widens his smile as his newly formatted fingers take the shape of sharpened claws, similar to the ones he attacked Mono with. The claws grow ever so slowly into Brahm's defenseless flesh, inching their way into his body at an excruciatingly leisured pace. The snapping and splintering of muscles, tendons and even bones give the Warden a pleasurable chill.

"OOOoooh!" he cries out with unadulterated glee. "The additional suspense! I say, how much more can the hero take?? I can hardly contain myself!" A deafening and heart stopping crunch ripples through the chamber as Brahm finally succumbs to the unrelenting force of the attack.

"Yeaaaahhh!" Brahm bellows in agony as his shoulder becomes completely crushed.

"Wowzers!" the Warden cries out again. "Yep! Oh my, I definitely felt that one!" he adds with some flavorful jest. Despite all the pain and added pressure, Brahm holds firm to his position.

"Not going to budge, are you?" the Warden says with slight disappointment. "How about this added surprise?" Suddenly, a sizzling sound emanates from his claws. A thick, caustic substance pours from the sharpened blades and flows into Brahm's open wound. A pungent smell of burning flesh erupts into the air. The pain becomes so overwhelming; Brahm feels his eyes trying to roll into the back of his head. His body begs him to give into the pain and surrender.

"How long do you plan on keeping that up?" the Warden cries, clearly losing interest in the game he plays. "You will die, you fool! You have so much more to live for! Just give up already! These scraps of life are not worth it! Let them die and fight me!" The poison continues to rush through Brahm's bloodstream, causing interference between his mind and body connection. The quivering pixel cubes in the tunnel start to vibrate even more violently, crashing down around the fleeing Seers without any warning of their structural compromise.

"Just… a… little… bit… longer!" Brahm grunts, desperately trying to hold balance to his tightrope situation.

"Enough!" the Warden commands. "You will fall to my poison! You will give in to this pain! You will crush those you wish to save! You will fail!"

"Aaaahhhh!" Brahm cries out again, this time the claws dive even deeper into his flesh. As more poison races down Brahm's arm, further dark swirls spring to life upon his skin in their wake. Steam radiates off his flesh as the caustic substance cooks him from the inside out. It flows through his body like nothing he has ever felt before. Even while using his inflated willpower to stop such a force, it barely acts to slow it down. He decides to divert the precious hand that governs the tunnel and grabs ahold of the Warden's wrist.

"Raaahhhh!" Brahm cries out with a triumphant battle roar as he rips the Warden's claw out of his battered body. He holds the devilish claw up over his head like a trophy. The poison still drips from the sharpened tips, trickling down into a sizzling puddle upon the floor.

"Ha! You lost!" the Warden exclaims with overwhelming pride. His words appear to ring true, as the questionable integrity of the tunnel inevitably gives way. The quivering cubes congeal like clotting blood as they race to seal up the open wound in the mountainside. With the Seers not nearly out of harm's reach, Brahm takes one more gamble in their game of survival.

"This is going to hurt!" he cries as he casts aside the Warden's appendages and points a single finger at the crumbling tunnel. With all his attention focused on a single lingering pixel cube, he commands its movement to race at full speed towards the opposing end.

Amidst all the surrounding chaos and impending doom, Tewari looks back and notices the speeding cube heading at him.

"S-Seriously—" is all he can say before the cube abruptly collides with his backside. Lifting him up off the floor, it sends him soaring into the air. One by one the other Seers pile on top of Tewari as they are all collected by the whizzing cube. Sucked back by the raging G-forces being imposed on their bodies, it's all they can do to hold on to one another for dear life. The newly freed serpent rushes unrestricted towards the Seers with the rage of the Warden fueling its pursuit. As the metal door at the end quickly becomes closer and closer, the Seers look back at the imploding tunnel and start to wonder if their survival rate has gone up or down.

"H-H-How does he expect us to survive this?" one of the men struggles to ask Tewari. The racing cube stops dead in its tracks as it reaches the end of the tunnel, flinging Tewari and his brothers through the air. The cube relinquishes its individualistic qualities and neatly merges back into the mighty mountain. The pursuing snake smashes into the closed-off tunnel, cut off from its elusive pray. Not quite out of danger yet, the still air-born Seers soar through the air with their quickly approaching brake pedal staring them down. The sound of flesh striking the unforgiving finish line causes a deep resonation to ring from the mighty door. One by one Tewari and his men fall from the door like lifeless flies off a rolled-up newspaper.

"Oi!" Mono cries, with a hand nursing the goose egg developing on his concussed head. He slowly scrambles to his feet like a midnight drunk. "Are you all right?!" he calls out to anyone who has maintained consciousness. Their stationary bodies cause Mono's heart to plummet into his gut; he is quick to assume the worst. Despite the aura of impending doom, Tewari is next to open his eyes, his shoulder is throbbing after taking the brunt of his impact. He looks to his men on the ground as they roll around and moan in agony.

"Ha, looks like that fool did it. We are going to be alright after all… oufff," he says, bringing his hand to his clearly broken shoulder. "Mostly."

∞

Brahm is hunched over, breathing heavily as he looks at the solid face of the reformatted mountainside. A brief smile swims across his face as the reality of the Seers' survival warms his soul. His attention is quickly diverted back to the wound in his left shoulder. He instinctively brings a hand to cradle the epicenter of pain. He can feel the poison in his body trying desperately to race into his heart and fully infect his being. It's as if the foreign substance has an intelligence of its own. Brahm concentrates his will power to isolate the poison's migration inside his body. He attempts to expel it out of the original entry wounds, but to his surprise, it won't leave. No matter how hard he tries, the substance springs back into his arm every time he makes the intention to remove it.

I can travel dimensions, challenge the rules of physical reality, but I can't relieve myself of this poison? He quickly becomes humbled by the Warden's power. *What is this stuff?* He is forced to resort to plan B of his poison management strategy. He uses his conscious energy to surround the momentary passenger of his vessel and locks it into place along his arm. The swirling black markings cease their squiggling movements and petrify their patterns upon the skin of his upper arm.

"I'll need to keep a constant check on this thing in me," he says to himself. "If I let my focus slip, this stuff will surely race back to consume my heart." He turns around and watches the Warden deal with his own shortcomings. The serpentine extension of his arm currently remains imprisoned in the reconstructed tunnel of the now very solid mountainside. The Warden snarls and tugs at his arm but the mountain won't give back what it has taken. He dawns his claws once again after a cry of unbridled rage. They slither from behind his humanoid fingertips and contort back into their very formidable formations. Brahm prepares himself for the Warden's next attack. Much to his surprise, the Warden unleashes his next strike on none other than himself. The claws rain down and slice the arm stuck in the mountain clean off.

"Woooo!" the Warden cries out happily. The slithering arm falls limp against the wall as the life is quickly severed from its animated form. "Glad to be rid of that useless mess," he says while rotating his shoulder like a baseball player warming up his pitch. A dark cloud pours from the Warden's mutilated arm. Like a magician concealing his trick with smoke and mirrors, a new arm emerges from the swirling cloud of darkness.

"Very clever," the Warden starts. "That energy you imbued that tunnel with was very unique. I got careless thinking I could leave my arm in there without consequence. It's a shame you look all out of gas. That last stunt of yours must really have taken a toll on you. Or… is that present I gave you finally starting to *sink* in?" he finishes with a devilish smile.

"This scratch?" Brahm says with a forced smirk. His arm pulsates with inflamed and radiating damage. "It's nothing. C'mon," he taunts. "Pain is only an illusion."

"You lie!" the Warden screams.

"Try me," Brahm says confidently.

"You have nothing left!" the Warden cries out, clearly tired of being taunted. His once pristine mohawk is starting to fray and fall into his face. "Just give in, you are clearly at the end of your rope!"

"Never!" Brahm grunts, as he brings his arms into a secure fighting position. The Warden takes the initiative and charges at his opponent. He raises his newly formed arm above his head and expands it to five times its original dimensions. Yellow eyes emerge in the slits of his knuckles and his skin adopts a scaly and armored texture. Leaping into the air, the Warden launches the full force of his mutated arm down upon Brahm's head.

"Raaahhh!!" the Warden screams. Brahm braces himself and catches the projected fist with both his hands above his head. He grasps the fist like a baseball catcher cradling the heat of a blistering fast ball. Veins burst from under his skin as Brahm's body rushes to fuel the excessive force needed to counter the brutal attack. The floor below him struggles to support the impact as several cracks and fissures sprout under his feet.

"Give in now or risk bringing this whole castle to the ground!" the Warden bellows.

"I'll bring this place down myself if I have to! Along with you!" Brahm yells back, sweat spraying from his pores. The extended veins in his neck and arms swell to the point of bursting. "I will show you. Aaggghhh!" Interrupting his next words comes the swirling poison in his arm slipping away from its concentrated prison. The caustic venom pushes him over the edge, proving too much for his depleting willpower to keep it at bay any longer. The devastating force of the Warden's fist above takes full advantage of the caving resistance and connects a devastating blow. "Oooof!" The fist drives him into the ground as if being hit by a runaway freight train. The force knocks the air from his lungs and burrows him deep into the floor below. Carving a tunnel of his own, the Warden drives his snake arm and his adversary down layer after layer of the castle tower. He increases the speed of his attack, driving his foe down through the castle until he reaches the ground floor. Brahm crashes hard into the ground, marking the symphonic crescendo of the descending destruction.

Quietly retracting his arm with a slithering recoil, the Warden molds his altered form back into his humanoid dimensions. He casually walks to the edge of the crater of his destructive attack. The loose rubble crumbles under his footsteps like the crunch of an early morning snow. Leaning his head over the gaping hole, he peers into the destructive path. The polished shoe of his left foot strikes an unsecured piece of stone from the floor. He watches the newly freed rubble fall through the unrestricted layers of Mune's disassembled fortress. The rubble, with all its building momentum, whizzes through the air before it strikes the waiting body below. The contact stirs no reaction from the bloodied warrior. Brahm's lifeless body remains sprawled out upon the rubble. He appears to have no more life stored in his vessel than the scraps of building material surrounding him.

Assured of his victory, the Warden brings his attention to the shifting walls around him. His final blow to Brahm has registered the same dismantling fate to the already structurally compromised castle. Resonating with no sense of alarm, he simply glides over to the place in the mountain wall where Brahm had sent the Seers. The building exhales its final breath of life, deteriorating itself into a destructive free-fall. The very floor the Warden walks upon disintegrates behind him like rippling waves crashing into oblivion. Striking the perfect cadence with his pace, each step he takes is just one step ahead of the flow of destruction nipping at his heals. He trots calmly through the sea of cascading devastation as if he is casually trail-blazing the raging infernos of hell.

Reaching the solidified stone entrance of Brahm's once-impressive tunnel, the Warden grips the rough exterior of the mountainside and holds on. He watches stoically as the compromised building finally dissolves all structural integrity, serving as the final topping to Brahm's grave. As the dust settles, the Warden takes in a heavy sigh with a surge of disappointment in his heart.

"I really thought you were going to be different than the others," he says, shaking his head. "No matter," he remarks cheerfully, turning to face the wall he clings to. "So, how do you suppose I open this thing back up again?"

CHAPTER: 36

The Fall To Rise Above It All

An electrifying sound of vibrating particles dance around Brahm's body. A translucent dome hovers over his lifeless frame, pulsating with frantic rhythms. The dome flickers with hues of red coursing through its electromagnetic structure. The fallen debris intended to bury the overwhelmed warrior now hovers above his head, suspended in-between the conflicting force of gravity and the repelling force of the pulsating dome.

"Oi," Beau grunts from his crouched position next to his fallen captain. "What the hell happened to you up there?" Beau peers down at his captain with growing concern in his eyes, giving no thought to his own disfigured appearance. Brahm lies motionless, his body serving as a memorial for the plethora of painful lessons his classroom in humanity has cost him. His blood pours effortlessly upon the unforgiving ground. It's no wonder why the Warden would have left him for dead. Beau pushes aside his own pain as he gives over his full sympathy to his captain.

"Y-you always run away when things get this bad," he grunts. "What could have ever possessed you to take on such suffering?" As he awaits Brahm's response, he involuntarily winces in pain. His knees and arms start to buckle as if holding up an increasingly heavy weight. With one knee upon the ground and his arms raised above his head, Beau looks to the red dome above them as if peering into a ticking timepiece. He puckers his lips, struggling to maintain the bioelectric barrier. Looking back down at his captain, his eyes lock onto the black swirling mark upon his shoulder. The mark slithers unrestricted down his arm and spills over onto his chest.

"That doesn't look good," Beau mutters to himself, still unsure as to what exactly he is watching. He takes a deep breath into his lungs. "Hee-yaaaa!" he screams, thrusting his arms up higher above his head, commanding the polarized energy to erupt through the many layers of debris above them. Holding onto his control of the energy, he takes his erected arms and thrusts them towards his sides. "Yaaahhh!" he repels the debris to either side of him as if parting the ancient waves of the Red Sea. Certain he has cleared all the compiled debris from above, Beau drops his arms and relaxes his energetic field. The fragments of Mune's discarded castle fall in sync with gravity, landing far away from Beau and his captain in a well-calculated orchestration. Taking another look at Brahm's deteriorating situation, the Warden's poison is quickly starting to consume all reaches of his body.

"I don't know what you got going on with you this time," Beau says to his unconscious captain, "but I know I can't fix this. I'm going to need you to come on back and take care of this one yourself." Rubbing his hands together, Beau closes his eyes and prepares to concentrate what energy he has left in his fatigued body. As his cyclic breath deepens, a faint green aura encompasses his hunched frame. A low hum can be heard resonating in the flowing waves of energy around his body. With a deeper breath brought into his lungs, Beau channels his buildup of healing imbued energy into the palms of his hands. It glows bright green and radiant, like a lone flame in a dark chamber. Slowly exhaling his concentrated breath, he places his palms upon his captain's chest. Reacting to the healing energy, Brahm's body leaps up off the ground as his heart abruptly restarts. The vital organ waists no time as it pumps blood and life back into the intricate veins that line his interior. As his body returns to the ground, Beau musters up borrowed strength to drive another surge of energy back into his captain's battered body. Catapulted into the air again, Brahm's lungs finally expand and engulf the much-needed air they have been starved of.

"Geee-aahhhh!" Brahm cries as he consumes his returning breath. With eyes wide and bloodshot, he pants with hungry breaths as he sucks down the surrounding atmosphere like a famished vagrant. "W-What happened?" Brahm asks his collapsing companion. "Beau! Oh no, are you... aahhhh!" Brahm's attention is quickly returned to the surging poison still flooding his body. He clenches his frame and falls back to the ground, rolling around in sheer agony.

"Get yourself together!" Beau shouts from his own deflated seat upon the ground. "Don't you make me regret reviving you! Fix this mess of yours! We still have work to do!"

"D-Damn you!" Brahm responds, rocking himself back and forth in a fetal position. "

H-Have you always been this compassionate, or have I just missed it all these years?"

"I'll truly be damned if your last words are a mockery of me!" Beau shouts back. "Hurry up and fix yourself and then see what energy you have left to talk smack!"

"Alright, alright, have it your way," Brahm responds with a childish tone. With a deep breath drawn into his lungs, Brahm concentrates his command upon his energetic life force. With eyes closed, he stops his frantic sprawl upon the ground and steadies his frame. Deep cyclic breaths give birth to immense tension within his body. His muscles contort and ripple under the overwhelming willpower being demanded of every fiber of his being. The free-flowing poison stops dead in its tracks, finally hitting a wall of willpower. Fighting back as hard as it can, the poison withers and flails in utter resistance to the growing restraint being imposed on it. Slowly but surely, Brahm channels his life force to entrap the foreign substance and brings it back to its concentrated position upon his left shoulder. Trying desperately to rid the entity entirely from his body, Brahm pours every ounce of his conscious attention into extracting the substance. However, a deep exhale reveals the task still appears too great for him. He opens his eyes and looks upon the now stationary and contained poison. It wraps around his shoulder and down his arm in the familiar pattern. Brahm shakes his head in disbelief as he looks to Beau who shares his same level of confusion.

"I don't know what this mess inside of me is," Brahm says. "It's taking so much energy to just contain it. No matter how hard I try, I can't get it out of me. I've never had to deal with something quite like this; something that harbors a stronger will than even my own!"

"Hey now," Beau says, halting his captain's train of thought. "As much as I have dreamt of the day that would humble you, now is not the time to start doubting your abilities. So what? You got into something you don't know how to overcome. You'll figure it out eventually. What is important now is that you have it contained. Did you forget we still have a mission to complete?"

"Ha, you are right," Brahm says with a warm smile. "It's funny hearing the old soldier talk in you coming out at a time like this," he says throwing himself down to rest next to his comrade. "'Mission to complete!' Ha! You must have had quite a time down here to bring that side of you out again."

"I'll have you know," Beau says in-between moans of exhaustion, "all that time you had to dilly-dally up there doing who knows what was all thanks to me. I gave that monstrosity quite a run for his money. Hung in there a lot longer than you did, I might add!"

"Whoa! Shots fired!" Brahm says, rearing his head back in laughter. "It was all thanks to you, huh? Say, Mr. I'm-going-to-take-all-the-credit-while-ignoring-the-elephant-in-the-room, so who's that you got dragged along by your side there?"

"Oh, this guy?" Beau says, playfully patting the passed-out giant beside him. "Oh, you know, maybe I can't take *all* the credit."

"You know that guy wanted to kill me," Brahm says looking down at the peacefully sleeping Jeeven. It took him a minute to recognize the beast without his cloak and heavy metal plate covering his face. Despite his altered physical presentation, his level of tranquility is what threw Brahm off the most.

"Well, that guy *did* try to kill me! But here we are, fighting side by side. Funny how that works out, isn't it?" Beau says, taking a vital sample of energy to turn his head and look his captain in the eye. "I would almost be convinced you knew this would happen."

"Eh, you give me too much credit, old timer," Brahm says, brushing off his friend's jest of endearment.

"So you are telling me you didn't?"

"Oh, get off it, Beau!" Brahm says with a childish wave of his hand before sinking his back deeper into the shifting pile of rubble the two men lean against. "I've realized lately there are far more things I *don't* know than I ever thought I knew. Regardless, it looks like you two did a good job staying alive together. That's all that really matters."

"I guess you're right."

"Hey Beau," Brahm says ominously.

"Hmm?"

"That guy, the one they call the Warden…"

"Yeah?"

"He knew my name."

"So? You've told a lot of people here your name."

"No, I mean my *birth* name. The *whole* thing."

"Oh," Beau says, forced into deeper ponder. "What do you make of that?"

"I don't know. He mentioned something about having a master… not having a will of his own. I don't think *he* personally knew me, but whoever is controlling him sure does."

"Hmm… your father had a fair number of enemies back in the day for what he did; could be any number of ghosts coming back to haunt you."

"Sure, you've told me about some of them. But I wouldn't have thought one of them would have found me out here, and so soon after leaving home! What do you make of *that?*"

"I don't know, but I don't like it. To think we thought Babel would be the worst of our worries out here. How foolish we were. We can always go back you kno—"

"Ha! Never!" Brahm shouts with excitement. "It's way too much fun out here to turn back now."

"Fun, huh? Ha, I had to at least try," Beau says, admitting his priority for Brahm's safety. "So then, what are you going to do now? As gung-ho as you sound, you look to be in worse shape than the two of us battered hunks down here."

"Simple. I'm going to go back up there and challenge that Warden guy again, beat him, and rescue Sophia."

"Interesting," Beau says, noticing Brahm's purposeful dismissal of his physical nature. "Do you even know where she is after all this time?"

"Yes," Brahm says softly. "I saw her right before falling here. She's safe for now, but not for much longer."

"Alright, lover boy, so how do you plan to put up a fight? I just brought you back from the verge of death, so I hope you have a better strategy than before!"

"With a dimensional bridge of course," he responds, with resounding excitement in his voice.

"Geeze, didn't think you would try that maneuver again so soon, let alone in the condition you're in. Need I remind you of the astronomically high risk of not having enough energy to return to your body? Let alone what your level of fatigue will have over your ability to control such power? You could seriously bring a rift to this world this time that would dissolve it into oblivion!" He looks to his battered captain who remains intoxicated with jubilation. Beau can't help but smile with silent resolve. "Ya know, I guess just some things will never change," he says with a defeated jab.

"Maybe so," Brahm says sitting himself upright and centering his spine. He stretches back and forth causing some of the dust and rubble to fall off his backside. "But then again, some things may have."

"Oh?"

"Yeah, I mean, I'm not about to sit here and tell you I understand everything that's happened since I've been here. But something happened during all this mess that made me realize how much I take the people I still have left in this world for granted."

"Go on," Beau says with intrigue. Brahm grabs a piece of rubble and rolls it around in his hand as he ponders the thoughts rolling around in his head.

"I realized I've been going about this all wrong," he finally says. "The whole thing that is. Life. My life here, or what I've stuck around for anyway." Beau shakes his head in sheer bewilderment at his young captain's words. "After father died, you stuck around to look after me. Instead of honoring that, all I did was give you hell…"

"Oh, don't beat yourself up about that. That's just what kids are supposed to do!"

"Please," Brahm says, deflating his companion's attempt to lessen his testimony. "If that's the case, I never grew up. I never stopped giving you a hard time, or anyone for that matter who tried to get close to me. I would always run away from this world when things got tough or unsettling. I disregarded any hardship that lay waiting for me in this world. I left that all on you to deal with. All I would do was come back for the fun stuff and run away when it got hard again. How selfish I am! Don't you see, Beau? I'm trying to apologize to you!" Beau looks to his captain, his friend, and his adopted child all in one, watching him in silence with waterlogged eyes. "I'm sorry, Beau, I really am. And it's time I find a way to apologize to everyone here for the mess I've stirred up. It's time I do something about it all. It's time I finally start to grow… not up, but… *inward*… I guess." Brahm brings himself to stand. He dusts off the debris from the remaining shreds of fabric hanging off his battle-worn frame. Beau watches him as a steam of sunlight cuts through the dense cloud cover overhead, shining down on his transfigured captain. The shredded top layer of his overalls hangs over the still tightly bound shawl around his waist. It flaps gently in the wind like a makeshift cape of a storybook superhero.

"You're going to need more than resolve to beat this guy," Beau says. "The danger of not being able to return to your body is the least concerning consequence if you really plan on doing your dimensional bridge."

"That's true," Brahm says flatly. "That's what I have you for. Sophia too, and all the others: Otto, Domino, Raja, Mono, Mufida, Tewari, and all the Seers!"

"That's quite a list you have there. How is it going to help?"

"Love. It is what will keep me here, keep me from failing," Brahm says with a tear welling up in the corner of his eye. "I've never stuck around in this world to even start to understand such a concept until now," he continues, trying to hold back a full sob. "Through all the pain I've experienced these last two days, it has really taught me why so many people go through with it all, and *how* they do it! It's love, Beau. They all have something or someone in this world they love, and it keeps them rooted here no matter what. This world seemed void of love to me because I never went looking for it. I never saw it was all around me all the time. It exists within the connections we build with one another... hidden in the connections we build with ourselves. It's always been hidden in plain sight!" He gazes down upon the shadow attached to his feet. The shadow gives him a cheerful wave and an enthusiastic thumbs-up from his two-dimensional vantage point. Brahm smiles at his shadow's antics before returning to his train of thought. "I needed so much energy before to return to my body because I never allowed myself to truly love *anybody*, not even myself!"

The stream of consciousness takes Brahm off guard as he is forced to pause and contemplate the words that just exited his mind. Beau shares the silent contemplative moment too. There rests a heavy weight on both of the men's hearts. "But now I have a better reason to come back," Brahm continues. "It won't matter how tired, exhausted, beaten, or battered I become. I'm confident I will be able to make my way back into my body no matter what! I will make it back for you, for Sophia, and for everyone. That I promise you."

"Enough already," Beau says, wiping a snotty, tear-infused blob of congestion from his face. "You've made your point already. No need to get all mushy with it."

"Ha, so you're not going to try and stop me?"

"Please, I've never been able to stop you," he says with a chuckle. "My only worry is how to convince you to take this useless old man with you when you go beat this guy."

"I thought you would never ask," Brahm says with a warm smile. He looks back to his companion, now mirroring the same teary-eyed mess upon his face.

"Oh, c'mon now! Get it together and get serious!" Beau shouts despite his own blatant hypocrisy.

"Never! These are the emotions I'm banking on saving us all, I'm tired of repressing them!"

"Ha! Are they now? I guess you really have changed," Beau says proudly. "Oh! Hey, so what about this guy here?" he says, tilting his head towards Jeeven. "I would hate to leave him here all alone after all we've been through."

"I couldn't agree more," Brahm says as he walks over and bends a knee next to the giant. He carefully picks him up and throws the Marionette over his right shoulder. His knees buckle under the giant's immense weight, but he stand strong. "Whoa! Big boy we got here!" he says with cheery vigor.

"Ya know, he might still want to kill you when he wakes up," Beau says as Brahm lifts him up onto his other shoulder.

"Yeah, guess that is just a risk I'm willing to take at this point," he responds with a smile. With his shoulders full of war-torn warriors, Brahm scans the mighty mountain before him, visualizing his final destination within. With a heavy inhale, he closes his eyes and brings conscious attention back to his remaining reservoir of life energy. He notices his personal well has nearly run dry. He searches for another source to draw power from. With a calm mind, he thinks back to his time with Mono and Babarossa. The web that connects all things drifts into his mind. He visualizes the web wrapping around the world and pulsating with its own heartbeat. Picturing himself within this web, he sees himself as a single aspect of the greater whole. Reaching deeper, he realizes he exists equally as not just one part, but as the whole unified field of reality. Everyone and everything exists separately on one level and completely connected on another. This realization opens a dusty and forgotten channel in his vessel. A river of energy now pours into him that flows from within and from without. He feels nourished and protected by the mighty web of life force. On his exhale, a swirling oval orb of energy erupts from his core and encircles the trio. Radiating colors of blue and red dance in swirling tandem, eventually merging into a deep purple glow. Once the polarized colors have united, Brahm nods to himself with approval, pouring another breath into his next move. The now audible hum of the vibrating orb of energy starts to intensify, allowing the triad of warriors to lift off the ground.

"You always were better at this maneuver than I ever was," Beau says with complementary endearment. He shakes his head with pride as he watches his pupil float through the air. "To have simultaneous control over the polar charges of your bio-field is… incredible. To think I ever taught you anything at this point is quite comical. I'm glad you still feel the need to keep me around."

"It just goes to show how good a teacher I had," Brahm says, very conscious of his companion's slip into self-doubt. "I could never have become the man I am today if it were not for you. I was never an easy student, but you never gave up on me. The lessons I need now more than anything have nothing to do with physical or energetic power. Where I falter most is the will of the heart. That has always been your strongest quality, Beau. I will always need you around to help me with that."

"Damnit boy," Beau says, falling back into a sloppy tear-spewing mess. "Just don't drop me, alright?" As the three soar through the air up towards the heart of the mountain, now stripped of all but her mighty Lotus crown, Brahm aligns his focus on getting his party inside the mountain. He is confident that if the Warden can un-marble himself, moving through a mountain should be no more difficult of a feat to replicate. Cutting through the thick fog of The Pearl, now mixed with the fluttering debris of Mune's fallen castle, Brahm picks up on a strange energy signature along the mountain. As he focuses his attention, he notices two familiar humans tethered together, dangling from one of the many jagged cliff faces.

∞

"This is the last one I got," Izak says to himself as he looks up at his final tether chord attached to the mountain. The chord runs all the way down through his hand, over his arm, and adheres to a canister along what's left of his disfigured exoskeleton. Stripped of his arsenal of gadgets, the weapon's master is left to place all faith in this remaining mechanical lifeline. The cord creaks and moans from even the slightest movement. The very expansion of his breath causes a ripple of foreboding tension. The only thing keeping him from slipping into complete psychotic despair is what rests in his other arm; he carefully looks down at his precious cargo, securely clenched with his super-human grip. He breathes a careful sigh of relief as he honors the silent moment he shares with the unconscious Ayananda. The gentle wisps of her green-tipped hair blow in the wind, tickling his nose. Her signature aroma fills his lungs and calms his anxious heart. Intoxicated by her presence, he remains thankful for what he imagines are his final moments of life. He holds her tightly to his chest with every remaining ounce of strength he has, never wanting to let go of her or this cherished moment.

"We sure fought hard back there," he says, reminiscing on their previous battle. "You really dug deep and brought that ferocious warrior out again. No matter how many times that snake demon came back to charge that tunnel, we sent it away every time. I don't know how we would have survived without either of you. I know you don't like it when that force takes over; I'm sure it wasn't easy to subject yourself to that again so soon. Who knows if I ever will be able to tell you how much respect I have for you, or how much pain I see you go through every day. You hide it so well… or you think you do at least. You never let your guard down long enough for me to tell you how I really feel about you. Ha, I realize I share the same problem…" The tether cord continues to creek as its tightly bound fibers grow exhausted.

"Maybe after all this is over, we can have another chance… in another lifetime. I don't know if it works that way, but it would sure be nice if it did. Different circumstances, different starting points, ya know? I don't know if that's anything you would want. I guess that would be the big unanswered question right there, but I would. I would be willing to come back and try again." Izak looks away from his fantasy and examines the continuing splintering of his tether cord. Izak fears they only have a few moments left suspended together.

"Guess this is it," he says, gripping Ayananda even closer than before. "Maybe I didn't get to live the way I wanted to, but being here with you, at least I get to die the way I dreamed of," he says with a budding tear in his eye as he takes what he thinks is the last look upon his secretly admired companion.

wwooOOOMMmmm … wwooOOMMmmm … wwooOOOMMmmm …

"What the hell is that?" Izak ponders out loud as he squints through the dense fog. A bizarre vibrating hum blares from behind the obscure wisps of fog, leading him to stretch out his neck in bewildered confusion. A faint purple glow can barely be made out from the overlay of gray tones. As the pulsating vibrations wash over the duo, the invigorating frequency triggers Ayananda to stir from her unconscious slumber. She opens her eyes and stares down into the dangling heights she is suspended from.

"Whaaat?" she screams, frantically flailing around in Izak's firm clutches.

"Be still, will you!" Izak bellows. "Get it together or you will be the death of us both!"

"Huh?" Ayananda says as she decides to look up and assess the rest of her situation. She quickly notices the failing binding that suspends them. She then looks down at the strong arm that rests securely along her waist.

"Hmmm," she hums, with an added shrug of her shoulders. "Not the worst way to go." She nestles her head closer into Izak's chest. She closes her eyes, appearing already at peace with her impending doom. Izak starts to pour sweat profusely, unable to hang on to a single thought swirling around the storm in his mind. His desperation to take advantage of this unforeseen moment leads him to overthink his situation to the point of mental paralysis. His only fixated concern is the protruding beat of his heart. His irrational worries lead him to believe his heart is beating so hard it could knock Ayananda back into unconsciousness.

"Relax, would ya?" Ayananda says while slowly bringing her hand to Izak's chest. "No use worrying about the things out of your control." Her soft touch drives the struggling man into even deeper disarray. With his heart somehow shifting into an ever more erratic beat pattern, he truly becomes worried that now he might die from a heart attack before the rope decides to snap.

"Aya, I…" Izak stammers, struggling to take a final shot at his emotional testimony.

wwooOOOMMmm … wwooOOMMmmm … wwooOOMMmmm …

"What in the world is that?" Ayananda says, sharply shifting her focus to the purple orb of light coming into view. "Oh! It's Je'! I can see him breathing! Big Je' is still alive! How wonderful!" Izak casts his eyes upon the same sight, letting out a deep sigh of disappointment. He hangs his despair upon the bubbly inflection of Ayananda's words as she sees their giant leader.

Izak's familiar feelings of jealousy, incompetence, and self-loathing come pouring back like a resurging tidal wave. The lowered walls of his heart begin to regret their vulnerable position and lock back into place, sealing off any genuine emotions. He shrinks back into his protective and familiar emotional armor. However, this time he has allowed an old wound to reopen while his defenses were down. The open wound rubs against his armor as an additional reminder of the necessity of such protection. He rolls his eyes in disgust over his carelessness and heartache. He begins praying that the rope just snaps any second, bringing a quick end to his dismal existence.

"Whoa, and who is that other guy carrying him?" Ayananda says, oblivious to Izak's pain. Izak lets out a deep sigh of initial disinterest, but quickly grows to share her curiosity. His eyes dilate slightly as he watches the angelic man erupt out of the dense fog.

Brahm's restless hair floats around in the purple orb completely intoxicated by weightlessness. His eyes are fierce and glow with white light pouring from within his cosmic apertures. An additional ball of light emanates from his face. It rests in the middle of his forehead, glowing with a deep purple hue. Izak can feel the light penetrating his barricaded soul and lifting his vibrational frequency out of any realm of fear or doubt. Having no qualms with the sheading emotional weight, he looks on with a clear heart, deeper into Brahm's face. The serious and content presence it displays appears to contradict the rest of his disfigured and mangled body. Still unsure of who is drifting towards him, Izak scans the rest of Brahm's body for further clues to his identity. It's only when Brahm floats directly in front of him does the gunslinger finally recognize the enigmatic figure.

"I can't believe it's you," Izak says, completely dumbfounded by his epiphany.

"You know this man?" Ayananda asks.

"Yeah. I mean… I *thought* I did," Izak says with his mind swimming in the past. He shakes his head at the memory of Brahm's first impression back at the lighthouse. "This is the guy we thought kidnapped Sophia." Brahm remains silent during the reveal of his identity. Izak takes a moment to look upon Brahm's other shoulder. He sees Beau floating just off his body, who gives him a warm smile and a feeble wave. With all animosity and lower vibrational energies draining from his body, Izak returns a genuine smile of his own. A splintering sound overhead quickly shifts his focus back to his basic survival. He looks to the failing rope with resurging concern. Ayananda, clearly intoxicated by the same warm and vibrant energy, looks up at Izak with tender eyes. The two gaze at each other with open hearts, wondering silently what change in their fate this man could bring. Looking back to Brahm, Ayananda is first to speak of the glowing elephant in the sky.

"I feel you are here to help us, but you have no more hands to carry any more weight," she says with resounding understanding and contentment. "I can tell you mean well, but I don't think you want to watch what will come next for us. We appreciate you showing us our captain is still alive. We can at least transition in greater peace knowing that." She stares up again at Izak for confirmation. He nods in agreement. "Is Sophia still alive?" Izak asks suddenly, the image of their Resistance leader popping into his head abruptly. Brahm nods silently. Heavy waves of emotion pour from his body. They resonate with a deeper sense of reassurance than any words could wish to capture. "Good," Izak says with a curled smile. "So the Resistance is not dead."

"And neither are you," Brahm finally says. The flow of his words overwhelms the dangling duo with emotion. Before either of them can speak another word, they watch as the glowing purple orb grows in size and envelops them into the weightless vortex.

"This is… incredible," Izak says, consumed with wonder. He looks one last time at his frayed rope as he releases his gridlocked grip from its fibers. He drifts slightly towards Brahm, floating effortlessly as if a buoyant cloud. His eyes widen and jaw aches with joy as he feels like a child again floating around in his mother's womb.

"Ahem," Ayananda nudges politely, tapping gently on Izak's arm that still holds her tightly. He looks down, having forgot their tight embrace remains intact.

"Oh, oh! So, sorry," he says as he reluctantly releases her into the weightless womb of light.

"No," she says, shaking her head slowly. "Thank you. There is no way I could have survived that battle without you."

"Uhh…Uhh…" Even with Brahm's overwhelming vibration of love and compassion coursing through his energetic body, Izak remains trapped by his reluctance to open his heart to such a depth of emotion. To add further conflict to his heart, he struggles to make sense of Ayananda's uncharacteristic kindness and softness while inside Brahm's bubble. He can hardly believe it is still the woman he admires without her coarse exterior.

"But don't let it go to your head, bucko," Ayananda jabs playfully, as if she can feel her comrade struggling with himself. Her jest lightens the mood and disrupts Izak's painful battle with himself. He is able to smile and return to enjoying their collective moment of gratitude.

"And thank you," Izak says, turning to Brahm. "Neither one of us would have made it off this rock alive if it weren't for you floating by."

"It wasn't your time," Brahm says matter-of-factly, giving no other explanation for his actions.

"Right," Izak says, his head now full of questions. "So, what exactly is this thing we are floating around in?"

"This is a polarized torus vortex that is a direct extension of my bioelectric field. It is fueled by the collective life force of this world and constructed by my conscious will. Within the confines of this expanded energy field, the polarized electromagnetic forces are inflated and manipulated."

"I see," Izak says, able to quickly process the information. "So, we are not actually reversing or altering the force of gravity?"

"Yes and no," Brahm responds. "The phenomenon of gravity is influenced in part by electromagnetic energy. I am reversing our bioelectrical attraction to the planet, causing us to hover above it. When the polarized forces are perfectly blended, the state inside this vortex appears to mimic weightlessness or anti-gravity."

"This is amazing," Izak says, looking around Brahm's energetic engineering. "It's a good thing Jeeven is out cold for this one," he chuckles.

"Why is that?" Brahm asks.

"Oh man," Ayananda chimes in. "This meathead over here loses his marbles at the sight of anything or anyone manipulating energy. He sees physical strength as the only thing of any merit. Somehow he can turn a blind eye to the energy manipulation Emmanuel uses. None of us are really sure why that is, so we do our best not to bring it up in conversation. He sees energy manipulation as a sign of… *cheating* in a way. He hates people like you!"

"Seriously?" Brahm asks, genuinely concerned.

"Yeah," Beau now jumps in. "It's amazing you can get anything done with this guy around, but hey, even people like us can see eye to eye if the common threat is great enough!"

"Good to know," Brahm says, taking time to factor this new information into his developing rescue plan.

"Whoa!" Izak shouts out abruptly. All the talk about Jeeven has drawn his attention onto his captain, leading to an unexpected discovery. "Big Je's wounds! Look! That scratch on his face! The one across his cheek! It's shrinking right before my eyes!" Ayananda whips her head around to catch the bizarre report of her comrade. "Am I seeing things? I mean… I know *I* could be, but are you seeing this too?"

"I see it too!" Ayananda responds. "Look! His other wounds too! I can see the bruises around his wrist fading! And my own!" she shouts, looking onto the cuts and burns upon her arms getting smaller and pain receding slightly. "What gives? This is unbelievable!"

"It's another consequence of the polarized vortex. Time spent within it causes our physical bodies to undergo an expedited healing process. It won't completely heal your wounds, but it will speed up your recovery rate greatly."

"Amazing," Ayananda responds, mostly distracted with watching her injuries recede back into her beloved polished skin.

"If you all don't mind, we must start moving on. There are still many others who need our assistance," he continues. "It is the Warden I plan to challenge. I realize now I can never guarantee Sophia's safety if he is not taken care of. I would not blame you if you did not wish to join me. I can drop you and your captain off somewhere safe before I encounter him again."

"Are you kidding me?!" Ayananda responds boisterously. "After just spending a few moments in this bubble I can feel my strength returning! I don't fully understand what you are doing, but keep it up, buddy! A little bit longer in this thing I'll be ready to kick some Warden ass. I'm dying to get another piece of that shape-shifting snake freak!"

"Yeah, count me in too," Izak says with compelling vigor. "I'll tell you, man," he continues. "I think I got you all wrong before. I'm starting to understand what Sophia saw in you the other day." A deep pulse of energy erupts from Brahm's core, shaking the integrity of the floating orb and everyone in it. He quickly regains his composure, smoothing his energy back out into perfected harmony. Everyone conscious looks to one another, wondering silently what just happened.

"Very good," Brahm says abruptly, completely disregarding his energetic hiccup. "Then let us continue. We don't have much time." Brahm closes his eyes, directing his attention back to pinpointing the exact spot within the mountain he aims to reach. With his path clear and in focus, he jets off without any warning.

"Hold on a second there," Ayananda feels the need to shout as she notices the glowing man heading right into the very solid rock face. "There is this thing called a mountain right here; I know you are Mr. Magnet Man right now, but maybe running into it isn't the best... oh." As the vortex connects with the mountain, sharp lines cut through the rock face, dividing the once rigid structure into malleable cubes. They float gently around the vortex and its patrons as Brahm continues his maneuvering through the mountain.

"Well, definitely wasn't expecting that," Ayananda says as they move into the apparently now very malleable mountain. She leans back into the weightless vortex and pops a piece of gum into her mouth. She chomps down on the hard exterior of the gumball as she watches the cubed blocks move as if parting for an important social figure. Izak and Ayananda look behind them and notice the cubes reforming back into the familiar mountains structure as if nothing happened.

As the fog-dusted sunlight becomes fully obscured by the reformatting mountain, the band of five rely on Brahm's glowing light to illuminate their way. Deep in meditative concentration, Brahm carries on his projected path to find Sophia with blistering pace. Cubes of carved mountain zip around them in all directions as they move out of the way for the energetic anomaly.

"I'm coming for you… all of you!" Brahm says out loud, causing a surge of emotion to flicker through the purple vortex once again. Everyone within its energetic boundaries can feel the love and determination bleeding from the angelic man's heart.

CHAPTER: 37

Second Sight

"J-Just look at this thing!" Mono says as he is overwhelmed by the magnificent beauty and scale of the giant iron door that stands before him. A single lantern hangs from above, shining light upon the intricate landscape carvings all over the door. Lush and prosperous imagery are showcased, which is something very uncommon in a land known to be barren and destitute. "Who do you think put this here, and how? Do you think this is still a part of Mune's castle?" Mono asks, turning around and facing Tewari.

"Anything is possible," Tewari says, walking closer to the iron door to further inspect it. He places his hand on it and glides his fingers over the indented carvings. So much detail envelops the magnificent structure. As his fingertips flow over a carving of a large tree, he picks up on a strong familiarity with the root structure. "Look at this tree, Mono, specifically the roots. Do they look familiar to you?" Mono scurries over to join in on the detective analysis.

"Whoa!" he shouts, jumping back with surprise. "That's definitely an elephant tree, no doubt about it!" he confirms with swirling pride. "Those trees don't grow anywhere else! If that really is one, then this door *must* have originated on The Pearl… and judging by the other luscious landscapes, it must have been done a long, *long* time ago!" He stands back to marvel at the newly depicted beauty.

"And look at this!" Mono says with compounding excitement as he points to a unique carving under the elephant tree. Centered on the door exists a mesmerizing symbol made up of seven identical circles. Six circles revolve around a seventh central circle. Each outer circle aligns its center point of origin along the circumference of the middle one. They are all evenly spaced, and their overlapping nature creates five peddle-like shapes.

"It kinda looks like a flower," one of the Seers says as he tries to make sense of the carving.

"I don't know, Sorovi," another Seer says. "Look, there is something else carved below it!" The excited Seer highlights another elegantly carved symbol of a dragon curled in a particular way, with its tail and head lifted and curving to either side as if mirroring one another. Above the dragon is a single circle with a dot in the center. Below the dragon is a small oval shape sprouting dueling olive branches on either side that bookend the carving.

"A dragon?" someone from the crowd asks blankly.

"And what's under it? An egg? A seed?" comes further inquiry.

"A seed?!" someone else shouts. "Why would a dragon have a seed? It's definitely an egg. Dragons lay eggs, right?"

"How the hell should we know what dragons do or don't do?!"

"Well, there is something written underneath it all," Mono points out. "Maybe it can help explain what these symbols mean." Running his fingers over the indented words, Mono reads aloud the ancient text:

> *"All who cross the threshold must tend to the Garden.*
> *Hold in hand the torch bearing the flames of Truth.*
> *Nurture the seeds that will bear the fruit of the Second Sun."*

"Second Sun? Now what do you think it means?" comes the question from the crowd.

"It means this place has more history than any of us ever imagined!" a jubilant Seer shouts proudly before diving into an impromptu dance. The energy of the dancing youth helps to lighten the elevating tension in the group.

"It also means it *was* a seed! I told you!" Comes a triumphant cry from the group. A wave of conversation rushes over the Seer's as they all become drunk on speculation and wonder.

"This is incredible," Mono says. "There is no way Mune put this here. This was done well before his time, even ours. Tewari! This place could predate Babel! These symbols could very well be some of the first clues regarding our ancestry in centuries! Do you think Brahm knew about this when he sent us here?"

"It was clear he sent us here to rescue the other members of our tribe. That much is *very* clear," Tewari says seriously while cradling his damaged shoulder. "But what this door, these symbols, and this place has to do with all that is still a mystery."

"Well," the jubilant Seer interjects while still engaged in ecstatic-dance, "why don't we just knock on the door and see if anybody answers?"

"Haha, brilliant!" Mono shouts. "Let's get to the bottom of this mystery the old fashion way!"

"Very well," Tewari says with a strong flavor of caution. "However, be on guard, we have no idea who or what is behind that door. Remember, the Warden is still very much alive. Be prepared for anything."

"Yee-oo!" the Seers bark in unison, allowing their battle cry to echo along the hollow chamber walls that extends beside them. The ominous path appears to go back to Mune's fallen castle, a direction no one is willing to venture towards at this point. The mysterious door is their only way forward, and the men stand ready to embark on their new path. Tewari gives a silent nod to his men while raising his able arm above his head. With a clenched fist, he turns towards the impressive barrier. He knocks with a commanding swing, hammering his fist into the cool iron door. The door bellows like an ancient gong, ringing as if a doorbell for the gods. It ripples and vibrates from Tewari's knock, transmitting its magnificent and otherworldly hum into the atmosphere.

The Seers can feel the profound vibrations coursing through their bodies, sending chills down their spines and tickling their brains. They all stand perfectly still and silent as they allow the powerful sound to wash over them. As the heavenly acoustics gently dissipate back into silence, the men take a deep breath, preparing for whatever consequences may come next. Some sloshing sounds of feet approaching can be heard from the other side, which puts everyone on guard. A slit on the door not noticed before starts to slowly slide open, breaking the seemingly impenetrable boundary the door possesses. The men crouch down to take an eager glance at the other side. However, they are quickly met instead with the receiving end of multiple rifles jutting out of the opening.

"Tewari! What is this?!" Mono shouts, as he jumps back from the threatening devices.

"I don't know," he responds calmly. "Just don't make any more sudden movements."

"Who's there?!" comes a gruff and muffled voice from the other side. The Seers look to one another before answering. The voice sounds clearly altered for some reason, which only confuses the already baffled bunch.

"My name is Tewari," their leader says while stepping into the line of sight of the protruding weapons. "I come with my Seer brothers, natives of this land in hopes to reunite with the sisters of our tribe. We come in peace and ask for any assistance you might provide." Tewari's words hang in the air for a moment before fading back into silence. Nervous anticipation grips the Seers, as they all stare intently at the stationary weapons still directed at them. Suddenly, without another word spoken, the rifles retract one by one and the slit in the door closes violently.

"H-Hey! What gives?!" Mono exclaims, expecting a very different outcome to Tewari's declaration.

"I don't know, just be patient," Tewari asks of the eager youth. Forcing his emotional state back into check, Mono stands at attention, silently praying for the patrons behind the door to help them in their cause.

The Seers are surprised to hear the unexpected unlatching of locks. They look with wide eyes as the enormous door begins to slowly swing open on its mighty hinges. The slight resistance the hinges impose on the weight of the door causes a resonating hum, similar to the profound acoustic ramifications of Tewari's knocking. The sound comforts the awaiting men who stand frozen with beating hearts in their throats. As the door reaches a wide enough opening to allow the light from the other room to shine through, three dark silhouettes can be seen standing in the doorway. The men are forced to shield their eyes as they look at the obscured figures standing still. Their rifles remain dangerously in hand. As the Seers' eyes adjust to the light, the humanoid shadows develop into a more recognizable presentation.

"Yahooo! You're alive! You are all really alive!" The men scream as they run into the arms of the unveiled shadows. Huddled around the party of three, the men embrace their Seer sisters with tears pouring from their eyes.

"I never thought I would see you again!" one man cries out.

"I never had any doubt we would find you!" another cries.

"Right!" the first man corrects himself. "That's what I meant to say!"

"I can't believe this is all finally over!" another chimes in.

"Alright, alright, alright!" one of the women says, compassionately pushing her emotional brothers aside. "We are happy to see you all too, very much so," she adds warmly. "But I need you all to get it together, there is still much work that needs to be done. We are definitely not out of the woods yet."

"Right, right!" the men say, wiping the tears from their eyes.

"Where is everyone else?!" one man asks.

"Yeah!" another says before an answer can be reached. "And how did you manage to escape?!"

"Did everyone make it?" fires yet another inquirer.

"Yes, yes, we all made it this far together without any casualties. You have that one over there to thank for it all," the woman says, taking the weight of all the questions and redirecting it to the center of the room. She extends a finger to pinpoint the source of answers. The men follow her finger and find Raja standing as the directed focal point. She stands consumed in conversation, surrounded by her mother who is talking in one ear as Raja is trying to listen to Sophia with her other. Her attention is so consumed, she has yet to notice the entrance of her brethren tribe. Mono doesn't waste another second and races to them.

"Raja! Mother! You are all right! Thank goodness!" he says as he pours all his energy into each step towards his family. His flailing and disruptive presentation finally draws the attention of his sister as she looks to the emotional wreck heading right to her.

"Mono!" she cries in sync with her mother. The three collide with a loving embrace, twirling around the room in ecstatic bliss. They all quickly fall into an emotional release, confiding in one another through wordless transmission. They swim together in their collective pool of grief, happiness, sorrow and relief. Their tearful silence says more than they could ever hope to convey in a lifetime. As the room starts to spin faster than they are, the three slow their twirl before they risk falling to the floor.

"I can't believe this!" Mono finally says, gazing back and forth from his sister to his mother, wondering if this could be an elaborate dream he is destined to wake from.

"Believe it!" Raja says cheerfully. Her energy resonates with an overwhelming level of confidence, balance, and power. Mono is taken aback slightly from the memory of a more chaotic and frenzy-fueled sister.

"What has become of you?" he asks his sister. "You appear to have grown up a great deal since the last time I saw you."

"A lot has changed since we last saw each other," she says solemnly. "It's been years since the Warden first came and took you and father. Is he—"

"They took him to the Ward," Mono responds heavily. He struggles to find any words to console his mother and sister. A deep and hollow breath fills his lungs.

"That is okay," Mufida says as she embraces her children. "Your father is a strong man. I'm sure he is still alive."

"That's right!" Mono chimes in, desperate to breathe hope back into their reunion. "He was the strongest of us all! Now we are one rescue mission closer to getting the whole family together again!"

"Mono," his mother exclaims, "you cannot be serious, can you? Have you learned nothing from your captivity?"

"Well," he responds cheekily, "I've just learned Raja is responsible for something none of us have ever accomplished since our imprisonment! Is it true, Raja? Are you really the one responsible for your escape?"

"It appears so," Sophia chimes in abruptly, ready to transition back to their earlier conversation, "and that's *exactly* what we were just discussing before you all showed up."

"Oh!" Mono says, now addressing the tall woman in a long beige cloak. "My apologies. My name is Mono, who are you?"

"I am Sophia, your sister and her tribe were the ones kind enough to release me from my prison. And in the process, managed to apprehend Mune and his forces. She was just telling me about how she managed to do it."

"Mune? You *apprehended* Mune?! For real? Is he here?" Mono asks as he twirls his head around and scans the room. His brothers, catching wind of what Sophia has just said, come to join him as they, too, look around at the unimaginable scene before them. Where Sophia once stood bound and shackled now resides the not-so-mighty Mune. His beady eyes look back at the unified tribe of Seers who send waves of emotional fury with their return gaze.

"Don't you dirty Bakuwan dare look at me like that you… abominations!" he threatens from his shackled state. "I am nobility! A worldly authority! I represent progress, you backward swine! By your actions here today you have declared war on Wisteria! Do you even understand the consequences of your actions?"

"Enough!" one of the Seer women shout as she aims the barrel of her newly acquired rifle at his face. Her head dons two neatly braided bands of hair that line either side of her head and flow down her back. Her clothes are worn and tattered, more so than some of the others. Her face is dirty, but her eyes glow bright. She forgoes her pain and smiles at the chance to meet face to face with the source of her physical suffering.

"You don't even know how to use that thing!" Mune tries to intimidate. The woman moves closer, placing the barrel tip right onto his forehead and her finger upon the trigger.

"Maybe I don't," she says calmly. "I was just going to push on this little trigger right here and see what happens. Think that is a good place to start?" she finishes with a playful wink.

"You wretched woman, get that thing out of my face!"

"Guess not. Just remember, we are only keeping you alive to send a peaceful message to the rest of the world. Don't think we have to stick to the script." Mune's muffled grumbling is enough of a confirmation for the woman to walk away for the time being. She sends a threatening glance to the rest of Mune's men who remain bound on the ground next to him. They are bundled together, tethered by a thick chain circumventing their midsections.

"Incredible!" Mono exclaims. "So how did you do it, Raja?"

"Yes," Sophia adds. "Please, tell us how you managed such an unbelievable task. I know you Seers are talented, but I never imagined you all to be this powerful."

"Neither did we," Raja says humbly, "Not until last night during the storm, did we know anything like what happened today could be possible." She takes a deep breath before diving into her eagerly awaited story. "There was this old man who sought shelter with us during Babel; he was kind, jovial, and seemed completely at peace with the storm. While we huddled together waiting for Babel to pass, he decided to tell us a story. He began talking about our past… the Seer past! We never even told him who we were, but we definitely didn't stop him from telling his story. He told us about how great our civilization was and how powerful we were due to our connection with the planet. He went on to confirm that we hailed great powers and abilities granted by Maia well before Babel. At the height of our power, he said there were those who possessed a special ability, that of 'second sight.' The old man was very excited to tell us about this ability. He said those chosen by the planet could move beyond the normal Seers' visions and see into the 'nature of all things.'"

"'Nature of all things?'" Sophia repeats quizzically.

"Yeah, he said with such an ability, one could see past the physical limitations of our world. He started talking about energy and vibrations… the power of our thoughts and how everything that appears physical is just one version of reality. We didn't really understand him, but his enthusiasm kept us wrapped up in his story. He said all the Seer leaders in the past possessed this ability and used it to create large temples, buildings, and incredible works of art. Meant to better the planet, this power was quickly abused for personal gain and led to the destruction of our people. It was a power too great to befall on those who could not respect it and was taken away. However, just as the storm was about to pass, he mentioned that it was prophesized one day this power would return and would be the key to rebuilding our civilization. He left before saying any more. His words had been racing through my head ever since. It's like he planted a seed in my mind that just kept growing and growing! Even when Mune's forces captured us, all I could think about was his story. I wasn't nervous or scared during that time; I was completely consumed by the idea of this 'second sight.'"

"This is so wild. How have we not heard of such an ability until now?" Mono says, scratching his head lightly.

"So much of who we are has been lost, Mono," Raja responds warmly. "There is no telling how much more is left to be rediscovered."

"I guess you are right," Mono says, trailing off into thought. All the time he spent finding himself locked in Mune's castle had never led him to such a revelation. "So, what do you make of it?"

"Well, it's difficult to really put into words. By the time I got to the prison, I was absolutely exhausted. After running for hours, beaten then dragged to our cage, I didn't think I had anything left to give. I laid there on the floor unable to even move my body. I found myself fading in and out of consciousness, wondering if I was dreaming or still awake. At that time, it didn't seem to matter. I felt myself drifting into a weird space where I knew I was in pain, but I didn't really feel it. I knew I was in a prison, but I didn't really feel trapped. I just *was...* you know? No labels, no judgment, just... *presence* I guess. It was very freeing despite my situation. Sometimes I wanted to remind myself I really was trapped, but I didn't have the energy to fight it. As I started to give into this feeling of freedom, I noticed the prison bars appeared to be dancing and playing. It was as if they felt free too!"

"Whoa!" Mono shrieks reflexively. "Did that really happen, or was that part a dream?"

"It's hard to say what is real after all this, but it's what I saw! It's what I felt and evidently, it's what came to be. It felt like the prison was reacting to my sensation of freedom. The more I leaned into it, the more vigorously the bars appeared to dance. Assuming it all had to be a dream, I asked the dancing bars if they really would let me be free. Next thing I know, I am being led to the lock on the cage door. My energy had returned, but I thought that could just be part of the dream. I saw the lock dancing like everything else. It sprouted a face and gave me a playful wink. Total dream right? Well, then the lock leapt off its clasp and fell to the floor."

"We may have not seen the dancing bars," one Seer sister remarks, "but, we sure heard that lock fall to the ground."

Raja looks up from her testimony and studies the wide-eyed and silent brothers that surround her. As the silence builds, doubt starts to creep into her mind. She wonders if her story sounds crazy or unbelievable.

"So?? What happened next?!" Mono yells, breaking the spell of doubt.

"Haha," Raja responds lightly. "What happened next is we left! Soon the guards were hot on our tail, and not knowing where to go, I prayed for a way to stay free. Just as that thought left my mind, I had a vision leading me to a certain painting of Mune. When we arrived, it seemed like a dead end. Not knowing what else to do, I put my hand on Mune's face. I could feel the painting start to give a little. After pushing harder, it gave way to the tunnel that brought us to the metal door behind us. We could hear commotion on the other side, so we decided to knock. Eventually, this metal slot opened up and a guard popped into view. It was hard to say who was more surprised. We acted quick and grabbed the guard before he had time to react. Looking past him, we saw we easily out numbered his forces.

Unfortunately, the door was still locked, so there wasn't much we could do with our situation."

"Yikes, going from one trap to another!" Mono exclaims.

"Yeah, it felt that way. As that feeling of being trapped returned, I tried to resist it, but I only felt worse. It... *physically* hurt, if that makes any sense. Not knowing what else to do, I decided to lean into it again, like back in the prison. As my heart softened, so too did the feeling of being trapped. So bizarre. Suddenly, I heard the lock spring open from the other side. I'm sure we were just high off our earlier escape, but we took our chance. We grabbed his gun, and ran into this chamber guns blazing. Before they knew what was happening, we had them all overwhelmed and overpowered. That's when we met this lady right here! Her and I were just starting to get to know each other when you all showed up!"

"Wow!" Mono says, filled to the brim with pride for his sister. "You are amazing, Raja! So that story the old man told you, does this mean, does this mean—"

"I don't know what it means yet," Raja says calmly. "All I know right now is I'm exhausted from it all and very thankful for everything that has happened. Right now, I just want to worry about getting everyone out of this place alive."

"I agree," Sophia says with an authoritative tone. "It looks like that iron door is the only way in and out of this place. We should get moving if we hope to prolong our survival."

"Hold on, just wait a moment," Tewari interjects.

"Wait?" Sophia repeats. "Wait for what? Wait for that Warden still lurking around here to find us? Wait for this whole mountain to collapse? Wait for us to become poisoned by radiation from that Power Pole beside us? What in the world do you suspect we wait for?"

"Did you ever stop to wonder what this place is?" he says, with no concern given to her exasperated tone. "The carvings on the iron door... the markings on the walls in here; this doesn't look like a place Mune would have built for himself. It looks nothing like the rest of his castle!" He twirls his gaze around to take in the full contents of the octagon chamber. They stand next to the stacked sculpture in the center of the room. He runs his fingers over a multitude of geometric carvings imprinted on the flat faces of the giant cube on the bottom. Many resemble the flower-like design he and his men saw on the iron door. His heart swells with familiarity, yet his mind forgoes any recollection of the symbols. The energy in the room appears to be perpetually building; it bounces off the perfectly cut walls, and reflects off the specific carved angles, enhancing the vibratory energy of all who reside within the chamber.

"These angles, these shapes, these symbols," he thinks out loud. "They are not here by coincidence; nothing is. Everything in this place is built so perfectly, so precise! It all must mean… something!" His eyes scan the myriad amounts of mural work that cover the walls. He prays to the gods to give him the ability to decipher such rich history.

"What difference does it make what this place is?" Sophia asks, growing impatient with Tewari's heartfelt exploration.

"What difference does it make? Lady, I don't know who you are or what you know about this land, but before Mune took control over The Pearl it was the Seers who ruled the land for centuries. Like Raja was saying earlier, much of what we know about our people has been lost forever. Our temple was built where Mune's castle stands now. He destroyed what we believed was everything left of our history. But this place…" he says, lingering for a moment as he scans the room once again in awe. "Ancient lore told us of an inner sanctum of the temple that the greatest Seer Sages would retreat to in order to channel their power and talk directly to Maia's spirit. As long as we lived in the Seer temple, we never found it. We thought it to be yet another story of legend that faded with time. But look around you now!" he says, addressing his people. "What does this place look like to you? Could this not be the very sacred inner sanctum we have been told about by our elders?!"

"Okay, okay, I get it. This might be the nostalgic cornerstone of your past history, but if that's true, how did a bird-brained, dunce-cap wearing weasel like Mune find it when your people have spent generations looking for it? Something doesn't add up."

"Well, let's get some answers," the woman who held the gun to Mune's head earlier says with a flash of joy. She moves closer to her captive and returns the gun's barrel to the quivering man's forehead.

"What?! What do you want?" Mune squeals.

"What do you think? Are you deaf *and* dumb?" the woman responds. "How did you find this place?"

"If I tell you, will you let me go?"

"Of course not."

"Well then," Mune says as he places his nose in the air. "What reason do I have to answer your questions?"

"Did you forget about my target practice?" the woman says, flicking the trigger of her weapon playfully with her finger. "If you don't prove some use to us then you are no better dead than alive."

"Damn you all," Mune grumbles. "Fine, but don't think you are going to get some elaborate story from me. It's simple. As I was destroying your pitiful excuse for a castle to make room for my own, I spent a good amount of time personally demolishing all the statues you had carved into this mountain of yours. All those important faces of antiquity, crushed and crumbled by my hands… lost to the sands of time forever…" Mune pauses as he enjoys the elevated fury his words bring to his crowd. "Now, where was I? Oh yeah, as I was taking a sledgehammer to your history, destroying it brick by brick, memory by memory…"

"Just get to the point," the woman says as she pushes the barrel of her gun deeper into his skull. Her voice cracks slightly as her emotions run rampant.

"Mmm," Mune hums, clearly proud of himself. "Guess you don't want to hear the good part. Anyway, as I smashed in the head of one of your statues, there was a cool breeze rushing from the hole I made. I ordered my servants to tear down the rest of the statue only to find this hallway behind it. I found this ugly room but thought it would make a good place to hide the Power Pole. It also seemed to be a safety bunker if you pesky fools ever decided to revolt. You lot clearly couldn't find it when you ran this place, so I was assured you would never find it when you didn't! It was working pretty good… well, until now."

"That just doesn't make any sense," Tewari says, falling back into ponder. "Why would the entrance to this place need to be carved out? How did the ancient Sages reach this room if there was never any door to it?"

"Well, think about Raja's story," Mono chimes in, trying to piece the puzzle together. "If she learned how to connect and communicate with the prison, maybe the Sages could do the same with the mountain! Maybe the higher Sages didn't have any need for doors if they could see the 'nature of all things.'"

"Maybe you are on to something, Mono," Tewari says, stroking his chin. "We need to find that old man Raja and Mufida talked to during the storm and get more answers!"

"Wonderful!" Sophia says, jumping back into the conversation. "I bet this old man is *not* in this room, so why don't you say we all finally make our way out of here! Then you can go run off and find this mystery man while the rest of us get as far away from here as possible."

∞

High atop the beehive ceiling, some dust falls from one of the many octagon depressions. The sound of anxious banter and commotion emanates from the seemingly arbitrary space. As the Seers and Sophia remain focused on deliberating their escape route, none of them seem to notice the unusual commotion stirring above them.

"Quit moving so much!" Domino whispers to his friend. "You are going to wind up falling! Or worse, pushing me off this ledge! Just sit still already!"

"But I can't see!" Otto says with a childish tone as he continues to shift around Domino to get a better view of the events below him. "Ah! There we go!" He pushes his friend out of the way. "Look! Look! Sophia is surrounded by all those other people, maybe this is finally all over! Even the rumbling has stopped!"

"That doesn't mean anything yet," Domino says as he tries to wiggle himself back into a comfortable position. "Plus, where is everyone else? Izak? Ayananda? Brahm? Beau? Demon Giant? Hey, what do you say Emmanuel? Do you see anything?"

"Oh, no jokes this time?" Emmanuel asks playfully.

"C'mon man, this is serious!" Domino fires back.

"Ahhhh, I do actually," Emmanuel hums as he scans the energetic surroundings. "Yes, this is definitely not over yet. There is a radiating force of energy moving through the mountainside heading in our direction. It's hard to make out exactly what or who it is; its energy source is incredible though. It moves through the mountain like it's swimming through water. Fascinating."

"That's cool and all, but you really don't know who it is?" Domino asks flatly.

"No, unfortunately I do not. I've never seen energy quite like this."

"I wonder what it could be," Domino says as he returns his gaze down below at the conspiring Seers. He plants his face into his hands and eagerly waits for the incoming anomaly to present itself.

"Well, I'm not waiting any longer!" Otto cries out triumphantly as he takes his prized rope off his shoulder. "Domino, help me find something to tie this thing on to."

"Do what?" Domino bellows, forgetting to keep his voice down. "You're going to climb down there after we went through all that effort to get up here?"

"All *that* effort?" Otto fires back. He is already working on finding a sturdy outcropping from the tunnel to secure his rope. "We decided to turn left instead of right when all that shaking was going on! Where is the effort in that? We got lucky! Or! Maybe we could have found a better spot! What good is this vantage point up here anyway? It's not like we can do something if things go wrong."

"Do something? What would be your brilliant service to the community if you were down there, hot shot? Huh? Make a mess?"

"Hey! At least I plan to do more than just stay out of the way the whole time!"

"C'mon boys," Emmanuel chimes in. "We all have our purpose in this situation. Everyone's place in it will unfold sooner or later."

"Yeah, and mine will unfold down there, thank you very much!" Otto says proudly as he ties the other end of the rope to his midline. "All those who wish to join me feel free! Otherwise—" A large explosion suddenly detonates from outside the iron door. The shockwave pulsates through the sanctum, shaking everything to its core. The reverberating sonic current forces Otto to focus on maintaining his balance rather than finishing his sentence. The boys look down from their high perch to examine what new addition has just arrived. Sophia and the Seers shift their attention to the door. The women, still caring firearms, lock their ammunition into place and march towards the door to inspect the new arrival. They move slowly, unsure as to what awaits them on the other side.

"Was this in your vision, Raja?" Sophia asks as she tries her best to prepare for what comes next.

"No, unfortunately, not. My vision only went as far as entering this chamber. Everything else must have still been in too great of a probability state."

"Probability state?"

"Well, as much as we know about how our visions work, we can only see what the planet wishes and what has condensed into a high enough degree of probability. Even with our regular visions, the future is still ultimately malleable. If there are too many… *mutable* factors leading up to an event, then we can't see the vision clearly or at all."

"Ah, that makes sense, I suppose. I guess that's the great 'mutable factor' knocking at our door," Sophia says as she reflexively burrows her hand into her now empty cloak pocket. A wave of concern washes over her. Everyone rushes to the door except Sophia, Raja, and the women keeping watch over Mune and his guards. One of the Seer women is first to reach the door and extends her arm out to open the viewing slat, but the giant door creaks open before she even touches it. The familiar sound of a gong resonates from the door throughout the chamber, amplified by the acoustic-friendly geometry. The group of Seers at the door take a step back, adrenaline pumping, as they await the sight of their unexpected visitor. As the light from the room shines into the dimly lit hallway, Mune stretches his neck to also catch the sight of the newcomer.

"It's about time you got here!" he calls out, making a point to shake the chains that bind him. As the room falls into a hush of gasps, Mune continues to address the tall figure now entering the room. "Hurry up and get me out of these damn chains! I can't believe you would let me fall into such a state! Make good on your servitude and fix this mess!"

"Very well," the Warden says with a disapproving huff of his breath. He casually walks past the armed women that remain at the door. They quiver in fear as they quickly recognize the devilish beast. The resounding fear clouds their consciousness. Driven by the primal desire for preservation, they make their unconscious move to attack the incoming threat. Quivering trigger fingers spring into action, firing the ominous declaration of war. As the smoke wisps out of the heated barrels, everyone looks onto the face of the now stationary Warden. He stands tilted to the side, with clear puncture wounds visible where he was shot at point blank range. A lingering moment of hope blankets the room, as the abrupt maneuver appears successful. However, that hope quickly fades as the Warden continues his reluctant path to Mune with his bullet wounds worn proudly. Not knowing what else to do, the women at the door scramble to reload their weapons, despite the clear uselessness of their previous attack. Everyone else tenses up, desperately trying to figure out how to best manage the overbearing threat before them.

"I said hurry! What good are you if you are just going to take your damn time and do whatever you want! You defective piece of crap, listen to me!" Mune bellows in a full temper tantrum. "I am your master! You have to do as I say!"

"Yeah, yeah," the Warden responds coldly. "Just don't get it twisted. You are no master to me; my *real* master has merely commanded me to assist you," he says dramatically with his hands held out in front of him as if bound by invisible shackles.

"You... useless, pompous, self righteous prick..." Mune mumbles under his breath. "Makes no difference to me!" He scowls as he notices the Warden has failed to increase his pace. "The first thing I will do when I make it back home is to trade you in for a functional unit."

"Will you now?" the Warden says, materializing directly in front of Mune like a plume of smoke.

"When did you..." Mune stammers, unsure how the Warden moved so quickly. "It doesn't matter! Just get me down from here already!"

"As you wish." He gently severs Mune's chains with his hand as if tearing wet paper. He looks down at the collection of guards and directs a skinny, slithering snake from within his suit towards their location. The snake curves across the checkered floor slowly and smoothly, taking its time to feast its eyes upon the helpless guards. It's deep yellow eyes and pronounced fangs appear more hungry than heroic. The men grow uneasy as the snake appears completely disinterested in securing their safety. The snake rises into the face of one of the guards, tickling his nose with its tongue. The helpless guard starts to lose all hope in being rescued.

"That's enough!" Mune commands. The snake maintains its ocular lock on the frightened guard while simultaneously breaking the binding chain with its tail. As the chains clank to the floor, Mune has his companions quickly rush to the circling band of Seers, eager to distance themselves from the devilish snake.

"Alright, you fools, the game is finally over," Mune commands with an inflated sense of power. "Drop *my* weapons on the ground and walk yourselves over against the wall. No funny business or it's not just me you'll have to answer to," he says as he ominously looks back at the Warden. Sophia and the Seers carefully comply with Mune's commands. The

Warden appears pitifully bored and unamused, but his threat is still real enough. They watch him huff and puff like a disgruntled child as he commands the chains upon the floor to fasten around their wrists. His deflated sense of purpose is almost painstaking to watch.

"Good… very good," Mune decrees happily as he rings his hands together greedily. "You all look like nice, neat packages ready to be delivered to the motherland! How pleased the High Family will be to see how I have succeeded in rounding up such wonderful specimens for their experiments! All right Warden! Lift them up and get us out of here. Let's leave this barren rock for Wisteria!" Hanging his head low in disgust, the Warden lifts his hands causing the binding chain to constrict and lift Sophia and the Seers off the ground. He slowly follows behind his commanding officer with the precious cargo as they make their way towards the iron door.

∞

"Mmmm," Emmanuel hums, coming back from another deep meditative dive.

"What is it this time?" Otto cries out, desperate for some good news.

"A new game piece has been introduced to the playing board."

"What the heck does that mean?" Domino demands, eager for some straightforward answers.

"You shall see," Emmanuel says cryptically as he brings a warm smile to his face.

"Game piece this, playing board that, a blind man telling me to see… this old fart over here just likes playing games!" Domino blurts out in frustration. "Whatever happened to straightforward communication?" he asks rhetorically as he slumps back into viewing position, waiting to see whatever Emmanuel has hinted at manifesting. "This better be good!" From below, a deep rumbling can be felt from underneath the inner sanctum.

∞

"Warden?!" Mune calls. "Is this your doing?" He flounders around the room like a fish out of water.

"No," the Warden says slowly, but the jubilant look on his face makes him appear more excited than concerned. He scans the energetic atmosphere like a hunting dog catching the scent of his prey. As the pulsating rumbling underneath them grows, so does his level of excitement.

"This should be good," the Warden says as he awaits the release of the growing pressure from below. Right in front of the convoy and before the iron door, the ground ripples and undulates like a bubbling geyser ready to erupt. The curved edges of the upheaving ground start to develop sharp edges, becoming more cube-like, popping off the ground like a boiling pot of water.

"What is the meaning of this?!" Mune cries out, somehow personally offended by this turn of events. "Warden! Stop this at once!"

"But sir," the Warden replies playfully. "*How* do you wish me to do that?"

"Do *something*, you buffoon! Don't try and weasel your way out of doing what you're told with your silly line of questioning!" Mune screams in exasperated frustration. "Put the ground back to how it was this instant! I know you have something to do with this!"

"Not this time," the Warden says seriously. "But I think I am going to enjoy dealing with it." As the Warden's words leave his lips, the bubbling ground finally reaches its climax and erupts into a splendid array of cubical confetti.

"The inner sanctum!" Tewari frantically exclaims. He is stricken with grief at the sight of his beloved historical landmark being destroyed by this bizarre eruption. Cubed fragments of mountain crash into the walls harboring the precious artwork. Tewari's eyes fill with tears as he imagines his own personal history being destroyed before him. "Wait, what is this?" he asks no one in particular while watching the waves of destruction retreat like the receding tide of the ocean. The various cubes of mountain sprawling all over the chamber start to playfully bounce back into the geyser hole, carving into the ground as if it were water. In a bizarre turn of events, the cubes dancing along the ground wash away any signs of damage in their wake. As the initial cubes roll back into place, they are replaced with new sprouting cubes that erupt with slightly less force than the first wave. Eventually the geyser-like activity dies down to a low murmur, bubbling gently as a few choice patrons rise out of the ground from within the hole. Entrapped by a glowing purple orb, Brahm, along with two Severed Marionettes, place their feet upon the checkered floor of the inner sanctum. He still holds two men atop his shoulders, one comically disproportionate in size. The last remaining bubbling cubes roll back into place, merging into the mountain and eliminating any lingering evidence of their bizarre behavior.

∞

"Whoa!" the boys cry out together.

"That was incredible!" Otto blurts out.

"That's Brahm! He is out of this world! He's got the others with him too! Oh man, he's going to take down that Warden for sure!" Domino adds in. "Is this what you saw?" He looks back to address Emmanuel, who currently looks very pleased with himself. "Why didn't you say it was Brahm?"

"I thought you might enjoy the surprise for yourself!" he responds playfully, while also letting out a heavy sigh of relief.

"So, everything is going to be okay now? Isn't it?" Otto asks with hopeful intentions.

"This, my friends, is something we will all have to wait and see how it plays out." Emmanuel says as he shifts his weight. "It's still anybody's game at this point."

"Again with the game talk?!" Domino nearly spits out of his mouth, "enough already, this is serious!"

"Indeed it is," Emmanuel agrees, preparing himself for the growing tsunami of energy brewing between the two powerhouses below.

CHAPTER: 38

Combine and Conquer

From inside his electromagnetic torus-field, Brahm looks through the glowing orb, assessing his new surroundings. Mune stands in front of him, glaring with fiery rage, yet frozen in disbelief. Behind him are the Seers and Sophia who are chained and shackled along their wrists. They are tethered to one another, paused in mid-march towards their impending doom. They remain mesmerized and gridlocked, still processing Brahm's reality-bending entrance. Sophia's eyes start to water as she begins to peel back the feeling of hope like a ripened banana. Everyone appears reluctant to be the first to cut the silent tension; all except for the Warden, who casually slides out from behind the prisoners and walks eagerly up to the newcomers.

Having taken in as much information as he needs regarding the occupants of the space, Brahm makes a quick scan of the rest of the room. He studies the dimensions, structure, location within space and time, as well as the bizarre pulsating pole of dark energy along the wall. The room resonates with an ancient charm much like the sound of an old instrument that's been dusted off and strummed for the first time in ages. After dragging a heavy breath into his lungs, he exhales with a firm acceptance of his daunting situation.

"Are you all able to walk?" He asks his conscious companions.

"We can do more than that!" Ayananda says with confidence as she shifts her body into a fighting position.

"Definitely. Let's finish what we started," Izak says as he stares through the crowd in front of him towards the light consuming Power Pole.

"Beau?" Brahm asks, as his companion has remained silent during the roll call.

"Go ahead and set me down, let's see what these legs are still capable of," he says with the grunt of an aging man. Brahm complies, using the manipulated forces of his vortex to move Beau through the air and gently towards the ground like a falling leaf from a tree. Utilizing the vortex yet again, Brahm looks to Izak and Ayananda and moves the still unconscious Jeeven into their possession.

"I trust you will keep him safe," he says while the giant is still floating through mid-air.

"I have already dedicated my life to this man!" Ayananda responds with overinflated flair, "I will die before I let anything happen to him."

"Yeah, yeah, don't worry about him or us," Izak says flatly, realizing he has transitioned into a supporting role. "You just worry about dealing with that monster."

"That settles it," Brahm says. "Prepare yourselves. I'm taking down the vortex." With a flick of concentrated willpower, the torus-shaped aura recedes back into Brahm's body. Beau's knees buckle for a moment as the resurging force of gravity returns, but he quickly recovers. Izak and Ayananda are not as graceful, as they fall flat under the returning weight of their sleeping giant. Brahm's eyes twitch as he notices the clear display of weakness was not missed by the eager Warden. The adversary stands pensively, studying their every move.

"Mmhmm," the Warden remarks, as if struggling to decide what item to select off a menu.

"Your fight is with me," Brahm says definitively, taking a step in front of his weakened party. He stands with radiating confidence and determination despite his body displaying an equal level of glowing frailty. This pleases the Warden greatly. Assured he has the Warden's full attention, Brahm lifts his arm and sends a gentle pulse of energy out into the atmosphere. It passes through all the people before him, having no more effect on their bodies than a fleeting emotion. Everyone looks around to see what has happened. One by one, the shackles around the prisoner's wrists start to unlock and drop to the ground with a resounding *clank*. The guns Mune's guards hold begin to vibrate down to the very core of their physical make up. They eventually dismember their structural integrity and fall to the ground as individual and harmless pieces.

"W-W-What is this?!" Mune exclaims, infuriated with his resurging lost sense of control. He looks to his empty-handed men, who look back with glances of helplessness and bewilderment. Shaking his head, Mune turns back to his last resort.

"Do something!" he commands the Warden, who has yet to dislodge his sights from Brahm since entering the room.

"Oh, I'm going to do something all right," the Warden replies, "but I think I'm going to leave the mess of those prisoners for you to clean up." He looks to Brahm with shivers of excitement running down his spine. "Ahhh, to think of how long I have waited to face a worthy opponent!"

"Perfect," Brahm responds as he nods his head to Beau and the Marionettes to go and assist the recently freed Seers and Sophia. Mune watches in horror as the wounded warriors march unopposed to his position in the center of the room.

"You defective, worthless excuse of a servant!" Mune bellows in rage, "I command you this instant to stop these fools and recapture my prisoners!" The Warden can feel the drive to comply surge into his programing, but the tantalizing dream of squaring off with Brahm remains enough of a force to counter the command.

"Not this time, boss, I have… greater needs to attend to," he says making his defiant step away from his commanding officer.

"That is it!" Mune fires back in blinded rage. "You leave me no choice!" He grabs the detonator from along his waist. He proudly holds it up into the air for everyone to see.

"I didn't want to have to use this, but your defiance has brought this upon yourself!" he says with heavy panting. "Do you want to take a guess at what this is?" he asks, trying to intimidate the Warden with his questioning.

"No, but I have a strong suspicion you will have to tell me eventually, so I'm not too worried about it."

"Grrr… you are making my decision to use this thing all the easier, you… you waste of resources!" Mune shouts. "This is the detonator to the bomb I have secured to that precious Power Pole of yours over there!"

"Oooh?" the Warden hums, displaying more amusement than concern.

"I knew from the start Wisteria sent me a defective Warden, so I had to take matters into my own hand to secure your obedience! You are proving to me that the power you draw from is becoming nothing more than a liability. A liability I can no longer afford! You either comply with my commands, or I blow up the very source of your life right here and now! Comply or die!" he shouts from the depths of his core, his arms quivering under the adrenaline rush of his procured proclamation.

"Seriously?" Izak says as he looks to Ayananda for confirmation. "Is he really going to do our job for us? This guy is nuts!" Ayananda shrugs her shoulders with genuine confusion.

"Go for it! Blow it to smithereens!" Izak yells from within the peanut gallery.

"Well then," the Warden says, clearly ignoring Izak's rogue comment. With a childish huff of his breath, he turns to face the infuriated Mune. "I guess you do make a compelling argument. Fine, I'll clean up your mess… again." Thinking quickly, Brahm decides to take advantage of the Warden's divided allegiance and uses himself as bait to regain his focus.

"Oh, so you can take your sights off of me that easily?" Brahm taunts as he widens his stance and straightens his spine. A resonating force starts to pulse from his chest like the Warden has never experienced before. It stops him in his tracks. He whips his head back around to feast his eyes upon his persuasive opponent. Bringing his hands together over his heart, Brahm pours all of his concentrated willpower into summoning his most risky energetic endeavor to date.

Fine-tuning his personal energetic frequency, the earlier pulse from his chest increases its resonating hum with each breath he pours into his body. Waves of higher vibrational energy flood the room, churning the life force energy of all the inhabitants like they are in a spiritual washing machine. Pulse after pulse, the energy only grows in intensity as it swirls and focuses around Brahm's radiating body. Flickering in and out of visual perception, Brahm's eyes roll into the back of his head as he dives even further into concentrated focus.

"What in the world is this?!" Mune exclaims as he tries to make sense of the bizarre sensations coursing through his body.

"Oh no!" Sophia exclaims, very familiar with this feeling. Earlier flashes of Brahm's preparation for his water golem transformation and his chariot flight into the sky come pouring back into memory. "This is…" she stammers, as she braces herself for the nauseating, disorienting, and reality-bending sensations she predicts will follow this coming transformation.

"This is it!" Beau says, looking to his captain and sending a silent prayer for his success. Everyone has their eyes glued to the flickering warrior standing before them. As the energy reaches a level of maxing capacity, a visual red orb of light emerges into sight just below Brahm's tailbone. It swirls and pulsates along with the same rhythm as the rest of the energy he commands. Next buds an orange orb near his pelvis, a yellow one at his core, a bright green orb above his heart, a blue light along his throat, a purple one blossoms from within his forehead, and finally an indigo light erupts from atop his head. Brahm takes a deep breath, signifying the near completion of his intended transformation. Tilting his head upwards, he takes in a deep breath and thrusts his arms above his head. He strikes a pose as if he is the conductor of the universal orchestra. Following his lead, the churning energy in the room springs to attention and races to meet the needs of his conducted direction. The energy twirls and crashes around his body and is channeled upwards like a reverse cyclone.

"Yeeeaaahhhhhh!" comes a triumphant yell from the energetic conductor. Brahm's flickering presentation vanishes from sight as he completely merges with the upward vortex of energy. Deafening silence fills the air following his departure as everyone struggles to make sense of their ocular perception.

∞

"W-What happened?" Otto stammers, as he creeps to the edge of his perch. According to his eyes, Brahm has completely vanished from the inner sanctum. "Did he just… leave us?"

"I-I don't know!" Domino says, unable to make any further sense of his senses. "Maybe… maybe he…"

The vortex of energy that erupted off into a skyward haven now comes crashing back down, pouring into the very position the vanishing warrior once stood. Like a waterfall blasting away at the bedrock beneath it, the ground quivers under the pressure of the heavenly light. Brahm's silhouette flickers into view as he gently fades back into his earlier position upon the ground. A pulsating wave erupts from his being just as the point of etheric cosmic energy and physical reality become one. The wave blasts through the room, subjecting all the unsuspecting patrons to the surge of energy that now courses in-between the very spaces of their organic particles.

∞

"Here it comes!" Sophia screams, buckling over in anticipatory agony. "I can't do this again! I-I-I can't believe this! I'm… *not* doing this again?" She stares at her hands and then to the rest of her body in disbelief. As the wave crashes over her and drowns her in the cosmic energy from Brahm's return, she can't help but feel absolutely giddy from the unexpected side effects. Waves of love, compassion, beauty, and completeness fill her emotional registry. All stagnant negativity is washed away and replaced with heavenly bliss. With tears streaming down her face, she looks around and locks eyes with her Seer companions who also bask in the emotional glory. She quickly scans the room for her Severed Marionettes, capturing each one in the room with individualized glances of love and appreciation. Her heart flickers as she notices Emmanuel is missing.

∞

"Oh wow!" Otto cries out in unrestrained bliss. "This is absolutely amazing! I feel on top of the world!" He stomps jovially atop his high perch. He grabs Domino's hands and twirls him around. Emmanuel can't help but crack a smile at the boys' display of joy. He sits back and basks in the waves of higher dimensional energy washing over them.

∞

"That fool!" Beau says with overwhelming joy in his heart. "He did it! A perfectly balanced dimensional bridge! And this doesn't feel anything like the previous dimensions he has bridged! My, my, my. I wonder, just how far did he go?" As the cosmic wave starts to bleed back into the baseline energetic resonance of the room, the patrons turn all their attention to the illuminated being. Radiating with blinding white light, Brahm's solid form stands in the center of the column of heavenly luminescence. From within the white light, they can see his physical form has been altered quite significantly.

The multicolored orbs at his energy centers remain a fixed feature. However, now surrounding the indigo orb above his head is a crown of floating eyes. Below the crown resides his head, which has gained the addition of two other faces. Each one of the new faces mirror his original one and rest on his right and left side where his ears used to be. All three pairs of eyes remain vacant, his pupils still rolled backwards. He now possesses four additional arms extending above and below the two that remain connected to his core. His feet hover slightly off the ground, as his body is overwhelmingly buoyant from the influx of higher energy.

"Now this is what I'm talking about!" the Warden nearly squeals with excitement. His breathing is quickened, and his body quivers with the desire to attack. As the unavoidable ripple effects of Brahm's transformation stabilize, Mune's baseline emotions return in full flavor. His rage, self-loathing, and thirst for power are desperate to regain their dominance.

"That's enough already!" Mune shouts, cutting the heavenly atmosphere with his abrupt negativity. He thrusts his detonator back into the air and waves it around like a flag. "Don't make me remind you again as to what I hold in my hand! Forget the light bulb freak over there and get me and my prisoners out of here!"

"Do it yourself, I'm done with you!" the Warden proclaims proudly, having fully taken the bait of Brahm's energetic fishing lure.

"Fine! Have it your way!" Mune says as he lifts his finger to strike the detonation button. Right before his finger makes contact, the surge of his vengeful, and killing energy erupts a heavy ripple into the cleansed and purified space. With the energetic sensitivity at an all-time high, everyone becomes infected by Mune's nauseating emotional content. His hostile intent even reaches the high perch of Emmanuel and the boys, disrupting their jubilant celebration.

∞

"Uggh!" Otto cries out as he slaps his hand upon his chest. "Uh… what is this?! I feel like something just stabbed me in the heart!" he cries out as he staggers around like a drunken bar patron.

"I don't know!" Domino responds, also suffering from Mune's negative vibration. "Ugh, hey! Watch out, will ya?" he calls to his disorientated friend. "You're getting awfully close to the…" he watches in horror as his friend's foot slips out of their sky-bound balcony. "… Edge!" Domino's eyes extend well past their physical limitations as he desperately tries to register the abrupt disappearance of his friend. Rushing to the edge of their perch, his heart sinks as he watches Otto plummet to the ground in a flailing fury.

"Otto!" he cries out, unable to do anything more to save his friend. As Otto continues his descent, his heart is thrust into his throat. The youth can't even scream as he races along the rip tides of gravity. Just as impact appears imminent, the anchor knot where he initially tied off his rope begins to constrict. Bringing resistance to the rope, Otto's momentum is redirected from the ground and swoops him towards the congregation in the center of the room. Saved by the security of his knot and his astute distance calculation, he barrels through the air just inches above the ground. Sophia is quick to spot the unexpected projectile and signals the Seers to avoid the incoming anomaly.

∞

"Get down!" she shouts, causing a flood of bodies to hurl themselves upon the floor in the nick of time. Triggered by the commotion behind him, Mune hesitates from his detonation plan for just a moment. Turning his head around, he locks eyes with the airborne Otto.

"What the—" his subconscious mind tries to fully verbalize, but it's too late. All he can do is watch the full force of the youth's flight pattern drive right into his back. Otto puts his arms out in front of his head to try and brace his impact as he crashes into the metal-plated exterior of his overlord. The collision lifts Mune up off his feet as he joins his airborne assailant. Time appears to slow as Mune's hands open, desperate to try and brace his upcoming collision with the ground. He watches in despair as his unconscious efforts cause his prized remote detonator to fly from his grasp.

His heavy metal armor collides with the ground, finally restarting the normal perception of time. Otto swings back and forth as the momentum dies down from his descent. Sophia rushes to tend to her concussed companion. Mune wastes no time as he scurries frantically on all fours, looking like a chubby baby crawling along the floor. He desperately tries to regain possession of his remote control.

"All... most... got... it!" he says in-between exasperated pants as he inches his way towards his prize.

"Oh, is this what you were after?" Mune can hear the Warden say. Without taking his eyes off the remote, he blocks out any distracting information until it's too late. Mune's heart drops as he watches the Warden's polished shoe soar down from above and pulverize his device right as his fingertips grace the edges of the detonator. The scattered circuitry disbands before any signal can be sent to the receiving end on the Power Pole.

"N-Nooooo!" Mune cries out like the spoiled baby he inadvertently presents himself to be. "How could you?!"

"Quite easily it seems. Now, where were we?" the Warden says proudly as he lifts his foot off the prized device and shakes free the lingering electrical components from his shoe. With a devilish smile, he turns back and faces the illuminated Brahm with all his undivided attention. Mune's childish temper tantrum serves no further distraction to the Warden's cold-blooded desire for unrestrained warfare. "I've been waiting a long time to test the boundaries of this body of mine... you appear to be the perfect test subject to finally go all out!" As his bloodlust radiates from his body, the Power Pole behind him surges with an invigorated rhythm like never before. The light in the room starts to dim as the Pole draws in light like a ravenous black hole. It beats like a heart, pumping radiated energy into the room from the power-lusting demands of the Warden. His physical muscles start to erupt from inside the well-tailored suit as he channels the alien energy source into his physical makeup. He begins to grow in size while his veins pulsate from under his skin. Each slithering venous extension harbors a similar light warping, anti-glow like the Power Pole. Dark black snakes start to multiply from under his feet, detaching themselves from his body and pouring onto the ground around him. They surround the Warden like a slithering shadow, merging as they lift him up off the ground onto a serpentine podium.

Breathing heavily, the Warden laughs uncontrollably as he takes inventory of the overwhelming power coursing through his veins. A single snake emerges from the base of his spine and slithers up his body until it blossoms atop his head. The sentient creature unfolds as a proud cobra before merging atop the Warden's skull like an Egyptian headdress. Licking his lips with his newly adopted split tongue, the Warden inadvertently shows off his extended fangs.

"Remember," Brahm says, assured his opponent has completed his stages of transformation, "your fight is with me. You leave the rest of these people out of it, and I promise I will give you a fight like you've never had before."

"Nonsense!" the Warden cries with unadulterated enthusiasm. "You're going to give me the fight of a lifetime regardless! I am now free! Even the high master gives no resistance to my desire. If these worthless excuses for life forms get in the way, then that is just something you will have to deal with!" he says with a slight slithering lisp.

"I expected as much," Brahm says with a heavy exhale. He turns his head around to address his companions. "Beau! Sophia! Get everyone out of here, now!" The blue orb around his throat pulsates with additional emphasis. Sophia is taken aback by his direct mention of her name. Until now, she felt like a grain of sand upon the beach of his boundless ocean. Taking a moment to gaze into Brahm's glowing eyes, she becomes lost in their endless beauty and otherworldly origins. Despite his altered appearance, she is guided into the frequency at the core of his majestic presentation. She looks past the white light and onto the man she met the day of the Fantuzzi Festival. He is still the same man who risked everything to warn her of the incoming storm surge, the same man who nearly drowned her, the same man who single-handedly went toe-to-toe with Babel, the same man who destroyed her trust, and the same man who is currently rebuilding it; rebuilding the trust she has in him, and in herself.

Nearly at the emotional saturation point, her heart races into her throat as she notices a once concealed detail up until now. As Brahm stands with his exposed back to her, she can finally see the wondrous hidden gem he has unknowingly kept from her all this time. The skin on Brahm's back bears a unique, animalistic birthmark of curving and meandering bleached lines that contrast his dark clay complexion. The lines intersect into a unique and harmonious pattern. Thirteen hexagonal-like shapes cover the

majority of his back with twenty-eight smaller, rectangular shapes surrounding them like a barrier. Upon first glance, his markings resemble the design of a flattened tortoise shell.

"Tiger…" she mumbles under her breath, her thoughts racing to the past. Her memories swirl around the noble Resistance leader and *his* trademark animalistic markings. Tears flood her eyes as her mind struggles what possible connections, if any, these two men in her life could possess. Aware that she needs to regain her composure, she takes in a deep breath of confidence as she turns to address her Seer companions as well as The Severed Marionettes.

"You heard the man!" she cries out. "We are getting out of this alive, and we are going to do it together. Everyone! Head to the door!"

"No!" Izak cries out as he reaches Sophia's inner circle with the other two Marionettes in tow. "The castle is destroyed! That way will only lead to a dead end!"

"C'mon! Think of something else!" Ayananda demands of her leader, harboring little patience in her tone. The two women lock eyes, each casting nonverbal waves of hostility.

"We don't have time for this!" Izak pleads.

"Wa-hahahaha!" the Warden bellows from above. "The little confused rats can't get out of their cage? I grow tired of your disgusting existence in the presence of a *god*!" As the last audible frequency leaves his lips, the Power Pole surges again under the Warden's demand for more power. With devilish glee, he raises his hand towards Sophia and the others. "Die!" he cries as his arm erupts into a river of snakes, charging through the air before rerouting to the ground. The individual snakes hold tightly together like a school of fish as they flow around his outstretched hand. Everyone on the ground can only watch hopelessly as the menagerie of snakes, merge together, creating a giant cobra racing towards them.

Remaining calm, Brahm finally opens his crown of eyes sending yet another strong pulse of thought-waves through the room. The whole inner sanctum ripples as if the chiseled stone was just turned into water. As the transformed Warden nears striking range of the others, Brahm twists one of his hands so that his palm faces upward. Swiping his open palm up and across his chest, it appears as if he is moving some unforeseen obstacle out of his way.

Unrestricted by the division of self and other, Brahm maneuvers the energetically altered room around him as if an extension of self. The swatting motion of his hand directly correlates to an upheaval of the floor between the incoming serpent and its desired victims. Like a tidal wave rising out of the sea, the floor leaps from its traditional composition and crashes into the Warden's projectile.

"Wonderful!" the Warden applauds from within his serpent cocoon. He turns to face Brahm as the tidal waved floor bounces back into place. The wave breaks off into the familiar dancing cubes, completing their return with a satisfying *plop!* Emerging from his cocoon, the Warden appears as a blended reptilian nightmare. Part dragon, part crocodile and part abomination, his distorted figure crawls with a multitude of insidious swirling snakes that form his new identity. With out warning, he barrels through the room, dismissing any gravitational pull from below. He flies right at Brahm with his dragon jaws open wide. Bringing two of his hands to his chest, Brahm takes a deep breath and draws in the raw energy from deep within the planet's core.

He channels the energy up through his root center, into his pelvis, igniting his core and settling it into his heart. His body trembles under the overwhelming energetic pressure. With one final inhale to stabilize himself, he thrusts his hands out in front of him with a heavy exhale.

"HAAAAA!" he screams as he releases the buildup of energy. The Warden is abruptly blasted into a myriad of individual snakes as he meets the receiving end of Brahm's channeled heart energy. A piercing green light barrels through the erupting serpentine amalgamation, ripping them apart with unrestricted ease. They shriek with eager desperation as they try to shield themselves from the blinding light. Blasting into the corresponding wall from its ejection point, the green beam burrows into the bedrock of the mountain, leaving an enormous crater in its wake.

"Nooo!!" Tewari cries out as his prized inner sanctum falls victim to the attack. Brahm pants with a moment of exhaustion stemming from his enormous expenditure of energy. Before shifting his attention, he flicks his wrist and reassembles the destroyed contours of the room.

"Oh thank god!" Tewari cries out, falling to his knees in gratitude.

"EEEEEAAAAKKKKK!" comes the shrilling sound of the screaming snakes as they slither upon the ground in agony. Unable to regain control over his beasts, the Warden rematerializes himself back into his humanoid form. He wipes his own smirk from his face as he looks upon Brahm with vengeful disgust. Now positioned in-between Brahm and the iron door, Sophia and the others finally have a clear barrier to hide behind as they continue their escape deliberation

"We are running out of time," Ayananda reminds Sophia. "Figure something out soon or I will figure out this mess myself."

"Patience," Sophia commands of her subordinate, striking a wave of fury in Ayananda's core. "We must do this right." She lightly taps the empty pockets of her cloak again, only to be reminded of Hanu's absence. With a quiver of borrowed hope, she looks to the presumed leaders of the Seers; "Tewari? Raja? Do you know of any other way out of here?"

"Unfortunately not. This is the first time the people of our generation have ever stepped foot in this place." Tewari responds.

"Yeah, my vision showed the iron door being the one pivotal structure in this whole chamber," Raja concludes.

"Wow boss, your plan is really starting to come together," Ayananda says with caustic flair.

"Well, what about up there?" Otto blurts out, pointing to the hole in the ceiling he just fell from.

"How in the world did you get up there?" Tewari demands as he shakes his head in confusion. "And what is an opening doing so far up there anyway?"

"I mean, I have no idea," Otto says, unsure as to why this line of questioning is important. "There are tunnels all through this mountain, leading so many different ways. We just happened to follow one that ended up there. Honestly, it felt like whoever was digging them had no idea where they were going either! Maybe Mune had his guys digging around to find more rooms like this? The good thing is that we know the one up there goes through the mountain and leads to an opening behind Mune's castle."

"Perfect!" Sophia exclaims, putting an end to any further questioning from Tewari. "Now it's just a matter of getting everyone up there! How confident are you, Otto, in your rope tying?"

"My whole livelihood has depended on my knots!" he says proudly. "Those knots have kept me alive this long, I know they will hold through this!"

"We are depending on you, Otto. Alright, everyone! Start climbing!"

"Not so fast!" the Warden says as he slithers from behind Brahm. Raising his hands above his head, a sea of snakes erupt once again from his body. This time they divide into every direction possible with the hopes of throwing off Brahm's defense. Closing his physical eyes and relying on the ocular crown atop his head, Brahm studies the energy at the core of the Warden's seemingly separate attacks. He notices the foreign energy of the Power Pole coursing through each of the flying serpents.

"This has got to be the same energy I noticed when I was detached from my body," Brahm ponders out loud. "Something this caustic shouldn't be able to exist in this world!" The particles of the atmosphere around the projectile serpent grow tumultuous and unstable. He notices a mild radioactive wake starting to ripple from behind the Warden's careless attack. Needing to first address the initial physical threat, Brahm rotates his hands and burrows them energetically into the room. Conducting the physical makeup of the inner sanctum like a marionette, he twists and twirls the still water-like stone to combat and deflect each individual strike.

Anticipating this same maneuver, the Warden does not let up, pouring more and more snakes into the air, attacking everything and anything in sight. He quickly notices that Brahm appears to alter every aspect of the room to block his attacks except for one spot. Attack after attack, the ground under the crowd of people has remained conveniently untouched. He smiles as he targets all his hostility above the ground Brahm refuses to manipulate.

"I have you now!" the Warden shouts with joy as he thrusts his radioactive energy in-between the cracks of Brahms defense. Realizing an adjustment needs to be made, Brahm shifts his attention to another means of manipulation. Crossing his six hands to arrange over his midline, he shifts them to circle in front of his face. He purses his lips and exhausts all the air from his lungs. Like a diver coming up for his first breath, he opens his mouth and devours the deepest breath he can indulge.

Suddenly, howling winds can be heard coming from behind the Warden. He shifts his head around and is taken aback when he sees a giant replica of Brahm's trifecta-face protruding from the contours of the iron door. The iron face mirrors Brahm's open mouth, the source of the ravenous vacuum.

The Warden is forced to dig his heels into the ground to keep from being drawn into the whirlwind gust of the new attack. As if channeling the howling winds of Babel herself, the iron face twists and contorts, commanding more and more atmosphere to be drawn into its orifice. Its unrelenting suction starts to disrupt the path of the radioactive snakes. One by one, the vengeful snakes fly through the air and become consumed by the deep cosmic inhale. Brahm notices Sophia and the others are starting to take effect from his suctioned pull, so he erupts a concentrated final gust to finish the job. The iron face slams its mighty mouth shut as it successfully consumes the last remaining snake. A muffled gulp resonates within the hushed silence of the chamber. The caustic snakes are forced into cosmic digestion, starting the transmutation process back to harmless energy.

The extended metallic face now turns its attention to the Warden's true form. It snarls its iron lips and chomps its oversized mouth, inching its way out of the door like a chained dog. As the Warden tries to leap out of the way, the iron face opens its mouth once again and draws another vortex of atmosphere into it. Taking advantage of the airborne state of its target, the Warden is easily drawn closer to the howling mouth. Having to think quickly, the Warden extends his elastic arms and thrusts them into the beehive ceiling. He burrows his fingers into the octangular grooves, momentarily keeping himself from being devoured. His efforts prove to be too little and too late as he is easily overcome by Brahm's attack. He is sucked down into the cosmic belly of the iron face like a well-sauced spaghetti noodle.

"Now's our chance!" Sophia commands as she directs her companions up Otto's unexpected escape rope. As the Seers are first to rise in single file order, Sophia studies the crowd. She comes to the unfortunate realization that not everyone may have the strength to maneuver the strenuous climb.

"This isn't going to work for everyone," Sophia says as she opens the floor to suggestions.

"Right," Ayananda ponders. "Boy, you said Emmanuel was with you?"

"Yeah, he's up at the top there," Otto says pointing to his earlier perch. Feeling the call of his name, Emmanuel sticks his head out of the opening above and gives Ayananda a playful wave.

"Ha! This is perfect," she says, thrusting the full weight of Jeeven onto Izak.

"Hey! What gives?" Izak cries, struggling to carry the unbearable weight of his captain.

"Just hold on a moment, I have an idea," Ayananda says as she scrimmages around her waist, unlatching her trusty chain dart. She stands composed, twirling her weapon around in the air.

"Do you plan to fight?" Beau asks, very familiar with his last run-in with the dangerous weapon.

"No…" Ayananda says, looking disappointed. "As much as I hate watching someone else fight my battles, now is not the time. Hey! Em'!" she shouts, redirecting her focus. "You got enough strength to play some catch?"

"Catch?" Emmanuel ponders out loud. "Oh! 'Catch.' Haha, yeah, I think I can play along. Go ahead and send them flying while we have this opening, I'll make sure you don't crush them!"

"What in the world are you planning?" Beau shouts with desperate confusion, "Are you going to fling people up there and hope that guy catches them?"

"Yeah, you got a better idea?" Ayananda says as she fastens her chain around a very unsure Seer.

"Trust her, Beau," Sophia says with a warm and compassionate tone. "I do." Ayananda looks back at her Resistance leader with wide eyes of surprise. Sophia notices the questioning glance and she responds with a silent smile of recognition and respect.

"Lord help us…" Beau says with a defeated twist of his head.

"Perfect, no time to waste! Here we go!" Ayananda says with a voice full of surging pride. She thrusts her grizzly strong legs into the ground to secure her footing before whipping her chain over her head. Around and around she swings, with the Seer in tow. She accumulates a build up of momentum before firing her chain high up into the air. The helpless Seer starts to see his own life flash before his eyes as he anticipates a full impact into the ceiling above. As he closes his eyes during what he thinks are his final moments, he feels a sharp shift in his direction. He opens his eyes once again to see a char-grilled bald man with silver tears pouring out of mutilated eyes.

"Demon!!" he screams. "You killed me! I've died and gone to hell!"

"Relax," Emmanuel says, trying to soften his gruesome exterior. "You are fine, but I can't hold you for long like this," he continues with his arms extended. The purple light around his hands slowly shifts to reflect a bright blue hue. The Seer immediately flies at top speed into Emmanuel and the two slide back from the impact. They tumble on the ground before coming to a stop further back in the tunnel.

"What did you just do to me?" the Seer cries.

"Well, other than save you," Emmanuel says while dusting himself off, "I was attempting to mimic the aura that man in the white light first displayed when he entered the room. Such an amazing display of manipulated energy, I wanted to see if I could do it!"

"You mean that was the first time you did something like that?" the Seer asks with growing concern.

"Well, yeah, but it's not my first time mimicking a technique! It's kind of my specialty," he responds with a tone of pride. The Seer prays to all the gods he can think of in hopes of thanking the one who just kept him alive. Without another word he runs as fast as he can down the tunnel to safety.

"Alright, Aya, hit me with another one! I think I'm getting the hang of it!" Emmanuel calls down to his comrade.

"You got it!" she responds, with another Seer already hooked up. Without a single word of warning, she sends the poor girl soaring through the air. Her screams bounce off the perfectly crafted stone walls like an amplified microphone. Her shrill horror finally takes a pause as Emmanuel reaches his aura out to grab her from the air, this time a bit more gently than the last one. The mastery of his energetic maneuvers remains debatable, but at least the safety of the patron is secured. Satisfied, Ayananda scours for her next human throw toy. She locks eyes with the man standing next to her and gives him a playful wink.

"You next, big boy?" she asks with an unnecessarily seductive tone.

"Um… no, thank you," the man declines politely. "I think I'm just going to climb that… um… rope over there," he says with growing confidence in taking his fate into his own hands.

"Suit yourself," Ayananda responds flatly. "Next!"

As the relief efforts are well underway, Brahm directs his attention to the light-warping Power Pole. Its unguarded nature begs Brahm to consider taking advantage of its vulnerable status.

"What's worse?" He mumbles to himself. "Letting loose that energy, or letting that monster continue his rampage?" Feeling he does not have time to weigh all the options, he decides to take a risk and target the caustic energy. "I was afraid to risk exposing this energy to the world. I realize now I can't let fear guide my decision. I saw the darkness that resided in that guard from earlier was the true enemy. I'm sure it's the same this time. I must trust this energy I borrow can handle whatever consequence comes next!" Extending his hands, he molds the surrounding chamber to his liking once again. Giant hands erupt from the well-painted walls around the Power Pole. They grow arms in their wake, appearing tattooed with Seer history. They lunge forward, preparing to crush the defenseless power source. As the humanoid extensions near their target, a bright flash erupts from the enigmatic anomaly. The spark of light quickly recedes into a consuming vacuum of darkness, effectively countering Brahm's attack.

"Interesting," Brahm ponders. "Is this energy source... defending itself?" As he continues to apply pressure, he is surprised to notice the dark energy effectively pushing back his attack even further. The roots from the Pole begin to contort, molding its raw energy into physical matter. The ambiguous aura of darkness quickly converges into competing colossal hands of its own. Crawling out of the darkness like an impatient infant, the Warden begins his rebirth into the room. Overwhelming his opponent's strength, the Warden burrows his fingers into Brahm's rock hands and crushes them into obliteration.

"Not again!" Tewari bellows in despair, watching his beloved history crumble to the floor. Hearing the cries of his companion, Brahm directs his focus into quickly rebuilding the crumbling walls that once served as his arms. The dust and rubble merge into the familiar dancing cubes. They playfully bounce around as they march seamlessly back into place.

"You dare let your guard down over some discarded trash?!" the Warden shouts. "How foolish!" Taking advantage of Brahm's momentary distraction, he sends an extended fist hurling towards his opponent. The speed of the attack is too fast to dodge. Confident he will be able to phase through it, Brahm decides to take the attack head on. Just before the fist penetrates his column of white light, he prepares his molecules to reconfigure around the strike. At first, Brahm is amazed to realize he is struggling to maneuver his molecules the way he wants to. Usually, vast pockets of space surround each individual particle of matter, but not this time. The Warden's attack has been imbued with gravitational properties fit for a black hole. With a checkmate established, Brahm takes the full impact of the Warden's infinitely dense strike. He can feel his energetic body being reduced to its third dimensional properties, crushing his bones and indenting his flesh as he is sent flying across the room.

"Brahm!" Sophia cries out, taking a step forward. Beau places his arm out in front of her, stopping her from rushing to his side.

"He will be okay," Beau says to her. "He has a job to do, and he intends to succeed. He is trusting you to do the same."

"Of course," Sophia says, abruptly shifting her attention back to the rescue operations. "I just didn't expect him to take such a hit."

"Me either," Beau says honestly. "That Warden is unlike anything we have ever come across."

With his heavenly column of light still raining down upon him, Brahm picks himself up out of the demolitioned wall. As he brushes himself off, he directs even the most minute of dust particles that were dislodged into their original alignment. The Warden watches eagerly as he studies his opponent's desire to maintain the integrity of their battlefield.

"How long can you keep this up?" the Warden cries out, beginning to reduce his size from his earlier gigantic manifestation. "You spend so much energy protecting others and rebuilding this room. It will be your downfall! Just let it go and fight me with all you have!"

"That's where you fail to understand the source of my power," Brahm replies. "My power comes from a tiny sliver of the divine light of our higher dimensions. A light that struggles to enter our world due to the dense negativity we are here to work through. It is only due to my intention to bring balance to your unnatural source of energy, that I have been allowed access to this small stream of light. This light is the ultimate source of love and can never be used maliciously or with impure intent. It is the source of all that is. It is only through love this energy is harnessed. Protecting these people and preserving this sanctuary, if anything, is what allows me access to such power!"

"Nonsense!" the Warden screams. "You have just proven it makes you weak! I can sense your bones are still crushed within that light body you hide behind! With your focus divided, I will make quick work of your neglected weakness. I see how much energy you have to put into maintaining that specific frequency of yours. Even the slightest deviation from your concentration could sever your connection! How long can you stay in such a state of mind? What will it take for you to destroy yourself with your borrowed power? I wonder… if a flicker of grief might be all it takes to bring you down," the Warden says as he looks out of the corner of his eye towards Sophia. She has returned her full focus back to the rescue mission, unaware of the attention being drawn towards her. A devilish smirk lathers the Warden's face as he extends a finger in her direction. In a flash, his finger sharpens itself to a point and fires at the unsuspecting Resistance leader.

The soft and subtle sound of impaled flesh seems to momentarily stop time within the chaotic chamber. Blood drips from the pulsating wound the Warden's finger now burrows through. A hush falls upon the crowd as they are shocked by the abrupt turn of events.

"NOOO!" comes a cry in Brahm's direction, as grief and disbelief reverberate in the sorrow-filled voice. The Warden falls into victorious celebration, assured that he exploited his opponent's greatest weakness. However, the sound of the cry doesn't strike his ear in the way he was expecting. Something is not right. He turns to face the being surrounded by the column of light and is met with waves of disbelief crashing over him.

"H-How is this possible?!" the Warden exclaims, as his eyes capture none other than the victim of his attack falling to her knees within the white light.

"How could you?!" she wails, bringing only further confusion to the Warden as she appears fully intact and in perfect health. Searching for answers, the Warden follows the path of his extended finger. Against all fathomable logic, it is Brahm who stands at the receiving end of his attack where Sophia once stood. Taking the attack head on, the Warden's finger clearly impales him along his lower abdomen. Blood drips to the floor like a wounded mortal, his higher dimensional light appearing nowhere around him.

"This... this is how it ends?" the Warden asks with disappointment. "You throw it all away for a meaningless sacrifice?"

"N-nothing is meaningless," Brahm grunts.

"Nonsense! As you fall to your wounds, you must know that nothing will stop me from killing everyone here! It was meaningless... meaningless! Why would you do this?" he asks, as if personally offended by Brahm's choice. "I don't understand!"

"I never thought you would," Brahm says as he winces from the pain. "Then again, you never could understand the source of true power."

"What in the world are you talking about? Spit it out before you fall to your death!"

"Ha! Don't you see? Ugh," he grunts as he pulls himself closer to the Warden, sliding through the impaling appendage. "Without a connection to our true life source, you could never see the vital importance our connection to others truly is. At the source of highest truth, we are and always have been connected as one. You and I are inherently the same! When you apply such a concept to the higher levels of reality, can you still believe that *you* have stabbed *me?*"

"W-What are you saying?" the Warden blabbers. "Of course I did! You put yourself right in front of my attack! I can see the blood pouring out of you! I can see the color fading from your face! You will be dead at any moment!"

"You were too focused on *me...* the me as an individual opponent defined by a flashy transformation." he says with a nod to Sophia's new position. "Is that really the Resistance leader? Or has that been me all along?" The Warden shakes his head in disbelief. "Tell me, where do any of us *truly* end and another begin?"

"Lies! You are just trying to trick me!"

"Hardly! I am trying to wake you up! If that power you utilize was grounded in any truth, then you would have realized the Law of Oneness is leading to your downfall!"

"Laws!" the Warden scoffs. "I am a free man! I abide by no laws!"

"I thought the same!" Brahm confesses. "But I woke up to the same lesson I hope you can now see! In this dimension there *are* laws! And yes, with enough power you can run from them, but that does not serve you in the end. They are here to help us! Guide us in this otherwise confusing dimensional layer. You see, we are *all* connected, that's what this Universal Law is based on. Our separation is only perceived on these lower dimensions. This whole room has risen to a higher dimensional frequency that brings us closer to that oneness. We are all one Warden, can't you see? Even as you stand there blinded by this collective reality, you too are no exclusion to it; only you have refused to accept it. It's that power of yours that separates you from the truth! It's not me that you have stabbed. It's not Sophia you have stabbed... it's..."

"Uh... oh my..." the Warden exclaims, the breath fading from his lungs as he finds it increasingly more difficult to draw in his next breath. His other hand floats to a growing source of warmth upon his abdomen. As he touches an unexpected puddle of moisture on top of his suit, he looks down to examine the source.

"B-Blood?" he murmurs in utter confusion.

"Your blinded rage has only brought harm to yourself, Warden. In the shadowless light of the higher realms, your actions could never damage the lives of those connected within this higher union. You and Mune have been the only ones holding on to separation since the light fell upon this chamber! That pain you wished to impose could only be manifested in yourself as you continued to try and separate from the light. The worst thing you could have done was to see me as an enemy. You've only been fighting yourself this whole time."

"Ugh, this really hurts," the Warden says as he brings himself to his knees. "I've never felt pain before. Why can't I heal myself?"

"It's because you still think your wound exists outside of you. You can't heal yourself if it is *me* you believe is wounded. Until you can realize the ultimate connection we all share, you will bleed out on the floor thinking I am the one who is dying. You must let go of your separation if you wish to survive!"

"Ha… hahahaha! What an unexpected realization! Twisty, twisty! So clever! So that's it, huh? This is how I die? How I wish I had more time to play," the Warden says childishly.

"Warden! You will only die if you want to. You could use your pain and learn what's been hidden from you all this time. Let go of the power you crave. That power only leads you into separation and disillusion. Discard it and embrace what tethers to humanity you still have left! It's what has been allowing your deviance and resistance to Mune all this time! It has been the source of your desire for freedom! There is still some human left in you! I know you can feel it! Let it save you!"

"Maybe so…" the Warden ponders pensively.

∞

As the Warden contemplates his fate, Mune decides to take advantage of the dramatic standstill. Convinced there is no use trying to salvage his plan to regain favor with Wisteria, he makes a mad dash to escape. Unwilling to believe his beloved castle has been destroyed, he scurries over to the iron door seeking salvation. As he creeps his way to the door, his clunky armor shifts with every ungraceful movement. Fearing his plan will be quickly discovered, he keeps glancing over to the others in the room to see if they notice him. Back and forth he looks, with paranoia and doubt creeping into his mind. Feeling the need to fully commit, he doubles down on his resolve and makes a mad dash for the door. His flapping armor crashes around him, sounding off like a trash can drum solo. Only now does this obnoxious rattling draw the attention of the Seers closer to him.

"Eek!" Mune cries out, realizing he has been spotted.

"Hey, wait," the Seer man tries to call out to Mune, but it's no use. Mune fires up the afterburners and starts sprinting even faster.

"You'll never catch me now!" he says, completely convinced he is still of some importance to anyone. "I will live to see another day, and then I will come back and seek my revenge! This is not the last you have seen of—" he is interrupted by an unexpected crunching sound coming from underneath him. Mune stops his sprint to gaze down at his foot. His metal-plated boot has just stepped on the remaining components of his damaged detonator. Grief and anger fill his heart as he thinks about how close he was to coming out victorious with such a device. As he stands there staring at it, he notices most of the detonator is still intact.

"I wonder if it could still work," he says. Shifting his weight slightly to examine the device further, he notices a spark fire from under his foot. "Odd," he thinks. "Must still be some juice left in it!" Another spark ignites again, this time latching onto the conductive surface of Mune's metal boot. The spark of electricity flows unrestricted, sliding neatly into one of the previously severed circuits. "Oh. Oh! Oh no—" is all he can murmur as the consequences of his actions literally blows up in his face.

Mune drops to the ground and curls himself into a tight fetal position. He rocks back and forth, perseverating upon the seemingly obvious consequence he never truly accounted for. He regrets ever devising such a plan that was just intended to be a bluff. As moments tick by, he begins to wonder why there has not been more destruction in the wake of his actions. Pulling on a sliver of confidence and courage he finds buried deep inside his being, he looks up from his fetal position to assess his situation.

"Whoa," he utters with his mouth fully ajar. His gaze remains transfixed upon the glowing warrior atop the room. A being he thought to be an enemy just a moment before has risen to become his savior. Brahm hovers in the air above the source of the explosion, all six arms extended wide as they channel a pulsating shield around the escaped energy. Creases of tense muscles ripple through Brahm's frame as he struggles to contain the erupted caustic force. The tension triggers a sharp pain that begins to flow through his left shoulder. He looks upon his persistent poison-filled tattoo as it wiggles under his skin. It appears to be undergoing a strong reaction with the energetic force he has captured in mid-air.

"I wonder if this energy is the source of the poison," Brahm thinks out loud before being forced to return his attention to containing the escaping energy. He can feel his strength slipping; even the borrowed powers of the higher dimension struggle to overpower this bizarre alien force. "Ahhh! I can't hold this forever. Now I know for sure I can't release this energy into this dimension! It would destroy everything it touches! For the Law of Oneness to hold true, this energy's existence *must* integrate at some level. But what is it!?" Brahm ponders. "Well, there is another Law I might be able to call upon, it's risky… but it may be the only way!"

"Warden!" Brahm cries down below to his still ailing combatant. "I have a plan, but you have to sever your connection with this power source!"

"Never!" the Warden blasts back with defiance. "As long as that power exists, I will always be connected to it! I don't even know what would happen if I cut the cord between us. I don't even know if I could, it's *who* I am!"

"It's not! Trust me!" Brahm says, remembering his time with Baba in the Void. "There is still human left in you! If you can let go of this outside force, you can finally realize the power within your humanity! Only then will you find who you really are!"

"Ha! Trust you? That would be a first!" the Warden jests. "And what do you plan to do anyway? You think you can destroy all that power all by yourself?"

"Destroy?" Brahm asks rhetorically. "No, it's too dangerous to even attempt! I'm going to *transmute* it!"

"Transmute?" the Warden ponders aloud.

"Yes! I'm going to assimilate this energy into my own life force in hopes to transmute it into something that will not harm this world! The Law of Perpetual Transmutation dictates that higher vibrational energy can consume and transform lower ones!"

"Ha! Hahahahaha! You think you resonate at a higher vibration than the force you can hardly hold in your hands?" the Warden bellows. "What is to keep that energy from consuming and transmuting *you*?!"

"Hope!" Brahm admits. "I have to try! That's why you need to cut ties with it! Otherwise, if I succeed, you could die! Draw now on your connection to humanity or risk losing everything!"

"Forget it, you are out of your mind!"

"Maybe I am," Brahm says, his multiple faces contorting under the demanding pressure to contain the escaping energy, "but it's now or never! I can't hold this any longer! Ahhhhhhhh!" Brahm unleashes a pounding battle cry, triggering a surging flow of higher dimensional light to pour back over him. The light reigns down upon him like an opened floodgate. His body glows with a brightness hardly perceivable to the human eye. Tying the knots between the higher dimensions, he weaves his bridge as tightly as he can. He makes his peace and releases the intention to consume the foreign energy. As his conscious thought and willpower trickle into the surrounding reality, his intention begins to manifest. The raging orb of energy contained at his fingertips begins to flow into his vessel like reverse osmosis.

"Ye-ahhhhh!" Brahm cries out in pain as the scornful force enters his body. With unwavering determination he continues to pull the energy into him. The energy from the Power Pole shifts violently back and forth, resisting the merger with all its might. Despite its own desire to avoid the transmutation process, Brahm's will overpowers it and continues the grueling endeavor.

"There is no way he can pull this off," the Warden says as he watches Brahm endure an unfathomable amount of pain and suffering. An unexpected wave of humility washes over him as he takes in the gravity of the situation unfolding. He looks to his hands, still covered in blood as he witnesses the familiar power source of his being starting to quiver and fade. "Can he really do it?" the Warden ponders openly.

"Ah-eh-yaaaaa-haaaa!" Brahm cries out again as the energetic merger is nearly complete. Brahm places all six hands on either side of the remaining Power Pole energy. With a final push of all his intention and willpower, Brahm shoves the radiating dark energy deep into his core. The weight of the foreign substance quickly becomes too heavy to remain airborne and he plummets to the ground below. He hits the ground with solidifying force, but remains propped up on one knee. He grimaces and contorts his body while struggling to contain and fully transmute the new energy within him. The poison tattoo races to greet its fellow energy source, causing the already dark mark upon his flesh to grow even bigger. A conflicting energetic battle rages within. The surging dark energy tries desperately to overpower the light of the higher realms. Brahm starts to notice the effects of his merger beginning to sever his connection with the dimensional bridge. Inspired by the additional risk of his situation, Brahm summons a final burst of cosmic energy.

Unable to fully transmute the caustic force with the time he has left, Brahm decides to contain it within his arm until he can summon enough strength to finish the job. The swirling, dark, fractal-like tribal pattern swells and grows on his arm as the new energy makes itself at home within his body. The markings shift and meander to resemble a spiraling river delta, a curving bolt of lightning, or the branch structure of a twisted old tree. He looks upon the markings and wonders what he has just done to himself. A sliver of doubt manifests within his heart.

"No!" he says aloud dismissing the negative belief. "I can do this! I must do this! Everything depends on my ability to harbor this energy until I learn what to do with it!" With that being said, a final burst of will power locks the energy into place, branding Brahm with the mark of the Power Pole. Standing up momentarily triumphant, he looks at the Warden who has slumped lifelessly upon the ground. Sensing the battle has finally been won, Sophia runs over to embrace the branded warrior. Noticing her approaching presence, Brahm turns and gives the emotional Sophia a warm smile as she collides with his still glowing form.

"You are always so reckless!" she says as she begins to sob. Her arms grip around Brahm's torso, squeezing him with all her might. He places one arm around her back and one gently behind her head. Pulling her closer into his chest, he loses himself for a moment in the warm embrace.

"I couldn't have done this all without you," he says.

"What are you talking about?!" Sophia says with her face still pressed against his chest, "I was powerless to help in any way! All I could do was watch you save us all!"

"No," Brahm corrects her. "I could have never connected with such power without your help. I've never felt strongly about existing in this world. With so much suffering everywhere, I always wanted to be somewhere else. It wasn't until meeting you, did I realize there was a purpose to this suffering. You showed me the power of being human and what it means to dedicate yourself to others. I can't thank you enough, Sophia. This is as much my victory as it is yours, and everyone who was here today. It was our collective connection that saved us all, and that's how it always has to be. I am finally starting to see that now."

"Hmm," Sophia hums, soaking in Brahm's words. His truth resonates deep into her core. It is as if he speaks the words that are already known in her heart. Disregarding the need for further conversation, the two bask in the heavenly white light that pours over them both. The warmth and love of the light blend them together as if they are existing momentarily as one being. Feeling as if time is standing still, Sophia is taken aback as an unexpected shift in energy disrupts her blissful satori state.

The warmth around her starts to dissipate slightly, leading her to lift her head and scan the altering surroundings. She watches as the white light begins to recede back into the higher realms, rising up out of the chamber and out of visual perception. The glowing man she holds flickers back and forth from his illuminated state until his physical body is all that remains. His knees buckle as the weight of the world returns to him. Sophia is ready and braces his fall.

"Looks like you didn't disappear this time," she says warmly.

"Another thing I have you to thank for."

"Geeze," Sophia says playfully, "I'm going to need a bit more compensation for all the work I seem to have done around here!"

"Ha!" Brahm grunts. "You joke, but it's true. Without a strong reason to come back to this world, it's always been hard for me to return to my body when I leave it. Thanks to you, a part of me felt like I was always right here." The weight of Brahm's words sinks deep into Sophia's heart. The implication of his declaration becomes too much for her to contemplate any further than at face value. Resurging emotions she has kept buried deep inside race to the surface in order to be expressed.

"You sentimental goof," she says, successfully pushing back and denying her emotions for the time being. "Let's get you out of here so you can get some rest."

"Yes," Brahm says with a heavy exhale following his response. He realizes and accepts that the time is not ready to bring more clarification to their connection. "Who do we have left in here?"

"Just the two of us," Sophia says with unintended warmth. "I told the others to go on without us. Just in case things went south here, I wanted them to get as far away from here as they could."

"Why did you stay?"

"I couldn't just leave you while you sacrificed yourself for everyone else. I felt it was only fair for someone to be here for you."

"Mmm, well, I'm glad it was you," Brahm says with a smile.

"Alright!" Sophia snaps sharply. "Let's just get out of here, shall we?" She's determined not to let her uncooperative emotions get carried away.

"Yeah, yeah, yeah, but let's not forget these other two," he says, looking back at the unconscious Warden and Mune.

"You want to bring them along too? Ha! Your heart has grown a little too big with all this white light sunbathing!" she jokes.

"What can I say? I'm a changed man!" Brahm responds as he goes over to pick up the two previous adversaries. As he lifts them into his arms, they return to their original state, void of labels and identity, neither friends nor foes, just brothers of the planet. Walking back over to Sophia, he looks up to their intended escape route and realizes the rope has been removed.

"So how do you plan on getting up there?" he asks.

"What, you mean you don't have any superpowers left in the tank?"

"Ha! I severely doubt it at this point," He says while sneaking a glance at the dark mark along his arm. "Am I going to disappoint you at the last moment?"

"Lucky for you, you get to rely on me for this one," she says confidently. "Well, Hanu to be exact," she corrects herself as she removes the reacquired Totem Wand from her cloak. "Fortunately, Mune never knew what potential he had with him this whole time," She remarks, thankful to finally have Hanu back safe and sound. With a flick of her wrist, the vibrant rainbow crow emerges from a stream of light protruding from the intricately carved wand within her hand. The bird soars to the ceiling of the chamber, flying back and forth as he stretches his wings out. His radiating prism light bounces off the ancient-angled walls.

"Hanu! Take us up to meet the others!" Sophia asks of her new companion. "Ca-karaaa!" Hanu cries out as he soars down to greet the humans below him. As he plummets to the ground, he begins to increase his size in order to meet the needs of Sophia's request. He stretches his beautiful wings, and beckons them to climb onto his enlarged feet. Like a gondola ride from the spirit world, Hanu lifts them off the ground and leads them up to the opening above. Flapping his wings to stabilize a stationary position in the air, Hanu extends his feet so Sophia and Brahm can easily enter the rooftop escape route. With their cargo in tow, the two look to the still-oversized rainbow crow.

"Thank you, Hanu!" Sophia cries with unrestrained appreciation. "Now show us the way out of here!" Circling around the vaulted ceilings one last time, Hanu reduces his size to that of a hummingbird and races into the tunnel. His radiating light illuminates the dark and twisty route; as he darts ahead, he calls back to remind the two to follow him.

"Quite a useful friend you got there," Brahm says as they make their way down the tunnel.

"Yeah, he sure is," Sophia says. "I seem to have come across quite a few of them on this trip." Side by side, the two follow in silent harmony. Led by the light, they weave themselves through the dark tunnels of the sacred mountain.

CHAPTER: 39

Reunion, Retribution, Reprieve and Run!

With a solid push, a small section of The Pearl's sacred mountain swivels out of place. It creaks on its weathered hinges as the not-so-secret passageway opens to release the last remaining travelers. Hanu is first to emerge. He soars up into the sky, thankful for the room to spread his wings. His dazzling glow blesses the gray-toned Pearl with his colorful rays of light. Dancing rainbows reflect off the rolling plumes of fog that race over the cobblestone streets. Sophia is next to emerge; she takes a deep breath of relief before looking up into the sky at Hanu. His light is so bright, it feels as if she were basking in the sun. Brahm hobbles out of the tunnel, his unconscious cargo lugged over his shoulders. Finally able to stand up straight, he gently stretches his back before walking over to stand next to Sophia. A moment of silence passes as the two begin to digest the gravity of events they have experienced. A simultaneous smile strikes both of their faces as the relief starts to set in.

Sophia turns to say something to Brahm but is caught off guard by the swirling tribal tattoo that covers the arm facing her. Her eyes widen as she notices it pulsating like a beating heart. Having been too distracted to notice such a change before, a wave of concern washes over her.

"Brahm," she says as she gently touches the pulsating design, "w-what happened to you?" Taken off guard, Brahm winces slightly at her touch, unsure what the consequences could be if she were to come in contact with the contained energy. Quickly realizing nothing came from it, he tries to casually play it off.

"Oh this?" he responds lightly. "It's a long story, but it's nothing to worry about! You could call it something like a… souvenir from our recent adventures!"

"Right," she says, clearly aware of his minimizing.

"Hey, I think your bird is trying to tell us something," Brahm points out, happy to change the subject. The pair look to Hanu who is flying repetitive cyclic patterns in front of them, similar to that of a dog chasing his tail. His playful behavior does beckon a strong call for attention.

"What is it, Hanu?" Sophia asks, taking a step closer to her spirit bird.

"Ka-aww!" Hanu cries into the air, shifting his cyclic momentum towards the Portala Plaza.

"I think he wants us to follow him," Sophia points out.

"Ka-aww!" comes Hanu's confirming call, clearly pleased with his master's quick deduction skills.

"Looks like our journey isn't quite over yet!" Brahm responds joyfully. The two carry on out of the valley of wreckage Mune's castle has been reduce to. The deconstructed castle is juxtaposed by the mighty Lotus desalinator still standing proudly atop the great mountain peak. The lingering totem of Mune's influence remains a scarring reminder of Wisteria's occupation of the divisive island. A sinking feeling grips Brahm and Sophia's chests, as they now must walk past the fallen souls who gave their lives to the recent battle. Young men, enveloped in the colors of a foreign land, cover the ground they fought blindly for. Their hollow sacrifice rings loudly in the two warriors hearts.

"Someday people won't have to die like this," Sophia says heavily.

"I hope to see that day," Brahm responds, his mind contemplating the amount of suffering the world still harbors.

"Then let's make sure we do. Eventually, people will see the power that exists within themselves. Only then will they no longer need a corrupt leader like Mune to tell them what to do. Until then, let us do what we can to show the world what is possible."

"I like that," Brahm says with a smile returning to his face. As the two rise out of the valley near the large stone entrance of the Portala Plaza, they begin to hear the commotion of a large crowd. They look to one another in confusion, unsure as to what could be causing such an uproar. They wonder if they should put themselves back on guard, but Hanu gives a comforting call from the sky to dispel any such worry. With a playful shrug, the two continue into the awaiting Plaza. With their steps nearing the entryway, the roar of the awaiting crowd begins to intensify. Just as they make their first step into the Plaza grounds, their eyes widen with disbelief as it appears that the entire population of the Pearl has come to greet them.

"Hurraaaaayyy!" The crowd shouts, throwing their hands up in the air. The cry of their celebratory chant rings throughout the plaza. Racing to meet Brahm and Sophia, they quickly encircle the two warriors as they continue to shout their praises. Quickly overwhelmed and mildly claustrophobic, the two warriors look to one another for hopeful suggestions on how to best manage their confusing situation. Individual blasts of praise from Pearlites are welcoming and appreciated, but equally unbelievable.

"Do you have any idea if what they are celebrating actually has anything to do with what just happened in that mountain?" Brahm whispers to Sophia.

"None at all!" she responds. "But they sure are happy about something!" Up ahead, a small pocket of people can be seen being pushed to the side. The Pearlites, uninterested in making way for the emerging party, are forcibly relocated as Domino comes bursting through the crowd.

"Domino!" Sophia calls out, very thankful to see a familiar face in the crowd of strangers.

"So good to see you!" Brahm responds, returning the same level of relief in his voice. "Is everyone else all right?"

"Yeah! Yeah!" Domino says, seemingly pressured by some unspoken urgency. "Eeekk! Is that the Warden?" he cries out with a shrill squeak as he notices Brahm's cargo.

"Ha, yeah, but he isn't going to be a concern to anyone but himself for now on."

"Right, whatever you say!" the youth says, completely unconvinced. "You're the one who would have to deal with him anyway. Now, quick! Come with me, I need you to see someone!" Domino concludes as he turns to jump back into the tightly woven crowd. Brahm and Sophia look to one another, curious as to how their larger frames will fair maneuvering through the dense sea of people.

"What are you waiting for? Do you want to be mobbed by this crowd or do you want to know why they are so happy?" Baited with the lure of answers, the two trudge through the rambunctious crowd, led to the center of the Plaza by the eager youth. The crowd starts to thin as they reach the center. It's as if a force field has erupted disrupting the chaotic flow of energy.

"This is nice," Brahm says as he basks in the comfort of the moment.

"Hey! We are not there yet. Keep moving, you two!" Domino calls from ahead, his target now becoming clear. Sitting along the edge of the Clam Stage is Izak, Emmanuel, Beau, the Seers, and Otto, who all sit next to a warm and bubbly Babarossa. Noticing the new arrivals, Babarossa shifts his attention to Brahm and Sophia. He stands, draped in his plaid blanket and greets the two with a warm toothless smile. His radiating presence gives a clear indication as to where the force field of calm and balanced energy originates. Everyone within a fifty-foot radius appears to be completely centered and at peace with themselves. Hanu takes this moment to dive into the warm and pleasant field of energy before perching himself upon Sophia's shoulder.

"Ha! I should have known you had something to do with this!" Brahm says playfully to the welcoming Seer Sage.

"Mmmm," Babarossa hums playfully. "I don't know what you are talking about!"

"I guess you don't know what has gotten everyone so excited around here either," Brahm responds, deciding to play along with the Great Sage.

"Well," Babarossa says with a deliberate pause, "it's true I might have had a *slight* hand in this, but it was all based on an idea you and Raja gave me."

"Really, how?" Brahm says as he decides to finally unload his cargo from his shoulders. He rests the two previous adversaries up against the stage and shifts his focus back to Babarossa.

"Remember that little stunt you pulled during the festival?" he asks, his words causing Raja to stand up and walk closer to the conversation.

"You mean the group vision?" Raja says, standing by Brahm's side.

"I sure do! It was such a wonderful idea, I loved it so much I figured it would be a great way to show everyone what a wonderful job you all were doing to help them."

"No way!" Brahm shouts out with glee. "So, you mean to tell me everyone here saw what was going on inside the mountain?"

"I figured it would be easier for everyone to understand if they could see it for themselves."

"Would someone like to fill me in on what's going on?" Sophia asks bluntly.

"Remember when I came to see you at the docks, to warn you about Babel?" Brahm asks.

"Hard to forget that."

"Right, well, anyway I went there because you missed out on Raja's vision! With a little bit of my help, she was able to amplify her gift and show the whole festival her vision of the incoming storm surge. She's the reason everyone was saved yesterday. So, it sounds like Baba over here just did the same thing to show everyone what went down in the mountain!"

"Wow," Sophia says, struggling slightly to grasp the reality of their battle being broadcasted to an entire island. "So they saw… everything?"

"Why don't you see for yourself," Baba says with a wave of his hand towards the crowd. The unseen force field lifts to allow one Pearlite to come running towards them with full, unrelenting, energetic frazzle. He comes to a screeching stop, inches from Sophia, Brahm, and Raja before throwing himself onto the floor.

"What is—" Sophia starts to say.

"Thank you!" the man interrupts from his prostration, his face buried into the stone with his hands outstretched towards the three before him. "I speak on behalf of all of us when I say you have our utmost gratitude and appreciation! We had no idea what kind of man we allowed to lead us! We would have never seen the light if it wasn't for all of you! Thank you for fighting for us. Thank you for freeing us. Thank you for not giving up on us. Thank you for… everything!" The man begins to sob uncontrollably as his last words leave his lips. Brahm and Sophia look to Raja who looks back at them with a puzzled expression. The two nudge their heads in the direction of the crying man, silently urging her to intervene. She gives a violent shake of her head, clearly not wanting the responsibility. Brahm and Sophia persist with aggressive head bobbing, insisting that she be the one to lift the man from the ground. With a huff of defeat, Raja looks to the man, bends a knee, and places her hand upon his shoulder.

"I-It's okay, you don't need to cry anymore. Please, stand back up and join us," she says warmly. The man is humbled by her gesture and slowly rises to face his saviors. He looks to Raja, with tears starting to swell back into his eyes.

"We have been so cruel to you and your people. What we have done is un… unforgivable." The man begins to get choked up again with his words.

"We understand the darkness of this world," Raja says, speaking for her people. "This whole endeavor has been eye-opening for us as well. We realize the path to freedom requires us to face this darkness. I am fortunate you now see us neither as your enemies nor as the reason for your shortcomings. We always have seen you as our brothers and sisters, so let us now live upon this land as the family we always have been."

"Such humble words," the man says in-between sobs. "Ahem!" he blurts out, clearing his throat and casting aside his water works for the time being. "Such words make what I am about to say that much easier." The man stands fully erect as if he is to address nobility. He looks around to the crowd just outside the unseen force field before turning back to address Raja. "We have had a lot of time to talk amongst ourselves while watching your battle in the mountain. We feel it is time to put the balance of power back where it should be." Bending a knee to the ground, the man continues with his proposition. "It would bring us the highest honor to have the Seers return as the leaders and watchers of this land!"

"What?" Raja says, blown away from the man's testimony.

"All those who are in favor of my words, let me hear you!" the man's voice booms as if suddenly amplified by a megaphone. Instantly, the surrounding crowd erupts with cheer and praise, showering Raja and the Seers with overwhelming support. The man stands back up and looks at Raja, eagerly awaiting her response.

"I-I don't know what to say," she admits, feeling like she is carrying the weight of her entire people with her decision.

"Just say yes," the man says warmly. In the wake of Raja's silence, Tewari comes and places a hand upon the young woman's shoulder. She stares up at him as he returns a silent smile. Her brother comes to join her, then her mother, then all the remaining Seers gather around to show their support.

"You are the one who can see clearer than all of us," Tewari says. "We trust your sight and your judgment. With that said, we leave this decision to you. Do you think we are ready to lead once again?"

"I-I don't know! I-I—," Raja starts to crumble under the imposed pressure.

"What does your heart say?" Brahm says, hoping to cut right to the core of the matter. Raja is instantly calmed by the words of her new friend. A moment of relief consumes her, allowing her to gain control over her racing mind.

"It says yes!" she cries out triumphantly. The crowd erupts into jubilant cheer once again. The man takes Raja's hand and lifts it over her head, causing the crowd to cheer even louder as they look upon the face of their new leader.

"I'm glad you have agreed, because we are in the works of putting together a celebration for you and your friends! There will be music and a feast where we will officially toast the returning leaders of the Pearl! Yahoo! Meet us all back here at dusk for the celebration of a lifetime!" The man turns back to the crowd. "You hear that? Everyone, step it up! We need everything ready before the sun sets!" The crowd rallies together as they all rush off to pour their exuberant energy into celebratory preparations.

"Why do they look to me as the next ruling Sage?" Raja asks as she looks back to Tewari for answers.

"Because with the gift you have been bestowed, there should be none other fit to serve such a role." Judging by the overwhelmed look of the youth, Tewari adds some additional comforting words. "Don't you worry. We will keep the seat warm until you are ready."

"Yes," Babarossa says as he makes his way next to Raja. "We have a lot of work to do if you wish to master that gift of yours."

"You… you knew all along this was going to happen?"

"What? Do I look like a fortune teller to you?!" he asks very brashly.

"Um… no sir, you don't," Raja responds, taken aback by the old man's sass.

"Good," he says with his nose tilted to the sky. "But I am someone who can train you. You will work with me until you have mastered your gift. Then you will lead this land. Yes?"

"Ha-ha…" Raja says nervously, "yes!"

"Good."

"Hey! Hey!" Otto and Domino cry out as they catch a whiff of Baba and Raja's conversation.

"Do you think you can teach us too; how to do that energy manipulation thing? Beau tried to show us, but you look like a better teacher. We want to master it too! Or is that just a Seer thing?" Domino's excitement quickly fades into disbelief as he starts to doubt the willingness of the Sage to teach him.

"Ha! I don't know about a better teacher, but there is one way to find out if you got what it takes, isn't there, boys?" Babarossa responds with a welcoming call. The boys jump for joy, linking arms and twirling around with shouts of relief. Brahm looks down and notices the dwindling number of unconscious adversaries at their feet. The Warden has managed to sneak off somewhere while Mune remains asleep, sawing logs like a peaceful lumberjack.

"Hmm…" Brahm ponders, wondering where the Warden has run off to. Before diving too far into that thought, he shifts his focus to the dethroned leader still in front of him.

"So, what do you suppose we do with this guy?" he asks Sophia about Mune.

"I'm positive word will soon get to Wisteria about the overturning of their appointed leader and their defeated Warden, wherever he is."

"Yeah, don't worry about him. He can't be far, I'll find him."

"Good. While you do that, I'll take Mune and put him in the plaza prison for the time being. He will be a good peace offering when the Wisterian representatives come searching for answers. Let's meet back here before sunset so we don't miss the festivities."

"Yeah!" Brahm responds enthusiastically. "Plus, I'm starving!" His youthful energy brings a smile to Sophia's face. She gives him a silent nod of her head before transitioning to her aforementioned plan.

"Any of you coming with me?" Sophia calls to her Marionettes.

"Yeah, we'll come with ya," Izak says as he speaks for himself and Emmanuel. The two men stand up to follow their leader.

"Good. Where are the other two?" she asks.

"Oh, when Jeeven woke up he ran off to the castle ruins to salvage his armor plates." Izak answers. "And, of course, Aya had to run after him like always to 'help,'" he says, holding his fingers in the air to mimic quotation marks.

"Let it go, love bird. Just help me get this guy where he belongs," she says as she makes her way to the prison, leaving Mune for the flabbergasted Izak to tend to.

"What did you… ugh, forget it. You got it, boss!" Izak says, first fumbling over his words before disregarding the need to challenge Sophia's observation. He picks up Mune from one side as Emmanuel braces the other. They follow their leader through the wisps of fog towards the prison. As everyone else makes their way to wrap up unfinished business before the start of the festival, Beau decides to have a word with his captain before they part ways.

"Are you going to go turn another enemy into a friend?" he calls after his captain.

"Ha, yeah. I don't know if I would go that far," Brahm says as he turns around to address his first mate. "I'm starting to learn just how challenging this being *human* thing can be. Now that I know a little bit about what he must be going through, I just want to make sure he is okay."

"You are one of a kind, you know that?" Beau says with a hearty slap across Brahm's back.

"Thanks Beau," he says as he slips into a pocket of self-reflection. "Thanks again for not giving up on me, I know looking after me isn't easy."

"Nonsense," Beau responds, "I wouldn't have it any other way. That's the beauty of watching someone grow up. If you look close enough, you realize the process never stops!"

"Nice words, old man."

"Hey," Beau says, shifting the energetic flow of the conversation. "That mark on your arm… it's grown since I last saw you."

"Yeah, I couldn't completely transmute the energy from that Pole like I thought I could. As of now, the best I can do is contain it inside me until I learn how to transmute the rest."

"You make it hard not to worry about you, ya know? I just hope we can figure out what to do before it tears you up from the inside out."

"Yeah, I agree," Brahm says with a growing concern for his own wellbeing. "So, what are you going to do now?" he asks, hoping to change the subject.

"Well, other than fantasize over what food I will devour first, The Serapis Bey could use some tender loving care after all she's been through.

I'll work on getting her seaworthy again before sunset. Meet you back here with the rest of them?"

"Sounds wonderful," Brahm says before returning to his search for the elusive Warden.

∞

Following the whim of his intuition, Brahm wanders down the winding streets he first climbed when arriving to The Pearl. He playfully jumps from one cobblestone to the next as if playing perpetual hopscotch. Focusing on being guided by the heart and not the mind, he lets his thoughts play freely, while he follows the intuitive pull of his core. His bare feet kiss the stones once again as they carry him to his unknown destination.

He floats past an elephant tree, its roots remaining steadfast in their grip to the rocky soil. The sharp sloping angle of his cobblestone path begins to point towards the bay. The rough waves crashing into the sandless shore start to resonate inside his ears. He looks down and notices a particular wreckage caught between the waves and the shore. The waves carry the remains of a torn bladder from a personal airship, draping it along the rocks of the beach. A multitude of ropes are still tethered to a shattered wooden ship hull. The battered ship sloshes back and forth with the rising tide.

A man sits hunched over by the wreckage playing with a rock in his hand. He twirls the stone around in his palm before finally casting it into the vast ocean. The stone skips steadily along the surface of the water before eventually sinking below. As the man watches the ripples from his stone bleed back into the surrounding waves, he takes his hands and adjusts the patch of deflated hair atop his head. He molds it into a very familiar mohawk. Pleased with the accuracy of his internal compass, Brahm races down to the shore to join the Warden.

"Fancy meeting you here," Brahm says as he brings himself to stand next to the once deadly adversary. The two share a moment of silence as they look out into the vast ocean. They listen to the sound of the repetitive lapping waves crashing around them. The ocean appears to stretch infinitely into the horizon, an enigmatic force that has almost consumed the entire planet.

"Even stripped of my power, you cannot trust me?" the Warden says without making eye contact. Instead of looking at the new arrival, he searches around his feet for another stone to cast. "I would understand if you came to finish me off."

"That's not why I came here," Brahm responds compassionately.

"Then why are you here?" he asks, tossing another stone into the waves.

"I know all too well what it feels like to have your power cast aside and to be left with what little humanity appears to offer."

"Ha! Do you now?" he says condescendingly, quick to cast aside any thought of someone understanding the pain that beats in his heart. Basking in a wave of silence following Brahm's statement, the Warden feels compelled to give him the benefit of the doubt. He no longer feels the need to pick a fight with the enigmatic warrior. "Yeah, well, I wasn't sure if I could even do it. I was so close to giving up." The Warden is surprised at the candid honesty that flows from his lips.

"Well, it looks like you *did* do it," Brahm responds cheerfully.

"Yeah," the Warden replies, feeling an unfamiliar rush of warmth and compassion washing over him. He starts to wonder what spell he has been cast under, but it does not stop him from continuing his testimony. "I was able to push aside Mune, but the main puppet master, I didn't think I could cut ties with."

"So how did you do it?"

"He cut me," the Warden says coldly, still unwilling to make eye contact. "In that moment where you held his power in your hand, ready to transmute it, I could feel him giving up on me. He cut me away like the entrails of a filleted fish. I was no more use to him."

"Looks like he ended up giving you the full freedom you have been craving all along."

"I guess so, but at quite the cost. I'm not even sure what I am anymore. I'm sure I was human at some point in my life, but I have no memory to fall back on. I have nothing… nobody. My only memories are of being a servant to another, powered by someone else to do their bidding. Fighting you I felt so alive for the first time, a part of me wishes I could have died back there. I feel I could have at least died with satisfaction in my heart. And now…"

"Now?"

"Ha, now who knows? I'm a man with no identity, no power, thrust into humanity with nothing but a handful of enemies. I've dreamt of freedom, never thinking of the weight those choices carry. I don't know who I am, let alone what I am supposed to do. Maybe with as fragile as this body of mine has become, death might not be the worst option to explore."

"Why not start over?"

"Easy for you to say."

"Nonsense. *Death* is the easy answer," Brahm says heavily. His heart swirls with emotions as he continues to look out into the ocean. The Warden finally turns his head to look at the man standing beside him. He tries to burn him with hostile eyes, but Brahm does not make eye contact. "Choosing to live despite the hardship, that's where the real work is. That's where you will find your true purpose." His words cut the growing tension. "Don't throw away the joy of finding out who you are just because it's hard. I can promise you that you will regret it. That power you had was never the real you in the first place, just something convenient to hide behind." Brahm looks at the softening eyes of the Warden after speaking his truth.

"So, let me get this straight. You won't kill me, and you don't want me to kill myself?"

"You got it."

"You know, you are taking a big gamble with sparing my life," the Warden says with an odd playfulness.

"Oh, and why is that?"

"Not only do you spare me, but you try to inspire me to find myself? What makes you think I'll go out there in the world and become a good guy, huh? You've seen what I've done, who I was. Who's to say the person I find myself to be isn't going to be worse off than who I was before?"

"That's the beauty of free will," Brahm says. "I hope whoever you find yourself to be, you embrace it for all that it is. Even if you turn out to be complete dumpster filth," he finishes with a jestful smile.

"Suit yourself. But don't think this makes us friends just because you came down here to give me a pep talk."

"I would never dream of such a thing!" Brahm says before bursting into laughter. The Warden cracks a smile of his own before bringing a hand to his face. Grabbing ahold of the frame of his dark sunglasses, he slowly lifts them off his face revealing the dark brown human eyes behind them.

"Guess I don't need these anymore," he says before casting the darkened shades into the water. Brahm watches the stylish spectacles sink into the lapping depths while a curious look manifests on his face.

"I mean… the sun does still get pretty bright. You probably didn't need to—"

"Enough!" the Warden snaps, clearly having second thoughts about his rash decision. "It was supposed to be symbolic."

"Oh! Right, right. I get it now. Yeah, that was… deep," Brahm says, trying to recover from his misstep.

"You are hopeless…" the Warden says with a shake of his head. As he starts to take off the tie that hangs around his neck like a noose, Brahm looks to him with a deep pondering glance.

"Hey, what you said before, about knowing who I am. What else do you know about me?"

"What I said?" the Warden asks, slightly puzzled by the question. "Oh, *that.* Ha, as much as I would love to take advantage of your vulnerability right now, I just don't feel up to it. The truth might sting just as much. I honestly don't know anything about you. That was the master talking through me. In this state, all I know is that you are a reckless fool." His words hang in the air for a moment as Brahm struggles to accept the empty lead he was hoping to uncover. Despite the Warden's desire to appear harsh, he decides to try and smooth over the downtrodden moment. "With a name like 'Freewater' hanging over you, I can see why you ran away from the world. That might be a tighter noose than the one I'm trying to get off *my* neck," he says playfully.

"Yeah, seems we are both in a bit of an identity crisis," Brahm says as he gazes up at the Warden with a smile. "Looks like the search continues." The pair stand in silence as they ponder the gravity of their own shoes they are meant to fill. "So, think I can convince you to come join us at the feast?" he asks, ready to change the subject.

"The feast in celebration of defeating me? No thanks."

"No, the feast to celebrate new beginnings. Everyone gets the chance to start over today. Why not join us?"

"Thanks, but no thanks. I'm going to take some time alone before I try to weave myself back into the rest of humanity."

"Fair enough," Brahm responds. "What are you going to do instead?"

"Well, now that I'm not going to sink myself at the bottom of the ocean, I might fix that ship of mine over there and see if I can get it to fly again. It's going to take some time with just these human hands, but it will give me something to do for a while."

"Mmm, that sounds like a nice place to start." The two men look back out over the ocean into the setting sun. Its warm glow dances off the reflecting waves of the ocean, finally displaying its radiant beauty from behind the rolling clouds above.

"Yikes!" Brahm exclaims, realizing he got himself caught up in the moment. "I'm going to be late! Are you sure you are going to be okay?" Brahm asks the Warden with a hurried expression.

"Yeah, yeah, go ahead and go. You don't owe me anymore of your time. You didn't even need to come down here in the first place."

"I know," Brahm says with a shrug of his shoulders. "I wanted to."

"Whatever, weirdo. Just remember, if our paths are to ever cross again, don't you go expecting me to harbor any gratitude towards you. I pledge allegiance to no one, especially a *Freewater*," he adds with a sarcastic flair.

"Good. I wouldn't have it any other way," Brahm says, his loose hair flapping in the sea breeze. He takes a moment to place his tattered hat back on his head before returning to the Plaza. Without another word shared, the Warden watches Brahm race up the cobblestone path to the festivities above. The lights and commotion have grown to the point where they can be heard all the way down by the bay. The Warden smiles to himself as he borrows a moment of curiosity, wondering where his path through humanity might take him.

Cutting it close, Brahm slides into the Plaza just as the cloud-draped sun kisses the horizon. He stares around at the sea of people searching for some familiar faces. He casually walks around aimlessly, hoping it will aid his search. Festive banners and decorations hang loosely from the buildings lining the plaza. A swarm of fire-lit lanterns hang in the sky, tethered to the surrounding windows as they bake the approaching darkness with their warm glow. Brahm finds himself drawn to the Clamshell Stage once again as the flickering flame in front of it has been lit once again. He can see the dancing shadows of people preparing something that are reflected along the inner wall. Over-inflated silhouettes of musical instruments dance alongside humanoid shadows, teasing Brahm with thoughts of future sonic delight. As he hastens his pace to check out what is brewing atop the stage, he bumps into Beau who appears to be looking for something as well.

"There you are!" Beau cries out, placing his hands upon Brahm's shoulders. "I've been looking all over for you! I thought your disregard for time got the better of you again! Hurry up, the feast is about to start!"

"The feast!" Brahm yells with joy. He decides to put down his interest in the brewing music scene for a moment to explore another blissful indulgence. "Let's go, it's been days since we've had a decent meal!" The two men race off to find their seats along the enormous table laid out for the celebration. Chairs line the extensive table that houses a plethora of culinary delights. Steam frolics off the freshly baked goods, filling the air with a delectable aroma. Brahm throws himself into the chair Beau points out to him as he grabs his utensils and scans the table for his first bite.

"Hey!" Beau shouts, slapping his captain behind his head. "Don't be rude! They haven't made the toast yet!"

"Toast? Why wait for toast when we have all this other food to choose from?" Brahm asks with a tone that does not clarify his sincerity. Beau just gives him a disappointing glare and reaches his hand up again with an open palm.

"Okay, okay," Brahm says, nursing his head unnecessarily. "Well, is everyone else here at least?"

"Everyone but Sophia, I don't know what she got caught up with, but the rest of them are over there." Beau points across the table to the band of Seers located near the head of the table. As Brahm shifts his focus, he catches sight of Tewari, Mono, Raja, and Mufida who notice his attention and give him a welcoming wave. They all have cleaned up and now don beautiful sky blue robes of elegant style. To their right are the Marionettes, still as dirty and war-torn as Brahm remembers them. Their disheveled appearance makes him feel more comfortable about his own. None of them seem to be interested in Brahm's arrival except Emmanuel, who gives him a casual wave. The rest are in deep conversation with Jeeven, who now wears his heavy metal plating once again. He seems comfortable covered in the weight of his plates, although he looks a little extra peculiar with the additional dents in his metallic exterior. There is one seat next to him that remains vacant. Brahm assumes it has been reserved for Sophia.

He settles himself into his seat and waits for the feast to begin, hoping Sophia will return soon. He takes this time to look for the boys, expecting them to be near everyone else. Anticipating Brahm's inquiry, Beau helps his captain out and points further down the table. His eyes widen as he sees an over-excited Otto with his arms around an elderly couple. He hugs them warmly before nudging them towards Domino. The four share a few words then rush to embrace each other. As Brahm brings his attention back to his plate, his eyes catch those of someone sitting next to the boys. An older man gives Brahm a drunkenly wink and lifts his prized drink to toast him personally. Brahm squints to make out who it could be, only to recognize the old drunk who he met during the festival. Brahm flashes a warm smile to the man, thankful he survived the recent turmoil. The sound of a metal utensil striking glass suddenly rings through the air. The man who was talking to Raja earlier in the Plaza stands at the head of the table, now asking for everyone's attention.

"It brings me great pleasure to see everyone sitting at this table, as we are about to share a meal together as one family. It has been too long that we have been divided on this land, tainted by the lure of an outside force. As challenging as these last few days have been for everyone, and how challenging these last few years have been for our Seers, we all now sit here together with a newfound perspective. Surrounded by a sea that has claimed the majority of the land of this world, we have more to be thankful for standing upon these shores than not. Let this celebration mark the beginning of a new era for The Pearl! An era defined by unity and resolution... rebirth and retribution. Let us raise our glasses as we extend our gratitude for our Seers and return the rightful protection of this land into their capable hands. We have been blinded for too long regarding our history, let us all open our eyes and see our future transpire together. Who's with me?!"

"Aaooouuuu!" the patrons at the table shout together as one. The triumphant bellow triggers chills to run down Brahm's spine.

"Yes! And let us all come together, as we officially announce the incumbent Seer leader, Tewari Mutatalla!"

"Aaooouuuuu!!!"

"He will hold the seat until their chosen one, the one talked about in legends is ready to rise up and guide us to even greater heights! Let us give thanks for our future leader of The Pearl, Raja Zooani!"

"Aaoouuuu! Aaooouuu! Aaoouuuu!" the Pearlites slam their fists upon the table as they praise their young leader to be. Brahm glances over at the overwhelmed youth who is doing her best to keep her composure.

"And let us give one more thanks to the noble Shakers who washed upon our shores only to save us from ourselves! Even though their origins and intentions upon our land may forever be a mystery, their selfless deeds we witnessed will forever be remembered! To all of you!"

"Aaooouuuu!" This time Brahm catches an eye with the Marionettes across the table. They share a reluctant bow of gratitude for one another before diverting their attention back to their earlier affairs. Brahm is swimming with sentimental emotions despite their obvious disregard for communion.

"Such an interesting bunch, aren't they?" Brahm asks Beau.

"I don't know what you saw in them initially," he responds, "but for everyone's sake, whatever it was, I'm glad you did."

"Okay! So, without further ado," the man at the top of the table decrees, "let the feast begin!"

"Aaooouuuu!" Brahm and Beau shout, deciding to join in on the collective roar of the table this time. As everyone dives into the plethora of food before them, they begin devouring the spoils like ravenous dogs. The delectable nourishment pouring into Brahm's body is almost too much for him to handle. As he becomes overwhelmed with bliss, he feels as if he is drifting off to heaven in a chariot sent by the food gods. Beau looks to his captain as he basks in this ray of delight and almost chokes on the bite in his mouth.

"Hey!" he cries out, noticing his captain starting to fade in and out of existence. "Cut that out!" he yells, slapping him upside the head once again.

"Whoa!" Brahm exclaims, shaking his head back and forth. "Thanks, Beau! This food is so good, I almost lost myself there for a moment!"

"I can't take my eye off you for one second!" Beau says with parental flair. The two glance at one another before each bursting out into laughter. As the sound of clanking silverware and delightful musings fill the air, Brahm notices a quiet patron coming to join the table. Sophia nears the place at the table intended for her but does not sit. She leans her head towards Jeeven and whispers something into his ear. The rest of the Marionettes bend an ear to her words and once she finishes what she has come to say, they all immediately put down their silverware. Wiping their mouths, the Severed Marionettes quietly remove themselves from the table and disappear into the darkness. Sophia is left at the table and directs an intense look at Brahm. She walks her way around the table to share her message.

"Are you not going to stay for the feast?" Brahm asks before she has a chance to relay her message. "And I think there is going to be music coming on soon!"

"No, I'm afraid not," Sophia says, clearly intending to say more but is disrupted by Brahm's childish desire to distract her from her purpose.

"Oh, c'mon! What's so important you have to leave *right now*? We've been through so much already today! Why not sit back and enjoy yourself!"

"I wish I could, but—"

"But what?"

"But, if you are smart, it's a luxury I doubt *either* of us can afford right now."

"What do you mean?" Brahm asks, finally putting down his forkful of food and taking Sophia seriously.

"I did a scan of the water when we went down to lock up Mune. Our telescope showed Wisterian ships already heading this way. They will be here within the hour by my calculations. I assume there will most likely be another Warden."

"Another Warden?" Brahm asks with heavy dread. He looks down at his ragged and beaten body, confident he does not have the energy to return to battle. "So what?" he tries to bargain. "We are heroes aren't we?"

"No, unfortunately, *we* are not. *We* are a band of rebels who have made a name for ourselves overthrowing underhanded plots from this broken global government system. Essentially, *we* are terrorists. And *you* are an accomplice in our terrorist actions. Overthrowing a Wisterian leader? Taking down a Warden? A punishable and unimaginable offence no matter how you cut it. However, for the people of The Pearl, it's a welcoming reprieve. As long as everyone here blames us for the overthrow, then we are the bad guys in this one. That shouldn't be a problem with everybody watching what went down today thanks to that Seer Sage. Everyone here will give the same testimony when questioned, which is perfect. The Pearl *should* be left alone for the time being… hopefully. That is, as long as we get out of here and not make it look like the people here are celebrating and harboring known fugitives!"

"So, what you are trying to say is…"

"You just became a wanted criminal, bucko," Sophia says flatly. "And unless you want to wage war with the current ruler of the world and bring havoc and suffering back to this island, I suggest you make a run for it… now."

"Fine," Brahm says throwing his utensils down at the table. Despite his dramatic intention to show his resolve, his eyes shift back and forth, studying his plate still full of food. He reflexively grabs the half eaten sandwich on his plate and stuffs it into his pocket. "I guess you—"

"Excuse me? Excuse me? Can I have everyone's attention please?" comes a booming voice from the Clam Stage. Brahm whips his head around to see the familiar quartet of musicians from the day before standing back up on stage.

"No way!" Brahm shouts, it's those guys again! Oh my, they were so good!"

"Thank you," the front man of the group says as he notices the surge of attention shifting towards them. "Before we get started, I want to thank those who put together this festival here to welcome us back on stage. It's an honor to play for you all, and we are so pleased to be able to be here for such an occasion. We travel the world to share our music, but what we got to see with all of you has been out of this world. So, to share this moment with *everyone* after such an experience means everything to us. This is our life and our passion to play music. We couldn't do it without all of you. We also want to give another shout out to the unnamed heroes who took down that Mune guy. We didn't really get to know him, but he seemed like quite the jerk. I'm sure there are brighter skies for this island's future. Well… you know what I mean," he back tracks, reflecting on the dismal grays skies that still populate the island.

"Oh, c'mon!" Brahm pleads with Sophia. "You have to stay and listen to them! They are amazing!"

"So, we are the Switchfoot Soul Shakers, and we are about to start off with a new song we just wrote. It was inspired by all the events that have gone down since we've been here," the front man continues.

"Absolutely not!" Sophia responds to Brahm's pestering question. "And if you have even an ounce of regard left for these people, you will leave right *now*!"

"Ugh, Fine!" Brahm says while pouting. He looks to Beau who stands ready to make their move. "Is the ship ready?"

"She's not perfect, but she should float."

"Good enough!" Brahm says as he scoops up another piece of his dinner to finish later. "Let's do this!"

∞

As the three race to the docks, Domino and Otto notice their not-so-sneaky exit and rush to intercept them. They scurry down the cobblestone street before being abruptly stopped by an extending hand from a darkened alleyway. The boys turn to scold the unsuspecting hindrance before they recognize the plaid blanket the hand extends under. Babarossa calmly walks out of the darkness and gives the boys a warm hug.

"I thought you two had a feast to attend to?" the Sage says to the boys.

"Baba! They are all leaving us!" Otto cries out.

"And without even saying goodbye!" Domino adds with tears starting to perspire from his eyes.

"Ahhh," Babarossa hums, gazing down the winding street. "You have come to care for them very much, haven't you?"

"Yes!" the boys scream through snot clogged noses.

"Do you have any doubt they also have carved a space in their hearts for you?"

"Well, no! Of course not! After everything that has happened, I know they care for us!" Otto says proudly.

"Well, they seem too far away to physically catch up to them. Maybe there is another way to connect."

"What?!" the boys ask together. "Well, if you are sure they made room in their hearts for you, maybe we can utilize that space…" The boys stare at the old man with puzzling and curious eyes.

"Trust in that connection," Baba says as he places his warm and gentle hands upon their backs, "and say what is in your hearts."

"Oooiii!" the boys scream at the top of their lungs, wasting no time.

The familiar voices race through the surrounding ether and booms from within Brahm's chest. Confused by this unique sensation, he whips his head back and forth to find the boys. His distracted descent towards the sea starts to leave a trail of food that falls from within his gluttonous clutches.

"Thank you for everything!" Domino yells, his voice bellowing from the chests of the retreating heroes.

"Yeah, and don't forget about us!" Otto declares within the sacred heart space. Sophia smiles to herself, unwilling to question the warm and bounding sensation in her heart. She stays committed to her task, forcing herself to continue running. Brahm beckons Beau to stop and go back to find the boys but is reminded that they have outstayed their welcome.

"We endanger everyone the longer we stay here!" Beau reminds his captain.

"Such a bummer," Brahm says childishly.

"We better see each other again!" Otto cries out, desperate to get some kind of response from his departing friends.

"You bet we will!" Brahm shouts back, making use of the heart-centered channel that connects their souls, showering the boys' with joy. Babarossa squeezes the boys' shoulders as he follows the triad of runaway fugitives with his eyes until they fade away from sight.

∞

"Yeah, so this song is called Truth or Dare, hope you all enjoy. Here we go!" the band announces to those still gathered at the Plaza. The song opens with an abrupt funky bass line, triggering a frenzy of fast beat drum kicks that gets even the most senior Pearlites tapping their feet. The bass continues to weave itself into the drumbeats, smoothing out the melody and adding meat and stability to the transpiring sonic manifestation. An angelic riff layers upon the building rhythm, powered by the addition of the six-stringed guitar.

∞

"Why domp hue sail wiff hus?" Brahm asks Sophia, his mouth stuffed with the remaining food he snagged from the table.

"Thanks but no thanks," Sophia says. "If this adventure has taught me anything, it's that I still have much to learn about myself." She thinks back to what Namaka said about how he knew more about her than she knew herself. Then the memory surfaces of Mune, who couldn't even consider her a threat without her Resistance members. She even brings herself to accept the feelings of futility that came with watching Brahm fulfill *her* mission. It all has been eating away at her. "I need to find *myself* out there. Not with the assistance of powerful allies, but I need to find my own strength… my own power. I want to be more than the *reason* a hero comes to save the day. I want to learn how to be my *own* hero. That I must figure out on my own."

"Oh," Brahm says, sinking into the disappointing reality of having to part ways. "Right, yeah… yeah, that makes sense I guess." The building musical remedy can still be heard from behind them. Its resonating beauty brings slight comfort to Brahm's deflated emotional state. "Come find us after you find yourself," he says as lightly as he can. He tries his best to hide his breaking heart.

"I might," she says playfully.

"I'm going to miss you," Brahm says to Sophia with a warm smile.

"Oh geez," she says, throwing her hands up in the air, disappointed with how quick her repressed emotions can resurface. "I can't believe I am going to do this," she says as she brings her run to a halt and throws her hand into her cloak pocket. Brahm looks to Beau and raises an eyebrow in excitement.

"I'm assuming you don't have a LRC?" she asks with high certainty of the answer to her question.

"A what?"

"A Long Range Com… ugh, I don't know why I even asked." She rummages in her coat pocket in search of her back up plan. "Hanu! Come out!" she says, holding her Totem Wand. Hanu soars into existence, dazzling the darkness with his unique glow before perching himself onto Sophia's shoulder. "Hanu, let me see one of your feathers." Hanu lifts a wing at the command of his master. Careful not to harm the rainbow crow, Sophia plucks a single feather from Hanu's outstretched wing.

"Thank you, Hanu. Now please return to the wand for now." Soaring into the air, Hanu quickly dives back down into the Totem Wand still in Sophia's hand, dissipating his light instantaneously. The only light that remains of him is in the single feather between Sophia's fingertips.

"Here," she says, handing Brahm the fluorescent feather. "As long as you hold onto this feather, Hanu will always be able to find you. He can transfer messages between us. If you ever need to contact me again, just channel your intention into that feather. Hanu will know you are looking for me and I can send him your way. And of course, it works the same if for whatever reason I need to contact you."

"Whoa! Cool! So, we can be like, pen pals… or bird buddies?" Brahm says with overeager enthusiasm.

"Hey! This is a big deal, okay?" Sophia yells back. "Make sure if you ever do it's important. Don't forget that I'm still the leader of one of the most wanted terrorist organizations on the sea!"

"Well now," Brahm says playfully, "don't you forget I'm an *accomplice* to one of the most wanted terrorist organizations on the sea! So, I'm a big deal too, ya know."

"You are something else," Sophia says as she shakes her head. Looking ahead, she notices the fork in the road they now face. "This is where we part ways, my ship is at the west dock. I heard yours was crashed over in the east. I hope it is ready to sail. Goodbye Beau, Brahm."

"Goodbye, Sophia," Beau says warmly. "And don't worry, our ship is ready to go. It's been a wild adventure. Thank you for all your help."

"Don't mention it."

Brahm takes his turn to bid the Resistance leader goodbye. He looks deep into her eyes, allowing himself to swim within their golden yellow glow one last time. She can feel the intrusion, but she decides not to look away. She steals her own farewell glance into the enigmatic apertures before her. His bicolored eyes flicker like homing beacons, taunting her heart to stay connected despite her determination to part ways.

"Goodbye, Sophia," Brahm says again, not willing to tease her any longer, "for now, that is." Freed from his distractionary gaze, she turns to head to her ship. The two men stand still as they watch her run off into the darkness. As she fades from view, Brahm places Hanu's feather in his hat and turns to Beau to give him a reassuring head nod. Just before they make their next move, Brahm hesitates once again. The music from above has reached an acoustic climax; he can hear the frontman stirring up momentum to drop something sonically spectacular.

"Hold on, just one more moment…" Brahm asks his first mate.

"C'mon Brahm! We have to go!" Beau says, grabbing his captain by the arm and dragging him to their ship. Not willing to give up so easily, Brahm secretly channels a little bit of manipulated energy. He uses it to distort his sense of hearing just enough to pick up the developing melody above.

Uhh… yeah… so we hand over our funds,
To the devious man,
Rich from his plan,
To keep our heads buried deep in the sand!

Shackled by debt,
We are left to fret,
And yet?
Let us not forget
What binds us,
What perpetually blinds us …

Yo! Our habit to get high off the fumes,
Of the societal gloom and doom,
Ideas that drive us to consume
A relief from the darkened despair
Of our skewed worldly affair.
But is this truth? Or do you choose DARE!?

Uh!

Dare to fend off the fear,
To look inside and clear
The scrambled mind,
And realize what is yours to find.

Hidden behind the lies
Exists a world left to realize,
One comprised of love and light
A brightness worth the fight:
The light versus the night,
What is wrong versus what is right.

It's a battle that rages within us all,
So listen to the call,
And worry not of the fall
From a false grace that holds no place
In the truth that sits in the center of your
Divine and heavenly face.

The face that reflects back,
Even when you think you live in lack.
It whispers the hard fact
That if you open your eyes,
You too can realize…

That the curriculum of these worldly classes
Are just schoolrooms designed for the masses
To teach the lessons of peace and prosperity,
Not of single solidarity,
Or punitive causality.
So don't go thinking you are alone,
That alone is the greatest fallacy!

Uh!

The angels above
Are always showering you with love,
Guiding you with a gentle nudge,
Not with a forceful shove.

So open your book,
And take a good look
At all who are here to teach the way,
Hear what they have to say.

Separate at first glance,
Stop and give them a second chance
And you too will see
What it is we are all meant to be.
Heavenly bodies by birth,
Led astray by the fears and lies planted
To lessen our worth,
But remember, this is our spiritual turf! Yeah!

We are all one and one is the all,
So don't take the bait and trip and fall...
Into the lies that aim to divide and control.
It's all they have to sell...

And all they ask is that you pay with your soul!